PRAISE FOR THESE
New York Times
Bestselling Authors

Barbara Delinsky

"When you care to read the very best,
the name of Barbara Delinsky
should come immediately to mind."
—*Rave Reviews*

An author "of sensibility and style."
—*Publishers Weekly*

Catherine Coulter

"Catherine Coulter has created some of the most
memorable characters in romance."
—*Atlanta Journal-Constitution*

"Coulter is excellent at portraying
the romantic tension between her
heroes and heroines."
—*Milwaukee Journal*

Linda Howard

"Ms. Howard can wring so much emotion and tension
out of her characters that no matter how satisfied
you are when you finish a book,
you still want more."
—*Rendezvous*

"Howard's writing is compelling."
—*Publishers Weekly*

Barbara Delinsky was born and raised in suburban Boston. She worked as a researcher, photographer and reporter before turning to writing full-time in 1980. With more than fifty novels to her credit, she is truly one of the shining stars of contemporary romance fiction! This talented author has received numerous awards and honors, and her books have appeared on many bestseller lists. With over twelve million copies in print worldwide, Barbara's appeal is definitely universal.

Catherine Coulter has enticed millions of readers with her bestselling novels. A versatile and prolific author, she began her writing career penning Regency romances. She has since garnered wide acclaim and earned a large and loyal following for both her historical and contemporary romances, and regularly graces the bestseller lists. Catherine continues to write her stories from the Northern California home she shares with her husband.

Linda Howard claims that whether she's reading or writing them, books have long played a profound role in her life. She cut her teeth on Margaret Mitchell and from then on continued to read widely and eagerly. In recent years her interest has settled on romance fiction, because she's "easily bored by murder, mayhem and politics." After twenty-one years of penning stories for her own enjoyment, Linda finally worked up the courage to submit a novel for publication—and has since met with great success! This Alabama author has been steadily publishing ever since.

Barbara Delinsky

Catherine Coulter

Linda Howard

Forever Yours

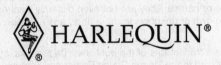

HARLEQUIN®

TORONTO • NEW YORK • LONDON
AMSTERDAM • PARIS • SYDNEY • HAMBURG
STOCKHOLM • ATHENS • TOKYO • MILAN • MADRID
PRAGUE • WARSAW • BUDAPEST • AUCKLAND

HARLEQUIN BOOKS
225 Duncan Mill Road, Don Mills,
Ontario, Canada M3B 3K9

ISBN 0-373-83460-8

FOREVER YOURS

Visit us at www.eHarlequin.com

Printed in U.S.A.

CONTENTS

Threats and Promises
Barbara Delinsky

PROLOGUE

The dark of night lay thick in the garden of the lavish Hollywood Hills estate where two shadowed figures conversed in low tones. Both were men. One was tall, broad and physical; the other was smooth, arrogant and cerebral.

"Are you sure? Absolutely sure?" the smooth one demanded, sounding less smooth than usual as his eyes pierced the darkness to bead mercilessly at his companion.

"She wasn't in that car," the tall one insisted quietly.

"You said she was. I buried her."

"You buried ashes of what we thought was her. We were wrong."

The smooth one's nostrils flared, but he kept his voice low. "And how can you be sure it wasn't her?"

"One of our men heard talk around the coroner's office. There was no evidence of a body, charred or otherwise. A burned purse and shoes, but no body. Unofficially, of course. Officially, at least as far as the heat's concerned, she's dead."

The arrogant one cursed under his breath. He pulled a pack of cigarettes from his pocket and barely had time to raise one to his mouth when the underling snapped a match with his thumbnail and lit it.

"No body," he muttered, squaring his shoulders. "So she got away."

The physical one had enough sense to keep still. He knew what was to come, knew he had his work cut out for him.

"I want her found," the smooth one growled. "I want her found *now*."

Still the physical one remained silent.

"She didn't have any family, at least none she ever told me

about. She wasn't in touch with anyone else, and her friends were mine." A long drag on the cigarette momentarily brightened its glowing red tip. "She must have had help." Smoke curled out with the words and dissipated into the air. "New identity, new location, money.... Damn it," he gritted out as the wheels of his mind turned, "she sold the jewels. There wasn't any burglary. The bitch took the jewels herself and sold them!"

"I'll find her."

"Damn right you will. Half a million in diamonds and rubies, not to mention another hundred thou in furs—no woman can steal like that from me!"

"Do you want me to bring her back?"

The tall man's boss pondered that as he stroked the closely shaved skin above his lip. When he spoke, his voice was low once more and as dark as the night. "She's a thief. And a traitor. I've given her a funeral fit for a queen. I won't suffer the embarrassment of having her materialize from the grave." He paused for a moment before continuing smoothly, arrogantly, cerebrally, in his own perverted way. "She's dead. That's how I want her. Make her squirm first. Let her know that I know what she's done. Get the jewels and whatever else you can from her. Then see that she's buried, this time with an unmarked stone."

Tossing the cigarette to the grass, he ground it out beneath the sole of his imported leather shoe. Then he straightened his silk evening jacket, thrust out his chin and walked calmly, coolly, back toward the house.

CHAPTER ONE

Lauren Stevenson looked at herself in the mirror. And looked. And looked. "It doesn't matter how long I stand here," she said breathlessly. "I still can't believe it's me!"

Richard Bowen grinned at her reflection. "It's you, and if I do say so myself, it's smashing."

She slanted him a shy glance. In the weeks during which she'd come to know this man, she'd grown perfectly comfortable with him as her doctor. But she couldn't ignore the fact that he was attractive; hence his compliment was that much more weighty. "I'll bet you say that to all the women you've worked on."

"Not necessarily. Some only look good. Some only look better than they did before. For that matter," he added with a wink, "some looked better before the surgery."

"You don't tell them that, do you?" she chided.

"Are you kidding? If it's vanity that's brought them down here, I'm not about to make an enemy for life. But it wasn't vanity that brought you here, Lauren Stevenson, was it?"

She shook her head. "It was sheer necessity." Once again she eyed herself in the mirror. "I'm amazed, though. I knew there'd be an improvement..." She faltered. Narcissism was foreign to her nature. Her cheeks grew red, her voice humble. "I didn't expect half this."

Richard's laugh was filled with intense satisfaction. "Cases like yours are the most gratifying. You had the makings of a real beauty when you walked in here. All it took was a little rearranging."

Very lightly, she ran her fingertips down her straight nose, then along her newly reformed jawline. "More than a little." Her hand fell to graze her hip as she turned back to Richard. "And I've put on ten pounds in as many weeks. Funny, but I would have thought that having my jaws banded together and drinking through a straw would make me lose weight."

"You couldn't afford to have that happen, which was why I put you on a high-calorie liquid diet. And now that you can take in solids, I want you to follow the regimen I gave you to the letter. You could still use another five pounds on that slender frame of yours, which means you'll have to work at eating. Remember, you'll be able to chew just a little at a time until the muscles of your jaws regain their strength. How's it been since we removed the bands?"

"A little sore, but okay."

"It's only been three days. The soreness will ease off. You're talking well. In some cases we have to bring in a speech therapist, but I don't think you have to worry about that." He rose from where he'd been perched on the corner of his desk. A soft breeze wafted from the open window behind him, bringing with it the gentle rustle of palms and the fragile essence of frangipani blossoms. "So what do you think? Are you ready to go home?"

Her sigh was a teasing one, and her eyes twinkled. "I don't know. Ten weeks in the Bahamas...body wraps, massages, manicures...sun and sand and sipping all kinds of goodies through straws.... It's not a bad life."

"But the best is ahead. When does your plane leave?"

"In two hours."

"Nervous?"

"About my debut?" She sent him a helpless look of apology. "A little."

"Will someone be meeting you when you land in Boston?"

"Uh-huh. Beth."

He squinted and raised a finger, trying to keep names straight. "Your business partner, right?"

Lauren smiled. "Right. She's dying to show me everything she's done since I've been gone. She rented the spot we wanted in the Marketplace, and from what she writes, the renovations are nearly done. We've got prints and frames on order and have been in close contact with the artists we'll be representing, so it's just a question of getting everything framed and on display.''

"For what it's worth, Lauren, you strike me as a patient but determined woman. I'm sure you'll be successful.'' He threw a gentle arm over her shoulders as she started for the door. "You'll drop me a line and let me know how things are going?''

"Uh-huh.''

"And you've got the name I gave you of the specialist in Boston in case you have a problem?''

"Uh-huh.''

"And you'll be sure to eat—and eat well?''

"I'll try.''

Releasing her shoulder, he turned to study her face a final time. His gaze took in the symmetry of her nose, the graceful line of her jaw and the now-perfect alignment of her chin before coming to rest with warmth on her pale gray eyes. "Smashing, Lauren. I'm telling you, you look smashing.''

"Thank you. Thank you for everything, Richard.''

"My pleasure, sweet lady.'' He gave her hand a tight go-get-'em squeeze, then turned back to his office. The last thing Lauren heard him say was a smug but thoroughly endearing "Good work, Richard. You done us proud this time.''

Laughing softly, she retrieved her suitcase from the reception area and headed for the airport.

"YOU…LOOK…*smashing!*'' was the first thing Beth Lavin could manage to say through her astonishment when, after Lauren had grinned at her for a full minute, she finally realized that it was indeed Lauren Stevenson who stood before her.

The two women hugged each other, and Lauren laughed. "You sound like my doctor.''

"Well, he's right!'' Beth's eyes were wide. Hands on Lauren's shoulders, she shifted her friend first to one side, then the next. "I don't believe it! Your profile is gorgeous, and you've filled out, and your eyes look huge and wide-set, and you had your hair cut.…''

In a self-conscious gesture, one of pure habit, Lauren threaded her fingers into the hair above her ear to draw the thick chestnut fall forward. Then she caught herself. With a concerted effort, she completed the backward swing, letting her hair swirl gently around her ears so that her face was free of the cover she'd hid behind for years. "I really look okay?" There was honest anxiety in her voice.

"You have to ask?"

Lauren gave an awkward half shrug. "I look at myself in the mirror and see a new person, but in my mind I'm the way I've always been."

"I'm no psychologist, but I'd say that's normal." Beth's expression brimmed with excitement and the touch of mischief Lauren knew so well. "A different person—think of the possibilities! What if you were to bump into someone you'd known before, someone like Rafe Johnson—"

"Macho Rafe?"

"Macho Rafe, who would never have thought to look at either of us, but all of a sudden he sees this gorgeous woman and makes his play. You could string him along, then reveal your true identity and cut him off dead. Ah, the satisfaction!"

"You're awful, Beth."

But Beth was staring at her again, this time with a touch of awe. "Maybe.... God, you look marvelous," she said, moments before her face twisted in mock horror. "And *I'm* going to look positively plain next to you!"

"Fat chance, Beth Lavin." Lauren hooked her elbow through her friend's and started them both toward the baggage pickup. She knew that Beth was attractive; she also knew that Beth had worn her dark brown hair in the same long, straight hairstyle for fifteen years and that her clothes—the round-collared blouse, wraparound skirt and flat leather sandals she wore now being a case in point— were as down-country as Lauren's own had always been. "Neither one of us is going to look plain by the time we're ready to open that shop. I learned a lot down there, Beth. There were seminars on hairstyling and makeup and dressing for success. I took tons of notes—"

"You would."

"So would you, so don't give me that," Lauren teased gently. "Tell me, what's the latest with the shop?"

Beth took a deep breath. "I finally got the ad to look the way I wanted it. It'll appear in the next issue of *Boston*. The workmen should be done in another day or two—which is good, because the prints have started arriving. Not to mention the order forms, sales slips and stationery. And the frames and hooks, wire and labels. I've got everything stashed in my apartment."

"How *is* the apartment?"

"I like it. It's compact and within easy walking distance of the shop. Beacon Hill is exciting." Beth paused to ogle her friend again. "I can't believe you!"

"In another minute I'm going to put a bag over my head."

"Don't you dare. I'm thoroughly enjoying riding on your coattails. For that matter, I still wish you'd let me take a bigger apartment so we could room together."

"Rooming together *and* working together, we'd get on each other's nerves in no time. Besides, you want the city, while I want the country. Lots of room, wide-open spaces, trees, peace and quiet."

"You're thinking of that farmhouse."

"Uh-huh."

"You'll be isolated!"

"In Lincoln?" Lauren crinkled her nose. "Nah. I'll only have three acres. When the trees are bare, I'll be able to see neighbors on either side. And the commute will be little more than half an hour."

"But that farmhouse is a wreck!"

"It's simply in need of loving."

"Tell me you've already put in an offer."

Lauren grinned. "I've already put in an offer." At Beth's moan, Lauren delivered an affectionate nudge to her ribs. "When I couldn't get the place out of my mind, I called the realtor. The purchase agreement is ready and waiting to be signed."

"Lauren, Lauren, Lauren, what am I going to do with you?"

Lauren's eyes twinkled. "You're going to put me up at your

place tonight. Then, tomorrow morning, you're going to take me on a grand tour of our pride and joy. After that we are both going shopping on Newbury Street."

"Oh?"

"Uh-huh."

"Could be expensive."

"That's right," Lauren agreed remorselessly.

Beth hunched up her shoulders and gave a naughty chuckle. "I love it, I love it." Then she abruptly narrowed her eyes and flattened her voice to a newspaper-headline drone. "Country bumpkins take city by storm. Effect transformation reminiscent of Clark Kent."

"Clark Kent?" was Lauren's wincing echo.

"Or Wonder Woman, or whomever. Of course, you know we're both a little crazy, don't you?"

"We're twenty-nine. We deserve it."

"I'll tell that to the creditors when they come calling."

Lauren Stevenson wasn't worried about the creditors. She wasn't a spendthrift, but she'd finally come to the realization that life was too short to be lived in a cocoon of timidity. Thanks to her saving prudently and the legacy she'd received when her brother had died nearly a year ago, Lauren had enough money to buy and renovate the farmhouse, pay what little wasn't covered by insurance for the corrective surgery she'd had, get a wardrobe befitting the new Lauren and establish the business.

"Here we go," she said as her luggage appeared on the revolving carousel. "Did you drive over or take a cab?"

"I drove. Your poor car was so glad to see me, I swear it got all choked up."

Lauren grunted. "Must need an oil change. On second thought, it needs to get out of the city. See, *it* wants to live in the country, too."

They left the enclosure of the terminal and headed for the parking lot. "Will you be driving north this weekend?" Beth ventured.

"To see my parents? I guess I'd better."

"I'd think you'd be excited—the new you and all."

Lauren grimaced. "You know my parents. For ultraliberals, they're as narrow as a pair of shoelaces. They didn't see the need for facial reconstruction. They thought I was just fine before."

"But medically, you were suffering!"

"I know that and you know that, and one part of them must know it, too. They're both brilliant, albeit locked in their ivory towers. I think they associate plastic surgery with vanity alone, and vanity isn't high on their list of admired traits. They said they loved me the way I was, and I'm sure they did, because that's what being a parent is all about. But let me tell you, I feel so much better now, even aside from the medical issue, I'm not sure they'd understand."

"Of course they would."

Lauren didn't argue further. Her trepidation about seeing her parents went far beyond the reconstructive surgery she'd had. She was starting a new life, and much of that life was being underwritten by her brother's bequest. Her parents resented that. Brad had been estranged from the family for eleven years preceding his death. Colin and Nadine Stevenson had neither forgotten nor forgiven what they'd considered to be their only son's abdication from the throne of the literati.

Lauren sighed. "Well, whatever the case may be, I'll see them this weekend. It may be the last time I'll be able to in a while." Lips toying with a smile, she darted a knowing glance at Beth. "I have a feeling that the next few weeks are going to be hectic."

"HECTIC" WAS PUTTING IT mildly, though the pace was interlaced with such excitement that Lauren wouldn't have dreamed of complaining. With the completion of the redecoration of the shop, she and Beth began transferring things from Beth's apartment. Prints were framed and hung on the walls. Large art folders, filled with a myriad of additional prints and silk screens, were set in open cases on the floor for easy browsing. Vees of mat board in an endless assortment of colors were placed on Plexiglas stands atop the large butcher-block checkout counter, behind which were systematically arranged frame-corner samples, each attached to the wall with Velcro to facilitate their removal and replacement. Bolts of hand-screened fabric were attractively displayed beside bins containing unstained-wood frame kits; matching pillows were suspended from the ceiling like bananas from a tree.

Lauren signed the agreement on the farmhouse in Lincoln and, since it was already vacant, moved in a short week later. Her enthusiasm wasn't the slightest bit dampened when she saw at firsthand the amount of renovation the place would need. She had only to stand on her front porch and look across the lush yard to the forested growth surrounding her, or to smell the roses that climbed the porch-side trellis, or to listen to the birds as they whistled their spring mating ritual, to know that she'd made the right decision.

And, more than anything, she had only to look in the mirror to realize that she'd truly begun a new life.

In keeping with that new life, she and Beth did go shopping. They bought chic slacks, skirts, bright summer sweaters and lightweight dresses. They bought shoes and costume jewelry to coordinate with the outfits, all the while feeling slightly irresponsible yet enjoying every minute of it. Neither of them had been irresponsible before in their lives, but now they had earned the luxury.

Three weeks after Lauren returned from the Bahamas, the print-and-frame shop opened. It was the second week of June, and the fair-weather influx of visitors to the Marketplace kept a steady stream of shoppers circulating. With sales brisk, Lauren and Beth were ecstatic, so much so that on the first Friday night after closing, they took themselves to nearby Houlihan's to celebrate.

"If business continues this way, we'll have to hire someone to help," Lauren suggested. They were sitting at the crowded bar nursing cool drinks while they waited for their table.

"Tell me about it," Beth complained, but in delight. "There isn't enough time during the day to do bookkeeping, so I've been taking care of it at night. And you're going to need time to work with printmakers and the framer."

"I'll call the museum. Maybe they'll know of someone who'd be interested. If not, we can advertise in the newspaper."

In slow amazement, Beth shook her head. "I can't believe how good things were this week. We really lucked out with the location. There are people all over the place."

"Summer's always a busy season, what with tourists in the city. The Fanueil Hall is one of *the* spots to see."

"Wintertime's supposedly as good. At least, that's what Tom next door—you know, at the sports shop—told me."

Lauren's lips twitched mischievously. "So you've befriended Tom, have you? See what a new hairdo and clothes can do?"

Raking a hand through wavy black hair that had newly been cut to shoulder length, Beth wiggled her brows. "Look who's talking. That guy over there hasn't taken his eyes off you since we walked in."

"He's probably in a drunken stupor and I just happened into his line of vision."

"That's a crazy thing to say. You don't believe how good you look!"

Beth was right. Lauren had been accustomed to being practically invisible where men were concerned, and old habits die hard. Now she dared a quick glance in the mirror behind the bar to remind herself of the woman she'd become. Even her smart cotton sundress of crimson and cream was an eye-catcher.

With a conspiratorial glimmer in her eyes, she turned again to Beth. "Tell me about him. I don't want to be obvious and stare."

Beth had no such qualms, but she spoke in little more than a whisper. "He's of medium height and build and is wearing a brown suit. His hair's dark, a little too short. He's got aviator-style glasses—must be an affectation, since they don't go with the rest of him." Her voice suddenly frosted. "Oops, there's a wedding band." She instantly swiveled in her seat and stared straight ahead. "Forget him. He'd only be trouble."

Lauren grinned. "Forgotten."

"Doesn't it bother you? I mean, I'm sure he'd make a play for you if you flirted a little, and the bum's married."

Shrugging with her eyebrows alone, Lauren took a sip of her drink. "I think you're making too much of it. I was probably right the first time. He's probably in a fog."

Beth grew more thoughtful. "We're going to have to do something about this situation."

"What situation?"

"Our love lives."

"What love lives?"

"That's the point. They're nonexistent. We have to meet guys."

"We have. There's Tom from the sports shop, and Anthony from the music store across the way, and Peter, who sells those super hand-painted sweatshirts, and your neighbors, those three bachelors... We could always reconsider and go to one of their parties."

Beth snorted. "We'd probably get high just walking into the room. I'm sure they're on something. Whenever I run into them, they seem off the wall. I'm telling you, we were smart to chicken out last time. We're so naive that the place could be raided and everyone would run out through the back and leave us holding the bag."

"Hmm. Maybe we'd meet a cute cop."

"I don't know, Lauren. I still think you should have gone out with that guy who came in on Wednesday."

"He was a total stranger, just browsing around."

"He was nice enough. And he did ask you out for drinks. For that matter, the fellow who came in this morning was even nicer and better-looking."

"He was a pest—trying to be so nonchalant about asking where I come from and where I live and, by the way, what my astrological sign is. I don't know what my astrological sign is. I've never been into that."

"You're scared."

Lauren hesitated for only a minute. "Yup."

"But why? You've dated before."

"That was different."

"You're right. This is supposed to be a new life you're leading!"

"On the outside it is. On the inside, well, I guess it'll take me a little longer to catch up. I don't know, Beth. Those guys seemed so...fast. So slick and sophisticated."

"You look slick and sophisticated."

"*Look*, not *am*. You know me as well as anyone does. I've lived a pretty sedate life. What dates I had were with quiet men, more serious, bookish types.''

''Bo-ring.''

''Maybe. But I'm not a swinger.''

''Maybe you're gonna have to learn.''

The hostess called their table then, but Beth picked up the conversation the instant they were seated in the glass-domed room just below street level. ''Maybe we should try a singles bar, or a dating service.''

''If we didn't have the guts to go to your neighbors' party, we'd never have the guts to go to a singles bar. And blind dates give me the willies.''

''Blind dates gave the 'old' you the willies. The 'new' you doesn't have anything to worry about. Besides, it's not really a blind date if you go through a dating service. You get to express your preferences and pick through the possibilities.''

''Just like they get to pick through us. Uh-uh, Beth. I don't really think I'm up for that.''

''Well, we have to do something. Here we are, two wonderful women who are bright and available, and we should be having dinner with two equally as captivating men.''

''Maybe we should put an ad in the paper,'' Lauren joked, then promptly scowled. ''Only problem is that we're cowards. All talk, no action.'' Her eyes grew dreamy. ''They say that good things come to those who wait. I'm more than willing to wait if one day some gorgeous guy who is bright and available and gentle and easygoing will walk up to me and introduce himself.''

''According to women's lib,'' Beth offered tongue-in-cheek, ''we shouldn't have to sit back and wait. We can take the bull by the horns.''

Lauren glanced over Beth's shoulder toward the table at which a lone man sat, just finishing his dinner. He wasn't gorgeous, but he was certainly pleasant-looking. When he looked up and caught her eye, he smiled. Curious, Beth turned also; he shared his smile with her.

''There's your chance,'' Lauren coaxed in a stage whisper filled

with good-humored challenge. "I don't want him, so he's all yours.
Go ahead. Take the bull by the horns."

Turning back to their own table, Beth opened her menu and
concentrated on its contents. Lauren followed suit. Neither woman
noticed when the lone man took his check from the waitress and
headed for the cash register.

CHAPTER TWO

The second week of the shop's existence was as promising as the first had been. Just as Lauren was wondering how she and Beth would be able to cope with the continued pace on their own, a free-lance photographer came in, peddling his wares. He was a young man—Lauren guessed him to be no more than twenty-five—and his pictures were good. He was also looking for part-time work to pay for the increasing costs of his materials and equipment. She hired him instantly, and neither she nor Beth regretted the decision. Now they could take an hour off here or there—albeit separately—to do paperwork, go out for lunch or shop through downtown Boston.

On one such occasion, a week after Jamie had signed on, Lauren returned to the shop with a new sweater in a bag under her arm and a faint pallor on her face. Beth quickly joined her in the back room. "Are you okay?"

Setting the bag on the desk, Lauren sank into a chair. "I think so. You wouldn't believe what just happened to me, Beth. I'd bought this sweater and was walking back along Newbury Street when a car lost control and veered onto the sidewalk. I was day-dreaming, feeling on top of the world, looking at my reflection as I passed store windows. I mean, I was so caught up in being happy that I wasn't paying attention to what was going on around me. If it hadn't been for some stranger who grabbed me out of the way in the nick of time, God only knows what would have happened!"

"Don't think about that. You're safe, and that's all that matters. Was the driver drunk?"

"Who knows? He regained control of the car and went on his merry way again. Didn't even bother to stop and make sure no one was hurt."

"Bastard."

"Mmm."

"The stranger who saved you...was he cute?"

"He was a she," Lauren snapped, but her annoyance was contrived. "And what kind of question is that to ask at a time like this?"

"Have to restore a little humor here. Just think how romantic it would have been if you'd been snatched from the hands of death by a tall, dark and handsome stranger. You could have fainted away in his arms, and he'd have lifted you, holding you ever so gently against his rock-hard chest while he gazed, smitten, upon your lovely face."

Lauren rolled her eyes. "Oh, God."

Beth wagged a finger at her. "Someday it might happen. Miracles are like that, y'know."

"Is this the same woman who was putting in a plug for women's lib not so long ago?" Lauren asked the calendar on the wall, looking back at Beth only when she felt a hand on her arm.

"Are you okay now?" The question was soft and filled with concern. "Want a cold drink or something?"

Taking a deep breath, Lauren shook her head. "I'm fine. It was after the fact, while I was walking, that the shakes set in. But I'm better now. I'd really like to get back to work. That'll keep my mind occupied."

It did, and by the time Lauren arrived in Lincoln that evening, she'd pretty much forgotten the incident. By the next day, it was lost amid more important and immediate activities relating to the shop.

That night she went home, changed into a T-shirt and jeans and made herself dinner, dutifully following the guidelines Richard Bowen had given her. It was an effort at times, since she seemed to be eating so much, but she'd gained three of the five pounds Richard had prescribed, and she had to agree that they looked good on her.

What with the time demands that the shop had made since her return from the Bahamas, she'd had precious little opportunity to organize her thoughts with regard to renovating the farmhouse. Now, pen and paper in hand, she walked from room to room, making lists of what she wanted to have done. The realtor who'd sold her the house had given her the names of a local contractor, a carpenter, an electrician and a plumber. Though she wasn't about to hire any one of them without checking them out further, she wanted to have her thoughts together before arranging preliminary meetings.

After more than an hour of taking detailed notes, she put down the pen and paper and went out to the front porch. The night was clear, the moon a silver crescent in the star-studded sky. On an impulse, she wandered across the yard and stopped at its center, then tipped her head back and singled out a star to wish on.

But what did one wish for when life was already so good? She was totally healthy for the first time in many years. She had a new look, which she adored. She had a new business, and it was well on its way to becoming a success. She had a home of her own, with potential enough to keep her happy for a long, long time.

What did one wish for? Perhaps a man. Perhaps children. In time.

Lowering her head, she started slowly back toward the house. A sound caught her ear. She stopped and frowned. It was a sound of nature, yet odd. It had been distinctly unfriendly.

When it came again, she whirled around. A low growl. She cocked her head toward the nearby trees, then narrowed her eyes on the creature that slowly advanced on her. A dog. She breathed a sigh of relief. Probably one of the neighbors' pets.

Pressing a hand to her racing heart, she spoke aloud. "You frightened me, dog. Is that any way to greet a new neighbor?" As she took a step forward to befriend the animal, it bared its teeth and issued another growl, this one clearly in warning. Lauren held her hands out, palms up, and said softly, "I won't hurt you, boy." She lowered one hand. "Here. Sniff."

Rather than approaching her, the dog growled again, accompanying the hostile sound with a crouch that suggested an imminent attack.

"Hey, don't get upset—" She barely had time to manage the

tremulous words when the dog was on her, knocking her to the ground, snarling viciously. Struggling to fend off the beast, she put her arms up to protect herself and kicked out. But as quickly as it had lunged, the dog retreated, galloping toward the trees and disappearing into the dense growth.

Trembling wildly, Lauren pushed herself up to a seated position. Then, not willing to take a chance that the dog might return, she stumbled to her feet and made a frantic beeline for the house.

Once inside, she leaned back against the firmly shut door, closed her eyes and dragged in a shaky breath. When the worst of the shock had subsided, anger set in. Had it not been so late at night, she would have called the Youngs, her neighbors on the side from which the dog had come. Then again, she realized, perhaps it was lucky it was too late to make a call. Furious as she was that anyone would let such a savage animal loose in even as rural an area as this, she was apt to say something she might later regret. She'd met Carol Young only once. She didn't want to alienate the woman, or her husband, or one of their teenaged boys. Better to let herself calm down. She'd call tomorrow.

Hence, from work the next morning, she dialed the Youngs' number and was relieved to hear Carol herself answer the phone. "Carol, this is Lauren Stevenson. We met several weeks ago when I moved in next door."

"Sure, Lauren. It's good to hear from you. How's it going?"

"Really well.... I hope I'm not dragging you away from anything."

"Don't be silly. One of the luxuries of working at a computer terminal out of my house is that I can take a break whenever I want. The boys have gone to visit their grandparents in Maryland for a week, so I've got more than enough time for a phone call or two. How's the house?"

"Pretty raw still. I've been so busy here at the shop that I haven't had much of a chance to look into hiring workers to fix things up. But that's not why I called." Lauren chose her words carefully, striving to be as diplomatic as possible. "I had an awful scare last night. I was walking out in the yard sometime around eleven when I was attacked by a dog.''

"*Attacked?* Are you all right?''

"I'm fine. The dog jumped me, bared its teeth and made ugly noises, but it ran off before it did any harm.''

"My God! I didn't think there were any wild dogs around here!''

"Then…it's not yours?''

"God, no. Is that what you thought?''

"It came from the trees on your side…. I'm sorry, I just assumed…''

"You should have called us last night. We might have been able to help you track it down. What did it look like?''

"It was big and dark. Short-haired. Maybe a Doberman, but it was too dark out for me to see the dog's exact coloration, and besides, I was too terrified to notice much of anything.''

"You poor girl. I'd have been terrified, too.'' Carol paused, thinking. "To my knowledge, no one in the neighborhood has a dog like that, certainly not one that would attack a person. Sometimes strange animals do wander into the area, though. Maybe you should call the local police.''

Lauren was lukewarm to that idea. As a new resident, she hated to make a stir. "I—I don't think that's necessary. As long as I know the dog wasn't from the immediate vicinity, I feel better. It's probably a watchdog that escaped and got lost. And it didn't hurt me, much as it looked like it could have.''

"Listen, we'll keep an eye out for it, and I'll mention it to some of the other neighbors. But if you catch sight of it again, you really should file a complaint. There's no reason why you should be frightened to walk on your own property.''

Lauren sighed. "I'll be on guard in the future. Thanks, Carol. You've been a help.''

"I wish I could do more. Let me know if something comes up, okay?''

"Okay.''

As Lauren hung up the phone, Beth straightened up from where she'd been leaning unnoticed against the door. "A dog? First a car, now a dog. Lord, the new you is attracting some pretty weird elements."

"Go ahead," Lauren teased, "have a good laugh at my expense."

"I'm not laughing." Beth rubbed her hands together in anticipation of high drama. "Maybe someone's out to get you...someone who lived in that old farmhouse a century ago and whose ghost will never be laid to rest until the rightful owner of the place returns."

"Beth..."

Beth held up a hand. "No, listen. Suppose, just suppose, the ghost is determined to run you out of town, so it plots all kinds of little 'accidents' designed to scare you to death—"

"Beth!"

"And then some gorgeous hunk arrives and just happens to have a secret weapon that can zap even a ghost and reduce it to—to a shredded sheet...."

Lauren sat back in her chair, helpless to contain the beginnings of a grin. "Are you done?"

"Oh, no. The best part comes after the ghost is shredded and you and the gorgeous hunk fall madly in love and live happily ever after."

"Why aren't you working?"

"Because Jamie's working."

"I think *you* should be working." Lauren pushed herself out of her seat. "I think *I* should be working." With a fond squeeze to Beth's arm as she passed, she returned to the front of the shop.

SEVERAL DAYS LATER, Lauren knew that she had to do something about starting the renovation work on her house. The garage door had unexpectedly slammed to the ground when she'd been within mere inches of it. Ironically, if the garage had been nearly as old as the farmhouse itself, its doors would have swung open from the center to the sides, and she would never have been in danger of a skull fracture. But the garage had been added twenty-five years before. Apparently, she mused in frustration, it had been as neglected by recent owners as the house.

She made several calls, setting up appointments to discuss repairs with the men whose names she'd been given. None of them had impressed her on the phone, though she reasoned that there was no harm in meeting with them before she sought out additional contacts. She wanted her home to be perfect, and she was willing to pay to make it so.

With that settled in her mind, she sat down on the living room floor, using the low coffee table as a desk, to write up orders for the framer. But she was distracted. Repeatedly her pen grew still and her gaze wandered to the window. It was dark as pitch outside. She was alone. Anyone could see in, watch her, study her.

Cursing both Beth for her fanciful imaginings and herself for her own surprising susceptibility, she returned to her work. But that night, to her chagrin, she fell asleep wondering if one-hundred-year-old ghosts were capable of sabotaging twenty-five-year-old garage doors.

SHORTLY AFTER NOON on the following day, Lauren saw him for the first time. She was working in the front window of the shop, replacing a framed picture that had been bought that morning, when she happened to glance toward the bench just outside. He was sitting there, quietly and intently. And he was staring at her.

With a tight smile, she looked quickly away, finished hanging the new print, then took refuge in the inner sanctum of the shop.

Fifteen minutes later, during a brief lull in business, she glanced out to find that he hadn't moved. One arm slung over the back of the bench, one knee crossed casually over the other, he appeared to be innocently people-watching—until his gaze penetrated the front window once more.

Again Lauren looked away, this time wondering why she had. There was nothing unusual about a man sitting on a bench in the Marketplace; people did it all the time. And this man, wearing a short-sleeved plaid shirt, jeans and sneakers, looked like a typical passerby. Though he wasn't munching on fried dough or licking an ice cream cone, as so many of the others did, she assumed he was enjoying the pleasant atmosphere. Or waiting for someone. Or simply resting his legs. The fact that he kept looking into the shop was understandable, since it was smack in front of him.

A telephone call came through from one of the printmakers she'd been trying to reach; then customers occupied her time for the next hour and a half. She'd nearly forgotten about the man outside until she left the shop to buy stamps, and even then she was perplexed that she should think of him at all.

He was nowhere to be seen.

AT HOME THAT NIGHT, Lauren was strangely on edge. She didn't know why, and for lack of anything better, she blamed it on the two cups of coffee she'd had that afternoon.

With a critical eye, she looked around the kitchen as she waited for the bouillabaisse she'd bought at a gourmet take-out shop to heat. She intended to do this room in white—white cabinets with white ash trim, white stove and refrigerator, white ceramic tile on the floor. The accent would be pale blue, as in enamel cookware, patterned wallpaper, prints on the wall. Perhaps she'd order a pale blue pleated miniblind—not that she'd originally planned to put anything on the windows, but it occurred to her that she might like the option of privacy for moments like these when the night seemed mysterious.

She was edgy. Too much coffee. That was all.

THE FOLLOWING MORNING, the man was back. Wearing a crisp white polo shirt with his jeans, he was sitting on the bench again, this time with his legs sprawled before him.

"Remarkable, isn't he?" Beth quipped, coming up beside Lauren.

"Who?"

"That guy you're looking at. Have you ever seen such gorgeous hair?" It was light brown with a sun-streaked sheen and was neatly brushed, but thick and on the long side.

"No."

"Or such long legs?"

"No."

"Wonder who he is."

"I don't know."

"Probably just another tourist. Why is it the good ones are here today, gone tomorrow?"

"This one was here yesterday."

"What?"

Lauren blinked once, dragging her gaze from the man to her friend. Absently she wiped damp palms on her slim-cut green linen skirt. "I saw him here yesterday."

Beth's eyes widened. "You're kidding! Do you think he's waiting for...us?"

"Come on, Beth. Why in the world would he be waiting for us?"

"Maybe he heard about these two terrific ladies who own the print-and-frame shop, and he's come to investigate."

"If he had any guts, he'd come in."

"If we had any guts, we'd go out."

"Well, we don't, and apparently he doesn't, either, so that's that." As the two watched, the man got to his feet and ambled off. "That's that," Lauren repeated, not quite sure whether to be relieved or disappointed. There had been something fascinating about the man, not only his legs and his hair but also a certain sturdiness. She wondered if he'd ever owned a black dog that snarled. Then she promptly pushed that thought from her mind, along with all other thoughts of the man—until she caught sight of him again that afternoon.

At first he walked slowly past the shop without sparing it a glance. A few minutes later he returned from the opposite direction, this time pausing near the door before heading for the bench. When Lauren saw him sink onto it, leaning forward with his knees spread and his hands clasped between them, she couldn't help but grow apprehensive. There was something definitely suspicious about the way he glanced toward the shop, then away, then back again.

"Who *is* that man?" she whispered to Beth, who promptly looked up from the VISA charge form she was filling out to follow Lauren's worried gaze.

"So he's back, is he?" Beth resumed writing but spoke under

her breath. "He's a little too rugged for my tastes. You can have him."

"I don't want him," Lauren grumbled from the corner of her mouth, "but I would like to know why he's been loitering around here for two days straight."

"Why don't you go and ask him?" Beth murmured, then, smiling, handed the charge slip and a pen to her customer. "If you'll just sign this and put your address and phone number at the bottom…"

Lauren whispered back in a miffed tone of voice. "I can't just walk out there and *ask* him! He's probably got a very good reason for being there, and I'd feel like a fool."

"Then stop worrying. I'm sure he's harmless."

Lauren wasn't so sure. The man was too intent in his scrutiny of the shop, and she felt the touch of his gaze too strongly to forget him.

When a customer approached her to buy a piece of fabric and have it stretched onto a frame, Lauren welcomed the diversion. When another customer selected a print and needed advice on its framing, she was more than happy to oblige. When a third customer entered the shop in search of several prints to coordinate with swatches of fabric and wallpaper, she immersed herself in the project.

By the time the closing hour drew near, Lauren was tired. She was in the back room, dutifully updating inventory cards and looking forward to a leisurely drive home, a quiet dinner and what was left of the evening with a good book.

"Lauren?" The low urgency in Beth's voice brought Lauren's head up quickly. "He's here, asking for *you*."

"Who—"

"Him." Beth's eyes darted back over her shoulder. "The guy from the bench."

Lauren put down the cards. "He's asking for *me*?"

"By name."

"How did he…he must have…where is he?"

"Right here," Beth mouthed in a way that would have been comical had Lauren been feeling particularly confident.

But she wasn't. This man was different. Not boring-looking. Not slick and sophisticated-looking. Very...different.

Beth made an urgent gesture with her hand.

"I'm coming. I'm coming," Lauren murmured unsteadily. She stood up, smoothing the hip-length ivory cotton sweater over her skirt and squared her shoulders. Then, praying that she looked more composed than she felt, she slowly and reluctantly left her refuge.

CHAPTER THREE

He was much taller close up than he'd appeared through the shop window. And broader in the shoulders. And more tanned. What was most surprising, though, was that he seemed just a little unsure of himself.

"Lauren Stevenson?" he asked cautiously.

She'd come to a stop several feet away and rested her hand on the butcher-block table. "Yes?"

As he studied her more closely, his puzzlement grew. "It's really strange. You're not at all as I expected you to be."

Lauren held her breath for a minute, then asked with a caution of her own, "What had you expected?"

"Someone…well, someone different."

If he had some connection to her past, she realized, not only was his puzzlement understandable but his tact was commendable. Still, she couldn't deny her wariness. The man had been staking her out for two days. "Do you know me? Should I know you?"

For the first time, he smiled. It was a self-conscious smile, endearing in its way. "My name's Matthew Kruger. Matt." He hesitated for a split second. "I was a friend of your brother's."

Lauren wasn't sure what *she* had expected, but it hadn't been this. "Brad's friend?" She was unable to hide either her surprise or her skepticism.

"That's right. I was with him just after the accident. I'm…sorry about his death."

"I am, too," she returned honestly, her brow lightly furrowed as she studied Matthew Kruger. He didn't quite fit into the mold she'd constructed of Brad and his friends. Strange that she'd never heard of him. Then again, perhaps not so strange. She hadn't been any closer to Brad before his death than her parents had been.

"But...it's been a year since he died." Silently she asked herself why this so-called friend of Brad's had waited this long to contact her.

"I know you weren't close, but Brad did mention you to me several times, and since I had to come east on business, I thought I'd look you up."

"What kind of business are you in?"

Another split second's hesitation. "I'm a builder. The development firm I work for has just contracted to do some work in western Massachusetts. I'm here to set things up—to get the ball rolling, so to speak."

She nodded. A builder. Given the pale crow's feet at the corners of his eyes, he was not a builder who directed things from his desk. He was a builder who got his hands dirty. And whose body was well-toned through hard physical labor. *That* she could associate with the image she'd formed of her brother's new life and friends, though if her parents' opinion had been valid, she would have expected someone far coarser. On the surface, at least, Matthew Kruger didn't appear to be coarse. "Clean and all-American" was a more apt description. Could the surface appearance be deceptive?

"I see," she said. Then, feeling uncomfortable, she averted her gaze. In truth, she'd known little about her brother and his way of life...and then there was the matter of this man's physical presence. He intimidated her. "Have you, uh, have you been in Boston very long?"

"A week."

She nodded.

"I'm staying at the Long Wharf Marriott."

"If your work is in the western part of the state, wouldn't it be easier to stay out there?"

"I have been, but our investors are here and there's some paperwork to do, so I decided to take a few days to sightsee." When he suddenly looked beyond her, Lauren swung her head around.

"I'm going to lock up," Beth whispered, darting a curious glance at Matt as she started to pass.

Lauren reached out and caught her arm. "Uh, Beth, this is Mat-

thew Kruger. He is—was—a friend of Brad's.'' Lauren still had
her doubts about that, but saying it simplified the introduction.
''Matt, Beth Lavin.''

Beth had known Brad Stevenson before he'd struck out on his
own, and since she wasn't a member of his immediate family, she'd
been more objective about his departure. Hands clasped tightly before her, she smiled shyly at Matt. ''I'm pleased to meet you.''

''The pleasure's mine,'' Matt said, returning her smile. His gaze
quickly grew apologetic when it sought Lauren's again. ''I don't
want to hold you up if there's something you should be doing
now.''

Lauren opened her mouth to say that she really did have work
to finish, but Beth spoke first. ''Oh, you're not holding her up. We
were pretty much done for the day when you came in. I finished
the inventory cards, Lauren. Why don't you and Matt take off? I'll
close up.''

The last thing Lauren wanted to do was to take off with Matt.
She wasn't convinced he was who he said he was, and even if it
was so, they were on opposite sides of a rift. Besides, he hadn't
asked her to ''take off'' with him.

As though on cue, he did. ''How about it, Lauren?'' He paused,
then took a quick breath. ''I heard there was a sunset cruise around
the harbor. If we hurry, we can make it.''

''Uh, I really shouldn't....''

''Go on, Lauren,'' Beth coaxed. Subtlety had never been her
forte. ''You haven't been out much. It's a beautiful night. The fresh
air will do you good.''

''I'd really like the company,'' Matt urged softly.

His last words trapped Lauren. If he'd come on strong, she might
have easily refused. But he sounded sincere, and she caught a drift
of the same unsureness she'd seen when she'd first faced him.
Though large and rugged-looking, he had an odd gentleness to him.
His eyes were brown, warm and soft. At that moment they hinted
at vulnerability; above all, Lauren Stevenson was a sucker for vulnerability.

Releasing the breath she'd subconsciously been holding, Lauren acknowledged an internal truce. "I'll get my things," she whispered.

Soon after, she and Matt were walking side by side toward the waterfront. He was as quiet as she, casting intermittent glances her way, and she wondered if he felt as strange as she did.

In an attempt to break the silence, she asked the first thing that came to mind. "How did you know I was in Boston?"

"Your parents told me."

"My *parents*!"

He sent her a sidelong glance. "Shouldn't they have?"

"No—yes—I mean, I'm just surprised. That's all."

They walked a little farther before he spoke again. "You're thinking that they wouldn't have willingly given your address to any friend of Brad's."

"I...guess that says it."

A muscle in his jaw flexed. "At least you're honest."

She shrugged. "How much do you know about Brad's reasons for leaving?"

"Only what Brad told me—that your parents couldn't accept his wanting to work with his hands rather than with his mind, that they flipped out when he left college and pretty much washed their hands of him."

Perhaps Matt had known Brad after all. "Spoken that way, it sounds cruel."

"It was, in a way. Brad was badly hurt by the split."

"So were my parents, yet none of the three tried to mend it."

"And you, Lauren? Did you do anything?"

Her gaze shot sharply to his, then softened and fell. "No," she admitted quietly. "I think I might have in time. Then time ran out."

"You regretted the distance?"

"Brad was my only brother. We had no other siblings. He was four years older than I, and his interests were always different. We weren't close as kids, but I like to think that we might have found common ground as we'd gotten older."

They had reached Atlantic Avenue. Matt put a light hand on her elbow as they trotted across to avoid an onrushing car. He dropped it when they reached the median strip, where they waited for a minute before finishing the crossing.

"Then you were seventeen when Brad left."

Lauren blew out a breath. "You really *do* know about Brad, don't you?"

"He told me he was twenty-one when he dropped out. If you were four years his junior..." Matt's voice trailed off and his features tensed. "Did you think I was lying about being his friend?"

"No. Well, maybe. I have to take your word for it that you knew him, since he can't verify it, can he?"

"Are you always distrustful?"

She looked him in the eye. "Only when I see someone lurking outside my shop for two days before coming in."

"Oh. You saw me."

"Yes." Was that a sudden rush of color to his cheeks? She wondered if it was guilt, or embarrassment. In case it was the latter, she softened her tone. "I assume you weren't trying to hide."

"Actually," he confessed, "I was trying to get up the nerve to come in."

That was a new one in her experience. "Why ever would you have to get up the nerve to approach *me*?"

"Several reasons. First, I knew there were hard feelings where Brad was concerned and I wasn't sure how I'd be received. Second, I wasn't sure if it was really you." His gaze slid from one to another of her features. Again that puzzled look crossed his face. "You look so different. Very...very pretty."

Lauren clutched the shoulder strap of her bag more tightly. "Brad had a picture."

"An old one. You were sixteen at the time."

For reasons she wasn't about to analyze, she didn't want to go into the matter of her reconstructive surgery. "It was a long time ago," she said quietly. "People change."

"I'll say," Matt drawled. "Still, it's amazing..." He seemed about to go on, and for an instant Lauren wondered just how much Brad had told him about her. She was saved when he looked up and announced tentatively, "I think this is it."

She followed his gaze toward where the wharf and its cruise boats loomed. "Looks like it. This is really the blind leading the blind. I went to college in Boston, but that was a while ago. I haven't been back for very long."

"Are you living here in the city?"

The glance she sent him held subtle accusation, but there was a whisper of amusement underlying her words. "What did my parents tell you?"

Reading her loud and clear, he fought back a grin. "Just the name of the shop. I assume they wanted to keep things on a strictly business level."

"I'm sure they did."

"And you?"

"And me what?"

He was suddenly serious. "Would you put me down because I don't have a Ph.D. in some esoteric subject?"

"I don't have a Ph.D. in *any* subject."

"You have a master's degree in art. I never went to college."

"But you're successful in what you do. At least, if you're traveling across the country, the firm you work for must be doing well...you must be valued." Having doubted his story such a short time ago, she amazed herself by coming to his defense. Suckers for vulnerability weren't always the most prudent. She took a deep breath. "No, Matt. I'm not like my parents. Brad wasn't the only one who had differences with them. It's just taken me a little longer to act on those differences."

Their conversation was cut short when they arrived at the ticket booth. Matt paid their fare, and they boarded the boat. Wending their way through the other groups that had gathered, they climbed to the top deck and found an empty place by the rail to look back at the city skyline.

"I love Boston," Lauren mused after several minutes of silent appreciation.

"Explain."

"It's bigger than Bennington and that much more exciting, yet smaller than New York and that much more manageable. You can understand it, get to know it. It's livable.''

''You have an apartment?''

''A farmhouse.''

''In the *city*?''

''In Lincoln—'' She caught herself and scowled at him. ''That was sneaky. You took advantage of me when my defenses were down.''

He grinned amiably. ''Sorry about that. Do you really own a farmhouse?''

Somehow further prevarication seemed silly. ''Uh-huh. It's old and needs a whole load of work before its potential can be realized, but it's on a great piece of land and has charm, real charm.''

''Old places are like that. History adds character. That's one of the reasons *I* like Boston. Wandering around, seeing where the Boston Massacre took place or where the Declaration of Independence was first read—it gives you goose bumps.'' He paused, staring at Lauren. ''Why are you grinning?''

''You and goose bumps. You're so big and solid. It seems a contradiction.''

''No,'' he said gently. ''The goose bumps I'm talking about have an emotional cause. Big and solid don't necessarily mean unfeeling.''

''I didn't mean—''

''I know.'' His point made, he left it at that.

They lapsed into silence, watching as the gangplank was drawn up and the boat inched away from the dock. Soon the engines growled louder. The boat made a laborious turn, then picked up speed and entered the main body of the harbor, moving at a steady, if chugging, pace.

''Would you like a drink?'' Matt asked.

Lauren drew herself back from her immersion in the scenery. ''No—uh, make that yes. A wine spritzer, if they can handle it, or lemonade. Something cool.''

With a nod, he made his way back across the deck and disappeared down the stairs leading to the lower level. Following his progress, Lauren had to admit that he was as attractive as any other man in sight. It wasn't that he was beautiful in the classic sense; his chin was too square, his nose a shade crooked, his skin too weathered. But he exuded good health and strength and competence. He'd crossed the shimmying deck without faltering.

The wind whipped through her hair as she turned to face the sea once more. She concentrated on the sights—the Aquarium, the Harbor Towers, the piers with their assortment of fishing boats and tankers, the waterfront restaurants. Only when Matt returned and she smiled did she realize how much nicer the setting seemed with him by her side.

"Two lemonades." He handed her one. "The spritzer was beyond the bartender, and the other drinks were heavier. There were some hot dogs down there, but they looked pretty sad." He took a bag of potato chips from under his arm, opened it and held it out. She munched one, then washed it down with a drink.

"Tell me about Brad," she surprised herself by saying.

Somber-eyed, he studied her expression. "I'm not sure you really want to know."

She attributed his hesitancy to her own obvious ambivalence. "You may be right. But...I guess I really am curious. I've never met anyone who knew him after he left. I'm not sure I should pass the opportunity by."

Matt tossed several chips into his mouth. "What do you want to know?" he asked between stilted bites.

"Did he work for your company?"

"No."

"Had he always been in San Francisco?" She knew that was where he'd died.

"He started out in Sacramento."

"As a carpenter."

"That's right. By the time he came to San Francisco, though, he was doing a lot of designing."

"Designing what?"

Matt hesitated for an instant. "Houses, mostly. Some office parks. As an architect, he was a natural."

"Is that how he was viewed—as an architect?"

"No. He didn't have the credentials. He was like a ghost-writer, presenting rough sketches to the company's architect, who then embellished and formalized the sketches."

"Were you familiar with his company?"

"We were competitors."

The words were simple and straightforward, yet something about the way they'd been offered gave Lauren the impression that Matt hadn't particularly cared for Brad's outfit. "But still, you were friends. How did that work?"

Matt seemed to relax somewhat. "Very comfortably. Our respective superiors held the patent on rivalry. Brad and I rather enjoyed fraternizing with the enemy."

"How did you meet?"

"In a bowling league."

Her expression grew distant. "Funny, I can't picture Brad bowling. But then, I can't picture him sweating on the roof of a house, either." She tore herself from her musings. "What else did you do together?"

"Ate out. Sometimes double-dated. We vacationed together— there were six of us, actually. We rafted down the Colorado, went on horseback through parts of Montana. It was fun."

"Very macho," she teased and was rewarded by a sheepish grin from Matt.

"I suppose."

Her smile lingered for a minute before fading. "Brad never married." She'd learned that when she'd been informed by the lawyer that she was the sole beneficiary of her brother's estate. "I wonder why."

"Maybe he never met the right girl, one who could accept him as he was."

"Have you ever married?" she asked on impulse. Matt stared at her for a minute, then shook his head. "Why not?"

"Same reason."

She pondered his answer quietly. "I can understand it in Brad's case. He grew up in an atmosphere in which intellectual excellence was the only valid goal. He struggled to keep up for a while, then simply threw in the towel. Neither my parents nor their circle of friends could accept his behavior. Long before he left, he was labeled a misfit. I'm sure he was sensitive about it."

"We all have our sensitivities."

"What are yours, Matt? Why would a woman have trouble accepting you as you are?"

He chomped several more potato chips and would have seemed perfectly nonchalant had it not been for the ominous darkening of his eyes. "I'm blue-collar all the way. I don't have a pedigree, or a series of fancy qualifying initials to put after my name. Over the years I've done well in my work, but that doesn't mean I aspire to own my own company, or that one day I won't decide to chuck it all and go back to building log cabins. If a woman thinks she's getting a future real-estate tycoon in me, she'd better think again."

Lauren couldn't miss the bitterness in his words. "You've been burned."

"Several times." He looked out over the water and his tone gentled, growing apologetic enough to defy arrogance. "I've always attracted women pretty easily. But physical attraction isn't enough. Not by a long shot."

"The grass is always greener..." she said softly. "There are those of us who'd *love* to have looks that would attract."

Matt eyed her as if she were crazy. "But you *do*! I can't believe there isn't a line of men waiting to take you out!"

It took Lauren a minute to realize what she'd said and why Matt had answered as forcefully as he had. She'd forgotten. That happened a lot. A slow warmth crept up her neck. Compliments were still new to her, and from as physically superb a man as Matthew Kruger... "I don't know about a line," she said simply.

"Then there's one man?"

She shook her head.

"You're a beautiful woman, Lauren. Surely you've had offers."

Again she shook her head, this time with a self-conscious half smile.

"Why not?"

At his bluntness, she burst out laughing. "You're almost as un-diplomatic as Beth."

"I'm sorry. I was just curious." He held up a large, well-formed hand. "Not that I'm saying you should be married. You're only, what, twenty-nine, and you're obviously building a career for yourself." A new thought hit him, and he frowned. "You said you haven't been in Boston for very long. Then the shop is a recent thing?"

"We've been open barely a month."

"And before that?"

"I worked in a museum back home."

He rubbed his forefinger along the rim of his paper cup. "Back home. That could explain it. Brad told me about back home."

"What did he say?"

"That it was stifling. One-dimensional. You were either an artist or an academician affiliated with the college."

"He was being unfair. Bennington's a beautiful place. Some fascinating people chose to live there. Brad just didn't."

"Nor did you, apparently. Why did you leave, Lauren?"

"Because I wanted to open the shop."

"But you could have opened a shop in Bennington."

She shook her head. "Too small a market."

"So you're going for the big time."

"I want the shop to be a success, yes," she said on a defensive note. "I may not aspire to put out one profound treatise after another the way Mom and Dad have, but that doesn't mean I can't aim to do what I do well."

There was a wistfulness to Matt's smile. "Now you *do* sound like Brad. He was so determined...." A flicker of uncertainty crossed his brow.

"So determined...?"

It was a while before Matt finished his sentence, and then it was with care. "To be successful. Recognized. I'm not sure he realized it, or realized what was driving him, but as often as he claimed that he was doing his own thing and didn't care what his family thought, I think he was kidding himself."

"Was he happy, Matt?"

Matt had to consider that. "In a way, yes."

Peering down at the bits of lemon pulp clinging to the sides of her cup, Lauren spoke more slowly. "All we were told about the accident was that he was supervising some blasting and got caught in the mess. Was there...anything more to it?"

"That was it."

He'd answered quickly and with finality. Not knowing why, Lauren was taken aback. "You saw him right after?"

"At the hospital." His tone was clipped. As he went on, its harshness eased. "Brad was lucid for a time, but between the internal injuries and everything else—well, maybe it was for the best. If he'd lived—and the chances of that were slim from the start— he would have been a quadraplegic. I don't think he would have been able to bear that."

"No," she whispered, and when she looked up, her eyes were moist. "I feel guilty about it sometimes."

"Guilty?"

"Everything I have now—the shop, the farmhouse, this—" she gestured broadly toward herself "—has come from the money he left me. Did you know that?"

Matt put his hand on her shoulder and massaged it gently. His voice was much, much softer, his focus shifted. "That was Brad's wish. I was the one who passed it on to the lawyer. Given the circumstances, Brad gained a measure of peace from it."

Lauren nodded, then somehow couldn't stop the overflow of words. "If it hadn't been for Brad, I'd probably still be back in Bennington. Even aside from the money, his death was a turning point for me. For the first time in my life, I stopped to think of my own mortality, of what I'd have to my credit when the time came, of what I'd be leaving behind. That was when I decided to move to Boston and open the shop. I only wish Brad could know how much better I feel about myself now."

"It's enough that you know, Lauren. If Brad were here to see you, I'm sure he'd be proud."

She looked timidly at Matt, then away, and took a long, shuddering breath. "It's too bad we can't have it both ways—too bad I can't have what I do and have Brad alive to see it."

Slipping his arm across her back, Matt drew her to his side. His warmth was the comfort she needed. "Life is cruel that way, filled with choice and compromise. Even those who reach the heights make sacrifices along the way. The best we can do is to decide exactly how much we're prepared to give up and move on from there."

As she raised her gaze to his, her cheek brushed his shoulder. It seemed a perfectly natural gesture. "But that's a negative view."

"It's realistic."

"Maybe I'm more of a romantic, then. I want to focus on the goals and face the hurdles as I come to them."

He shrugged. "And I want to be prepared for the hurdles. It's just a different approach. Who's to say which one is better?"

She didn't answer. Her gaze was suddenly locked with his, lost in his, and she struggled to cope with the intensity. He was a virtual stranger, yet she'd told him things she'd never told another soul. Was it the fact that he was a link to her brother, or that he was a good listener, or that he'd shared his own thoughts with her? She'd been wary of him at first; she still was, in some respects. And yet...and yet she was drawn to him....

The sudden blast of the boat's horn made them both jump. They looked around to find the bulk of the passengers crowded on the other side of the deck, waving to a passing tall ship. Without releasing her, Matt moved to join them.

"Impressive," he breathed, taking in the towering masts and ancient fittings of the proud vessel. "Too bad she's not under sail."

"Mmm. It's almost disillusioning. There weren't any motors in the old days."

"Or Sony Walkmans." He pointed to the sailor perched on the rigging, headset firmly in place. Lauren smiled at the sight, then shifted her gaze to the airport.

"If I had a downtown office with a view of all this, I doubt I'd ever get any work done. I could sit for hours watching the planes take off and land."

"Not me. Even watching gives me the willies. I'm a white-knuckle flier."

Lauren stared at him in disbelief. "A big guy like you?"

"Big guys crash harder."

She suppressed a smile. "I suppose you've got a point. But you do fly."

His expression was priceless, a blend of revulsion and resignation. "When necessary."

"Which is far too often for your tastes."

"You got it."

Her eyes took on an extra glow. "I don't think I could ever fly too often for my tastes. Not that I've flown that much, but I've always been so excited about getting where I'm going that I just sit back and relax. That's about all you can do, y'know. Once you're in the air, you're in fate's hands. It's not as if you have control over anything that might happen to the plane."

His grunt was eloquent. "That's what bothers me. I *like* to be in control. Just like measuring hurdles...."

Lauren narrowed her eyes playfully. "I'll bet you're the type who checks over every blessed inch of a new car before you venture to slide behind the wheel."

"I also sample the whipped cream, then the nuts, then the hot fudge, then the ice cream before I take a complete spoonful of a sundae."

"But where's the surprise, then?"

"The surprise is in the perfect blend of ingredients. The way I do it, y'see, I minimize the chance of disappointment. If something's not quite right, I can get it fixed, and if I can't do that, at least I'm prepared, so my expectations are on a par with reality."

"You're a man of caution."

"Quite."

"Another reason why you sat outside my shop for two days." She tipped her head. "Tell me, what would have happened if I'd looked exactly like that picture you'd seen?"

"I'd have come in the first day."

Lauren had wondered if he would ever have come in. "I don't understand. My looks made you *cautious*?"

"That's right."

"But...I look better than I did in the picture, don't I?"

"You look gorgeous."

"Then?" Mired in confusion, she made no protest when he turned her into him and crossed his wrists on the small of her back.

"Gorgeous women intimidate me. I've been burned, remember?"

His smile didn't ease her this time. Her eyes widened. "Do you think I'm after your *body*?"

He winced and shot an embarrassed glance to either side. "Shh."

She grasped his arms to push him away. When he held her steady, she whispered, but vehemently, "Is that what you think? Well, let me tell you, *I* didn't ask you to walk into my shop. I didn't ask you to take me on a cruise. I don't want any part of your body! And even if I did, that wouldn't be all I'd want. Before I ever got around to your body, I'd make sure that I wanted the rest." She snorted in disgust and turned her face away. "Of all the self-centered, arrogant—"

"That wasn't what I meant, Lauren. You're jumping to conclusions. Has it ever occurred to you that you can intimidate a man?"

"*Me?*"

"Yes, you. I'd expected to find a quiet—" he hesitated, then cleared his throat "—rather thin and plain-looking young woman living an equally quiet life in the country. At least, that was what Brad had implied. If he could only see you now! You own your own shop—in the city, no less. You're beautiful. You dress smartly. You're bright as all get-out. And you're sure as hell not falling at *my* feet." He took a begrudging breath. "Yes, I'm intimidated."

Lauren had felt suspended during his short speech. Now she realized how absurd her own attack must have sounded. "Funny," she managed to say in a small voice, "you don't look intimidated."

He squeezed his eyes together. Even before they relaxed and opened, a smile had begun to form on his lips. "I guess I'm not now, at least not as much as I was before. For someone who is beautiful and chic and super-intelligent, you're really pretty normal.''

She smiled self-consciously, averting her gaze. "I think we're missing the sunset."

"I think you're right."

They returned to their own side of the boat, then switched when the vessel made a slow turn and headed back to the docks. Neither of them said very much. Lauren, for one, was lost in her own thoughts.

In spite of Matt's explanation, she still felt stunned that her looks had put him off. Initially her pride had been hurt. The thought that she'd drastically improved her appearance only to find that it kept men away was unsettling; hence she'd lashed out.

Or had she simply been searching for a wedge to put between Matt and her?

He was too attractive, too easy to be with, too firmly aligned with Brad and a way of life that she'd been indoctrinated to frown on. No, she wasn't exactly frowning now, but neither could she turn her back on the disappointment of Brad's long-ago desertion. And then came the guilt. She'd acceded to her parents' view of Brad as a failure, yet she'd accepted his money—lots of it. Did an architect masquerading as a carpenter earn that much money? Had he banked every spare cent for some eleven years?

She realized that there were many more questions she wanted to ask Matt about Brad. In hindsight, she wondered if he'd been evasive when talking about her brother's work. His answers had been short, his expression solemn. He'd opened up more about Brad's personal life, yet she couldn't help but wonder if there were some things he hadn't said.

The boat pulled alongside the dock, its lines were secured, and the gangplank was lowered.

"You must be starving," Matt said. "Want to catch a bite at my hotel?" The Marriott was only a short distance from where they stood, but Lauren quickly shook her head.

"I'd better be getting home. It's been a long day."

"Are you sure?"

This time she steeled herself against the cocoa softness of his gaze. She needed time to acclimate herself to his appearance in her life. He was a figure from Brad's past, yet the immediacy of him unbalanced her. What she craved was the solid footing of her own home.

"I'm sure," she said with a gentle smile. "But...thank you, Matt. This has been lovely."

"At least let me walk you to your car. It's pretty dark."

"And the path to my car is well lighted all the way. Really, I'll be fine."

Matt straightened his shoulders and nodded. "Well, take care, then."

She started off, half turning as she walked. "Good luck with your work. I hope it goes well."

He nodded again and waved, then turned and headed for his hotel. Lauren didn't look back until she'd crossed Atlantic Avenue, and by then he was gone.

THE LATE-AFTERNOON SUN glanced brilliantly over the Hollywood Hills, but the shades in the study were drawn as its proprietor entered, strode across the tiled floor to the desk and picked up the telephone.

"Yes?"

"We're on our way."

"It's about time. I'd assumed I would have heard from you sooner."

"She's a clever girl. Covered her tracks like a pro—almost. I still don't know who helped her out of L.A., but you were right about the Bahamas. She went back to the same clinic she visited when the two of you were vacationing on the islands last fall. That was her only slipup."

"Then you've found her?"

"She had plastic surgery, just like you thought she would. Not much. Subtle changes. There was a phony 'before' shot stuck into the doctor's files and a bunch of misleading medical reports, but the 'after' shot had just enough similarity to the real thing to give her away. Her hair's different now, darker and shorter. And she's taken a different name.''

"We knew she would. Where is she?''

"Boston. She just opened a little print-and-frame shop.''

"With the money from the gifts *I* gave her. A print-and-frame shop. That's priceless.''

"You'd be amazed if you saw her. She's the image of innocence. Dresses just so—stylish but understated, nothing flashy like before. Drives a Saab she must have picked up secondhand. Has this woman working with her who looks nearly as snowy-pure as she does, and a young guy who's probably eating out of—''

"What about the jewels? Have you located the fence?''

"No. No sign of the jewels at all. She may have started with the furs. They'd be easy to sell and nearly impossible to trace.''

"Have you made contact with her?''

"Got a good man on it. She's already had a couple of little 'accidents'—nothing to hurt her actually, just set her to wondering.''

"Is she?''

"Yeah. She's looking nervously around her front yard each time she leaves the house.''

"The house?''

"An old farmhouse she picked up outside the city.''

"*With my money!*''

"It'll all come back to you. Between the shop and the house, she's made investments that'll come back with interest.''

"I want you to find the jewels.''

"We're looking. She doesn't have them at home. I went through the place myself today.''

"Ransacked it?''

"Nothing that obvious. Just moved little things here and there. She'll suspect someone's been snooping, but she won't be sure enough to call the cops.''

"She wouldn't *dare* call the cops. She knows how long my arm is, and she wouldn't do anything to risk blowing her cover. So where do we go from here?''

"I've got a few more mishaps up my sleeve. You want her to squirm. I want her to squirm. She's gonna squirm."

"You're having fun, aren't you?"

"You could say that. I feel like I let you down before, and it was her fault. This is my revenge."

"It's *my* revenge, and don't you forget it."

"No way, boss. No way."

CHAPTER FOUR

Beth was lying in wait for Lauren when she arrived at work the next morning. "Well? How did it go? What happened? Your parents would *die* if they knew you were dating him, but I think it's great! A sunset cruise... I've never heard of anything so romantic in my life. He may be rugged, but he's got style. Was he nice? Did you invite him back to Lincoln after the cruise? I almost called you, but I didn't dare. *Tell* me, Lauren. Tell me *everything*!"

Closely shadowed by her friend, Lauren continued through to the back room and plunked her purse in the bottom drawer of the file cabinet. "How can I tell you anything if I can't get a word in edgewise?"

"Okay. I'll shush. Give."

Lauren only wished she could. She'd spent a good part of the night thinking about Matthew Kruger, and she still didn't know what to make of him. "Yes, he was nice. Yes, the cruise was nice. Romantic? Well, I don't know about that. And no, I did not invite him back to Lincoln."

"Why not?"

"Because it wasn't called for. And we weren't on a *date*. He was my brother's friend. That's all. We talked a little about Brad and a little about other things. Period."

"Did he explain why he'd been hanging around outside for so long?"

For the first time that morning, Lauren smiled. Dryly. "If you can believe it, he was trying to get up his nerve to come in. Brad had shown him a picture of me. I wasn't quite what he'd expected."

"That's marvelous!" Beth's eyes grew rounder. "The handsome prince was so taken with your beauty that he was actually awestruck. I love it!"

Lauren screwed up her face and carefully enunciated her words. "Handsome prince? Taken with my beauty? Awestruck? What *have* you been reading, Beth?"

"Come on. I think this is great. Are you seeing him again?"

"I don't know."

"What do you mean, you don't know?"

"Just that. He didn't say anything about seeing me again, and I wasn't about to put him on the spot." Lauren reached for a can and began to spoon fresh coffee into a filter.

"'Put him on the spot.'" Beth snorted. "Straight from the mouth of the old you. The new you is sought-after. You'd be doing him a favor to *consider* seeing him again.... Well?"

"Well, what?"

"Are you?"

"What?" Lauren measured out water and poured it into the top of the coffee maker.

Beth sighed in frustration. "Considering seeing him again."

"I don't know."

As coffee began to trickle slowly into the carafe, Beth rolled her eyes and muttered, "This is absurd. We're going in circles. Do you or do you not want to see the man again?"

Lauren turned toward her friend. "I don't know! Damn it, Beth, how can I give you a better answer if I don't have one myself? Yes, I liked him, and under normal circumstances I'd be glad to see him again. But these aren't exactly normal circumstances. In the first place, the man lives on the West Coast. He's only here doing business, most of which keeps him in the western part of the state. He'll be going back to San Francisco and he hates to fly. I don't exactly have the time to zip out to see him every weekend— not to mention the money, when there are so many other things I have it earmarked for." She sucked in a breath. "And in the second place, he was Brad's friend. You're right. My parents would go bonkers."

"You're an adult. They didn't want you to go to the Bahamas, but you did it. They didn't want you to leave Bennington or open this shop, but you did both. You don't need their permission. You can do whatever you want and see whomever you want."

Lauren sighed loudly. "I know that, Beth. I'm not asking their permission for anything. I have qualms of my own about seeing Matt again. He was a friend of Brad's. He sees me and my parents through Brad's eyes. And he's a confirmed bachelor who loves taking off with the guys and shooting the rapids for a week. So what's the point?"

"The point," Beth murmured, wiggling her brows, "is that he's single and gorgeous."

"I thought he was too rugged for you."

"For me, yes. For you, no. The two of you looked great walking out of here together last night. I'm telling you, see where it leads."

"You have a one-track mind," Lauren grumbled, brushing a wisp of hair from her low-belted, apricot jersey dress.

"And you're in a lousy mood. Where's your sense of humor? Hey, I'll bet Matthew Kruger would be the *perfect* one to ward off the ghost that's hanging out at your farm."

"Humph. I'm beginning to think I need something. That ghost was at work again."

Beth blinked once, then again. The coffee continued to trickle in the background, its rich aroma wafting from the carafe and spreading through the small room. "Excuse me?"

"That ghost. I swear it went through my things yesterday."

"Wait a minute, Lauren. There are no such things as ghosts."

"You're the one who's been touting them."

"I was teasing."

"Then I guess you've teased once too often. I'm almost becoming a believer."

"You're not serious!"

"Well, maybe not. But still…it was weird." She made a face accordingly. "I could have sworn I'd put certain things in certain places at home, and they were still there, just…shifted somehow."

Beth leaned back against the desk and crossed her arms over her chest. She might have been a psychiatrist for the indulgent tone of her voice. "I think you're going to have to be more specific. In what ways were they 'shifted'?"

"Small ways. A bottle of perfume turned around so that the sculpted bird faced the wall. A pair of shoes neatly set in the closet, with the right shoe on the left and the left one on the right. A pair of underpants perfectly folded, but inside out. I always turn them the right way before I fold them. *Underpants*." She shuddered, then whispered in dismay, "Can you believe it?"

"Maybe you should call the police."

"I thought about that, but I feel like a fool! I mean, it's not as if anything were taken. The locks on the doors were intact, and as far as I could tell, none of the windows had been jimmied open. Ruling out a breaking and entering, I'd say someone might have just walked in, except that I'm the only one with a key."

"How about the realtor who sold you the place?"

"I had the locks changed right after I moved in." Lauren gave a guttural laugh. "That's about all I've done, but it does preclude a human visitor." She took a deep breath. "So either it *was* a ghost, or I'm simply not as meticulous about things as I used to be. Maybe that's it. I mean, I suppose I have been preoccupied with the shop. It's very possible that I wasn't paying attention when I put the perfume bottle back or took the shoes off or folded the laundry." She looked beseechingly at Beth. "So what are the police going to say?"

"Mmm. I see your point. Maybe you should get a dog."

"One encounter with a dog on my property was enough."

"Then a burglar alarm system."

"A burglar alarm isn't going to stop a ghost. And it sure isn't going to improve my own absentmindedness, if that's what it was." She reached for a clean mug and poured herself some coffee. When she looked up to find a smug smile spreading over Beth's face, she scowled. "Now what are you thinking?"

"That I was right all along. Matthew Kruger may be just the one to protect you. All you have to do is to coax him along. Before you know it, he'll be thinking of that farmhouse as his second home."

"Matt is going back to San Francisco. How many times must I tell you that? And even if he wasn't, I can't use the man that way."

"Seems to me he'd get something out of the arrangement."

"Humph. When—and if—I take a live-in lover, it'll be because I truly adore whoever he is, not because I need him as a body-guard."

"You could truly adore your bodyguard."

Lauren sank into a chair and raised her mug. She spoke slowly and distinctly, as though her friend might not understand her otherwise. "I am going to drink my coffee now and gather my thoughts. Then I am going to face this new day with a bright smile and a free mind." She closed her eyes, brought the mug to her lips, sipped the coffee, then sighed.

Somewhere between the sip and sigh, Beth gave up on her and left the room.

THE SHOP GREW BUSIER as the noon hour approached, and Jamie's arrival at one was a relief. Beth ran out to pick up sandwiches, returning shortly thereafter with news far more interesting than that the rye bread had caraway seeds.

"Have you looked outside lately?" she murmured excitedly to Lauren as she passed on her way to the back room.

Lauren had been helping a customer decide which of two silk-screen prints to buy. She glanced toward the front window.

Matt. Sitting on the bench she was coming to think of as his. Reading a book.

Reading a book? That was a novel approach! Not that she doubted he was a reader; he looked more than comfortable with the paperback in his hand. But reading a book in the middle of the bustling Marketplace and on that particular bench? What was he thinking? What did he want?

She returned her attention to her customer, pleased that in the minute she'd been distracted he'd decided on the print she'd originally recommended. Decisions on its framing proved to be more difficult, what with so many different mat boards and frames to choose from, but Lauren didn't mind. This was the part of the job she really enjoyed, and the shop made far more money on matting and framing than on the sale of the prints themselves.

It was only after she'd written up the customer's order, taken a deposit and let her gaze follow him to the door that she glanced again at the bench outside.

Matt was still reading.

Beth, who'd finished her lunch and come to relieve Lauren, was perplexed. "What's he doing out there?"

"Reading, obviously."

"But what's he *really* doing?"

"Beats me."

"Aren't you curious?"

"Sure."

"Aren't you going to satisfy your curiosity?"

"I'm going to have lunch. I'm famished."

"You're hopeless, is what you are," Beth declared. Lauren merely shrugged as she headed for the back room.

"Hopeless" wasn't exactly the word for it. She was flattered. Matt couldn't have chosen that bench by chance. But she was also puzzled. If he wanted to see her, wouldn't he simply come into the shop?

Did she want to see him? She still wasn't sure. There was something intimidating about him, and she couldn't quite pinpoint its cause.

Unwrapping her sandwich, she ate it slowly, sipping occasionally from a can of Coke. By the time she was finished, her curiosity had risen right along with her energy level. She *did* want to know what Matthew Kruger was up to. What right did he have to monopolize that bench? What right did he have to distract her? What right did he have to make her feel *guilty* for not acknowledging his presence?

Without further thought, she crossed through the shop, breezed out the door and approached the bench. Matt didn't look up. She stood there for a minute, then quietly eased herself down on the bench several feet away from him, far enough to preclude any implication of intimacy.

While he continued to read, she studied him closely. Other than his eyes, which moved rhythmically from one line to the next, his features were at rest. His lean cheeks were freshly shaved. His tawny hair was clean and vaguely windblown, haphazardly brushing his forehead and collar. He wore his usual jeans and sneakers, but today he'd put on a pink oxford cloth shirt. If she'd ever thought pink was feminine, she quickly revised that opinion. With his sleeves rolled to just beneath the elbow, and with the bronzed hue of his forearms, neck and chin contrasting handsomely with the shirt, he looked thoroughly male. Almost rawly so.

Reaching out, Lauren removed the book from his hands. She caught a brief glimpse of his startled expression before she turned the book over, carefully holding his place with her fingers, and examined the cover.

"*A Savage Place*," she read aloud. "It's a good one. But some of Parker's other books are set more in Boston. His descriptions of the city are priceless. You really should read them."

"I have," Matt answered. His liquid brown eyes caught hers when she lifted her head. "I've been a Parker fan for years."

Any indignance Lauren might have felt when she'd marched out of the shop had vanished. For that matter, she couldn't remember what doubts she'd had about Matt yesterday, last night, this morning. She couldn't seem to think of anything except the fact that his eyes were the warmest she'd ever seen and that his smile did something strange to her insides.

With a determined effort, she refocused on the book. "Like mystery and a little bit of violence, do you? Or is it Spenser's machismo that intrigues you?" The softness of her tone kept any sting from her words.

"Actually, it's Parker's writing style I enjoy. It's clean and crisp. Fast-paced. Filled with wit and dry humor."

She nodded. So it hadn't been an act, Matt's immersion in the book. He obviously knew his Parker and appreciated him.

"Why this bench?" Lauren asked suddenly. Her eyes had narrowed and were teasing in their way.

Matt stared at her, opened his mouth, then promptly shut it again.

As she watched, his expression grew sheepish, filled with a boyish guilt that tugged at her heartstrings. When he finally did explain, she knew she was lost.

"I like this bench because it's close to your shop. I guess I was hoping you'd come out. What I was *really* hoping was that you'd take off with me for the afternoon and we'd rent a sailboat and join the others on the Charles. I got a view of the Basin from the thirty-second floor this morning. It looked so inviting." His voice fell, along with the expression on his face. "But you have to work. I know. It's not fair for me to come along and expect you to drop everything you're doing. You have responsibilities. I accept that, and respect it."

Lauren didn't know whether to hug him in consolation or hit him over the head with his book. "How can you *do* this to me, Matt? It's not fair!" That he should be a lovable little boy in a virile man's body. That he should be a stranger, yet so very familiar. That he should offer excitement in such a gentle and undemanding way. None of it was fair.

"Then you'll come sailing with me?"

"You were right the first time. I can't."

"But you would if you could."

"Yes."

He smiled and relaxed against the bench. "I guess I can live with that." Almost as soon as he'd sat back, he came forward again. "How about tonight? There's a Boston Pops concert on the Esplanade. We could pick up something to take out and eat while we listen."

Lauren knew that an hour later, or two or three, she'd find all kinds of reasons why she shouldn't go. At the moment, however, she couldn't think of a one. "That'd be fun. I'd like it."

"Great! What time can you get off?"

"What time does the concert start?"

Matt's eyes widened. "I hadn't thought that far." He jumped up, staying her with his hand. "Don't move. I'll be right back."

She watched him sprint toward Bostix, the ticket and information booth adjacent to Fanueil Hall, where he managed to wedge himself through the crowd at the window. Within minutes, he had trotted back to her.

"Eight o'clock. They suggested we get there early for the best spots on the grass, but the music carries pretty far, so if you can't get away from the shop until later—"

"I think I can convince Jamie to give Beth a hand until the shop closes. If we want to allow time to walk over the hill... How about your coming by at, say, seven? I'll call in an order for dinner—"

"Let me take care of that. I'm on a quasi vacation, remember? My work is done for the day, while you've still got more to do."

With a shy smile, she stood up. "Okay, then. I'll see you later?"

"Sure thing."

She nodded and had started for the shop when Matt called out to stop her. "Uh, Lauren?" Brows raised in question, she looked back. His gaze dropped from hers to the book she still held in her hand. She blushed, hurried back and gave it to him.

"Sorry. I'd forgotten I was holding it."

"I hadn't. If I can't go sailing this afternoon, I'll have to keep myself occupied somehow. Even aside from Parker's style, I suppose there is something to be said for mystery and a little bit of violence. And as for machismo—"

"Don't say it," she interrupted with a teasing glint in her eyes. "I don't think I want to hear it. A girl can take only so much, y'know." She'd pretty much reached her limit already. Another minute or two, and she'd chuck the shop and run off to the Charles with Matt. And that she would certainly regret. The shop was lasting. Matt wasn't. She'd have to remember that.

It was hard for her to remember much of anything that afternoon—other than the fact that Matt would be coming by for her at seven, of course. Beth teased her mercilessly when she rang something up wrong on the cash register, then again when she began to stretch fabric on a frame backside-to.

She thought seven o'clock would never arrive, but it did, bringing Matt, a blanket "compliments of the Marriott" and a large brown bag filled with all kinds of promising goodies. They walked over Beacon Hill, past the State House, the Common and the Public Garden, then across to Storrow Drive and the Hatch Shell.

They weren't the first to arrive, but they found a patch of grass within easy viewing of the raised stage. In truth, Lauren could have sat half a mile off under a tree by the water. The fact of the concert was secondary to that of the pleasure she felt being with Matt. She didn't analyze it, didn't stop to wonder why she was letting herself get so carried away about a man who'd be gone before she knew it. She simply wanted to enjoy, and enjoy she did.

Matt doubled up the blanket and spread it on the grass; then, after they had both sat down, he pulled out one container of food after another. He'd brought spinach turnovers, chicken salad with grapes and walnuts, Brie and crackers, fruit and a tumbler of frothy raspberry cooler. Lauren wondered where they'd ever put such a feast and told him so. He merely laughed, then laughed again when they'd eaten nearly everything. The concert was well under way by that time. He stuffed the remains of their picnic back into the bag, then sat close to Lauren with one arm propped straight on the grass behind him.

The assembled crowd was far from quiet; esplanade concerts were that way, informal evenings geared toward lighthearted company and relaxation. Families with children, young couples, middle-aged couples, elderly couples, mixed groups—all shared the pleasure of an evening along the Charles with the sweet smell of the outdoors, the gentle breeze, the exquisite blend of strings, horns and percussion.

As the evening progressed, Lauren and Matt sat closer and closer together. Lauren couldn't remember ever having felt so replete, and the dinner was only partly responsible. Matt was with *her*. Not with the pretty blonde to their right or the adorable redhead to their left. He was with *her*. She had only to drop her eyes from the stage to see his strong legs stretching endlessly before him. He'd changed into a white shirt and a pair of tan slacks that were more tailored than the jeans but no less sexy. His thighs were solid beneath the lightweight cloth, his hips proportionally lean. She felt the warmth of his shoulder as it gently supported her back; felt the goodness of its fit and its strength. His arm cut a diagonal swath to her hip, beside which his hand was flattened. His hand…long, tanned fingers, fine golden hairs, a well-formed wrist…

One song ended on a round of enthusiastic applause. When another began, the applause never quite stopped, for this song was a popular one with a heady beat, and the temptation to clap along was too great to resist. Too great, at least, for everyone but Lauren and Matt. They grinned along with the others, but neither seemed to want to disturb the physical closeness they'd captured. It seemed natural, and right, and very, very special.

Bidden by a silent call, Lauren turned her head to look up at Matt, and what she saw made her breath catch. His eyes were dark, drawing hers with a magnetic warmth, and his expression was one of gentle but insistent hunger. She might have been frightened by it, had her own body not been as insistently hungry. A glowing sun seemed to have risen inside her, radiating sparkles that speeded up the beat of her heart and her pulse and gave the faintest quiver to her limbs.

Lowering his head just the fraction that was necessary, he shadow-kissed her, openmouthed, not quite touching her lips. He drew back for an instant, dazed, then tipped his head and kissed her the same way, but from a different angle. The first kiss had been tantalizing enough for Lauren, but the second one was devastating. Acting purely on instinct, driven by the ache of desire, she opened her mouth in the invitation he'd been waiting for.

When he lowered his head this time, there was nothing shadowy about his kiss. It was full and binding, caressing her with a passion she'd never have believed mere lips to be capable of. She smelled the faint musk of his skin, tasted the fresh, fruity tang of his mouth, felt the sensual abrasion of his tongue as it swept through the moist recesses she offered.

She was about to turn into him, wrap her arms around his neck and draw him closer, when he dragged his mouth from hers and pressed it to her forehead. Though he didn't speak, the harsh rasp of his breath was eloquent and comforting, since Lauren was working equally hard to suck in the air she needed. Eyes closed, she gradually regained control.

Matt shifted and drew her back against his chest, fully this time, with her head resting on his opposite shoulder and his arms wrapped tightly around her waist. They stayed very much that way until the last encore was over. Then, with reluctance, they got up, gathered their things together and let the leisurely movement of the crowd carry them back the way they'd come.

Matt held the folded blanket under one arm. His other arm was draped over Lauren's shoulder. She held tightly to the hand that dangled by her collarbone.

They were nearly at the State House before he spoke. "I've got to be heading back to Leominster."

"When?"

"Tomorrow morning. Early. I have a nine o'clock appointment and probably should have driven out tonight, but I wanted to be with you."

She nodded, not knowing what else to say.

"I'll have to be there through Sunday. I'm sorry. It would have been nice to do something together on the weekend."

"That's okay. The shop's open seven days a week. I've forgotten what a weekend is."

"You have to have *some* time off each week."

"I will, once things get more settled. We weren't sure how soon we'd be able to hire extra help, but business has been going so well that we're trying to convince Jamie to work full-time so Beth and I can stagger days off for ourselves."

"That'd be nice. There must be things you need to do."

"At least a million. Sundays are a help—we're only open from one till six—but I'd really like a day off in the middle of the week once in a while. If I don't start hiring people to fix up my farm-house, it's apt to give a final groan and crumble at my feet."

"Maybe I could help with that."

"With the farmhouse? But you're leaving."

"I've got some good contacts, and while I'm in Leominster I can check around for more. What do you need?"

"You name it. Plumber, electrician, roofer, carpenter. Actually, I was exaggerating before. The structure of the house is sound. I had that checked out before I bought the place. But I want to do extensive modernizing inside, and I need good people I can trust, since I won't be able to stand around and supervise."

He gave her hand a squeeze. "Got it. I'll see what I can do."

They walked on in silence for a time. Lauren felt simultaneously content and unsettled, if that were possible. Finally she couldn't help but ask, "When will you be flying back to San Francisco?"

"Not for another week or two. I'll be here in the city early next week, then back in Leominster.... Where are you parked?"

She pointed in the direction of the garage. "You don't need to—"

"I insist."

"But it's out of your way."

"What else do I have to do?" he teased.

"Sleep. You'll have to be on the road very early to get to Leominster by nine."

"It's okay. I'll sleep tomorrow night."

All too soon, they had reached the garage, climbed to the third level and found her car. Reluctantly, she unlocked the door and opened it, only then turning to Matt. "Can I give you a lift back to the hotel?"

He shook his head. "It's out of your way."

"But this was out of yours."

"I'm on foot. It's ten times harder by car, what with one-way streets and all."

"I don't mind. Really—"

Any further words she might have said were stopped at her lips by the single finger he placed there. The dim light of the garage couldn't disguise the way his eyes slowly covered her face. They were hypnotic, those mellow brown eyes, and they conspired with the unmistakable vibrations from his body to suspend Lauren's thought processes once more.

His finger slid to her chin, where it collaborated with his thumb to tip her face up. He kissed her once, then again, then brushed his lips over her cheeks, eyes and nose. Lauren was entranced. Her own lips parted, then waited, waited until he'd completed the erotic journey and returned home.

But if she'd thought what he'd already done was erotic, she was in for an awakening. The tip of his tongue flicked out to paint her lips in the rosy hue of passion, and if she hadn't been clutching the top of the car door, she might have collapsed. She'd never experienced anything as electric, and the hardest part to believe was that the only points where their bodies touched were his tongue and her lips.

When he severed that connection, she stood still, eyes closed, mesmerized by the lingering flicker of a sweet, sweet longing. With regret, she finally opened her eyes.

"Can I come out to see you when I get back to town?" he asked. There was a trace of hoarseness in his voice.

Clearly implied was that he wanted to see her in Lincoln. Without a second thought, she nodded. "I'd like that."

He smiled, then cocked his head toward the car. "Get in. I might not let you leave if you wait much longer."

"Is that a threat or a promise?" she quipped softly, but she was already sliding behind the wheel. One part of her was tempted to wait much, much longer. The other part knew that things were happening quickly and that there were too many considerations to be made before she dared Matt to follow through.

After he had shut the door, she locked it, then started the car and backed out of the space. Matt stood to the side, watching. He gave a short wave as she began the slow, twisting descent. Soon he was lost to her view.

Lauren smiled all the way down Cambridge Street. She was still smiling when she curved into Storrow Drive and was ebullient enough to ignore the harsh beam of headlights from a car following too close on her tail. When she crossed the Eliot Bridge onto Route 2 and the same car remained behind her, she indulgently assured herself that if she was patient, the car would turn off soon.

It didn't.

She passed through Fresh Pond, circled the far rotary and moved into the right lane of what was now a comfortable superhighway. The car stayed with her. She tossed frequent glances in the rearview mirror and frowned. The traffic wasn't heavy. Surely whoever it was could move to the left and pass her, rather than tail her at forty-five miles per hour.

The highway was well lighted. She could see that the car was a late-model compact and that the driver was alone. Some kid having fun? There was no weaving to suggest he was drunk. Neither was there any hint that he was trying to tell her something, such as that her car had a flat tire or was on fire. He was simply following her and succeeding in making her extremely nervous.

Lauren pressed her foot on the gas pedal, pulled into the middle lane and held steady. The other car accelerated, pulled into the middle lane and held steady. She moved back into the right lane. The compact followed suit. She pumped her brakes lightly in an attempt to signal the driver to pass her, but he only slowed accordingly, then resumed speed when she did. In a last-ditch attempt to free herself of the tail, she flicked on the signal lights, moved into the breakdown lane and came to a cautious stop, prepared to floor the gas pedal if the other car stopped.

It swung to the left and passed her.

Breathing a shaky sigh of relief, Lauren sat for several minutes to recompose herself. Since she'd realized she was actively being followed, her imagination had taken her to frightening places. Too many little things had happened to her lately—the near accident on Newbury Street, the vicious dog in her yard, the garage door's fall, the subtle suggestion that someone had been in her home—for her to dismiss summarily this instance as a prank.

Yet as she entered the driving lane once more, that was exactly what she forced herself to do. A prank. A dangerous prank.

Then she crested a hill and saw taillights in the breakdown lane. She passed them by, instinctively speeding up, but within minutes the same car was behind her once more.

She swore softly, but that did no good. The car remained in pursuit. Five minutes went by. She searched the road for a sign of a police cruiser she might hail, but there was none. Another five minutes elapsed, and her knuckles were white on the steering wheel.

She approached her exit and held her breath, praying that when she turned off, the driver of the compact car would consider the game not worth any further effort.

He exited directly behind her and proceeded to follow her along the suddenly darker, narrower road.

Praying now that her car wouldn't break down and leave her at the mercy of the nameless, faceless lunatic, she drove along the road as fast as she dared, heading directly for the center of town.

For the first time she blessed every chase movie she'd suffered through in which the dumb innocent was pursued up and down hills, around corners and through dark alleys without grasping at the simplest solution. Lauren Stevenson was no dummy. She had no intention of heading off into a side street, much less leading someone to her farmhouse, where she would be totally unprotected.

She headed for the police station.

What she hadn't expected when she pulled up in front was that the car that had been on her tail all the way home would swing smoothly—with no qualms or hesitation—into a space in the parking lot. Between two police cruisers.

Lauren quickly shifted into drive and headed home.

She was mortified. Apparently she'd imagined the worst for nothing. Yes, she was angry. For an officer of the law, plainclothes or otherwise, to have behaved in such an irresponsible fashion was inexcusable!

But what could she do? If she marched into the police station and complained, she'd be making a certain enemy. Policemen protected their own, and if what she'd read so often in the newspapers was correct, they weren't beyond administering their own subtle forms of punishment. Someday she might need them, really need them. Could she risk turning them off to her now?

Moreover, what could she say? That she'd been terrified because so many strange things had happened to her of late? They'd think she was nuts. A wild dog. A garage door that went bump. A ghost in her underwear. Maybe she *was* nuts.

No one was following her now, but then, she hadn't expected that anyone would be. Some cop had been playing his own perverse game, perhaps simply practicing up on the technique of the chase. It must be boring being a cop in as peaceful a town as Lincoln. No doubt he'd enjoyed the excitement of his little escapade. At that moment he was probably sitting in the back room with his police buddies, having a good laugh.

Lauren put the car in the garage, then all but ran for the side door of the farmhouse. No doubt about it, she was spooked. She'd left her pursuer at the police station. She'd reasoned away all of her other little near-mishaps. Still, she was spooked.

Coincidence and imagination were a combustible combination.

Turning on every available light, she walked from room to room before satisfying herself that everything was the same as when she'd left that morning. That morning seemed so very far away. And that evening had been so very special, but somehow tarnished by the terrifying experience she'd just been through.

After leaving a single bright light on downstairs, she went up to bed, thinking about the outside floodlights she would have put in when she finally found an electrician. Perhaps she *should* consider a burglar alarm. God, she hated that thought. One of the reasons she'd bought a home in the country was to avoid the stereotypical city fears.

She was making something out of nothing, she reminded herself for the umpteenth time as she lay in the dark of her bedroom, afraid to move. She was letting Beth's wild imagination get to her. She was letting her own wild imagination get to her. Maybe Beth was right. Maybe she did need a bodyguard. The thought of Matt Kruger—strong, capable of protecting her, capable of thrilling her with a kiss—brought some measure of relaxation, so that at last she was able to fall asleep.

THAT WEEKEND, working around the hours when the shop was open, Lauren met with three different general contractors to discuss what she wanted to do with the farmhouse. None of the three impressed her.

The first was too traditional in his orientation. What she wanted wasn't exactly restoration, she tried to explain. Yes, she wanted the outside of the farmhouse to look much the way it always had. But she wanted the inside to be a modern surprise of sorts.

Unfortunately, number one didn't have much imagination when it came to modern surprises.

Number two was both patronizing and condescending. "I know exactly what you want," he informed her, then proceeded to tell her what he'd do to the farmhouse. It was exactly what she didn't want.

Number three was not only late for the appointment, but both he and his truck were filthy. That said a lot in her book. She could just picture hiring the man and having him show up for work when the mood suited him. He'd probably leave a mess behind every day for her to trip over, and then she'd have to hire a team of workers to clean up after him.

She'd gone to the contractors first in the hope of finding someone who would then issue subcontracts for things like plumbing and electricity. Now, having struck out, she debated calling the plumbers and electricians herself. Lord only knew she desperately needed to get the job done.

She decided to wait for Matt to return. He'd help her. And she trusted him. She'd never seen his work, but she somehow knew that any recommendations he made would be solid.

By Sunday night, she was thinking of Matt more and more, wondering when he'd be returning and what would happen then. She liked him—very, very much. She wanted to believe that his finest qualities—his gentleness, honesty and spontaneity—were indicative of the way Brad had been, too. She still wondered about Brad, still had questions for Matt to answer. But when she was with Matt she wasn't thinking brotherly thoughts. Matt intrigued her. He excited her. He seemed to take the best of both worlds—brain and brawn— and emerge superior. He wasn't quite like anyone she'd ever known before.

Nor did he kiss like anyone she'd ever known before. Not that she was anywhere near to being an expert on kissing. But she'd dreamed of feeling things in a kiss, and Matt had taken her far, far beyond those dreams—so much so that the restlessness she felt was no mystery.

Knowledge of the cause of a problem was not, however, a solution in itself. And since the solution was for the present out of reach, Lauren did the next best thing. Leaving a light burning in the living room, which had become a habit, she headed upstairs to treat herself to a long, soothing shower.

"Treat" was the operative word. As with most everything else pertaining to the farmhouse, the hot-water heater was small and outmoded. Even with its thermostat set on high, the "hot" was negligible. She'd quickly learned that she couldn't take a shower and then expect there to be enough hot water for the laundry. But she wasn't doing laundry that night, and she fully intended to indulge herself until the water ran cold.

Tossing her clothes into the hamper, she took a fresh nightgown from her drawer and went into the bathroom. The shower was little more than a head rigged high in the bathtub, but it served the purpose. She turned on the water, drew the curtain, waited until steam rose above it, then stepped inside.

Heaven. Just what the doctor ordered. Eyes closed, she tipped back her head and let the warmth flow over her hair, shoulders, back and legs. Soap in hand, she lathered her body, then turned, inch by inch, to rinse off. Relaxation seeped through her. She rocked slowly to the pulse of the water.

Then she heard a noise. Her head shot up and her eyes flew open. The slam of a door? Or was it her imagination? She lingered beneath the spray, listening closely. She thought she felt vibrations.

Without pausing to decide whether the vibrations were footsteps or her own thudding heart, she reached back and quickly turned off the water. Then she grabbed her towel and, with jerky movements, began to dry off. Under the circumstances, she did a commendable job, though her nightgown didn't realize that. It stuck so perversely to the damp spots she'd left that she was all but screaming in frustration by the time she finally managed to get it on properly.

Holding her breath, she peered around the bathroom door into the bedroom. When she didn't see anyone there, she dashed out to her closet and grabbed the first weapon she could find. The heavy, workhorse of a Nikon camera, which she hadn't used in years, would certainly serve as a makeshift club, particularly when heaved from its strap.

She tiptoed to the wall by the open bedroom door, flattened herself against it and listened. And listened. Nothing.

She took a deep breath, then yelled as forcefully as she could, ''I've already connected with the police department and they're on their way! Better get out while you can!''

Silence.

Of course, she hadn't connected with the police department. They'd think she was a fool. Old houses made noises all the time, and she wasn't sure she'd lived long enough in this one to be able to identify all its characteristic moans and groans. No, she wasn't convinced there was an intruder.

On the other hand, she wasn't convinced there wasn't one, either.

Figuring that she'd need every precious moment if someone should storm in, she reached for the light switch and threw the room into a darkness that was broken only by a faint glow from the bathroom. Then, moving as silently as she could, given that she was more than a little unsteady on her feet, she wedged herself behind the bedroom door and peered through the crack, waiting for someone to creep up the stairs or emerge from one of the other two bedrooms.

No one did.

Noiselessly, Lauren sank to the floor, her gaze never once leaving the narrow slit of a peephole. She waited and watched and listened, growing stiff with tension but not daring to move. Five minutes passed, and there was nothing. Ten minutes passed, and she continued to wait, her temple now pressed wearily to the wall. By the time fifteen minutes had elapsed, she had to admit that she'd very possibly jumped to conclusions.

She wasn't convinced enough to leave herself unprotected, though. To that measure, she carefully closed the bedroom door, carried over a chair and propped it beneath the knob. Then, with the strap of the camera still wound around her hand, she climbed into bed and lay stiffly, listening, waiting. The only thing she was sure about as the hours crept by was that she very definitely would have a burglar alarm system installed when the house was sufficiently readied for it. Nights like this she didn't need.

Unless, of course, she had that bodyguard.

CHAPTER FIVE

When the phone rang early the next morning, Lauren jumped. She was in the kitchen, trying to force down a breakfast she didn't really want, and the unexpected sound jarred her already taut nerves. Snatching up the receiver after the first ring, she gasped a breathless "Hello?"

"Lauren? It's Matt."

Hand over her heart, she let out a sigh of relief. It wasn't that she'd actually expected someone menacing to be on the other end of the line but, rather, that the sound of Matt's voice was an instant and incredible comfort. "Matt," she murmured. "I'm so glad...."

There was a slight pause. "Is something wrong?"

"No, no. Just me and my imagination." She put her hand on the top of her head and found herself spilling it all. "I had the worst time last night. I was in the shower and thought I heard a noise. It turned out to be nothing, but the weirdest things have been happening lately, Matt. You wouldn't believe it. After I left you the night of the concert, some car tailed me all the way home. Well, not all the way, but almost. And before that the garage door had missed me by inches, and the dog had attacked me, and the car had swerved into the sidewalk—"

"Whoa, sweetheart. Slow up a bit. It doesn't sound like it's all been your imagination."

"No, but my imagination has been connecting all these little things that have nothing to do with one another and could really have happened to anyone—"

"But they happened to you." His voice was low and distinctly grim. "When did this all start?"

"I don't know...maybe a week and a half ago. It's like every few days something happens. I never thought I was accident-prone, but I'm beginning to wonder. Beth thought it was a ghost—''

"A ghost? Come on!''

"I know, I know, but if someone's trying to scare me out of this farmhouse, he's doing one hell of a job.''

Matt was silent for several long seconds. "Listen, I'm still in Leominster, but I'll be driving back later this afternoon. Why don't I meet you at home? If I get there before you do, I can take a look around.''

Lauren was without pride at that moment, and self-sufficiency was a luxury she couldn't afford. "Would you? I'd be so grateful, Matt! I've never been one to be spooked, but I'm as spooked as they come right about now. I don't think I slept more than two or three hours last night, and that was with a chair propped against the bedroom door and a camera nearby.''

"You were going to take pictures?'' he asked in meek disbelief.

"I was going to hit whoever it was over the head! My camera was the closest thing to a weapon I had. And then this morning I crept around the house looking for signs of an intruder. Crept around my own house in broad daylight—I must be getting paranoid!''

"Shh. Don't say things like that, Lauren. I'm sure there are perfectly logical explanations for everything that's happened.''

"That's what I've been telling myself, but it's getting harder to believe. I mean, I can't deny that a car nearly ran me down, or that a dog attacked me, or that the garage door fell…but someone going through my lingerie?''

Matt cleared his throat. "Someone going through your lingerie?''

"See? You think I'm crazy, too!''

"I do not think you're crazy. Never that. You strike me as one of the most together women I've ever known.''

"But you don't know me. Not really.''

"Well, we'll have to do something about that, then. Tonight?''

"Promise you'll come?''

"I promise.''

Lauren gave him directions; then, for the first time that morning, she smiled. "Thanks, Matt. I feel better already."

"So do I, sweetheart. See ya later."

LAUREN ARRIVED HOME from work that night to find a car in the drive. It was a brown Topaz and had local license plates. She assumed it was Matt's rental, but, seeing no sign of him, she felt a momentary tension. The car that had tailed her the Thursday before had been of a similar size, and though she'd had only glimpses of it when it passed beneath lights, she'd guessed it was either maroon or brown.

Staying where she was, safely locked inside her car with the motor running just in case, she leaned heavily on the horn. Then she waited. She seemed to be doing a lot of that lately.

This time she didn't have long to wait. Within a minute, Matt opened the front door of the house and loped out to greet her. The relief and sheer pleasure she felt upon seeing him eclipsed the fact that he'd somehow entered her house without a key.

Killing the motor, she scrambled from the car and threw herself into his arms. It seemed the most natural thing to do and, given the way Matt's arms wound tightly around her, he appeared to have no objections.

When at last he set her down, they exchanged silly grins.

"You look wonderful," he said. "A little tired, maybe, but a sight for sore eyes."

"I could say the same." Her hands were looped around his neck, her lower body flush with his. He looked positively gorgeous, sun-baked skin, slightly crooked nose, too-square chin and all. "Thanks for coming, Matt. I really needed you here. Did you have any trouble finding the place?"

"Nope. Your directions were perfect. I got here a couple of hours ago. It's a nice place, Lauren. I can see why you bought it. It does have charm."

"But does it have ghosts? That's what I *really* need to know."

Taking her hand, he started with her toward the house. "No ghosts. Just lots of things that need repairing." He cleared his throat. "For starters, the lock on one of the back windows is broken. I had no trouble climbing inside."

So that was how he'd done it. Simple enough. "But I tested all the locks. I was sure they worked!"

"Oh, this one works, all right. Until you raise the window. The wood around the screws has rotted. The entire lock simply slides up with the window. Close the window and the lock is in place again." He paused. "Which means that there's good news and bad news."

"Mmm." She dropped her purse on the chair just inside the front door. "The good news is that there's no ghost. The bad news is that the moving around of things inside the house was caused by a human intruder."

"Right. Hey, don't look so down. Every other lock in the house is solid, so it's just a matter of fixing this one. I've already been to the hardware store and picked up larger screws and packing. That'll hold the lock until the wood can be replaced."

"Oh, Matt, you didn't have to."

"I did it for my own peace of mind, if nothing else. Besides, fixing things is my speciality." He eyed her apologetically as they entered the kitchen. "I'm not sure I did as well with dinner. I picked up some things in town, but I'm afraid I'm not all that good a cook."

"I could have taken care of that."

"You'll still have to. I made a salad and husked some sweet corn, but I didn't know what in the hell to do with the chicken. At home I douse it in barbecue sauce and throw it on the grill, but you don't have a grill, and for the life of me I couldn't figure out how the broiler in that stove of yours works." His eyes shot daggers at the appliance in question.

She laughed. "It doesn't. The stove has to be replaced along with the refrigerator, the hot-water heater, the furnace—I could go on and on."

"So what do we do with the chicken?" Opening the refrigerator, he removed the plastic-wrapped package.

"We bake it. And I've got a super sauce. You'll think you're eating the best of barbecue.'' She looked toward the single cabinet on the wall beside the sink, then down at her sleeveless beige jump suit. ''I'd better change first. By the way, was that a bottle of wine I saw in the refrigerator?''

He nodded. ''California's finest, already chilled. I'll pour while you change. Then we can talk.''

Talk. For a minute she'd forgotten what they needed to discuss. She felt so good, so safe, with Matt that the last thing on her mind had been her series of recent misadventures. But she wanted to tell him. Matt was levelheaded and straightforward. She trusted that he'd be honest with her and let her know if she was making a mountain out of a molehill.

She trotted upstairs to her bedroom, changed into a pair of jeans and an oversize gray shirt that she knotted at the waist, then returned to the kitchen in record time.

Matt stood at the kitchen window, looking out at the field beyond. He spun around in surprise when she breezed into the room, then stared at her and swallowed hard.

''I...is something wrong?'' She glanced down at herself.

''No. Not at all. It's just that I've never seen you in play clothes.''

Lauren could have kicked herself for not having taken the time to touch up her makeup and brush out her hair. In the past those things had never mattered. She'd looked as good—or as bad—with or without the primping. She'd forgotten that she had something to work with now. But it was too late.

Self-consciously, she reached up to finger-comb her hair toward her cheek, but Matt crossed the room in two long strides and stayed her hand. ''Don't. Don't do that.'' Releasing her hand, he used his own fingers as a comb to smooth the hair back. ''You look so pretty. I want to see your face.''

You look so pretty. I want to see your face. So hard to believe. So...strange. ''I look tired. I should have done something.''

''You look beautiful—and with only two or three hours' sleep.'' Dipping his head, he brushed a kiss on her cheek, another closer to her mouth, then another closer still. His hand was curved around her jaw by the time he reached her lips, though Lauren wouldn't have pulled away even if he hadn't held her. His nearness was drugging, his kiss intoxicating. His breath mingled with hers, seeming to bring her to life as she'd never lived it before. She forgot all else but the sweet sensation of closeness, of awareness, of longing that the caress of his mouth inspired.

"Ahh," he breathed against her lips at last, "your kiss takes me…"

"You have it…the wrong way around."

"Then it's reciprocal, which is why it happens to begin with."

"This is getting confusing."

"Mmm." He smacked his mouth to hers, then set her back and put his wineglass in her hand. She sipped the wine, perfectly content to drink from his glass while he laid claim to the second he'd poured. "Now, let me watch you make this super sauce of yours. I want to see what you put in it."

She grinned. "Cautious, Matthew. Hungry but cautious."

"Quite" was all he said, but the grin he gave her stole her breath almost as completely as his kiss had. Fearing for the state of her health, she quickly set to work mixing the ingredients of her super sauce, then indulged Matt by offering him the spoon for a taste.

"Mmm." He licked his lips. "Not bad. Not bad at all."

"Don't give me 'not bad.' It's *super*. At least," she added in a demure undertone, "that's what it was called in the cookbook I took it from."

"Ah, a cookbook reader." He glanced around. "But I don't see any cookbooks."

She flipped open the cabinet and pointed.

"Two cookbooks? That's all? A cookbook reader is supposed to have a huge collection."

"I'm, uh, I'm a little new at it." She unwrapped the chicken and rinsed it under the faucet.

"You didn't used to cook?"

"I didn't used to eat."

Matt chuckled and scratched his forehead. "That picture. I'd forgotten. You were pretty skinny back then—no offense intended."

"None taken. You're right, I was pretty skinny. It's just recently that I've been forcing myself to eat. I don't dare tell that to many people, mind you," she added, patting the chicken dry with a paper towel. "Most of them get annoyed."

"Jealousy, plain and simple."

She sent him a mischievous grin, then knelt down to remove a baking dish from the lone lower cabinet. That took some doing on her part. Pots were piled on top of pots, which were piled on top of pans, which were piled on top of the baking dish. "Top priority in this kitchen," she announced, rising at last, "is new cabinets, and plenty of them."

"Cabinets—easily done. What else?"

As Lauren dipped the pieces of chicken, one by one, into the sauce and placed them in the baking dish, she outlined her concept of the perfect kitchen, only to find that Matt's suggestions and additions made her plans more perfect than before.

"Why didn't *I* think of a center island?" she asked as she shoved the baking dish into the oven.

"Because you're not a builder."

"And you do this kind of thing?"

His shrug was one of modesty. "The development we're planning in Leominster is a cluster-home type of complex, a planned-community thing. Modern and elegant but also practical. Island counters in the kitchens are an option. They can be used for storage underneath and eating above, or for a sink and a stovetop. Lord only knows, this kitchen's big enough to handle an island."

"And you know people who can do this for me?"

He patted the breast pocket of his shirt. "Names and numbers, already checked out."

With exaggerated greed, she put out her hand. "Gimme. I'll make the calls tomorrow." She proceeded to tell him of the contractors she'd interviewed herself; well before she had finished, he'd closed her fingers around his list. She promptly secured the piece of paper with a decorative magnet on the refrigerator door, then reached for the foil-wrapped loaf of French bread Matt had brought.

He clasped her wrist. "Set the timer for twenty-five minutes. That'll be plenty early to put the bread in the oven." While she did so and then put a pot of water on to heat for the corn, he refilled their wineglasses. "Come on. Let's go out back. I want to hear more about your...escapades."

With vague reluctance, since she'd enjoyed talking with Matt about lighter subjects, Lauren led the way through the back door to the yard. A weathered bench under the canopy of an apple tree provided them with seats. Sunset approached; shards of orange and gold sliced through the trees and threw elongated shadows on the grass.

"Okay," he said. "Start from the top. I want to hear about each thing as it happened."

Encouraged that at least he was taking her seriously, she turned her thoughts to the days that had passed. "The first incident took place more than a week and a half ago, I guess." She related the Newbury Street story. "I don't know if the driver was drunk. I don't even know if it was a man or a woman."

"How about the car? Size? Color?"

She shook her head. "It came from behind. I don't think it was red or yellow. Nothing bright—that would have stuck with me. It must have been some nondescript color. As for the size, God only knows."

"Did you go to the police?"

"What could the police do? The car was gone."

"Maybe there was a witness who caught the license number."

"If there was one, he or she certainly didn't come forward. I just assumed I'd had a close call with a freak accident and left it at that."

He nodded. "Okay. What next?"

"Next was the dog. My run-in with him was...I don't know, maybe two days after the incident with the car." She described what had happened. "As soon as I was down on the ground and thoroughly frightened, he took off. Like he'd simply lost interest."

"You said it was a Doberman?"

"I said it *might* have been a Doberman. It's the same with the car. You're so stunned when it happens that the details slip by you. And anyway, it was dark.''

''Was the dog wearing a collar?''

''That's the last detail I'd have noticed.''

''Not if your hand had hit something when you tried to push him away.''

''My hands were busy protecting my face. I kicked out with my legs—pretty ineffectively, I'd guess. If that dog hadn't wanted to leave, he wouldn't have.''

Matt seemed about to say something, then stopped and took a breath. ''Did you call the police?''

Lauren shook her head. ''The dog was gone. It hasn't been back since.''

Even in the fading light, the tension on Matt's face was marked. ''Then what?''

She took a drink of wine for fortification. On the one hand, Matt's grim concern was reassuring. On the other, it seemed to make the situation all the more real and, therefore, ominous. ''Then the garage door crashed down. It's an old garage, an old door. I'd simply assumed it would hold.''

''I checked it out. There's no apparent reason why it didn't. The chains are strong. So are the coils.''

''Then what could explain it?''

He looked off toward the shadowed trees and didn't speak for several minutes. ''There are ways to rig a door like that.''

''But it worked perfectly the next day, and every day since!''

''There's rigging—and unrigging.''

Apprehension made her gray eyes larger. ''You're suggesting that whoever might have tampered with it before it crashed down went back and fixed it again? But why would anyone *do* that?''

''What happened next?''

Lauren stared at him. He hadn't attempted to answer her question. Not that he ought to have an answer when she didn't, but at least he could have tried to soothe her. Brows lowered, she looked away. What had happened next? ''I'm not sure about the next thing. It wasn't as obvious as the others…I mean, it could have been me.''

"What was it, Lauren?"

She took a short breath. "After we'd gone on the cruise that night, I came home and noticed that some things were out of place in my bedroom. At least, they seemed out of place to me, but it might have been my own carelessness." When his silence demanded further explanation, she told him about the perfume, the shoes and the underwear.

"Nothing was taken? Money? Jewelry?"

"I don't have much of either lying around, but no, nothing was taken."

"And it was only the bedroom that was touched?"

"As far as I could tell."

"Did you go through the other rooms?"

"Of course I did! And nothing was touched—*as far as I could tell*. Honestly, Matt! I mean, it's possible that the spoons in the kitchen drawer were rearranged, but I don't set them up in any special pattern, so how would I know?"

He held up a hand. "Okay, okay. Take it easy."

Even the softening of his tone did little to calm her. "How can I take it easy? I feel like I'm at an inquisition, and the implication is that you think I've been irresponsible. Well, I haven't! Taken separately, not one of these incidents is particularly unusual. People on the streets have close calls with cars all the time. Wild dogs get loose; they attack innocent victims. Garage doors malfunction. And as for my personal effects, that could just as well have been my own fault. I'm not perfect! I might have been distracted! And *don't* ask me if I called the police, because I didn't!"

"I didn't ask," he said. His words were gently spoken; his gaze was solicitous. "And I'm sorry if I sounded critical. It's just that I'm concerned...and I'm a stickler for details. I like to know exactly what I'm facing." He slanted her a lopsided smile. "You were supposed to know that already."

Immediately ashamed of her outburst, Lauren sent him a look of apology. "I forgot."

"Well, don't," Matt went on in the same soft voice. "I'm looking for any possible detail that would give us some clue to whether the things that have happened are unrelated or not.''

She shivered at the latter thought. ''I know. And I appreciate your listening to all this. But I don't know in which direction to turn at this point.''

''Which is why you should tell me everything.'' He paused. ''All set?'' When she nodded, he released a breath. ''Okay. Some things were amiss in your bedroom. Possibly your own fault. What was the next thing that happened?''

''The car followed me home.''

''Did you see where it picked you up?''

She shook her head. ''It could have been anywhere. I was on Storrow Drive when I first noticed the headlights in my rearview mirror.''

''Make of the car?''

She shrugged and shook her head.

''Color?''

''Dark. At the time I thought it was maroon or brown, but it was hard to tell.'' Her eyes widened. ''Do you think it could have been the same car that nearly hit me on Newbury Street?''

''I don't know. There are a hell of a lot of maroon and brown cars on the road. Without a make and model, we're clutching at straws.''

''I'm sorry,'' she murmured. ''Cars aren't my thing. I'm no good at identifying them.''

''That's okay, Lauren. Do you remember when it finally dropped away?''

''It didn't, in a sense.'' She explained how she'd headed straight for the police station, where the car had nonchalantly pulled into a parking space. When Matt remained silent, she feared that he would chide her for not entering the station and complaining; she still wondered if she should have done that. ''Well?''

''It's odd,'' he said at last. ''Could have been a policeman having a little fun on his way to work, but all the way from Boston? And he stopped, then picked you up again.''

''But he had to be harmless if he was a policeman.''

"If, and that's a big if."

"Matt, he pulled into that space as if he knew just where he was going!"

"He may have pulled out just as smoothly once you drove on."

"And if I'd gone in to file a complaint?"

"He could have driven off anyway. You would have led the officer on duty to the parking lot, only to find that there wasn't any car there."

"Mmm. And the officer would have thought I'd dreamed the whole thing up."

"Possibly. Okay, the only thing left, then, is the matter of strange noises last night. Tell me exactly what you heard."

She did. "By the time I came out of the shower, there was nothing. Maybe I imagined it all."

"Maybe."

Then again, maybe not. "If someone had gotten *in* the house, wouldn't he have had to get *out*? I was so spooked that even the tiniest creak in the floorboards would have sounded like thunder to me. But there was nothing. I'm sure of it."

"And when you got up in the morning, there was no sign of an intruder?"

"Nothing."

"No window partway open? No dirt tracked onto the floor?"

"Nothing."

"And is that it? No other suspicious incidents in the past few weeks? Anything that, with a twist of the imagination, might seem odd?"

She thought about it, going back over the days with a fine-tooth comb. Eventually she shook her head. "Nothing."

Matt sat back on the bench, deep in thought. Sandy brows shaded his eyes. His mouth was drawn into a tight line. Lauren studied him, waiting to hear what he had to say. When he stood up abruptly and began to walk back toward the house, she was mystified.

"Matt?" She bolted to her feet, jogging to catch up. He looked at her almost in surprise, and she wondered where his thoughts had been.

"Oh. Sorry. I thought I'd put the bread in the oven now."

"But the timer—"

"We wouldn't have heard it." Sure enough, as they mounted the back steps they caught the insistent buzz.

Biding her time with some effort, she watched him open the oven door, flip over each piece of chicken, then slip the prebuttered loaf onto the lower shelf. Without missing a beat, he carefully dropped the husked ears of corn into the now-boiling water.

Finally she couldn't wait any longer. "Well? What do you think?"

"Mmm. Chicken smells good."

"Not the chicken. My *predicament. Is* someone after me?"

Straightening, he leaned back against the chipped counter and studied her. "Is there a *reason* that someone should be after you?"

She couldn't believe the question. "Of course not! I haven't done anything. I haven't hurt anyone. To my knowledge, I don't have any enemies. I'm amazed you'd even ask that!"

"Just ruling it out. It's as good a place as any to start."

"Well, we've started. A more probable possibility is that these incidents have something to do with the farmhouse. Everything began after I moved in."

"When, exactly, did you move in?"

"The first week in June."

"And the car incident took place, what, at the end of the month?" He thrust out his jaw. "The delay doesn't make sense. If someone legitimately didn't want you living here, the incidents would have started while you were first looking over the place, or certainly as soon as you'd moved in. Besides, not all of the things have happened here. Nah, I don't think they have anything to do with the farmhouse."

"That'd be the most plausible explanation," she pointed out. "And it'd be the easiest one to follow up. I've considered the possibility that one of the neighbors doesn't want me here, but the few I've met have been pleasant enough, and I can't think of any reason that my presence would be objectionable. I know nothing about the former owners, though. I could speak with the realtor and go through the records of who has lived here in the past. If necessary, I could call in a private investigator, or even the police—''

"Don't do that," Matt interrupted, then quickly gentled his voice. "Not yet, at least."

Though Lauren herself hadn't been anxious to call the police, she was surprised by his vehemence. It occurred to her that he might be indulging her in her fancy while not quite taking it to heart. "What do you suggest?" she asked more cautiously.

"Let's consider the possibilities." He squinted with one eye. "Are you sure you can't think of someone who might get his jollies by scaring you?"

"Like who?"

He shrugged. "An old boyfriend?"

"An old boyfriend who'd come all the way from Bennington in search of a little mischief?"

"Then maybe someone you might have met since you've been here. Someone who asked you out. Or followed you around. Or just...looked at you for hours on end."

"You're the only one who's done that," she replied with a smirk. "Maybe you've got a Jekyll and Hyde thing going."

The twitch of his nose told her what he thought of that idea.

"Well," she went on, thinking aloud, "it could always be a random lunatic."

He shook his head. "Too persistent. Your average random lunatic may hit once, even twice, but not six times. Your average random lunatic wouldn't have access to a trained attack dog—"

Horrified, Lauren interrupted him. "Trained? Do you think that dog was trained?"

Matt gnawed on his lower lip, as though regretting what he'd said, but the damage had been done. "It's possible. If it was trained to respond to a high-pitched whistle that our ears can't detect, that would explain why it retreated so abruptly."

"Just enough to frighten me...not enough to harm me. What kind of insanity are we dealing with?" Her voice had reached its own high pitch.

He gave her shoulder a reassuring squeeze. "We don't know anything for sure, except that so far you haven't been hurt."

"But I *could* have been. If I'd been a little slower in leaving my garage that night…if there'd been no Good Samaritan near me on Newbury Street that day…"

Responding to the sudden pallor of her skin, Matt drew her against him and slowly rubbed her back. "Don't think about what might have been," he murmured. "Nothing's happened, and if I have any say in the matter, nothing will."

With her head pressed to his heart, Lauren believed every word he said. She didn't stop to ask him how he intended to protect her. She didn't stop to ask herself why she, who valued her independence highly, welcomed the protection. She only knew that Matthew Kruger filled a spot that, at this particular point in her life, was open and waiting for him.

He drew back from her to ask, "Think that chicken's almost ready?"

"The chicken!" Pushing herself away from him, Lauren flung open the oven door, reached for a pair of mitts and pulled out first the chicken, then the bread. "Thank goodness it's not burned! I'd forgotten all about it!" She teased him with a punishing glance. "And it's *your* fault."

"My fault?" He was the image of innocence. "You said *you* were the cook around here."

"But you've kept me preoccupied. I haven't even set the table!" The item in question was of the card-table variety, albeit inlaid with cane, and there were folding chairs to match. She'd picked them up to use until she bought regular furniture.

"Then you do that while I toss the salad," Matt suggested. He was already draining the sweet corn. "I picked up a creamy cucumber dressing—unless you've got a super dressing of your own."

The twinkle in his eye brought fresh color to her cheeks and a momentary curl of warmth to the pit of her stomach. "Creamy cucumber's fine. Super sauce I can handle; super dressing is still a way down the road." As she reached for the dishes, she said, "It's amazing…"

"What is?" Matt asked, removing the salad from the refrigerator.

"That you can take my mind off things. Not only dinner, but everything else. One minute I can be worried sick about what's been happening; the next, I forget all about it."

"Maybe you've been worrying for nothing," he ventured quietly. "Maybe all that's happened really *is* a coincidence."

"Maybe…but it's crazy. Everything's been so wonderful. I left Bennington. I have a new job, new home, new look—" The last had slipped out. She rushed on. "Maybe it's all too good to be true."

Matt poured dressing on the salad and began to toss it. "I'm sure that whatever's been going on can be taken care of."

"But how can it be taken care of if I don't know what it is?"

"In time, Lauren. In time. Let's get back to the random-lunatic theory. Lunatic, perhaps. Random, unlikely." He held the salad tongs in the air for a minute before resuming his tossing. "Are you absolutely sure you can't think of anyone who might be behind it?"

Lauren set the silverware on the table with far greater force than necessary. "Yes, I'm sure. I've told you that, Matt. I don't know anyone who'd be capable of doing what has been done. Why do you keep harping on it?"

He hesitated. "Because the only other possibility is that we're facing someone who is neither lunatic nor random, but who has a very specific ax to grind. Maybe someone who has a grudge against your family."

Her jaw fell open, then snapped back into place. "If you knew my parents, you'd never even suggest that. They are utterly harmless. They live in an insulated little world. There may be competition within the academic community, but my parents have been so well accepted for so long that I can't begin to imagine anyone's acting out of jealousy, much less trying to seek revenge. And if someone did, he or she sure as hell wouldn't do it through me. I've declared my independence in ways that have my parents climbing those ivy-covered walls of theirs—'' Her voice broke abruptly, and for a minute she wished she could retract what she'd said. Then she realized that there was no point in being coy. Matt, more than anyone, would understand.

He brooded for a minute as he placed the salad on the table, then reached for the wine. "What do you mean?"

Lauren opened the foil-wrapped bread with care. It was hot. "What I'm doing with my life isn't exactly what my parents had wanted me to do."

"In what sense?"

"Oh," she began, juggling the steaming loaf into a bread basket, "they would have preferred that I stay in Bennington and work at the museum. I'd be surrounded by culture, attend plays and lectures, take part in a weekly reading-and-discussion group. Then I'd marry some nice, pale-faced fellow whose interests lay in Babylonian astronomy or medieval art or comparative linguistics. I'd go on to have sweet little children who would take up the cello at age four, read Dostoyevsky at age eight, write a novel at age twelve and beg for college admittance at age fourteen."

"And you? What would you prefer?"

"Me?" She set the bread basket on the table and looked up at him pleadingly. "I want to be happy. I want to do well at whatever I choose to do. I want to feel good about myself."

"And a husband and children?"

Shrugging, she brought the plates to the stove. "I haven't thought that far yet."

"Sure you have. Every woman dreams."

"Every man does, too," she countered.

"But I asked you first. What do you want in a husband? What do you want for your children?"

She put two pieces of chicken on Matt's plate, a single piece on her own. "The same thing I want for myself, I suppose. If a person is happy, and feels good about himself, everything else falls into place." She added an ear of corn to each plate before bringing both to the table.

"How can your parents argue with that?"

"They believe that certain things make a person happy. We just disagree on what those things are."

Matt was standing with one hand on his hip as he watched her. Straightening suddenly, he tilted a chair out and gestured for her to sit. "Brad's philosophy was similar. It's amazing how alike you are in so many ways. Then again, there are differences."

"Tell me more about him, Matt. Did he really feel the same way I do?"

Matt slowly seated himself and didn't speak until he'd pulled his chair in and spread a napkin on his lap. His expression was pensive. "He felt that what your parents wanted was different from what he wanted. But you already know that. I think he would have been surprised that you agree with him. He saw himself as the black sheep of the family."

"So much so that, regardless of what he did, it didn't seem to measure up?" she asked.

Matt frowned, then shifted in his seat. He drew the salad bowl toward him and prodded the lettuce with the tongs. In a sudden spurt of movement, he began to pile salad on Lauren's plate. "Is that the way *you* feel? That nothing you do can measure up?"

"Hey." She put her hand on his and pushed the tongs toward his own plate. "That's enough."

He served himself. "Do you feel that way, Lauren?"

"No. I'm pleased with what I'm doing. Brad tried to meet my parents' expectations, failed, then took off. I went along with their wishes and was fairly successful at it before realizing that it wasn't what I wanted. I left because I chose to. Brad left because he had to. I could have gone on forever up there, I suppose. Brad couldn't have survived." She took a breath. Her fork dangled over the chicken. "It wasn't that he didn't have the brains for it, but his temperament was totally different. He was more impulsive, more restless. Hyperactive, my parents always said, but I think they were wrong. He just wanted to use his brains for things other than scholarly pursuits."

"He did that," Matt drawled under his breath, but there was no humor in his expression. When he saw Lauren staring at him, puzzled, he spoke quickly. "Designing houses, interesting houses, takes brains, although it's not considered a scholarly occupation. It's too bad your parents couldn't have seen some of the work Brad did."

"They never even knew about it" was her sad reply. "They didn't know who he worked for or what he did. They were shocked at the amount of money that came to me when he died." She rolled her eyes. "For that matter, so was I."

Matt's hesitation was a weighty one. "They didn't begrudge it to you, did they?"

"No." She snorted. "The only thing they begrudged was what I *did* with it." Spearing a tomato wedge, she waved it for an instant. "Family interrelationships are weird things. Expectations are often so unrealistic. It's as if we have blinkers on. I suppose I'm not that much more understanding of my parents than they are of me, but it's a shame. I'm an adult now. They're adults. Wouldn't it be nice if we *liked* one another?"

"It's not that simple. You're right. Unrealistic expectations can stand in the way. Or ego needs. It must be difficult in a situation like yours, where it would be impossible for you to rise above what your parents have done. They've been so successful in their fields. Maybe that's why both you and Brad felt the need to strike out on your own."

"Maybe. I hadn't thought about it that way." Lauren mulled over the prospect for several minutes, but what lingered with her was how insightful Matt was. "What about you? Are you close to your family?"

"Very."

"Are they in San Francisco, too?"

He shook his head. "L.A. I guess I needed a little distance, just as you do. The pressure coming from my parents was a more traditional one. They're retired now, but for years they both worked in a factory. They wanted my sister and me to rise higher, to advance socially. Unfortunately, there wasn't much money for college. I suppose I could have tried for a scholarship, but I wanted to work. Once I got going, I discovered that I could get the education I needed on the job. I've taken business courses here and there, and I've advanced, so I can't complain.''

"How about your sister?"

Matt warmed Lauren with a grin. "Maggie's a speech therapist. She *did* go for a scholarship, won it and wowed 'em all at UCLA. I'm really proud of her. We all are.''

"I can see that," Lauren said. His grin was contagious, or was it the way his cheeks bunched up and his eyes crinkled? Whatever, she was grinning back at him, wondering how a man could be so gentle and giving, yet so wickedly attractive. "Tell me more," she urged. "About when you were a kid, what you were like, what you did.''

He made a face and tilted his head to the side. "It's really not all that exciting.''

"Tell me anyway." She perched her chin in her palm and waited expectantly.

"Only if you eat while I talk. You haven't had more than a bite, and the chicken is fantastic.''

Listening to Matt and watching him drove all thought of food from her mind. But if eating was his precondition, well…

He talked and she ate. She made observations and asked questions while he ate, then resumed her own meal when he talked more. By the time they'd had seconds of just about everything, including wine, she'd learned that, though a mischievous Matt had received his share of spankings as a boy, he'd grown up in a house filled with love. She'd also learned, but between the lines, that what Matt craved most was his own house filled with love.

When he offered to help her clean up, she accepted. It wasn't that she needed the help or that she was liberated enough to demand it. She'd thoroughly enjoyed the way they'd worked together getting the dinner ready, and she wanted to draw out the evening as long as possible.

Apparently Matt had the same idea. When the kitchen was as spotless as one that age could be, he suggested they relax for a few minutes before he left. They settled in the living room, which, aside from Lauren's bedroom, was the only room with furnishings. There was one sofa and two side chairs. They shared the sofa.

Lauren felt peaceful and happy and tremendously drawn to the man beside her. His arm was slung across the back of the sofa, his fingers tangling in her hair. The clean, manly scent that clung to his skin heightened her senses, while his warmth bridged the small space between them with its invisible touch.

"This has been nice," she told him, slanting a shy glance his way. "I'm glad you came."

His voice was like a velvet mist. "So am I." Sliding his arm around her shoulders, he drew her closer even as he met her halfway. His lips touched one corner of her mouth, then the other, then her cupid's bow, then her lower lip. He'd opened his mouth to kiss her fully when, unable to help herself, she laughed.

He drew back and stared at her for a minute, then cried in mock dismay, "Lauren! What kind of behavior is that? Didn't anyone ever tell you not to laugh in a man's face when he's about to kiss you?"

"I'm sorry… It's just that…you were tasting me one little bit at a time…. You really *are* cautious!"

His eyes danced mischievously. "Caution's gone" was all he said before he covered her mouth with his and proceeded to deliver the most thorough kiss she'd ever received. No part of her mouth was left untouched by any part of his, and by the time he buried his face in her hair, she felt totally devoured. She might have told him so had she been able to speak, but her breath was caught somewhere between her lungs and her throat, for his hand was sliding over her waist, over and up, ever higher, and anticipation had become as tangible as those long, bronzed fingers. When at last they reached her breast, she let out a soft moan and succumbed to the exquisite sensations shooting through her.

Lauren had never been touched this way, yet there was nothing demure in her response. Both mind and body said that what she was experiencing was right and natural; instinct, goaded by desire, set her fingers to combing through his thick hair, running over his broad shoulders, splaying eagerly across his sinewed back.

"Lauren." His voice was hoarse. "Lauren…I have to…we have to stop.…"

"No," she whispered. She held his head with one hand, pressing it to her neck. Her other hand covered his at her breast. "Don't stop."

A groan came from deep in his chest. "Do you know what you're saying, sweetheart? What it does to me?" His voice was thicker now, foreign to her ears yet exciting. She held her breath when he transferred her hand to his own chest and slowly slid it lower.

Lauren could feel the strength beneath her palm, the tautness of his stomach, then the stunning rigidity beneath the fly of his jeans. She wanted to hold him, explore him, let him satisfy the ache that had taken hold deep in her belly, but the newness of it all brought a measure of sanity. With a shuddering breath, she sagged against him.

"Yes. Do stop," she whispered. She was shocked by her own abandon, not quite sure what to make of it. "Everything…everything's happened so fast…and there's still the other matter." Of her own accord, she retreated from him, taking refuge in her corner of the sofa and clasping her hands tightly in her lap. The aura of arousal, a telltale quiver, lingered in her body, but thought of that "other matter" gradually put it to rest.

Matt, too, retreated to his corner of the sofa. He shifted in an attempt to get comfortable, finally hunching forward with his elbows on his knees. His fingers were interlaced, not quite at ease. He cleared his throat. "Yes…that other matter."

"We didn't reach any conclusions."

A pause. "No."

"What do you think?"

Another pause. "I don't know."

"Should I call the police?"

"No." Emphatically.

"Why not?"

He didn't answer, but studied his hands and frowned. "I have to ask you this, Lauren. I know it may sound terrible…but you did mention that your parents were against your coming here—"

"My parents? You think my *parents* could have been behind what's happened?" Vehemently she shook her head. "No. Absolutely not. They may disagree with me, but they'd never try to harm me."

"Maybe just scare you into going back—"

"No." She was still shaking her head. "Not possible! They wouldn't be capable of conceiving of violence."

"Maybe not violence, but if they've already lost one of their children—"

"Forget it, Matt. It's simply not possible…. I think I should call the police."

"No."

"You've been very firm about that. Why, Matt?"

He offered the longest pause yet. "Maybe it's…premature."

"Premature? Then you don't think there's a connection between the things that have happened?"

"I didn't say that. I just think we ought to give it a little time. Let me see what I can do."

"What can you possibly do? Neither of us knows where to begin!"

He didn't argue with her; neither did he agree. Instead, he scowled at his hands.

"Matt, I'm frightened." As much by the strangeness of his response as by everything else, she told herself. "I haven't been hurt so far, but maybe I've just been lucky. What if the next time—"

"You won't be hurt," he gritted out, raising his dark brown eyes to hers. She tried to read his feelings, but they were shuttered. "I'll stay here. If something happens, I can take care of it."

Lauren stared at him. "You can't stay here! My bed's the only one—and—and anyway, you can't be with me every single minute of the day. You have to work. So do I. How can you anticipate when something will happen?"

"If something happens."

She bolted from the sofa and began to prowl the room. She was confused and upset. "You think I'm paranoid. I know you do. You think I'm making something out of nothing." Whirling to face him, she stuck her fists on her hips and glared. "The little lady with the rampant imagination. The fanciful little woman to be indulged— that's the macho attitude isn't it? That's where *you're* coming from!"

Matt's face paled. He sat up straight, then rose and began to walk stiffly toward the front door. His voice was flat. "I think I'd better leave. If that's the way you feel…"

Lauren watched him open the door, then close it behind him. What had she said? Had *she* put that look of hurt in his eyes? Had she been responsible for draining the emotion from his voice, that very same voice that had always been so wonderfully expressive?

Her gaze flew to the window. It was dark outside. Once Matt left, she'd be alone. Unable to take back the ugly words she'd said. Open prey to her own impulsiveness and…

The growl of his engine hit her ears as she wrenched open the front door. "Wait!" she cried, arms waving as she tore down the walk. "Matt, wait!" The car was halfway down the drive. Thinking only that she needed him with her, she flew in pursuit. "Don't go, Matt! I'm sorry! Please…don't…go!"

The taillights went on at the end of the drive, and the car slowed, about to turn onto the street. Lauren's steps faltered. She came to a tapering halt. She'd lost him. He was gone.

The car began to turn, then stopped.

She held her breath, then started running again. "Matt! Please! Wait!"

His tall figure emerged from the car but didn't move farther. Again she faltered and stopped. But the hesitation was only momentary. She knew what she wanted, knew what she needed. With a tiny cry of thanks that she'd been given a second chance, she raced forward.

CHAPTER SIX

Flinging her arms around him, Lauren hung on for dear life. "I'm sorry—so sorry, Matt!" She pressed her cheek to the warm column of his neck. "I didn't mean what I said. I was nervous and frustrated. I took it out on you." Slowly she eased her grip on him and met his gaze. Her voice grew softer. "Don't go. Please?"

"I don't disbelieve you, Lauren," he stated quietly.

"I know that. I accused you unfairly. I expected you to have answers where I didn't. It was wrong of me."

"Nothing's changed. I still don't have answers."

"I know that."

"And you still have only one bed." His hands came to rest lightly on her hips, fingers splayed. "If I were a saint, I'd offer to sleep on the couch, but I'm not a saint."

His words and the look in his eyes sent ripples of excitement through her. "I know that," she whispered.

"Then you know what I want?" he asked as softly.

Unable to speak, she nodded.

His gaze held hers captive for a minute longer; then he grabbed her hand. "Get into the car."

"What—?"

He was urging her into the driver's seat, his hands on her shoulders. "Slide in. Over a little. That's it." He was mere inches behind her, then flush to her side. "I'm not taking the chance that you'll change your mind." Tucking her arm through his, he put the car in reverse and sped backward up the drive. Then he all but swung her from the car, fitted one strong arm over her shoulder and half ran to the house.

"Matt?" She was laughing, breathless.

"Shhh."

Once inside, he continued up the stairs, straight to her bedroom. The light was off. He made no attempt to alter the darkness, and Lauren was relieved. She knew that she wanted what was about to happen. She also knew that the darkness added to its dreamlike quality. That a man like Matt wanted *her* was mind-boggling. Surely if he turned on the light, he'd have second thoughts; she'd have second thoughts....

He took her in his arms and kissed her until the only thoughts she had were how wonderful he was, how unbelievably desirable he made her feel, how lucky she was to have found him. She gave herself up to his kiss, to his hands as they unbuttoned her shirt and unclasped her bra, to his fingers as they charted her flesh, branding her woman with fire and grace.

A soft moan came from deep in her throat, and she arched her back to offer herself more fully. Acceding to her wordless plea, he stroked her with gentle expertise. His fingers made firm swells of her breasts; his thumbs, tight buds of her nipples. And all the while his tongue correspondingly familiarized itself with every nook and cranny of her mouth.

His hands left her only to free himself of his shirt, and then he was back, crushing her close. His chest was warm and lightly furred. Its texture exhilarated her, though she wondered if it was simply the closeness, male to female, that pleased her so. There was something very, very right about what she felt. There was something very, very right about Matt. At that moment she didn't know how she'd ever doubted him.

While he held her lips captive, he reached for the snap of her jeans, released it, lowered the zipper. She gasped for breath when he knelt and eased the denim from her legs, then did the same with her panties. She clutched his shoulders for support and shivered, though her blood was hot, her body aching for completion. Modesty was nonexistent; she wanted him too badly.

"Please," she whispered shakily, "I need you, Matt."

For an instant, he buried his face in her stomach while he caressed the backs of her legs and her bottom. His breath was ragged, his hair damp against her hot flesh. She drove her fingers into the thick, sun-streaked pelt and held him closer, then urged him upward.

He didn't need much urging. Standing, he shed the rest of his clothes, then came to her naked, pressing her to him, graphically showing her that the need wasn't hers alone. She thrilled to the knowledge, unable to be afraid when Matt was all she'd ever wanted, all she'd ever dreamed about. The fact that she could arouse him to the state he was in was as heady as the state of arousal he'd himself brought her to.

He moved from her only to tug back the spread before lowering her gently to the sheets. "Lauren…God, Lauren…" he murmured, then kissed her again. He caressed and teased with his hands, his lips, his tongue, but the play took its toll. His body seemed on fire, trembling under the strain of the heat, finally unable to withstand it. Threading his fingers through hers, he anchored them by her shoulders and positioned himself between her thighs. With one powerful thrust, he surged forward.

Lauren arched her back against the sudden invasion, and a tiny cry escaped her lips. When he stiffened, she wrapped her arms around him to draw him close to her. He resisted.

"Lauren?" His voice was little more than a throaty whisper.

"It's okay…don't stop…don't stop."

His breathing grew all the more labored and he pressed his forehead to her shoulder. "I couldn't if…I wanted to," he finally managed, "but I can be more…gentle."

"Don't be!" she cried, for the instant of pain was gone, leaving only that swelling knot of need low in her belly.

But he was gentle and caring, moving slowly at first, letting her body adjust to his presence before he adopted the rhythm designed to drive her insane. What he didn't realize was that even his initial, cautious movements were delicious. His fullness inside her gave Lauren an incredible sense of satisfaction; the idea of receiving a man, of receiving Matt in this way, was the sweetest delight.

By the time he moved faster, Lauren was right with him. She adored the way his thighs brushed hers, the way their stomachs rubbed. When he bent his head, she strained higher. His mouth closed over her breast and began a sucking that pulled at her womb from one direction while the smooth stroking of his manhood pulled at it from another. Her hands roamed over and around his firm body, but even had she not touched him, she would have been intimately aware of every hard plane and sinewed swell he possessed. Their bodies were that close, working in tandem.

He murmured soft words of encouragement and praise. "That's it, sweetheart...ahhh...your legs...yes, there...so good..."

They moved as one then, each complementing and completing the other. Lauren experienced a beauty she'd never imagined. She was drawn beyond herself into Matt, sharing, collaborating, merging with him into a greater being for those precious moments of emotional and physical bliss.

After the climax had passed, it was a long time before either of them could speak. They gasped for air, alternately panting and moaning, laughing from time to time at their inability to do anything more. At last Matt slid slowly to her side, leaving one leg and an arm over her in a statement of possession she had no wish to deny. His head was beside hers on the pillow, his cheek cushioned in her hair.

"How do you feel?" he asked in a thick whisper.

"Stunned," she whispered back. "I never imagined..."

"*You* never imagined..."

She forced her lids open and looked at him. "Then...it was okay?"

"It was more than okay," he teased in throaty chiding, "but you had to know that."

"No. I didn't."

His grin faded, replaced by a look of tender concern. He brought a shaky hand up to smooth damp strands of hair from her brow. "I'm sorry if I hurt you, Lauren. If I'd known, I might have been able to make it easier."

"It couldn't have been easier. I've never felt so wonderful in my life."

"Even at the start?" His arched brow dared her to deny the moment of pain she'd felt.

"Even then. If I hadn't felt a thing, something would have been lost. I wanted the pain. Does that make any sense?"

He didn't answer. Instead, he traced her eyebrow with his finger. "Why didn't you tell me, sweetheart?"

"I didn't think it mattered." She paused, experiencing a frisson of apprehension. "Did it? I mean, we're both adults. I knew what I was doing."

"Did you?"

"Yes!" She didn't understand what he was getting at.

"Lauren, I didn't do anything to protect you. It's possible I've just made you pregnant."

Her jaw slackened only slightly. Then, unable to control herself, she burst into a smile. "What an exciting thought!"

Matt closed his eyes for a minute. "You're supposed to be worried, sweetheart." He propped himself up on an elbow and looked down at her. "You're supposed to be thinking about this new life you have, the shop, your independence."

"But a baby!" Her eyes were wide. "I could adjust to that. It would be marvelous!"

"I didn't know you wanted a baby so badly."

"Neither did I." She scrunched up her nose. "But it probably won't happen. Just once, Matt. And it's the wrong time of the month." She brushed the strands of hair from his forehead and left her fingers to tangle in the wet thatch. "Are *you* worried?"

"Of course I'm worried. Babies should be planned, the logistics worked out. Everything should be clear from the start."

"There you go again. So cautious." She tugged playfully at his hair. "If I were to become pregnant, I'd manage. One way or another I would, because I'd want the baby enough to make everything fall into place."

"Such a romantic," Matt murmured, but there was a sadness in his eyes.

Her smile faded. "You're thinking that you'll be leaving soon."

"Sooner or later I will."

"It's okay, Matt. There are no strings attached to what happened tonight. I won't ask any more of you than you want to give."

He snorted and flopped back on the pillow. "That's cavalier of you."

"Would you rather I demand marriage?" she asked, confused. "Times have changed. Just because we made love doesn't mean you have to make an 'honest woman' of me. I don't feel dishonest. I feel…lucky."

He turned his head on the pillow so that he faced her again. "Explain."

"I never expected what happened tonight. What I felt, what I experienced, were so much more than I've ever dared to dream."

"Why not? That's what I don't understand. I don't understand why you were a virgin. You're beautiful, charming and intelligent. And you're right. Times have changed. Women your age are rarely inexperienced."

"Would you have had me throw myself at just any old man for the sake of experience?"

At the sound of hurt in her voice, he rolled over to cover her body. With his large hands cupping her face, he spoke gently. "No, sweetheart. Of course not. I'm the one who's been lucky tonight. To know that you've given me what you've given no other man…that was one of the reasons I couldn't stop when I realized what was happening."

"One of the reasons?"

Even in the dark she caught his sheepish grin. "The others are right here." He dropped a hand to her knee and lifted his body only enough to permit that hand a slow rise. He touched each and every erogenous zone before tapping his finger against her temple. "All of you—mind, body, soul. You turn me on, Lauren."

"Oh, God" was all she could whisper, because his tactile answer had set her body to aching again, and she hadn't believed it could be possible. She didn't know whether to be pleased or embarrassed, but that was her mind talking. Of its own accord, her body shifted beneath his with a story of its own.

As she'd already learned, Matthew Kruger was a good reader.

When the last page of this second chapter had been turned, she fell asleep. Her body was exhausted yet replete, her mind at peace.

She was totally unaware that Matt lay awake beside her for long hours before curving his body protectively around hers and at last allowing himself the luxury of escape.

LAUREN AWOKE the next morning to a strange sensation of heat running the entire length of the back of her body. Her lids flew open and she held her breath. Only her eyeballs moved, questioning, seeking, finally alighting on the large, tanned hand flattened on the sheet by her stomach.

Matt.

Shifting her head, she followed a line from that hand, up a lean but powerful arm to an even stronger shoulder.

Matt.

Quietly, almost stealthily, she turned until she faced him, and her heart melted. He was sound asleep, tawny lashes resting above his cheekbones, his mouth slightly parted, lips relaxed. Unable to help herself, she let her gaze fall along his body. Last night she'd savored him with her hands; this morning it was her eyes' turn to feast.

He was magnificent. Soft hair swirled over his chest, tapering toward his navel, below which the sheet was casually bunched. His hips were lean, as she'd known they'd be; the sheet was nearly as erotic a covering as the air alone might have been.

A self-satisfied smile spread over her face. She felt good. Complete. All woman. Giving in to temptation, she leaned forward and kissed his chest. He smelled of man, earthy but wonderful. Eyes closed, she drank in that essence as she continued to press the lightest of kisses into the warmest of skin.

When a hand suddenly tightened around her waist, her head flew up. Matt's eyes were still closed, but he wore the roguish shadow of a beard on his cheeks and a faint smile on his lips. "Am I dreaming?" he whispered.

In answer, Lauren shimmied higher, slid her arms around his neck and kissed his smile wider. She was further rewarded when he rolled onto his back and hauled her over him. Only then did he open his eyes.

For long minutes, they simply looked at each other. She wasn't sure what her own eyes were saying, but Matt's quite clearly spoke of pleasure. And affection. They made her feel special.

"Hi," he whispered at last.

She swallowed the lump of emotion in her throat. "Hi."

"How'd you sleep?"

"Fine."

"No ghosts?"

She shook her head.

"No strange noises?"

She shook her head. "Beth was right. She said I needed a body-guard."

He closed his hands around her bottom and gave her a punishing squeeze. "So that's why you did it? Because you wanted a body-guard?"

"You know better than that." She sucked in a breath when his hands pressed her intimately closer. "Matt?"

He was grinning. "It's your fault. You started it. In case you didn't know, a man's at his peak in the morning."

"I thought a man was at his peak in his twenties, and you're a mite beyond. You're shocking me."

"You're the one with the bag of surprises. A virgin is supposed to be shy and demure."

She grinned. "I'm not a virgin anymore, so my behavior is ex-cusable."

Rolling over, he set her on her back, then held himself up so that he could look at her. Just as hers had done moments earlier, his eyes touched her body as only his hands had done the night before. "You are beautiful, Lauren. God, I can't believe it." He met her gaze. "No regrets?"

Still basking in his approval, which both stunned and thrilled her, she shook her head. "How about you?"

One long forefinger drew a bisecting line from the hollow of her throat to the apex of her thighs. "No," he answered, but gruffly. "Not about this. About not having the answer to your problem, yes, I have regrets."

"Don't think about that," she whispered, feeling a strange urgency not to let anything intrude on this precious time with Matt. "Not now."

His grin was lopsided, slightly forced, and his eyes lingered on the soft curves of her body. "I think I'd better. It's either that or ravish you again, and I imagine you're going to be a little sore."

"Me? Sore?"

"Yes. You, sore."

"Oh."

With a deep growl, he gathered her into his arms and held her tightly. When his grip loosened, it was with reluctance. "I could use a shower and some breakfast. It's a workday, or had you forgotten?"

"Oh, my god!" She twisted toward the clock on the dresser, then pushed herself from his arms and bolted out of bed. "I'll take the shower first," she called over her shoulder. Remembering her sadly deficient water heater, she added, "Real quick."

Lauren was true to her word, but by the time she had returned to the bedroom, Matt was nowhere in sight. For a split second she panicked. Then she caught sight of his clothes on the floor. "Matt?" Wrapped in her towel, she headed for the stairs. "Matt?"

The aroma of fresh coffee filled the air, but he didn't answer. She was halfway down the staircase when the front door opened and Matt strode through, carrying a large leather suitcase. He was stark naked.

"Matthew Kruger! Where is your sense of decency? If one of my neighbors saw you—"

He'd taken the stairs by twos, and the smack of his lips on hers cut off her teasing tirade. He continued upward. "The trees were my cover. It's a gorgeous day outside."

Lauren couldn't think to argue. He was spectacular. Tall and straight. Broad back, narrow hips, tight buttocks. If it hadn't been for the time, she'd have followed him into the shower just to touch him again. The mere sight of him took her breath away.

But time was of the essence. She blow-dried her hair and put on makeup while Matt showered and shaved; then she dressed quickly and hurried to the kitchen. They were seated side by side, finishing off the last of the scrambled eggs and toast, when Matt laid out his plans for the day.

"I've got meetings set for ten and two. We can take my car into Boston, meet for lunch, then grab something on the way home tonight. Sound okay?"

His words were offered gently, not at all imperiously, yet they brought back to Lauren the crux of Matt's present mission. He intended to protect her as he'd promised, which meant that he was going to stick as close to her side as possible. On one level, she was thrilled with that prospect. On another...

"About my problem, Matt. Are we just going to...wait?"

"Pretty much. It'll be interesting to see if my presence here makes any difference."

"But if nothing happens, we won't know if you've scared someone off for good or simply put him off for a while. And you can't stay here forever."

"I know." He looked away. "I'm going to make some calls today."

"What kind of calls? To whom?"

"People who may have more insight than we do." There was an edge to his voice, but his gaze was soft when he glanced back at her. "Let me do the worrying for now, Lauren. You've done your share."

"But it's my problem! I can't just dump it on your shoulders and wipe my hands of it. That's not fair to you. You don't owe me anything."

For a minute he looked as if he would argue. He gnawed on the inside of his cheek, then lifted his mug and drained the last of his coffee. "Let's just say I owe it to Brad, then. He was my friend and you're his sister. The least I can do is to help you out when you need it."

That wasn't quite the answer she wanted, but she knew she'd have to settle for it.

"Anyway," he added with an endearing grin, "I've got broad shoulders. I can handle it. Maybe it's the Spenser in me coming out, after all."

"Better you than Robert Urich. But are you sure?"

"Very sure. Hey, as far as work on the house goes, are you going to call those names I gave you or would you like me to do it?"

She winced. "Got a cold shower, did you?"

"Well..."

"I'll do it. You're doing enough. I'd love it if you were here when I meet with them, though. I have a feeling some of those guys show more respect when a man's around." The last had been offered on a dry note. She paused, then asked cautiously, "How long will you be here?" She envisioned two or three days, and the thought left her feeling empty.

He rubbed the back of his neck. "I was thinking about that last night. I have to be in Leominster on Thursday and Friday, but I could almost commute from here." He took a fast breath. "Unless you'd rather have the house to yourself again. I'll understand, Lauren. It's okay, really it is—Hey, crumpled napkins in the face I can do without first thing in the morning!"

"Then don't give me that little-boy pout," she chided as she carried their plates to the sink. But when she returned to the table, she gave him a hug from behind. "Of course I want you here," she murmured with her cheek pressed to his. "For as long as you can stay. Besides, you *do* owe it to me."

His hands clasped hers at the open collar of his shirt. "I do?"

"Uh-huh. You've awakened me to some of the finer points in life. Seems to me there's got to be an awful lot I still don't know."

"Then you *are* after my body! I knew it all along!"

"Could be," she answered with a grin. "Could be."

DURING THE NEXT FEW DAYS, Lauren and Matt spent every possible minute with each other. They drove to and from Boston together. They met for lunch each day. When Matt wasn't working but Lauren was, he was parked so frequently on the bench outside the shop that Beth suggested they charge him rent.

"Either that, or hire him part-time."

Lauren wrinkled her nose. "After all we went through to convince Jamie to start full-time next week? No way. Besides, what does Matt know about art?"

"What does he know about *other* things?" Beth drawled suggestively. "That's what *I* want to know."

"Oh, quite a bit" was all Lauren would admit. She knew Beth was fishing. She hadn't made a secret of the fact that Matt was staying with her in Lincoln. But some things were sacred, not to be discussed with even the closest of friends, and for more than the obvious reasons. Lauren felt she was living a fairy tale. By her own admission, Beth was envious. The last thing Lauren wanted to do was to rub it in.

"Well," Beth said with a sigh, "at least he's managed to keep you safe."

"That he has."

Since Matt had been with her, there'd been no accidents, no close calls, no questionable occurrences. Indeed, Lauren felt safe enough almost to forget there was a problem.

Almost, but not quite.

Tuesday evening she asked Matt if he'd made any calls to those "people who may have more insight than we do." He said he had and that the ball was rolling. His tone was light. She hadn't dared ask more.

Wednesday evening, though, she couldn't help herself. As gently as she could, she inquired about it again.

"Have you heard anything yet?"

"No. It takes time."

"Time to do what? I don't understand."

"Questions can be asked, people consulted. Trust me, Lauren. Please?" Put that way, with an eruption of tension dissolving abruptly into beseechfulness, she'd surrendered.

But much as she tried, she couldn't shake the conviction that the things she'd experienced were linked and that, despite Matt's protective shield, they were bound to resume at some point. And she was frightened.

THURSDAY MORNING Matt crawled out of bed at dawn, showered, shaved and dressed, then woke Lauren to say goodbye. She was groggy. It had been another late night of sweet, prolonged loving.

Only the realization that Matt was leaving brought her from her self-satisfied stupor.

"You should have wakened me sooner," she whispered, reaching up to touch his freshly shaved cheek. "I'd have made you breakfast."

"No time. They'll have coffee and doughnuts there."

"I wish you didn't have to go."

"I'll be back tonight."

"I know, but I've been spoiled. Leominster seems so far away."

He sighed. "I agree." He pressed his lips together, then forced a smile. "You take care of yourself, sweetheart, you hear? Drive carefully, and be sure to lock the doors."

"I will."

Lifting her in his arms, he hugged her before setting her back with a kiss on the tip of her nose. She knew not to ask for more. Where temptation was concerned, they were both decidedly weak.

"Good luck, Matt. I hope everything goes well."

He waved as he left the room. Climbing from the bed, she crossed to the window and watched him slide into his car, start the engine and drive off. In an attempt to parry the unease that settled over her, she took a shower and dressed, then forced herself to make breakfast for one and eat every last bit.

Only when she'd finished did she permit herself to sit back and think. She missed Matt. Already. After only two full days together, she'd gotten used to his presence. More than used to it. Addicted to it. Breakfast wasn't the same without him. Neither would lunch be. For that matter, she'd miss being able to look up at odd times and find him on the bench outside the shop.

She wished he could stay forever, but that was an unrealistically romantic thought if ever there was one. Today he was off to Leominster. Next week, or soon after, he'd be back in California. What then? Would they talk on the phone? Visit each other from time to time?

She knew it wouldn't be enough for her. She wanted him in Lincoln with her. Whatever initial reservations she'd had about his background, his occupation or his character were nonexistent now.

His background was blue-collar and strong, his occupation solid, his character sterling. She'd never once glimpsed anything coarse in him. Rather, he'd proved to be unfailingly gentle and giving. Even his reticence about discussing Brad had ceased to matter. He was simply protective, skirting around what he knew to be a sensitive subject.

And he'd brought out a new side of her. Since she'd met him, she'd matured as a woman. He made her believe in both her looks and her sexuality. Whereas her confidence had come from looking in the mirror when she'd first returned from the Bahamas, now it came from the reflection of admiration in Matt's eyes. She didn't care what anyone else thought of her. Only Matt mattered.

So where was she to go from here? Sighing, she rose from the table. She'd clean up the kitchen, go to work and come home. Soon after that, Matt would return. She wasn't even going to think about tomorrow.

One day at a time. All she could do was take one day at a time.

Cleaning up the kitchen was no problem at all. Going to work was another matter. When she tried to start her car, the engine refused to turn over. Not one to beat a dead horse, she returned to the house, called AAA, then sat waiting for half an hour until the tow truck arrived.

"Battery's dead" was the mechanic's laconic diagnosis.

"But that's impossible. This battery's barely four months old!"

"It's dead."

"How can a four-month-old battery die?"

Taking jumper cables from his truck, the man set to work recharging the battery. "Maybe you left the headlights on."

"I never do that."

"Anyone else drive this car? A kid? Maybe he forgot and left 'em on."

"There's no kid, and I'm the only one who drives the car. It's been sitting in the garage since Tuesday morning—" that was when Matt, in fact, had put it away, but he wouldn't have left the lights on "—but it's sat for longer than that without any trouble."

"No sweat, lady. The battery looks okay otherwise. I'll have it working in no time."

He did, and Lauren was only fifteen minutes late for work, but she was bothered by the incident. It occurred to her that the same person who'd sabotaged her garage door might have entered the garage during those days when the car was idle, switched the lights on for a good, long time, then switched them off without her being any the wiser. She decided to discuss it with Matt that night, but the sense of solace in that resolution wasn't enough to prevent a certain nervousness when she returned to the car after work. She found herself glancing around the large parking garage and into the back seat of the car before she dared climb into the front.

She held her breath. The car started. She drove to Lincoln without any trouble.

Matt wasn't due back until nine at the earliest, so she took the time to stop for groceries before arriving at the farmhouse. It was still light out, and she was grateful. She imagined herself being watched and knew that, had it been dark, she would have been terrified.

Relief came in small measure after she was locked safely inside the house. Focusing determinedly on Matt's return, she stowed the groceries, prepared all the fixings for dinner, then poured herself a glass of wine and took refuge in the living room. While lights were burning in the rest of the house, she chose to sit in the dark. Hiding. Brooding. Wondering. Worrying. She knew that her imagination was getting the best of her, but that didn't stop it from happening.

Minutes seemed to stretch into an eternity, though it was barely after nine when finally she heard a car whip up the drive. Hurrying to the window, she peered cautiously out. Her relief was immediate and considerable when Matt climbed from the car. Even before he'd stepped over the threshold, her arms were around his neck.

"Matt, it's wonderful to have you back!"

He had one hand at the back of her head, the other arm around her waist. "Mmm. You're good for my ego. Such a welcome, and I haven't even been gone fourteen hours."

"Close. Thirteen and a half." She lifted her face for a kiss that was instantly comforting and thoroughly satisfying. "How did it go?"

"Very well. I think we've finally worked out the last of the bugs with the locals, so we can get the permit we need, which is great, since we've got everyone else lined up and ready to go."

"Good deal!"

"And I spoke with Thomas." Thomas Gehling was the general contractor whom Lauren had called on Tuesday. "He's looking forward to meeting with us Sunday morning."

"But if he's going to be involved with your project, will he have time to do mine?"

Matt threw an arm around her shoulder and drew her into the house with him. "You have to understand construction lingo. When I say that everyone is lined up and ready to go, it means that if we're lucky, we'll have broken ground within six weeks. And then there's the heavy work that has to be done first—blasting, digging, pouring foundations. The plumbers and electricians and carpenters you'll need won't be required at our site for three months minimum. Thomas will have more than enough time to oversee work here— that is, if you find that you like him and what he has to say. You're under no obligation to use him. There are other names on that list."

"Of the ones I spoke with, I liked him the best. Call it instinct, or whatever, but something meshed even on the phone." She was well aware of the fact that Matt's using Thomas Gehling for his own work might have slanted her view. She trusted Matt's judgment. But she had liked Thomas. He spoke intelligently and seemed perfectly comfortable dealing with a woman.

"I think you'll be impressed when you meet him." Having reached the kitchen, Matt went directly to the sink, turned on the water and squirted a liberal amount of liquid soap on his hands. "So how was your day, sweetheart?"

"Fine—I mean, okay. God, I can't believe it happened again."

"What?"

"I've been a nervous wreck all day, counting the minutes until you got back so I could tell you what happened. Then you walk in here, bringing a sense of security, and I forget all about it."

He stared at her over his shoulder. "What happened?"

"My car wouldn't start this morning. The battery was dead. I had to get a truck here to jump-start it."

"The battery was dead? Didn't you say you'd gotten a new one just before you left Bennington?"

"I did. That's what's so weird. The man from the garage suggested that I'd left my lights on by mistake. I'm sure I'd never do that."

A thick cloud of suds coated Matt's hands, but he paid it little heed. His brows knitted low over his eyes. "I was the last one to drive your car. I put it in the garage Tuesday morning before we left for Boston in mine. I'm sure the lights were off. There'd have been no reason for me to turn them on to begin with, and the car started perfectly, so they couldn't have been left on the night before."

"That's what I figured." She was standing close by the sink. "The only logical explanation is that someone's been tampering in the garage again."

He shot her a sharp glance. "Was anything else wrong with the car?"

"No, and it started perfectly when I left work tonight."

Bending over the sink, Matt splashed soapy water on his face. Lauren reached into a drawer and had a clean towel waiting by the time he'd rinsed and straightened up. No amount of wiping, though, could remove the concern from his features.

"It may have been a fluke," he suggested quietly.

"Do you believe that?"

He hesitated. "No."

"Matt, don't you think it's time we called the police? I mean, when it was only a couple of incidents, they might have thought I was crazy, but at this stage the situation has to be considered suspicious. At least if the police were aware of the possibilities, they could patrol the area more closely."

Matt's expression grew more troubled than ever. "The police might scare him off, and then he'd only wait for things to die down before starting again. What we need to do is to catch him."

"Come on, Matt," she chided, "I was only kidding about playing Spenser."

"It wouldn't be too hard to rig up some booby traps." His eyes were growing animated; he was obviously warming up to the idea. "I think I could manage it, with a little help from a friend."

"From what friend?"

"One of the guys I met in Leominster. He works at a nearby lumberyard." Matt gave a mock grimace and scratched the back of his head. "Seems to me that he mentioned something about having done time."

"A convict? You're going to enlist a *convict* to save me?"

"An ex-convict. And he's been straight for ten years."

"Matt, what *is* this?"

"His specialty was breaking and entering, and he was a genius at it."

Lauren narrowed her eyes. "How long did you spend with this guy?"

"Not long. Can I help it if he's proud of what he's done?"

"Not only after, but before." She grunted, then muttered under her breath, "I can't believe I'm standing here listening when I should be on the phone talking to the police."

Matt put his hands on her arms and stroked her coaxingly. "Come on, Lauren. It's worth a try. You know how the police are—"

"I don't know how the police are. I've never had dealings with them before, contrary to *some* of your friends."

He kissed her forehead. "The police ask millions of questions and then get their minds set on an answer that isn't the one you've given or the one you want to hear. These local departments just aren't geared to taking the offensive, and they sure as hell wouldn't call in the state police or the FBI in a situation like this." His voice softened, taking on a hint of teasing that was reflected in his eyes. "If you were worried about contractors being chauvinists, just wait until you've met the police. They'll treat you like a sweet little thing who's slightly soft in the head." He cupped said item in his hand and gently massaged her scalp. "And even if they decided that you just might be on to something, there's the matter of red tape. They could step up their patrols, but that'd be all. They'd have trouble getting authorization for much else. More than anything, they'd be reluctant to do something that might backfire in court.''

Lauren was having trouble fighting him when he was so close and touching her so gently. ''You're not reluctant,'' she stated, but the accusation she'd intended came out sounding more like admiration.

''Not one bit.'' His thumbs traced the delicate curves of her ears. ''I want whoever's been harassing you to be caught. I have to believe that once we find out who it is, we'll find a motive as well.''

''You're seducing me,'' she breathed.

''Me?''

''Don't look so innocent. You're seducing me.''

''I am not. I'm simply trying to convince you to let me have a go at it.''

''At what? That's the issue.'' Her voice was whisper-soft, not seductive in itself, simply...taken. ''Do you want a go at playing cops and robbers, or at making love with me?''

''I'll make you forget, Lauren,'' he murmured, lowering his head until his lips feathered hers. ''I'll make you forget everything else.''

She caught her breath when he nipped at her lower lip. He was already making her forget, damn him—bless him. At this moment, she wanted to forget.

''I'll make you forget everything else,'' he repeated hotly against her neck. ''And that's a promise. Word of honor.''

MATT MADE GOOD on his promise. Right there, propping Lauren against the kitchen counter, he made love to her with such daring that she forgot everything else but what she felt for him, with him.

He also made good on the promise to call his friend, the breaking-and-entering expert, who showed up at the farmhouse bright and early the very next morning with a carload full of booby-trap makings the likes of which Lauren had never imagined. She had to leave for work before the last of the snares were set, and remarked only half in jest that she'd never make it back into the house alive.

Matt called her from Leominster in the middle of the afternoon to say that he was going to have to attend a dinner meeting and that he wouldn't be back until late. Disappointed but fully appreciative of the demands of his work, she decided to stay in the city after the shop closed to have dinner with Beth and then see a movie.

"Nervous about going home?" Beth teased.

Lauren chuckled—yes, nervously. "It'll be dark, and they've hooked up so many gadgets that it's very possible I'll be the first one caught. You wouldn't believe it, Beth. There's a gizmo on the garage door that has to be deactivated, or else a huge black net descends on an intruder. And once the net falls, *it* sets off a god-awful clanging. The doors to the house have hidden latches that are attached to electrical devices that deliver a shock powerful enough to stun, and the shock in turn sets off an alarm."

"You're right in the middle of a spy novel. I love it!"

"You wouldn't if you had to negotiate everything yourself. There are even hidden snares along the edge of the woods. You'd think we were trapping mink."

"I'm telling you, you've got all the makings of a best-seller. Just think, when this is over, you can write it up. Before you know it, you'll be signing autographs and doing the talk-show circuit."

"Thank you, Beth. I'll settle for catching one man and turning him over to the police."

"But what if it isn't *one* man?" Beth tossed out with imaginative anticipation. "What if there's a whole syndicate that's got some kind of grudge against you? What if you catch one man and another takes over where the first leaves off, so you catch the second? Meanwhile, the first dies mysteriously in jail, so the second decides to sing, and before you know it, there's enough evidence to convict the *entire* syndicate. You'll be a hero!"

"Heroine," Lauren correct dryly. "And I don't believe we're dealing with any syndicate. What would a syndicate have against me?"

"Maybe it was using your vacant farmhouse as its headquarters, and then you came along and, boom, moved in lickety-split, and there's still some very valuable and potentially condemning material stored in the cellar—''

Lauren scowled at her. "What happened to your theory about the ghost of inhabitants past?"

"Too passé. I think I like the syndicate idea better."

"I don't like *either* of them, and if we're going to have dinner together, you'll have to swear you won't go on like this. You're making me nervous."

"I thought you were already nervous."

"You're making me *more* nervous."

Beth patted her arm, then squeezed it. "I'm just teasing, Lauren. You know that. Just teasing."

THAT WAS WHAT LAUREN told herself when, later that night, after the movie had let out and she and Beth had gone their separate ways on the streets of Boston, she had the uncanny sensation of being followed.

CHAPTER SEVEN

The sensation was vague at first, and Lauren wondered if her imagination was simply working overtime. She glanced over her shoulder, then faced forward again. There were people around—she wished there were even more—but none appeared to be suspicious. At least, no one had ducked into a doorway when she'd looked back.

She had walked a bit farther and turned a corner when the sensation intensified. A prickling arose at the back of her neck, accompanied by a frisson of fear. Instinctively she quickened her step, mentally charting the course she'd have to take to reach the garage. It consisted of main streets for the most part, with a single alleyway at the end.

She darted another glance behind her and saw the same outwardly innocuous people—several couples, a handful of singles, all staggered at intervals. If someone grabbed her, she'd yell. There were plenty of bodies to help.

She walked on. Fewer people were ahead of her now; some had turned off toward the subway stop. She assumed the same was true for those behind her, and the thought added to her unease.

She turned another corner. There was no one ahead of her now, and she didn't dare look back. Unbidden, she recalled her childhood. There'd been a dog in the neighborhood, a large German shepherd of which she'd been terrified. Her mother had always instructed her to walk calmly past it on the theory that dogs could smell fear. Could people smell fear? Lauren wondered now. She was sure she reeked of it.

Imagination. That was all it was. Imagination getting a little out of hand. The sounds she heard not far behind weren't footsteps. They were the knocking of the air-conditioning unit in the building she passed...or the creaking of heat as it escaped from the engine of a newly parked car alongside the curb...or...

Eyes wide, she shot a frightened glance over her shoulder and gasped. There was a man. He was very tall, large-set, dressed in black, and he was not twenty feet behind and gaining steadily on her.

Uncaring if she was jumping to conclusions, she began to run. She turned another corner and ran even faster. Her heels beat a rapid tattoo on the pavement, merging with the thundering of her heart to drown out all other night sounds of the city.

She passed another long—agonizingly long—building, then reached the alley, in actuality a single-lane driveway. At its end stood her salvation, a guard booth.

She was breathless and shaking, terrified of looking back and losing time, tripping or slamming into the wall. She cursed her side, which ached; cursed the shoes she wore and the heat that seemed to buffet her and slow her progress. By the time she reached the booth, she felt as though she'd run a marathon.

"Thank God," she whispered, panting as she sagged against the thick plastic enclosure. Then, with a burst of energy, she scrambled to the booth's opening. The guard, a young man with a punk hair-style at odds with his uniform, sat balanced on the back legs of his chair. A dog-eared magazine lay open on his lap. The heavy beat of rock music thrummed from the stereo box by his side. He was chewing gum; the vigorous action of his jaw only enhanced the indolence of his stare.

"Someone was following me," Lauren gasped and darted a frantic glance toward the alley through which she'd run.

Looking thoroughly bored, the guard followed her gaze. There was no one in sight.

"He must have turned away when he saw me heading toward you," she explained, trying to calm herself enough to think clearly. "Listen, I need a big favor."

The young man blew a bubble, popped it and licked the gum back into his mouth. "Depends what it is."

"Could you walk me to my car?"

He gave a one-shouldered shrug. "I'm on duty."

"I know, but there aren't many cars leaving the garage now. With the gate down, they'll wait. It won't take you long—two, maybe three minutes. Just until I lock myself in."

He fingered his earlobe, which sported a crescent of multiple studs. "I'm not supposed to leave this booth."

"But I'm in danger!"

Slowly, his head nodding in time with the music, he looked back toward the street. "Don't see anyone."

"He may have taken the stairs. Please! I need your help!"

After what seemed forever, the front legs of the chair hit the floor. "So. Chivalry calls." The guard stood up, yawned, then pushed his shoulders back.

The show was wasted on Lauren, who saw right through it to the scrawniness of his physique. Not much to protect her with. But he wore a uniform. There was safety in a uniform.

"I'm the new guy on the block," he drawled. "I was given specific instructions—"

She felt sweat trickling down her back. "Look, I'll argue on your behalf if you get into trouble. It seems to me your boss would reward you for helping a regular tenant."

"You're a regular tenant?" His gaze drifted down her body.

"Yes." She sighed in exasperation, feeling suddenly tired. Instinctively she knew she was safe standing at the booth with even as unlikely a guard as this, but there was still the threat of the inner garage to overcome. She wanted nothing more than to be locked in her car and on the road, headed for home. "Please. Just walk me upstairs. You could have been up and back in the time you've spent talking with me."

He grinned. "Yeah, but talking with you beats sitting here by myself." He cocked his head to one side. "Sure. I'll walk you upstairs."

Lauren jerked her eyes toward the thick pipes overhead. "Thank you," she breathed. By the time she looked down, the guard had let himself out of his cage and was swaggering toward her.

She glanced worriedly back toward the exit, but it remained empty.

"Come on, love. Up we go." He took her elbow and she jumped, wondering for an instant if she'd leaped from the frying pan into the fire. Unfortunately, she was the proverbial beggar who couldn't be choosy. So she clamped her mouth shut and let her cocky gallant lead the way to the stairs.

He dropped her elbow to open the door. Her apprehensive gaze examined every nook of the stairwell as they started up.

"Floor?"

"Third." Had the stairwell always been this narrow?

He chewed away at his gum. "Work around here?"

"Yes." Had the stairwell always been this confining?

"Kind of late leaving, aren't you?"

"Yes." He wouldn't try anything. He wouldn't dare. She knew where and for whom he worked.

"Hot date?"

"Yes...he'll be waiting for me on the corner as soon as I leave here."

They climbed the last set of stairs in silence. Though Lauren didn't look, she could feel the smirk on her companion's face. He hadn't believed her. She'd hesitated too long, then spoken too quickly. Damn, but she wasn't good at this.

He swung open the door, then stood aside to let her through. "Always park on the third floor?"

She was looking nervously from side to side, trying to see into corners where a tall, large, dark form might be lurking. "It depends," she offered distractedly. With no assailant in sight, she blindly fumbled in her bag for the keys.

"Where's your car?"

She pointed. They reached it half a minute later.

"There," he announced as she unlocked the door, checked the back seat, then all but threw herself behind the wheel. "Safe and sound."

She locked the door and rolled her window down, just enough

to murmur a heartfelt "Thank you. I do appreciate what you've done."

"How about a ride down?"

"Uh…" Dumbly, she looked at the passenger seat, then leaned over and tugged up the button on the opposite door. Already striding around the front of the car, the guard let himself in.

She had her window up tight and the car started before he'd closed the door, and she took the ramps at breakneck speed. Her passenger didn't seem to mind. She suspected he enjoyed the daring ride.

She brought the car to an abrupt halt by the booth, let the guard out and quickly relocked the door. By the time she'd straightened up, he was at her window and making a rolling gesture with his hand. Again she lowered the window several inches.

"Your card?" he asked with an impudent grin.

"Oh." She rummaged in her purse, drew out the card and handed it over. While he studied it, her gaze alternated between the rearview mirror and the windows on either side.

"Looks okay…Lauren." Chomping briskly on his gum, he returned the card, then winked. "Drive carefully now." The last word was muted through her reclosed window. He twisted backward in a move she was sure he practiced regularly on the dance floor, pressed a button and released the gate.

Without another word, Lauren stepped on the gas. She held her breath and didn't expel it until she'd reached the relative safety of Government Center.

With great effort, she forced her rigid fingers to relax on the steering wheel. She took long, deep breaths, feeling safer with each block she put between herself and the parking garage. No one appeared to be following her. To double-check, she swung from one lane to the other, then, a block later to the first lane. She annoyed several drivers, but she didn't care. All that mattered was that the headlights in her rearview mirror were ever varied.

During the drive home, her emotions ran the gamut from fear to confusion to anger. It was the latter that was dominant by the time she pulled up in front of her own garage. She left the engine running and the headlights on; she had a death grip on the wheel again, and her teeth were clenched. She barely had time to debate whether she should sit this way until Matt returned—she didn't expect him for a while yet—when a pair of headlights pierced the darkness behind her.

She sucked in a breath. It was *him*! He'd followed her after all! Frantic, she struggled to decide on the best course of action. The other car neared. She had to think quickly. She could make a mad dash for the safety of the house, but it would take time for her to work around the booby traps.

Too late.

She could run from the car and head for the woods in an attempt to make it to a neighbor's before being overtaken, but the woods, too, were booby-trapped, and that man had been large and ominously physical-looking.

Too risky.

She could lean on the horn in the hope that the noise would either scare him off or arouse someone's attention.

That seemed her only option.

Her hand was on the horn, about to exert force, when the car behind her sounded its own horn in short, repetitive blasts. Her fear-filled gaze snapped to the rearview mirror.

Matt! It was *Matt*!

Lauren had never felt so relieved, or so foolish, or so furious in her entire life. Storming from her car, she met him halfway between the two. "I cannot *take* any more of this!" she screamed, hands clenched by her sides.

"Lauren, what—"

"It's gone on too long! Why *me*? What have *I* ever done to deserve this—this torture?"

"Take it easy, sweetheart—"

"I've *had* it, Matt!" She took a step back, eluding the hands he would have put on her shoulders. "This isn't fair! I'm a nervous wreck. I'm getting a permanent crick in my neck from looking over my shoulder. Someone's following me. Someone isn't. Someone's been in the house. Someone hasn't. Someone's sicced a dog on me.

Someone hasn't. I don't know who to trust and who not to. For all I know, *you* were the one who stalked me in Boston!''

"*Me?* I just this minute got back from Leominster!''

"But how do I know that?'' she fired at him. She was visibly shaking; the emotional strain was taking its toll. "How do I know *anything*? It's always in the dark. *I'm* always in the dark. I'm afraid to pull into my garage for fear I'll become a sitting duck in a big black net. I'm afraid to go into my house for fear I'll be electrocuted at the front door.'' Her voice grew as wobbly as her knees. "I can't live this way.'' She ducked her head and withered into herself, whispering, "Damn it, I can't live this way.''

She didn't have the strength to elude Matt this time. He put his arms around her and held her while she cried softly.

"It's okay, sweetheart,'' he murmured. "Let it out. You'll feel better, and then we'll talk.''

"I won't feel...better....''

His arms tightened, hands gently kneading her back. "Sure you will. You're upset now. Sounds like you had a bad day.''

"Bad night....''

"Come on. Let's go inside.''

A short time later, Lauren was huddled in a corner of the living room sofa, holding the glass of brandy Matt had pressed into her hand. He drew one of the side chairs close and propped his elbows on his knees. "Okay. From the top. What happened tonight?''

"It's not just what happened tonight. It's *everything*.''

"But tell me about tonight. I need to know, Lauren.''

She studied the rim of the brandy snifter and shrugged. "I panicked.'' Painstakingly, she explained how she'd walked back to the garage. "Then there was that awful last stretch when only one man was behind me.''

"Did you see what he looked like?''

She tipped the snifter until the brandy came perilously close to its rim. "Not really. I glanced back once and got the impression of someone big and tall and dark. Then I started running and didn't look back again.''

"He didn't follow you once you ran?''

"I don't know. I didn't look. By the time I reached the garage, I couldn't see him. I conned the guard into walking me up to my car."

"Smart girl."

She snorted. "Fine for you to say. You didn't see the guard."

"It was still smart. A paid guard wouldn't try anything. He'd never get away with it."

"That was what I figured, not that I had much choice at the time."

"But you made it to your car safely. Did you see anyone when you were driving away from the garage?"

"I wasn't looking." She paused to take a healthy swallow of brandy, made a face, recovered, then went on. "I just locked the doors and drove. No one followed me home, at least no one I could see. I was checking for that." Her voice rose. "But when I got here, I didn't know what to do. Everything was dark, and I was sure that if I tried to get into the house, I'd get caught in one of your snares. Then you drove up, and I thought it was *him*—but I really don't know if there *was* a him. The man I saw could have been after me. Then again, he could have been minding his own business."

Matt closed his hand over hers and urged the snifter to her lips again. The brandy was doing its thing; at least she'd stopped shaking.

"I'm sorry I frightened you," he said.

"I thought you'd be later."

"I left Leominster as soon as I could. I was worried."

The eyes Lauren raised brimmed with discouragement. "What am I going to do, Matt?" she whispered. "I can't go on this way."

"I know, sweetheart. I know." His expression was grim. "Do you think someone's keeping tabs on you during the day?"

"While I'm at work, you mean?"

He nodded. "Have you ever gotten the feeling that you're being followed in broad daylight?"

She thought for a minute. "No."

"Ever remember seeing anyone who might fit the description of the man you saw tonight?"

Again she pondered his question, then shrugged in frustration. "There have to be dozens of tall, large-set men who wander through the Marketplace each day. I've never noticed anyone special...other than you." When he glowered at her, she added a sad "That was a compliment," and his glower promptly faded.

"Oh. Thank you."

"What *am* I going to do?"

"I'm thinking. I'm thinking." It was a while before he spoke again, and then it was almost to himself. "You haven't gotten any strange phone calls, heavy-breathing type of thing? And there hasn't been any direct contact, like a note or anything?"

She shook her head, but Matt's attention was on the floor. His brows were knitted together, his lips clamped into a thin line.

"I think," he said at last, "that you should finish your brandy and get to bed. You've had a frightening—"

"Finish my brandy and get to bed? That won't solve anything!"

"There's nothing to be solved tonight. You're safely locked in, and I'm here."

"But tomorrow! I have to go to work tomorrow! You can't be with me every minute, and I don't even want that. I've never been helpless or clinging before, but it seems that lately I'm throwing myself at you the instant you get here."

"I don't mind," he volunteered with a half grin, only to be cut off.

"Well, I do! I don't like what I've become, Matt. I can't continue living this way. I won't!"

What had existed of a grin was wiped clean from his face. "I agree, Lauren. Something has to be done. It's simply a matter of deciding what. Just...just let me sleep on it, okay?"

"I know what should be done. The police should be called in."

He took her hand. "Do you trust me?"

"Of course I trust you. I just think that—"

"Do you *trust* me?"

She knew he was testing her. There was nothing of the little boy about him now. He was all man. Eyes locked with his, she nodded.

"Then let me sleep on it. Give me until morning to figure out what the next step should be."

At that moment, Lauren came out of herself enough to see the lines of fatigue that shadowed Matt's face. He was tired. And worried. "But it's not your responsibility—"

"Till morning?"

She clamped her lower lip between her teeth, then let it slide out. Her nod was slower in coming this time, but when it did, it conveyed the trust he sought.

MORNING ARRIVED, and Lauren awoke to find that Matt was no longer in bed. Tossing her robe on, she hurried off in search of him. He was just replacing the telephone receiver when she entered the kitchen.

"Matt?" She halted abruptly and stood suspended on the threshold. There was something about the tired slump of his shoulders that filled her with dread.

He covered the distance between them and took her in his arms. His words came out in a rush. "I have to go back to California for a couple of days, Lauren. I've just spoken with the airline and made a reservation."

For a minute she couldn't say anything. She'd known that sooner or later he'd be leaving, but... "Now?" she whispered through a tight throat. "Why *now*?"

"It's important. You know I wouldn't leave if it weren't."

"But...what should I do?" The instant she said the words, she hated them, hated herself, hated the situation.

"I think you should consider visiting your parents."

"No."

"What about Beth? You could sleep over at her place."

"No."

"Then take a room at a hotel. Maybe the Bostonian, or the Marriott. Something close to work."

"No!" She freed herself from his grasp and wrapped her arms

around her waist. "I'm not running away. I won't be forced out of my own home!"

Matt ran a hand through his hair, which looked as if he'd done that more than once. For that matter, between the creases on his brow and the weary look in his eyes, she wondered if he'd slept at all. He seemed to be exerting a taut control over himself, but then, so was she. She refused to fall apart, to be reduced to a simpering weakling. No strings, she'd told Matt, and no strings there would be.

"It's very important that I go, Lauren."

Her chin was firm. "It's all right. You can go."

"I don't want to."

"But it's all right. I'll be fine." Hadn't she always been before?

"It's just for two or three days."

"I understand."

"No, you don't. You think I'm running out on you."

"I think just what you told me, that it's important for you to fly back." She was feeling distinctly numb. "When does your plane leave?"

He glanced at his watch. "In two hours."

"I can drop you at the airport on my way—"

"You'll be late. I'll drive myself and leave the car at the airport."

She nodded. Without another word, she turned and retraced her steps to the bedroom. She thought of nothing but getting ready for a regular day's work.

Matt showered while she dressed. They said little to each other during breakfast. Only when she had swung her pocketbook to her shoulder did she look at him. Even her self-imposed anesthetization couldn't fully immunize her against the swell of emotion that hit her.

"Have a safe flight," she whispered.

He walked her to the door. "You know how to work the latch for this thing?"

"Yes." He'd reviewed the process in detail when they'd entered the house last night.

"Be sure to reset it once you've let yourself in or out."

"I will."

They passed through and headed for the garage. "And this one?"

"Yes. I've got it now."

"Lauren, I really wish—"

"Shh. Please, Matt. You have to do your thing, and I have to do mine." She pressed the hidden switch that allowed her access to the garage without mishap, but before she could enter the car, Matt stopped her. He put both hands on her shoulders and looked her straight in the eye.

"I know you're angry, Lauren, and hurt. Believe me, I'd never be leaving if I didn't think it was absolutely necessary."

She stared up at him, saying nothing because there was nothing she would permit herself to say. Only when he tugged her close and wrapped his arms tightly around her did she allow herself a moment's softening. Closing her eyes, she leaned into his strength. By the time he'd released her, though, she was on her own again.

"Be cautious, Lauren," he said. His voice was thick, his gaze clouded. "When in doubt, go with your instincts. They're good. Trust them."

For a split second, she wavered. Her instincts told her that Matt shouldn't go, that she needed him here, that whatever it was that drew him back to California wasn't as important as what was happening between them in Massachusetts. Her instincts told her that his trip would bring no good where they were concerned.

But reason ruled. Matt's home and job were in San Francisco. She had no claim on either. She was right in what she'd told him; he had to do his thing and she had to do hers. And hers was to carry on with her life, just as it had been before Matthew Kruger had entered it.

"Take care," she whispered, then slipped into her car. She didn't look back to see Matt by the garage door after she'd backed out and around, or to see him still standing there when she drove down the drive and turned into the street. If she was aware that she'd left part of herself with him, she put that particular ache down to the general upheaval her life had gone through in the past few weeks. Doggedly she kept her sights ahead.

As THE DAY PASSED, Lauren had less control over her emotional state than she might have liked. Much as she tried not to, she thought of Matt. *He's arriving at the airport now. His plane is taking off now. He's over Pennsylvania, Illinois, Kansas, Utah.* Out of the blue, she'd feel tears in her eyes, and though she cursed her preoccupation, she knew that it was diverting her mind from other thoughts.

Beth, who'd been quick to sense something amiss, tried to get her to talk, but all Lauren would say was that Matt had been called back to his home office for a few days.

"But I thought he was here for another week at least."

"Things come up."

"And he didn't elaborate?" There was an undercurrent of accusation in Beth's words.

Lauren, who was carelessly flipping through the morning's mail, ignored it. "Other than to say it was important that he go." She frowned. "I don't believe it. Another letter for Susan Miles."

"Who's Susan Miles?"

"Beats me. But it's addressed to her, care of this shop. There was one yesterday, too."

"Mark it 'return to sender, addressee unknown' and stick it back in the mail."

"I would if I could, but I can't. There's no return address."

"Postmark?"

"Boston. If whoever sent it doesn't get an answer, he'll just have to show up here to see what's wrong."

"He? How do you know it's a he?"

Lauren held out the letter. "Look at the handwriting. It's heavy. And messy. Has to be a he."

Beth donned her imagination-at-work look. "A he. Hmm, I smell possibilities in this one. You've already got a guy, so forget you. Let's concentrate on me. Suppose, just suppose, some fellow was given the name of a girl he was told worked here. A blind-date kind of thing. Only either he got the girl's name screwed up or the friend who set him up was playing a joke."

"Why would a guy *write* to set up a blind date?"

"Maybe he's too shy to call. Or he's simply taking a new approach. A new approach—that's it." She eyed Lauren through a playful squint. "Not all that different from sitting on a bench for two days, or sitting on it for hours a third day just reading."

"Point taken," Lauren admitted dryly. "I suppose this guy's gorgeous and witty and bright."

"Naturally."

"Then why does his handwriting look like a thug's?"

"It's not like a thug's. It's...creative."

"Ahh. Then whatever is inside this envelope," Lauren said, waving it, "must be equally as creative."

"I'm sure it is." Beth's voice dropped conspiratorially. "Let's open it."

"We can't do that, Beth. It's not addressed to us."

"It's addressed to our shop."

"And what if your gorgeous guy comes in to collect the letters he's incorrectly addressed? He'll be mortified."

"He'll be so taken with me that he won't have time to be mortified. Besides, we can say we threw the letters out. So what harm is there in opening them first? Do you have the other one?"

"Yes, but, Beth, I don't think this is a great idea."

"Don't think." Snatching the gray envelope from Lauren's hand, Beth quickly opened it. She removed a sheet of matching stationery, unfolded it, then turned it over, puzzled. "Blank. There's nothing on it."

Lauren, too, stared at the blank sheet. "Maybe he lost his nerve the second time around."

"Where's the first?"

Lauren fished the envelope from a drawer in the desk and, her own curiosity piqued, opened it. "The same. The paper is blank. What's going on here, Beth?"

"Who knows?" Beth continued the game, but her enthusiasm was waning. "Maybe his tactic is to be mysterious for a while."

"So we have to wait for the next installment to find out who the mad letter writer is?"

Beth shrugged. "Looks that way." She headed for the front of the store, leaving Lauren to dispose of the blank love letters as she saw fit. For some reason Lauren herself didn't understand, she folded both sheets back into their envelopes and tucked the envelopes into the drawer.

This activity had provided only a temporary respite for Lauren, as did most of work that day. Unfortunately, by the time she knew that Matt had landed and been swallowed up in his own life again, she could no longer free herself of those other, more ominous thoughts.

"How'd you like a roommate for a night or two?" she asked Beth when they were getting ready to close the shop. She'd tried to sound nonchalant, but the gesture was lost on Beth, who knew better.

"I'd love it, Lauren. You know that. You're welcome to stay at my place whenever you want."

"I know you have a date—"

"No, I don't."

"Listen, it's okay. I just don't feel like driving back to Lincoln. You can go out. I'll make myself at home—"

"I don't have a date, Lauren."

"But that fellow Joe—"

"Asked me out and I refused. He wanted to go camping. Overnight. I didn't have equipment, and I'm not keen on camping, and I'm even less keen on Joe."

"How do you know? You've just met the guy."

"Exactly. Have you ever heard of camping overnight for a first date?"

Lauren shrugged. "Might have been interesting."

"Maybe for you and Matt. No, chalk that." Beth grunted. "Matt might have left you stranded in the woods while he raced off to scale some nearby peak. How could he simply abandon you this way, Lauren? I still can't believe it."

Lauren kept her voice calm. "He has his own life."

"But he's barged his way into yours—"

"He didn't barge his way in anywhere."

"Okay, then he wormed his way in. He's made himself nearly indispensable—"

"He has *not*. I can do just fine without him."

"Mmm. That's why you can't bear the thought of going home."

Lauren's gaze lowered to the scrap of fabric she was fraying. "It's not that. But after last night I feel…uncomfortable." She'd told Beth earlier about the episode near the garage. "It's still too fresh in my mind."

"Matt wasn't around then, either. Why do men do this, Lauren? Why aren't they around when you need them?"

"It's not a question of need," Lauren rationalized. "I'm independent. I can take care of myself."

"You should go to the police. I think what you're facing is more than even Matt can handle. Why is he so vehement against it?"

"He has good reasons. He may be right."

"Maybe his reasons aren't so noble."

Lauren tensed. "What do you mean?"

"It's occurred to me that much of what's happened to you has been since Matt showed up."

"That's not true! Three of those incidents happened before he ever got here!"

"No," Beth returned, determined to make her point. "If my memory's correct, three of those incidents happened within mere days of his first introducing himself to you. He said he was here in Boston on business. For all you know, he was here in the city that very first time, when the car just missed you on Newbury Street."

"I'm not sure I like what you're implying."

"I'm not sure I do, either, but it may be worth considering."

"Absolutely not! What could Matt possibly have to do with those incidents? What reason could he have to wish me harm?"

"Maybe something to do with Brad?"

"That's impossible. Don't even think it, Beth. It's out of the question."

No more was said about it, but Beth had accomplished her objective. Lauren fought it. She told herself that Beth was either playing the game she played so well or simply jealous. Lauren closed her mind to it while she and Beth walked over Beacon Hill to Beth's apartment, where they shared a congenial dinner and evening. Later that night, though, while Lauren lay quietly on the sofa bed trying to fall asleep, unwanted thoughts flitted in fragments through her mind.

Ironically, Matt's phone call didn't help. It came at two in the morning, shortly after Lauren had fallen into a restless sleep. The phone was on the table by her head. She nearly jumped out of her skin when it rang.

"Hello?"

"Lauren! I've been worried sick! When there was no answer at the farmhouse, I started calling hotels. You said you *weren't* going to Beth's!" He sounded angry. That was all Lauren needed.

"Why, Matt, how good of you to call in the middle of the night. I'm fine, thank you. How are you?"

"Lauren, you said you weren't going anywhere!"

"I changed my mind."

"Damn it, you could have let me know. I was sure something had happened!"

"How could I have let you know? I don't know where you are, much less at what phone number."

"I'm at home, and I'm the only Matthew Kruger in the San Francisco book!"

"How did I know you'd be trying me? You didn't say anything about calling."

She heard a deep sigh at the other end of the line. "Right. I'm sorry. It was my fault. Are you okay?"

"I'm tired, Matt." *And confused. Very confused.* The sound of Matt's voice, imperious, then gentle, only added to her confusion.

"I'm sorry to be calling so late. I started trying the house an hour and a half ago. When there was no answer, I figured maybe you'd gone to another movie or something, but when you didn't return, I started imagining things and it all began to spiral. You are okay?''

"Yes, I'm okay."

"Nothing happened today?"

"No, nothing happened."

"Thank goodness."

His voice clearly held relief. For that matter, Lauren mused, everything about his voice was clear. He could just as well be calling her from around the corner....

"Well," he went on, less sure of himself now, "I just wanted to hear your voice. And to tell you that I'm going to try to catch an afternoon flight out of here tomorrow. By the time I get into Logan and on the road, it's apt to be pretty late. It may be easier if I go to a hotel—"

"No!" she interrupted. She could hear the fatigue in his voice, and it pulled a string somewhere deep inside her. This was Matt, the man she missed, the man she wanted to see, to be with. "No. Meet me in Lincoln. I'll be there."

"But you may be sleeping. I'll frighten you."

"Just give a honk like you did the other night and I'll know it's you."

"Are you sure?"

"I'm sure."

"Okay, sweetheart." His voice lowered. "I miss you."

"Me, too, Matt."

"See you tomorrow night, then?"

"Uh-huh."

"Take care, sweetheart."

"You, too. Bye-bye, Matt."

She replaced the receiver and sank back to the bed, only then realizing that she hadn't even asked how he was doing. Maybe she hadn't wanted to. Maybe she'd been afraid he'd give her an evasive answer. He hadn't spelled out the reason for his abrupt return to San Francisco—if indeed he was there. Was his business on the West Coast shrouded in mystery, or was her imagination at work again?

After tossing and turning for better than an hour, she finally fell back to sleep. When she awoke on Sunday morning, she felt weary and tense. Even Beth's lighthearted chatter didn't lighten her mood; irrationally, perhaps, she blamed Beth for having planted the seeds of doubt in her mind.

Driving to Lincoln in broad daylight was accomplished comfortably. Lauren arrived there moments before Thomas Gehling pulled up. She liked him instantly, finding him easygoing, intelligent and polite. As they walked through the house, they discussed a wide range of possibilities. She hired him on the spot.

That was the high point of her day. The tension, the confusion, the worry, were back in full swing by the time she'd returned to Boston. Work at the shop was a blessing, but a short-lived one. All too soon she was headed back to Lincoln. This time around, she was a bundle of raw nerves.

A confrontation was imminent. She felt it in every fiber of her being. By nature she was a peaceful, accommodating sort, but the events of the past few weeks had upset her equilibrium. It was one thing to suspect that an unknown lunatic was after her, yet quite another to suspect that it was Matt. He was either with her or against her. She had to know one way or the other.

Arriving home at dusk, she was assailed by every one of the fears she'd been free of that morning. Glancing anxiously from side to side, she incned her way up the drive. Her first thought was to leave the car outside, but she knew that its protection, and hence her own, came from the trap that was set inside. Dashing quickly from the car to the garage, she fumbled to disengage the alarm and raise the door. That done, she quickly brought the car inside, lowered the door and reengaged the snare, then tackled the front door of the house. Beads of sweat were dotting her upper lip by the time she'd finally closed the door behind her and reset the alarm.

Then she made dinner, ate practically none of it and waited. She picked up a book, turned page after page without absorbing a word and waited. She dozed on the living room sofa, awakening with a jolt at the slightest sound—though most were in her dreams—and waited.

Midnight came and went. Then one o'clock. It was nearly one-thirty when she finally heard a car approach. This time she didn't rush to the window. She didn't so much as shift on the sofa. She sat quietly in the dark, waiting.

CHAPTER EIGHT

Lauren held her breath when she identified the click and scrape at the front door as the disengagement of the makeshift electrical alarm. Her eyes pierced the darkness, never once leaving the broad oak expanse as, with an aged creak, the door slowly opened. The man who came quietly through was tall, very tall, and large-set. Though he could have doubled for the man she'd seen behind her in Boston on the previous Friday night, there was no doubt in her mind that this time it was Matt.

"You didn't honk," she accused in a voice that shook.

His head twisted. "Lauren!" Setting his suitcase on the floor, he groped for the light switch. The weak glow that subsequently filtered into the living room from the hall was enough to reveal her position on the sofa. "What are you doing up, sweetheart? I thought for sure you'd be in bed."

"You didn't honk."

He paused, turning his head slightly. "The thought of it seemed jarring at this hour. I really didn't want to wake you up." He stood backlighted in the archway of the living room, his face in shadows. "But you weren't sleeping, were you?" Crossing the room, he hunkered down and curled his fingers lightly around her arms. Her skin was cold. "Why aren't you in bed?" he asked softly.

"We have to talk."

"You sound strange. What's wrong?"

She didn't move. "I'm not sure. That's one of the things we have to discuss."

He frowned at his hands, dropped them to the sofa on either side of her hips, then met her gaze. "What is it, Lauren?"

"I've been sitting here thinking. I've spent most of the day thinking. And last night, too."

He sank back on his heels, hands falling to his sides. "About what?"

"You. I want the truth, Matt." It was a struggle to keep her voice steady when so much was at stake, but she managed commendably. "I want all of it. No evasion. No seduction. I want to ask questions and have them answered."

"I don't understand. I've always given you answers—"

"They were never enough, but that may be my fault. Maybe I haven't *asked* enough."

"I don't know what you're getting at."

She tucked her legs more tightly beneath her. "Three weeks ago I was happy. My life was shaping up so beautifully that I had to pinch myself to make sure it was real. Then certain things started happening, and I'm suddenly stuck in the middle of a nightmare. Someone is after me. I don't know who or why."

"What's this got to do with *me*?"

"You showed up right after it all began, Matt. By some coincidence, you appeared out of nowhere. You claim to be a friend of my brother's, but my brother has been dead for a year, so I can't ask him about it. You have biographical facts about Brad, any of which you could have picked up by reading a standard job résumé. You have insight into his character, most of which you could have gained in one night of heavy drinking with him, even if he'd been a total stranger up until then."

"I don't believe this," Matt muttered, but Lauren was just beginning.

"That first night when you introduced yourself to me, you said you'd been in Boston for a week. It was during that very week that I was nearly run down by a car on Newbury Street. Nothing about the car registered with me. It could very easily have been a nondescript rental, just like the one you've been driving."

"Lauren—"

"Then a dog attacked me. You were the one who suggested it might have been trained to pull away when a special whistle was blown. That thought wouldn't even have occurred to me, yet it did to you. Why?"

"It's common knowledge—"

"And then my garage door crashed down." Despite the warmth of the night, her hands were freezing. She tucked them more deeply in the folds of her shirt. "You're a builder. You seemed familiar enough with the workings of that door to be able to rig, and unrig, a malfunction."

"This is absurd, Lauren! Do you know what you're saying?"

"I'm not done," she declared. "Let me finish."

He was on his feet, prowling the room. "I can't wait to hear the rest."

She ignored his sarcasm, knowing only that the time for silence had passed. "There was the matter of an intruder in my house. You found the problem immediately. A lock on one of the windows was broken. In fact, you used that very window to get into the house, supposedly to scout around. How can I be sure it was the first time you'd entered the house that way?" When Matt took a sharp breath to defend himself, she rushed on. "The car that followed me all the way home from Boston was compatible in both size and shade to your rental. And the timing was perfect. You could have left me at my garage, picked up your own car—even on another floor of the same garage—and tailed me out. Then there was the night when I heard strange noises. You said you were in Leominster. It was a convenient alibi, but I have no proof, do I?"

"I'll give you names and numbers—"

"My car battery went dead; you were the last one to drive the car. Someone followed me late at night in Boston; you conveniently arrived here within minutes after I did."

"I was in *Leominster*—but I told you that once before, didn't I? I thought we agreed on it."

"That was what you wanted, for me to agree on it."

"I wanted you to trust me."

"So you told me. Many times. And I've been completely taken in, because I thought you were one of the most sincere, straightforward men I've ever met. Maybe I was wrong, Matt. Maybe I've been playing into your hands all along."

He stood before her then, hands on his hips, his face a mask of steel. The oblique light from the hall did nothing to blunt his obvious irritation. "What brought all this on? That's what I'd like to know. You did trust me. At least, I thought you did. Where did I go wrong?"

Lauren's composure was beginning to slip. If Matt was innocent—and his reaction was far from conclusive on that score—she was going to hate herself for the accusations she'd made. On the other hand, if he was guilty as charged, she was in a lot of trouble.

"You went wrong," she began with a shaky breath, "when you took off for California on Saturday morning."

"You *were* angry."

"No. But I was puzzled and maybe a little hurt, because the trip was so sudden and you were so tight-lipped about it. And that got me to thinking, and suddenly there were more questions than ever. I'm an intelligent person, Matt. 'Together,' to quote you. You could have told me anything and I'd have understood. Okay, what happens with your work is your business. But you've shared other things with me, which I realize in hindsight you've been very selective about. Why discuss some things and not others? Unless you're hiding something. Unless there's something you don't want me to know."

He threw a hand in the air. "It's Beth. You've been listening to Beth. This sounds like one of her harebrained plots."

Lauren stared him out. "Days ago I wanted to go to the police. Any person in his right mind would do that in a situation like mine. But I didn't go to the police, because you told me not to. You've been adamant about it! *Why?*"

"You want to know why?" Matt raged suddenly. His eyes were narrowed, his head thrust forward. "I'll tell you why! Because your brother, Brad, was up to no good during the last few years of his life, and if I'd gone to the police when I suspected that Brad's boss was behind what was happening to you, it would have all come out. *You'd* have been hurt. I was trying to protect *you!*"

Lauren sat in stunned silence as the warm summer night crowded in on her. One minute she felt smothered, the next chilled. In the third, she was stifling again and began to sweat. Dropping her gaze to the floor, she pressed a finger to her moist upper lip, frowned, then looked back at Matt. "What did you say about Brad?" she asked in a timid whisper.

Matt stood with his feet braced apart, one hand massaging the taut muscles at the back of his neck. At her question, he lowered his head, put two fingers to his forehead and rubbed. "Brad was in trouble." His voice held a blend of sadness and defeat. Lauren knew he'd have to be a consummate actor to produce such a heart-wrenching tone on cue.

"What kind of trouble?" Her stomach had begun to jump. She pressed a hand to it.

"Please. Lauren, you don't want—"

"What kind of trouble?" When he didn't answer, she repeated the question a third time. *"What kind of trouble?"*

Matt sighed in resignation. "He'd been padding invoices and expense vouchers, then pocketing the difference."

"I don't believe you."

"Maybe that's just as well. Brad's dead. Nothing will ever be proved one way or another. Just rumors. Lousy rumors."

"You believe them."

"I knew Brad." He took a quick breath. "Please, don't misunderstand me. Brad and I were close. He was a loyal friend. I respected him in many, many ways."

"But?"

"But all along I knew there was one part of him that was unsettled. It was as if he was looking for an opening, and his boss unwittingly gave him one. Chester Hawkins was a crook. We both knew it. We discussed it many times. Bribes, kickbacks—you name it, Hawkins did it."

"But padding expense vouchers—that's small-time stuff. What could Brad have hoped to gain?"

"It's not small-time when it's done over and over again."

"For how long?"

"Two years, maybe three. It adds up."

"But *why*? Why would he have done it?"

Matt dropped into a side chair. "Maybe he felt it was poetic

justice, stealing from a thief. More likely he felt that an accumu-
lation of wealth was the only way he could prove his worth.''

Lauren moaned softly. Her head fell back against the sofa and
she closed her eyes. When she spoke, her voice was wobbly. ''I
knew there was too much money. It didn't make sense. Right from
the start I wondered, but I took it. I took it and I used it.''

''Which was exactly what you *should* have done!'' Matt sat forward and spoke with renewed force. ''Brad earned every cent of
that money. He was overworked and underpaid for years. What he
did might have been punishable in a court of law, but there was
still a certain justice to it. He gave Hawkins his life, for God's
sake, and there was only a piddling insurance policy on it! Hawkins
wasn't big on employee benefits. He gave the bare minimum. Brad
earned that money, Lauren. And he wanted you to have it.''

Lauren swallowed hard, trying to ingest all that Matt had told
her. ''Did he really? Or did you tell me that just to make me feel
better?''

''He said it. Believe me—ah, hell.'' Matt flopped back in the
chair. ''Believe what you want. The fact is that you've put the
money to good use. No one can ever take it away from you.''

They were back to square one. ''Someone's trying. Is it this
fellow, Hawkins?'' she asked nervously.

''He claims not.''

''You *spoke* to him?''

Matt was out of his seat, pacing again. ''What did you think I
went to San Francisco for?''

''I didn't know! I assumed it had something to do with your own
work. You didn't volunteer any details!''

''I went to confront Hawkins.''

''And?''

''He says he's innocent.''

''Do you believe him?''

''I'm not sure.'' Matt stopped his pacing and stared at her. ''On
the one hand, he wouldn't dare try anything. I wasn't the only
friend Brad had. If Hawkins tries to pin something on Brad, even

posthumously, any number of us will cry foul. Hawkins can't risk that. There's too much that can be pinned right back on him.''

"On the other hand..."

He took a deep breath. "On the other hand, I wouldn't put it past him to try something on the sly. He and Brad had reached a stalemate. Each knew what the other was doing, so it was a form of mutual blackmail. Hawkins didn't dare fire Brad for fear he'd squeal. But Brad's gone now. It's possible that Hawkins thought he'd go after some of that money—''

"By terrorizing *me*?"

"Sick minds work in sick ways. Besides, Hawkins wouldn't do it himself. He'd hire someone. If he's discovered that you've invested the money between the shop and this place, he may be out for his own private form of revenge.''

"So we're back where we started.''

"Not...quite," Matt stated with such quiet thunder that Lauren's pulse skipped a beat before racing on. "There are still certain allegations you've made that have to be resolved. Y'know, you're right." He cocked his head and eyed her insolently. "I may well be the man Hawkins hired, playing you now just as I've played you all along—orchestrating events, then showing up and explaining them away.''

"But why *would* you?" she cried.

"You're the one with the answers." He flung himself back into the chair. "You tell me.''

"I don't *have* the answers. That's what this—this is all about! I don't have *any* answers. My mind is running in circles!''

"Could be I'm getting paid a pretty penny for this.''

"You don't want the money," she protested. "You're not ambitious that way! You told me so the first time we met!''

"Could be I was lying. Could be it was all an act." He jacked forward in the chair. "And since you're hurling accusations, I've got a few of my own. You were a virgin for twenty-nine years. Then you met me, and within a week we became lovers. Strange things were happening to you. You were frightened. You needed protection." He snorted. "Pretty high price to pay for it, I'd say.''

She felt as though she'd been slapped. "No! I didn't—"

"Then again, maybe you were truly infatuated. I was different from the men you'd known. More physical. Brawny. But now that you've gotten what you wanted, you're scrabbling for reasons to put me off."

"No, Matt! How can you—"

"I don't meet your high standards. Is that it, Lauren?" His eyes bore into hers. "You're prepared to believe the worst because you just don't think I'm good enough for you?"

Unable to bear another word, Lauren sprang up from the sofa and rounded on him. "That's not true!" she screamed, grabbing his shoulders and shaking him. It was a pitiful gesture, since he was so much larger than she, but her fury was beyond reason. "It's not true! And I wasn't *prepared* to believe the worst!" His face blurred before her eyes. "But I had to know—had to know. I'd never been with another man, because no man had meant anything to me until you came along!" Tears trickled unheeded down her cheeks, and her hands stilled, impotent fingers clutching fistfuls of his shirt. "I've been dying, slowly dying for the past two days, grasping at straws, wondering if it was possible that—that I'd made a big mistake and given you everything and that you were really on the other side."

Her knees gave out then, and she sank to the floor between his legs. Her head was bowed. She wept softly. "It hurt so to...to think that, and I knew I had to get...get it out in the open, but that hurt, too...and...and..." Her fingers curved around his knee, gently kneading in a silent bid for forgiveness.

Matt put a tentative hand on her hair. "And what, Lauren?" he asked softly.

Her head remained down, her muffled voice punctuated by sniffles. "I love you...and I've hurt you...and somehow this new life that was supposed...supposed to be so wonderful is all messed up!"

With a low groan, he slid to the floor. His thighs flanked hers as he took her into the circle of his arms. "Oh, baby. Sweetheart, shhh.'' He rocked her tenderly. "You've just said the magic words. Nothing's messed up. Everything's suddenly clear."

She shook her head against his chest, too upset to comprehend.

He spread a large hand over the back of her head, buried his face in her hair and pressed her closer. "It's all right," he whispered between soft kisses. "Everything's going to be all right."

Lauren let her tears flow. They were a purging of sorts. It wasn't that she agreed with Matt or understood things as he seemed to, but being held in his arms this way, absorbing his strength and incredible tenderness, she felt herself slowly emerging from the hell she'd been living for the past few days.

He rubbed her back, caressing her gently. He whispered soft words of endearment and encouragement; with each one the darkness receded and she moved closer to the light. The warmth of his body thawed her inner chill. She fed on his strength like a creature starved for it.

Then he tipped her chin up and kissed her, and the last of her anguish broke and dissipated like a fever at the end of a long illness. She felt suddenly free, lightheaded and very much in love. Shaping her hands to his cheeks, she gave herself up to his kiss; but because she offered as much as she received, Matt was as aroused as she by the time they finally parted, panting.

While she strung slow kisses along the line of his jaw and his chin, she worked at the buttons of first her shirt, then his. His hands were already in full possession of her breasts before she'd finished the latter, and when she came to her knees to press closer, the squeeze of her thighs against the mounting ache between them was a necessity.

From numbness such a short time before to this rich blossoming of the senses, Lauren reeled. Everything about Matt turned her on, from the vitality of the thick, sun-burnished hair through which her fingers wound to the musky scent of the rough, sweat-dampened skin beneath her lips to the virile cords of muscle straining against the rest of her body.

"I love you," she whispered against his mouth. "I love you, Matt." Her hands slid from his head down his chest, savoring the journey. But urgency was quickly mounting. She released the snap of his jeans, then the zipper, and worked her way beneath the waistband of his shorts until her fingers found what they sought. He was thick and hard, needing her in the same way that she needed him.

He gave an openmouthed moan and whispered her name, then set her back and shoved his jeans lower. "Hurry," he rasped as Lauren rocked back on her bottom and tore her own jeans off in jerky movements. He reached for her with urgent fingers, bringing her close until she straddled his thighs.

"Love me, Matt. Please, love me…"

"God, yes…"

His hands covered her buttocks, urging her downward even as she guided him inside her, and there was nothing then but paradise. His hands on her body, stroking…inflaming…lifting. His tongue wet and greedy on her throat, her collarbone, her breasts. Her own hands clutching his bronzed flesh, molding…straining…her mouth rapacious, her hips meeting his every thrust with matching ferocity.

They brought each other to near-peak after near-peak of exquisite sensation, and when the final climax hit, their cries were simultaneous, prolonged and distinctly triumphant.

For long moments, Lauren was aware of nothing but the state of heavenly bliss in which she floated. Then came Matt's ragged breathing. It took her a minute longer to realize that her own throat was contributing to the rasping sound.

Very gradually the gasping eased, then ended, yet neither of them made a move to leave the other's arms. Their bodies remained joined, and Matt defied the limpness of his limbs to hold her even closer.

"I love you, Lauren," he murmured hoarsely. "Please, please don't doubt me again. I think it would—" His voice broke. "It would destroy me."

Her face buried in the warm crook of his neck, she whispered his name over and over again. Her arms, too, had taken on a strength that denied passion's drain, and she held him with no intention of ever letting go. "I'm sorry" came her muffled cry. "I shouldn't have suggested those awful things."

"No, it's good you did. You were right. They had to come out in the open." He tipped her head back and looked into her eyes. "We need the truth, sweetheart. Both of us. There are so many things we can't figure out, but the situation becomes only more complicated if we can't be honest about ourselves and our feelings." With one arm supporting her back, he gently smoothed damp tendrils of hair from her cheeks. "I have insecurities. Lots of them. They hit me like a ton of bricks when I first met you, and they've kept me a little off balance ever since."

"You didn't need to worry about *anything*!"

"But I did. At the start I worried that you'd associate me only with Brad and that you'd transfer the rift between you and him to me. I worried that you'd turn down your nose at my occupation, that you'd categorize me and put me in a slot and wouldn't like the things I suggested we do. Then, when I began to realize how I felt about you, I was afraid you wouldn't feel the same." He slid his cheek against her temple. "And all the time I was worried about what was happening to you. I imagined Hawkins might be behind it, and I was reluctant to tell you the truth. Maybe I wouldn't be able to protect you or catch the bastard before he really hurt you."

"You'll be dead long before I will if you keep up that worrying," Lauren quipped softly, "and *then* where will I be?"

"Do you love me?"

"I do love you."

"And you're not bothered by who I am and where I come from?"

"Only that you come from the opposite coast, and that's much too far away."

A tremor shot through his body and he gave her a bone-crushing squeeze. "God, you're wonderful. You're beautiful and bright and warm and giving. What did I ever do to deserve you?"

Lauren was thinking the very same thing, but with the pronouns reversed. "I love you," she whispered. She'd never tire of telling him so, and with that knowledge and the intimate closeness of his body, her insides began to quiver. She tightened her lower muscles and was rewarded by the faint catch in Matt's breath; then, as he grew inside her, she began to move.

It was much, much later, after they'd finally sought out her bed, that she turned in his arms. "Matt?"

His eyes were closed. She was wondering if he was asleep when she heard his low "Hmm?"

"Do you realize what we did?"

He shifted his hips and smiled smugly. "Mmm-hmm."

"But without anything." After that first night, Matt had taken the responsibility of protecting her. "Aren't you worried?"

"You told me to stop worrying."

"But if we make a baby…"

His eyes opened slowly, but the smugness remained on his face. "If we make a baby, we'll have it. It'll be beautiful and bright and healthy."

"But the planning, the logistics…"

The light in his eyes grew brighter. "I love you, Lauren. If a baby comes out of that love, I think I'd be the happiest man alive."

With a soft sigh of elation, she nestled more snugly against him. "Oh, Matt, I love you so." Basking in a special glow, lulled by the strong and steady beat of his heart, she fell into a deep and untroubled sleep.

COME MORNING, Lauren and Matt awoke together, showered together, dressed together, cooked and ate breakfast together. Neither seemed to tire of touching the other, or smiling, or whispering those three precious words.

It was only when they were getting ready to drive into Boston that Lauren permitted herself to think beyond the fact of their newly shared love. Matt sat sideways on the sofa, sorting through papers in his briefcase. Curling an arm around his neck, she slid onto his lap.

"We can't go to the police," she began quietly. "You're right. If they start looking into things and somehow come upon Brad's dealings, his memory will be sullied. I'm not sure my parents would care, but I would. So that leaves us back where we began. What should we do?"

Matt finished straightening a pile of letters, set them in the brief-case and snapped it shut. "I think maybe it's time to call in some help. Not the police—someone private." He slipped an arm around her waist. "That way we can control what comes out. Hawkins may be behind this, or it may be someone totally unrelated to him."

"In which case the motive is still a mystery."

"We need a fresh ear, someone who might ask questions we haven't thought of or see things from a new angle." He paused. "Should I get a name and make a call?"

"Yes. We have to do something. I don't want to live with a shadow hanging over me, especially not now."

Matt was in total agreement. Through one of the corporate pow-ers he'd been dealing with in Boston, he contacted a reputable private investigator by the name of Phillip Huber and set up a meeting for the following morning. In the meantime, he stayed as close to Lauren as he could, returning to the shop between business meetings of his own, taking her to lunch, then dinner. When they finally arrived back in Lincoln, it was late. Given the minimum of sleep each had had—not to mention the strain of jet travel on Matt, about which Lauren teased him unmercifully—they were both tired.

Absently she picked up the mail and flipped through it. Gas bill. MasterCard bill. Advertisements. She lifted the next piece of mail, a disconcertingly familiar gray envelope, and stared at it.

Susan Miles. Addressed directly to the farmhouse.

Fingers trembling, she tore open the flap, pulled out the statio-nery and unfolded it. A separate piece of paper floated to the floor, but once again, the stationery itself was blank. Stooping, she lifted the paper that had been enclosed. Roughly cut at the edges, it was a picture of a gleaming fox fur coat, apparently taken from a mag-azine. The model had been unceremoniously decapitated.

"Matt?" she called faintly, then louder: "Matt!"

He appeared at the top of the stairs, his shirt unbuttoned, its tails loose. Lauren's anxious expression brought him trotting down im-mediately.

She spoke quickly. "Last Friday and again on Saturday we re-ceived a letter at the shop addressed to a Susan Miles. Neither Beth nor I know anyone by that name. We assumed it was simply a mistake. Now there's a letter addressed to Susan Miles *here*." She held out the piece of stationery and watched him turn it from front to back.

"It's blank."

"So were the other two. The only difference is that this one came with a magazine clipping." She offered it as well. "Just a picture of a fur coat. Nothing else."

Matt studied the clipping, frowned back at the blank sheet of stationery, then took the envelope from her hand and examined the raggedly scrawled address. "There's got to be a message here," he said at last. "We may not be understanding it, but there's got to be one. You say the other two letters were exactly like this one, but without the clipping?"

"That's right. Same gray stationery."

"Same handwriting on the envelope?"

"Yes. And the same Boston postmark. I didn't think much of the first two. They were addressed to the shop. It could have been a simple mistake. Taken with this last one, though, there has to be something more personal in it. Whoever sent them knows my home address. He's got the name wrong, but he knows where I work *and* where I live."

Much as Lauren's stomach was doing, Matt's jaw clenched. "Right." He rubbed his forehead with his finger. "Is it possible that you've been mistaken for someone else? For this Susan Miles, perhaps?"

Lauren didn't say anything. Her heart was hammering, and the knots in her stomach had tightened painfully.

Matt's focus remained on the pieces of paper he held. "Mistaken identity…that would make sense. All along you've had no idea who would have a reason to threaten you. We know there's a chance it could be Hawkins, but if it's not, this might be something to go on. If we could identify and locate this Susan Miles…" He looked up and caught Lauren's stricken expression. "Sweetheart?" When she swayed, he held her arms to steady her. "What is it?"

"I don't believe this is happening," she whispered. Her eyes were wide, dry but filled with the horror of conviction. "I don't believe it. I knew it was too good to be true."

Matt ducked his head, bringing his face level with hers. Every one of his features broadcast love and tenderness, and his voice was filled with hope. "It's okay, sweetheart. It's good, in fact. At least it's another lead to follow, and now that we've contacted an investigator—"

She covered her face with her hands. "My parents were right. I shouldn't have done it. I played with what fate had decreed, and now I'm paying for it."

"Lauren, what—"

"My face, Matt!" she cried. "It didn't always look this way. When I was a very little girl, my bones developed improperly. I was ugly. You saw a picture! You know!"

"My God," he whispered, finally putting the last piece of the puzzle into place. "I thought it was just a bad picture. I never dreamed…" Seizing her wrists, he drew her hands from her face and clutched them to his chest. His eyes slowly toured her features. "You had surgery," he said in amazement.

She nodded. "My chin was practically nonexistent, and my jaw was so badly misaligned that I had trouble eating. That's why I was so skinny."

"And you're so beautiful now. It's incredible!" He took her chin and turned her face first to one side, then the other. "No scars," he announced excitedly. "It must have been done from the inside. When, sweetheart?"

"This past spring, right before I came to Boston. I went to a clinic in the Bahamas. The recuperative period was ten weeks. Part of that time I stayed in a rented apartment and returned to the clinic on an outpatient basis."

"Unbelievable." Done with its journey, his gaze coupled with hers. "Just this past spring. So if I'd come six months before, I'd have found you in Bennington looking exactly as I'd expected. It all makes sense now—your inexperience with men, your talk of a new life, a new look…" His eyes lit with pleasure at a new thought. "Part of Brad's money went toward this, didn't it?"

"Some. Insurance paid for most of the surgery, since it had become a legitimate medical problem."

"And you feel better?"

"Physically *and* emotionally." She hesitated. "What about you, Matt? How do you feel?"

"How do I feel?" he echoed, puzzled.

"About what I did. Having plastic surgery and all."

"I think it's marvelous! If you'd looked this gorgeous much earlier, you'd have been snapped up before I could have found you."

"But what do you think about the surgery itself? Does it...bother you?"

"Of course not! Why would it bother me?"

"It bothers my parents. They were against my doing it."

"Hell, it's no different from a kid wearing braces on his teeth to correct a bite problem that would become troublesome in time. Or someone having his nose fixed to correct a deviated septum."

Lauren blushed. "I had that done, too."

"You did!" He grinned. "What did it look like before? The picture I saw was a head-on shot."

"It was crooked," she admitted sheepishly. "And lousy for breathing. I used to snore something awful."

"You sure don't now. I love your nose." He ran a finger down its smooth slope. "It looks so—so natural. The whole thing looks so natural! I'd honestly decided that the picture was just a bad one. Either that, or you'd simply come into your own as you'd grown older."

"Then Brad didn't say anything specific?"

Matt's voice mellowed. "No. It wasn't often that Brad spoke of home, but when he mentioned you, there was always a certain tenderness in his voice. In spite of the rift, you had a special place in his heart. He worried about you. Wow, if he could only see you now!"

"Yeah," Lauren drawled wryly. "I've got a new face that apparently looks so much like someone else's that an enemy of that someone else is out for blood."

"Hey, we don't know that!"

"Well, maybe not blood, but something, that's for sure." She sent a pleading look to the ceiling. "I don't believe this. I just don't believe it. It's like something only Beth could have dreamed up, but she didn't." She arched a brow at Matt. "You do agree that the mistaken-identity theory is the strongest one we've had?"

"Mmm. Not that I'm ruling out Hawkins. But, given the letters for Susan Miles, this theory is more plausible."

"What could the newspaper clipping mean?"

"I don't know. If the letters were real letters with writing and all, it wouldn't be so bad. But three blank sheets of stationery— that's odd."

Lauren sighed. "So, we look for Susan Miles."

"It's the way to go. Seems to me that'd be right down our investigator's alley."

IT SHOULD HAVE BEEN. Lauren and Matt met with the detective at a small coffee shop in Boston early the next morning. They told him everything, from a detailed account of each of Lauren's mysterious incidents to their theories involving, alternately, Brad's boss and Lauren's new face.

Phillip Huber went off in search of Susan Miles. Unfortunately, after a full day of poring through State House and registry records, he could find no evidence of anyone by that name living in the area.

The next day he went through the records of the local and state police, and the day after that he made use of his considerable network of contacts to broaden the search to include the rest of New England and New York.

By Thursday night, Lauren and Matt were no closer to finding Susan Miles than they'd been at the start, and by Friday afternoon, the search was temporarily abandoned.

LAUREN LEFT THE SHOP shortly before four, intent on getting to the bank and back before Matt came for her. He'd been her shadow for most of the week, and she'd loved it. But that day he'd had business to attend to, so she set out on the errand alone.

With the luxury of Jamie's working full-time, Lauren was taking off early. It was a beautiful day. She and Matt planned to return to Lincoln to change, then drive one town over, rent a canoe and explore the Concord River.

She walked at a confident pace, buoyed by the anticipation of the outing, lulled into security by the peaceful week it had been. Since Monday, when the letter for Susan Miles had arrived at the farmhouse, there had been no incidents. Of course, Matt had been close at hand, a visible deterrent to mischief, and Phillip Huber had taken his turn when Matt had been busy.

Lauren had barely turned down the side street on which the bank was located when a car slid smoothly to the curb. Its door opened, and she was jostled inside by a burly hulk that had come from nowhere on her opposite side. Before she knew what had happened, she was seated in the back seat of a car that would have been roomy except for the two giants who crowded her between them.

She tried to squirm, but she was solidly pinned. "What—what is this?" she cried between attempts to free herself.

"Sit still, pretty lady," the man on her left said. "You know what it is."

"I—do—not." She was trying to elbow herself out of the human vise, only to find that the vise had tightened. "Let me out of this car!" she gritted. She began to pound at the thighs flanking hers but succeeded only in having her wrists immobilized by a single beefy paw on either side. "You can't do this!"

"We've just done it," the same man pointed out. His voice was calm, matter-of-fact, infuriating.

"Well—" she kicked out "—I'm not—" she writhed lower in the seat "—having it!" She managed to hike herself forward but was pitched back by the arm of steel that crossed her collarbone and tightened. She bit at the arm and heard a low grunt. Before she could struggle free, she was slapped viciously across the side of her head. Sharp pain radiated through her entire skull, rendering her utterly dazed. She sagged limply against the seat and fought to catch her breath.

"That's better," the man on her left said. "Now sit there and *don't move*."

She couldn't have moved if she'd tried, and she couldn't even try. The blow had robbed her of what little strength had remained after her futile attempt to escape. Her head lolled against the up-holstered seat, and for long moments she could do nothing but hope to regain her equilibrium. Her jaw hurt something fierce, and she felt a momentary flash of hysteria. If they'd broken her jaw after all she'd gone through to set it right, after all she was going through because she *had* set it right...

"You've got the wrong girl," she managed to mumble through stiff lips.

"Mmm" came a hum from her left. "Somehow we knew you'd say that."

"You do." Gingerly she worked her jaw. It was sore, but at least it functioned. "I don't really look like this...I had repair work done to correct a problem..."

"We know the problem."

The one on the left was apparently the designated speaker. She dared a glance at him. He was dark-haired, dark-eyed, dark-looking in every respect. His eyes were focused straight ahead, following the course the driver was taking.

"If you know the problem," Lauren ventured, "then you know this is all a mistake."

"The problem is that you didn't want to be found." He looked at her then, and she cringed under his scrutiny. "It's subtle, I have to say that much. You're clever. Didn't do anything drastic, thought we'd be off looking for someone *completely* different. Or maybe you just thought what you had was too beautiful to tamper much with. You always were a haughty bitch."

"You've got the wrong woman," Lauren pleaded in a shaky voice. "As God is my witness, I'm telling the truth. The surgery I had was to correct a problem I've had from childhood. You can contact the clinic. My doctor will tell you."

The man was looking forward again, a smug look on his face. "We've already been to the clinic. That was a fancy job you did with the records, and if we were stupid we might have been put off. But we're not stupid, Susan. I think it's about time you realize that."

"I'm not Susan! I know you think I'm Susan Miles, because that's the name on those envelopes, but *my* name is Lauren Stevenson! Lauren Stevenson, from Bennington, Vermont. I have family and friends still there—you can check."

"Lauren Stevenson." He rolled the name around on his tongue in a way that made her want to vomit. "It's as good an alias as any."

"It's *not* an alias!"

Dark eyes glittered dangerously back at her. "Keep your voice down. I have a headache."

"I'll talk as loud as I want—" she fairly shouted, only to have her words cut off by the human mitt that clamped over her mouth. It had come from the right, but the voice, as always, came from the left.

"I'll gag you. Is that what you want?"

"No," Lauren answered the instant the mitt had left her mouth. She had to be able to communicate if she was to get anywhere.

"Then keep your voice down. And talk with respect." The last had been tacked on almost as an afterthought, but the man appeared to find immense satisfaction in it.

She wasn't about to argue. Physically, she was outsized and outnumbered. All three men—one on either side of her, plus the driver—were huge. Their sedate business suits did nothing to disguise the bulk of their physiques. Intellectually, though, she had to believe she was at least on a par with them, if not above. Yes, she was terrified, and terror had a way of fudging the workings of the mind. But if she could stay cool and somehow control her fear, she had a chance.

In keeping with that, she considered her captor's command. If it was a respectful tone he wanted, a respectful tone he'd get. Far more could be accomplished with sugar than with vinegar.

"Who are you?" she asked quietly, directing her efforts solely to the man on the left.

"Now, that is an insult if I ever heard one. You know who I am."

"I don't."

"I sure know you." He tilted his head to the side and studied her lazily. "You're looking good, Susan. Hair's a little shorter. Face looks good. Makeup's different. Easing up on it, are you?"

"Where are you taking me?"

He gave a careless shrug. "I'm not sure."

"What are you going to do with me?"

"I'm not sure."

"You must have a plan."

"Oh, yes."

She waited, but he said nothing more, so she dropped her gaze to her lap. "The plan is to make me nervous. Just as you've been doing for the past two weeks."

He puckered his lips, then relaxed them in acknowledgement of her perception. "Very good."

"But you do have the wrong person," she argued, albeit in a respectful tone. "The first few things you did didn't even make me nervous, because I had no reason to suspect there was anything to them."

"You wised up."

"Not really. It was the mail for Susan Miles that pulled it all together. Up until then I couldn't imagine what anyone would have against me." The issue of Chester Hawkins was irrelevant. "That's when I realized it had to be a case of mistaken identity."

"Sure," he drawled.

Lauren felt a movement in the arm that was pressed against her right side, and she looked sharply toward the hulk connected to it. The man was laughing. Silently, but laughing nonetheless. On the one hand, she was livid; on the other, she was more frightened than ever. They were obviously prepared for her denials, which practically defeated her efforts before they'd begun, but she wouldn't give up. There had to be *some* way out of this mess—if only she could find it!

CHAPTER NINE

For the first time since her abduction, Lauren looked beyond the confines of the car to the outside world. If she'd expected to see narrow, unfamiliar streets, she was mistaken. The car was on Storrow Drive, taking the very same route out of the city that she traveled every day.

She wished she knew what her wardens were up to, but she hadn't gotten that far yet, so she thought of Matt. Surely he'd have arrived at the shop. Surely he and Beth would be getting nervous when she didn't return from the bank. The bank!

"I have money," she exclaimed in a burst of hope. "If it's money you want, I'll give you all I've got." She fumbled in her purse for the envelope containing the cash and checks she'd been on her way to deposit, but her offer was immediately denied.

"We don't want money. The boss pays us plenty."

"Who's the boss?"

"Come on, Susan. We're not really as dumb as you'd like to think."

"I don't think you're dumb at all," Lauren declared quietly. "You've just made an innocent mistake. I'm not Susan, and I don't know who 'the boss' is. And *because* you're not stupid, you'll realize that I'm telling you the truth before you do anything drastic. If you go ahead with whatever you're planning, sooner or later someone *will* call you stupid—because you'll have done whatever you're planning to do to the wrong person."

He shot her a sidelong glance. "You've gotten quick with words. You never used to talk this much."

"Maybe Susan Miles didn't, but I always have. Look, there are any number of people—people who've known me for years—who can vouch for my identity."

"Like the medical records in that clinic did?" His question dripped of sarcasm.

"If you don't believe the records, that's not my problem."

"But it is. Seems to me it's very much your problem."

He was right. She had to take a different tack. "Okay. So you don't believe the records and you won't believe my friends. You tell me. Who am I supposed to be? Just who *is* this Susan Miles?"

"You want to play games? I'll play games. Susan Miles was the boss's best girl. He gave her everything any woman could want—" his eyes pierced Lauren's and his voice grew emphatic "—like a safe full of jewels and a closet full of furs. Where are they, Susan? We haven't been able to find them yet. Did you sell everything to bankroll that little shop you've got, or the house?"

"Jewels?"

"And furs."

"That clipping," she murmured, horrified. "Matt was right. There was a message in the clipping, but we just didn't get it."

The man on her left said nothing.

"I don't have jewels *or* furs. I bought the shop and the house with a legacy from my brother, who died a year ago." In other circumstances she'd never have volunteered that information, but these were unusual circumstances, to say the least.

"A legacy from your brother. Touching, but not terribly original, although I suppose it is different from the dead-uncle or maiden-aunt story, or that of the parents who were tragically killed in an automobile accident."

"My parents are alive and well and living in Bennington, Vermont. Check it out in a phone book. Colin and Nadine Stevenson."

The man on her left was silent.

"How *else* would I get money to open that shop? I've never had anything of my own like that before."

"Oh, please."

"I did?"

"How quickly you forget."

"What was it? What did I own?"

"A charming little boutique in Westwood Village. Actually, you were running it into the ground. After you died, the boss put one of his own men in charge, and it's begun to turn a pretty profit.''

"I *died*?" Lauren felt as if she were in the middle of a slapstick comedy, only nothing was funny. She was totally bewildered. "But if I died, what am I doing here and why are you after me?"

The man on her left seemed to weary of her questions. "You didn't die," he growled. "You just made it look like you'd died. You took off with the jewels and furs, changed your face, bought your shop and your house and thought you could get away scot-free." His expression grew even darker. "Well, let me tell you, no one does that to the boss and gets away with it. And no one does it to *me*!"

"What did I do to you?" she whispered fearfully.

"You made a fool of me. I was the one who reported that you burned to death in that car."

"Oh."

"Yes, 'oh.' It's been a sweet pleasure putting you through hell these past couple of weeks. What was it like, Susan, knowing someone was on to you?"

"I *didn't*. I told you—"

"I'll bet you didn't believe it at first. You always were arrogant, with your pretty little nose stuck up in the air."

"It's not my nose—"

"When you finally admitted to yourself that you'd been found out, did you think of running? It wouldn't have done you any good. We'd have been right on your heels." He sniffed loudly. Lauren decided he had a deviated septum of his own. "I've enjoyed it. And the best is yet to come. What I've got planned for today will singe your hair. I mean *really*, this time. Think about *that* while we take our little drive."

Their "little drive" had already taken them to the outskirts of Lincoln. Lauren stared out the window and swallowed hard. *Singe?* She began to shake. What was he planning? Did he intend to kill her? She had to escape. And soon. But how?

They turned off Route 2 and began the drive down the street she took each night. She would have stiffened in her seat, or sat straighter, but she had precious little room to move in and barely more strength. Her arms and legs were beginning to ache from a combination of tension and the steady pressure applied from both sides. Her face hurt. Her stomach was knotting.

"Where are we going?" she asked in a small voice.

"Don't you recognize the streets?"

At that moment they turned down the very road that would lead to her house.

"Thought you might want to take a last look."

"A...last look?"

The man on her left said nothing.

"This is a mistake. It's all a mistake. I really am Lauren Stevenson. *Really.*"

"Sure."

She took a quick breath. "Look, you can come inside the house and I'll show you everything. I have identification—a birth certificate, college diplomas, even pictures of my family." Her captor's snort told her what he thought of the validity of that identification. She barely had time to wonder how one could possibly forge family pictures when another thought hit her. "I have a passport! Picture and all!" It didn't take a snort from her left for her to realize she'd struck out again. The passport would do her no good. If there'd been various point-of-entry stamps recorded over a period of time, she might have proved that Lauren Stevenson had existed long before Susan Miles had supposedly died. But Lauren's passport had been issued shortly before her trip to the Bahamas. Ironically, she hadn't needed it; it had never even been stamped. And yes, the picture was of her "before" face, but the files in the clinic had contained a similar picture, which these men had written off.

"So much for identification," she muttered under her breath. Then her head shot up. "My car! The registration!" Her face dropped again. "I reregistered it when I came to Massachusetts."

The man on her left seemed to be enjoying himself. "Keep thinking, pretty lady. See if you can come up with something we haven't already looked over. Don't forget, we've been through most of your belongings."

Lauren's nostrils flared, and for a minute she forgot herself. "You know, it wasn't so bad that you sampled my perfume and fiddled with my shoes. If that's what turns you on, okay. But my *underwear*? I mean, there's kinky and then there's—ahh!" Her arm had been wrenched up sharply against her back. She twisted to ease the pain. "Please," she gasped out in a whisper. "Please—that hurts!"

"I don't have to take your smart mouth. You're not calling the shots around here—*I* am!"

"Please," she begged, then gasped again when her arm was released. She hugged it close and alternately rubbed her elbow and her shoulder.

By this time the car was approaching the farmhouse. Lauren held her breath as she peered out the window, praying that Matt might be there, though she knew he wouldn't be. He was in Boston, waiting for her, maybe out looking for her by now.

The driver slowed in front of the garage, shifted into reverse, backed the car around and headed for the street again.

"Weird place," the man on her left said. "Pretty run-down. I really thought you had more class."

Lauren bit her lip and said nothing. She gazed longingly out of the window, hoping to see a neighbor walking along the side of the road, in which case she'd force some sort of ruckus inside the car that would attract attention. But she saw no one. The road was as quiet and peaceful as it had always been.

To her amazement, they drove on into the center of town. She marveled at the gall of her keepers, until she realized that she couldn't have made a stir if she'd tried. Large hands suddenly manacled both of her arms, just as burly legs had gripped her calves. She might have bucked in the middle, but no one outside the car would have noticed. And if she yelled—

"Don't even think it," the man on her left advised. "Mouse here has a mean right hook. It'll be even meaner the second time around."

"But if you're going to kill me anyway, why would it matter?"

He grinned. "The pain, Susan. The suffering. It'll be bad enough for you as it is. If you want it worse, well, then, go ahead and scream.''

Lauren didn't scream. But she did decide that this man's grin had to be the ugliest thing she'd ever seen. And she vowed that if she ever escaped, she'd take great pleasure in personally wiping if from his smug face!

They passed the police station, and she stifled a cry. They passed the market, and she bit her lip. ''You won't get away with this. There are two good men who are probably on our trail right now.''

''Two good men? Well, I know about the dick you hired. I suppose he's a good man, but he won't find a thing. As for Kruger, haven't you figured that out yet?''

''Figured what out?''

''He's one of ours.''

She didn't even blink. ''You're lying.''

The man on her left shrugged. ''Suit yourself. Cling to romantic illusion if you want.''

''You can say anything else and it might make me nervous. But Matt—one of *yours*? Not by a long shot.''

''What do you think his quickie trip to the coast last weekend was for, if not to check in with the boss?''

''I know what his trip was for, and it wasn't your boss he was checking in with.''

''You're awfully sure of yourself.''

''Where Matt's concerned, yes.''

''Why? What proof do you have that he's not with us?''

She knew she'd be wasting her breath to mention things like love and trust. ''He has the proof. Or, if you want to be crude, it was on my sheets the morning after we first made love. I was a virgin. If Matt had been with you, he'd have known something was strange. Unless, of course, your boss is some kind of eunuch.''

''A virgin,'' the man on her left mused. ''Kruger didn't mention that to us.''

''Of course not. He doesn't know you from Adam.''

When he shrugged again and simply repeated, ''Suit yourself,'' Lauren knew she'd scored a point.

That was the last bit of satisfaction she was to have in a while. They left Lincoln behind and drove along backcountry roads with no obvious destination, at least none obvious to Lauren. Her mind jumped ahead, touching on possible stopping places and possible forms of punishment in store for her, then recoiled in fear, seeking refuge in more purposeful thoughts.

"Did she have any birthmarks?" Lauren asked suddenly.

The man on her left frowned at her.

"Susan Miles. Did she have any distinctive birthmarks? There had to be *some* way I can prove I'm not her."

"Birthmarks. That's an interesting thought. I could ask the boss about it. Do *you* have any distinctive birthmarks?"

"No."

"Are you sure?"

"Yes."

"Maybe we should pull over to the side of the road. If you strip, I can check you out."

He was goading her. She looked away. "I don't have any birthmarks," she muttered half to herself as she shriveled into the seat. Her arms and legs had been released once they'd left Lincoln proper, but she might as well have been shackled for the little freedom she'd gained. Shoulders hunched, she tried to minimize contact with the bodies on either side by making herself more narrow. It was a token gesture; the more she narrowed, the more the two men spread.

They drove on and on. She lost track of their direction, and much of the scenery was unfamiliar. With each mile, though, she grew more edgy. They couldn't drive forever. Sooner or later they'd have to stop. And what then?

"Y'know," the man on her left offered, "you really blew it. You had it all. The boss adored you—"

"Who is he?"

"Oh, Lord."

"What's his name? If he's the one who's behind all this, don't I have a right to know his name?"

"You don't have *any* rights, pretty lady. You gave them up when you double-crossed him."

"I didn't double-cross anyone!"

His nonchalance faded. "I'd watch my tone if I were you. It's getting uppity, and if there's one thing Mouse can't stand, it's uppity women. Right, Mouse?"

Mouse grunted.

"I'm sorry," Lauren said as conciliatorily as she could. "I didn't mean to sound uppity. It's just that you assume I know everything, but I don't, and I feel as if this whole thing has to be an awful joke, except no one's laughing, and I'm sitting here trying to figure out a way to prove to you who I am, but my mind is getting all foggy and…and…" She'd begun to shake. Tucking in her chin, she closed her eyes. "I don't feel very well."

"Throw up in this car, lady, and I'll make you lick it up."

She swallowed hard against the rising bile and took several deep breaths through her nose. The strain was getting to her. Her insides continued to shake; she wrapped her arms around her middle as though to hold them still, but it didn't work. She was hot and tired and positively terrified.

"It's amazing," the man on her left said. "You're quite an actress, after all. Funny, you should be such a flop in Hollywood."

"I thought you said Susan had a boutique," Lauren murmured weakly.

"Yeah. But she was like everyone else in that town. Between running the boutique and pleasing the boss, she read for every bit part she could. Had a couple of walk-ons." He sent her a look of ridicule. "She wasn't much of an actress, at least not on the silver screen. What she's doing now is remarkable."

"I have never been, nor had the slightest desire to be, an actress."

"Sure."

Lauren didn't have the strength to argue further, and they didn't stop driving. Dusk fell over the landscape. She thought she'd explode if something didn't happen soon. Once she cast a glance over her shoulder. The man on her left picked up on it instantly.

"Sorry. No one's following."

She grew defensive. "Aren't we stopping for dinner or something?"

He simply laughed.

"Or the bathroom? Don't any of you need one?"

"We're like camels. You'd better be, too. No, we're not stopping. Sorry, but you'll have to think of some other way to escape."

She tried. Oh, Lord, she tried. But, imprisoned in the car between two dark-suited sides of beef, she was hamstrung. There was no hope for escape unless they stopped, and it terrified her to think of where that would be and what they had planned for her then.

Just as she was beginning to bemoan the darkness, she noticed that the car was heading back toward the city. Of course. It made sense. Psychological torture. The purpose of the long ride had been to set her further on edge.

"Look, you've accomplished what you've wanted," she confessed without pride. "I'm thoroughly frightened. You can drop me off anywhere. I'll even take my chances and thumb a ride home."

"Is that what you thought, that we'd just let you go? Susan, Susan, how naive you are."

"What are you planning?"

The man on her left made a ceremony of debating whether or not to tell her. He moistened his lips, scratched the back of his head, then shrugged. "I guess it's time you knew. We're gonna do what we thought had been done months ago."

Lauren's heart was slamming against her breast. "What was that?"

"Your car plunged off the road and burst into flames. There was nothing left but ashes. The ashes were supposed to be you, so the boss gave you a fine burial." He sighed. "In this case, the burial came before the death, so we're kinda doing things ass-backward. But you will burn, Susan. Take that as a promise. You will burn."

Where Lauren got the breath to speak was a mystery. Perhaps the source was her desperation. "It's a threat, and you won't get away with it."

"Oh, we'll get away with it, all right. We're not novices at this type of thing."

"You're killers, then. Hit men. Is your boss connected with the mob? Well, let me tell you, if the mob kills its own, that's one thing. But I've got nothing to do with the mob or your boss or Susan Miles or you, and that makes me an innocent victim. I swear, you won't get away with it!"

The man on her left laughed. "Ah, pretty lady, that's priceless. Tell me, what do you intend to do once you're dead? Haunt us?" He laughed again.

Lauren gritted her teeth, no mean feat since they were chattering. "You'll get yours. So help me, you'll get yours."

When his laugh only came louder, she lapsed into silence. She'd save her strength, she decided. At some place, at some time, she'd glimpse a chance to escape. She'd need every resource she had when that time came.

Unfortunately, she couldn't seem to glimpse that chance to escape. After they had arrived back in Boston, the car drove down Atlantic Avenue, parallel to the harbor. It turned into a darkened path, continued to the end and stopped.

"Let's go," the man on her left said.

Before he'd even left the car, the man on her right had seized her. His arms were like cords of steel around her legs and shoulders. She was literally crunched into a ball with her face smothered against his chest. As she was carried from the car, she called on those resources she'd saved to try to free herself, but her bonds only tightened. Her scream was a pathetic sound muffled against the man's shirt, and she grew dizzy from the lack of air.

Terror was a driving force, though. Frantically she fought against the arms that held her. Futilely she tried to turn her head and gasp for air. While the doomed battle waged, she was carted up a flight of stairs, then another and another. Her captors' footsteps hammered against the wood planks, each forceful beat driving another nail into her coffin.

Then she was released, dumped unceremoniously onto the floor of a cavernous room. Gasping and trembling, she pushed herself up and looked around. It was dark, but she knew she was in a warehouse—rank and decaying, abandoned warehouse.

The two men loomed over her. Their bodies were straight, their legs planted firmly apart. Their stance was aggressive, but it couldn't have intimidated her any more than she already was.

The man who'd been on her left abruptly hunkered down. She inched back on the floor, but she couldn't escape his hand when he took a strand of her hair between his fingers. He spoke with lethal quiet. "Your final resting place, pretty lady. Take a look around. Try to find a way out. It'll keep your mind busy."

"Where are you going?" she whispered.

"I've got a call to make."

"To whom?"

He let the strand of hair sift through his fingers. "Who do you think?"

"Your boss?" A sudden flare of fury gave her voice greater force. "You tell him for me that he's an idiot! You tell him that he's murdering the wrong woman and that he'll pay—"

When the man raised his hand, palm up, she ducked her head and shrank back. But he didn't hit her. Instead, he slowly lowered his hand until it gently brushed her cheek. "Such a pretty face," he murmured. "Such a shame—"

Her lips moved in a mere whisper. "You know I'm telling the truth. You do."

"I know you'd like to think that. It's okay. Hold on to the hope if you want. It won't be much longer. We'll be back soon."

"And then?" The devil made her ask that. Her eyes were wide with pleading.

"Then," he answered quietly, ever calmly, "we will sprinkle you with gasoline and set you on fire." She gasped and began to shake her head, but he went on. Too late, she realized she'd played into his hands by asking what he planned to do. Clearly, he took pleasure in her horror. "We'll watch you burn, Susan. This time there will be no doubt that you've died."

"Someone…will find me."

"I think not. Y'see, there's a contract out on this building. The man who owns it wants to build condominiums here, like those others along the waterfront, only he's a little strapped for money." The man glanced at his watch. "Roughly two hours from now, one of Boston's best torches will set fire to this place. It'll go up so quick that by the time the fire department gets here, the floor you're on will have long since fallen through. Your ashes will be hopelessly scattered. There's no way anyone will know you've been here, much less be able to prove you died here."

"Please," she cried, feebly grasping the lapels of his jacket, "please don't do this."

"Are you sorry, Susan? Do you finally regret what you've done?"

Lauren was weeping softly. "I haven't done anything...you *have* to believe me...*I'm not Susan Miles*!"

The man threw back his head, took a deep breath and stood up. Together with his sidekick, he made the long walk across the rotting floor. At the door, he looked back.

"You can scream as much as you want. No one will hear you. And Mouse will be right outside this door in case you decide you want to take a walk." He glanced at his buddy. "I think he'd like to get his hands on you again. Right, Mouse?"

Lauren never heard Mouse's answer. She found herself alone, trembling wildly and feeling more frightened than ever. For long moments of mental paralysis, she remained where she was. Then the bottom line came to her. It was do or die. Life or death. Scrambling to her feet, she began to explore her prison, seeking any possible hole or loose plank or trapdoor that might offer escape.

THE BOSS WAS LOUNGING by the pool when his houseboy brought out the cordless phone. He took it, nodded at the boy in dismissal, then put the instrument to his ear. "Yes?"

"We have her. She's safely tucked away. And she's dying just thinking about dying."

"Good. When will you do it?"

"Soon. Uh—did you get the pictures I sent?"

"This morning."

"What do you think?"

"With her hair that way and the clothes, she looks a little younger, more innocent, but it's Susan, all right."

"Are you sure?"

There was a pause. "Aren't you?"

"I thought I was until we picked her up today. Somehow, close up, she seems different."

"That was her intent."

"No. Not just in looks, but in character. The woman we've got does seem more innocent. Susan would have tried a come-on. She'd have promised us all kinds of little favors if we let her go. This one hasn't done that—like it's never occurred to her that she's got a marketable commodity. She's terrified, but half of it seems to be that we won't believe her story. Either Susan has suddenly become one hell of an actress, or we've been tricked."

The boss lit a cigarette and took a long drag. "You think it's someone else?"

A pause. "I'm not sure."

"Is it possible that Susan could have set up someone else to smoke us out?"

"Possible, but not probable. This one claims she had her face fixed to repair a medical problem, just like the clinic records said. If she's telling the truth, it'd be just too convenient that Susan would have happened to find her, looking so similar and all. And if she knew about Susan, she'd have squealed by now. She's scared, really scared."

"So it wasn't a setup. It has to be Susan."

"Or someone who looks like her."

Silence dominated the next half minute. Then, "It's not like you to get cold feet."

"That's what I've been telling myself, but something just doesn't feel right. If we do have the wrong woman, we'll be in trouble."

"I thought you had it arranged so that no one would know."

"I do. It's foolproof."

"So what's the problem? If it's really Susan, she'll be getting her due. If it's not Susan, but someone she set up to take the fall for her, let her take the fall. That'll get Susan to shaking all the more.''

"And if it's simply a case of mistaken identity?"

"I can't believe that. The resemblance is too strong."

"But we'll never know. That's the problem. Once this one's dead, we'll never know for sure whether we've taken care of Susan or not."

"Damn it, what do you suggest?"

"I suggest…that we let this one escape and then continue to follow her for a while. If she suddenly runs from Boston and tries to change her looks again and sets herself up somewhere else, we'll know for sure that she's Susan. She won't have a head start on us this time. We'll be watching her constantly."

"I don't like this. I want Susan dead."

"So do I. But I want to make sure it *is* Susan who's dead."

"I thought this was all clear-cut. You'd found her. You'd been tormenting her. You've got her set to fry. It's all very neat. I don't like waffling."

"It's your decision, Boss."

The silence this time was the lengthiest yet. It ended with a low growl of frustration. "Ah, hell. Let the girl go. Then follow her. Do you understand? *Follow her.* If you lose her, so help me, you'll die right along with her!"

"Right."

"*And let me know what's happening.*"

"Right."

LAUREN WAS AMAZED by the simplicity of her escape, although she assumed anything would have seemed simple in comparison to what she'd been through and the fate she'd so vividly been made to envision. After a lengthy search of the room, she'd found old planks sealing up a shaft. She'd pried them off—most had crumbled in her hands—and discovered a door leading to what was a cross between a dumbwaiter and a freight elevator. After climbing onto the platform, she'd pulled and tugged on a fraying cord of rope until she'd lowered the platform to its base. Then she'd shouldered her way through the rotting wood of the door and burst into a run along the street floor of the warehouse. Moments later, she was in the summer night's air.

Smelling vaguely of dead fish and other refuse, the air was the sweetest she'd ever breathed. But she didn't pause to savor it. She continued running out to Atlantic Avenue, veered left around the corner and didn't stop until she'd reached the first of the waterfront restaurants. She barged inside and made her way to the maître d's desk.

"I need a phone," she gasped, hunching her shoulders against the pain in her chest.

The maître d' smiled politely and gestured. "Right over there, in front of the rest rooms."

"No! I don't dare!" She shot a glance at the phone by his hand. "You've got one here. I'm being followed, and if I go back there, they're apt to catch...me again and I can't risk it...because they want to kill me and I...have to make this call. Please?" Her breath was coming in agonizing gulps, but she was beyond caring.

"This phone is reserved for—"

"Please!" she whispered. "It's critical!"

"I could call the police for you."

"Let me...please?"

Whether he acquiesced because, in her disheveled state, she didn't look like a troublemaker, or because he had a hidden streak of protectiveness in him, Lauren would never know. As soon as he reached to turn the phone her way, she snatched up the receiver and began to punch out the number of the shop. It was the closest place Matt might be, unless he was out searching. She had to try three times before her shaking fingers hit the right buttons.

"Lauren! My God, where *are* you?" Beth exclaimed. "We've been looking all over for you! Matt's half out of his mind, and the police won't do anything about a missing person for at least twenty-four—"

"Where is he? I need him, Beth. Where is he?"

"You sound awful!"

"Where's Matt?"

"He's out looking for you. He calls in here every few minutes. We've got Jamie stationed at your house."

Lauren's fingers had a death grip on the ridge of wood running around the top of the maître d's desk. "I'm at Fathoms. The restaurant. On Atlantic Avenue. Tell him to come *right away*."

"Where have you been? Are you all right?"

"Just tell Matt. I have to go." Lauren set the receiver back in its cradle, looked up at the maître d' and said, "You can call the police now." Then her knees buckled and she sank to the floor in a dead faint.

By the time she came to, she was lying on a couch in the manager's office. It took her a minute to get her bearings; then she bolted up, only to be restrained by two firm but gentle pairs of hands.

"It's all right, miss. You're safe. The police are on their way."

She recognized the maître d' but looked warily at his companion.

"I'm the manager, and you're going to be just fine."

"Matt...Matthew Kruger...he'll be looking for me."

"It's all right," the manager assured her. "The police will be here any minute. We won't let him get to you—"

"No! He's my—my—he's okay. He's not one of them. I need him."

The two men exchanged a glance before the manager spoke again. "Then we should let him in?"

"Yes!"

He nodded toward the maître d' who turned and left. When the door opened several minutes later, two uniformed officers entered. By this time, Lauren was sitting upright, sipping shakily from a glass of water. One of the officers sat down beside her on the couch; the other knelt before her and began to ask questions. Lauren barely heard the questions, much less her answers. At the slightest movement or sound, her eyes flew toward the door.

After what seemed forever, but was probably no longer than fifteen minutes, Matt burst in. His eyes were wild, his tanned skin was pale and his entire body was trembling, but that didn't stop him from catching Lauren when she rocketed into his arms or from crushing her tightly to him.

Brokenly, he whispered her name. He took her weight when her legs seemed to dissolve from under her and melded her body to his. She was crying softly, clinging to his neck, unable to say anything for a very long time. At last he lifted her and carried her back to the couch, which the seated officer had vacated for that purpose. Taking her onto his lap, Matt began to stroke her hair, her back, her arms.

"It's all right, sweetheart. Everything's going to be all right. I'm here. Shh." His breath was warm on her forehead, her ear, her cheek.

"Oh, Matt...you have...no idea..."

Framing her head with his hands, Matt examined her closely. "Are you all right?" His gaze focused on the faintly discolored side of her face, and his voice came out in a croak. "What happened to your cheek?"

"He hit me. It was Mouse, but he wasn't the one in charge."

Matt looked up quickly at the manager. "Can we get some ice for this?"

The man nodded and hurried out, but Matt's attention was already back on Lauren. "Can you talk about it, sweetheart? From the beginning?" His thumbs stroked the tears from beneath her eyes. "The officers will listen. You'll have to go through it only once."

Nodding, Lauren slowly launched into her tale. It was interrupted from time to time—when the ice arrived; when she began to cry again; when Phillip, who'd been out searching for her, too, joined them—but she managed to get through it all before she collapsed, emotionally drained, against Matt.

It was Phillip, soft-spoken and dependable, who turned to the officers. "You'll look for the car?"

"You bet," the older of the two answered. "And if the warehouse hasn't already been torched, we'll search it." He grimaced and rubbed his neck. "I'm afraid we don't have much to go on. Dark blue Plymouths are pretty common. But we'll check out the local rental agencies and the hotels. Three oversize men might be remembered, particularly if they've been here for a while. Of course, they could be staying somewhere other than at a hotel.''

Matt was cradling Lauren against his chest. "We'd be grateful for anything you can do. And we'd like to be kept informed."

"Can we reach you at—" The officer flipped back several pages in his notebook and read off Lauren's Lincoln address.

Matt caught Phillip's headshake. "No. They know the house. I can't take the chance they won't return. We'll be at the Long Wharf Marriott. You can either call us there or leave a message at the print shop."

With a nod, the policemen left, followed several minutes later by Phillip. Matt studied Lauren with tender concern. "Feel up to moving, sweetheart?"

When she nodded, he helped her to her feet, then wrapped an arm around her waist and guided her out. Less than half an hour later, they were in a spacious hotel room overlooking the harbor. Despite her exhaustion, Lauren insisted on taking a shower. She felt dirty all over. With her eyes closed or open, she could smell the men who'd abducted her.

She scrubbed herself until her skin was pink, while Matt stood immediately outside the shower. He helped her dry off, tucked her in bed, then sat down beside her. If she'd ever doubted his love, she doubted no more; it was indelibly etched on every one of his features.

"Want some aspirin?"

She shook her head and managed a wan smile. "We don't have any, anyway."

"I could call down for some."

"I'm okay." She reached for him and whispered, "Just hold me, Matt. Just hold me."

He did. After a time, he moved back to shed his own clothes, then climbed under the sheets with her and held her for the rest of the night.

Come morning, Lauren had recovered to the point where she

could think more clearly. Matt had been at that stage from the moment she'd fallen asleep in his arms.

They were sitting cross-legged on the bed, dressed only in white terry velour robes. She'd begun to gnaw on a strip of bacon when she set it back down. "I've been thinking, Matt. Theoretically, those guys are still after me. But something's odd. I escaped too easily."

Matt wasn't eating, either. "I know."

"It took me a while to find that shaft, but the one who went to make a phone call hadn't returned. No one heard me tearing off the strips of wood. No one heard the elevator. No one chased me down the street. Considering the way they manhandled me earlier and spelled out exactly what they planned to do to me, it just doesn't make sense."

"Maybe the terror they put you through was the end point of the exercise."

She thought about that for a while as she leaned against the headboard and sipped her coffee. "I suggested that to him, and he denied it. Maybe I managed to convince him that I wasn't Susan Miles, or at least plant some doubts—"

"In which case he *let* you escape. If only we knew for sure whether your escape was deliberate or accidental. I have no intention of assuming that you're off the hook until I have proof of it, which means either finding those thugs or—"

"Finding Susan Miles."

"Right. If we could find her and convince her to go to the police, they could question this boss of hers. At least then he'd know he had the wrong woman in you, and we could breathe freely."

Lauren sat forward and reached for the bacon. Matt's presence, his commitment to her cause, the fact of the two of them working together to resolve the problem—all gave her a sense of optimism that, in turn, awakened her appetite. "So," she said between bites, "we have to find Susan Miles, which may be easier said than done. No doubt she's using a different name, and she's probably had plastic surgery to alter her looks, so that's where we'll begin."

He nodded. "The clinic in the Bahamas."

"Right. That's where the boss found out about me, though how he knew to check out that particular clinic is a mystery. I wonder if Susan had been there before, or if she'd mentioned it to him at some point."

"If that was the case," Matt reasoned, "I doubt she'd be stupid enough to go back there when she was trying to flee him. On the other hand, the boss may have had some information we don't. Airline tickets, hotel reservations, something. I think we should fly down and talk with your doctor. Can they spare you at the shop?"

"They'll have to. The shop means a lot to me, but my own health and safety mean more. Between Beth and Jamie, things will run smoothly."

Matt popped a cube of cantaloupe into his mouth. "That Beth is a character. You wouldn't believe some of the stories she came up with to explain your disappearance. She even dared to hint that Brad had come back from the dead and taken you off to some hideaway to heal old wounds!"

"Did she really say *that*?" Lauren grimaced, then sighed. "She's got an unbelievable imagination. I think she's incurable."

"I think she's also incredibly devoted and loyal. She refused to budge from that shop yesterday because she wanted to be there if you called, and when you finally did, she all but sent out the cavalry to find me. She called Jamie to pass on your message in case I contacted the farmhouse first. She got in touch with Phillip—he has a phone in his car—and sent him looking for me. She was ready to tell the police I'd stolen her car so they would go out in pursuit. You're lucky to have her for a friend, Lauren."

Lauren reached out and touched his cheek. There was warmth in her fingers and love in her eyes. "I'm lucky about a lot of things. Very, very lucky."

THE POLICE weren't so lucky. They had nothing to report to Matt except the fact that shortly before they'd arrived to search it the night before, the warehouse had gone up in flames. The fire marshal's office was investigating arson, but that case had little to do with Lauren's, and there was no sign whatsoever of either the dark blue Plymouth or the three oversize thugs.

Accompanied by a pair of officers from the Lincoln police department, Lauren and Matt returned to the farmhouse at noontime on Saturday, packed their bags and headed for the airport. Matt took a few minutes to phone Phillip to keep him abreast of their plans. Then he and Lauren were airborne, en route to the Bahamas.

To the best of their knowledge, they hadn't been followed.

CHAPTER TEN

Upon landing, Matt took Lauren directly to one of the plush hotels on the island. It had become clear to him in the course of the flight that she was suffering a delayed reaction to what had happened the day before. She'd been shaky and restless, unable to do more than pick at the meal that was served. She'd dozed off, then awakened with a start to a fit of uncontrollable trembling. He'd teased her, saying that *he* was the one who was supposed to be nervous, but his fear of flying took a back seat to her upset. He'd known that what she needed most was a peaceful restorative night.

First thing the next day, though, they went to the clinic. Purposely, they didn't call in advance. They knew that the boss's men had been there, and they weren't sure how they'd be received. Lauren was convinced that the doctor would not have willingly colluded with thugs, but Matt reserved his own judgment until their meeting.

Richard Bowen was in surgery. They insisted on waiting in the room just outside his office and caught him the minute he returned. Richard was surprised and pleased to see Lauren, doubly pleased to find her with Matt. After the brief introductions, he ushered them into his sanctuary. Neither Lauren nor Matt missed the subtle blanching of his face as she explained what had happened.

"They made it very clear that they'd seen your files," Matt concluded for her when he sensed that Lauren wasn't sure exactly how to confront the doctor. She obviously liked and trusted him, and she was loath to toss accusations his way. Matt had no such qualm. "Did you show anyone those files, or know that they'd been seen?"

To Lauren's relief, Richard was not offended and deeply shared their concern. "My files are confidential. The only way I'd have shown them to anyone would have been if Lauren had specifically requested it.''

"Then how—" Lauren began, only to be interrupted.

"About a month ago there was a break-in here. My file cabinets were forced open and the files rifled. Records of hundreds of patients were left scattered all over the office. Nothing was taken that I could tell. Until now I've had no idea what the burglars were after.''

"And Susan Miles?" Matt prompted. "Have you treated a patient by that name?''

Richard widened his eyes for an exaggerated second. "Treated, no. Spoken with, yes. Oh, yes. She came by to see me last fall, maybe early winter. She wanted to discuss having some minor work done. It never got past the discussion stage, so I don't have a file on her, but I'll never forget her face. She was stunning. A real beauty.'' He cast an apologetic glance at Lauren. "Yes, Lauren, you do look a lot like her now.''

"Did you do it intentionally?" Matt growled. It was obvious that Richard Bowen had been taken with Susan Miles's looks. For him to try to form another woman in her image might have been conceivable, if infuriating and possibly unethical.

Richard chuckled. "I'm a plastic surgeon, not a miracle worker. It's only in the movies that one face can be completely altered to look like another. No, in Lauren's case, it was pure coincidence. The hair's the same in texture and color, and the figure is complementary, now that Lauren's put on weight. The eyes were alike all along. But, if I remember correctly, and I'm sure I do, Susan Miles wore much more makeup. As for the rest—the nose, the cheekbones, the jaw—they all just came together. You have to understand that in cases like Lauren's, the end results are sometimes a mystery even to the doctor until everything's done. Reconstructive work can go this way or that in the healing process.'' He smiled ruefully at Lauren. "Yours went the way of Susan Miles.''

"From what you say, I should be happy about that," Lauren mused, "but given all that's happened...''

"There are differences," Richard pointed out, "but mostly I

think they come from within. The woman I spoke with had a harder edge to her. She was very much like so many of the others I treat, women whose inner tension does things to their faces that no amount of plastic surgery can correct.''

"Then she didn't really need plastic surgery?'' Lauren asked. She looked at Matt. "Maybe she was planning on disappearing even back then.''

Richard spoke before Matt could comment on that supposition. "There were a few things that could have been touched up, but basically they could have gone another five or ten years without attention. People would have thought her beautiful if she'd done nothing.''

"Did you tell her that?'' Matt inquired. Richard gave him a wry, what-do-*you*-think look. "But she didn't come back.''

"No. I never saw her again.''

Lauren sat forward. "We have to find her. We know she came from the L.A. area and had a boutique there. Did she say anything to you—drop any names—that might give us a clue?''

Richard sat back in his chair and frowned, trying to absorb all that Lauren had told him. "I don't think so.''

"She was probably with a man,'' Matt offered. "A very wealthy and powerful man.''

"Wealthy and powerful men are a dime a dozen on the islands. She did say that she was here on a pleasure trip and had heard about the clinic from a friend.''

"No name?'' Matt asked.

Richard shook his head. "Fully one-third of my patients have been from the West Coast. They like coming here for the ambience, and for the distance. They can go on an extended vacation far from home, then return looking positively marvelous with no one the wiser.'' His frown deepened, and he chafed one eyebrow with the knuckle of his forefinger. "I can picture her sitting here talking with me. I'm sure I asked her where she way staying—it's standard small talk in a place like this—and I don't think it was one of the large hotels, because I would have formed a mental image of her there. Maybe a smaller—no—'' He hesitated, concentrating. ''A boat. I think she mentioned something about the marina.''

Matt grunted. ''There have to be dozens of marinas. She didn't say which one?''

''If she did, I don't remember.''

''Then it'll be like finding a needle in a haystack, and we don't even know which haystack to search.''

''How about other clinics on the islands?'' Lauren asked.

''There are none I'd recommend, and I doubt a woman like that would go to a second-rate place.'' Richard held up a hand. ''No conceit intended.''

''None presumed,'' Matt offered in his first show of faith. ''Can you tell us anything else about her—how she wore her hair, any distinctive jewelry or style of dress?''

Richard closed his eyes as he called back the full image from his memory bank. ''Her hair was pulled away from her face in a chic kind of knot. She was wearing gold jewelry—large hoops at the ears, a chain around her neck. She had several rings, maybe one with a stone, and she was wearing white silk slacks and a blouse. Oh, and high-heeled sandals. I noticed that because her toenails were polished to match her fingernails, and the pink was the same color as the sash around her waist.''

''You were very observant.'' was Matt's wry comment.

Richard laughed good-naturedly. ''It's my business to be observant when it comes to women's looks, and this woman was well worth the look. I remember thinking how elegantly she'd coordinated everything. She was stunning. Truly stunning.''

Matt pushed himself from his chair. ''The description may prove to be helpful somewhere along the line. I hope.'' It went without saying that they were still at the very start of that line. He held out a hand for Lauren. ''Come on, sweetheart. We'll have to rethink our strategy.''

Richard walked them to the door. ''I'm really sorry I have no more information. If only—'' His brow rippled. ''Wait a minute. There is something. I mean, it'd still be a long shot, but—''

Matt and Lauren had turned hopeful faces his way. "What is it?" Lauren asked, holding her breath.

"She smoked. I remembered thinking that in time her face would show it. It does, you know."

"But where does that get us?" Matt prodded.

"She was using a little green box of matches. Not a matchbook, but a little green box. I remembered thinking, 'Ah, she's been to Terrance Cove.' It's one of the more showy restaurants around here. Just the place for the wealthy and powerful."

Matt and Lauren exchanged a look of excitement. "Let's try it, Matt," she said. "We've got nothing to lose."

It was Matt who turned to shake Richard's hand and thank him. Belatedly, and purely on impulse, Lauren gave the doctor a hug. "You've been great, Richard. How can we ever thank you?"

His grin was crooked. "You can find Susan Miles and get both of you out of danger. Her friends don't sound very charitable."

Lauren agreed, then slid her hand into Matt's.

A taxi took them to Terrance Cove, which, fortunately, had just opened for lunch.

"What are you going to say?" Lauren asked. "If Susan Miles was with the boss, who presumably made the reservations, the people at the restaurant would have no way of knowing, much less remembering, her name."

"But the face," Matt cooed. "Ah, the face. Susan Miles had a memorable face. And, sweetheart, you've got that face. *I* always knew it was memorable, but then, I'm slightly biased."

Lauren pinched him in the ribs, but she was buoyed. She held her head high when they entered the restaurant, and tried to look every bit the boss's woman while Matt did the talking. His story sounded conceivable enough.

"My fiancée is looking for her identical twin. They've been separated for two years, and we just got word that she was here last winter. Her name is Susan Miles." He looked at Lauren affectionately. "And this is her face. Does it look at all familiar? Ring any bells? Susan might have had her hair pulled back, and she was probably wearing more makeup and jewelry. But the similarities are marked." He paused. "She might have been with a rather impressive man, and if we can find him, we can get a lead on her."

The maître d' stared at Lauren long and hard. "I'm sorry," he said in crisply accented English. "I don't recognize her. But I only work afternoons. The man who was working evenings last winter was recently retired. He is living in Miami with his daughter and grandchildren."

"It's very important that we reach him," Lauren urged. "We have no other leads. Do you have an address or a phone number?"

The man seemed to waver. His indecision came to an end when Matt pressed a folded bill into his hand. "Wait here, please. I'll see what I can do."

As soon as he had disappeared, Lauren leaned close and whispered to Matt, "Why does that always work?"

He whispered back, "It doesn't, at least not always. I was prepared to give him another. He sold himself cheap."

"That was quite a story. *Identical twin?*"

"Beats the other explanation."

Neither of them commented on the fiancée part of the tale.

Within minutes the man returned with a small index card on which he'd printed the name of the former employee and his Miami address. Matt pocketed the card, and he and Lauren headed back to the hotel.

"To Miami?" Lauren asked.

"To Miami."

"When?"

Matt glanced at his watch. "As soon as we can get a flight."

They both knew that the personal visit was a must. They could easily get the man's phone number and call him, but Lauren's face was the key. So they put back the few things they'd taken out of their suitcases, returned to the airport they'd landed at less than twenty-four hours before, and caught the first plane to Miami.

The flight was short and uneventful. As always, they were watchful, alert to any face that would be familiar, or threatening, or in any way suggestive of a tail. As always, they saw none.

After the plane had landed, they took a taxi straight to the address printed on the index card—a modest house on the outskirts of the city. Various bicycles and toys littered its driveway. Instructing the driver to wait, they approached the door.

It was opened by a gentleman in his early seventies. The children crowding behind him called him "Papa," but his actual name was Henry Frolinette.

Matt repeated the story they'd given the maître d' at Terrance Cove, stressing simultaneously their regret at disturbing him and the urgency of their mission. The man nodded, looked closely at Lauren and nodded again.

"I don't know the name," he admitted, "but I do remember the face. They came to the restaurant more than once."

"They," Matt echoed. "Then she was with the man."

"Oh, yes. A dapper sort, and a generous spender. There were usually eight or ten in his party, though the individuals differed— except for the woman. Miss…Miles, you say?" When Lauren nodded quickly, he went on. "Miss Miles was always with him. And Mr. Prinz always picked up the check for the entire group. He paid in cash, too, I might add."

Lauren's gaze met Matt's. "Prinz," she breathed.

Matt was already looking back at Henry. "Do you know his first name?"

"Oh, yes. He's been quite a presence in the islands over the years. Theodore Prinz, from Los Angeles. Not that everyone speaks highly of him, mind you. There have been rumors about the nature of his work. I never believed them, personally. He is a good-looking man, very well behaved and dignified, and he was always more than gracious to me."

Unfortunately, Henry Frolinette was unable to give them any specific information on Susan Miles. Lauren and Matt discussed it that night over dinner at the beachfront hotel they'd checked into.

"At least we have the boss's name," Lauren mused, "but that's about all. I suppose we could show up on his doorstep and tell him he's made a mistake, but—"

"He wouldn't believe us, and we'd only be putting ourselves right back in his hands. No, if anything's going to stick, we have to find Susan Miles. If Henry had been able to pinpoint a marina, maybe we could have gone back and found someone who might give us a clue to where she went when she left Prinz. But to use Theodore Prinz's name alone would only be asking for trouble. Word is bound to get back to him, and if he's half as powerful as I suspect, we'd be playing with fire.''

"So?''

''We call Phillip, who can use his contacts to get the lowdown on Prinz. If Prinz is involved enough with that boutique to have his own man running it, the name of the place will be sandwiched in there with the rest of the information. At least, it will be if Phillip is worth his salt, and from what I've seen, he is.''

Lauren didn't understand. ''But what good will it do to know the name of the boutique? We can't show up there, any more than we can show up at Prinz's home. If we start asking questions of nearby shopkeepers, they're apt to call Prinz. Besides, I'm sure he had his men question everyone in sight when he started looking for Susan himself.''

''True. But what if we go further back? What if Phillip can get hold of the original papers for that shop?''

''What if Prinz bought it for her in the first place?''

''Maybe he did and maybe he didn't. If he didn't, there might just be some information—even data on loan applications—that could lead us to where she came from—or even to a friend or a family member whom she might have contacted when she relocated.''

''But wouldn't Prinz have done that?''

Matt's eyes were filled with excitement, and his voice held a kind of restrained glee. ''Prinz went forward. He obviously felt he knew Susan well enough to anticipate what she'd do. He must have known of her visit to the clinic when they were in the Bahamas. That's why his men went there right away. They found what they were looking for, so why look further?''

''But you'd go backward,'' Lauren stated with sudden comprehension. And admiration. ''Cautious Matt. Wants to know the ingredients before he takes a taste.''

"It makes sense, doesn't it?"

"Sure does. And in spite of the danger, you're enjoying yourself."

"Sure am. I read somewhere—maybe not in a Spenser novel, but somewhere—that private investigators often locate people who've been missing for years by staking out the graves of their parents. Unless this Susan Miles is truly made of ice, she's been in touch with someone from her past, and more likely than not, that someone is a family member." He straightened in his seat and sighed. It was as though he'd suddenly set down the mystery novel he'd been reading and returned to reality with a jolt. "All *we* have to do is find that family member."

"WHAT'S HAPPENING?"

"They flew back to Boston. Looks like she's not trying to disappear. Kruger's with her constantly. They're staying in a hotel in town, but that may be because workmen have started tearing up her farmhouse."

"Tearing it up?"

"Remodeling. At least, that's what it says on the side of the truck parked out front. I don't think she's planning to abandon the place, Boss."

"Then she's not Susan."

"Looks that way. She's still pretty nervous, y'know. Looks all around her whenever she goes out, and, like I said, she doesn't go anywhere alone. More than that, the police are in and out of her shop."

"Susan wouldn't have dared call the police."

"Right."

"So. She's not Susan. Do you think she's given up the search for Susan?"

"I don't know. Word has it that the detective's been doing some research."

"About what?"

"The boutique."

"You have to be kidding! How did they find out about that?"

"I told her."

"Not smart. Not smart at all."

"It was when I had her in the car. I thought she was Susan then."

"They'll get my name."

"They've already got it."

There was a pause, then an arrogant "No problem. The boutique's on the up-and-up. You'll just have to be doubly careful with Susan's demise."

"What about Lauren Stevenson? And Kruger? And the dick, for that matter? If they do manage to find Susan for us and then something happens to her, they'll know who to blame."

"But Susan's death won't be traceable to us. It could be an accident; it could be part of a larger scheme. If it looks like someone else kills her, that's not my worry. And if a whole bunch of people shoot each other to bits, so much the better. I don't care how you do it, but keep us clean. I pay you good money to handle things like this. Do what you have to. Don't bore me with the details. I want Susan dead!"

"WE'VE HIT PAY DIRT!" Matt exclaimed with a broad grin as he set down the telephone. He was seated at the desk in the back room of the shop, and Lauren was propped expectantly at its edge.

"What did he say?" The call had been from Phillip. She'd known that much, but had been unable to follow the conversation, which had been distinctly one-sided in favor of the detective.

"He said," Matt began slowly, savoring the suspense, "that Susan bought the boutique herself and she financed it with a loan from a local bank. The loan application listed two people as references, neither of whom are named Miles, but both of whom are from Kansas City."

"Kansas City. Where she grew up?"

"Either that, or where she was living before she hit L.A. It doesn't really matter. At least we have contacts." He patted the scrap of paper on which he'd jotted the two names.

"But what if these contacts are somehow related to Prinz? What if one or the other of them was the instrument of Susan's introduction to him?"

Matt was shaking his head. "According to Phillip, neither of the names has shown up in any of the information he's gathered on Prinz. There's still that possibility, but I think it's remote. And even if it's not, neither one has any direct association with Prinz now, which means that we'll be safe.'' He lifted the receiver again and called the airport. Within hours, he and Lauren were headed for Kansas City.

"Poor Matt," Lauren mused when they were airborne again. "For someone who hates flying, you've done your share in the past few days."

He leaned close to her, denying the steel arm between them. "It's worth it. Every hateful minute."

Lauren smiled and whispered. "You are a wonderful man."

"Nah. I'm just along for the ride."

"That's one of the reasons I love you." She kissed his too-square chin. "You didn't ask for any of this."

"But I asked for you," he murmured deeply. "All my life I've been asking for you, and now that I've found you, I'll take any ride, as long as you're along." He sought and captured her lips, kissing her thoroughly. "And when this is all over," he whispered against her mouth, "we are going to take a vacation to beat all vacations. We'll fly somewhere and stay put for two weeks, just the two of us. Sun and sand and moonlit nights…"

"Sounds wonderful, but you'll have used up all your vacation time by then."

"So I'll take more."

"And if your boss objects?"

"I'll quit."

She grinned. "Mmm. I'd like that. San Francisco's too far away."

"My thoughts exactly." He kissed her again, softly, deeply. His mouth was just leaving hers when the flight attendant came by with lunch.

Beneath the lighthearted teasing, Lauren had been very serious. San Francisco *was* too far away. But she couldn't think about the future. Not yet. There was still too much to be done to ensure that she had a future at all.

BRIGHT AND EARLY the next morning, Lauren and Matt showed up in the office of one Timothy Trennis. The office was done in obvious taste and at obvious cost; the man was in his early forties, neatly dressed and pleasant-looking. When he saw them, his mouth dropped open. His eyes were riveted to Lauren's face.

"Susan?" he asked uncertainly.

"Almost," Lauren said gently, "but not quite. I am looking for her, though. We thought maybe you could help us."

Timothy continued to stare at her, then slowly shook his head. "The resemblance is remarkable. It's been a long time since I've seen Susan. I could have sworn—" He seemed to catch himself, and his cheeks reddened. "But you'd know, wouldn't you?"

Lauren nodded. "It's very important that we reach her. Do you have any idea where she might be?"

"Is she in trouble?" he asked with genuine concern.

Lauren looked hesitantly at Matt, who took over. "She may be if we don't find her. Someone else is looking for her. It's critical that we find her first."

"It's that Prinz guy, isn't it?"

"Do you know about him?" Lauren asked.

Belatedly, Timothy gestured for them to sit. When they'd done so, he lowered himself into a chair near his desk. "Susan and I dated for a time. I always knew she had greater ambitions—ambitions that went beyond Kansas City, I mean. When she decided to move to Los Angeles, I wasn't surprised. We kept in touch for a while, so I knew she was seeing Prinz. I made it my business to find out about him, and when I tried to caution her subtly, she pretty much severed all contact between us."

"When was the last time you heard from her?" Matt asked.

Timothy thought about that for a minute, making rough calculations in his mind. "It had to have been more than three years ago."

"And there's been nothing since then?"

Timothy shook his head.

"Is there someone she *might* have contacted? Someone she's kept in touch with—family, maybe?"

"If there is, I don't know about it. Susan rarely talked about family. There was an older sister, and her mother. The father died when she was a child, and the mother remarried. Susan detested her stepfather. She left as soon as she could."

"Do you know where the mother lives?" Lauren asked.

"Susan grew up in a small town in Indiana. Whether the mother's still there is anyone's guess. I don't even know her married name."

"How about the sister?" Matt queried.

"The sister was older by five or six years, took off after high school and got married. Susan never mentioned her. I simply assumed they'd lost contact, too."

Matt looked at Lauren. "Another strikeout." He fished the scrap of paper from his pocket. "What about, uh, Alexander Fraun? Do you know him?"

Timothy nodded. "Susan worked for him. He owns a pair of dress shops in the area. Nice-enough fellow. You could try him. He may have information I don't." As Lauren and Matt stood up to leave, he added, "I hope you find her. I always wished her happiness."

Lauren smiled warmly. She liked this man and felt he'd given them the first positive picture of Susan Miles to date. "We'll tell her that when we find her," she said. *When*, not *if*. Pessimism had no place here; there was too much at stake for all of them.

"THEY'RE IN KANSAS CITY."

"Kansas City? Clever. Susan was from Kansas City. They *are* looking for her."

"Will they find her?"

"In Kansas City? No. She wouldn't go back there. It's too obvious." There was a pause. "It is possible, though, that she's contacted one of her old friends there." A smug smile. "And if that's the case, Kruger and the girl will find out. They're doing our legwork for us."

"Seems to me I'm doing it anyway, following them around like this."

"You're not stupid enough to let them see you, are you? After that little kidnapping stunt, the girl would recognize you instantly."

"Don't worry. We've got Jimbo tailing them close, and she never saw him, so we're safe."

"But you're not far."

"No, sir."

"Good. I don't trust Jimbo to do the heavy work."

"Neither do I, and I have a personal investment here, too. Susan's kept us running in circles. That kind of thing inspires revenge."

"Mmm. I like that. Very good."

ALEXANDER FRAUN was harder to reach. When Lauren and Matt arrived at the address Phillip had given them, they were told that Fraun was at the other store. When they arrived at that one, they were told that he'd gone to a luncheon meeting and would be back at the first store that afternoon.

They went to lunch themselves, then returned to the first store to await the elusive Mr. Fraun. Shortly before two o'clock, he entered the small outer office in which they sat. He had started to pass through into his own office, after glancing briefly their way, when he did a double take on Lauren and came to an abrupt halt.

"Susan?" he asked uncertainly.

"Almost," she said gently, "but not quite." She felt she was living a broken record and quickly moved to free the needle from its cracked groove. "My name is Lauren Stevenson. And this is Matt Kruger. We're looking for Susan and thought you might have some idea as to her whereabouts."

"Come into my office," the man said with a broad wave of his hand. He was as different from Timothy Trennis as night from day. Not only was his office a disaster area, but the man himself looked as though he'd seen better days. Lauren estimated that he was in his late fifties. His bald pate was scantily covered with strands of gray that had been called to the rescue from somewhere just above his ear. He had chipmunk cheeks and a multitiered chin, both of which coordinated perfectly with his girth. There was something about him, something strangely genuine, that made Lauren like him on the spot.

"Now," he said, scooping a pile of ancient magazines from the torn vinyl sofa so that Lauren and Matt could sit down, "what's this about Susan?" He propped himself on the edge of the desk. The wood groaned.

"We're trying to find her," Matt explained. "We were told she worked for you once."

"What do you want with her?" Fraun shot back with such suspicion that Lauren, for one, wondered if Prinz's men had reached him first.

Matt did the talking, apparently taking the man's suspicion for protectiveness. He explained just why he and Lauren were anxious to find Susan.

Fraun shifted his gaze back to Lauren. "You look just like her. For a minute when I walked in, I thought she'd come back."

"We know that she went to Los Angeles when she left here," Lauren offered, "but we were hoping that you might have heard from her."

"She's not still there?"

Lauren shook her head.

The wrinkles on Fraun's brow echoed higher on his bald head. "I thought she was. Last thing I heard from her, she had her own boutique." He smiled. "Susan was good. She had a way with color and style." He gave his head a little toss. "She was wasted here. I told her so. I mean, my goods are nice enough, but she needed high fashion to make the most of her talents."

"When was the last time you heard from her?" Matt asked.

Fraun suddenly scowled at him. "How do I know you're on the up-and-up? How do I know you two haven't come to do her harm?"

Lauren, too, saw protectiveness this time. As briefly but meaningfully as she could, she told him where she'd come from and where she worked, then did the same for Matt. "We don't wish Susan any harm. We have no reason to do her harm. If Matt and I can locate her, Susan and I stand to benefit—Susan, because she'll be aware of the danger and be able to do something about it; me, because if Susan does something about it, I'll be out of danger, too.''

Fraun tugged a slightly warped pad of paper from beneath a haphazard pile of letters. "I'm going to write down your names and addresses. That way, if anything happens to Susan, I'll know who to call.''

"Then you know where she is?'' Lauren asked in excitement.

"Driver's licenses, please.''

Lauren and Matt exchanged a glance and dug into their respective pockets for identification. Only when the man had taken notes to his satisfaction did he put down the pad and face them.

"No, I don't know where Susan is,'' he admitted. "The last time I heard from her was nearly two years ago. She sounded fine then. Why did she leave L.A.?''

"We're not sure,'' Matt answered. "But we do know she left. We'd hoped she'd contacted you, or someone else she knew before.''

"You could try Tim—''

"We already have. He suggested we try you.''

Fraun sighed and gave a shrug that made his belly shake. "I don't know what to tell you. I can't believe Susan's in trouble. She was always honest, and a hard worker.''

"She probably still is,'' Lauren speculated. "It's just that she had the ill fortune to get mixed up with a man who's probably neither of those things. Can you think of anyone she may have contacted? Timothy said she wasn't close to her family, but there's always a chance she could be in touch with one of them.''

Fraun shook his head. This time his jowls shimmied. "Tim was right. She wasn't big on her family. She did mention the sister from time to time.''

"Do you know her married name,'' Matt asked, "or where she's living?''

"Nah— Wait just a minute.'' He bounced off the desk and tugged at the drawer of a file cabinet. It resisted his efforts, yielding at last, but with reluctance. Lauren understood why. The drawer was nearly as overstuffed as was the man rummaging through it.

"How can you find anything in there?" she asked on impulse.

"I find. I find. It just takes a little time."

It took a good fifteen minutes, during which Lauren and Matt sat by helplessly, glancing from each other's faces to the man at work to the calamity of his office.

"Here we go!" Fraun exclaimed at last. He held up a sheet of paper that had a permanent press running diagonally through it. "Susan's original employment application. You see," he cried victoriously, "it sometimes pays not to clean out drawers." Holding the paper at arm's length, he ran his eyes down the form. "Aha! Person to call in case of emergency: Mrs. Peter—Ann—Broszczynski. Relationship: sister." Proudly, he offered the form to Lauren. "St. Louis. Think you can get there?"

Lauren looked from the form to Matt and grinned. "You bet we can." When she returned her gaze to Alexander Fraun, she realized that, with a beard and a little more hair, he would have reminded her of Santa Claus.

ANN BROSZCZYNSKI was not living at the address listed on the employment application, which was understandable, Lauren and Matt told each other, since the application had been filled out seven years before. The people presently living at that address didn't know what had become of the Broszcynskis, but the telephone company did.

A phone booth with its book miraculously attached and intact gave them the information they needed, and a taxi delivered them to the right address. It was another apartment, but a nicer one, more a garden complex. Lauren felt a certain pleasure that Susan's sister had moved up in the world.

The door was answered by a teenage girl who reminded Lauren of the guard at the garage where she parked. Definitely a music fan. If the net of lace banding her curly hair, the penciled mole just above her lip, or the abbreviated top and minuscule straight skirt hadn't given her away, the fingerless lace glove on her hand would have.

"Mmm?" the girl mumbled.

"We're looking for Ann Broszczynski," Lauren explained. "Is she in?"

The girl tilted her head back and hollered to the ceiling, "Mom!" A minute later she stepped aside to make room for the woman who approached.

Ann Broszczynski was a clean and attractive representative of middle America. She wore jeans, a sleeveless blouse and an apron, the latter serving at the moment as a towel for her wet hands. Her hair, a little lighter than Lauren's, was shoulder-length and swept behind her ears. Even devoid of makeup, her face was lovely.

It was also momentarily stricken. Her eyes were huge. She opened her mouth, then closed it and stared at Lauren in puzzlement.

Lauren smiled. "I look a lot like Susan, I know, but my name's Lauren Stevenson. This is Matt Kruger. We wonder if we could talk with you for a few minutes."

"Are you friends of Susan's?" the woman asked, more wary than curious, a fact that Lauren attributed to the distance between the sisters.

"Indirectly, yes," Lauren answered. "May we come in?"

Ann didn't budge. "Susan and I don't see each other," she returned a little too quickly. "We go our own ways."

"I know that. But we need to talk with you. No one else has been able to help us."

"Why do you need help?" Ann shot back.

Matt, who'd been silent up to that point, suddenly understood the problem. "We don't wish Susan any harm, Mrs. Broszczynski. If anything, the contrary is true, which is why we're here. Susan is in danger. Apparently you know that, or at least you know she's living somewhere new under an assumed name and that there's a potential for danger if she is discovered. What you don't know is that Lauren was mistaken for Susan by Theodore Prinz's men. For weeks they've put her through hell, using one scare tactic after another. Last week they abducted her and came very close to killing her. It was during the time she was being held that she learned about Susan.'' He spoke with soft urgency. ''We need to find your sister. She must be told that she's being hunted. We have to convince her to go to the police. Between her testimony and Lauren's, we know that something can be done about Prinz.''

Ann was pale. She gnawed at her lower lip and clutched the folds of the apron in her fists.

''May we come in?'' Lauren asked again, this time pleadingly.

After another moment's hesitation, the woman nodded. Shooing her daughter away, she led them into a small, modestly furnished living room. None of them sat; the air was too tense for that.

''I'm not sure if I know what you're talking about,'' Ann burst out. ''I'm not involved in Susan's life.''

''We realize that,'' Matt said quietly, intent on convincing her of the legitimacy of their mission. ''We've just come from Kansas City, where we spoke with both Timothy Trennis and Alexander Fraun. Do those names ring a bell?''

After a pause, Ann nodded.

''Do you trust them?'' he asked. When, after another pause, Ann nodded again, he went on. ''Alexander Fraun was the one who found your name on Susan's old employment application. He was obviously fond of Susan and wouldn't have given us your name unless he trusted us.'' Though he raised a hand to emphasize his point, his voice remained soft. ''We wouldn't be bothering you if we had anywhere else to turn, but no one seems to know where Susan is or what she's doing. Prinz doesn't seem to be aware that Susan had any family, which may explain why no one has reached you sooner. But it's simply a matter of time before he gets to you, and then to Susan, because it may well be that you're the only one who knows Susan's new name and address.'' He paused, gentling his voice all the more. ''Will you tell us, Ann? We only want to help.''

''I wish my husband were here,'' Ann wailed softly, hands tightly clenched before her. ''I'm no good at things like this.''

''You're Susan's sister. It's your decision, more so than your husband's.''

''But things are so tenuous between Susan and me,'' she argued.

"For years we had very little contact. She was in one world, I was in another. There was no middle ground between us. I don't want to do something that will anger her, or worse, put her in danger."

"Then you have to tell us where she is," Lauren urged. "*None* of us will be safe until we find her and convince her to go to the police with us. For all we know, Matt and I are just one step ahead of Prinz's men right now."

Ann pondered Lauren's words nervously, her gaze shifting from one spot in the room to another. Then she brightened. "Why don't you let *me* call Susan? I can tell her everything you've told me—"

"Do you think she'll believe you—or that we're legitimate?" Matt cut in. "She'll run, Ann. She's done it before, and she'll do it again if this isn't handled right. She needs to *see* Lauren and the physical similarity between them in order to believe what's happened."

Ann looked from one face to the other. "You're asking an awful lot."

Lauren nodded. "We know."

"If you turn out to be the bad guys—"

"We're not! You can call the police back home, either in Boston or Lincoln. They'll verify everything that's happened to me."

"And Fraun took precautions of his own," Matt added soberly. "He has our names and addresses. He knows where to send the police if anything happens to Susan."

"I'll never forgive myself if she's hurt because of me!"

Matt put every ounce of feeling into a single, last-ditch plea. "*No* one will be hurt if we reach her in time. But time is of the essence, and we can't reach her if we don't know where she is."

Ann worried the issue for several minutes longer, her eyes filled with concern, her lips clamped tightly together. Her gaze slid from Lauren to Matt and back to Lauren, asking questions for which there were, as yet, no answers.

Just as Lauren was about to scream in frustration, Ann straightened her shoulders, took a deep breath, let it out in a sigh and surrendered.

CHAPTER ELEVEN

A single long shadow stretched across the grass behind him as Ted Prinz stood in his garden staring out over the hills. Absently he lit a cigarette and dragged deeply on it. Pensive, he narrowed his eyes through the tunnel of smoke.

So Susan was in Washington, D.C. That made sense. He could picture her trying to hook up with a politician who had enough clout to protect her.

He grinned. She'd never make it. His men would make sure of that. At this very moment Kruger and the girl were being staked out at the Hay-Adams House. When they moved, his men would, too.

And Susan would regret the day she'd been born.

"WHADDYA THINK?" Matt asked, looking at his watch. "Should we make a stab at it tonight?"

Lauren pressed a hand to her chest. "My heart is pounding. I can't believe we've found her."

"Don't believe it until you see it. There could be a catch yet."

But Lauren was shaking her head. "Ann said she'd spoken to her just last week. Oh, she's here all right. I can *feel* it."

Slinging an arm around her shoulder, Matt tugged her close. "My eternal optimist." He popped a kiss on her nose. "So. What will it be? Tonight, or tomorrow morning?"

Lauren pondered the choice. "If we go tonight, it'll have to be to her apartment. Ann said it's a nice place, which means there will be security guards—"

"Who call up to announce your arrival and get permission to let you in. Susan doesn't know us. She'll never allow it. No, I think we'll have to take her by surprise. Any advance announcement of our presence will put her on guard and, in turn, put us at an immediate disadvantage.''

"On the one hand," Lauren mused, "I hate to wait. The sooner we get to her, the sooner we'll all breathe freely. But another twelve hours, after all this time…it can't hurt.''

Matt nodded his agreement. "We know where she works. If we surprise her there tomorrow, she won't have a chance to turn us away sight unseen. And if she gets scared and tries to run, we can stop her.''

"But we need time with her, time to explain what we're about.'' Lauren ran her tongue back and forth over her lower lip, then expressed her thoughts aloud. "She's a beauty consultant, Ann said. That figures. From what we've learned, she has a way with makeup and color and style. What if I call first thing in the morning and make an appointment? If we just drop in, she's apt to be with a client. On the other hand, if I can guarantee us a piece of her time…''

A slow grin spread over Matt's face. "Smart girl. I *knew* there was a reason why I brought you along.''

Lauren grabbed his ears, tugged him down and kissed his yelp away. She lingered to savor his returning kiss, her fingers tangling in his sun-kissed hair. At last she dropped her arms to his waist and pressed her cheek to his chest.

They were silent for a time, enjoying the closeness. But Lauren's thoughts of the day to come refused to stay in abeyance for long. "Poor Susan. If she only knew tonight what was in store for her tomorrow.''

"Save your sympathy, sweetheart," Matt murmured. "Susan Miles may still put us through an ordeal. Confronting her is one thing, convincing her that we're on the level is another, but selling her on the idea of going to the police may be a different can of worms entirely.''

MICHELE SLOANE, as Susan now called herself, had set up her business in fashionable Georgetown. Lauren got the phone number from directory assistance and started calling at eight-thirty in the morning on the chance that the shop opened early for the prework set. It wasn't until nine that she got through.

Luck was with her. Michele had a cancellation and could see her at eleven-thirty.

The minutes ticked by with agonizing slowness as Lauren and Matt pushed their breakfasts around their plates in the hotel dining room. Then, to expend nervous energy, they went out for a walk. But while the White House, the Mall and the Lincoln Memorial should have inspired awe, they were too preoccupied in anticipation of the coming meeting to award these sights their due.

Ten o'clock came and went, then ten-thirty. Back in their hotel room, Lauren began to pace the floor. By eleven she was ready to jump out of her skin, but it wasn't until eleven-ten that she and Matt left the room, rode the elevator in silence, walked calmly through the hotel lobby and climbed into the cab that the doorman had whistled up. They'd calculated well for the traffic. It was eleven-thirty on the dot when the cabbie pulled up at the address they'd given him.

For a minute Matt and Lauren stood before the stately brownstone on the ground floor of which was Susan's shop. The sign on the front window, a contemporary logo in burgundy, read "Elegance, Inc." Smaller letters, far below, advertised fashion advice and salon services.

Taking a collective breath for courage, they crossed the sidewalk, descended three steps to the door and entered the shop. An aura of quiet dignity surrounded them instantly. The reception area was done in shades of a soothing pale gray and peach. Soft pop music hummed in the background, low enough to create a modern mood yet be unobtrusive.

A woman sat in a chair reading a magazine, apparently awaiting her appointment. Lauren and Matt made their way directly to the receptionist.

"May I help you?" she asked politely.

"Yes. My name is Lauren Stevenson. I have an eleven-thirty appointment with Michele Sloane."

The receptionist consulted the large book open before her, put a tiny dot next to Lauren's name, then smiled up at her. "Why don't you have a seat? Michele is just finishing up with another client. She'll be with you in a minute."

Lauren thanked her and settled into one of a pair of chairs farthest from the receptionist. She crossed her legs, folded her hands in her lap and leaned closer to Matt, who'd taken the chair immediately on her left.

"When was the last time you were in a place like this?" she whispered in an attempt at levity.

His soft grunt was the only answer she got, the only thing that betrayed his mood. He looked self-confident and composed. Taking her cue from him, she breathed deeply and straightened her shoulders. They were so close, so close....

Moments later another woman entered the shop, checked in with the receptionist and was sent directly through to one of the back rooms. Lauren stared after her, noting a long hallway sporting two doors on the side she could see. She assumed another two doors were on the opposite side.

Just then, from that blind side came the soft murmur of conversation. It was immediately followed by the appearance of two women, but Lauren's eyes homed in on only one of them.

Susan Miles was everything she'd been built up to be. She was indeed stunning. Very much Lauren's own height and build, she wore a pale yellow dress whose shoulder pads gave a breadth that narrowed, past a hip belt, into a pencil-slim skirt. Chunky beads hung around her neck. A coordinated bracelet ringed her wrist. Whether she wore earrings was not immediately apparent, for her chin-length hair was a mass of thick waves that framed her face in haphazard tumble.

The entire look was chic without being ostentatious. Lauren, who mere moments before had felt sufficiently confident in her own stylish tunic and slacks, was envious.

She was also puzzled. Susan Miles looked very much like her, yet very different. Apparently the receptionist had missed the resemblance. Now, studying Susan, Lauren could understand why.

Susan's hair was far lighter than Lauren's, for one thing. It had obviously been colored, though there was nothing obviously doctored about the blond, sun-streaked tangle. It blended perfectly with Susan's skin tone and makeup and looked completely natural.

Makeup. Yes, another difference. While Lauren wore it lightly and for simple enhancement, Susan's makeup sculpted her face, shading and contouring with a skill that was remarkable. Plastic surgery? Lauren doubted it. Yet there was something about the nose...a small bump...

The woman who'd been with Susan left. Susan bent over the desk to examine the appointment book, then followed the receptionist's finger to Lauren and Matt. She smiled as she straightened and approached them, but her smile wavered as she neared. Lauren thought she saw a faint drain of color from Susan's face. The smile remained but was more forced.

Lauren stood up, finding solace in the warmth of Matt's body by her side. If Susan was playing a part, she herself was doing no less. She held out her hand, willing it not to shake. "Michele?"

Susan met her clasp. "Yes. You're Lauren. And..." Her gaze slid to Matt.

"Matt Kruger," he said with a smile.

Susan nodded, but she was already looking back at Lauren. She folded her hands at her waist, hesitated a minute too long, then cleared her throat. "Well. You're here for a consultation. Why don't you come back to my office?"

They followed her down the hall to the last door on the right. The office they entered was simply decorated and furnished, exuding the same quiet dignity as the front room had. Large semiabstract watercolors—one of a woman's face—hung on the walls. Had it been another time, Lauren would have paused to admire the pictures themselves, if not their matting and framing, but she was too busy trying to organize her words and thoughts to handle anything else.

They were all three seated—Susan behind her desk, Matt and Lauren in comfortable chairs before it—when Susan spoke. "What can I do for you?" she asked. Her tone was thoroughly cordial, even warm. The wariness in her eyes was subtle enough to go unnoticed by any but the most watchful of observers. Lauren and Matt were that.

Lauren went straight for the heart. "You've noticed the resemblance, haven't you?"

Susan frowned. "Resemblance?" Her expression was one of confusion, but it was studied. A second, almost imperceptible drain of color from her face betrayed her.

"I have a problem," Lauren explained softly, her eyes never once leaving Susan's. "I was hoping you could help me. Several months back I had plastic surgery, reconstructive work, actually, to correct a long-standing medical problem. The work was extensive, and when it was done, I looked like a new person. But after I returned to the States—the clinic where I had the surgery was in the Bahamas—I ran into trouble. Things started happening. Odd things. Dangerous things." She gave several examples, then paused, looking for a reaction in Susan. But the latter, aside from her underlying pallor, remained composed, so Lauren went on.

"Matt and I put two and two together when I began to get letters addressed to Susan Miles. We realized that I was being mistaken for someone else, but we couldn't find a Susan Miles in the area and we didn't know what to do next. Then, just about a week ago, I was abducted, forced off the street into a car by two men who firmly believed I was Susan Miles."

Susan blinked. That was all.

"They drove me around for hours, finally brought me to an abandoned warehouse and told me their plan. They meant to set me on fire and watch me burn. They had every intention of seeing me dead, as their boss wanted me to be." Lauren paused again, this time out of necessity. Her voice began to shake, whether from remembered terror or the utterly bland look on Susan Miles's face, she didn't know.

Matt came to her aid. "Lauren managed to escape. But we don't know if they're still out looking for her or if they actually let her go because she managed to convince them she wasn't Susan. The police have nothing to go on, at least nothing that's leading them anywhere, and Lauren can't live under guard indefinitely. We realized then that our only hope was in finding Susan.''

For the first time, Susan stirred. She propped her elbow on the arm of her chair and rested her chin on her knuckles. Her fingernails were beautifully shaped and painted a sheer pink noncolor. ''I'm not sure I understand. I'm a beauty consultant, not a detective. Why have you come to me?''

Lauren resumed speaking, more calmly, now, and briefly sketched the course of their search. She concluded with a soft ''Ann Broszczynski sent us here.''

Susan's eyes were blank and she was shaking her head, but her knuckles had curved into a fist. ''None of those names mean anything to me. Ann—whoever she is—must have been wrong. I have no idea why she sent you here.''

''I think you do,'' Matt challenged. ''You saw the resemblance to your old self the minute you looked at Lauren, and we saw the resemblance the minute we looked at you.''

A hoarse laugh tripped from Susan's throat. ''This is ludicrous! I don't know why I'm even sitting here listening to you.'' But she didn't move. ''Do you really expect me to swallow the story you've told? I'm sorry. Even if I believed it, which I don't, I don't know why someone would have sent you to *me*. And as far as the resemblance is concerned, you're mistaken—''

''No.'' Matt spoke softly, trying his best to understand her fear as he tamped down his own impatience. ''We're not here to hurt you. You have a problem, and because of that, Lauren has a problem. I, for one, don't think it's fair that she's been saddled with it. She did nothing but try to correct a medical deficiency, and now she's being punished. We know that Theodore Prinz is at the root of the problem. We also know that unless you agree to go to the police and testify along with Lauren, he'll snake his way free.'' Susan's telephone chirped melodically. Matt ignored it. ''It's only a matter of time before he finds you—Ann realized that—and he may well kill Lauren along the way.''

When the phone on the desk chimed a second time, Susan picked it up. Her every movement was carefully controlled. ''Yes?... She's back?... No, no, don't let her go. I'll be there in a second." Replacing the receiver, she rose from her seat and headed for the door. Matt was instantly on his feet, but she held him off with a hand. "There's a problem at the front desk. I have to see to it, but I'll be back. Please don't go anywhere. I'd like to hear more about this Theodore Prinz."

With that, she left the office. The door had no sooner closed behind her than the phone rang again, that same soft tinkle. Matt stared at it and frowned. When he made a move toward it, Lauren was one step ahead. Their lines of sight merged on the keyboard. A red dot flashed beside the bottommost number, one that was separate from the others, one totally apart from that marked "X" that would connect the interoffice line.

"Damn it," Matt barked, heading for the door, "she's gone! That wasn't the receptionist. It was someone on her personal line, someone who's calling back now to find out what in the hell she was talking about." He was in the hall, looking first one way, then the other, with Lauren by his side. "I'll take the back, sweetheart. It probably leads to an alley. No, you take the back. I'll circle around and head her off." He burst into a run toward the front of the shop.

Brushing past the white curtain at the end of the hall, Lauren raced through the back room, threw open the door and dashed up the steps. Yes, there was an alley, a long, long alley strewn with trash cans and miscellaneous other debris. Susan Miles was about halfway down its length and running.

"Michele!" Lauren screamed as she, too, broke into a run. "Wait!"

Susan wasn't waiting. She was running as if the devil himself were at her heels, and would have long since made it to the end of the alley had it not been for the dodging the obstacle course demanded.

"Michele! Wait! It's dangerous!"

But Susan had no intention of stopping. Had it not been for Matt's timely appearance at the end of the alley, she'd have escaped. As it was, when she saw him, she whirled around, saw

Lauren, whirled again and made for the nearest doorway. Matt reached her before she made it.

Capturing her bodily, he swung her up and wrestled her back until he'd pinned her to the nearest brick wall. "I am *not* going to hurt you, Susan," he gritted out between breaths, "but nei-ther…neither am I going to let you get away. Not…after all we've been through to find you, not after all Lauren's been through *be-cause* of you."

Lauren came to a breathless halt just as Susan sagged lower against the wall. Matt simply shifted his grip, veeing his hands under her arms and propping her right back up. She'd tricked him once. Lauren agreed with his caution.

"It wasn't my fault," Susan gasped. Her composure had van-ished. There was near panic in the eyes that skipped from Matt's face to Lauren's and back. "I'd been with Ted for two years before I discovered who he really was. I wanted to leave him then, but he wouldn't hear of it. For a year, a whole year, I tried, but he threat-ened awful things and I kept giving in until I hated myself nearly as much as I hated him. I was desperate…so desperate that I tried to kill myself."

"A suicide attempt?" Matt drawled. "We knew about the ac-cident, but that's a new twist to the story."

"Why else would I drive over a cliff? You thought I wasn't in the car when it went over the edge? I was. *I was.* But I was thrown free when the car began to roll." Trembling, she shoved the hair from her forehead. Just below her hairline was a three-inch scar. "I broke an arm and several ribs, but I could breathe and think and feel, and it was then that I realized I'd been given a second chance. So I let them think that I'd died, and I ran. Don't ask me what hospital I went to—it was in some godforsaken town in northern Arizona."

"How did you get there?"

"I hitchhiked."

"Talk of ludicrous stories!"

"It's the truth. At the time, nothing was more dangerous than staying where I was."

"Why didn't you go to the police? If Prinz threatened you—"

"Ted *owns* the police, or half of them, and what he doesn't own he has connections to. I know what I'm talking about. I've seen him buy his way out of serious investigations. That was what tipped me off in the first place!"

Lauren entered the conversation at that point. She was beginning to feel sorry for Susan. While she understood Matt's anger, she wanted to put the other woman at ease. They still needed her co-operation. "Okay," she said gent-ly. "You felt you couldn't go to the police. Where did you go? What did you use for money? The two men who kidnapped me mentioned furs and jewels."

"I had both. Ted had given them to me. As far as I was con-cerned, I'd earned them."

"But how did you get them? You'd have to have gone back to Los Angeles."

"A friend did it." Susan's voice softened. "He was a little old man who used to sell flowers on a street corner not far from the boutique. I liked him. He reminded me of my father—or what my father would have been like if he'd lived beyond forty," she added in a whisper. "Sam was kind and gentle. I knew he'd do anything for me." She averted her gaze. "Maybe it was wrong of me, or arrogant. I knew Sam was dying. He'd told me that he'd been given six months to live. I figured that he wouldn't mind the risk, that he'd take pleasure in helping me out." Her eyes met Lauren's. "And he did. He told me so in a note he stuck inside the pocket of one of the coats."

"An old man, breaking into your apartment and stealing your things?" Matt was clearly skeptical.

"He didn't steal them," Susan shot back. "He simply returned to me what was mine. As for breaking into my apartment—he had friends who would have done anything for him, just as I would have."

"But you never got the chance," Matt concluded sarcastically, only to be instantly corrected.

"I did. After I sold the very first ring, I sent him a large chunk of the money. I know he received it, because I called him to make sure.'' Susan took a ragged breath. ''Whether he lived long enough to enjoy it, I'll never know. I've tried to call him again, but there's been no answer. He may be using the money to travel, or he may be…well, I'll never know.''

Matt stared at her. ''Prinz's men may have had him killed.''

''Do you think I don't know that?'' Susan cried. ''I've *seen* Ted in action—''

''Isn't it about time you did something about it?''

The air between the two sizzled. Lauren set about diffusing it. ''We're getting ahead of ourselves. Did you come directly to Washington from Arizona?''

Susan was leaning against the brick on her own now, Matt having released her and stepped back. She took several calming breaths. ''I made a few stops. I wasn't sure where I wanted to settle. But each time I stopped, I felt I was still too close to Ted, so I kept going. When I reached Washington, it was either stay or swim. So I stayed.''

''What about your nose?'' Lauren frowned as she leaned to the side for a profile view. ''We assumed you'd have plastic surgery to change your looks. Prinz's men assumed the same, which was how they got onto me.''

''I figured they'd think that, so I avoided it.'' Susan gave a self-conscious half shrug. ''My nose had been broken in the accident, and I didn't trust the doctors in that hospital to do more than tape it up. When the bandages came off, I saw the bump. It was subtle enough to change my profile just that little bit. I told myself it'd give my face character.'' She snorted. ''Obviously it didn't fool you.''

''We started with an advantage.'' It was Matt speaking, more gently now. ''We had your name and knew where to find you. Even before you walked into that reception area, we were primed to see Susan Miles.''

With an air of helplessness, Susan raised her eyes to the sliver of sky above. ''Well, you saw her. And you have her cornered. I suppose I knew that someday someone would find me. In some ways, it's a relief that it's you.''

"Then you do trust us?" he asked.

Her gaze met his. "Trust? Maybe that's going a little too far."

Lauren grasped her arm. "But you do believe that what we've told you is the truth."

Susan studied her for a long time. "The resemblance...it's amazing. What did you look like before?"

Dropping Susan's arm, Lauren glanced awkwardly at Matt, who nodded. "I was awful." Lauren proceeded to paint a brief, if blunt, picture of her former self. "Richard took care of it all, bless him." She winced. "Then again..."

Matt curved his hand around her neck. "No, no, sweetheart. From a purely medical standpoint, it is a blessing, what he did. And as for this other, we'll work it all out. Susan will go to the police with us—"

"Whoa. I never said that."

"But you have to!" Lauren cried. "It's your only chance. Sooner or later those guys will find you—"

A deep voice cut her off with an ominously sarcastic "Hel-lo, hel-lo."

All three heads jerked around. Lauren and Susan gasped in tandem. Matt grew rigid.

"What have we here?" drawled the man whose face and voice Lauren would never in a million years forget. He stood several yards away, a human wall with a gleaming gun in his hand. "Matthew Kruger, Lauren Stevenson...and if it isn't the elusive Miss Susan Miles."

"What do you want, Leo?" Susan demanded. Her eyes were hard, glittering more with disgust than with fear.

Leo grinned, that ugly grin Lauren remembered so well, and looked first at Mouse on his left, then at another thug on his right. The eyes he refocused on Susan were nearly black. "You know what I want. I want you."

"I'm not available."

"Seems to me you are." He cocked his head toward Lauren and Matt. "These two don't want you, that's for sure. You've been a thorn in their sides."

"I'd pick her any day—" Lauren began, only to be silenced by the restraining hand Matt put on her arm, and by his own retort.

"You've got the three of us, and you know damn well that if you so much as touch Susan, we'll go straight to the police. Do you plan a triple murder?"

"Wouldn't bother the boss any. I have his okay."

"Think, Leo, think," Susan urged. "There are too many people involved now. If you do something to Matt and Lauren, someone *else* will go to the police. This isn't another one of your little in-house jobs. If you kill one of your own, you're doing us all a favor. But to kill me—and these two, who are totally innocent... The police will get you one day, Leo. And if you think Ted will come forward on your behalf, you're crazy."

Leo laughed. "The police won't get me. I'm good at what I do. We'll have it arranged so it looks like you shot the others, then killed yourself. Very clean."

"Very simpleminded," Susan retorted. When Leo made a move toward her, she slipped into a half crouch, arms raised. "I think it's only fair to warn you that I've learned karate."

Lauren and Matt glanced at each other, then at Susan. Leo threw back his head and laughed louder. "Talk of simpleminded. That threat's the oldest in the book, and in your case it's empty. You haven't had the time to learn enough karate to protect yourself."

"I'm a quick study."

"Against a gun?"

Susan had no answer for that, and Matt and Lauren said nothing. They were concentrating on the gun, measuring the distance between Leo and his accomplices, peripherally evaluating the potential weaponry within reach.

"Gotcha there, don't I?" Leo said. He took a step back. "Okay, I want the three of you to start moving. Straight to the car at the head of the alley." He gestured at Susan with the gun. "You first."

Lauren swallowed hard. She had no desire to be in a car with Leo and company. She knew the helplessness of that. No, if a move was to be made, it had to be now.

Matt's hand remained on her arm, but it was steadily tightening. He agreed with her. She waited for his signal.

Slowly Susan moved forward. She hadn't taken two steps, though, when her ankle turned and she buckled over.

"Ah, hell," Leo moaned. "That's the corniest move I've ever seen. It won't get you anywhere, Susan, and if you think I'm going to carry you, you're nuts."

"These heels," Susan gasped. "They're too high."

Matt's hand tightened all the more on Lauren's arm. They both knew from personal experience how well Susan could maneuver, high heels or no. Internally coiled and ready, they watched her unstrap the thin buckles and remove the shoes.

"Come on, come on. We haven't all day—" Leo's words were abruptly cut off by a totally unexpected, lightning-quick move. As Susan straightened, she hiked her slim skirt high on her thighs, spun around and delivered a kick that would have made her instructor proud.

The gun went flying, as did Matt, who barreled into Leo's midsection, knocking the burly man to the ground. Susan, meanwhile, turned her attention to the other men, throwing strategically placed kicks with such speed that they barely knew what hit them. When Mouse doubled over in pain, she whirled around and into his pal, and by the time she was done with him, she was aiming lethal chops at Mouse again.

Lauren came to her aid. Grabbing a heavy shovel from its resting place beside a nearby trash bin, she slammed it repeatedly against the back of whichever man Susan wasn't battering. Each slam vented a little more of her anger, and she might have actually enjoyed herself if she hadn't shot a glance at Matt.

He and Leo were fighting hand to hand, tumbling on the filthy pavement, each landing his share of punches.

Dropping the shovel, Lauren scrambled along the alley, returning seconds later to put an end to the fray. *"That's it!"* she screamed. *"Enough!"* She stood a safe distance back with her feet planted firmly, both hands curved around Leo's gun. The fact that she didn't know how to use it was secondary to the proprietary air with which she held it. Her chest was heaving, the only part of her that betrayed any weakness.

Later she realized that if she'd had to shoot, she'd never have been able to separate Matt from Leo, so fast were they shifting. But her strident yell brought all heads up in surprise. Matt took advantage of the precious seconds to free himself and stumble to her side. He grabbed the gun and turned it on the trio.

"Susan! That's enough!" he ordered. She'd been poised to deliver another side-handed slice to Mouse's head, and only with reluctance did she lower her arm and move back.

Matt motioned with the gun toward the three. "Okay, up! And if you think I don't know how to use this, think again. I'm an avid hunter." His knees were bent; both hands were on the gun, holding it aimed and steady. Not once did his eyes leave the men. "Lauren, go back inside the shop and call the police—"

The sound of shoes clattering on the pavement interrupted him, and seconds later the police themselves rounded the corner and entered the alley with their guns drawn. Slowly Matt straightened. He didn't lower his arm until each of Prinz's men had been handcuffed.

"Mr. Kruger?" one of the officers asked. He was the only one not in uniform and was obviously the man in command. "I'm Detective Walker. Phil Huber gave me a call and told me to keep an eye out. He sensed there might be some trouble."

"How did you know where to come?" Matt wondered. His voice shook. He shot a glance behind him to make sure Lauren was safe.

Walker smiled and cocked his head toward Susan, who stood warily at the side. "Miss Miles's receptionist gave us a call when she found out that something had gone awry with your, uh, beauty consultation. Sorry we didn't get here sooner." He studied Matt's face. "We might have spared you a little of that."

Gingerly Matt fingered his cheek, then his mouth. In the next instant, he reached out for Lauren and hauled her close. She was eager to support him; he'd fought valiantly and had to be uncomfortable.

"Those three thugs intended to kill us," he said.

Lauren pointed. "Those *two* were the ones who kidnapped me back in Boston."

"No doubt," Matt added, his eyes filled with venom, "the third is another of Prinz's men."

"His name is Hank Ober, but he's called Rat," Susan stated stiffly. "The one with the ugly nose is Leo Charney, and the other, Mouse, is Malcolm Donnia." She watched as the three men were hustled off. "What will you do with them?"

The detective faced her. "Book them for attempted murder."

"Then what?"

"They'll be arraigned, and if they can post bond, they'll be released until their trial."

"*Released!* Do you know what they'll do once they hit the streets? They'll disappear. But before they do that, they'll finish off one or another of us, if not all three!"

"Susan…" Matt took her shoulder with his free hand. "That won't happen. The police won't *let* it—"

"The police! If they're not already in Ted's pocket, they will be soon!"

"Just a minute now," Walker growled. He took a menacing step closer. "I have never been, and will never be, in anyone's pocket, and I can safely vouch for three-quarters of my men."

"And the other quarter?"

"They won't be allowed anywhere *near* this case. The Ted Prinzes of the world would like to believe they can buy their way out of trouble, but it won't work here."

"You know of Ted?" Susan asked, wavering.

"Every major law-enforcement officer in the country knows of him. It will be one of the greatest thrills of my career to nail him, but I can do that only if you're willing to testify."

"You have to, Susan," Lauren begged. "Once and for all, it has to be put to rest."

Matt echoed her sentiment. "Lauren's right. If the three of us work together, we can do it. Lauren and I alone…well, it'll be tougher."

"He'll still come after me. It won't matter if he's in prison."

Walker spoke up. "He won't *dare* come after you. Nor will he send anyone else. He knows we'll be watching his every step. I've seen how these men work, Susan. Revenge may eat them alive, but in the end they opt for survival. Prinz will be signing his own death warrant if he comes near you again. He'll know that. Believe me, he'll know it."

Susan swallowed and looked from the detective to Matt and Lauren. "I want to believe. Really I do."

"Trust him," Matt urged. "Trust *us*. But then, you already do, don't you?"

"What makes you think that?" she returned, but there was a softness in her tone.

Matt smiled, then winced when his bruised lip protested. He soothed the spot with his finger. "You really do know karate, but you don't try it on me. One kick, and you'd have escaped. The fact that you didn't try it had to mean something." He ventured a second smile, this one more carefully. "How *did* you learn it so quickly?"

Susan shrugged and gave a tentative grin of her own. "Like I told Leo, I'm a quick study."

Matt chuckled softly. Reaching out, he drew Susan to his side at the same time that his arm tightened around Lauren. "You'll work with us, Susan, won't you?"

Susan moistened her lips, but it was Lauren she was looking at. "After all you've gone through for me, I guess I'll have to." She jerked her head toward Matt. "Where did you even find this big lummox, Lauren? Do you think maybe he has an identical twin stashed away somewhere?"

Lauren grinned up at Matt. "I don't think there's another man like him on the face of the earth. He's pretty special, isn't he?"

Purpled cheek, bruised lip, battered ribs and all, Matt sucked in a deep breath and threw back his head. "Ahhhh. Paradise. One pretty lady on the left, one pretty lady on the right...if only my buddies at the beer hall could see me now!"

"THE BEER HALL? You never talked about a beer hall. For that matter," Lauren said, scowling, "you never said you were an avid hunter.'' They were back in the hotel room after spending the afternoon at the police station. Lauren had insisted that Matt take a long, hot bath to soothe his aching body, but now she had him in bed, exactly where she wanted him.

Matt looked up at her through one half-lidded eye. ''Where did you think construction workers went for fun?'' He steeled himself against an attack that never came.

''Did you get drunk?'' Lauren asked.

''On occasion.''

''What were you like…drunk?''

He shrugged the shoulder she wasn't leaning against. ''I don't know. I was too far out of it to tell.''

She grinned. ''And the hunting?''

''Wooden ducks at an amusement park. We should go sometime. I'll win you a huge stuffed teddy bear.''

Lauren settled onto him, gently and with a sigh. ''Thanks, but I've already got one.'' She rubbed her ear against the tawny hair on his chest and stilled only when he began to stroke her back.

''You're pretty special yourself,'' he murmured. ''The way you thought to go for that gun, and then the way you held it…I thought for a minute that *you* were the one with experience.''

''All a bluff. I've never held a gun in my life.''

''Not even a water gun?''

''Nope. My parents were pacifists. Dead set against weapons of any kind. That's one of the things that drove them crazy about Brad. He used to make guns out of whatever toys he had handy. Some of them were pretty creative.''

''Lauren?''

She took a deep breath, inhaling the clean, male scent of his skin. ''Mmm?''

''What will your parents say about me?''

''That depends,'' she said softly and raised her head. ''It depends on what I tell them first.''

''How about you tell them that I love you and want to marry you?''

"How about I tell them that you're fearless and strong, or that you've got brains as well as brawn, or that you saved my life?"

"I didn't save your life. You escaped from the warehouse on your own. Then, today, you were the one who saved all of our lives."

"You saved my life."

"How did I save your life?"

"You gave it deep, deep, lasting meaning. A good job is fine. So's a good house, even a pretty face. But the thing that really pulled it all together was you. I love you, Matt. Love is what counts. Always has been, always will be."

Matt cleared his throat, but his voice still came out hoarse. "How about you tell them that I love you and want to marry you?"

"They'll hit the roof, but you know something?" Lauren asked, pushing her chin out. "I don't care! If they love me—and I'm sure they do—they'll come around in time. So. Any other questions?"

"Just one. Aren't you worried about where we'll live?"

She turned the tables on him. "Are you?"

"No."

"Why not?"

"Because I've already decided that if my boss won't open a permanent Boston office, I'm quitting. I've made enough contacts here to get another job. And I love the farmhouse in Lincoln." He paused, narrowing his eyes. "But you knew that. You've known all along. You're too smart, that's what you are. You've got me wrapped around your little finger. Y'know, maybe I ought to re-think this. If I'm going to be led around by the nose for another fifty or sixty years—"

Lauren's lips silenced him, and within seconds he was fully involved in the nonverbal give-and-take of love. Belying the punishment he had taken that day, he rolled over to cover her with his body. Hands buried deep in her hair, hips poised above hers, he whispered thickly, "...for another fifty or sixty years, I'll love it...every...sweet...minute."

The Aristocrat
Catherine Coulter

PROLOGUE

The New York Astros' offense stood helplessly on the sidelines, gripping their helmets, their eyes glued on the players on the field as the Steelers' field goal kicker, Karpatian, sent a high, slicing kick from the forty-third yard line toward the uprights. Brant Asher watched the ball sail inside the right goalpost by no more than inches and watched tensely for the signals.

The kick was good.

Guy Richardson, the Astros' kicker, threw his helmet to the ground and stomped his feet in disbelieving frustration. "*Damnation!* I don't believe it, for God's sake! He couldn't get the other two up in the air! Fifty-three yards!"

Karpatian jumped a good three feet in the air and disappeared into a mob of teammates.

"*The fans here in Three Rivers Stadium are going bananas!*" screamed the excited field announcer. It felt, Brant thought blankly, as if the stands were trembling.

Brant heard some vivid cursing from his teammates, but most of them stood quietly, their heads lowered. He looked over at the final score flashing on the electronic scoreboard: 24 to 21. This play-off game was over; it was history. Their chance at the Superbowl was down the tubes. He shut out the noise from the crowd, clutched his helmet tightly in his hands and made his way to Sam Carverelli, the Astros' coach. He looked as rotten as Brant felt. His bushy gray eyebrows nearly met over his forehead, his shoulders were slumped, and his lips were a thin white line.

"Jesus," Brant heard him whisper. "Now I've got to go congratulate that polecat Howard! A damned fluke! Karpatian is the biggest mistake he ever made!"

Brant wrapped a muscled arm around his coach's shoulders. "Luck's the next best thing," he said, for want of anything better.

Sam Carverelli pulled himself together by a thread and blinked up at his prized quarterback's face. "Hell, Brant, it isn't fair. Our second winning season—oh, what's the use? Let's get over there before this crowd goes ape."

Most of the Astros were already on the field, congratulating the Steelers. The tension was over. The Steeler fans would soon forget this football game, for they had another game to think about in only a week. The Astros would be home watching the rest of the play-offs and the Superbowl on TV.

They'd played well today, for the most part, Brant thought as he jogged toward the center of the field to congratulate Joe Marks, the Steelers' quarterback. If Eddie Riggs hadn't fumbled in the second quarter on the Steelers' thirty-eight yard line, if he hadn't thrown that one interception in the first quarter. Too many damned ifs. He'd had twenty-four completions today, including two for touchdowns to Lloyd Nolan, and Washington Taylor had rushed for over a hundred yards. But it hadn't been enough. He was deaf to the incredible noise as he trod over the football field, unwary now of the uprooted clumps of turf that could easily trip up a quarterback. There would be no more football until next summer.

Joe Marks was so euphoric that he didn't at first recognize Brant. "Lordie, Lordie," he shouted over and over again, clapping Brant on the back until he realized who he was. He doused his elation and clamped down on his competitiveness. He was the winner. "We lucked out, Brant, didn't we?"

"Sure did. Good game, Joe." *How sweet it is.* He almost grinned at Jackie Gleason's famous quote. Sweet for Joe and the Steelers.

The two longtime competitors shook hands, and Brant stepped back, letting Joe return to his moment of glory. The locker room scene with champagne soaking sweaty uniforms, plastering every-one's hair to their heads with booze, would be his today.

Brant fell in with a group of his silent teammates on their trek to the Astros' locker room. He was thirty-one, at the height of his career. He thought for one depressed moment that maybe it was time to retire from football, retire with dignity. Then he thought of Kenny Stabler, the Snake, still out there, taking on all comers. He wondered how the Snake felt, seeing those huge young men on the field, eager to stomp all over him. Age, he'd begun to realize once he reached thirty, wasn't a relative thing in football. Even at thirty-one, he faced men eight years his junior. He grinned for a brief moment. He imagined that Joe Marks, over thirty himself, wasn't thinking about being at all old right now.

The locker room was subdued. Suddenly Brant wanted to yell at all his glum teammates that losing in the play-offs wasn't the end of the world, for God's sake. They'd had their second winning season in a row. The owner might be crying now, but he'd made a lot of money with the Astros the past two years.

Brant Asher, all-pro quarterback, jumped on one of the benches and shouted, "All right, you turkeys! Before the press breaks down the doors, I want you to stop acting like I've just screwed your wife!" At least I'm getting their attention, he thought, willing the bummed-out athletes to respond to him.

"There wasn't a damned thing we could do about Karpatian's kick. At least the man still has a job—next year, anyway."

A laugh came from Nolan Lloyd.

"He can't even speak English," growled Guy Richardson, "and he's got a beer gut."

"And a lucky foot," Brant said. "Listen up, you guys, we're going out winners. George, give a towel to Lance. I saw a *person* of the press out there, and we don't want Lance to scare her. Give the lady something to wonder about."

Good, Brant thought as he stepped off the bench, seeing a few grins. He briefly turned an eye toward the horde of reporters filing into the locker room. He watched Lance Carver, a huge lineman, quickly wrap his towel around his waist.

Because he'd won and lost countless games since high school, and been on the receiving end of endless pushy questions during his first three years in pro ball with a consistently losing team, Brant fielded the press's questions with aplomb. He saw from the corner of his eye that one of the media people had managed to get Tiny

Phipps, only twenty-two and a rookie, in a lather of emotion. He quickly answered several more questions, then made his way to the young linebacker, clapped the two-hundred-seventy pound player on the back and said to the reporter, whose microphone was inches from his nose, "You'll be seeing Tiny next year, folks. This guy's got a helluva future." In Tiny's ear he whispered, "Don't give them what they want, Tiny. Just give 'em a victory sign and send it to your mother."

It was a good forty-five minutes before the press left the team in peace. Brant stood under the shower, letting the hot needles of water soak into his sore muscles. His right arm was in agony. Maybe he'd need an operation next season, maybe he'd lose his famous snap... *Stop it, you fool! Why don't you listen to your own speech!*

It was close to another hour before he was free of his teammates and out of the Astros' locker room. They were flying back to New York tonight, and he wanted the quiet of his hotel room for a couple of hours.

But he wasn't going to get it. The press *person* he had spotted earlier was waiting for him. She was a forceful, no-nonsense woman, and her eyes fastened on him like a vulture's who'd just trapped her prey. She was elegant-looking, of course. All the female press corps who covered sports were.

"Mr. Asher," JoAnn Marrow said, her pencil poised over an open notebook. "I wanted to speak to you just a moment." She gave him a wide smile, and he noticed that her front teeth were so perfect they defied nature. She gave a high, grating laugh. "I guess you'll want to be called Viscount Asherwood now!"

He blinked at her. It was a moment before he saw her TV crew stealthily ease up behind her. Before the microphone was hooked up, he said, "What did you say? Viscount?"

Her artificial laughter floated upward, picked up by the microphones. "You didn't know? It just came over the wire service. Your great uncle has just died in England and left you an estate and a title."

"Hey, Brant," one of the crew called out, "you're an English aristocrat!"

There was good-natured laughter.

"Make that the top of the line: 'Brant the Dancer—Aristocrat!'"

"Brant the Dancer runs for ten yards in the House of Lords."

"What do the English call that book of theirs? Oh yeah, De-Bretts. You're a star, Dancer, and not in the Football Hall of Fame!"

"I can just hear them on the tube next season: 'Now, folks, our star quarterback, my lord Asherwood'!"

Brant stared vacantly at the lot of them, faded memories flooding his mind. Asherwood. Lord Asherwood, an ancient old relic who'd more or less commanded his appearance in England last year. He hadn't gone, put off by the obnoxiousness of the old man's letter to his heir. Now he was dead. He'd never had a whit of interest in England, or his father's unobtrusive relatives, unobtrusive at least until a year ago. Brant's grandfather, Arthur, had come to the United States in the early twenties and shortened his name to Asher, and Brant had never thought of himself as anything but an Asher and an American. Good God, he thought blankly, who the hell cares if I'm Lord Asherwood or Count Dracula?

There was a microphone in front of his face. JoAnn Marrow was waiting for his comment. He pulled himself together and said pleasantly, "I haven't heard a word about this. But," he managed a thin smile, "I am not surprised that you are way ahead of me. The press always has the jump on everyone else. I'll have a statement when I find out exactly what has happened."

"But you knew, didn't you, Brant, that you were heir to an English title?"

He gave JoAnn as big a white-toothed smile as she was bestowing on him. "Yeah, I knew. I'll be certain to invite all of you to a big bash when I get everything straightened out."

He wasn't allowed to get away that easily, but finally, by dint of simply shutting himself in his rented Corvette and revving the powerful engine, he blocked them out. He knew he couldn't go back to the hotel. They'd be waiting for him. He drove around

Pittsburgh, not really seeing the sights, until he had to return to his hotel and pack for the return flight.

He managed to sneak in the back way. On the way out of the hotel, buried in a group of his teammates, he saw the six o'clock news blaring loudly on a color TV in the lobby. He shook his head in disbelief as he watched himself and JoAnn Marrow. Lord Asherwood had upstaged the game! He felt the nudge of an elbow in his ribs and gave Nolan Lloyd a bemused shake of his head.

Brant was feeling closer to sixty than thirty-one when he finally drove into the underground parking garage of his west-side New York condominium. His muscles were stiff, and a bruise on his ribs from a crunching tackle throbbed. He focused his thoughts on his Jacuzzi as he retrieved his suitcase from the trunk of his Porsche. And then bed, to sleep for a good twelve hours. He would turn on his answering machine and bolt the front door. No press, no questions until he could call his mother and sort out what had happened. Who, he wondered, had spilled the news to the press?

His two-bedroom condo was on the thirty-fifth floor, and the elevator had never seemed slower. Two residents were in the elevator with him, and they were solicitous about the loss to the Steelers. They said nothing, bless them, about his newly acquired dignities.

He unlocked the front door, stepped inside and firmly closed it behind him. Home, he thought as he fastened the extra chain-lock in place. He strode through the living room, not bothering to turn on the lights as he flipped on the answering machine and went straight to the immense bathroom. He'd stripped off his clothes and lowered his grateful body into the hot swirling water of his Jacuzzi when he heard a noise. He cocked one eye open and turned toward the open door of the bathroom.

Marcie Ellis stood there, her tall, charmingly formed body silhouetted in the bathroom light. He started to smile, but didn't have the chance, because she said abruptly, "I can't believe you didn't tell me, Brant! I look like an utter fool with that bitch JoAnn Marrow getting the jump on me!"

"Marcie, I was kind of busy with the game, just like everyone else. Who cares who interviews the loser, anyway?"

"I'm not talking about the ridiculous game. You an English lord and I knew nothing about it!" Her dark brown eyes flashed magnificently, and she tossed back her thick auburn hair with an impatient hand.

"Ridiculous, Marcie? I promise my body doesn't agree with you, at least at the moment. It is how I make my living, you know."

Marcie flushed and lowered her eyes. She knew Brant well enough to realize that when he spoke very quietly, his voice nearly emotionless, he was angry. "I—I'm sorry, darling. I was dreadfully disappointed that the Astros lost. I know how much it meant to you and the team." She shrugged slightly, one thin strap of her nightgown falling down her arm. "You'll make it next year; I know you will."

"Yeah, it's possible," he agreed. "What are you doing here, Marcie? You know that I'm half-dead after a game."

She rarely considered deception, particularly with Brant, because he had an uncanny ability to see through it. "I hadn't intended to come," she said truthfully, "but after I saw the news, I wanted to know why the hell you hadn't told me yourself."

That was one thing he liked about Marcie, other than her exquisite sensitivity in bed. If suitably encouraged, she could be frighteningly blunt. It was a quality that made her an excellent reporter. "I really never thought about it," he said with equal honesty. "I knew the old bird was getting older, but I don't care about English titles. Good God, I'm as American as the stadium hot dogs. In fact, I can't believe the media are making such a fuss about it."

"Don't be stupid," Marcie said sharply. "It's not like you're Joe Schmuck from Kansas!"

"I'm not Joe Montana from California, either."

"You're still famous, and people eat up a story like this. I can just see JoAnn's headline now: *Athletic Aristocrat*. It isn't fair. If only I'd known!"

A lot of things weren't fair today. "I think I'd prefer something less cutesy, like nothing at all."

"You can take your preferences and flush them, Brant. It'll take a good week for all this to cool down."

The other strap fell, and the gown slithered down a good three inches. He felt his muscles ease miraculously. Lord, he loved her breasts. "Tell you what," he said, rising from the tub and reaching for a towel, "I'll give you an exclusive interview when I find out what the hell is going on. Okay?"

Marcie forgot her snit for a moment as her eyes traveled down his body. "There's an ugly bruise on your ribs," she said.

"Yeah," he said, giving her a wide grin. "Do you think you can limit yourself to the north and south?"

"Primarily south," she said on a slow smile.

CHAPTER ONE

Daphne Claire Asherwood sat cross-legged on her blue flowered beach towel, watching the tourists, mainly German, board the small motorboat tied to the dock of the Elounda Beach Hotel. They were off for a day of fishing and swimming on one of the many deserted islands off the northeastern coast of Crete.

As usual, the Greek sun was so hot she could feel her knee caps beginning to burn after only thirty minutes. Blast her fair complexion, she thought, reaching for her bottle of sunscreen. As she rubbed the thick cream into her warm flesh, she smiled ruefully at the two brief strips of bright orange nylon that covered her. Uncle Clarence would have had a seizure if he'd seen her in something so very revealing.

Uncle Clarence, dead now, and with no more control over her life. She felt little grief at his passing at ninety years of age, only an occasional expectation of hearing his voice, commanding in his querulous way for her to fetch something for him. He's a lonely old man, she'd told herself when she'd felt the familiar spurt of resentment. He really can't help that he's hateful and treats me like a housekeeper, nurse and servant, a possession to be at his beck and call at any time, day or night. I owe him because he took me in when my parents died. It was a litany that had become more difficult over the years. Now she was free of him. She sighed and carefully fastened the cap on the sunscreen. Aunt Cloe would tell her roundly to stop dwelling on those long, empty years at Asherwood. "Life," Aunt Cloe would say grandly, "life, my dear little egg, awaits you!"

Well, Daphne thought, thrusting her chin upward, I'm ready for it…I think. But how did one go about grasping life if one had no notion of what to grasp at? What was she going to do when she returned to England? I am an adult, twenty-three years old, she told herself yet again, a new litany in response to the thorny question. An adult always thinks of something. She looked down her body at the bikini and shook her head, bemused. She would never forget the look on Aunt Cloe's face when she'd emerged from the posh dressing room in an Athens department store, slinking forward, her hands furtively trying to cover herself.

"Merciful heavens!" Aunt Cloe had exclaimed. "And here I thought you a skinny little twit! Goodness, love, what a bosom! Now that I think of it, your dear mama was marvelously endowed. I shan't despair, no indeed, I shan't despair."

Despair about what? Daphne had wondered. It was true about the bosom, hidden for so many years beneath her loose jumpers and oversized windcheaters. She personally thought she looked lopsided, particularly since the rest of her was so skinny.

"No, love, not skinny," Aunt Cloe had said sharply, demolishing Daphne's tentative observation. "Fashionably svelte! Like a model, at least from the seventh or eighth rib down."

And now here she was in Greece, on the island of Crete, a place she'd dreamed for years of visiting, sitting on a beach and looking like a model, from the ribs down. Eighth rib.

Why, she groaned silently, running one hand distractedly through her long hair, did I let Aunt Cloe talk me into this? Not that Crete wasn't one of the most beautiful places Daphne had ever seen, for it was. Aunt Cloe had known for years that Daphne had spun dreams of visiting the Acropolis and the Greek isles, and particularly King Minos' palace, now partially restored, on the outskirts of the capitol of Crete, Herakleion. And, of course, Aunt Cloe knew she would simply adore the exquisite small village of St. Nicholas with all its colorful fishing boats and quaint canals. "Well, little egg," Aunt Cloe had said to her in mild exasperation when she'd dithered, "do you intend to rot here by yourself at Asherwood until you're booted out by the new viscount? It's time, my girl, to do something for yourself!" Daphne had let Aunt Cloe sweep her away from England after Uncle Clarence's funeral. I'm like a limp noodle, she told herself in silent disgust. Always bending to the stronger will. But at least Aunt Cloe wanted her to have fun.

Suddenly aware that a man was looking her way, his dark eyes resting with a good deal of interest on her bosom, she eased herself quickly into a robe and skittered from the beach. Men, she thought, another problem. What did one *do* with them?

Where the dickens was Aunt Cloe?

Cloe Sparks was busy making an appointment with the French hairdresser in St. Nicholas, Monsieur Etienne.

"She has looked the *jeune fille* for all her life, *monsieur*," she was explaining. "Now she is twenty-three and still looks fourteen. You know, too gamine. We must have something dramatic, scintillating, oh, something *je ne sais quoi*!"

"I understand, *madame*," Monsieur Etienne said, the veil of boredom glazing his dark eyes. These pushy Englishwomen and their deplorable, heavy-handed French! Undoubtedly this gamine was a squat, depressingly plain girl who was probably better off just as she was. "When would you like to bring the young lady to me?" He picked up his appointment book and gave her one of his special intimate smiles.

"Tomorrow at nine o'clock," Cloe said firmly. On the taxi ride back to the Elounda Beach Hotel, Cloe chewed her lower lip, painfully chapped from the relentless Greek sun. She'd forced Daphne into this trip, whirling her willy-nilly away after the old curmudgeon's funeral to Athens, then on to Crete. She'd taken advantage of the girl's sweet biddable nature, just as the old curmudgeon had always done. But, dammit, it was for her own good. Yes, she thought, resolutely, Daphne had to have her chance. She wasn't plain, not by any means. She still had to get Daphne out of those ridiculous glasses of hers and into contacts. She drew a deep breath. One thing at a time, Cloe, she told herself. Everything was right on schedule. She had to remember, she reminded herself, to send a cable to Reggie Hucksley in London. She needed another week, at least.

Brant hugged his mother tightly. "Peace and quiet at last, lots of tender loving care, and no hassles. It's so good to be home. You look beautiful as ever, Mom.'' She usually teased him when he told her that, because he was her masculine counterpart in looks.

Alice Asher said nothing for a few moments, feeling an equal surge of affection for her splendid son. Thank heaven he wasn't like his father, embarrassed to show his feelings, as if that would make him less than a man. "Welcome home, Brant. It's so good to see you again. In addition to tender loving care, I've made you your favorite dinner—stuffed pork chops and homemade noodles.''

"My body will think it's died and gone to heaven with a home-cooked meal, Mom.'' He gave her another hug and released her.

"There's lots to talk about.''

Her eyes searched his face for a moment. He looked tired and, oddly enough, wary and uncertain. "Yes, I imagine there is. But first, honey, why don't you just relax for a while?''

Brant sat down and leaned back against the soft cushions of his mother's infinitely old and comfortable velvet sofa. He grabbed one of the cushions, shoved it behind his head and closed his eyes.

"It's been a hard several days I would imagine,'' Alice Asher said, her eyes, as brilliant a blue as her only son's, resting sympathetically on on his tired face. "I'm glad you managed to get here in secret. The press has been hounding me, too. Luckily, they haven't managed to track Lily down.''

"She's cruising the Aegean, right?'' Brant asked, cocking an eye open.

"Yes, this time with her husband,'' came the tart response.

"It is her honeymoon, Mom,'' Brant said, grinning at her.

"Her third! And of all things, Danny, Patricia and Keith are staying with *his* mother.''

"Don't fret,'' Brant said. "I like Crusty Dusty, and so do the kids. Lord knows he's rich enough to give her whatever she wants.''

"He's closer to my age than Lily's!''

"You know as well as I do that Lily needed someone like Dusty, someone older to keep her in line.''

"You should hear his Texas accent!''

"I have. You're not turning into a snob, are you, Mom, just

because you're now a dowager viscountess, or something? The way the nobility address each other is craziness.''

Alice Asher smiled ruefully. "You're right. I'm a regular old fool, and I sound like an obnoxious mother-in-law." She sighed deeply, clasping her hands in her lap. "I wonder what your father would say to all this."

"He'd laugh, a big belly laugh, and tell them to go shove it. The ridiculous title and the moldering estate."

"Moldering?" Her fair left eyebrow shot up. "What do you know that I don't, Brant?"

He felt a surge of restlessness and bolted up from the sofa. He said over his shoulder as he strode to the bow window that looked into the beautifully landscaped front lawn of his mother's Connecticut home, "I spent several hours yesterday with my lawyer, Tom Bradan, and a *solicitor*—as they say—who'd come all the way from London to 'inform me of my good fortune,' which is exactly what he said in that affected accent. Fellow's name is Harlow Hucksley, of all things! About my age, I'd guess, acts like a pompous nerd, and covers himself with tweed. And skinny as your azalea stems, not a muscle on him."

Alice Asher laughed, picturing Harlow Hucksley with no difficulty. Her splendid athletic son didn't think much of men who were "soft as mulch." She imagined that with his teammates he would be far more specific and excessively graphic.

"He was the jerk who spilled the beans to the press, dam—*darn* him."

"You gave him a tongue-lashing, I suppose."

Brant turned and gave her a crooked grin. "Well, Tom did run a bit of interference for the guy. I tried to outflank him, but it didn't work. He expected me—no, he really *demanded*—that I fly to London and get everything squared away."

"You will go, of course," Alice said calmly.

"Why the...heck should I?" Brant said sharply. "It makes no difference to me what happens to any of it."

Alice Asher gave her son a long, thoughtful look. "I know your father never spoke much about his English relations, and neither did your grandfather, for that matter, but England is a part of your heritage, honey. You are more than half-English, you know, because I've got a drop or two in there somewhere. Remember that letter he wrote you last year? The old man knew a lot about you.''

"Obnoxious," Brant said.

"Perhaps. I reread the letter, you know, after you phoned me. It was really rather pathetic.''

"Mom, listen. Harlow told me very little, but I gather there are no estates, and no money. Just this moldering old house in a place called Surrey, and maybe some worthless acres surrounding it.''

"The house is called Asherwood Hall, and its located in a quaint village, East Grinstead.''

"And don't forget that the title had to come to me, so Harlow Hucksley says. The old coot had no choice about that. The rest of it he probably willed to me because it's worthless, and he realized that the American branch had some money and would pour it back into his tomb of a house.''

"Well, son," Alice said logically, "you do have money. It really wouldn't hurt for you to at least go see the place. The season's over, after all. You are at loose ends for a while, aren't you?''

Brant shrugged. "I'm supposed to do a commercial for a sporting goods company, but not right away.''

"At least it's not shaving cream!''

Brant laughed. "True. Lily told me she'd never speak to me again if I bared my face to the world covered with white sh— stuff.'' He shot his mother a guilty look from the corner of his eye.

"Don't feel guilty about your...lapses, dear,'' Alice said, rising. "I expect it'll take you a while to get yourself under control. Last year, if I remember correctly, it took about two months. As for your sister's lan-guage—'' She shrugged, slanting her right shoulder just as her son did.

"Look, Mom,'' Brant said, fighting what he knew was now a losing battle, "maybe you should go. You could take charge of things and tell me what you think.''

"Brant,'' she said, her blue eyes sparkling with mischief. "I already have culture. It's time you acquired some. Roots, Brant. They are important. As a personal favor to me, honey.''

"Damn," he muttered. "It's not as if I didn't have any culture, for God's sake! I have been to Europe, and I did go to college."

"Yes, dear, I know."

"I didn't have to be tutored like a lot of the athletes!"

"Yes, dear, of course."

"My degree isn't totally worthless. Communications. Maybe I'll go into announcing when I retire from football."

"Yes, dear, an admirable choice."

"Duke isn't a second-rate college."

"Of course not. You exhibited tremendous foresight. I am quite proud of you, as was your father, of course. Now, why don't you think about it for a while? I'm going to go stuff the pork chops."

He gave up the battle and said, mimicking her, "Yes, dear, an excellent idea."

Brant was feeling full and mellow when he answered the phone after dinner. Lily, exuberant from a distance of five thousand miles, yelled over the phone, "Lord Asherwood! As I live and breathe! Lordie, does that make me a countess or something, brother dear?"

"Hello, Lily," Brant said. "How are Athens and Dusty?"

"Both unbelievably warm, darling," Lily said, laughing deeply.

"Yeah, I bet. When are you coming home?"

"To Connecticut or to London, darling?"

"Texas. That is where your husband lives?"

"Houston, Brant. It's hot there, even this time of year. I don't know if I could take it." She giggled. "All right, stop screwing up your mouth. I can just see you now! How can you be so disapproving, and you a jock? Of course, it's only because I'm your sister, I know. Maybe an English lord should be straitlaced, but—"

"Lily," Brant broke in, "as a personal favor to Mom, I'm going to London, all right? The end of next week. Do you want me to buy you anything?"

Brant had to hold the phone away from his ear at her crow of delight. He could hear her yelling to Crusty Dusty in the background. "I've talked him around, lovey! All he needed was some good reasons for—'' Thankfully, he couldn't hear the rest of what she said, because Dusty Montgomery grabbed the phone away from his bride.

''Good, Brant,'' he said in his slow, measured drawl. ''Hey, boy, sorry about the play-off game. It'd be a lot easier for you if you played for the Dallas Cowboys. But I'll tell you, that pass to Nolan in the second quarter was mighty impressive. And that draw play, what a call!''

''Thanks, Dusty. It was a good game, despite the outcome.''

''Damned foreigner and his toe,'' Dusty said, and Brant could picture him shaking his head in mournful disgust.

''Yeah. Well, you guys having a good time?''

''There ain't no other kind around your sister, Brant. Place is old, though. Not an oil well around. Maybe we'll see something on the cruise. These ruins are getting to me.''

Speaking of ruins… No, I can't say that, even as a joke, Brant thought, and quickly asked about the islands they were going to visit.

''Thank you, honey,'' Alice Asher said to Brant after she'd spent some ten minutes more talking to her daughter.

''No reason to thank me,'' Brant said.

''Yes, of course there is. I know you're going for me, and I appreciate it.'' She paused a moment, wiping her hands on her apron. ''Will you take Marcie with you?''

Marcie, beautiful Marcie, who'd decided only a week ago that it would suit her just fine to marry a somewhat famous jock who was also an English viscount. ''No,'' he said, surprised, ''of course not.''

''She's called twice today.''

Brant ran his hand through his thick dark hair, the color of his mother's mahogany piano, she'd always told him. ''I was hoping she'd cool down a bit.''

''You're thirty-one, Brant. Marcie is serious, isn't she?''

''You hoping for another grandchild, Mom? I promise you, Marcie isn't into children. After all, she does have a dynamite career, to be fair about it.''

"Yes, that's true enough," Alice said with the utmost composure. "But that really isn't the point. I've never been particularly blind, Brant. So many years now you've gadded about like the gay bachelor. So many women."

"Yeah, most of them out to have their names and faces in the paper with a famous jock."

"And a very handsome and kind man. It's too bad, you know, both for those women and for you. I think you've gotten the least bit cynical. It's understandable, I suppose. I'm glad you're going to England. Come here a moment. I want to show you a family album that you haven't seen in years. I dug it out of the attic just before you arrived."

"You didn't need to drag out the album, Mom. You knew you'd convince me without it."

"It never hurts to have reinforcements, just in case."

Brant sat beside his mother on the sofa, balancing a cup of coffee on his knee.

"So many people that we never even met."

There were faded photographs of great uncle Asherwood, looking irascible and formidable, even in those old pictures from the twenties. He looked as unremittingly stern as any hellfire minister, but no more stern-faced than the flock of females surrounding him, whoever they all were.

"This is your poor Uncle Henry, who died in World War II when he was only twenty-one years old. And your Aunt Loretta, who passed away in 1976, I believe it was. She never married. So, you see, your great uncle had no one left in his direct line. And this is Asherwood."

Brant was surprised that it was so impressive looking. But it looked dark and uninviting with all the tangled ivy covering it. There was an unpaved circular drive, and an old 1940's car parked in front of the house. He felt absolutely no sense of his touted roots as he stared at the house.

"Here's your grandfather, Edward Charles, as a little boy."

Brant laughed. "He certainly improved with age!"

"Indeed he did. Incidentally, you were the picture of him at the same age."

"You know that's not true!" Brant laughed. "You've always told me I'm the spitting image of you. You can't have it both ways, Mom."

There were more pictures of children, dressed in styles suited to the twenties. There were no pictures of Brant's grandfather as a young man.

"Why?" he asked his mother.

"Well, he came to the United States in 1919, just after the war, with his English bride, Melanie. I think there was some sort of falling out between the two brothers shortly after your great grandfather died. He never talked about it."

"Asherwood must have been furious that his title would pass to an unwashed American, particularly if he and my grandfather weren't speaking to each other."

"Yes, I imagine he was somewhat disappointed."

"I suppose all that damned ivy has roots, anyway," Brant said slowly, his forefinger tracing over the photo of Asherwood Hall. "Are you sure you don't want to come with me, Mom?"

"No, Brant. They're not my roots, just yours. I'm almost pure Bostonian, remember? A provincial colonist of no worth at all."

CHAPTER TWO

I can't believe it's really me!" Daphne Asherwood stared at herself, openmouthed, in the mirror. Her contacts had been tinted according to Aunt Cloe's instructions, and her eyes shone back at her a vivid green. A fake green, she thought rebelliously, but only for a moment. She'd never known a moment's vanity in her entire twenty-three years, until now. She rather liked it.

"It's you, my pet," Cloe said, quite pleased with the results. Cloe, in fact, couldn't believe it was the same young woman. "Your green eyes are lovely with your tan and your blond hair."

"Streaked blond hair, Aunt," Daphne said. "Monsieur Etienne, well, he was most thorough, wasn't he?"

"Oh, indeed, my pet, most thorough, but look at the result! I'm glad he left your hair long; it's so lovely. Are the contacts comfortable?"

"I don't even feel them," Daphne said, rolling her eyes about and blinking rapidly. "And the doctor says I can wear them for a full week or so without even taking them out."

"I won't remind you of all the witless arguments you gave me, my pet. Now that you see I'm right, we're off to pick up your clothes from Mademoiselle Fournier."

"I haven't been to Paris since I was fifteen," Daphne said. "Then it was only for three days. Uncle Clarence let me come over one summer with the rector and his family. It's so very lovely, isn't it, Aunt?"

Actually, Cloe thought, gazing for a moment at the heavy dark clouds, Paris in February was a rather dreadful, dank place, and bloody cold to boot. "Yes, indeed, love," she said. She efficiently flagged down a taxi outside the eye doctor's ornate office on the

Champs Elysee and directed the driver to the Place Opera. *"Numéro quatorze,"* she said in ringing tones.

"Bien," said the French taxi driver, not looking up.

As he zipped them through the snarled traffic in a most intoxicating fashion, Cloe listened to Daphne's expressions of delight at everything in sight. Poor child! Three days with the rector! Good lord, how utterly like Clarence, her impossible father. How dare that old man keep Daphne in that damned tomb of a house, denying her everything! Friends, school, fun. She'd pleaded with him to let her take Daphne to Scotland to live with her, but he'd refused.

"Impossible!" her father had roared more than once. "She'd come back to me one of those insufferable modern chits! I won't have it!" She thought of the terms of his will and stilled her niggling guilt. Only she and Reggie knew what was afoot. She pictured the photos she'd studied of the new viscount as she'd sorted through everything Reggie had found out about him. Utterly handsome fellow. Lord, think of the things he could teach Daphne! She flushed at her thoughts, but only slightly. After all, she wasn't that old. She'd decided irrevocably on her present course after Reggie had told her the terms of the will and asked her advice on how to proceed with Daphne. "The girl's not up to snuff, Cloe. I haven't the foggiest notion of how to carry on."

But Cloe did. In a flash of inspiration she had realized exactly what she must do. Then Reggie had given her the report old Clarence had prepared on young Brant Asher. "Here you are, Cloe, all the information old Lord Asherwood gathered on Brant, including newspaper articles and photos of him. He's no brainless fellow, as one might expect from an athlete, particularly one from America. Quite the virile bachelor, I'd say. Look at the women he's with in this picture. He's got money, though, and that might prove to be a problem."

"There's no such thing as having too much money," Cloe had said firmly. "He'll come through. And don't you dare get cold feet, Reggie! I'm going to have enough problems with Daphne!"

But what about Lucilla? Damn Clarence anyway! Why Lucilla? Obviously he wanted the same thing I want. Why couldn't he just let me handle everything? No, she thought, I won't worry about Lucilla; there's no need. Maybe. And she turned to smile complacently at Daphne.

To Cloe's utter delight, when she handed the surly taxi driver the requisite francs for the fare he didn't even count them, his eyes fastened like a dazed famine victim's on a succulent Daphne.

Hoorah! She'd always thought of French cab drivers as the most blasé men in the world.

There can be no more dismal a place than London in February, Brant thought, trying to make out details of the landscape below as the 747 circled Heathrow. It looked cold, foggy and depressing. He didn't think about the blackened snow that had made Boston look equally depressing when he'd left. It had been a smart move, leaving from Logan. The press had expected him to take off from Kennedy.

The man seated next to him was still dozing peacefully when the plane swooped down at Heathrow. One of the flight attendants, ever-smiling Laurie, was more observant, and Brant caught her eye on him, studying him closely. He quickly put his sunglasses back on.

At least in London, he thought, he could lose himself in the crowd. He grinned, thinking he'd have to buy himself a tweed sports coat to ensure that he'd blend right in.

He was met as he left customs by none other than Harlow Hucksley himself. He wondered briefly if all Englishmen were so tweedy and twirpy. The designer glasses he wore were the final touch.

"Ah, Lord Asherwood, such a pleasure to see you again!"

"Mr. Asher is just fine, or Brant."

"Then call me Harlow. I fancy we're going to become quite chummy before all of this is settled." He laughed, and his protuberant adam's apple bobbed.

"Fine, Harlow."

An underling appeared at an unobtrusive nod from Harlow, and Brant's luggage was taken away. Brant arched a thick brow.

"Old Frank will see to it, nothing to get uprooted about," Harlow said.

Brant was greeted outside the airport by a blast of Arctic air and swirling snowflakes.

"Bloody awful weather we're having," Harlow said, unconcerned.

"Yes, bloody dreadful," Brant said.

"London's knee deep in muck, but it won't bother you. The limousine is at your service, of course."

"First class treatment," Brant said, eyeing the gas-guzzling black car that pulled up alongside the curb.

"Certainly," Harlow said over his shoulder as he climbed into the back seat and unfolded his long, skinny legs.

"Compliments of the firm, Harlow? Didn't you tell me there was no money involved in my inheritance?"

"Scarce a sou, old chum," Harlow said. "Even so, my father insisted that you be treated appropriately."

"Very nice of him," Brant said.

"Not really, just good business. At least, that's what he told me. The Old Man's always alert. By the by, Brant, I had thought this car monstrous, but with you in it, it looks like one of those little German boxes. Most impressive, your size."

"I'd have been in trouble if I weren't this size."

"Are all American rugby chaps as big as you?"

"Football, Harlow, football it's called. Actually, I'm something of a shrimp compared to the men on the line. A mere one hundred ninety-five pounds."

Harlow fell into intense thought. "That's a goodly number of stone."

"Probably a whole bagful. What's a stone?"

"A stone is around fourteen of your American pounds," Harlow said. "Equates to the size of Jonah's whale, in your case. Odd business, this." Before Brant could seek clarification, Harlow continued blandly, "Yes, indeed. Who would have imagined an American athlete claiming an English title? You'll be in for some raised brows, old boy. Talk's already around, you know. But don't worry, no one knew exactly when you were to arrive. The Old Man insisted that mum's the word!"

"Good for the Old Man," Brant said. "I assume he's your father?"

"Indeed. Reginald Darwin Hucksley. Very proper sort, and no relation to *the* Darwin," he added.

Brant stared out the limousine window at the cramped, boxlike rows of houses they were passing. The light, swirling snow made them look quite quaint, but he imagined that when the snow melted the black smoke that belched from the pot-shaped chimneys, their charm dwindled fast.

"The Old Man's been trying to round up your relatives."

"Relatives," Brant said sharply, turning to face Harlow. "You said nothing about relatives in New York."

"Well, no, actually. We weren't quite certain how many there were, or where they were. The Old Man doesn't like to spring things without being certain of his facts. I told him they'd be dribbling out of the lamp shades if there was any money involved, which of course there isn't, at least not enough to fill a hat, so my father told me."

"My mother didn't mention any relatives," Brant said. "Who are they?"

"You Yanks do spread yourselves out so, don't you? Lose track of people, and all that. Well, let me see. There's an aunt legging about somewhere in Scotland. Glasgow, we think."

"An aunt," Brant repeated blankly, beginning to feel like a damned parrot.

"Righto. An adopted daughter of old Lord Asherwood, married a chap named Sparks, Carl Sparks, a Scot. Dashed ridiculous name I told the Old Man, but there you have it. Sparks, Cloe Sparks, widow. She was an Asherwood, of course, until she married this bloke, Sparks."

"Any more relatives hanging about in the wings?" Brant asked.

"Quite. There's a young female in there, your father's younger brother's wife's first cousin's offspring."

Brant was silent, weaving his way through this morass of genealogy. Uncle Damon, whom he'd never met. He'd died when

Brant was a young boy. His wife's first cousin's kid. "And what, may I ask, is her name now?"

"Ah, she was a Bradberry, but after her parents were killed in an auto accident in 1974, old Lord Asherwood took her in and had her name legally changed to Asherwood. Can't remember what her first name is. The Old Man will know. She grew up at Asherwood. Then, when your great uncle cocked up his toes, she popped out— to Greece, we believe."

"I can't believe the old coot forced her to change her name to Asherwood!"

"Well," Harlow said reasonably, "it certainly gave the girl a leg up, you know. Asherwood's a much more cushy name than Bradberry."

"Still, it seems to me that people are entitled to keep their true names."

"I don't know, old chum, look at your name. Asher, not Asherwood. Incidentally, there's one other female, a *femme fatale*, if you get my meaning."

"Yes, I get it," Brant said. He was startled that Harlow could manage a leer. Did Englishmen poke you in the ribs when they made a dirty joke?

"She comes off one of the old bird aunts. Loretta, I think, or maybe not. I'm really not certain. Named Lucilla. Dashed goer from what I hear."

"Does she have a confounding last name?"

"Oh no, changes her names like her jumpers. She's married to a rich German industrialist by the name of Meitter and lives in Bonn. That's the lot of them. Doubt you'll have to worry about them barging in and queering your lay. No money and all that, just the bloody house."

"Hall," Brant corrected blandly. "Asherwood Hall, I believe."

"Quite, old boy, quite!"

"Where are we now?" Brant asked.

"Coming up to Westminster Bridge. The Old Man said I should show you some of the sights. He wants you to feel at home. That gray matter swishing down below is the Thames."

Brant perked up to take in Big Ben and all the government buildings. The driver gave them a quick spin along Downing Street, then turned back onto Horse Guards Road.

"St. James Park, old chum. Thought you'd like to see it. Soon we'll be coming up to Buckingham. The queen's in residence now."

Traffic was incredible. Much like New York, Brant thought, except all the cabs were black and on the wrong side of the road.

"Here, Brant, is Hyde Park. See over there…"

Brant closed him out. He was tired, beginning to feel wrung out from jet lag, and wanted nothing more than to sack out for a while, without any "quites" or "indeeds" sounding in his head.

"Your hotel, old chum. The Stanhope. Quiet, and quite private. No nosey blokes hanging about here. You can walk in Hyde Park and sort out your mind and all that."

Curzon Street, Brant read silently. It was a beautiful tree-lined street, calm and restful. The snow fell like a lacy white curtain, obscuring anything that might di-lute the serenity. The Stanhope was small, old and reeked of Victorian atmosphere. The lobby was empty, which was just as well, because Brant couldn't imagine very many guests managing to weave their way through the dark, heavy stuffed sofas and chairs. A thin, tweedy clerk was at the desk. He eyed Brant with a good deal of interest.

"They don't get many foreigners here," Harlow said kindly. "Particularly blokes your size. Here now," Harlow continued to the clerk, taking charge, "this is Lord Asherwood. Reservations for your best room."

Brant handed over his passport and signed his name to an ornate old-fashioned register. From the corner of his eye he saw a hunched old man struggling with his luggage.

"Let me help you with the elevator," Brant said, striding over to the old trouper.

"Eh?" the grizzled old man asked.

"The lift, old chum," Harlow said. "I had the same trouble in America. I kept asking for the loo! Wouldn't believe the tooty looks I got."

Brant closed his eyes for a moment, wishing he'd never come to England. He turned and stuck out his hand to Harlow. "I think I'll tuck up for a bit, Harlow." He grinned, liking his choice of words. If it wasn't English slang, it should be.

"Righto, Brant. Follow the fellow upstairs. I'll send the limousine for you tomorrow, say about ten o'clock?"

"To see the Old Man?"

"Quite," said Harlow.

"Welcome to London, my boy! Sit down, sit down! Betty, fetch a cup of tea for Lord Asherwood."

Brant felt as though he'd stepped into the last century. The law offices of Hucksley, Hucksley and Maplethorpe on Salisbury Court, were somber, dark and, Brant guessed, admitted only male solicitors through their staunch portals. As for the Old Man, he was heavily jowled, nearly bald, and wore stiff wire-rimmed glasses. They were anything but designer frames. He wore a very conservative dark suit, the jacket buttoned and stretched over his ample stomach. Brant had no difficulty picturing him with one of those curled white wigs on.

"Mr. Hucksley," Brant said, shaking the older man's hand. "A pleasure to meet you, sir."

Brant was aware that he was being scrutinized closely and bore up without shifting a muscle.

Mr. Hucksley said to his son, "You didn't tell me Lord Asherwood was such a demmed good-looking sort. The girls will be swarming all over him, starting with pop-eyed Betty."

Pop-eyed Betty did gape at him a bit, but nothing more obtrusive than that as she handed him his tea. Thank God, Brant thought, staring at the repulsive brown liquid, he'd drunk two cups of black coffee for break-fast.

There were amenities to be sorted through and Brant stilled his impatience. Oddly enough, by the time Mr. Hucksley sat back in his huge leather chair, Brant felt relaxed.

"Now, my boy," the Old Man said, his voice shifting gears to a businesslike tone, "it's time to discuss what's to be done with you."

Brant cocked a thick dark brow. "Done with me, sir? I'm afraid I don't quite understand. Harlow has told me that there's only the house and nothing to go along with it, except, of course, the title."

Reginald Hucksley picked up a gold pen and began to tap the side of his impressive nose with it. "That's correct, to a point." He sent a bland look toward his son.

"Point, sir?" Harlow asked, popping forward in his chair like an eager schoolboy.

Brant had the sudden feeling that this scene had been played through many times between them in the past. Obviously the Old Man kept some things, probably some very important things, to himself. Poor Harlow looked for all the world like an eager puppy waiting for a meaty bone from his master.

"Well, you see, there are some stipulations in the late Lord Asherwood's will."

"Stipulations?" Harlow asked, as if on cue.

Brant said nothing. What the hell is going on, he wondered. He felt himself tensing.

The Old Man's gold pen moved more slowly over his nose. "I assume, my lord, that Harlow here told you about the three women?"

"Yes," Brant said. If Hucksley senior wanted to make a drama out of this, he didn't feel like helping him.

"Humph," said Reginald Hucksley, the only sign that he was at all disappointed by Brant's cool reaction. "Actually, only the two young ones are of any concern. Daphne Claire Asherwood and Lucilla Meitter. Both distant cousins of yours, my lord. More disparate females I've yet to see. Rather than read you your great uncle's will, which I must admit is a bit difficult to grasp, I'll explain it to you."

"I understood from Harlow," Brant said slowly, "that there was really nothing to be concerned about. And I will be frank with you, sir, the only reason I came to England was as a favor to my mother."

"Perhaps I should begin with an apology, my lord. I must admit that I have held some things back, as per the late Lord Asherwood's instructions. You see, your great Uncle Clarence most seriously desired that you come to England, and I was to use any means at my disposal to get you here.''

"Then I suggest, sir," Brant said very quietly, "that you get on with your explanations. I expect I'll be leaving London soon, quite soon."

"Well, yes, indeed, my lord," the senior Hucksley said. "First, dear, sweet Daphne Claire, a very properly brought up young lady. Lucilla Meitter, on the other hand, well, she's a bird of very different plumage! Just received word yesterday that she's indeed free and clear of her German husband—indeed, she was back in business before the old lord passed on—and is wending her way back to London after getting over her, ah, disappointment in the South of France.''

"You didn't tell me!" Harlow said, looking much aggrieved. "I told Brant she was still married!''

"Ah, didn't I? Well, now you know, my boy."

"What," Brant asked, his voice ominously quiet, "do they have to do with me? And with these stipulations?"

The gold pen slowly descended from the Old Man's nose, and he sat forward in his chair. His shrewd eyes glittered from behind his glasses.

"The long and short of it is, my lord, that old Lord Asherwood did leave a bit of money. After all the taxes, it comes to about 400,000 pounds. That would be about half a million dollars."

"Sir!" Harlow nearly shouted, jumping up from his chair. "You didn't tell me!"

"Well, my boy, now you know. Do sit down. Now, my lord, you will inherit all the money and Asherwood Hall, if—"

"*If?*" Brant wanted to leap over the Old Man's desk and throttle him. Of all the ridiculous charades!

"If you marry Daphne Claire Asherwood, the dear, sweet young lady.''

Brant stared at him, one incredulous brow raised a good inch.

"Isn't that clear, my lord?"

That's ludicrous! He nodded, tight-lipped.

"Very good. Now, listen carefully, sir. This is, ah, rather detailed and quite specific. If, my lord, you refuse to marry Daphne, you will get nothing, Daphne will inherit a mere five hundred pounds, Lucilla gets half the money and the Hall, and the other half of the inheritance goes to the old lord's favorite charity, the Foundation for Abandoned Foreign Children."

Brant wished at that moment that old Lord Asherwood was there. That old fool!

"Is that clear, my lord?"

That's even more ludicrous! "Oh, yes," Brant said, "quite clear." He sat back and crossed his arms over his chest. "I can't wait to hear the rest of it."

Hucksley Senior ignored his sarcasm. "Now then, if, on the other hand, the impossible happens, and Daphne refuses to marry *you*, then you get nothing, Daphne receives only one hundred pounds, and Lucilla inherits everything."

Brant's stare became more pronounced. Suddenly he threw back his head and burst into laughter.

"I say," the Old Man said, looking shocked, "surely you understand! Really, my lord, you must realize that the estate isn't entailed. Old Lord Asherwood could do anything he wished with it."

So, Brant thought, sorting through this maze of insane information, if he married Daphne the Dog—Daphne, the dear sweet young lady—he got the money, the Hall and a wife. If he refused to marry her, he got nothing and Daphne got practically nothing. Ah, Lucilla! If Daphne refused him, he still got nothing and she was out on her ear with one hundred pounds in her pocket. "Jesus," he muttered, "my great uncle must have been insane!" He raised his eyes to the Old Man and asked, "What does entailed mean?"

"Ah, you Americans!"

"It means, Brant," Harlow said, eager to be able to contribute to the unfolding drama at long last, "that old Lord Asherwood didn't have to bequeath anything except the title to the next male in line. By law, he could do whatever he pleased with his money and the Hall."

"Perhaps you know why my great uncle made such a ridic—ah, unusual stipulation?"

"He didn't want the future viscountess of Asherwood to be an American. He wanted his bloodline to continue."

"But a viscount who's an American is all right?"

"In that, he had no choice," Hucksley Senior said primly. "But after all, your blood isn't entirely diluted."

"Quite good," Harlow said. "All the pitter-pattering little feet should have British blood."

Pitter-pattering little *what*? Jesus, I've got to wake up soon! But nothing occurred to end the scene, and Brant asked, "And what happens to the money if both I and my far-removed cousin refuse to marry each other simultaneously?"

"Everything goes to Lucilla. Understand, my lord, that old Lord Asherwood wanted Daphne cared for."

Is she incompetent? A half-wit? "That, sir, is quite obvious. It's also blackmail of the lowest sort." He felt another surge of anger at his great uncle well up in him. Not for himself, but for his whatever-degree cousin, Daphne. He didn't give a damn about the wretched house or the money. But to leave the poor girl stranded if either of them didn't cooperate with the insane will…! He said with furious irony, "It is obvious that my great uncle was truly fond of this Daphne. So fond of her, in fact, that he's trying to condemn both of us, with me the villain if I don't marry her! This is unbelievable!"

"Now, now, my boy," Hucksley Senior said, adopting his most placating tone, "I must admit that old Clarence did go a bit far. As for Daphne, my lord, I can't frankly consider her refusing to marry you. And, as you say, if you do the refusing, well, as you know, both of you lose everything. And Daphne, I'm afraid, would be left penniless and homeless."

"But what if we find each other equally repellent?"

"Not possible," Harlow said firmly. "It isn't as though you parade about looking like a gnome."

Brant bit back a wild surge of sarcastic laughter. "Another question, sir. What if I had already been married? What would have happened to all these stipulations then?''

"Old Lord Asherwood knew you weren't married. It never came up.''

"What if I were to tell you that I'm already engaged to be married—to an American?''

There was a moment of stunned silence. "Surely you are jesting, my lord,'' the Old Man said, his eyes narrowing in disapproval. "Of course the old lord had you thoroughly, er, investigated, as I believe you Americans put it. We know that you're seen with a lot of women, but no one woman in particular.''

Brant rose from his chair. "I think, sir, Harlow, that I'm going to pay a visit to the Tower of London. Check out all the torture devices and see if the block is still there. Good day, Harlow, Mr. Hucksley.''

"But—''

"I say, old chum—''

"I'll talk to you later,'' Brant said over his shoulder.

"Don't miss the royal jewels!'' Harlow called after him.

Brant turned suddenly in the doorway. "It sounds to me like my great uncle wasn't playing with a full deck. That means queer in the attic,'' he added at the blank expressions. "Loony, off his rocker, ready for Bedlam.''

"Ridiculous!''

"Not to be thought of. Really, my boy, four hundred thousand pounds isn't to be sniffed at!''

Brant sniffed, wheeled about and strode from the room.

"The boy's a bit upset,'' said the Old Man.

CHAPTER THREE

Harlow, you're pushing me, you know.''

"Now, old chum, it's but another hour and we'll be there!''

"That's not what I mean, and you and the Old Man know it! I've given this entire…mess a good deal of thought. I am quite willing to settle some money on Daphne. She won't be destitute then, and she can go on with her life without—''

"Good God, Brant! You can't do that! I mean, it's not what the Old Man, that is—''

I'm getting tired of arching my eyebrows, Brant thought.

"Ah, Brant, you can't think of legging it now! You'll love the old place, you'll see. You've got to see it before you decide anything, and Daphne—''

"Have you ever seen it, Harlow?''

"Well, actually, old boy, that is…''

"I thought not. I, on the other hand, have seen a photo of the place, and it didn't turn me on.''

"Turn you on?''

"I was indifferent to it, Harlow. I could probably shine it on without a second thought.''

"Shine it on?''

"Dismiss it, ignore it, send it to hell.''

"Ah, well, just another forty-eight minutes.''

Brant sat back in the comfortable limousine and closed his eyes. The scenery was beautiful, but he didn't want to gaze at another perfect quiltlike field or another perfectly trimmed hedgerow. Hucksley Senior, the old devil, had held him in London for a full week before insisting that he come to Surrey to see his *ancestral home*. Every damned play he'd sat through in Drury Lane he'd already seen in New York. You're being a jerk and an ugly American, he told himself, and not honest. Westminster Abbey had moved him deeply, as had, oddly enough, the British Museum. Who wouldn't be moved at seeing an original of the Magna Carta? Whenever he could shake the ubiquitous Harlow, he'd roved all over London, enjoying Great Russell Street just as much as Piccadilly. Even Madame Tussaud's on Marylebone Road had fascinated him.

Asherwood Hall. Old, bringing back the dim past. Hucksley Senior had duly filled him in on the history of the place over a formal black-tie dinner at the Savoy. Unlike Harlow, the Old Man had visited Asherwood Hall on many occasions.

"Old red brick, my boy, mellowed in tone, contrasting so well with the green things that clothe or neighbor it. What charm! The River Wey winds all about the place in the most romantic fashion. As to particulars, Brant, Sir Richard Worton was granted the land by that old demon, Henry VIII. There was an immense brangle with the king and Anne Boleyn, but the family survived, even prospered under Elizabeth. The Wortons died out in the direct line in 1782, and a gentleman of Herefordshire, John Gebbe, took over the name. Ah, the transoms and the mullions. Some of the best examples of Tudor architecture in all of England. There are even some painted glass windows with the rose *en soleil*, don't you know, from Edward IV."

"*En soleil?* Why, how unusual! You're certain it's not a fake?"

"Really, old chum," Harlow had said, frowning at Brant's sarcasm, "there's nothing like it, believe me!"

"How many rooms are there?" Brant had asked when the Old Man paused in his monologue to eat his mushroom soup.

"It's not large at all, actually. Not more than twenty rooms."

"Hardly enough room for pets," Brant had agreed.

After that night at the Savoy, Brant simply couldn't contemplate leaving, for there was to be a formal reception for him, given by the Earl and Countess of Rutherford.

"I say, old chum," Harlow said, tugging at his suede jacket. "That's the Wey. Dashed lovely, eh?"

"Utterly dashed," Brant said, eyeing the sluggishly winding river, its water brown from the winter mud.

"We're now driving through Guildford. Be there in just a sec!"

Guildford was another sleepy little village with lots of sturdy, leafy trees and quaint pubs set around a common green. There were even ducks strolling about the brackish pond in the center of the green.

Brant felt restless. He wanted to go home. He didn't even want to meet the dog, Daphne.

He asked suddenly, "You said that Daphne is in Greece?"

"That's what the Old Man told me."

In that case, Brant thought, the girl could be anywhere!

"And she doesn't know the terms of the will?"

"That's what the Old—"

"Yes, what the Old Man told you."

"Ah, we're here! I think."

The limousine turned into a drive between two high stone pillars. Overhead on a rusting circular iron grill were the scrolled words, Asherwood Hall. The wide graveled drive was surrounded on either side with more sturdy, leafy trees. Oaks, he thought, or maybe beeches. Suddenly, out of nowhere, he felt a very odd sensation, as if he'd been smashed by a lineman in the stomach. It was something of a déjà vu, an inescapable feeling that he'd been tied to this place, somehow, in the distant past.

He stared at the huge house. Slowly he climbed out of the limousine, his eyes never leaving the graceful old structure before him. It was three stories high, not quite square, with ivy climbing up to the chimney pots on the sloped roof and twining about the many steep gables. A surge of pride, of possession, washed through him. He wanted suddenly to scrub the dirty panes of glass in the mullioned windows until they sparkled. He wanted to cut away the ivy and bring light into the rooms. He wanted to lovingly replace each of the torn slates on the roof.

I'm turning into a senile fool.

He wanted to run his hands over the huge oak double doors and peel away the rot, then stain them to their former splendor. He wanted to polish the huge brass griffen-head door-knockers.

I'm losing my damned mind.

He drew a deep breath. Suddenly the doors were pulled open, and he heard them creak on their hinges. They have become warped through the years, he thought. How will I fix that?

A scrappy-looking old woman emerged, wiping her hands on her apron. She looked for all the world like an over-the-hill wood sprite. "Eyuh?" she said, staring at Brant and Harlow warily, as if they were there to collect on an overdue grocery bill.

"Mrs. Mulroy, I believe," Harlow said. "This is Lord Asherwood."

"Eyuh," Mrs. Mulroy said. To Brant's surprise, she dropped him a curtsey. "Welcome, my lord." Her voice sounded as creaky as her old bones likely were. Brant heard himself mutter something.

"You were expecting us, weren't you, Mrs. Mulroy?" Harlow asked.

"Oh, uh," said Mrs. Mulroy. "'Tain't much of a homecoming for his lordship, but me and two girls from the village been cleaning out the muck, just as Mr. Reggie instructed. As for Mr. Winterspoon, he's still on holiday. Old Maddy agreed to cook for a bit until his lordship could find someone permanent. It'll taste like fly paper, but ain't nothing for me to say about it. My, but you're a grand fellow, my lord! I ain't never seen a lord as big as you, if you don't mind my saying so."

"No, I don't mind." The front stone steps were chipped. He supposed there were masons in England. He hoped they'd know what to do about that, and where to find the right kind of stone.

"Well, righto! Do you want to see the inside, Brant?"

"Yes."

He was aware that Harlow was looking at him somewhat oddly, but he didn't care. Indeed, Harlow barely impinged on his conscious thoughts.

The old wood sprite scratched her thin gray bun and led the way into the huge, black-and-white marbled entryway. Were there special cleaners to shine up the marble squares? Brant wondered. The ceiling was simply the underside of the roof, some forty feet above. Directly ahead was a beautiful old oak staircase, winding to the second-floor landing. He drew closer and ran his fingers over the smooth old wood. He swore for a moment that he could feel the warmth from hundreds of years of hands that had touched the bannister.

"This here's the Armor Hall," Mrs. Mulroy said, not a hint of awe in her voice as she creaked toward the open doors to the left.

Brant turned reluctantly and followed her, Harlow behind him. He stepped through the twenty-foot-high double doors and sucked in his breath. He'd never before imagined that a room like this could exist. It appeared to be at least forty feet long and some twenty-five feet wide. It had thick beamed ceilings, a huge fireplace against the far wall, tall narrow windows that gave onto the front drive, and a very odd mix of furnishings. Suits of armor, many of them missing parts, were both standing and sitting along the walls like an array of drunken soldiers. Maces, lances, long bows, battle-axes and other pieces of assorted medieval fighting equipment whose names he didn't know were affixed to the paint-peeling walls above the drunken soldiers. One battle-ax had obviously fallen at some time, conking a suit of armor on the head, and had been fixed back on the wall with a crooked knot. Brant moved forward to examine a medieval-type chair, caught the toe of his shoe in the threadbare carpet, and went flying.

"Yoicks!" Harlow shouted. "Careful there, Brant. The place isn't quite all up to snuff!"

Brant picked himself up and grinned at the wizened guffaw that erupted from the old sprite. He shook off Harlow's hand and began a closer examination. Lord, the work he'd need to do in here! How did one replace armor parts? He couldn't imagine wandering into London's equivalent of Macy's and asking for a steel arm, circa 1500. The fireplace was huge enough to roast a whole cow, and so blackened that it looked like an immense dark cavern. The heavy, hewn-oak furniture looked as if it hadn't been polished for at least two centuries.

"Eyuh, my lord," Mrs. Mulroy said in a commanding voice,

"'tis time to see the rest of the place. Can't be spending an after-noon in each room. Those lazy girls are in the kitchen, likely drink-ing tea without me to tell them what to do."

He was tempted to give the old sprite a salute.

There were ten odd more rooms on the ground floor: a long, narrow dining room that would be a perfect setting for candles and ghost stories; a large ballroom that boasted haphazard groupings of heavy Victorian sofas and chairs; and the Golden Salon. Again Brant felt that odd, unsettling feeling when he walked into the room. He knew next to nothing about architecture, but in this room he felt generations of loving care. There was no decay here, no musty smell or peeling paint. It was light, spacious and, he noted, would be wonderfully airy if the damned ivy were cleared away from the wide windows. There were cherubs and other such things along the molding in the ceiling, and an exquisite light marble fireplace that some fool had painted gold! The furniture was grouped in small conversational arrangements, each grouping from a different bygone era. Delicate white and gold pieces by the win-dows; heavy dark mahogany pieces he suspected were Victorian; and even some light-wood sofas and chairs from this century. There was bric-a-brac everywhere, and a line of photographs on the man-tle. His feet drew him forward, and he studied the faded black-and-white pictures. So many people he'd never known! There were several more recent photos: one of an older woman who had fas-cinating eyes that seemed to mock the world, and another of a young woman who was squinting at the camera through ugly thick glasses, had her hair scraped back from her face in a fat bun, and wore a shapeless, dowdy jumper. Suddenly he smiled. The signa-ture at the bottom of the photo was "Daphne Asherwood." The dog! Then he stiffened. He was supposed to marry *that*? His hands felt clammy and he thrust them into the pockets of his corduroy trousers. As he followed Harlow and the old sprite from the room, he noticed that the floors were in awful shape. How, he wondered, would he be able to bring them to their former beauty?

"Eyuh, my lord," Commander Wood Sprite said, "time for the upstairs."

The next thirty minutes passed in rather a daze. The half-dozen rooms on the second floor were in depressing shape, but each one of them fascinated Brant. There were endless little nooks and cupboards, even a priest's hole that the old wood sprite pointed out proudly. There was a long, narrow portrait gallery, filled with centuries of paintings, many of them so dark that the faces were difficult to make out. Brant gulped. It would cost a fortune, he guessed, to bring in an expert to clean them up. *It would eat well into the 400,000 pounds.*

There was only one bathroom on the entire floor and it was a shrine to the inefficient opulence of the last century. He was still fretting about how to modernize the bathroom when Mrs. Mulroy led the way into old Lord Asherwood's suite.

My God, Brant thought, still somewhat dazed, this is my room! It was as rich and splendid as the Golden Salon downstairs, a strange combination of styles that fascinated rather than repelled. He immediately strode to the heavy burgundy draperies along the west wall and jerked them open.

I've got to paint the walls a light color, and get rid of that ridiculous dark wall paper.

"Aubusson, they call it," Mrs. Mulroy said, pointing at the beautiful red carpet that stretched a good twenty feet in each direction. The bed was canopied, a monstrosity that was raised, of all things. Brant suddenly pictured himself climbing into the thing, and smiled. The crimson spread would have to go. Moths had taken their yearly meals here for two generations at least.

"I hope you're not too disappointed, Brant," Harlow said as they wended their way back downstairs. "The place is in dreadful shape, something the Old Man didn't mention to me. But it's filled with tradition—"

"Yes, roots."

"I hope you're not too disappointed."

Disappointed! Brant stared at him as if he were crazy. "It is perfect," he said simply, and turned away, his mind buzzing with plans.

CHAPTER FOUR

I don't see a photo of my cousin, Lucilla Meitter.''

Mrs. Mulroy sniffed loudly. ''She ain't here often,'' she offered by way of an answer. ''Two years ago it was Outrake, and before that, Vargas.''

Brant grinned. ''A woman of international tastes. No photo of her?''

''If it 'tain't there, 'tain't one, I don't imagine. His old lordship was vastly amused by Miss Lucilla, used to tell her without a husband, she was like a cup of tea without the lemon. Why, look ye here! It's Mr. Winterspoon, my lord.''

Winterspoon?

''My lord!''

Brant stared at the short, very chubby little man whose bald head came even with his chin.

''I'm Winterspoon, my lord, Oscar Winterspoon. I was the old lord's valet.'' His bright blue eyes took in every inch of Brant. ''I'm here, my lord, to take care of you.'' Goodness, his look said clearly, do you ever need it! ''I do apologize for not being here when you arrived yesterday, but I was on holiday. Bath, you know.''

''Stuffy sod,'' Mrs. Mulroy sniffed under her breath.

Winterspoon drew himself up to his full height, looking so dignified that Brant had the momentary urge to salute. ''Are all your things upstairs, sir? If so, I'll see to your unpacking.''

A valet, Brant thought blankly. Then he smiled, remembering one of his favorite authors, Wodehouse, and the inimitable valet, Jeeves. I hope this vintage dapper doesn't think I'm mentally incompetent. He stuffed the hand that wanted to salute into his jeans pocket and said, ''I'm not certain actually, er, Winterspoon, that

I'll be here at Asherwood Hall all that long.'' His eyes fell on the peeling paint around the floorboard, a detail he hadn't noticed on the first tour he'd taken the previous afternoon. *I've got to scrape that and stain it.*

"Certainly, sir, but doubtless you'll remain until Miss Daphne arrives?''

"And Mrs. Cloe, don't forget,'' Mrs. Mulroy snapped.

"Indeed, Mrs. Sparks. And Mrs. Meitter also, I understand.''

"I say, what's all this?'' said Harlow, stifling a yawn as he strolled into the Golden Salon. "Just who, my good man,'' he asked, staring hard at Winterspoon, "are you?''

"Winterspoon, sir.''

"My valet,'' Brant added smoothly.

"My father didn't tell me about the valet,'' Harlow said.

"Well, Winterspoon,'' Brant said, turning to the dignified little gentleman, "let us say that you stay on as long as I'm in England. All right with you?''

"Yes, sir. Most proper. In my last position, with Lord Culpepper, I also acted in the position of butler, sir, when his lordship's finances took something of a downturn.'' He cast a deprecating eye toward Mrs. Mulroy. "Since Mr. Hume, his late lordship's butler, won't be returning, perhaps you would like me to assume his responsibilities now?''

"Eyuh!'' Mrs. Mulroy said. "As if I can't answer the door!''

"Perhaps,'' Brant said to both his retainers, "it would be best, Mrs. Mulroy, if you spent your time getting the house to rights. I imagine it will be up to Mrs. Meitter to decide about the future disposition of Asherwood Hall.''

"Mrs. Meitter!'' Mrs. Mulroy exclaimed. "What about poor Miss Daphne?''

Brant didn't wish for the moment to strangle himself in explanations, and said only, "We'll speak of it later. If you would both see to your responsibilities for the moment...''

The vintage dapper and the wood sprite left the room, Mrs. Mulroy calling over her shoulder that breakfast was ready in the breakfast room.

"We'll be right there," Brant said.

"Where," Winterspoon asked with awful calm, "is Mr. O'Reilly?"

"Who is Mr. O'Reilly?" Brant asked as he entered the breakfast room.

"His old lordship's cook, my lord."

Brant bent an eye toward Mrs. Mulroy. "He bagged it," she said. "Took a case of his old lordship's best brandy with him. Bloody blighter!"

"He is Irish, my lord," Winterspoon said by way of explanation. "I trust, Mrs. Mulroy, that the kitchen is in competent hands?"

Mrs. Mulroy drew herself up, looking like a bantam-weight fighter.

"I'm certain that all hands are competent enough," Brant said quickly.

"Did you sleep well, Brant?" Harlow asked once they were alone.

"Yes, I slept very well."

"No ghosts or strange noises?"

"No..." *It was like coming home and sleeping in my own bed. Only better.* "It was a noble experience sleeping in a huge bed three feet off the floor."

Over a rather uninspired breakfast of one egg, too well-done, soggy toast and weak coffee, Harlow said, "The Old Man wanted me to tell you that expenses for the staff would be picked up by the estate, until...everything was finally settled."

"Too bad O'Reilly bagged it," Brant said, wincing as he gingerly took another sip of coffee.

"If you like, Brant, I can call up an agency and see about getting you a proper cook."

Brant's attention was on the stained and faded wallpaper in the breakfast room, and the hideously dark wainscotting. Lord, he was thinking, this room could be flooded with light. I must do something with it soon, since I'll be eating three meals a day in here.

"I say, old boy, is that all right with you?"

"What? Oh, certainly, Harlow. Tell you what, drive me back to London this morning and I'll rent a car for myself."

"You don't mean you're leaving Asherwood today!"

"I'm coming back. There's so much to be done, you see. Oh, one thing you can do for me, Harlow. I want you to contact an agency or whatever, and find me a cook."

Harlow chewed thoughtfully on his toast, wondering if it were an American trait to be witless in the morning. He said only, "For what period of time, Brant?"

"Make it two weeks, why don't you?" He glanced at the wallpaper, smiled to himself, and said, "No, a month."

My God, what has happened! Daphne stared openmouthed as the cab drove through the gates of Asherwood. The drive was cleared; there were two men trimming bushes; and another was mowing the dead winter grass. The thick ivy was gone, all of it, and the windows sparkled in the bright February afternoon sun. She saw another man, wearing old, faded jeans, a wool shirt and sneakers, high on a ladder, doing something to the roof.

"This is the place, Miss?" the cab driver asked, turning to see the young lady staring fixedly at the house.

"What? Oh yes, thank you! Please, just put my suitcases on the drive."

None of the men turned, and she realized they couldn't hear the taxi over the low roar of a buzz saw. She stood in the drive a moment, staring about her, wondering yet again why Aunt Cloe had insisted that she had things to do in London and had sent her on ahead.

Brant didn't know what made him turn on the ladder, but when he did he saw a taxi leaving through the front gate, and a gorgeous young woman standing in front of the house, looking blankly about her.

Lucilla Meitter, he thought. Lucilla the Vamp, he added to himself. Lord, what a face and figure! He climbed slowly down the ladder, jumping the remaining few feet to the soggy ground. He stared at her a moment, taking in the waving streaked blond hair that fell softly to her shoulders, the incredible wide green eyes, and her endless stretch of legs. She was wearing a soft blue wool coat that was belted at her narrow waist.

"What," Daphne asked, eyeing the staring man, "are you doing?"

Brant gave her a crooked grin, knowing he was gaping at her like a horny goat. "The gutter was filled with leaves and other things. I was cleaning it out."

"It appears that the new viscount has taken control. The house looks so different, quite lovely, really, without all that tangled, depressing ivy."

"Thank you, ma'am. I—we are all doing our best."

Daphne studied the man more closely, suddenly aware of his strange accent. He was a lovely looking man, too, and it pleased her that he was smiling at her. "Are you a friend of Lord Asherwood's? You sound American, I think."

"Oh yes, we're quite close." Brant thrust out his hand. "Actually, we're one and the same person."

Daphne blinked at him, and gave him her hand without thinking. His grip was warm and firm. "Oh, I'm sorry! I suppose I hadn't expected you to be clambering about on the roof. You're the football player."

"That's right." He paused a moment, clasping her hand a bit tighter, and said, "I don't think I have to ask your name. You're my cousin, Lucilla Meitter, right?"

Lucilla!

She gave him a thin smile and removed her hand. "Why do you think that?"

Brant thrust his hands in his jeans pockets, and Daphne's eyes followed his movements. She gulped. He was a beautiful man, and so well put together! *But he thinks you're Lucilla.* He gave her another lovely smile, and she just looked at him, waiting.

"Well, actually, it didn't require a great deal of intelligence on my part. I was informed that my cousin Lucilla was the beauty, and, of course, I've seen a photo of my other cousin, Daphne."

Daphne thought of the single picture of her in the Golden Salon and winced. Ugly, ugly, ugly! Still, he didn't have to be so...

"I understand that Daphne has changed a good deal," she said, clutching her purse tightly, and wishing her newfound self-confidence weren't plummeting to her toes.

"Has she? Well, like this house, I imagine that any change would improve matters. Do you know her well?"

"Oh yes, quite well, as a matter of fact."

"Then you also know the terms of the infamous will?"

Daphne shook her head. "No, I didn't stop in London to see Mr. Hucksley. Aunt Cl—that is, I imagine I'll find out soon enough."

"Good grief!" Brant said. He began to laugh. "Well, since Asherwood Hall will doubtless be yours quite soon, may I recommend that we adjourn to the Golden Salon? Unfortunately, the old spr—er, Mrs. Mulroy is in the village right now, so I can't offer you any refreshment."

Brant picked up her suitcases and strode to the open front doors saying over his shoulder, "I'm expecting a cook shortly. I was informed by Mrs. Mulroy that O'Reilly bagged it with a case of his old lordship's brandy."

For a moment Daphne simply stared after him, not attending to his words. What did he mean that Asherwood would shortly be Lucilla's? Impossible! It was his; it had to be.

She followed him numbly into the house, at first not noticing the shining marble floor. Then she did, and blinked.

"Come on in here, Lucilla," Brant said. "I just finished the Golden Salon two days ago. I started there first, since there wasn't too much to be done. I've also been working on the breakfast room. Hopefully, you'll approve my changes. If you don't..." He shrugged.

She couldn't think of a word to say. If the house was Lucilla's, why was he doing all this work? She paused in the doorway and looked around. The large room was filled with clear winter sunlight. The walls had been repainted a cream color, and the furniture had been reduced to the Regency settings. All the heavy mahogany pieces that she'd hated were gone, as were the piles of ugly bric-a-brac.

"It's beautiful," she said. "And the carpets are so clean! I never realized they were so lovely."

"Thank you. I'm glad you approve. I was surprised myself that they came out so well. I was certain they'd have to be replaced. Here, let me help you off with your coat."

He slipped it off her shoulders and placed it on a chair back. "Won't you sit down?"

Daphne sat in her favorite chair, a small, high-backed blue satin-covered affair that had been relegated, before Uncle Clarence's death, to the far corner.

She crossed her legs, unaware that Brant was studying each exposed inch.

"So," he said, forcing his eyes to her lovely face, "you don't know about your good fortune?"

"No," she said, "I don't. Perhaps you'd be good enough to tell me about the will."

She didn't have the look of a swinger, he thought. Nor did she look old enough to have gone through three husbands. She looked fresh as sunshine, and...

"The will?"

"Forgive me," Brant said. "It's just that you're something of a surprise. I knew, of course, that you were...lovely, but I thought you'd be older."

"I take good care of myself," she said, trying to keep her voice light. *Tell him who you are, you fool!* But she said nothing more.

"Ah, the will. Shouldn't we wait for Hucksley Senior?"

"I don't see why we should."

"It's quite complicated, actually, and in my opinion, odd in the extreme. Basically, it all boils down to this: I inherit all the money and Asherwood Hall if I marry my cousin, Daphne Asherwood."

"Marry Daphne! Why, that's ridiculous!"

"My feelings exactly," Brant agreed in a dry voice. "Evidently old Lord Asherwood wanted her taken care of. Why he didn't leave her the money to take care of herself is quite beyond me! From what I've heard, though, it's likely the girl doesn't have a notion of what to do."

"But what if you don't wish to marry Daphne?"

"Ah, then the fun begins! If I refuse, then you, Cousin Lucilla, and a charity, split everything, and poor little Daphne is out with only five hundred pounds in her purse. If she refuses to marry me, then we're both out, and this time it's all yours."

Everything fell into place. The scales have fallen from my eyes, she thought, utterly distracted. Uncle Clarence muttered something about taking care of me, but this! Oh no, it can't be true! Aunt Cloe must have known; she must have! Why else would she have insisted that I needed to be redone, top to toe? "How much money is there?" she asked.

"If you're not a rich woman now, Lucilla, you soon will be. The estate amounts to four hundred thousand pounds."

"Four hundred thousand pounds! But why didn't Uncle Clarence spend some of that precious money on the Hall? I begged him and begged him not to let it fall into ruin! Oh, that impossible old man! I'd like to strangle him!"

"You're a bit late," Brant said.

"Daphne is supposed to marry you," she repeated blankly. "But I…she doesn't even know you! And you don't know her!"

"I can't say I'm particularly looking forward to our meeting," Brant said.

"Why is that?"

Brant shrugged. "I think that is rather obvious. The will, my great uncle's ridiculous stipulations, Daphne herself…"

"What," she heard herself asking in a shrill voice, "about Daphne herself?"

"I've seen a photo of her, as I told you," Brant said with disarming frankness. "She is not what I ever envisioned my wife to look like, nor do I expect her personality to be particularly invigorating. I've heard her referred as 'that poor, sweet young lady.'"

Conceited, arrogant beast! Jerk! Cad! Her mental list of insults came to a grinding halt. Ah ha, bastard!

And true, all of it!

"Why, if you have no intention of marrying Daphne, are you spending your time here, doing all this work?"

Brant clasped his hands together between his thighs. "I don't know," he said, honest puzzlement in his voice. He raised his eyes to hers. "I didn't even want to come to England. I didn't want to see this house, but when I did..." He shrugged. "It's like I've been here before, long ago, perhaps. I have these pictures in my mind of how it should look. Sounds dumb, doesn't it?"

"No," she said. "No, it doesn't, not at all. I'm delighted that you kept the Regency furniture in here. It is my favorite. Many times I've pictured myself reclining gracefully on that sofa, pretending to be a rich, beautiful lady of 1810, dressed perhaps in a soft muslin gown—oh! You must think I'm bonkers!"

He was smiling at her, open approval and liking lighting his blue eyes. "I don't think either of us is dumb or bonkers." He rose and paced across the room, Daphne's eyes following his progress. "Then you feel the draw of the house, too?" he asked.

"Draw? Oh, do you mean that I feel an affinity toward it? Why, yes, I suppose that I have always felt that way. That's why it always made me so angry that Uncle Clarence was letting it fall down around his ears." She added, without pause, "You don't look like a viscount."

He thrust his hands into his jeans pockets, drawing the pants down further, which made her mouth feel strangely dry. "Wait until you meet my valet, Winterspoon. Likely he's hiding in a closet right now, bemoaning the fact that I'm such an ugly, informal American, but just wait until evening. He turns me out in fine fashion, whether I want it or not."

"Winterspoon is here? How marvelous. I've missed him."

Brant sent her a quizzical look. "I wasn't under the impression that you'd visited Asherwood Hall all that often."

Daphne forced herself to shrug. She couldn't believe that she was actually carrying on a conversation with a man. It's what Lucilla would do, she told herself. Daphne would sit huddled up, looking and acting like a tongue-tied fool.

"Perhaps you'll like Daphne," she heard herself say.

"Fat chance!"

"What?"

"Very unlikely. I suppose I'm not being very kind, but I've thought of her as a double bagger."

"A double what?"

"American slang. Forgive me. To be blunt, then, a dog. Probably a very sweet dog, but a dog nonetheless."

She was trembling. It's all your own fault, she was repeating silently to herself. It's like eavesdropping. You never hear anything good about yourself. But a *dog*! "Just maybe," she said viciously, "she'll think *you're* a double bottle."

"No, double *bagger*. You could be right. I shouldn't be saying things like that to you, her cousin. It's just that I'm damned mad about the whole situation." He raked his fingers through his thick hair. "Are you here to stay? Since you will be the owner, I should stop with all my plans. They should be your plans."

The bitterness in his voice made her blink. He had indeed fallen in love with the Hall. Well, to hell with him! Lucilla would get the "dump," as she'd always stigmatized Asherwood Hall. She rose jerkily to her feet.

"No," she said, "it's not up to me, I can assure you of that!"

"I tell you, I won't be marrying Daphne! I'll be returning to the United States shortly, and it'll be all yours."

"None of it will be mine, since I'm not—"

There came a gasp from the open doorway. "Miss! Lawks, you're home! And just look at you—what a stunner!"

"Mrs. Mulroy," Daphne said, smiling at the beaming old woman. "How good it is to see you again. His lordship has been telling me that Winterspoon is here, also."

Brant was seized by a very funny feeling. Something was wrong here, quite wrong. He looked from Lucilla to Mrs. Mulroy and back again.

"You're not Lucilla Meitter?" he said in a very low and controlled voice.

"No, I'm not, my lord!" She swept him an insulting bow.

"Mrs. Meitter!" Mrs. Mulroy gasped. "Certainly not, my lord. This is Miss Daphne!"

"Yes," Daphne said with furious calm, "the double bagging dog."

Brant flushed deeply, and cursed very softly and very fluently under his breath.

CHAPTER FIVE

They faced each other across the dining table in the formal dining room. Brant was dressed according to Winterspoon's notions, in a dark suit and white dress shirt. Daphne wore a dark gray wool dress that Aunt Cloe had insisted upon in Paris. It hugged her body like a York glove, and gave additional oomph to her magnificent bosom with its small pleats splaying downward like an opened fan from a circular neckline. She wore no jewelry; she had none. For once Daphne didn't feel like hunching her shoulders forward. She sent Brant a studied, insolent look, one that she'd been practicing, and sipped from her wineglass.

She'd walked out on him that afternoon, and this was the first time he'd seen her since their debacle. He'd managed to whip himself into a fine state, and her nasty silence egged him on.

He said, his voice as cold as her stare, "You should have told me immediately who you really were. Your behavior was infantile, like a schoolgirl wanting to write her own Shakespearian scenes, with all the silly mix-ups and people at cross-purposes."

Daphne's fingers tightened on her glass. Oddly enough, for the first time in her twenty-three years she didn't feel at all embarrassed or intimidated by being in a man's company, alone. She was too furious. She pulled back her shoulders, with the result that her breasts could not help but draw his attention. "I," she said finally, in an equally cold voice, "have never thought much of Lucilla's looks." *Lord, what a lie! I've been jealous of her since I was ten!* "On the other hand, my lord, you were just as I knew you'd be: brash, rude, insulting, arrogant, conceited—"

"Well, that certainly must cover it!"

"—and you were wearing disgusting American clothes!"

"So you liked my jeans, huh?"

"I don't know how you could bend over! What's more—"

"Don't strain your brain for more charming adjectives!"

"I never *strain my brain*."

"Perhaps you should consider straining it a bit more in this particular instance. I repeat, Miss Asherwood, your behavior was every bit as ridiculous as mine, no, more so. And yes, I admit that I was out of line."

"Is that to be construed as an apology?" she asked sweetly.

"Construe it as you like," he said, and forked down a bit of leathery roast beef. "Surely you can't take exception to my clothes this evening. Winterspoon assures me that this is what the well-dressed English lord wears to dinner."

"Clothes," she said, "do not make the lord."

"But clothes," he said, eyeing her bosom with lecherous interest, "do tell me a lot about what a woman has to offer."

She choked on her roast beef, too angry to think of a retort, and frowned at the taste. "Oh, how I wish O'Reilly were here!" she exclaimed. "This is terrible. How have you managed to survive?"

"I keep asking for hamburgers. They're hard to screw up."

"Who would want to screw a hamburger?"

"I've never wanted to screw a hamburger. What I mean is that hamburgers are hard to ruin, to mess up."

"Oh."

"Now I suppose you'll tell me that I can't speak proper English."

"Oh no. It appears that you already recognize your...lacks, at least in that area."

Brant dropped his fork and leaned against the high-backed chair, folding his arms over his chest. "Why don't you tell me why the hell you don't even remotely resemble that *double bagger* in the photo? Was it all some elaborate joke? Who is that girl?"

Daphne toyed a moment with a slice of bread. "I'm not certain to which photograph you are referring."

"The one of the girl who looks frumpy, dowdy, unappetizing, completely without style, with a face that could sink a thousand ships—"

"Now, I believe *you* can cease with *your* sterling adjectives! Actually, that photo is of Lucilla, taken when she was much younger. Her first husband saw to it that she was done over. I haven't seen her for quite a while, but I've heard that she looks much different now."

"Just why is the photo signed Daphne Asherwood?"

She looked at him with wide, innocent eyes, and stared limpidly into his suspicious, narrowed ones. "Is it? Well, perhaps it was added as a joke, you understand."

"And why are you referred to by everyone as 'poor, sweet, little Daphne'?"

She surprised herself by giving him a saucy grin. "Well, it does appear as if I now am poor. What is it, five hundred pounds?"

"Only if I refuse to marry you!"

"And I'm certainly sweet."

He stared at her breasts. "But not little!"

I will not let him embarrass me! "I'm not all that tall," she said blandly, surprising herself even more.

"Perhaps," he said, with a wolfish gleam in his eyes, "we'll see just how you size up."

"Size up?"

"How you fit against me."

Her eyes widened; she couldn't help it. She felt a flush rising from her neck to her cheeks. "Are all Americans so abominably conceited and rude?"

"Do all English women turn into little red roses when they can't stand the heat?"

"Little red roses! What heat?"

"You're blushing, and you haven't retorted with much aplomb," he said. "Thus, I applied the heat, and you couldn't handle it."

"Have I mentioned how very muscular your chest looks with the shirt buttons straining so...so provocatively?"

He threw back his head and laughed deeply. "Bravo! My little English rose is getting into the swing of things!"

Where is Daphne? she wondered for a brief moment, marveling at herself. She should be under the table by now. "I very much enjoyed watching you thrusting your hands in your jeans pockets.'' She rolled her eyes. ''What a treat!''

''I'm glad you thought so. I think I'd prefer *your* hands thrusting in my pockets, though.''

Her eyes fell from his face as fairly specific images flitted through her mind.

''Gotcha!'' he said. ''Now, if you're through fencing about with me, a poor mortal man, perhaps we can get serious.''

''Serious about what?'' she asked, relieved that he'd changed the subject. But then again, she felt so alive, so sparkling...

''Serious about why my Great Uncle Clarence produced such an outrageous will.''

She set to crumbling her bread into small bits. ''I believe he thought me incapable of doing anything on my own.''

Brant shook his head. ''Was he blind? You're beautiful, you're witty, and I can see you being capable at anything you tried.''

The string of compliments, said quite seriously, stunned her for a moment. Am I really beautiful and witty, she wanted to ask him. ''You don't understand,'' she said, sighing a bit. ''I came to live at Asherwood when I was very young. I grew up here, alone, except for Uncle Clarence and the servants, of course.''

''Surely you went to school.''

She looked stricken for a brief moment, a look not lost on Brant. ''Uncle brought in a tutor, an obnoxious little man who treated me like a half-wit. He left when I turned seventeen. Uncle had other uses for me then.''

''Like what?''

She swallowed and forced her voice to indifferent calm. ''Oh, I sort of ran things here at the Hall. You know, housekeeper, fetcher, bill-payer, gardener, and anything else he wanted of me.''

''General all-purpose slave, in fact.''

''Nothing quite so...degrading. And, of course, he let Aunt Cloe come to see me on occasion. I even went once to Scotland to visit her.''

''You must have died of excitement,'' Brant said. Miserable old codger!

"Aunt Cloe loves me. In fact, she took me to Greece just after the funeral."

"Where is Aunt Cloe?"

"In London, I think. She sent me on ahead. She said something about business with Mr. Hucksley."

"Ah."

"Ah, what?"

He didn't reply for a long moment. Instead he gazed at her, a thoughtful expression on his face. "That is your photo, isn't it?"

"Yes," she said, "it is. I lied about Lucilla; she's been beautiful since she was born. I was the one who needed doing over, and Aunt Cloe saw to it, I guess you'd say."

"She couldn't have achieved this result if all the ingredients hadn't been lurking about, ready to come together."

"My eyes aren't really such a vivid green. They're kind of a washed out hazel. These are colored contacts. Aunt Cloe insisted."

"Confession time? Your lovely hair…is that a wig?"

"No, it's mine. Monsieur Etienne streaked it."

"And your clothes?"

"Aunt Cloe took me to Paris."

"This transformation began just after the funeral?" At her nod, he continued. "Look, Daphne, I'm delighted someone cared enough about you to do something. Obviously, all you needed was a bit of a boost."

"You are kind to say so."

"No, on the contrary, I'm being honest." Suddenly he grinned. "Obviously your Aunt Cloe knew what she was about, as did Reginald Hucksley, I'll bet."

Daphne's eyes drew together. "I don't understand."

"Don't you, yet? I would imagine that she and the Old Man—Hucksley Senior—plotted this together. You see, Aunt Cloe wanted you to have your chance, to present you in all your glorious new plumage to the new Lord Asherwood."

"That's…ridiculous! I don't know you! You're an American!"

"I wondered why Hucksley kept insisting that I remain in England," Brant continued, ignoring her spate of words. "He ran me all over the place, then insisted that I come here, to Asherwood Hall.''

Daphne didn't reply. She was thinking about what he'd said, and she knew he was right. They'd planned to truss her up like a Christmas goose and present her on the new viscount's platter! Her hands flew up to her face, and she pressed her palms against her cheeks.

"This is awful! Why, you don't even like me!''

"I don't?'' he asked blandly.

"No! And I think you're...well, I won't insult you! But what about me and my feelings?''

It was a wail of fury and chagrin.

"Eyuh! You all finished, my lord?''

Brant cast a distracted, impatient eye towards Mrs. Mulroy. "Yes," he said shortly, "we're finished. Coffee in the Golden Salon, if you please.''

Daphne pulled herself together with an effort. "It was quite fine, Mrs. Mulroy. Thank you.''

"Well, little Miss, you didn't eat much," said Mrs. Mulroy, judiciously eyeing Daphne's plate.

"It must be all the...excitement," Brant said. "Will you come along now, Daphne?''

"But I made some singin' hinnies for you, Miss Daphne!''

"Singin' what?'' Brant asked, bending a fascinated eye on the old wood sprite.

Daphne said smoothly, "They're scones. Very fattening, indigestible, and really quite delicious. Just wrap them up, Mrs. Mulroy, and we'll enjoy them tomorrow.''

"Eyuh,'' said Mrs. Mulroy, and left them, shaking her head.

Daphne rose and took Brant's proffered arm. "Perhaps you can tell me what 'eyuh' means,'' Brant said, smiling down at her.

"It's an all-purpose word that can convey anything from dire chagrin to immense joy. I meant to tell you,'' she continued after a brief pause, all too aware of the strength of his arm beneath her hand, "the entranceway looks marvelous.''

"Yes, it does, doesn't it?'' he said smoothly. "Stop a moment, Daphne.''

She did, looking up at him, a question in her eyes.

He drew her toward him, very slowly, very gently. "You aren't too tall, even with your heels on. A nice fit, though, a very nice fit. Probably perfect in your bare feet."

He saw the surprise in her widened eyes, then the uncertainty. "Come along," he said. "Let's continue our discussion over coffee, such as it will be."

Once Brant managed to remove the old wood sprite from the room, he sat back on the sofa and said, "Won't you sit down? You're prowling about like a caged tiger. Tigress, rather. Not that I'm not enjoying the view, of course."

"No, I don't want to sit," she snapped at him. "I'm too mad."

"Oh? You didn't seem at all mad in the entrance hall."

"Stop drawing me! You have realized their…plot! But what about me? Am I supposed to fall into your arms and beg you to marry me? I don't even like you!"

"As I recall," Brant said, eyeing her closely, "I believe you were even referred to as being dreadfully shy. Odd, I haven't noticed any shyness in you at all." *Except when I brought you against me.*

Daphne drew up short, her hands on her hips, her head cocked to one side. "You're right," she said, her voice puzzled. "I am shy, dreadfully so, as you said. At least, I always thought I was. Uncle Clarence always called me his bashful little peahen. I don't understand…"

"I imagine that starting out our relationship as Lucilla the Vamp helped you get over it. And then you were so angry with me, you forgot to act like the old Daphne. Incidentally, Uncle Clarence was a complete and utter idiot and fool."

She frowned and waved a dismissing hand toward him. "But why did he write his will in such a way? I guess he knew you weren't married, but you must have friends, women friends."

"Yes," he said, "I do, but no one terminally serious. Undoubtedly Uncle Clarence did something of a work-up on me. As Harlow told me, he must have believed this the ideal way to have pitter-pattering little British feet running about Asherwood Hall. You, I take it, are all British?''

''Yes,'' she said absently. She flopped down into a chair and crossed her legs. ''What,'' she said, raising her eyes to his face, ''are we going to do?''

I think I should get the hell out of Asherwood Hall and out of England as soon as I can, he thought, pulling his eyes away from those glorious long legs. Instead he said coolly, ''Let's not worry about it now. You've just arrived. Perhaps I can draft you into helping me with the house. There's a great deal to be done.''

''Lucilla's house? Why bother? As soon as she takes ownership she'll turn it over to the National Trust. That or sell it.''

''Perhaps you're right,'' Brant said. ''Still, I don't have to be back in the U.S. for another month. It amuses me to work on the house. Besides, I'll bet you've got some great ideas.''

''Why would you bet that?''

''You love it,'' he said simply. ''It must have made you furious to see it go to rack and ruin.''

''I planted the rose garden in the back. It's not impressive now, but wait until spring.''

''Roots,'' Brant said.

''Yes, of course rose bushes have roots.''

''No,'' he said smiling as he rose, ''I meant roots as in where a person hails from, belongs.''

''You're rooted in the United States, aren't you?''

''I'm not quite certain. Actually, I'm really not certain about a whole bunch of things right now. Are you ready to sack out?''

''Sack what?''

''Go to bed, sleep.''

''Yes,'' she said without guile or wiles, ''I would like to go to bed. It's been a terribly enlightening day, hasn't it?''

''Frighteningly so,'' he agreed. ''Incidentally, do you have any idea where I can find replacement parts for the armor?''

She burst into merry laughter. ''I worried about that for the longest time! I told Uncle Clarence that I wanted to reassemble them, taking parts from one knight to make another one whole." She paused a moment, a sad glint in her eyes. "He didn't let me."

"Screw Uncle Clarence," Brant said.

"As in screwing hamburger?"

"As in damn and blast Uncle Clarence, and let's forget him."

"You Yanks have the oddest way of talking," she said, grinning up at him. "Screwing this and screwing that, all with different meanings! How do you keep it all straight?"

"That particular expression," he said, appearing much struck, "does have many different meanings. There's one special one, though, that tops them all."

"And what is that?"

"Perhaps," he said slowly, "I'll tell you, someday."

CHAPTER SIX

Y ou had the *nerve* to criticize my jeans?"

Daphne skittered to an abrupt halt in the doorway of the Armor Room at the sound of Brant's teasing voice. "Oh dear," she said, feeling suddenly as if she were on display, "I shouldn't have used that as an insult." She wanted to cover herself somehow, but she didn't know where to put her hands.

"No," he agreed, gracefully coming to his feet. "You shouldn't have." His eyes traveled from her bulky cream wool sweater to the very new designer jeans she was wearing. Not wearing, he thought, dazzled by the sight. Poured into was more like it. Endless long legs, lovely shape, no bulges, no... He shook his head and said abruptly, "You ready for some breakfast?"

She nodded, saying impishly, "Maybe Mrs. Mulroy has put out the singin' hinnies!"

"Lord save us!"

She fell into step beside him. "Or maybe some kedgeree, or some bangers, or—"

"How 'bout some plain eggs and bacon?"

"Impossible! Too provincial. I think I'd prefer some angels on horseback."

"You got me on that one," he said, grinning into her twinkling eyes. "All right, what are angels on horseback?"

"Oysters wrapped in bacon. But, if you substitute prunes and chutney for the oysters, you have devils instead of angels."

"How about a combination of the two? Too much of one or the other would be boring."

"I have this odd feeling that you're no longer talking about oysters."

"No, and you're not boring. Not at all."

She gave him a sudden, dazzling smile, revealing small white teeth. "Nor am I shy," she said proudly, and blinked.

He wanted to kiss her, run his hands over her bottom and up under her sweater. He wanted... "Oh no," he said, "more soggy toast."

"Shush," Daphne giggled. "Mrs. Mulroy will hear you. Old Maddy does try, Brant, truly she does."

"The new cook is arriving today, hopefully. Winterspoon agreed to pick her up at the train station. Then we can pig out."

"Pig what?"

"Make gluttons of ourselves, eat until we're stuffed."

"We can't. We wouldn't be able to get into our respective jeans. Aunt Cloe told me I shouldn't do anything but drink tea when I wear these."

I'd just as soon see you out of them anyway. "Good point."

"It's raining," Daphne said, looking toward the fogged up windows.

"We've got plenty to do in the Armor Room. You up for fitting armor puzzles together?"

"I'd adore it." She fell silent, dipping pieces of her toast into a cup of tea, tea laced with milk, for God's sake, he observed, wincing at the sight.

"What's the matter?" he asked after a moment. "Your jeans hugging a bit too close?"

She smiled, but only briefly. "Lucilla. Perhaps we shouldn't be changing things, since Asherwood Hall will be hers."

"There is that," he agreed. "I like your hair," he added abruptly.

She smiled tentatively, as if surprised by the compliment.

"And your scrubbed face."

Her scrubbed face fell. "You mean I look like a prim school-girl."

"No, that isn't at all what I meant. I don't like much makeup on women. And you're lucky. You don't need it."

"I am wearing eyebrow pencil," she said, thrusting up her chin. "My eyebrows are too light without it. Aunt Cloe told me so."

"I'll have to take a closer look to see if I approve."

She remembered in very specific detail how he'd been quite close for those few moments the night before. Her breathing quickened. She said, her voice full of reproach, "You're making sport of me."

"I? Surely not. I'm merely trying to keep your self-confidence up." Just as I'd like to pull your jeans down. How, he wondered silently, surprised at himself, could he be so horny? Daphne—ridiculous name—was lovely, no doubt about it, but take Marcie, for instance. Now, she was beautiful, perfect body...and full of herself.

"Brant, what is football?"

He grinned, waving his fork at her. "Football and baseball are the two most popular American sports. It's similar to rugby, I guess, though I don't know too much about rugby."

"I don't either, so we're even. But what do you do in football?"

"I'm a quarterback," Lord, where to begin? "Tell you what, Daph, I'll call up my mom and have her send over a couple of films of my games. We can rent a projector somewhere around here, can't we?"

"Certainly. You're not in the wilds, Brant. Are you famous? Like a cinema star?"

"I'm not exactly a household word, but I'm fairly good at what I do."

"And you love it."

"Yes, I do. Immensely. But I'm getting old."

"Old! What a silly thing to say. What are you? Thirty?"

"Thirty-one. In football, that's getting up there. It's a very rough contact sport. And every year I get older and my competitors get younger. I've probably got four or five more years, barring any serious injuries."

"Oh no! You get hurt?"

He grinned wryly. "The opposing team loves nothing more than to cream the quarterback. That is," he added, quickly translating, "their objective is keep me from gaining yardage. If they can bury me under a pile, they succeed. Pile of bodies, that is."

"Have you ever been hurt?"

He unconsciously flexed his throwing arm. "On occasion. My teammates are good about protecting me."

"It sounds like the Romans and the Christians."

"It does a bit, doesn't it? In my early professional days I was quarterback for a consistently losing team. I was usually sore all season. No big deal, really," he added, seeing her eyes darken with concern. "I realize it's difficult for you to understand until you see the game. I'll explain everything to you then. Okay?"

She sighed, sitting back in her chair. "While you were playing this game and making money, I was rotting here, wondering what was going to happen to me when Uncle Clarence died."

"And you still wonder?"

"Of course, wouldn't you? Five hundred pounds won't last long, after all. I don't have any skills."

Her voice was matter-of-fact, not an ounce of bitterness or self-pity, which he would have expected. He said lightly, "You'll probably marry a nice young Englishman."

"I'll miss my rose garden," she said, ignoring his words.

"I'd like to see it."

"Not today. I don't have a brolly big enough to keep us from drowning."

"Brolly?"

She looked startled. "You know, Brant, one of those things you raise over your head when it's raining."

"Ah, an umbrella."

"Exactly," she said, giving him an approving look. Like I'm a bright schoolboy, he thought.

"You finished?" he asked, rising. "Ready to attack the knights?"

"Onward!"

They worked throughout the morning, assembling matching arms and legs to form a half-dozen proper suits of armor. Their laughter floated out of the room, reaching Mrs. Mulroy's ears as she dusted in the entrance hall. She smiled benignly.

"Oh, you've a spot of smut on your face." Daphne raised her hand and rubbed his cheek with her fingertips.

Brant felt an alarming jolt of desire at her touch. She was so close he could see her contact lenses. Slowly he raised his own hand and stroked it through her hair. Silky smooth, he thought, and so thick.

Daphne's hand dropped. She looked at him, confusion written all over her face.

"I was just checking to see if you had any spots of smut," he said smoothly, leaning away from her. He had no intention of seducing the castle maiden.

"In my hair?"

"One never knows." He jumped gracefully to his feet and stretched. "I'm ready for some exercise. How 'bout you, Daph?"

"Daph? Is that a common nickname in America?"

Her voice sounded a bit breathless, for she was watching the play of muscles as he stretched his arms over his head.

"No, it's my own. I've never known a woman named Daphne before. It's nearly stopped raining. Why don't you get the um...brolly and let's take a look at your rose garden."

"Righto," she said. "I'll be back in a moment."

He watched her walk gracefully from the room; he couldn't seem to take his eyes off her swaying hips.

Daphne found him a few minutes later in the Golden Salon, standing in front of the fireplace.

"I'm ready," she said.

He turned, and she saw that he was holding the god-awful photo of her in his hand. "I think we can burn this," he said quietly.

"But she still exists, I'm afraid."

"Does she?" He handed Daphne the photo. To his delight, after staring at it for a moment, she giggled. "Goodness," she said, raising eyes brimful of laughter to his face, "what a double bagger!"

They spent the evening seated on a carpet in front of the fireplace. It was cosy, intimate and utterly enjoyable.

"I talked to my mother. She's sending a couple of films express. You want a bit more brandy?"

"I'm already tipsy. I'd better not."

"I like your dress. I know, Aunt Cloe insisted that the English Rose should wear peach silk."

"It is silk, my very first silk anything. And yes, conceited man, she did insist. At the time I thought it a bit..."

"Sexy? Too revealing?"

"I'm not in the habit of exhibiting myself to such an extent," she said tartly. Her hand moved to cover the deep V of the neckline.

"No, don't," he said, and grasped her hand, drawing it down to her lap. "I'm a simple man, and the sight gives me pleasure."

She flushed, embarrassed, pleased and confused by his manner and his words.

As for Brant, he thought, I'm acting like an idiot. I won't seduce her. Nothing could be more stupid than that. She's not the seducible type. She's revoltingly innocent. I'm leaving England shortly. I'll never see her again. Not those beautiful breasts, not those gorgeous legs...

"Do you have any brothers or sisters?" she asked, turning slightly, so her breasts weren't directly in his line of vision.

"One sister," he said easily, leaning back against the chair. "Her name's Lily, and she's a character. I also have two nephews and a niece. They all live in Texas with Lily's new husband. He's an oilman."

"Just like on the telly? Is he another J.R. Ewing?"

"I'd heard *Dallas* was popular over here." At her excited nod, he continued. "I call him Crusty Dusty. I imagine he's ruthless enough if the situation calls for it. But he loves my sister, and that's good enough for me. I told him before they married that Lily needed a keeper more than a husband, and Dusty drawled that as long as she was housebroken, it was fine with him."

"Housebroken? You mean like a burglar?"

Brant groaned. He clasped her hand and drew it to his mouth, kissing it lightly. "No, not like a burglar. Have you ever had a puppy?"

"Yes, when I was a little girl."

"Well, housebroken means that you train the puppy not to relieve himself on the floor or on the carpet or anywhere in the house. Like breaking a horse, I guess. Get him tamed and under control.''

''I'm beginning to get quite fond of American. How long do you think it would take me to speak it fluently?''

''It would all depend on your teacher, I expect.''

''You said that you're going home in a month. Will you play football?''

''No, it's the off-season. Practice starts in the summer. No, when I go back, I'm making a commercial for TV.''

''For the telly! Oh, I am impressed. Whatever will you be selling?''

''I'll be pushing sports equipment.''

Daphne came up on her knees, resting her hands on her thighs. ''Do you want to know a secret, Brant?''

He arched a thick brow at her, forcing himself to keep his eyes on her face.

''It's about my Aunt Cloe. Well, you mustn't tell her I told you, but she adores young men. I remember her nearly choking when she saw a poster of one of your American athletes wearing nothing but sexy undershorts.''

''Ah, and did you nearly choke, Daph?''

''I was too busy watching her reaction. When she noticed that I'd noticed, she hauled me away.'' She grinned at him, shaking her head. ''I can't wait to see what she does when she lays eyes on you!''

''Shall I greet her in my underwear?''

''She'd love it, but perhaps you'd better not.''

Would you love it? ''I can see it now,'' he said lightly. ''English Viscount Arrested for Indecent Exposure. Aunt Cloe in Hospital for Severe Palpitations.''

Daphne was still laughing when she rose to her feet. ''Well, we'll soon know what she thinks about you. She should be coming here soon. Now, my lord, I'm off for bed. My weak head is spinning from that wicked brandy.''

''I'll walk up with you,'' Brant said. He laid his hand lightly on her shoulder when they reached the bedroom. ''Do you ride?''

"Of course. Every Englishwoman who lives in the country rides, I'll have you know."

"Fine. If this blasted rain stops and it's not too cold, shall we go out tomorrow morning?"

"I'd love to. I'll even wear my new riding togs."

"I know, Aunt Cloe insisted."

"No, I did. I can't imagine getting on my mare, Julia, in my new jeans."

"I can," Brant said, patted her on her cheek, and walked down the corridor to his room.

The morning was cold, but not overly so, and the sky was overcast, but there was no rain. Brant's mount, borrowed from a neighbor, was strong and fast, and Daphne, astride her Julia, looked good enough to eat in her tailored tan riding pants and jacket. An Englishwoman to the tips of her riding boots.

They galloped and cantered, and he saw her life through her eyes. A circumspect life, he thought. A limited world. She took him into East Grinstead, and he saw the fondness of the locals for her, and their surprise at her appearance. They dismounted and walked along the River Wey, talking about nothing in particular.

"Daphne," he said abruptly as they readied to return to Asherwood, "have you ever dated?"

"Me?" He saw a fleeting glint of anger in her eyes, but it was so quickly gone that he might have imagined it. And there was light amusement in her voice as she replied, "Well, there was the rector, Mr. Theodore Haverleigh. Uncle Clarence let him into the house a couple of times and allowed him to take me to a church picnic."

"Did you like him?"

"Theo? Goodness no! He had no shoulders and no chin, and he was terribly puffed up with himself. I'm sure at the time he honestly believed he was doing me a favor, and perhaps he was...."

"At the time. Now, he'd probably start slobbering at the sight of you."

She gave him a pert salute. "Very true," she said, and lightly dug her heels into Julia's fat sides.

She felt marvelous. Full of humor, full of life. Until they reined in in front of the Hall.

"Oh dear," Daphne said. "That's Lucilla."

Brant gazed toward the woman standing on the front steps looking toward them. She was tall, with raven-black hair, immense blue eyes, and a figure that would stop a train.

"Indeed," he said. "Shall we take the horses to the stable?"

Daphne nodded numbly. She'd seen the admiration in Brant's eyes. Life as she'd known it for the past two days was over. She wanted to howl her disappointment. Instead, she followed Brant to the stables.

CHAPTER SEVEN

Darling! How good to see you again! My, don't you look the smart bird! Whatever happened?"

Daphne suffered herself to be hugged and pecked on her cheek. "Hello, Lucilla. You're looking well. This is Brant Asher, the new Viscount Asherwood."

She's responding to him just as I would if I only knew how, Daphne thought with a stab of resentment.

Lord he's handsome, Lucilla thought as she calmly shook his hand, but her eyes were wide with admiration as she took in every inch of him. "Welcome, my lord, to England and to Asherwood."

She's already acting like the queen of the castle!

"Thank you, Lucilla. May I call you that?"

"Certainly, Brant. Has our little Daphne been showing you around?"

"We've been out riding, if that's what you mean, Lucilla," Daphne said. *Condescending bitch! Why do I feel as if I've just gained weight in my thighs, got greasy hair, and my contact lenses have turned red?*

"Why yes, dear, that's exactly what I meant. I hope," she continued, her eyes on Brant, "that you don't mind my dropping in unannounced?"

"Since Asherwood Hall will belong to you, Lucilla, how can we mind?"

"Oh yes," Lucilla said slowly. "The will."

"As you say," Brant said. "Shall we go in, ladies?"

It would all be extremely amusing, Brant thought, as the three of them sat over tea in the Golden Salon, if Daphne weren't losing her self-confidence by the second. It wasn't that Lucilla was obviously unkind to her. On the contrary, she was all that was gracious, as if she were addressing a sweet, but simple child.

Lucilla said over her tea cup, "The changes you've made, the improvements, Brant, are remarkable. The old tomb looks marvelous. Daphne, would you please hand me a biscuit? Thank you, dear. The entranceway is so very tip-top sparkling. And what you did to the suits of armor—why I would have tossed the lot out!"

"His lordship is quite creative," Daphne said dryly.

"What a lovely thought," Lucilla said, giving him a long, intimate look.

"I expect you saw Mr. Hucksley in London?" Brant asked.

"Oh yes. It's all too remarkable, isn't it? You mustn't worry, dear," she continued to Daphne, gently patting her hand. "I'll see that things are put right. I thought about it all the way up here. Perhaps a trade school, or a try at interior decorating, now that you've got yourself together. You'd enjoy that, wouldn't you, Daphne? Why, there's even business. You'd make an adorable secretary."

"Actually," Daphne said, getting a firm grip on her insecurities, "I think I might try my hand at modeling."

"Why, my dear girl, what a remarkable idea!"

If she says remarkable one more time, I'll yank off her panty hose and strangle her with them! Instead Daphne said, drawing herself up a bit straighter, "Not so remarkable. I certainly have the figure for it."

"Do you, dear? Well, I suppose I must wait to see you in a dress. Riding clothes are so…minimizing, aren't they?"

"I believe, ladies, that it's time for lunch," Brant said, rising. He looked toward Daphne, but her eyes were on Lucilla, who was gazing raptly at the zipper on his jeans.

At the sight of an unappetizing lunch of slipshod-looking sandwiches and thin potato soup, Brant said, "A new cook is arriving this afternoon."

"It's just as well," Lucilla said gently. "It will help us girls keep our weight down, won't it, dear?"

"Quite," Daphne said.

There were several minutes of blessed silence. Lucilla asked, "How long will you remain in England, Brant?"

"Another month, perhaps less."

"I understand from Mr. Hucksley that you're an athlete?"

"Yes, I play professional football for the New York Astros."

"How remarkable! You've certainly the…build for it. I thought you'd probably look grand in your title."

Daphne choked on her soup.

"I also understand that you've a *chère amie* waiting for you in New York, a lovely, independent career woman?"

Brant started to tell her that he had several gorgeous women waiting for him in New York, but he was aware of Daphne's eyes searching his face. "I'm fortunate to have many friends, both men and women."

"And all American, too. You must find our ways very strange."

"Not at all," Brant said pleasantly. Lord, is she playing both sides of the fence, he thought. "Though I will admit that Daphne is giving me quite an education."

"Daphne?" Lucilla's beautiful arched brows arched a bit more over incredulous light blue eyes.

"Yes," Daphne said, goaded. "I think Brant looks charming in his title too."

Lucilla laughed merrily. "My little peahen—as Uncle Clarence so sweetly called her—is changing before my very eyes! How utterly remarkable. Haven't you done something with your eyes, dear?"

"Yes," Daphne said, "I've finally learned to see with them."

"Well, I'm very proud of you, dear." She turned to Brant. "I talked of Daphne to my husband, you know, and he wanted to meet her, take her in hand and all that."

"You're too late, Lucilla," Daphne said. "Aunt Cloe already did."

"Dear Mrs. Sparks. I imagine that she'll be arriving here soon. To keep an eye on her investment, so to speak?"

Why do I feel like the sacrificial goat? "The more the merrier," said Brant. "Now, if you ladies will excuse me, I want to do some planing on the front doors. They're a bit warped."

Daphne's eyes followed his progress from the room. She stiffened when Lucilla said in a pitying voice, "Such a temptation, Daphne, but surely you have some pride?"

"What do you mean, Lucilla?"

"Surely, dear, you wouldn't consider marrying a man who only wanted you for money and Asherwood Hall? A good deal of money, I might add."

"Why not?" Daphne said, angry color staining her cheeks. "After all, it's either that or…trade school! I'll call Mrs. Mulroy to show you to your room, Lucilla."

"A marriage of convenience, dear. Really, what an appalling thought."

"Haven't you done it three times?"

"Why no, dear, not entirely. All three husbands were remarkably virile, you know. Just like Brant. I imagine that he knows every trick to make a woman swoon for him. Don't you agree?"

"Excuse me, Lucilla."

"Remember, Daphne," Lucilla called after her, "Brant is quite experienced with women. I do hope you won't make a fool of yourself over him. Seriously, dear, have a care. Hasn't he already turned your little head, just a bit?"

No, he's just made me feel very good about myself.

Daphne left the breakfast room and went immediately upstairs to change into her jeans and a sweater. Afterward she found Brant working on the front doors.

"Hi," he said, glancing up at her briefly. "Did you survive the first salvo?"

"What's a salvo?"

"A burst of rapidly firing artillery."

Daphne worried her lower lip for a moment, then burst out, "Do you need money, Brant?"

"Ah, that's very stiff cannon fire. No, as a matter of fact, I've got quite enough money."

"But I've heard that Americans view money as a sort of god, that they can never get enough of it."

"I wasn't aware that view was confined to the United States," he said. "As you well know, Daph, this estate runs about four hundred thousand pounds. Nearly a half million dollars. That's not chicken feed. Hand me that piece of sandpaper, will you?"

"This thing? Lucilla's so beautiful."

"Yes, she is. How old is she, anyway?"

"About thirty, I'd say."

"Listen to me, Daph. She's got a tremendous potential investment, all of it riding on what you and I decide to do. Don't let her rile you. If you were in her shoes, you'd likely do the same thing." He grinned at her. "Only not as well."

Daphne sighed. "Why do I feel as if I'm thirteen again, and fat and plain and dowdy?"

"She's quite good. Why don't you just sit back and enjoy her machinations? You might learn something useful."

"You're cynical, aren't you?"

"A bit, I guess. I just want you to use your wits and not get all sullen and defensive. You have got wits, you know, plenty of them."

"So, in other words," Daphne said slowly, "you want to keep her in...suspense?"

"I hadn't thought of that in particular. But it just might be fun. And, Daph, don't worry about your future. I won't let you starve. I'll see that you're set up in whatever you want to do."

"Marvelous," she muttered under her breath. "No, thank you, Brant. It's time, I think, that I looked after myself."

She walked away. She heard the grating sound of the sandpaper against wood cease, and knew he was looking after her.

If Brant felt like the main meal with Lucilla, he definitely felt like a very fattening dessert with Aunt Cloe. She'd examined every inch of him in great, interested detail, a dreamy look in her eyes. He noticed, gazing at her across the dining table over a delicious meal prepared by Mrs. Woolsey, that she was a tall, big-boned woman, with a strong nose and chin, and penetrating light blue eyes. When they looked at him, they both sparkled and looked speculating. She wore her thick salt-and-pepper hair the way his mother did, in a classic chignon. Her humor was dry, her smile charming. She has a lovely voice, he thought, listening to her speak of her trip.

"Ah, what a delight Paris was. All that gray sky and muzzling rain, but no matter. Such a relief to be home again. In the bosom of my family so to speak. I must say, Brant, you're everything I expected."

"I hope your expectations weren't set too high, Aunt Cloe," he said dryly, grinning at her. She'd arrived but three hours after Lucilla. He wondered if she'd hotfooted it here, knowing that Lucilla would be doing her best to making things unpleasant for her little chick, Daphne.

"Dear boy," Cloe said, wishing she were thirty years younger, "when you've lived as long as I have, you learn to be wary in what you expect. Photos help, of course. I must say, I like to see a man togged up for dinner. Very elegant."

"How long will you be staying, Aunt Cloe?" Lucilla asked, her voice as flat as her enthusiasm. "You must have so much waiting for your attention in Glasgow."

"What an excellent gunner you would have been in the war, Lucilla. Such marksmanship, such precise…yes, well, you know, I've been thinking that I will visit America. I will wait, of course, until Daphne gets settled in."

Brant blinked at her double-edged words. Lucilla gritted her teeth.

Daphne said, "That shouldn't take long, Auntie."

"Yes," Lucilla said. "We will all move her into a nice flat in London. Not long at all."

"Perhaps I'll study to be a carpenter," Daphne said. "I learned today how to plane a door."

"Or," Brant added, "you could work for the British Museum, keeping their armor exhibit in good shape."

"I thought that was probably your idea, Daphne," Lucilla said. "As I said, I should have tossed the lot."

"Oh, I don't know," Brant said. "I suspect the new owner of Asherwood might be delighted at such antiquity."

Cloe gave him a bland smile. "Indeed, my dear boy."

"But then again," he added, shooting her down, "one never knows, does one?"

He wished he'd kept his mouth shut, for Lucilla gave him another one of her patented intimate smiles. He wondered if he should lock his bedroom door tonight. He forked down another bite of the delicious Yorkshire pudding, listening to the well-bred backbiting going on between Aunt Cloe and Lucilla.

"How did you leave your dear third husband, Lucilla?"

"I left him, period, Aunt Cloe. I would have sworn you knew that."

"German men are so fierce and dominating, don't you agree?"

"Basically, Carl was a dear. But," Lucilla added, shooting Brant a honey-coated smile, "he was too old for me. Why, his daughter was Daphne's age, and his son, Dieter, well, such a possessive young man." She gave a little shudder.

"And Brant's age?"

"A bit older, actually. I just hope he doesn't follow me here."

Brant studied Daphne from beneath half-closed lids. She was toying with the fresh peas on her plate, eating little, saying even less. She'd reverted to the old Daphne, he suspected. Withdrawn, shy, all self-confidence obliterated. He wanted to shake her, to draw her into his arms and comfort her. No! If he had half a brain, he knew he'd leave in the morning, early.

"I say, a jolly good dinner," Aunt Cloe said. "Shall we have coffee in the sitting room?"

I've got to get Daphne alone, Cloe thought, as she watched her rise from her chair and walk from the dining room, like a prisoner going to the gallows. I've got to knock some sense into the girl!

To her utter delight Brant said, "Unfortunately, Daphne and I haven't time for coffee. We're going into the village to see a movie. Are you ready, Daphne?"

Daphne stopped dead in her tracks, wondering if she'd heard right. He was rescuing her! She turned and gave him a dazzling smile. "I just have to get my coat." She was off like a shot, nearly running up the stairs.

"I hope you'll forgive us, ladies, for leaving you on your first night here."

"Not at all," Cloe said. "Not at all."

Lucilla was frowning, but just for a moment. She said with just an exquisite touch of wistful disappointment, "I suppose one must keep one's promises. It's very nice of you, Brant, to see to Daphne."

Daphne was looking at herself in the mirror. I don't look like a frump, she said under her breath. I won't let Lucilla make me feel like a refugee from a turnip patch. I won't! However, when she returned to the entrance hall, there was Lucilla, her hand on Brant's arm, laughing up at him. And he, damn him, was smiling down at her.

"Ah, here you are, dear," Lucilla said, turning to give her an approving look. "How lovely your coat is. I've always thought brown such an enduring color, and wool so very wearing. Now, Brant, don't keep her out too late, will you?"

As if I'm some sort of backward adolescent!

Aunt Cloe gave her a quick hug, whispering in her ear, "Don't you dare regard anything she says, love! You look charming, make no mistake about it."

"You ready, Daph?"

"Yes. Good night, Lucilla, Auntie."

The evening was clear and cold, a quarter moon lighting the drive. "I've always liked enduring things," Brant said, grinning down at her. "Would you drive, Daphne? I still don't trust myself on the wrong side of the road."

She nodded and slipped behind the wheel. "It's a lovely evening," she said inanely.

In response Brant sighed deeply and leaned his head back against the leather seat.

"What's the matter, Brant? Too many salvos?"

"For sure," he said, his eyes closed. "I've never before felt like a duck in hunting season."

And I'm one of the hunters, she thought, suddenly depressed. He must despise the lot of us. "What movie do you want to see?" she asked, forgetting there was just one cinema house.

"Turn on the heater and let's go parking."

"Parking? You mean, stop the car?"

He gave her a long, lazy look. "Yes, find a nice spot with something of a view to liven things up and pull over."

She drove on in silence.

"I told you that you shouldn't let Lucilla get to you."

Her hands gripped the steering wheel. "You invited me out because you didn't want me to continue making a fool of myself. You were feeling sorry for me," she said flatly.

"No, I was feeling sorry for myself. And you're a cute fool."

"Ha! I thought men just loved so much female attention!"

"At least you've got your sharp tongue back."

She shot him a look of pure dislike.

"Also, I invited you out because I'd like to beat some sense into you. Good, I've got your attention. Watch out for that ditch! This looks like a good spot. Pull over here."

She obeyed him and turned off the engine. Daphne had stopped on a slight rise overlooking the Wey. Naked-branched beech trees surrounded them.

"Now, turn around and look at me. I've got lots of things to say to you."

"You sound just like Uncle Clarence," she said, her voice as nasty as she could manage it.

"Do I? Unlike Uncle Clarence, I won't ask you to do anything you don't want to do. Well, maybe that's not totally the case. Why the hell did you regress again? I thought we'd straightened all that out after our memorable lunch."

She stared at him, unable to find the words to explain her feelings.

"How do you expect to get along if you can't handle all different kinds of people, and that includes women who patronize you?"

"I'll get along," she said. "Why do you care, anyway?"

"Sometimes I think you need a keeper."

He sounded mildly angry, and that surprised her. "Things are different with Lucilla here," she said slowly, trying to explain it both to him and to herself. "Before, with just the two of us—"

"Daphne," he interrupted, his voice impatient, "Lucilla's really a great deal of fun if you'd just forget all your old stored up envy of her. There's a whole world of people out there that you have to deal with."

"Just stop it!" she hissed at him. "Just leave me alone, okay? I don't need you to tell me what's wrong with me. And I'm not envious of Lucilla!"

She twisted the ignition key, and the engine turned over. Suddenly his hand was over hers, and the engine died. "Damn you," he said, and pulled her into his arms.

Daphne was too surprised to resist. She opened her mouth to say something—what, she didn't know—and felt his lips cover hers. She stiffened at the attack, and immediately he gentled the pressure. His tongue glided lightly over her lips; his hands stroked up and down her back.

"You taste like Yorkshire pudding," he said against her cheek. He returned to her mouth, gently nibbling, tasting, and slowly she began to relax, and respond.

"That's it," he said softly. "You're a beautiful, intelligent woman, Daphne, and I don't want you to forget it again." *And you're such an innocent I feel like I'm being unfair even kissing you.*

He released her and smiled at the dazed, uncertain look in her eyes. He gently rubbed his thumb over her jaw. "This," he said, "is what we Americans call parking."

"It's...different."

"You sound a little out of breath. Let's try again. Trust me and relax."

She did, without a second thought. He was careful, very careful, well knowing she didn't have a bit of experience. He didn't want to frighten her or put her off. He kept his hands on her back and his kisses light, undemanding. He broke off and gently pressed her face against his shoulder. He thought her breathing was a bit faster.

He stroked his fingers through her soft hair. I've wanted to do that since I've met her, he thought. He leaned his cheek against her temple and breathed in her sweet womanly scent. He heard himself say, "I want to make love to you, Daphne."

She raised her face and gave him a puzzled but glowing look. "You mean, you want to go to bed with me...and..."

He grasped her upper arms, cursing himself silently. "No, that isn't what I meant to say." He dashed his fingers through his hair. "I want you to realize that you're a marvelous person who can do anything she wants."

"Then why did you kiss me?"

Because I'm horny and any port in a storm!

But that wasn't true. He wanted her, only her. He had no idea why. His idea of a good time had never been the company of a repressed female with the experience of a Victorian maiden.

"Did you kiss me because you thought that would give me self-confidence?"

"Yes," he said without thinking.

Slowly she pulled away from him. "Lucilla's right," she said. "And I'm a fool."

"We're both fools," he said in a distracted attempt at humor. "And Lucilla's been right about only one thing I can think of."

"What is that?"

"She's afraid of you," he said slowly, studying her face in the dim shadows. "And she has a right to be."

Daphne shook her head, an abrupt, angry movement. "I just don't believe this. Everything revolves around you; at least, that's the way you see it. All of us are like hens bowing and scraping in front of the cock! Well, I don't care! I intend to see to myself, do you hear? I don't want your help, or Lucilla's help, or Aunt Cloe's! What I would like from you, my lord, is your refusal to marry me. That way I'll get five hundred pounds rather than just one hundred dred."

Brant clenched his jaws together. How dare she fly off the handle at him like that! Damn her! Accusing him of being some kind of a conceited sheik with a harem! He wanted to help her; he wanted to make her realize how much she had to offer, to... He said quietly, very quietly, "I doubt you'd even know what to do with fifty pounds. I doubt you would even know a checkbook if it bit you. You'd probably last no longer than one week on your own. You want five hundred pounds, lady? Fine, you've got it!"

CHAPTER EIGHT

Brant opened his bedroom door quietly, not bothering to turn on the ancient overhead light. He was still angry with Daphne—ridiculous Victorian name—and her dumb accusations. Why should he care, anyway? What she did with her life had nothing whatsoever to do with him. Hell, he'd be home soon, and good riddance to all of them!

Cock, indeed!

He turned on a Victorian lamp with a red velvet shade that sported thick red fringe, and methodically began to strip off his clothes. At least Winterspoon wasn't waiting for him. The thought of his valet helping him out of his pants was unnerving.

"I knew you'd look marvelous in your title."

His fingers stilled over the zipper. He turned slowly to see Lucilla wearing a tight silky thing, lounging pajamas, he supposed, a saucy smile on her lips.

"How 'bout title and trousers?"

"Sounds like the name of a painting," she said. "Perhaps we could frame you and put you up for the Royal Academy."

He grinned at her. "What are you doing in here, Lucilla?"

She shrugged, and one of the straps slipped off her lovely shoulder. He suddenly had the image of Marcie in his mind, standing in his bathroom doorway, wearing finally, after both straps had fallen, nothing but her enticing smile.

"It occurred to me, after seeing you in person, of course, that there were more options, shall we say, than the simple ones presented."

"I think," he said, "that you'd better explain that."

She shrugged again, but fortunately for his peace of mind and body, the other strap stayed put.

"You love this house," she said simply.

"Yes," he agreed, "I do. I'm not certain why, but I do. It's as if," he continued thoughtfully, trying yet again to put his feelings into words, "the house has been waiting for me, as if the house needs me, just as I need it." Roots, his mother would have said.

"The house also needs quite a bit of money to reinstate it to whatever its former glory was," she said dryly, giving him an odd look, one he was certain he deserved. It did, he admitted to himself, sound a bit crazy that he'd feel so strongly about what, after all, was only a pile of brick, windows and stone. He mustn't forget the chimney pots that were in dire need of scrubbing down.

"That's true, too."

"I will inherit the house and more than enough money."

Only if I don't marry Daphne.

"I see," he said only.

She chewed on her lower lip a moment, as if uncertain how to proceed. "I think perhaps," she said finally, "that you and I could join forces."

"In what way, Lucilla?"

"I think a nice start might be a vacation to, say, the South of France. St. Tropez, perhaps, or Nice."

"To get to know each other better?"

"Much better. We might just discover that we could do quite well together, Brant. Yes, quite well indeed. You are, I think, a man who appreciates a woman who knows her way about, a woman who would please you and appreciate you also. You are a very nice-looking man, Brant."

And I'd look just dandy on your arm, huh?

"Thank you," he said aloud.

Lucilla walked nearer—glided was more like it, he thought, watching her warily as she came to a halt a half inch from him. She placed her hands on his bare chest. "Very nice," she murmured, stroking him lightly. One hand dipped down, her fingers slipping beneath his shorts.

"Lucilla," he said, grabbing her hand and pulling it away, "I don't think this would be such a good idea."

"Why not?"

He watched her tongue glide over her lower lip. *Because Daphne's in the house and she would find out and she would be hurt.*

"I have a headache," he said.

She burst into merry laughter, but didn't move away from him. "Well, why don't you think about it, Brant? We could, I think, make very nice music together."

He said nothing, and her forehead furrowed into a slight frown. "Daphne, you know," she continued in a sincere voice, "is a very English sort of girl. I do think it a pity that Uncle Clarence kept her so tied up, but what can one do? In fact, I can't imagine taking Daphne to the South of France. And in America she would be lost as a lamb, and desperately unhappy. You know how shy she is."

"Daphne seemed to do okay in Greece," he said in a neutral tone.

"With Aunt Cloe telling her what to do and when and how to do it, she should have done all right. But in your society, Brant? In your particular group of friends? No, it wouldn't do at all, you know. Not at all."

But Daphne wasn't at all shy, he thought, not until you came. He wanted to tell her that Daphne wasn't retarded but she was sliding her hands up his arms to lightly clasp his shoulders. "I fully intend to take care of little Daphne. You mustn't feel guilty about it."

She stood on her tiptoes and kissed him. He felt her darting tongue probe at his closed lips, felt the length of her pressed against his body, and he responded. But just for a moment. His breathing was a bit heavy when he grasped her arms and set her away from him.

"I don't have to leave you tonight, Brant," she said softly, her eyes luminous in the dim light.

He got a hold on himself. This was ridiculous, damn it! He didn't want to make love to Lucilla; he wanted to make love to… Oh no, you don't, he nearly shouted at himself. Oh no.

"I don't think so," he said finally. "I think you should leave now, Lucilla."

"Ah, I was forgetting about your headache. Will you think about things, Brant?"

"You can be certain of it," he said. He didn't move until she had quietly closed the bedroom door behind her.

"Here is your coffee, my lord."

Brant cocked open an eye to see Winterspoon standing patiently by his bed, a tray on his outstretched arms.

"You don't sound too approving," he said, yawning mightily.

"You are an American, my lord."

"I agree. In that case, it should be black and thick and grow hair on my chest."

"The hair is there, my lord—on your chest, that is—so I assume it is all of those things."

"You don't have to wait on me, Winterspoon," Brant said as he sat up and leaned against the thick pillows. "I could have gone down to the breakfast room."

"I don't think that would be such a good idea, my lord."

"Do you know something I don't?"

"Doubtless there are many things, my lord, but it is my job to...protect you from unpleasantness."

"Unpleasantness, huh? Is there a cat fight going on over the scrambled eggs? Delicious coffee. I needed it."

"Cat fight?" Winterspoon shuddered delicately. He looks just like Jeeves must have looked, Brant thought, when Bertie said something gross. But so tolerant.

"I shouldn't have phrased it exactly like that, my lord. But if you're referring to the ladies, I suggest you keep to your room for a bit longer."

"That bad? Well, what can they be doing?"

"I believe, my lord," Winterspoon said very carefully, his eyes trained on the spot above Brant's left shoulder, "that Mrs. Sparks was accusing Mrs. Meitter of trying to—" He cleared his throat and looked heavenward.

"Trying to what, Winterspoon?"

The amusement in his voice earned him a reproachful look. "Mrs. Sparks saw Mrs. Meitter go into your room last night, my lord."

"Ah." His amusement suddenly died, and he stiffened. "Was Miss Daphne there?"

"Yes, my lord."

"Oh no. Damn it!" He pulled back the covers, spilling the remains of his coffee. Winterspoon quickly handed him a robe, his eyes on Brant's adam's apple. "I set out pajamas for you, my lord," he said.

"I can't stand them," Brant said shortly, shrugging into the robe and belting it.

"I noticed, my lord. His old lordship was very fond of that pair. He never wore them, in fact. Saving them for a special occasion, I suppose. I've drawn your bath, my lord."

"I'd give a bundle for a shower," Brant grumbled. "Who wants to sit in their own dirt?"

"I couldn't say, my lord. What will you be requiring by way of dress?"

"Just jeans, shirt and my sneakers. I've got a lot of work to do, and I don't need to wear a tux."

"Very good, my lord."

Thirty minutes later Brant walked with a rather lagging step into the breakfast room. Only Aunt Cloe was there, waiting for him, he quickly realized.

"Good morning," he said.

She gave him a long look. "Handsome is as handsome does," she said.

"I didn't sleep with Lucilla."

"Didn't you? Lucilla didn't give that impression."

"I told her I had a headache."

Cloe wanted to be furious with him, but that calm, rueful string of bluntness made her break out in laughter. "You didn't!" she gasped. "How marvelous! That's called turning the tables, I'd say!"

"Am I forgiven?"

Cloe was shaking her head. "If only Mr. Sparks—my late husband, you know—if only he'd had your sense of humor! When he didn't want to make...well, that is...Yes, my boy, you're quite forgiven. Sit down. Mrs. Mulroy left your breakfast on the sideboard. I," she added handsomely, "will be delighted to serve you."

She was still chuckling when she handed him a plate loaded with scrambled eggs, several strips of crispy bacon and something else he couldn't identify. "What is this?"

"Oh, those are bloaters. Smoked herring, you know."

Brant gingerly tried one and nodded in approval. "Tell me about Mr. Sparks," he said, giving Cloe a boyish, teasing grin.

"Don't be impertinent, laddie. Now, tell me, Brant, what are you going to do?"

"I'm going to hang new wallpaper in this room today. I selected it myself."

"That," she said, frowning, "isn't what I meant! What color wallpaper? Something light, I hope. I always hated this grimy stuff. So depressing, but father wouldn't ever listen to me. Wouldn't listen to Daphne, either."

"It's light yellow, with white and pale blues in it. I hope it will make the room look nice and airy, a perfect setting for bloaters. Where's Daphne?"

Cloe didn't miss a beat. "Out riding. And it should make the room look very livable."

"She couldn't stand the heat, huh?"

"If you mean by that nonsensical American slang, was she upset, yes, she was. She's used to going off by herself when she's upset. She must be broken of that habit."

"And, of course," Brant said blandly, crunching down on a bite of bacon, "you want me to do the breaking."

"Certainly, my boy. You aren't stupid; at least, you don't give me the impression of stupidity. Of course, I could be wrong, I suppose. I remember what I thought of Mr. Sparks when he was courting me. Well, I changed my mind on our wedding night. Do you know what he did...? No, you aren't stupid. I want you to marry her. She'll make you a grand wife. And she loves this house.

It was only her Uncle Clarence she detested, and with excellent reason.''

Brant said very slowly and calmly, "Cloe, I don't even know Daphne, nor she me. What's more, she's very English and I'm very American. She's also—''

"Opposites attract, I always say," Cloe interrupted serenely. "You'd be good for each other. You would help her grow, and she would do you proud. She's quite the lady, gentle, kind, and she does have a sense of fun. Most pronounced, really, when she's not…what do you Yanks say? Oh yes, not…in heat."

Brant choked on his eggs and quickly downed half a glass of orange juice. "No, not quite that, Cloe. It's called can't stand the heat. Incidentally, Daphne informed me quite plainly last night that she thought I was a conceited jerk and she wanted nothing to do with me. I think if she could, she would have punched me out. She wants me to refuse to marry her so she can get five hundred pounds rather than just one hundred."

"Such passion from my little egg. I'm very pleased."

Brant could only stare at her. "Where," he asked, "is that place you Britishers call Bedlam?"

The wallpaper was hung and the breakfast room looked fantastic, at least it did in Brant's modest opinion. He'd been left alone all morning to do the job, and he supposed he'd been pleased about it. Where was Daphne? he wondered for the dozenth time.

She wasn't present at lunch. Lucilla and Cloe complimented him at least as many times as he wondered where Daphne was. He finally made his escape and went to the stables. Her horse was back in its stall.

There was a chill wind, and he zipped his sheepskin jacket all the way up. He called her name. She wasn't in or around the stables.

He wandered to the back of the Hall to her garden. She was there, on her hands and knees, digging furiously in the hard ground. She was wearing a brown knit stocking cap pulled down nearly to her eyebrows, an old pair of slacks and a thick short coat.

"Coward," he said, standing over her, his legs spread.

She spun about and tumbled back on her bottom. Brant dropped to his haunches in front of her. "Coward," he repeated.

"Go to hell," Daphne said.

"Good grief!" He slapped his hand over his head. "The Victorian maiden has uttered a profanity. What is the world coming to?"

"Go to hell in a handbasket."

"I didn't know you Britishers had that phrase."

"We don't. I heard it in an American movie."

"Really? Which one?"

"I don't remember. Would you please leave?"

"No. And you are a coward."

"I had no intention of watching you and Lucilla making obscene faces at each other!"

"Obscene? Goodness, I've never tried that."

"It isn't funny! I had it up to here—" She poked at her eyebrows and dislodged her knit cap. "Well, anyway, you can do just as you please. I don't care."

"Thank you for your permission. It means everything to me. And I didn't sleep with Lucilla." At her incredulous look, he continued blandly, "Cloe believed me. Isn't your bottom wet from the cold?" He rose and stretched out his hand to her.

She took it, and he pulled her to her feet. "If Cloe believed you, it's because she likes men, young men. She'll believe anything they say, if they're slick enough."

"I guess I was slick enough, then." He studied her closely for several silent moments. "How bad are your eyes without your contacts?" he asked finally.

"Without them you'd be a pleasant blur, which, I might add, wouldn't be at all a bad thing!"

"Can you sleep in them?"

"Yes. I can wear them an entire week. Why?"

Because when I make love to you I want you to see my face very clearly.

"Just wondered, that's all. Would you help me sand down some of the molding in the library?"

"Why not?" She sighed, swiped off her bottom and fell easily into step beside him.

"I promise you a reward for your help."

"What kind of a reward?"

He grinned at her suspicious tone. "Here's a down payment." He leaned down and quickly kissed her. He gave her no time to react, merely began walking again. "First we need to drive into the village. I need a special fine sort of sandpaper."

CHAPTER NINE

Brant and Daphne worked in companionable harmony for several hours in the library.

"You're quite good at this," he said. "Just be careful that you don't scratch up your hands."

"Aunt Cloe isn't going to be pleased about my fingernails," Daphne said. "I can't seem to keep them as long as she would like. Maybe it's a lack of calcium or something."

"Let me see," Brant said, sitting on the floor and holding out his hand.

She shot him another one of her patented suspicious looks and tentatively placed her hand in his.

"No ridges on the nails. They look good to me." He gave her a wicked grin. "Personally, I prefer short nails on a woman; it's safer."

"It's true," she said on a sigh. "I'm always scratching myself."

"My point exactly."

"It probably isn't, but I dread to know just what your point is."

"Perhaps you'll find out. Oh, the film of one of my better football games came this morning. You wanna watch it with me?"

Her eyes sparkled. "Oh yes, that would be great sport."

"Let's do it now. We'll finish up in here tomorrow."

The rented projector and screen were in Brant's bedroom. "Safe from interruption, I hope," he said when she gave him another suspicious look. He got the film threaded and turned up the volume. Soon the big screen was filled with his teammates.

"My God! They're so big! Is that you, Brant? You look so different!"

"Yes, now pay attention. You see me calling the toss? I won and chose to receive the football. That means that we're on the offense. You can only score when you have the ball."

"Like ping pong," Daphne said.

"Exactly, but not really."

To Brant's surprise and delight, Daphne's eyes were glued to the set. Suddenly she jumped and clapped her hands. "That was great! So graceful. How can you throw the ball so far?"

"That's not so far," he said modestly. "Only about thirty yards. My prime receiver—a player whose main job is to run down the field to receive or catch a pass—is Lloyd Nolan. You'd like him, I think."

There was a touchdown pass a few plays later, and Daphne clapped her hands, as excited as any Astro fan. "Marvelous! Such precision. I never imagined—wait a second, Brant. They knocked you down. Are you all right?"

"Sure. I didn't get creamed too many times in this game. The Patriots' defense couldn't get to me. Just once or twice. Now you see the score is 6-0. Watch Guy Richardson kick the extra point. It's good. That is, it goes between the goalposts. That gives us another point. We're winning now, 7 to 0."

They got through nearly to halftime.

"Well, hello. What is this?"

Daphne's hands curled into fists. She was shocked at the degree of disappointment and downright jealousy she felt.

"It's a film, Lucilla, of one of Brant's football games."

"How delightful! Do you mind if I join you?"

She did, but Lucilla stayed anyway, and the third quarter passed in stiff discomfort. Brant's explanations grew shorter and shorter, and Daphne's questions fewer and fewer.

"Goodness," Lucilla said, "it's time for tea. Can we watch the rest of the game some other time, Brant?"

"Daph?" Brant asked.

"Sure. I'll join you downstairs soon. I have to wash off my dirt."

"Yes, please do, dear."

Daphne left them to go to her room. "How is your headache, Brant?" Lucilla inquired, shooting him a smile.

"It's under control. How do you like the new wallpaper in the breakfast room?"

"It's lovely." She slanted him a questioning look. "But didn't I tell you I like it? Well, never mind. I was thinking, how would you like to drive down to London? We could take in a play and have a superb dinner. We could even stay the night, if it got too late."

Brant's first thought was why not? It just might make Daphne jealous. He drew up short, appalled at his devious reasoning.

"I don't think it would be a good idea, Lucilla," he said.

"Why not?" she asked, taking the bull by the horns.

"Lucilla," he said, drawing her to a halt beside him on the stairs, "how well off are you financially?"

"Very well," she said; then, realizing the import of her words, she quickly added, "That is, I doubt I'll starve. But taxes in England, you know. They're dreadful. I try very hard to live off my limited income, of course, but—"

"But you were offering to bankroll Daphne."

"Bankroll? Oh, you mean loan her money?"

"No, give her money."

"I could afford it, of course, and I will when I receive my inheritance."

"I see," he said. "Ah, Cloe. Have you been in the library?"

"Yes, Brant. A marvelous job you and Daphne are doing. Where is she?"

"Washing off her dirt," Lucilla said, in such a tone as to imply that Daphne was covered with muck.

"Well, she'll be here in just a moment, then. Cook has made some marvelous scones. They're biscuits, Brant, flaky and not too sweet. You spread them with butter and jam."

He knew well enough what scones were, but he said nothing. Thank God for Cloe, he was thinking, and her timely appearance. Of course, he realized, she had probably been on the lookout for him and Lucilla.

After an appallingly stiff tea time, with honeyed salvos flying back and forth between Lucilla and Cloe, Brant set down his tea cup and rose. "Daphne and I are going for a ride. Come along."

She hesitated, and he added, "I need to discuss our plan of action for the library tomorrow."

"All right," she said, the first two words she'd uttered since tea had begun.

Lucilla looked as if she'd object, but Cloe said quickly, placing a hand on Lucilla's arm, "Did I ever tell you about the lovely Greek hairdresser I met in Crete? Let me tell you, Lucilla, he was utterly magnificent! And those dark, snapping eyes!"

Brant escaped. "Where are you going?" he barked when Daphne turned to go up the stairs.

"To rub on some dirt."

He grinned. "Why is it you only find your acid tongue for me?"

She smiled back, unable to help herself. "You," she said, suppressing a giggle, "are a wretched man!"

"And you," he said softly, the words coming out before his mind approved, "are an adorable woman."

"But my fingernails are too long."

"I'll make sure they're trimmed when the time comes."

"And I'm stupid."

"Only around Lucilla."

"Aunt Cloe calls me her little egg."

He considered that for a moment, stroking his fingertips over his jaw. "I'll have to ask her what she means by that. I don't think she can mean you're hard boiled. Now, come along."

It was very cold, and the wind was blowing strong from the east. There wasn't an ounce of sun to provide any warmth.

Brant knew it was too cold, but he didn't want to return to the house. Their jackets were no match for the wind. He remembered an abandoned, tiny house toward the back of the property, and smiled to himself.

Daphne said nothing as he guided his horse directly toward the house. When it was in sight, he said, shivering dramatically, "Lord, it's cold. I think I'm coming down with pneumonia. Hey,

Daph, see that house over there? Do you think the people would mind if we came in for a moment and warmed up?"

"No one lives there. We could stop there, I suppose, and warm up."

Ah, he thought, such innocence.

They tethered their horses outside, and Brant pushed open the wobbling front door. There were only two rooms, a small kitchen of ancient vintage, and a living/sleeping room. "How long has the place been abandoned?" he asked.

"For as long as I can remember," Daphne said, moving to the center of the living room. "I guess we could light a fire if you're really cold."

"Let's."

Daphne proved more adept then he, and soon there was a blaze in the fireplace, and a goodly amount of smoke puffing out into the room.

"You know, we could have gone back to the Hall. It was just as close as this place."

"I didn't want to see you turn into a defensive madonna again," Brant said smoothly. "Come on, let's sit down."

They sat cross-legged on the floor in front of the fire.

"Are you still angry at me for last night?" he asked after a few moments.

"No, not really," she said, keeping her profile toward him.

"I didn't mean to sound like a conceited jerk."

"Probably not. It just comes naturally?"

He grinned. "Maybe. Would you have been upset if I'd slept with Lucilla?"

She slewed her head around and blinked at him. "No! It has nothing to do with me!"

"Not even a little bit upset?"

"Well, maybe a little bit."

"But not more than just a tad?"

"If a tad is an American thimble, then you've got it about right! Oh damn. Lucilla's so lovely, I don't know how you could resist, particularly when she turns on that sexy look of hers."

"You ain't so bad yourself, lady. And I was noble as hell."

"And profane as well."

"Lord, are your ears going to turn red when you meet all the jocks on my team. It isn't really cursing, you know. It's just part of the general idiom."

She gave him a long, thoughtful stare, then said very quietly, "I don't know how I'd ever meet your jock teammates, Brant."

Brant jumped to his feet, thrust his hands into his jacket pockets, scowled at her and said, "Oh, hell, Daph, let's get married."

He took a step back, but his eyes remained on her face. She'd flushed a deep red.

"I don't appreciate your notion of a joke, Brant," she said in a voice so cold it could have rivaled the outdoors.

"It isn't a joke, damn it! How can you think that? You're blushing."

Daphne pressed her palms to her cheeks. "Why?" she asked in a bewildered tone.

"Why not?" he snapped.

"But I can't *do* anything!"

"You can be my wife." He removed his hands from his pockets, his body as well as his mind beginning to warm to the idea. Why not indeed? he thought. She was beautiful, witty, not at all shy with him, and he wanted to take her to bed. "I think you could do that quite well."

"Do you really think so? Despite everything?"

He dropped to his knees in front of her and cupped her face between his hands. "Yes," he said, smiling into her eyes. "Despite everything. I think it would benefit both of us equally."

"A marriage of convenience," she said slowly, pursing her lips, and he swooped down and kissed her.

He pulled her up to her knees and enfolded her in his arms. "Part your lips," he said, and she did.

Brant felt her arms tentatively clutch at his shoulders. He deepened his kiss, but kept a firm control on himself. She tasted so sweet; and so surprised. He raised his head and smiled gently down at her. "You've got to breathe through your nose. Then you can kiss until the cows come home."

"Show me," she said.

He did.

"Are the cows here yet?" Her voice was shaky, her eyes somewhat dazed.

"I thought I heard a moo just a second ago. I'm very fond of you, Daph. Do you think you could become a bit fond of me?"

"As in a tad?"

"As in whole bunches. As in let's get married. We'll spend the greater part of the year in the U.S., and the remainder here, at Asherwood. There's so much we can do together."

She scooted away from him, for his nearness made her mind shift into reverse. She said more to herself than to him, "I guess what I feel about Lucilla is jealousy, at least when she monopolizes you. And I do like for you to kiss me. That's very nice."

She paused a moment, and he said, "Continue thinking out loud. That way, there won't be any unanswered questions between us."

"We've not known each other very long. And I'm not entirely a dolt. Your proposal just now, it popped out, didn't it? You didn't mean to ask me to marry you."

"That's true. I do know that I wanted to bring you here so we could be assured of being alone. I also know that I want to make love to you so badly I hurt. I've never felt that way about a woman before."

"You don't love me. You're talking only about sex."

"I don't think fondness and sex are a bad start, do you?"

She rubbed the end of her nose, her expression a combination of bewilderment and confusion. "I might not be any good at sex, Brant. Then you'd be stuck with me."

"I'm willing to take my chances. You're looking ferocious. What are you thinking now?"

"I'm thinking that if Uncle Clarence hadn't written his will the way he did, you wouldn't look at me twice."

Brant looked away from her into the leaping flames, clasping his arms around his knees. "I thought you were gorgeous when you stepped out of that taxi and I looked at every inch of you I could manage before I knew who you really were. But that's not really the point, is it? I think, Daph, that it's impossible to answer that objectively. In any case, I can't. The will does exist, and I wouldn't be honest if I assured you that I didn't give a damn about it, because I do. I love Asherwood, and the money that comes with it will enable me—us—to fix it up exactly as we wish." He sighed. "I just don't know about that. But I do know that we have a good shot at making it work. What do you say?"

He'd said he thought she was gorgeous, Daphne thought, gazing into his eyes. She couldn't imagine a man more lovely than Brant. "Would you teach me how to use a checkbook?" she asked.

"I'll teach you everything you want to know."

But it all sounded so wretchedly lopsided, she thought. She supposed that her dowry of the house and money was something of worth, but it wasn't from her, it was from Uncle Clarence.

"If Lucilla were me, would you have proposed to her instead?"

"No," he said emphatically, with no hesitation. "That I can be quite certain about. I think I would have taken to my heels and been on the first plane back to the U.S."

She chewed over his words, and believed him. She'd always thought of herself as plain and dowdy. It was difficult to adjust to his image of her. She said slowly, "I've never been to America. I realize we'd live there—"

"And you feel like you'd be traveling to another planet?"

"Something like that. What if your friends don't…like me? What if your mother thinks I'm an adventuress?"

Brant leaned toward her and cupped her face between his hands. "I love it when you talk nineteenth-century to me. An adventuress. I like the sound of that, but everyone will think I'm an adventurer. My friends will love you. And I'll tell you something else, Daph. We're going to take a nice long honeymoon. By the time we return to New York, you're not going to have an unselfconfident bone left in your body."

"Just how do you imagine you'll achieve that?"

"You'll see, sweetheart. You'll see. Now, say yes, then we can neck for a while."

She pursed her lips and tilted up her face. "Yes."

CHAPTER TEN

Brant pulled Daphne into a close embrace behind a thick yew hedge that bordered the drive. He kissed her quickly and said, "I want you to wear something gorgeous tonight. I want you to smile, look at me like I'm the living hunk of your life, and not fall apart when Lucilla blows a fit. Okay?"

She gave him a smart salute and a forced smile.

He patted her bottom. "Good girl. Go get 'em, tiger."

But I'm a woman, not a girl, she thought briefly, then quickly forgot it, trying to match his stride to the house. He left her at her bedroom door with another quick kiss.

"I want you to look gorgeous, too," she called after him.

"Winterspoon will see to it, I promise."

Forty-five minutes later Winterspoon was admiring his handi-work. "Excellent, my lord. Just excellent." He lightly brushed a speck of lint from Brant's tuxedoed shoulder.

"Miss Daphne and I are going to get married," Brant said.

Winterspoon didn't look even remotely surprised. "Congratula-tions, my lord. His old lordship would be so pleased, indeed he would. Miss Daphne is a most charming young lady."

Brant gave him a wide grin. "My sentiments exactly."

"When is the happy occasion, my lord?"

"As soon as I can manage it. You'll have to tell me how I go about things."

"It will be my pleasure, my lord."

Brant added on a rueful note at the door, "Wish me luck, Win-terspoon. I have the distinct feeling that this evening won't be en-tirely pleasant."

"You will do just fine, my lord. As my father used to say, 'keep your back to the wall'."

I've just been advised by a pro, Brant thought as he strode down the stairs. Winterspoon had probably seen just about everything. He paused a moment before entering the Golden Salon, squared his shoulders, and walked in. His eyes immediately met Daphne's. She looked remarkably beautiful in a gown of obvious French design. It was floor length, of a pale green silky looking material, and accentuated her narrow waist and beautiful full breasts. She'd piled her hair on top of her head, and several tendrils curled about her face. He felt very proud of her, and assured himself again that he was doing the right thing. Yes, everything would work out just fine.

"Good evening," he said. "Cloe, Lucilla, you're both looking great. Shall we go in to dinner?" He took Cloe's arm and winked at Daphne.

When Mrs. Mulroy had finished serving the soup, he called her over a moment and requested a bottle of champagne.

"Eyuh," she said, "so that be how it is."

"That be how it is, yes," Brant said.

When Mrs. Mulroy left the room, Aunt Cloe asked brightly, "Where did you and Daphne ride this afternoon?"

"It got a bit chilly, so we warmed up at that abandoned house at the north end of the property."

"Oh?" Lucilla asked, her soup spoon pausing in mid air.

"Daphne makes a great fire," Brant added blandly.

As for Daphne, she was studying the contents of her soup bowl with intense concentration. Little coward, Brant thought.

"My little egg has so many talents," Cloe said.

"Aunt," Daphne asked suddenly, "why do you call me your little egg?"

"I say, love, I'm not entirely certain. Mr. Sparks used to call me that when we were...well, in moments of fondness."

"I'm going to London tomorrow," Lucilla said. "Would you like to come with me, Brant?"

"First, here's the champagne. Thank you, Mrs. Mulroy." Brant rose and filled everyone's glass. He was aware that Cloe was regarding him with fascinated eyes, that Daphne still had her eyes trained on her plate, and that Lucilla was clutching her fork.

322   THE ARISTOCRAT

"I have an announcement to make," he said, holding up his glass. "Daphne has agreed to marry me."

"Oh, how marvelous! Congratulations, Brant, Daphne."

The silence that followed Aunt Cloe's excitement was deafening.

"Well," Lucilla said, sitting back in her chair and folding her arms over her breasts, "you're willing to marry a man who doesn't love you, Daphne. I'd thought you'd have more pride."

"Thank you, Lucilla, for your kindness." Daphne's chin was up, and her eyes gleamed bright lime green.

"And as for you, Brant, I would have thought that if you'd wanted money, you could have found a woman who was a bit more—"

"In addition to everything else," Brant interrupted her smoothly, "Daphne and I have discovered that we are quite fond of each other. I trust both of you ladies will come to the wedding. It will be as soon as possible."

Lucilla wanted to howl in fury and disappointment. How the hell could he want Daphne, for God's sake! I will not make a spectacle of myself, she thought. She rose from her chair, carefully placing her napkin beside her plate. "I hope everything works out for both of you as I think it will." With that obscure parting shot, she left the room.

"That wasn't so terrible, was it?" Brant asked Daphne quietly.

"No, it wasn't. It's odd, but I feel bad for her."

"Lucilla won't starve, sweetheart. Cloe, you'll stand up with us?"

"With the greatest pleasure, my boy. We should go to London and see Reggie. Mr. Hucksley, that is. He'll want to get everything in order."

Daphne had the funniest feeling that she'd just been filed away under All Went According to Plan. She heard Aunt Cloe ask Brant if he intended to have a civil service and wondered why she wasn't the one being asked. Because you're a stupid twit and nobody cares what you have to say. She said aloud, her voice shrill, "I want to be married again in the United States. It's not fair to Brant's mother not to be at her son's wedding."

Brant shot her a surprised look. "That would be fine," he said slowly. "My mom would appreciate that, I'm sure."

"And your sister and her husband and children."

"Okay. We should be able to work that out."

"Where are you planning to honeymoon, Brant?" Aunt Cloe asked.

"Hawaii...if that's okay with Daphne," he added.

Her eyes sparkled. "Hawaii!"

"Yes, the island of Kauai, to be exact. I own a condo there. I think you'll enjoy it, sweetheart."

"Goodness!" Cloe exclaimed, rising from her chair. "There's so much to be done! I must make a list. Come along, Daphne."

Every last item on Cloe's list was marked through by the time Brant and Daphne were married in the office of the Registrar General. The ceremony lasted only five minutes.

Daphne was in a daze.

Brant was quite pleased with himself.

Cloe wanted to shout her triumph, and did, to Reggie Hucksley.

Lucilla had left for Italy three days earlier.

Both the Old Man and Harlow rode in the limousine with Daphne, Brant and Cloe to Heathrow airport.

"Yes, indeed, my lord," the Old Man said for the third time, "everything is in order. There are funds in the bank for the work on Asherwood Hall to continue on schedule."

Harlow, who had never seen Daphne before, continued to stare at her in unabashed admiration. "Lovely wedding ring, Mrs. Asher," he said.

"Yes, thank you," Daphne said, staring for a moment at the huge diamond surrounded with sparkling emeralds.

"Hawaii," Aunt Cloe said. "That's an awfully long trip, isn't it, Brant?"

"We'll fly to New York, take a connecting flight to Los Angeles, then fly to Honolulu." He didn't add that there was another connecting flight of forty minutes to be made to Kauai. He hadn't thought about stopping; he always slept on airplanes. Now he realized that he hadn't asked Daphne her opinion. Well, it was too late now. All the arrangements were made. He wanted his wedding night to be in Hawaii. It satisfied his imagination. The balmy weather, the sound of the waves washing onto the beach, Daphne wearing a see-through something.

My God, Daphne was thinking, staring out the window, what have I done? I'm leaving my home. I'm married to a man I scarcely know. She was nearly incoherent with anxiety when Aunt Cloe kissed her goodbye. "I'll come see you in New York, little egg," she assured Daphne. "But I'll give you two time to yourselves first."

"Yes, that's marvelous. Please, Aunt Cloe…yes, do come."

Brant shot a look of indulgent surprise at his bride. He shook hands with the Hucksleys, kissed and hugged Aunt Cloe, clasped his bride around her waist and led her through the tunnel to the plane.

They were flying first class. Suddenly, Daphne paled and said, "I forgot my Dramamine!"

"You get airsick?" Brant asked with awful foreboding. At her mute nod, he jumped from his seat and collared a flight attendant. He had ten minutes until the plane took off. He made it back with three minutes to spare. He watched Daphne swallow the pill, and prayed that it would be effective so close to take-off.

His prayer was answered. She was in a drugged sleep within thirty minutes.

Nearly twenty hours later, they landed at the Lihue airport on Kauai, the time change making it not too many hours after they'd left London. Daphne was in a state of numb exhaustion, and so doped up from all the Dramamine Brant had forced down her that she could barely put one foot in front of the other. As for Brant, he'd gotten his second wind and was raring to go. He breathed in the sweet, clean air, then directed Daphne to a seat inside the small terminal. Thirty minutes later he helped her into a rental car. He loved Kauai and kept up a nonstop monologue about everything they would see and do as he drove down Highway 50 to the southern end of the island. Daphne was asleep when they finally arrived at the Kiahuna Planation on Poipu Beach.

He pulled the Datsun into the space in front of the condo and turned to look at his wife. She was slouched down in the seat, her eyes closed, her face pale with exhaustion. He felt a pang of guilt. Damn, he should have stopped over in New York, or Los Angeles.

So much for your romantic wedding night, old buddy.

"Daphne." He gently shook her shoulder. "Come on, sweetheart, wake up."

"No," she said quite clearly, her eyes remaining tightly closed.

He looked bemused for a moment, then shrugged. He took their luggage upstairs, unlocked the door and turned on the overhead fans. He shot a wistful look at the big queen-size bed in the single bedroom. Forget it, old man, he told himself.

He carried Daphne upstairs and gently eased her down on the bed. Her hair was tangled, her lovely cream-colored dress wrinkled to death. He tried again to wake her, but she didn't budge. He took a quick shower, changed into shorts and a golf shirt, and went out to forage for some dinner.

When he returned nearly an hour later with some carryout Chinese, the first thing he heard was the shower. Her clothes lay in a trail from the bedroom to the bathroom. He looked at her panties and bra, and felt a flood of desire. She was in the shower, naked, and she was his wife.

The bathroom was divided into two small rooms. The door to the shower and toilet was closed. "Daphne," he called, lightly tapping on the door. "Are you all right?"

Daphne raised her head at the sound of his voice and stared dumbly through the glass shower door. She'd come suddenly awake thirty minutes before, aware that something was wrong. It took her a good five minutes to discover it was the sound of the ocean and an overhead fan. She felt dirty, rumpled, and her head ached. She had stared around the bedroom at the rattan furniture and looked up at the whirling fan overhead. I'm in Hawaii, she thought, bemused, and I'm married.

She'd called Brant's name, but there had been no answer, which was an enormous relief. She had dragged herself out of bed and

THE ARISTOCRAT

begun to strip off her clothes, her only thought of drowning herself in the shower.

She heard him call her name again and forced herself to call out, "Yes, I'm fine. I'll be out in just a bit."

"I've brought us some dinner."

"Okay."

She sounded as if he'd said he'd brought worms, he thought, staring at the closed bathroom door a few minutes longer. It was dark, but the third floor condo faced the ocean, and the half-moon cast a romantic light, making the ocean waves silvery. He carried the food, plates and forks to the small table on the deck. He opened a beer, sat down, and let the warm air and the sweet smell from all the flowers flood his senses.

"Hi. Here I am."

He slewed his head about and smiled at his wife. Her thick hair was damp from her shower, falling about her shoulders. She wore a sexless cotton robe.

"How do you feel, Daph?"

"More alive now, thank you."

She still looked awfully pale, her movements sluggish. He said, as he served her some sweet and sour pork, "We'll hit the sack after we eat. A good twelve hours will put you to rights again."

Daphne found she was starving. She consumed at least half the three Chinese dishes nonstop, and a half-dozen fortune cookies. "Life in this body still exists," she said, and sat back in her deck chair. "I love Chinese food. This place must be heaven, Brant. I never imagined anything so beautiful." She stretched, drawing his eyes to her breasts, then rose to lean over the balcony.

Doesn't she know that I want to rip her clothes off and make love to her until she... Stop it, you fool! Brant drew a deep breath, and said, "Do you like the condo? I bought it about two years ago. Most of the year it's rented out to tourists. We really lucked out. We've got it for two uninterrupted weeks."

She mumbled something, and Brant continued, "The kitchen's fully stocked; we've got color TV; and the beach is at our back door. Do you snorkel, Daph?"

"Yes," she said, turning. "I learned in Greece."

The soft moonlight behind her made her look like a fairy princess, Brant thought, somewhat dazed. Her hair was dry now, and looked like spun silk. "That's good," he said. "Why don't you come here a moment, Daph? Then we'll go to bed."

She cocked her head at him, watched him lightly pat his bare thighs, and said, "When you told me to bring all my summer things, I really couldn't imagine wearing them. You look nice in those shorts, Brant."

"Thank you. Come here, just for a minute."

"Yes, it's so warm," she mumbled and took several slow steps, coming to a halt in front of him. He gently pulled her down on his lap.

"Just relax, sweetheart." He pressed her head against his shoulder, then settled his hands around her waist. "Listen, I'm not going to make love to you tonight. You're too tired, and jet lag is beginning to hit me, too. We'll start our official honeymoon tomorrow, okay?"

She nodded her head, her soft hair sliding over his chin. She felt enormous relief and, she admitted to herself, just a hint of disappointment. Brant didn't seem at all crazed with desire for her.

"I'm going to take very good care of you, sweetheart. Will you trust me?"

He held her quietly for some minutes, the only sound the lapping waves beneath them, splashing against the shore. He smiled, realizing that she was fast asleep. Just as well, he thought. Less temptation. He rose, clutching her in his arms, and took her into the bedroom. He gently slipped off her robe and pulled the sheet over her.

My wife, he thought again, staring down at her. He took off his own clothes and got into bed beside her. His last thought before he fell asleep was that he'd never before just *slept* with a woman.

CHAPTER ELEVEN

Daphne awoke at dawn, a bemused smile on her lips and smooth male skin under her palm. She became even more bemused when she realized that she was pressed tightly against Brant, facing him, one of his legs between hers, one of his arms thrown over her back. Her nightgown was up around her waist, and she could feel his belly pressed against hers.

She didn't budge. He felt so different from her, and very nice. Oh dear, she thought, jerking slightly, did he make love to me and I don't remember? Was I too sleepy to know what was happening? She frowned against his shoulder and lightly stroked her fingers down his back. He moved in his sleep, and his hairy leg moved upward between her thighs.

How dreadful! She hadn't lived through her wedding night, so to speak. But she didn't feel any change in herself. Surely she should feel *different*.

She thought about this for a while as she listened to her husband's even breathing and the steady thudding of his heart. From the books she'd read, the films she'd seen, she knew that she couldn't possibly be lying naked against him and he not have done anything. No, that was impossible. She'd been made love to, but she'd been too drugged to be aware of it. She groaned softly. I must look different, she thought. Slowly she eased herself away from him and came up on her knees on her side of the bed. He mumbled something in his sleep, flung one arm above his head and fell onto his back. The single sheet was around his knees. Daphne gulped. She'd never before seen a naked man. She'd seen a couple of pictures in a racy magazine once, but not *everything*.

Well, I'm seeing everything now. Lord, was he gorgeous. He wasn't covered with hair like many of the men she'd seen on the beach. Just enough, she thought, her hand tingling to touch him. Her inquisitive eyes followed the lovely line of hair down his belly to his... She pressed her palms against her cheeks in pleased embarrassment. She even loved the tuft of hair under his raised arm.

It must have happened, she thought again, and quietly scooted off the bed. She trailed to the bathroom and stared at herself in the mirror. Her hair looked like a bird's nest, her nightgown rumpled and ratty. But she looked like that most mornings, she thought. She touched her breasts, wondering if he'd felt her there.

She remembered the feel of his muscled leg between hers and gave a delicious shudder. It had certainly felt nice when she'd awakened.

She turned and looked back toward the bed. There was no door to the bedroom. In fact, the only door in the entire condo was the one to the shower. He'd moved slightly again, spreading his legs. She gulped, turned quickly away and pulled off her nightgown.

After a quick shower and shampoo, she crept out of the bathroom and looked at him again. He hadn't moved. Maybe, she thought, smiling slightly, she'd exhausted him. Weren't men supposed to be exhausted after making passionate love? That made her feel pleased.

Why don't I feel exhausted? But she didn't; she felt marvelous. Completely rested and full of her usual morning energy. She dried her hair and quickly dressed in a pair of shorts and a matching top. She wandered onto the deck and sucked in her breath at the sight of the rising sun over the ocean. It was every bit as beautiful as Crete. A balmy breeze caressed her cheek and ruffled her hair. And all the flowers! Plumeria, bird of paradise, bougainvillae in whites, bright reds and pinks. She wondered if she'd be able to grow these beautiful flowers in her new home. Brant had told her he lived primarily in New York City. She wondered if he had a good-sized garden. She hoped so.

"Good morning."

She whirled around. Her husband gave her a sleepy smile and ran his hand through his rumpled hair. He'd put on a pair of running shorts.

"Hi," she said, her breathing quickening a bit.

"You're a morning person?"

"Yes, disgusting, isn't it?" Was he looking at her intimately?
She hunched her shoulders just a bit.

Brant yawned. Nothing intimate about that, she thought, somewhat disappointed. She straightened again.

"Do you like Kauai so far?"

"It's beautiful. I like it; truly. It's still awfully early. Would you
like to go back to bed?"

He gave her a slow, wicked smile. "I can't think of a better way
to wake up."

"Oh!"

He watched her turn various shades of red. She jerked her head
up from looking down at her bare feet and blurted out, "I don't
remember anything!"

He cocked his head at her, wondering what the devil she was
talking about. He wasn't at his best in the mornings.

"I'm sorry," she said, flushing more deeply. "I was hoping I
would remember something, but I don't. I even thought I'd look
different, but I can't see any changes."

He scratched his hand over his stomach. Finally he understood.
At least, he thought he did. He grinned at her. "You were great,"
he said, his voice a deep caress. "You cried out and held onto me
and told me you loved it."

She heard only the intimacy, missing the teasing in his voice.
"It isn't fair," she said. "Why didn't you pour coffee down me
or something?"

"I didn't think about it. You seemed to be having such fun. Did
you enjoy the...view this morning?"

"Yes," she said. She suddenly felt inordinately relieved that it
was over and she'd responded so well. "You looked very nice."

"Sprawled on my back with my legs apart?"

"That, too. But you see, Brant, I wasn't sure anything had happened, so I didn't look at you all that long. That would have been
like invading your privacy."

It was on the tip of his tongue to tell her that nothing at all had happened, but he laughed instead. "Tell you what, sweetheart, why don't we have some coffee and go back to bed? Now that you know everything, it will be even more fun for you. And you can look at me as long as you like. I'd definitely love to invade your privacy. Will you make me some coffee while I shower? I bought some stuff last night for breakfast."

She gazed at him somewhat somberly for a long moment. She said slowly, thoughtfully, "I won't be embarrassed now, will I? There's no need to, is there?"

"None at all," he said. He hugged her briefly, and kissed her lightly against her temple. "No, none at all."

"Well, that's a relief," she said, and smiled up at him.

In between arias in the shower, Brant found himself grinning inanely and wondering if he should tell her the truth. No, he decided. Now he wouldn't have to fight her inherent modesty. He felt a leap of desire and quickly soaped himself, then turned on the cold water for a moment.

After drying his hair, he wrapped the towel around his waist and joined Daphne on the deck. She smiled at him and handed him a cup of coffee. "It's thick and black and very American," she said. "Winterspoon told me that was the way you liked it."

"Did Winterspoon tell you anything else about me?"

She sipped her own very blond coffee. "Just that you were, in his opinion, a nice man, despite your being American. He even admitted that you had some wit."

"Quite an accolade." His gaze flitted from her soft hair downward. "You have a very nice figure, Daph. Yes, very nice."

"Did you tell me that last night?"

"I must have. Now, why don't we go back to bed and I'll tell you again?"

He looped his arm around her shoulders, leaning down to nibble her ear. "I'll kiss every inch of you...just like I did last night. You loved that, Daph. Every inch."

She turned in his embrace, wrapping her arms about his back. "I must have," she said against his shoulder. "It sure sounds nice right now."

He grinned over her head and said lightly, "Have I created a monster? A sex fiend?"

"Well, I do have some of Aunt Cloe's blood, and she, I think, adores sex, or at least she must have when Mr. Sparks was alive."

Brant found that the few steps to the bed had made him so taut with downright lust that he was breathing hard. His wife, he thought. She was his wife. For life, not just a brief fling. He realized how important it was to make everything nice for her. He couldn't imagine his life without sexual satisfaction, both for himself and for his partner. Go slowly, old man, he told himself.

He tumbled her onto her back and came down over her, balancing himself on one elbow. "Hi, wife," he said, and leaned down to kiss her. "Open your mouth. How could you forget so soon?"

"You must have short-circuited me," she said, and parted her lips.

He didn't touch her below her shoulders for a good ten minutes. It felt strange to be so methodical and, in a sense, Machiavellian, but he held himself in check and continued his slow assault. He felt her ease, then respond to him. "That's it, sweetheart," he whispered into her mouth. "Just relax with me. Nothing new, you know."

Daphne wriggled beneath him. She wanted him to touch her, but she was embarrassed to ask him. What had she done the previous night? "Brant," she said finally, her voice ragged, "please." She thrust her hips upward; and gasped at the hard feel of him.

Brant eased off her and quickly pulled off her top. "Good God," he said, staring down at her. "You are so bloody beautiful." Tentatively, he touched her full breasts. So white they were, her breasts appearing almost too large for her slender torso. Her nipples were already taut and darkened to a dusky peach. He began kissing her again as he gently stroked and caressed her breasts. He laid his palm flat for a moment and felt her heart pounding. Slowly he kissed his way down her throat to her shoulders, then took her nipple into his mouth. She cried out, arching her back upward.

He felt her hands frantically kneading his back. Her breasts were very sensitive, and it delighted him. So much more of her to go, so much to anticipate, to appreciate.

"What do you want me to do?" she gasped.

He was gently stroking his tongue over her. "Just lie still and enjoy. This is what a man likes best to do."

He covered her belly with his leg and gently pressed. Daphne was beginning to feel frantic. She wanted to feel him, all of him, and began to wriggle to face him so she could jerk down his shorts.

"Slow down, sweetheart. You first." He pulled off her shorts and panties, then raised himself up on his elbow. She was very fair complexioned. Her waist was narrow, her belly flat. His eyes locked on the tuft of dark blond hair, and he felt himself begin to tremble with need. Slowly he stroked his hand from her breasts downward until he was lightly cupping his palm over her. He looked into her eyes, watching every expression, as his fingers gently probed. He sucked in his breath. She was damp, her delicate woman's flesh swelled and beautifully warm.

He began to rhythmically stroke her. "You like that," he said softly. "Remember?"

"I—I feel urgent. It almost hurts, Brant."

He eased his fingers away and stroked them down her slender thighs.

He eased himself up and pulled off his shorts. Daphne stared at him, her eyes growing wider. "Oh dear," she managed. "I liked *that*?"

It took him a moment to gather his wits. He looked briefly down at himself. Asleep this morning, he imagined he'd looked nothing like this. "Yes," he said, "you did. Very much." He slid his hands between her legs and eased them apart. Slowly he eased down on top of her. He made no move to enter her, though he felt himself straining against her. Hey down there, you've got no brain and no sense! Cool it!

He pressed against her, and she responded. He felt a rippling shudder go through her body. He covered her and began to kiss her, his tongue thrusting into her mouth. He felt her arms tighten almost painfully around his back. All the way, he thought. Yes, all the way. He eased himself down her body, pausing to enjoy her breasts, then her belly. She stiffened, and he raised his head.

"Listen, sweetheart. You wanted to know what you could do for me. I want to kiss you and love you, and I want you to relax and enjoy it. You did…last night."

When his mouth closed over her, Daphne lurched upward. She felt no embarrassment now, assuming that all her embarrassment had happened last night. It felt so good. "I like that," she gasped, tangling her fingers in his thick hair.

Brant did too. She tasted fresh and sweet and… Suddenly she gave a deep shudder, crying out. He felt the tension in her legs, and her release. Her breathing was ragged, and he felt her uncontrollable trembling. He loved the convulsive little shudders, the soft sounds from her throat. He eased his rhythm, then began again.

Daphne felt dazed. She felt as though she'd been on a roller coaster. It came down, finally. Then it started upward again. She was stunned, but eager. Brant felt it and used every ounce of his expertise to bring her up again. He felt her tense, heard her moaning softly. He quickly reared over her, and with one single thrust, entered her. There was no maidenhead, thank God, but she was very small. He felt her stiffen and press her hands against his shoulders. "Easy, sweetheart," he said. He buried himself deeply within her, then eased down over her, his eyes on her face. "It's okay, Daph. Just a little while longer and any discomfort will be gone. I won't move. Get used to me."

"All right," she whispered. She buried her face against his shoulder. Slowly he felt the tension drain from her, and he began to move within her. He bit down on his lower lip, hoping the brief pain he'd given her would tighten his control. He'd never made love to a virgin before, and it was a heady experience. He could feel her muscles clutching him, and he groaned. "Daphne," he gasped, "no!"

She didn't know what he was talking about. "Brant, please," she said, her voice high and urgent. He slipped his fingers between them and found her.

To his delight and near insanity, she arched upward, drawing him deeper. She yelled his name and nearly bucked him off in her frenzy.

He gritted his teeth and gave her release before he allowed himself to let go. He felt swamped with feeling, feeling so strong that he shook with it.

He collapsed on top of her, his face next to hers on the pillows.

"I'm going to die," she moaned.

He managed to gather enough energy to raise himself on his elbows and look into her dazed eyes. He stroked her hair off her forehead. "You were marvelous," he said. "And you aren't going to die, although I can just see the headline: Sex-Starved Bride Succumbs."

"How about: Bride Buried Smiling?"

She closed her arms about his back and squeezed. "I'm glad we got married. This is such fun."

"You think so, huh? Not bad, I'd say, for your first..."

Her eyes flew open and narrowed on his face. "My first what, Brant?"

He kissed her very seductively, but she was sated and tenacious. "What, Brant?"

He gave her a lopsided grin. "We didn't make love last night, Daph. I'm not into unconscious women."

"You...you crook!"

"Why did you think we had?"

"I woke up all tangled together with you and my nightgown...well, it was up, and not down where it should have been. And you are a crook, and dishonest, and a dreadful tease—"

"Yes, but you weren't embarrassed, were you?"

She chewed a moment on her lower lip, and he quickly kissed her again.

"Still..." she began.

He kissed her once more. "The very pleasurable result," he said with a disarming grin, "justified the means, as the Prince is supposed to have been taught."

She lowered her thick lashes. "Well," she said finally, "maybe.

Just maybe. Brant, did I react normally? I mean, I didn't disappoint you, did I?"

"If you'd reacted any more, I'd be dead." He paused a moment, enjoying the feel of her soft body beneath his, "I don't think you could ever disappoint me, sweetheart, not in a thousand and one nights."

"What about a thousand and one days?"

He moaned loudly and collapsed on his back.

CHAPTER TWELVE

Do you remember the song, 'Puff the Magic Dragon'?''

"Oh yes, it was quite popular in England."

"Well, old Puff was from Hanalei, and that's a town on the northern shore of Kauai. We'll go swimming up there and do some snorkeling."

Daphne sat back, sated from a delicious bacon cheeseburger, and patted her stomach. "Is the drive long enough so I won't sink like a fat whale when I hit the water?"

"Finish your planter's punch and you'll go down happy."

Brant leaned back in his chair and looked out over the Kiahuna Golf Club course. The back part of the restaurant was a roofed patio, and the air was redolent with the sweet scent of flowers and freshly cut grass. He felt good. He'd discovered that he enjoyed the freedom of being married, enjoyed the growing intimacy between him and Daphne. He sent her a sleepy glance, watching her slurp up the final bit of planter's punch. He'd made sure she was well-coated with sunscreen and in the past two days she'd just gotten a bit red, but no sunburn. She'd french-braided her hair this morning, and the plait lay heavy and lustrous between her shoulder blades. She looked fresh, sweet, and so inviting that he felt his body react yet again. He closed his eyes a moment, picturing her in that outrageous orange bikini Cloe had bought her. It was a wonder, he thought, that she hadn't been attacked on the beach in Crete. His presence was the only thing that saved her here.

"When do we take the helicopter ride? You did tell me that a lot of the *Thorn Birds* was filmed here. I want to see the beach where Father Ralph made love to Meggie."

"Inspiration?"

"That," she said, "I don't need."

"I like being married to you," he said, stretching lazily.

"Me too."

"I guess it's time we did something. That is, I guess it's time to show you the island." His eyes fell to her breasts, and his gaze was so intent that Daphne quivered.

"I'll never see it if you keep doing that," she said, her voice shaky. "You, Brant, are very addictive."

"So are you. Maybe I'll leave you alone in fifty years or so."

"So soon? I can just picture you, a little old man, placing your cane carefully by the bed, then creaking in between the sheets."

"And drooling all over you." He looked up to see the waitress grinning down at him. "Our check, please," he said. Out of habit, he watched her walk away and cataloged her finer points.

"You are a dirty young man!"

"Old habits are hard to break."

They left the golf club and walked the quarter of a mile back to the Kiahuna Plantation. "Do you want to learn how to play golf?" he asked.

"It seems rather a silly game, but I'll give it a try. What are we doing this afternoon?"

He gave her a long look. "Why don't we discuss it in bed?"

But they didn't. Her back was arched, the thick braid hanging over her shoulder. Brant let her control the depth of his penetration, let her determine the pace. It drove him wild to see the lightly tanned parts of her and the utter white of her breasts and belly. He felt her thighs hug him, and he gasped. He pulled her down on top of him. "Lie still," he said, gritting his teeth.

Daphne couldn't hold still. She cupped his face between her hands and kissed him deeply. "I love the way you feel inside me," she said between gasping breaths into his mouth. She felt him tighten his grip on her hips, holding her still.

"Sweetheart, I—"

She straddled him again, drawing him deep, and it drove him crazy. He closed his fingers over her and watched the surprised look in her eyes when the building sensations swamped her. Her muscles tightened convulsively, and he let himself go.

He drew her down against him and stroked her nape and back, reveling in the sheet of perspiration on her smooth flesh. "You're so bloody sexy," he whispered in her ear. "And I love the way you look so incredulous just before you start making all those cute little noises."

She was incapable of answering him for several minutes. Slowly she came back to life as she used to know it. It seemed the past two days that she'd been in a kind of dazed fog. "If," she said finally, arching up a bit so she could see his face, "you ever get a headache, I'll never forgive you. It just keeps getting wilder and wilder." She lowered her lashes a moment. "I like being on top. You were so deep."

He felt himself swelling again and groaned. "Let's eat some Macadamia nuts; they're supposed to help."

She giggled and kissed his chin. "They've got such a sweet taste, and such a crisp bite...roasted to perfection, dipped in rich creamy...ouch!"

He rubbed the hip he'd just smacked. "You, Daphne Asher, are a smart-mouthed...creamy..."

She moved over him, and he couldn't have found another word if his life depended on it.

At four o'clock they finally strolled to the beach and fell asleep in the sun.

"Below are the Wailua Falls. If they look familiar it's because they're in the opening scene of *Fantasy Island*."

Daphne snapped three pictures as the helicopter swooped down over the double waterfalls.

"Below is the Huleia National Wildlife Refuge. It's gotta look familiar; it's where part of *Raiders of the Lost Ark* was filmed. Everyone, even you mainlanders, has seen that."

"Damn," Daphne muttered. "I'm out of film."

Brant patted her knee in commiseration, the sound of the helicopter blades made it hard to talk and be heard.

"We'll go up again if you like," Brant said when they'd landed. "Did you like seeing the nurses' beach from *South Pacific*?"

She bubbled with excitement. She skipped beside Brant. "Oh

yes. And I can't get over Waimea Canyon. Just like the pictures I've seen of the Grand Canyon! And all the waterfalls, Brant! And the wettest spot in the entire world!''

He smiled down at her, enjoying her enthusiasm. When she'd finally completed giving him a rundown on what they'd seen, he said, "Tonight, Daph, we're going to the Sheraton for a luau. Are you into pig?''

"Just as long as I don't have to watch it being roasted.''

"You don't. The entertainment isn't bad, either. And, I swear, there's plenty of planter's punch to keep you afloat.''

Brant stopped in Koloa on their way back to Poipu Beach and parked in front of a line of shops. They picked her out several muumuus, not the shapeless ones, but exquisitely fashioned fitted ones. He left her to pay while he went to another shop, and for the first time since their arrival in Kauai she felt an unwelcome jolt of reality.

"I'm sorry, ma'am, but I'll need your husband's signature on those traveler's checks.

Daphne realized that she didn't have a cent. And all the checks were in Brant's name. "But I have the same name,'' she said

"I'm sorry, ma'am,'' the sales person repeated, "but I can't break the rules.''

"I understand,'' Daphne said. She left her packages on the counter and wandered outside to sit on the steps to the store. It wasn't that she was used to having her own money, because she wasn't. It just felt odd and somehow embarrassing that she, a married woman, was utterly dependent on her husband for everything.

"Hi, gorgeous,'' Brant said, sporting a new straw hat. "What's up, sweetheart? Where are your clothes?''

She looked up at his handsome face, so deeply tanned that his eyes looked even bluer. "I couldn't sign your traveler's checks,'' she said evenly.

"Oh, that, I'll be back in a minute.''

He pulled off his straw hat and flipped it to her, frisbee style.

Daphne didn't go back into the store. She was looking at postcards of Spouting Horn when Brant came out carrying several big shopping bags. "You're going to look gorgeous, lady. I like the gold one that's got the thin straps best."

It's not his fault, she thought, forcing a smile. She said formally, "Thank you, Brant. The dresses are lovely. I appreciate them."

He cocked a dark eyebrow at her. "That sounded like a recording. What's up, sweetheart? You change your mind about the dresses?"

She didn't reply until they were seated in the car. She turned slightly and asked, "Brant, there's something I don't understand. The inheritance from Uncle Clarence, is it yours or mine?"

He sent her a startled look. "It's ours, of course. We're married, you know."

"That isn't quite true. Did you inherit the money, or did I?"

"I did. But what difference does it make? What's mine is yours, Daph."

"And what's mine is yours, only I don't have anything to share with you. Nothing."

Brant pulled the car off the road and switched off the motor. "Okay, what's the matter? And don't give me any runaround bull."

She gnawed on her lower lip and shook her head.

"Daph, were you bothered because the traveler's checks were all in my name? If you were, I'm sorry. I just didn't think. Tomorrow I'll flip over to the Waiohai and have some made in your name."

"Thank you."

"Your enthusiasm is deadening," he said, his eyes narrowing on her face. He shrugged. "Look, I guess I'm just used to being on my own, and," he added on a wicked grin, "even when I wasn't on my own, no one ever complained when I picked up the tab. When we get home to New York, I'll set up a checking account for you, in your name, okay?"

"It's still your money, not mine. It's like an allowance that you'd give to a child."

His hands clutched the steering wheel, and he said acidly, "Don't be an ass. You're my wife, my responsibility—"

"An encumbrance, a parasite, a—a dependent."

He cursed softly, started the engine and screeched back onto the narrow highway.

Brant parked the car in their parking space, and they walked up to the third floor in silence. Brant unlocked the door, then stepped back for her to enter first.

"Come here and sit down," he said. "I want to get a few things straight."

She wanted to tell him to go to hell, but the habit of obedience was strong, the habit of bending her will to the stronger. And, after all, what had he done wrong? Nothing, she thought, her shoulders slumping in depression. She sat down.

"I thought," Brant said, standing in front of her, crossing his arms over his chest, "that we understood and agreed on our respective roles. That is, I would bring home the proverbial bacon and you would be responsible for our home. However, if not having your own money bothers you, I'll sign over half the money from the inheritance. Is that what you want? It will make you independent. You can have all the bloody traveler's checks you want in your name."

"I didn't earn that money," she said, thrusting up her chin just a bit.

"Like hell you didn't! You were the old man's slave for how many years? Did he pay you a salary for all the work you did? Let's consider your half of the inheritance as back pay. You can spend it; you can invest it; you can stuff it under your mattress."

"You're very...kind."

He shot her an exasperated frown. "Daph, for God's sake, I want you to be happy. You're my wife. You will have our children."

She stared at him, her face paling under her tan. "Children?"

"I haven't been using any birth control. Have you?"

She paled even more. "I didn't think about it." She rose jerkily to her feet, clasping and unclasping her hands in front of her.

Every bit of irritation disappeared in an instant. He grasped her shoulders and gently drew her against him. "I'm sorry, sweetheart. I was making decisions for you. I just assumed...well, I'll be responsible for birth control. When we get home, we can discuss what you'd like to do. All right?''

She wished for just a brief instant that he would yell and holler and call her an idiot, just like Uncle Clarence had with great regularity. But he was so reasonable, so kind. He was really trying to be nice to her. It was almost depressing. She felt like a fool, an overreactive ass. She felt in the wrong. ''All right,'' she whispered against his shoulder. ''I'm sorry. Please forgive me.''

''It's not for you to apologize, turkey. It appears that our conversations haven't hit on some very important issues. And that's your fault, of course, for being so delectable that my mouth is kissing you all the time and not talking.'' He kissed the tip of her nose. ''Is that a band of freckles I see?''

She smiled and wrinkled her nose. ''I don't know about a band. I think I'd prefer a sprinkle.''

''Or a gaggle or a herd?''

She punched him in the stomach, and he obligingly grunted. He cupped her hips and lifted her against him. ''We've got a couple of hours before we need to go to our luau,'' he said, nuzzling her neck. ''You got any ideas on how to spend them?''

''How about the beach? Maybe I can get a herd of freckles.''

''Forget it,'' Brant said.

The luau was a major production, Daphne realized as they pulled into the special parking lot at the Sheraton. There were a good one hundred people, much laughter and high spirits. There were no individual tables, so they sat with two other couples. One older man from Ohio recognized Brant, and Daphne sat back and watched her husband wrap everyone at the table in his own special brand of charm.

''Are you newlyweds, dear?'' the older man's wife asked Daphne while the men were discussing the Astros' chances for the Superbowl in the upcoming season.

''Yes, we are.''

''You're English, aren't you?''

''Yes, ma'am, I am.''

''Call me Agnes. Is this your first trip to Hawaii?''

The other woman, a stunning brunette from Seattle, soon joined in, and Daphne forgot her shyness.

"What a wonderful evening," Daphne said later to Brant, her voice just a bit fuzzy from the mai tais.

"I was proud of you, Daph," he said, hugging her against his side. He'd been a bit concerned that she'd clam up meeting strangers, but she hadn't, much to his delight.

"Brant," she said when they were sitting out on the deck a few minutes later, "have you called your mother?"

He was glad it was dark and she couldn't see the flush on his face. "Yes," he said. "I called her a couple of days ago when I was over at the Waiohai."

She felt herself stiffen a bit, wondering why he hadn't called her from the condo. "What did she say?"

He caressed the nape of her neck. "After she got over the shock she started singing hallelujahs." It wasn't precisely the truth, but close enough. Actually, he had been able to see her mind working, wondering just why he'd married an English girl so quickly. He'd ended up telling her the terms of the will. "She can't wait to meet you, sweetheart, and is delighted that you want another ceremony for her and the family. You wanna marry me next month?"

She gave him such a sweet, radiant smile that he froze for a moment, taken aback at the odd, twisting emotions that smile evoked. "Yes," she said, "I think I've compromised you enough without a minister's blessing."

"Are you certain that you weren't a Victorian maiden in your past life? Compromised? I love it."

There were no more snakes in the garden for the remainder of their stay in Kauai. Brant told her about every one of his teammates, his intention being to ease her shyness when she met them. They discussed Asherwood Hall, coming to agreement on all the renovations. Three days before they left Daphne discovered she had no worries about being pregnant, and Brant, groaning, told her he was going to have to live in the shower, under a steady stream of icy water. His joking eased her embarrassment, as he intended it to.

It started as a joke on their return flight to Los Angeles. "Why not have Winterspoon come to New York and be our majordomo?"

And it ended up as a plan. "I can't wait for Marcie to get hold of that item," Brant said. "An English valet in residence with a football player!"

"Who's Marcie?" Daphne asked, latching immediately on this heretofore unmentioned name.

"Marcie?" Brant repeated carefully. "Just a friend, sweetheart. She's a reporter for a newspaper in New York."

Ah, Daphne thought, a woman who's done something with her life other than live it at the orders of someone else. But that wasn't true, she chided herself. She would do something. She wouldn't sit around Brant's house doing nothing.

Their arrival in New York's Kennedy Airport was a nightmare. Brant's mother was there, along with a group from the press. A flashbulb went off in Daphne's face, and she shrank against him. "Damn," he muttered, then forced a smile to his lips. He knew she was practically insensible from all the Dramamine. How the hell had the press found out when he was returning?

The afternoon paper turned her into a silent ghost.

"Football Pro Gains Title and Rich Bride." The byline was Marcie's.

CHAPTER THIRTEEN

"How is she, Brant?" asked Alice Asher when her son came back into the living room.

"Asleep. She was so doped up to begin with and this—" he flung a disgusted arm toward the newspaper "—this didn't help. How did the press find out, Mom? Do you know?"

"Marcie called me last week and, fool that I am, I told her you'd gotten married in England and were in Hawaii. That's all."

"Of course all she had to do was call the airlines and find out which flight we were coming back on." Brant sat back, pulling a thick sofa cushion behind his head. "And, of course, she called some of her buddies in England. Well, it's done. I'll call Marcie later; you can be sure of that."

"I like Daphne, Brant," said Alice. "She seems unlike all the other women in your life, so—"

"Sweet? Guileless? Innocent as a lamb?"

"Perhaps. We'll get her over this…this nastiness."

Alice went into the kitchen and made some coffee. When she returned to Brant's very modern living room, she saw him standing in front of the large glass window, staring down on Central Park. "May I ask you something personal, honey?"

"Sure, Mom, everyone else does without even asking my permission." He turned to face her, and she saw the weariness on his handsome face.

"Did you marry her because of the will?"

"In part," he said honestly. "As she did me. But I'm fond of her, as she is of me. We both love Asherwood. We both want it restored to what it was years ago. By marrying, we got the house and ensured there'd be enough money to fix it up. She's guileless as hell, it's true. And young and inexperienced." He gave her a lopsided grin. "Well, maybe not so inexperienced about some things now."

"I gather," Alice said dryly, "that you handled that quite well."

"I guess there's something to be said about raising a girl in the bowels of the country. She'd had no chance to learn everything she shouldn't like or shouldn't do."

"Is that your oblique way of telling me that Daphne enjoys the physical side of marriage?"

"Yeah." He grinned. "She's very natural and loving."

Alice was silently relieved about that. She said, "Incidentally, Lily and Dusty are ready to fly up from Houston whenever you give them the word."

"Good. Give me some time to get Daph back in shape, then we can arrange everything. Just family and a few friends, okay, Mom?"

"No problem, honey. I've already talked to Reverend Oakes."

"Mom, I don't want you ever to think that I would marry just for money. But you know that's what the press is going to continue pushing."

"I know you would never do such a thing. I was thinking, Brant, once Daphne gets out and meets people, everyone will see what a lovely person she is. And, of course, she's very beautiful."

Brant drank some of his coffee, but didn't sit down. He began pacing and Alice watched him, a question in her eyes.

"Mom," he said abruptly, "I don't know much about birth control. That is, I know about it, and Lord knows I've been very careful in the past. I just don't want Daphne taking anything that could possibly hurt her. What do you think?"

"I would suggest that you call the medical society and ask for a woman gynecologist."

"Woman?"

"I think it would make Daphne feel more comfortable, don't you?"

"Yeah, probably. Thanks for coming, Mom. It's late. Are you ready to turn in?"

"Yes." She rose and hugged Brant. "Everything will work out, honey, don't worry."

"I'll try not to." He grinned down at her. "Would you be willing to make breakfast tomorrow morning? I'll help you. Daphne isn't too much of a marvel in the kitchen."

"Sure thing. After all, I spoiled you rotten for thirty-one years. Why stop now?"

Brant didn't turn on the bedroom light. He could see Daphne's outline in his large brass bed, and it gave him a warm feeling. He'd sleep next to her every night and wake up next to her every morning. It added a completeness that he'd never really realized wasn't there until he had it.

She murmured softly in her sleep when he eased in beside her. He kissed her lightly on her ear and pulled her into his arms.

"Brant?" Her voice was fuzzy and blurred.

"Shush, sweetheart. Go back to sleep."

"Can we go see the Spouting Horn again tomorrow?"

She was still in Kauai. "Sure thing." He stroked her hair lightly and pressed her cheek against his shoulder. "We'll do whatever you want."

Daphne was a morning person, awake and alert the moment she opened her eyes. But this morning she woke up slowly. She was aware that she was in a strange place, and she reached for Brant. He wasn't there. Slowly she sat up and stared at the expanse of bed. Brant's bedroom, she thought, shaking her head clear of confusion. Brant's home, no, she corrected herself, his condo. What a strange word! She remembered the events of the previous evening and cringed. She'd acted like Daphne the shy, insecure, dowdy, double bagger, and fallen apart in front of Brant's mother.

"You're full of rubbish," she said aloud to the empty room. "How odd," she added softly. Unlike the living room, which was a study in modern glass, chrome and stark furnishings, the bedroom was a study in elegant antiques. She quickly recognized an original eighteenth-century French armoire, and several heavy Spanish chairs. There was a scroll-armed sofa that reminded her of the Regency period, but she wasn't sure. The rug was a thick rich coffee color and covered the center of the polished hardwood floor. She climbed out of bed, pausing a moment to touch the beautiful brass headboard. She found herself wondering how many women had slept in that bed with Brant.

She giggled. With the lights off, it would take two people a good deal of time to find each other in that huge bed. She trooped into the bathroom and stood a moment, gaping at the incredible, utterly decadent tub. It was circular and deep, and there was some kind of a motor settled against one side. She hadn't the foggiest notion of what to do with that, and was thankful there was a separate shower stall. She quickly showered, then set about drying her hair and putting her face to rights.

Forty-five minutes later, dressed in wool slacks and a fitted long sweater with a gold belt at the waist, Daphne opened the bedroom door and peered out. She heard voices and laughter. Brant's mother was there, she thought, squaring her shoulders. She stepped into the small dining room.

"Hi," she said. "Forgive me for being so late. It took me quite a while to get my engine started."

Brant rose and came to her, smiling. "Morning, sweetheart. We've kept breakfast warm for you. You hungry?"

She nodded, flushing when he lightly kissed her in front of his mother.

"Sit down and get acquainted with your dragon mother-in-law, and I'll get you some eggs and bacon."

"Good morning, Daphne," Alice said. "Just ignore the Son of the Dragon and his big mouth. Are you feeling better today?"

"Yes, ma'am. Oh! I hadn't realized it yesterday, but Brant looks so much like you!"

"I'll take that as a compliment if it doesn't include huge shoulders and five-o'clock shadow. Now, tell me how you liked Kauai."

Brant stayed a bit longer in the kitchen than necessary, giving the two women time alone together. He heard the tension ease in Daphne's voice, heard her laugh. Such a sweet, clear sound. It made him feel good.

"Service from the chef," he said, setting her plate in front of her. "There's even tea, Daph."

She grinned up at him. "You the chef? I have this terrible feeling that we're going to starve."

Under Alice's skillful handling Daphne found herself talking about her life in England, Aunt Cloe, Lucilla and the minions at Asherwood. "Did Brant tell you we're going to invite Winterspoon to come over?" she asked, shyly smiling at her husband.

"Talk about culture, honey," his mother said, laughing at him. "I remember reading that all English valets were born with taste and snobbery."

"True enough," Brant said. "Even though you're a dowager something, he'll probably politely turn up his nose at you."

Alice encouraged Daphne to talk more about Hawaii, listening to her guileless enthusiasm and watching her closely when she referred something to Brant. They'll be quite good for each other, she thought. If Daphne wasn't yet in love with her husband, it would be just a matter of time. As for Brant, he seemed so…indulgent, gentle, protective.

Oddly enough, Alice felt herself wanting to protect this charming girl. No, Alice, she told herself sternly. She can't remain a girl. To live in Brant's world, she's going to have to be a woman and stand on her own two feet.

"Now," she said, when there was a lapse in the conversation, "let's talk about your Connecticut wedding."

Later Brant escorted the two women on a brief tour of New York. To avoid any vulturous press, they ate dinner at one of Brant's favorite Spanish restaurants down in the Village. Unfortunately, when they returned home, there were two men waiting for them in the underground garage. There was no way they could escape them.

"Glad you're home, Brant," one of the men said good-naturedly, easing his way carefully forward. "Is this the heiress? Hey, Mrs. Asher, give us a big smile!"

Daphne froze as a flashing light went off in her face. Suddenly she felt Alice Asher squeeze her hand. I am not Daphne the double bagger, she told herself fiercely, but somehow she couldn't make her muscles move into a smile. Alice said quickly, "My new daughter is very much enjoying New York and her new home. Everyone has been so, so…kind, haven't they, dear?"

Daphne nodded mutely. Why did her hair all of a sudden feel so stringy?

Brant tucked Daphne's hand through the crook of his arm. "Anything else, gentlemen?"

"Yeah. Mrs. Asher, Brant here got a real good deal when he married you, right? Would you like to comment on that, ma'am?"

Brant wanted to smash the man's face in, but he said calmly enough, "We both got a great deal, boys, but you're right. I don't think I've ever seen a prettier lady, have you?"

"Sure, Brant," one of the men said. He said in a carrying voice as he and his partner walked off. "If you like rich girls who are mutes."

Daphne felt tears sting her eyes. She'd let Brant down. Again. She'd acted like a stupid parrot who couldn't talk. I might not look like a double bagger, she thought, her shoulders slumped, but I still act like one.

"It's all right, dear," Alice said, patting her shoulder. "It will just take a bit more time for you to get used to things."

"She's right, Daph. Don't worry about the grubby bastards."

"I'm sorry," she mumbled.

"Don't be an ass," Brant said, ignoring his mother's gasp. "You're shy, Daph. I'll protect you. Just don't get depressed about it. Okay?"

She blinked back tears and nodded. Damn, she wasn't shy around Brant. Why did she have to be such a fool with strangers?

The ride up the elevator was a silent one. When they entered the condo Brant said in a too-hearty voice, "You haven't told me how much you like my house, Daph."

"I like your house a lot," she said.

"What I meant was our house, Daph. If you'd like to change anything, just let me know."

"I just wish there was a garden," she said, walking over to the huge picture window that looked out over Central Park. She gave a self-conscious laugh. "I'd been picturing acres of land. I didn't realize that New York was all buildings. Stupid of me, after all the pictures I've seen."

He frowned at the back of her head. "I suppose we could get a house in the country," he said.

It was a generous offer, but Daphne quickly shook her head. They already had a house in the country, in England.

"Well, my dears," Alice said, smiling at them. "I think I'm ready for bed. I'll see you both in the morning."

Brant kissed his mother good night, then turned toward his wife, who was still standing, staring out the window.

"The lights are beautiful, aren't they?" he said.

She nodded. He pulled her against him, gently kneading her shoulders. "Are you ready for bed, sweetheart?" He leaned down and began nibbling at her ear lobe.

She felt a surge of desire, but it was quickly dashed by her own feelings of inferiority. Was he just humoring her in bed? Was she as much of a failure making love as she was dealing with people? Angry at herself, and anxious to prove to herself that she could do something right, she turned in his arms and crushed herself against him. She stood on her tiptoes, cupped his face between her hands and kissed him.

Good Lord, Brant thought, a bit dazed by her enthusiastic attack. He locked his arms around her, cupping her hips in his hands to draw her closer. He felt her move her hips against him, and moaned into her mouth. "I want you now," he said. He picked her up in his arms and carried her into the bedroom, casting one eye toward his mother's room, thankful that the door was shut.

When he set her on her feet, she didn't let him go, but pulled him down on top of her on the bed. He didn't understand her urgency, but he was feeling near desperation himself, so it didn't matter. He pulled up her skirt, jerked off her panty hose and panties, and gave her what she needed. When she was trembling in the aftershock of pleasure, he jerked down his zipper and entered her warm body.

He lay heavily on top of her, rather stunned at his own violent reaction. He nuzzled her throat and said, "Will you let me go long enough to take my clothes off now?"

"All right," she said. Suddenly she hugged him tightly to her. "I was so afraid."

He eased up on his elbows so he could see her face. "Don't be afraid of those stupid media people. They're not worth it."

"No, not them," she said, biting down on her lower lip.

"Of what, sweetheart?"

"I was afraid that I would fail at everything. I did give you pleasure, didn't I?"

He felt a wave of pity for her, but forced himself to grin at her. "You wanna feel my heart? It's still galloping fast enough to be in the Kentucky Derby."

"So is mine," she said. "You are so nice, Brant."

"Don't forget it, Mrs. Asher. Now, how about taking a shower with me?"

"I think I'd prefer the tub with that engine in it."

Alice Asher left for Connecticut the following day to set the wedding plans into motion. Brant and Daphne would come the following weekend, as would Lily and Dusty. "To do the Deed," Brant said. "Again."

That evening, Brant and Daphne went to a formal dinner party given by a vice president of the ad agency doing Brant's sporting goods commercial. Daphne was wearing a new long gown of soft white chiffon and an emerald pendant Brant had bought her at Tiffany's. Mr. Morrison's house was on Long Island, and as Brant drove his Porsche out of Manhattan, he told Daphne about the people they would meet.

"Morrison's a short, balding, very nice man," he said. "The president of the sporting goods company is named Dicks, and the man's a shark. I just met him once, but not, thank God, in an alley or at the Stock Exchange. Speaking of the Stock Exchange," he continued nonstop, looking briefly toward his silent wife, "we'll go to the bank tomorrow and get your checking account set up. And you'll need credit cards in your name. Then we'll talk to my lawyer about transferring half the inheritance to you. Did I tell you how gorgeous you look tonight?''

''Yes,'' she said, turning slightly to give him a tentative smile. Like a damned puppy who's just wet on the carpet, he thought.

''Look, Daph, I know Max the doorman showed you the damned paper. Would you please just forget those toads? You'll like most of the people you'll meet tonight, I promise. Just be yourself, but don't treat any of the men like you do me, okay?''

That made her smile real. ''None of them could look nearly as lovely as you do. In fact, I sometimes have fantasies that you're starkers under your coat.''

''Sometimes…'' He laughed. ''I like that. You're going to be changing the New York idiom, sweetheart. Will you promise me one thing?''

I'd promise you anything you wanted, she thought. ''What?''

No, he thought quickly, don't caution her any more. He gave her a leering smile. ''Don't fall out of your gown. Your beautiful breasts are only for me.''

She flushed, laughed, and moved closer, sliding her hand up his thigh. She felt his muscles tighten under her fingers.

''Watch what you're doing lady, or we might find ourselves arrested for doing indecent things on the freeway.''

Forty-five minutes later they pulled into the large circular drive of the Morrisons' East Hampton home. They stepped through the front door and were inundated with noise from close to fifty guests. ''Just remember,'' Brant whispered in her ear, as their host and hostess approached them, ''you're the most beautiful woman here, and you're my wife.''

Daphne was reserved, but Mrs. Morrison decided that quality was typically English, and she smiled her approval. All that garbage in the newspapers was just that, she thought. Brant stuck to Daphne through all the introductions, and was relieved when she smiled up at him, completely at ease, and told him she was going to the loo.

Brant patted her arm and watched her walk gracefully to a maid and speak to her. She was doing so well. Her natural sense of humor was coming out, and the women as well as the men were warming to her. He began to look around for Marcie. He'd seen her earlier, and he wanted to talk to her. He couldn't find her.

Daphne was repairing her makeup in the large bathroom off the master suite when she heard a woman's cold voice say, "Well, if it isn't the little English flower. Alone at last."

Her hand jerked, and the lipstick ended up on her cheek. She turned slowly to face a gorgeous redheaded woman, gowned in silver lamé that accentuated every beautiful curve of her body.

"Hello," Daphne said as she wiped off the lipstick.

She's so damned young and pretty, Marcie thought, feeling a stab of jealousy, disappointment and fury. But what had she expected? A troll? "My name is Marcie Ellis. I'm a very close friend of Brant's."

"A pleasure, ma'am. My name is Daphne."

"Ma'am? I'm not that much older than you are. Daphne. What a...clever name, so unused nowadays." Marcie tossed her hair, a studied movement that showed off her long, graceful neck. "Oh yes, I know who you are. You're the stud's little bride."

Daphne felt every muscle in her body stiffen alarmingly. Marcie must be one of Brant's lovers. No, ex-lovers.

"So odd," Marcie continued, wishing she could toss a bottle of pink paint on Daphne's hair. "Brant marrying you so quickly. But then again, he always moves quickly when he wants something, whether it's a new car, a new woman or a good financial deal."

"If you'll excuse me, Miss Ellis," Daphne said, clutching her purse and inching toward the door.

"Tell me, Mrs. Asher, what do you do...profes-sionally?"

"Nothing," Daphne said flatly.

"Ah, the little house *frau*." She laughed. Her lower teeth weren't very straight, and it made Daphne feel better. There was a flaw. "I'll give Brant three months, and then, my dear, you'll be just like any of Brant's other possessions, and you can sit around with his silly antiques and gather dust."

"His antiques are lovely!"

"His lovely brass bed as well? Have you played in his Jacuzzi yet? He enjoys that."

She's treating me like Lucilla does, Daphne thought; she's nasty and condescending. She wanted to rage at the woman, but she could easily picture her in that awesome tub with Brant, frolicking about, and that wiped out any smart retort she could have made. How could he possibly want anything from her except the money? She felt flat-chested, dumpy and stupid. "I don't think you're very nice," she said, and fled from the bathroom, Marcie's laughter ringing in her ears.

Brant was in close conversation with two men, and she didn't consider interrupting him. She slipped onto the lighted patio and cursed herself silently. It was frigidly cold, but she didn't notice.

"Here now, Mrs. Asher. Don't want you to take a cold."

Mr. Morrison gently drew her back inside. "Someone has upset you," he said, eyeing her pale face. He caught a glimpse of Marcie Ellis and heaved a deep sigh. He wanted to comfort Daphne and tell her everything would be all right, but he wasn't stupid, and knew that was the last thing she needed. He said matter-of-factly, "You know, Mrs. Asher, your husband is in a high visibility position. And you, Brant told me, have lived all your life in the country. Most people, you know, are kind, and those who aren't usually have a reason. For example, take Marcie Ellis." She gave a start, but he continued blandly. "She is really a nice woman, but Brant's marriage gave her a nasty start. She and your husband were close, I suppose, but that has nothing to do with anything now. You have two choices, ma'am. Either you turn the other cheek and let her exhaust her venom, or you make a fist and punch her out. If you choose the latter, I hope you won't do it here," he added, giving her a wide grin. "I have high blood pressure, and such a sight just might topple me into the hereafter."

Daphne laughed, unable to keep it in. "Brant told me how kind you were, Mr. Morrison, but he didn't tell me how funny you were!"

"Call me Dan."

"I think you're safe tonight, Dan. I shan't punch her over."

"Out, Mrs. Asher. American slang."

"I'll remember that. You're very kind, sir. The habits of a lifetime are difficult to break, I think.'' She drew a deep breath and straightened her shoulders. ''It's time I stopped hiding behind Brant. I am, after all, a grown woman.''

''Quite grown, I'd say,'' Dan Morrison agreed.

Brant looked up to see his wife in close conversation with Dan Morrison.

''Well, Brant, is your wife that desperate?''

''Hello, Marcie. I tried to get you yesterday, but you were out. How's the news business?''

''All right, I suppose. You haven't given me that exclusive you promised, Brant.''

''How badly do you want it?''

She looked at him closely. He was tense, and his eyes glittered brightly. ''A knight in football armor, Brant? My, how ferocious you are! I gather you want to make a deal?''

''Yes, you could say that. No more crap, Marcie, and no more ridiculous attacks on my wife, or innuendos about the circumstances of our marriage. The straightforward, unvarnished truth. That's my deal.''

Marcie flinched when he said wife. ''I'll think about it,'' she said finally. ''You sure you want the unvarnished truth? As I understand it, unvarnished, it makes little green eyes a gold digger, and you, well...'' She turned to go, but couldn't resist saying over her shoulder, ''I personally found your *wife* about as interesting as a head of cabbage.''

Brant didn't ask Daphne about her conversation with Dan Morrison, and she didn't mention her scene with Marcie Ellis.

The next afternoon Brant was busily showing Daphne how to write a check and maintain a checkbook. He looked up at the sound of the doorbell, and frowned. ''Who the hell—'' he began.

When he opened the door, he took a step back at the sight of most of the Astros football team, complete with wives and champagne.

''Surprise!''

CHAPTER FOURTEEN

Have another glass of champagne, Daph.''

She smiled up at Tiny Phipps and thrust out her glass.

"I've always thought Brant's condo was huge," she said in some bewilderment. "Now, with all of you, it looks like a Liliputian's house bursting with Gulliver's."

"Yeah," said Lloyd Nolan, "we can't even run plays in here. You should see the place when all the players drop in."

"There are more of you?"

"Oh sure. It's the off-season now, and we couldn't round everybody up. So, Daph, what do you think of New York?"

"And football?"

"Yeah, you gotta see Dancer strut his stuff. We brought some tapes over for you"

She nodded enthusiastically. "I'd love it. Brant showed me just one back home."

"Lloyd wants you to admire *him*, too," said a lovely black woman, as she poked Lloyd in the ribs. "I'm Beatrice, his better half, but you don't have to remember it this time. You've got name overload, right?"

"Oh yes," Daphne said happily. "He's really called Dancer? He never told me that, although he was quite graceful when we danced a bit in Kauai—"

There was a hoot of laughter. Daphne felt a huge arm go around her shoulders and hug. "Ignore the fools, Daph," said "Choosy" Williams, a defensive lineman. "Your old man is called Dancer because he can scramble out of the pocket as well as Fran Tarkington. He doesn't want to get his beautiful body wrecked."

"I see," said Daphne with wide-eyed seriousness. "He does have a splendid body."

This guileless observation brought on fresh gales of laughter. Brant, in conversation with his coach, Sam Carverelli, looked over at the group surrounding his wife.

"You look like a fatuous bull," said Sam. "Lovely girl, Brant. And so at ease with everyone. I think Tiny is smitten."

She was at ease, completely at ease, Brant thought, and with a bunch of football players. And their wives, he added to himself, as he watched Cindy Williams lean over to whisper something in Daphne's ear. He couldn't believe it. He heard more champagne corks popping.

He blinked when his wife and a dozen or so players and wives left the living room.

"We're going to show her one of your famous plays, Brant!" Guy Richardson shouted across the room. "You know, the one where you tried a quarterback sneak and got creamed."

When Brant entered the den nearly a half an hour later he saw his wife sitting cross-legged on the floor in front of the TV, surrounded by the women. The men were draped over every piece of furniture in the room.

"Watch this pass, Daph," Lloyd was saying. "Sixty yards and right into my arms."

There was loud cheering when Lloyd trotted across into the end zone for a score, with Daphne's voice one of the loudest.

"How does he keep the ball from wobbling when he throws it so far?" she asked.

"Technique, darlin', technique," Lloyd said.

"He's got lots of that!"

"He sure seems to," said Daphne.

"Come on now, Nolan," Sam Carverelli scolded. "Look, Daphne," he said, showing her a football he'd pulled from the closet. "You have to handle the ball like this. See the seam? Look how I'm holding it. Here, you try it."

"Right over here, Daph," called Lloyd, backing to the far corner of the den.

She flung the ball at him, and he caught it against his chest. He gave a mighty "Ummph," and staggered backward.

"If he hadn't caught it, it would have ended up in Central Park," said Tiny, the self-appointed champagne pourer.

"Talented lady," Beatrice said to Brant.

He grinned. "Small hands, but yes, very talented."

"I love it when you talk dirty, Brant," Tiffy Richardson giggled.

Brant looked over her very pregnant stomach and said blandly, "Talk is cheap, by the looks of it."

"Look at that sweep around the right end!"

Brant blinked. The words had come from his English wife's mouth, and her eyes were glued to the TV screen.

"Oh, Brant, watch out!"

"Sorry, old buddy," Ted Hartland, the center, said, wincing as Brant was tackled by three of the Patriots' players.

"What a mess that play was," said Sam. "You nearly got a cracked rib out of that one, Brant."

Daphne turned to stare up at him. Brant dropped to his haunches. "I wasn't hurt, love. Just a bit black and blue. It's all part of the game, particularly when these idiots turn blind and clumsy on me."

"She doesn't want you to hurt your splendid body, Brant," said Nolan.

"All of you have splendid bodies," Daphne said. "You must be more careful, every one of you. Don't you agree, Beatrice?"

"I sure do. I can't count the times Lloyd comes home looking like a reject from a bruise factory."

"I bet he moans a lot to get sympathy," said Sam.

A good-natured argument between the men and women ensued about machoness and how it lasted only until the players got home. "Then he dissolves like a little boy," said Tiffy. "And Guy hardly ever gets tackled, 'cause he's the kicker."

"But the pain, watching the rest of the guys taking blows," Guy said, rubbing his ribs.

Brant sat on the floor beside Daphne, but he let the other guys tell her about the plays. She's like a sponge, he thought, seeing first confusion in her eyes at an explanation, then understanding. And if she didn't understand, she asked. This is my family, he thought, and she fits right in.

"Hey, Brant, you got a chalkboard?"

He looked up at Lloyd Nolan. "Sorry," he said. "Why?"

"Daph wants to see a double reverse."

"We'll wait for a nice day, then show her everything she wants to see in the park. Would you like to learn touch football, Daph?"

Tiny beamed at her when she nodded enthusiastically.

"You really lucked out," Tiffy Richardson said in a lowered voice to Brant. "We were all so worried."

Brant cocked an eyebrow at her. "Show of support? Or did all of you want to see if I'd married a cretin for money?"

"Well, the most obnoxious innuendoes were from Marcie, of course, and everybody figured she would slant things in the worst possible light. Daphne is..." Tiffy paused, then continued thoughtfully. "She brings out the protective instincts in one, doesn't she? I've never seen the guys so, well...careful. She seems like a lovely girl, Brant."

"Yes," he said, "she is."

"I love listening to her talk. I guess most Americans get off on an English accent."

"Particularly when she talks about a sweep around the right end?" He tried to mimic her accent, and they burst into laughter.

"Oh, Sam," they heard her call out to the coach, "you shouldn't pull your hair like that! It's just one play that went awry."

Guy Richardson showed her the final few minutes of the playoff game they'd lost to the Steelers, all the while explaining to her how their...darned kicker had missed two field goals before this.

She was indignant, hissing with the rest of them at the loss. "That's disgusting! You're the much better kicker, Guy. I'm so sorry." She turned to her husband and hugged him fiercely, surprising him. "Next season you'll demolish them. I promise."

The Astros didn't leave until nearly midnight. Tiny ordered in a dozen pizzas, and Brant watched with the fondness of a proud parent as Daphne laughed when they teased her mercilessly about the anchovies.

Nor did they leave until the wreckage was cleaned up. Daphne was hugged until her ribs ached. When the door closed for the last time she turned to Brant and flung her arms around his waist. "I'm so happy! I've never met so many nice people."

"You're tipsy," he said, running his hands up and down her back.

"Not that tipsy," she said, raising her face, her lips parting.

He kissed the tip of her nose and led her into the bedroom. When she was naked, her turned her onto her stomach, smiling when she looked at him questioningly over her shoulder. "Trust me," he said, leaning down to nip the nape of her neck. He moved deeply into her, and she moaned softly, wriggling beneath him as his hands stroked her breasts and belly. He realized vaguely that she didn't have her doctor's appointment until the following day, but when he tried to pull out of her, she twisted onto her back and held him deep within her.

"Sweetheart," he said desperately, "don't move." But his fingers found her, caressed her, and she jerked upward. "I can't stop," he said, his voice ragged.

"I can feel it," she gasped. "I'm filled with you."

Rippling, wild feelings surged through him, making him oblivious of everything except the warmth of her and the mindless depth of his pleasure.

"Only with you," he said. "Only with you."

In the next instant he was asleep.

What, Daphne wondered, dazed by her own passion, had he meant by that? She curled against him, listened to her galloping heart slow to normal, and fell asleep, replete with happiness.

"I would like to write you a check," Daphne said to the clerk in Lord and Taylor. She and Brant had just come from her doctor, and he had told her they should celebrate. The diaphragm would be ready in two days. The boots on sale in the display window drew them both in. Daphne's were a wreck.

"Certainly, ma'am," the saleswoman said. "Wouldn't you like to have a Lord and Taylor credit card? It's much easier, you know."

Daphne wondered where Brant was. He'd quickly approved her selection of the new leather boots, then wandered off.

"A credit card," she repeated. She'd never owned a credit card in her life. Suddenly it seemed the most important thing in the world. "Yes," she said, "I would like one."

"Excellent. Ah, Mrs. Asher, I'm certain your credit will be approved." She directed Daphne to the sixth floor. That was where Brant found her some twenty minutes later.

She was sitting very straight in the chair opposite a rather tired-looking man whose glasses kept slipping down his nose. He heard the man say, "You will need your husband's approval, Mrs. Asher, and, as I said, his signature."

"But all you have to do is speak to Mr. Edward Caufield, the broker. The card is for me, as I told you, not for my husband."

"Mrs. Asher..." The man was beginning to sound out of patience. "Ma'am, it's policy. You have no income of your own."

"Is there a problem?" Brant asked, stepping into Daphne's line of vision.

The man looked ready to embrace Brant with relief. "Mr. Asher? You're the football player, aren't you? A pleasure, sir." He quickly rose and shook Brant's hand. "We just need your signature, and some information for the application form."

Brant had two major credit cards, and had no wish for another one, but he saw the strained look in Daphne's eyes and quickly succumbed. "Of course," he said, seating himself beside his wife.

He realized that he'd totally misunderstood the situation when she said abruptly, "I want the credit card in my name, not his."

Mr. Reeves sighed and tried again. "Mrs. Asher, I can't imagine that credit is handled that differently in England. Of course you can have a card in your name; it is just that the major account will be in your husband's name. It is his responsibility—"

"No, Mr. Asher doesn't want a Lord and Taylor card. Only I do! *I* will be writing you checks to pay for purchases, not him."

"Ma'am, you have no major, steady source of income." He sent a pleading look at Brant. "You have no job and no credit record."

Damnation, Brant thought, what the hell was he supposed to do now? Daphne looked ready to spit nails. He said as calmly as he could, "My wife does have an income of her own. A thousand dollars a month is deposited into her account. Now, let's get this bloody application filled out.''

She was back to an allowance. Although she had over two hundred thousand dollars in investments, arranged two days previously by Brant's broker, all she could prove was that she had quarterly incoming interest from the investments. She bit her tongue, rage flowing through her. Rage at herself for being so utterly worthless. She rose jerkily to her feet, clutching her purse in front of her like a weapon. "I don't want your credit card, Mr. Reeves. I am going to go downstairs and write a check for my purchase."

"Daphne, wait," Brant began, but she was marching out of the office, her shoulders squared like a militant…whatever.

He looked back at Mr. Reeves. "Maybe some other time," he said, and left. The man's commiserating look made Brant want to strangle Daphne.

Daphne wished she had never even seen the damned boots, but she wrote out the check, her very first with elaborate care, and thumped it next to the saleswoman's cash register.

"May I please see your driver's license and a major credit card, Mrs. Asher?"

Daphne looked at her blankly. "What?"

"Since you don't have an account with us, ma'am, I need to see ID with your check. It's store policy."

Brant arrived in time for this exchange. He closed his eyes a moment, wishing he were playing football in California. Hell, he'd even settle for Alaska. It was his own fault. It hadn't occurred to him that she would need ID to write checks.

"I don't have any ID," Daphne said through gritted teeth.

The saleswoman looked at her helplessly. "I understand, ma'am, that you're new in this country. Let me speak to the manager, unless, of course, your husband could provide—" She broke off at Daphne's furious glare and fled.

She was smart enough to escape the impending eruption, Brant thought. He gently laid his hand on Daphne's arm. He could feel her trembling through her coat sleeve. "I forgot," he said. "I'm sorry. We'll get you ID this week."

Her contacts itched with the wretched tears welling up, and she dashed her hand across her eyes, inevitably dislodging a contact. A lime green dot of plastic fell on the counter. She cursed, and Brant was so surprised that he laughed.

"I hate you," she said, her voice low and trembling. "I don't want these damned boots. I don't want anything, do you hear?" She managed to pick up the contact, then left him standing at the counter, feeling like an utter fool. He was aware of pitying glances from other customers.

"I'm sorry, Mr. Asher," the saleswoman said, "but I will have to have your check instead. Or a credit card?"

Brant silently wrote out a check. When the boots were packaged, he went to stand outside the women's room. His wait was a long one, and he was beginning to think that Daphne had left before he'd gotten there. Five minutes later she emerged, her head down, her knitted hat pulled low over her forehead.

"Let's go ice-skating," he said, taking her arm in a firm grasp.

"You have an appointment, don't you?" she asked, not looking up at him.

"The appointment can wait. I'll make a phone call."

They went ice-skating at Rockefeller Center, and Brant watched her take all her frustration out on the ice. She was a very good skater, very graceful, and he was thankful. On the taxi ride back to their building he said calmly, "Tomorrow we're going to get you a New York driver's license."

"I'm sure you won't mind my taking the test in your Porsche?" she said sarcastically.

The thought of anyone but himself driving the Porsche in New York traffic chilled him, but he said nothing.

"What if I wreck your bloody car? I don't have any ID. I don't have any auto insurance. And they won't even accept my check!"

Thank heaven the cab pulled up in front of their building at that moment, and he was saved by having to search for the cab fare.

He said nothing until they were safely inside the condo. He tossed the package containing the infamous boots on the sofa. "All right, we're going to talk, Daph. No more snide remarks from you, no more infantile behavior.''

She had the utter nerve to walk away from him into the kitchen. How anticlimactic to argue in front of the sink, he thought, glaring at the back of her head. He watched her drink a glass of water.

"Are you quite through now?" he asked.

"No. I want to go to the bathroom."

"Convenient cause and effect," he muttered. He followed her through the bedroom and stopped abruptly when the bathroom door was slammed in his face.

A wife, he thought, striding back into the living room, is a pain in the butt. He was trying to smooth things out for her, and all he got in return was childish anger and scenes. He was well lathered up when she came into the living room some ten minutes later.

"I'm fed up with you," he said, erupting. "I should have married a woman, not some naive, silly girl whose only claim to anything is her performance in bed." Unfair, he raged at himself once the words were out, but he wouldn't take them back. He'd finally gotten her attention.

Daphne stared at him, her eyes darkening with anger.

"If you start on me again, I'm leaving. Now, do you want to talk like two reasoning adults or continue to carry on? And don't you shake your head at me!" He grasped her shoulders and shook her slightly. "Well?" he demanded.

"I should go get dinner started," she said.

"Oh? Burned tuna casserole? Cold scrambled eggs?" He plowed distracted fingers through his hair. "Damn it, I'm sorry, I didn't mean that. Come here and sit down. Now."

She curled up at one end of the long sofa and looked straight ahead at a pink marble sculpture of a naked woman on a side table.

"Daph," he said, drawing on his patience, "what happened today was unfortunate. There was no reason for you to freak out like that. It's no big deal. We'll get your ID, and you'll be free to shop anywhere you want to and write a zillion checks. What else do you want?"

"I want to go home," she said, then realized how stupid it all was, and gave a nervous laugh. "No, that's not true. I just feel so...useless."

"Useless! You're my wife! Or are you beginning to regret marrying me now?"

"No, it's not that," she said unhappily, feeling stupid and inarticulate, and guilty. It wasn't his fault, after all, that she couldn't do what any normal adult person could. How could he ever think that she'd regret having married him? He was the one with the cross to bear. She licked her dry lips. "It's just—" Just what? she wanted to yell at herself.

"Please spare me any psychological crap about not knowing who you are and wanting to search out your identity in the scheme of life."

"All right, but it's not psychological! I'll spare you everything. Don't you have an appointment soon?"

"Yes," he said, rising abruptly. "I do. When I get back, we'll go out to dinner."

She watched him helplessly as he shrugged into his beautiful leather coat and slammed out the front door.

She wandered around the house before settling in the den. She turned on the VCR and put in a video of one of Brant's football games. She felt pleasure begin to flow through her at the excitement of the plays. "That," she said to the empty room, "was a draw play. It didn't work, but it was a good call."

CHAPTER FIFTEEN

Welcome, my dears," said Alice Asher, embracing first Daphne, then Brant. "The house is filled to bursting! Come in quickly, it's so cold outside. Isn't the snow lovely? Here, let me take your coats. And, Daphne, I have quite a surprise for you."

Surprise wasn't the word for it. Daphne stared first at Winterspoon, then at Aunt Cloe, and burst into tears.

"Little egg!" Cloe exclaimed. "What is all this nonsense? Come here and let me give you a big hug. I brought you a reminder of England, that's all. Hush now." She held the slender body tightly against her, meeting Brant's eyes over Daphne's head. He shrugged and said, "Welcome, Aunt Cloe, and you, Winterspoon. I hope your trip wasn't too tiring?"

"Very tolerable, my lord," Winterspoon said.

"Actually, Brant," Cloe said, a pronounced twinkle in her eyes, "Mr. Winterspoon and I inbibed freely across the Atlantic and arrived with vacuous smiles on our faces! Thank you so much for sending the tickets."

Daphne turned in Cloe's arms to look at her husband. "You arranged for them to come?"

"Yes," he said, his eyes intent on her face. "I thought it would please you."

All she could do for the moment was gape at him. In the next instant she hurled herself against him, burying her face against his throat. "That's more like it," he whispered against her temple. The past three days had been tense and strained, except when they were in bed, and Brant had decided the more time in bed, the better. He'd held off since they were married, giving her time to adjust to him sexually. But not during the past three days. To his delight and relief, she'd responded enthusiastically, even though he knew she must be sore. When he'd pointed out that fact she'd moaned softly, telling him she didn't care.

"I don't hate you anymore," she whispered back. "I think you are a very nice man."

"Thank you, love. You've ravished my poor body at least ten times during the past few days. Maybe you should continue hating me. I like the result."

"I'll ravish you even more now, I promise."

"All right, you two love birds," Alice Asher said. "In an hour we're going to have Lily, Dusty and the kids invading us from Houston."

"How are they getting here from New York, Mom?"

Alice laughed. "Silly question, Brant. By limo, of course. Now, I would suggest that you and Daphne get unpacked and prepare yourselves. Cloe, Mr. Winterspoon, why don't we have a cup of tea?"

"Oscar, ma'am."

"Good heavens, Mr. Winterspoon," Cloe said exuberantly, "what a bloody noble name!"

"Thank you, Mrs. Sparks."

"Cloe, sir. After all, we are in America now."

Brant nibbled Daphne's ear as they walked upstairs to his old bedroom. "You didn't forget your diaphragm, did you?"

She slanted him a look that made him instantly horny. "I think," she said primly, "that it's going to be worn out by next week."

"Lord, wouldn't that be a trip! Just think of the look on your doctor's face. I'd have to fight her off with a two-by-four."

"She's fifty-five, Brant."

"With a stick, then?"

"Conceited jerk."

"Just think of it—I'd probably be written up in medical journals. How's this for a title of the article?" He leaned over and whispered in her ear.

"Ten hard what?" she said.

Alice, downstairs in the living room, smiled at the sound of her son's hearty laughter.

* * *

The dining room was crammed with food and laughter, adults and boisterous children.

"You're much more beautiful than Brant led me to believe," Lily said after she'd spooned a good helping of green beans on her daughter's plate.

"What a thing to say, darlin'," Dusty said. "I think the good ole boys in Houston would go stark raving mad at the sight of her."

"Well, I didn't mean it the way it came out," Lily said.

"You never do," said Brant. "Lily's got an uncensored brain," he added to Daphne.

But Daphne was gazing at Dusty, fascinated by his accent. "Could you say something else, please, Dusty?"

"After dinner I'll sing y'all a western song, how's that, ma'am?"

"His favorite is 'Flushed Down the Toilet of her Heart' or something exquisitely literate like that."

"This gal ain't got no taste," Dusty said, drawling even more to please his English audience.

"I'd love to hear you sing anything," Daphne said.

"Have some more chicken, dear," Alice said. "You've scarcely touched your dinner."

"I agree," Brant said. "You've got to keep up your strength, sweetheart."

She smiled at him happily, but turned to Cloe. "You must go to Hawaii, to Kauai! It's so beautiful, and everyone is so nice!"

"I bet you wrung their withers in that orange bikini," Cloe said.

"Lord," Brant said, "I had to hire an armed guard to keep the men away."

"Did you really, Uncle Brant?" eight-year-old Keith asked, his fork suspended between plate and mouth.

"Sure I did. All women."

"Brant, don't lie to him," Lily said. "Only half the guard were women, Keith."

"I say, madam," Winterspoon said politely, "this is a very tasty dish. I trust you will give me your recipe."

"Certainly, Oscar," said Alice Asher. "You plan to cook for Brant and Daphne?"

"Of course. Her ladyship was rarely allowed near the kitchen at Asherwood."

"Now, Winterspoon," Brant said firmly, "no more lordships or ladyships. This is America. Plus, it's damned embarrassing."

"I love it," said Lily. "Oh dear, I forgot to curtsey!"

"When does training begin, Brant?" Dusty asked.

"Too soon, I'm afraid. In about four months. We'll be training in upstate New York, and the humidity is enough to knock your socks off."

"How 'bout that commercial, brother?"

"You'll be seeing my handsome puss on TV next week, I think. And, Lily, it's sporting goods, not underwear or shaving cream."

"Well, underwear might be okay. What do you think, Daphne? Would you mind millions of women seeing Brant in his European boxers?"

"Oh no," Daphne burst out. "He's so beautiful—" She skidded to a stop, color flooding her cheeks.

Brant leaned over and whispered in her ear, "But, love, you've rarely seen me in underwear."

"What are you saying, Uncle Brant?" asked Patricia.

"I was just telling your Aunt Daphne that she's got great taste."

"Daphne sure is a funny name," said Danny.

"You can call me Daph. Your uncle does."

"That sounds like Daffy Duck," said Keith.

"Who's Daffy Duck?" asked Daphne.

The English contingent listened with great interest to Keith's convoluted description before Dusty interrupted, chuckling, "Let's keep your new aunt out of cartoons, okay son?"

"Are you and Uncle Brant going to have kids soon?" Patricia asked.

The green beans suddenly lodged in Daphne's throat, and she grabbed at her glass of water. Brant lightly thumped her on the back.

"Yeah," Keith said, adding his two cents. "We'd like some cousins."

"You all right, sweetheart?" Brant asked. At her strangled nod, he turned to his nephew and nieces. "Hey, you guys, it's hard work. What do you think, Daph?"

The ball's in your court, his wicked look told her. He loved her scarlet flush, the curse of all blondes. To his surprise she said, "Actually, I'd love some kids. But your uncle is a very busy man, you know. You'll have to be patient with him."

Brant was so surprised, he blurted out, "But I didn't think that you wanted...that is, you seem to..."

"He did the same thing on the first ten takes for the commercial," Daphne said, lying fluently as she patted his arm. "When he gets nervous, or excited, or surprised, he can't cope with words."

"Good grief, boy," Dusty said. "I never knew that. Always thought you were as slick as a pair of wet boots."

"I did, too," said Brant. His voice held humor, but there was none in his eyes as they searched his wife's face.

Alice cleared her throat. "Tell me, Cloe, how long do you plan to stay with us?"

"Well, I simply must meet all those lovely football players. If they all look like your son..." She gave a delighted shudder, her eyes sparkling.

"They are all marvelous, Aunt Cloe," Daphne said.

"As in huge with great...physiques?"

"Yes, ma'am. But I'm not sure you should meet them all at once."

"Yeah, we don't want you to have cardiac arrest, Cloe," Brant said.

"Dead right, sir," said Oscar.

Reverend Oakes's wedding ceremoney, held in the ultramodern presbyterian church in Stamford the following morning, was simple, elegant and blessedly short. Daphne wore a pale yellow wool dress, and Brant a dark suit. "Do you feel doubly married now?" he asked as he lightly brushed her lips at the close of the service.

"I feel scared to death," Daphne said.

"Why? You know what I'm going to do to that gorgeous body of yours." She didn't laugh as he'd expected her to, but he didn't have time to ask her what was going on in her lovely head.

The children, on their best behavior up to this point, could no longer contain themselves, and clutched at their uncle's arms.

"Mom said you'd never get married, Uncle Brant," Keith said. "Now you've done it twice."

"And to the same lady," said Patricia.

"Yeah, Mom said you like to play the field, but I told her you had to 'cause you're a football player."

"Out of the mouths of little heathens," said Lily. "Congratulations, Daphne," she said, hugging her sister-in-law. "Are you going to drag Brant back to Hawaii?"

"Actually," Brant said, "I'm going to drag her back to England. We've got lots of work to do on Asherwood. What do you think, sweetheart?"

"Yes," she said quietly, not meeting his eyes.

"You and I are going to have a nice, long talk," Brant said firmly. He turned away to speak to Reverend Oakes.

Because they weren't, strictly speaking, newlyweds, Brant spent the afternoon showing Cloe and Winterspoon over Stamford and the surrounding area. He and his bride had no time alone until late that evening.

"No," he said, watching her from the bed, "no nightgown. You won't need it. I'll keep you warm." He patted the bed beside him. "Come here, Daph."

She started to slip off her bra, then leaned over to flip off the bedroom lamp. "No," Brant said, "leave it on. I want to see you."

She hesitated perceptibly, and he frowned. "Daph, I know your body almost as well as my own. What's the matter, sweetheart?"

She shook her head, and turned her back to slip out of her underwear.

"Nice view," he said. "I love those long legs of yours and that cute little—"

"Brant!" She quickly moved into the bed and pulled the covers to her chin.

He was balanced on his elbow, studying her profile. "All right," he said seriously, "enough. No more jokes. Tell me what's wrong."

She shook her head, not looking at him.

"Daph, I'm not going to ravish you until you tell me what's in that mind of yours."

Without warning she threw herself against him, burying her face in his shoulder. He felt her trembling, felt her hands clutching at his back.

"Sweetheart," he said quietly against her hair. "What's all this? Please, talk to me."

She whispered against his throat, "You went through the ceremony today like…like you really wanted to."

He became very still, his hands halting their stroking down her back. "Of course," he said. "What did you expect? That I'd take one look at you and call a screeching halt? We're already married, Daph. This was for my mother."

"You're making the best of a bad bargain."

His hands cupped her buttocks, drawing her closer. "If this is a bad bargain, then certainly pigs will fly, quite soon."

"You'd enjoy sex with any woman, and you know it. You'll be bored with me soon enough."

"Why?"

She raised her head at his bald question. His eyes were resting intently on her face, his eyebrow arched upward. "Because I'm stupid, and make you furious and you're stuck with me."

"You're anything but stupid, yes, and like glue."

"You want to go back to Asherwood because I embarrass you here."

He whistled softly. "So that's what's going on. You're such an idiot, Daphne. Sexy, sweet, but an idiot. I want to go back to Asherwood because I love the place, and I thought you did, too. It's our other home now, and I don't want to neglect it. I never did get to refinish the wainscotting in the library."

"But I'm useless! You don't want to have children with me because that would mean you'd have to stay married to me!"

He didn't say anything. She felt his fingers stroking down her belly to between her thighs.

"What are you doing?" she gasped.

She felt his finger easing inside her, and she tried to jerk away, confused.

"Hold still," he said sharply. "Ah, just a bit further. Here we go. A pity, now we won't have the chance to wear out your diaphragm. I was kinda looking forward to being a new entry in the *Guinness Book of Records*."

She heard it thump onto the floor.

"I don't understand! Why did you do that?"

"We're going to make a baby so I'll be stuck with you forever."

"But you don't want to! You're just doing this because...you're honorable!"

"God, you're warm and soft." She squirmed as his fingers moved downward again, gently probing, stroking, driving her crazy. "Brant!"

"Stop bleating and kiss me. I love to feel you, and in just a few minutes, after you calm down, I'm going to kiss every inch of you."

"You make me sound like a goat," she giggled.

"I'm definitely the goat. I've wanted you all day, Mrs. Asher."

She felt him hard and velvet soft against her thighs. "What was it you said about ten hard—"

He kissed her deeply, easing between her legs and pressing upward.

"You," she gasped, feeling the swamping sensations build in her belly, "are an oversexed man."

"Lord yes," he said. "Aren't you glad?"

Her soft moan was her answer, and he smiled, loving the glazed look in her eyes. "There's quite a bit to be said about awakening a sleeping beauty."

He moved inside her, and felt her muscles tighten convulsively around him. He cursed softly and withdrew from her, his breathing ragged. She tried to bring him into her again, but he whispered,

"No, love, not yet. You've blasted my control. I'll leave you if I'm inside you."

"But—"

"Hush, let me make you feel as I do." She opened to him as he caressed her with his mouth, knowing that the marvelous feelings would build and build until she wanted to die with the force of them. When her whimpers became cries, she felt his hand gently covering her mouth. Then his mouth replaced his hand as he eased over her, and she was frantic with the feel of him deep inside her. She moaned into his mouth, whispering brokenly.

Daphne thought the world a most perfect place when she stared up into her husband's face as his own pleasure overtook him. He moaned through his gritted teeth, his head thrown back, his body arched upward.

Brent knew his weight was too much for her, but he didn't have the strength to move. "You are my wife," he said, the simple words mirroring the warm, incredibly tender feelings welling up within him. "My wife."

"Yes," she said, pulling him down to kiss him again.

They listened to each other's breathing slow and even out. Brant said, "I've never made love to another woman in this bedroom."

"I trust not," she said dryly.

He rolled off her onto his back, and turned off the light. When he felt her head on his shoulder, he said, aloud, "No."

"No what?" she asked on a satisfied yawn, snuggling closer against him.

"No, we can't leave for England right away. Aunt Cloe's got to meet the Astros."

"Do you think they'll survive her?"

"I can't wait to find out."

CHAPTER SIXTEEN

Tiny Phipps looked shell shocked. He grabbed a beer and threw back his head. Daphne stared at his massive neck, fascinated by the play of muscles as he downed the entire can.

After he lowered the bottle and swiped his mouth with the back of his hand, Daphne asked, her expression deadpan, "Did you enjoy meeting my Aunt Cloe, Tiny?"

"Daph, she patted my butt and told me I was really a cute hunk!" He looked like a little boy who couldn't quite grasp the complexities of the adult world.

Daphne laughed heartily. "Well, you are, Tiny. My aunt has excellent taste. She just learned the word 'hunk' and is simply practicing it on all appropriate males."

"But she's old enough to be my mother. My grandmother!"

"The term 'dirty old man' applying here, guys?" Brant asked.

"With a change in gender," Daphne said. She looked over at her aunt, who was now in avid conversation with Lloyd Nolan and Sam Carverelli. "They'll all survive," she said. "In fact, Sam is giving her the same look he gave Gus Colima after you guys beat the Rams."

"What a game that was," Tiny said. "Brant passed for over three hundred yards."

"I know," Daphne said. "And a seventy-two yarder for a touchdown."

"How 'bout another drink, Daph?" Beatrice asked.

"Not for me or I'll fall asleep before everyone even gets here. Wonderful party, Beatrice. I love your house. It's so rustic and homey and huge."

"Thank you. Lloyd has always had this thing for rocks and glass. It was close, but I managed to talk him out of a rock bathtub."

She rolled her eyes. "But the glass, well, have you seen the bedroom?"

"I thought I'd haul Daphne in there in a little while and give her a demonstration," Brant said.

"What kind of demonstration would you do with glass?" Daphne asked. "You mean glass blowing?"

There was a spate of laughter, and Brant moaned.

"Little egg," Cloe said, "what's all this about mirrors in bedrooms?"

"Well," Daphne said, "I'm not really sure. I'm being laughed at; that's the only thing I'm really certain of."

Cloe said to Tiny, "Why don't you show me? Come, my boy, let's do it now." She thrust her arm through Tiny's and dragged him away. "What lovely, monstrous muscles, my dear," Daphne heard her say fondly to her captive.

The doorbell rang. "More folk," Beatrice said. "Excuse me, guys."

Daphne was admiring the beautiful view through the French doors when she felt Brant stiffen beside her.

"What the hell!" he said softly. She turned to see Marcie Ellis come into the living room on the arm of a man she'd never seen before.

"Who is he?" she asked, but her eyes were on the beautiful woman at his side, who looked both flamboyant and elegant in a moss-green jump suit. She felt her hair begin to turn stringy, and her front teeth turn crooked.

"Matt Orson, the defensive coach. It looks like Marcie is really doing a number this time. Oh...damn! They've brought along a photographer."

He shot Daphne a worried look, and she knew he was concerned that she'd shatter again under pressure. And make him look like a fool. And make her look like a moron.

"Well, it looks like old home week," she heard Marcie say to Beatrice.

"We've got a couple of new faces," said Lloyd. "Have you met Daphne? And her aunt, Mrs. Sparks, here from England to visit?"

"Immigration seems to be getting out of hand," Marcie said in a carrying voice as her eyes met Daphne's. "I suspect all things foreign will return home soon enough. Perhaps I'd best do my interview with Brant here, before he's turned loose on New York's women again."

Oh God, Lloyd thought, so that's the lay of the land, is it? Spare me a cat fight. He shot a look at Matt Orson, who merely shrugged. Lloyd wondered if Matt knew he was being used. Probably so, he wasn't a fool.

"Little egg, how very fascinating, to be sure," said Cloe, coming up behind Daphne. "She's quite lovely, of course, but nothing compared to you," she added, not missing a beat.

"I agree," said Brant easily, but he looked as tense as a man facing a firing squad.

"I can't wait to talk to her," Cloe remarked. "Perhaps she'll be more of a challenge than Lucilla. More wit, I think. Buck up, Daphne! It's about time you realized you had my outrageous blood in your veins."

"She was Brant's lover before he came to England," Daphne said in a low voice to Cloe.

"So! Dear boy, please fetch me a glass of white wine. Thank you." After Brant moved away reluctantly, Cloe continued, "I never thought Brant would bed a woman who wasn't a looker. If you'd but realize it, little egg, this could be most amusing. You are the wife, you know."

"Yes," Daphne said slowly, her eyes widening, "I am, aren't I? And I can also write checks and balance a checkbook. I'll have my driver's license soon. And a Lord and Taylor credit card."

"Sounds like the top of the heap to me," said Cloe.

"Well, well, so the wolf left the little shepherd unprotected."

"Hello, Marcie," Daphne said. "This is my Aunt Cloe, from England."

"Scotland, actually," said Cloe. "You're a journalist, aren't you, Marcie?"

How did Aunt Cloe know that? Daphne wondered.

Fluttering old lady, Marcie thought. She smiled. "Yes, and I hope to get the true story from Brant today. His being suddenly a lord, a husband, and a castle owner.''

"I dare say Daphne here can tell you all about it," said Cloe, her voice utterly complacent. "I can't say exactly what Brant thinks of being a lord, but he adores being a husband and a castle owner." Cloe shook her head and patted Marcie's hand in a fond, maternal gesture. "I've never before seen a man so smitten. Of course, he had to cut out all her admirers first."

Daphne did her best not to drop her jaw in surprise at her aunt's words.

"I suppose it's natural enough for an heiress to have many men around," Marcie said. She didn't want to revise her opinion of the old lady, but...

Daphne laughed. "An heiress! That's one thing Brant should have corrected immediately. I'm surprised, Marcie, that Brant didn't tell *you*, of all people. I didn't have a *sou*, a dime even."

Marcie, who had pulled a pencil and pad out of her purse, looked as if she'd just swallowed the eraser. "What do you mean?"

"Why, just what I said, of course." Daphne gave her what she hoped was an evil smile. Her pulse was racing, but not with fear.

"But Brant told me before he left for England that he'd inherited only the title and a moldering old house."

Maybe a bit of fear, then. She shrugged. "English solicitors are notorious for keeping little tidbits of information back until they meet their clients face to face. Brant didn't know about me, either."

"I see," said Marcie, who didn't see at all. She watched Brant approach, a glass of wine in his hand.

Cloe laughed indulgently. "It took him little time to rectify that situation. Ah, my boy, thank you for the wine. Daphne here was just telling the journalist lady that she was poor as a beggar, and not the heiress everyone thought. Love at first sight it was when Brant laid eyes on her. I really didn't believe such a thing existed. Of course, when I met Mr. Sparks, and he took me for a drive in the moonlight, well..."

"Very nearly," Brant said easily. "Remember, Daph? I was

working on the roof and turned to see your gorgeous legs coming out of a cab? I nearly expired in the gutter.''

Marcie, who was endowed with a pair of the nicest legs in New York, said tightly, ''But you always were a leg man, weren't you, darling?''

Brant grinned. ''That and other things.'' He wrapped his arm around Daphne's shoulders. ''All of which my beautiful wife has, in abundance.''

Marcie was aware of the old lady's eyes resting on her face and started. The old bird was looking at her with pity! Marcie wanted to spit. ''What do you intend doing now that you're in America?'' she asked Daphne.

''Get a driver's license and run Brant's Porsche into the ground.''

There was a crack of laughter behind Marcie. Matt Orson said, ''What's this, Brant? You never let anyone drive the Porsche.''

Brant, who had no great enthusiasm for Daphne's plans, merely shrugged. ''You should see her behind the wheel. She stops traffic.'' He looked thoughtfully at his wife. ''Perhaps I should get you your own car.''

''A station wagon to cart around all the kiddies?'' Marcie said, wishing that she could leave this wretched party and forget that she ever decided to marry Brant herself. Could he really have fallen in love with this vacuous girl? Well, she had seemed vacuous, she amended to herself. Now she seemed to sparkle with confidence. Was one born with those unbelievable green eyes?

''No,'' Daphne said with great decisiveness, ''that will be the third car.''

''Come along, love,'' Brant said. ''It's time I showed you all that glass in the bedroom, particularly since I'm beginning to envision myself in the country, surrounded with infants and autos.''

Matt took himself off to the bar, and Marcie was left with Mrs. Sparks, the devious old lady.

''My dear Daphne is getting quite good at launching smart retorts, don't you think? Brant calls them salvos. I'd hoped you'd be a bit more up to snuff, Marcie. Your insults dwindled into catty nothings.''

Marcie said ruefully, ''She didn't have a word to say for herself when I saw her the first time. Damn it, she was a dolt, and I couldn't imagine Brant putting up with that.''

''Things change, I've always found.'' Cloe patted Marcie's shoulder. ''Buck up, my dear. Forget and forgive. You're a bright girl; don't continue swimming upstream with the salmon.''

Marcie uttered an obscenity under her breath.

''I know. Did that help?''

''You're a wicked woman, do you know that, Aunt Cloe?''

''Me? Ah, I remember how Mr. Sparks used to say that…well, that's neither here nor there, is it? There's that gorgeous boy, Tiny. What an odd name, to be sure. Excuse me, Marcie. And remember, you're too smart a girl to keep plowing in a field that's no longer fallow.''

Brant watched his wife lying on her back, staring up at the mirrored ceiling. ''Getting any lascivious ideas, sweetheart?''

''Oh yes,'' Daphne said enthusiastically. ''I could see all of you while you—'' She broke off and gave him a come hither smile.

He shuddered slightly, easily picturing himself covering her, her white legs wrapped around him, her arms clutching his back. To distract himself he said, ''You handled Marcie quite nicely.''

''Yes,'' she said, her voice surprised. ''Yes, I did.''

''You didn't need me at all.''

Daphne cocked an eyebrow at him. ''I thought you were tired of playing knight errant to my damsel in tongue-tied distress?''

Brant ran his fingers through his hair. ''I'm crazy. Ignore what I say.''

Daphne came up on her knees on the bed. ''I think I hear Lloyd shouting about a videotape of one of your games. Let's go see it, okay?''

He cocked his head at her. ''You really like football, don't you?''

''I can't wait until August for the exhibition games. I'll be cheering myself hoarse for you. But there's still so much to learn. I've got to talk to Matt Orson. There's lots I need to understand about the defense, particularly how they know what to do when the quarterback does an audible.'' She continued talking as she walked out of the bedroom, assuming that he was following her.

Brant shook his head. She was changing so quickly that he was having trouble keeping up. He remembered the girl he'd met not two months ago and shook his head again, bemused. Who the hell had told her about audibles? He pictured her driving his Porsche and shuddered.

The following evening, as they left a French restaurant on the east side, a flashbulb went off in their faces. Brant's arm immediately went around his wife's waist, to bring her protectively close. It was the same two men who had trapped them in the garage some time before.

''Hey, Mrs. Asher, you got anything to say this time?'' one of them called out.

Brant felt a surge of anger, and his hand clenched. He had no time to do or say anything. Daphne, a snide smile on her face, said, ''Hi, guys. Nice to see you again. You've stopped lurking in garages?''

The man ignored that. ''Everyone's gotta eat,'' he said. ''I suppose you heiresses are used to dining in the best spots?''

''Tomorrow night Brant is going to take me to a Mexican restaurant. I love tacos. What's your favorite food?''

Ah ha, she thought when he had no answer, satisfied that she'd taken him totally aback. The man's partner snapped another picture.

''What do you think of all your husband's women, Mrs. Asher?''

''He has excellent taste,'' she said blandly. ''I've been meaning to send out letters of condolence.''

''Gentlemen,'' Brant broke in, ''I think you've shot your wad. Daph, let's go home.''

''All one has to do is feel good about oneself,'' Daphne said, trying to snuggle closer to Brant, but unable to in the Porsche.

He revved the engine, saying nothing as the Porsche screeched around a corner in Central Park. She'd handled the men like a pro. You want her to fit in, not to be afraid and tongue-tied around people, he chided himself. But somehow he felt as though he'd lost control. Stop it, you're acting like a dog who's lost his own private bone.

When they finally got home they found that Winterspoon and Aunt Cloe were still out. Brant turned to his wife, "Let's go to bed."

"All right," she said, her eyes twinkling up at him.

Brant didn't wait for her to undress. He stripped her, tossed her onto the bed and turned every bit of his uncertainty into wild passion and, he realized vaguely as he thrust into her, a show of complete control and dominance. His savage moan of release filled the silent bedroom.

"Damn," he muttered as his breathing eased. He hadn't given a damn about her feelings, and now he felt like a complete and utter bastard. Her eyes were closed. "Daph," he said softly. "Sweetheart, forgive me." He pulled away from her and yanked off the rest of his clothes. Gently he eased her under the covers and pulled her against him. "I won't let you retreat from me," he said, anger at himself in his voice.

"I don't understand," she said finally against his shoulder.

"I don't either," he admitted. "But I'm going to try my damndest to see that you forget what a jerk I just was. Did I hurt you?"

"No, but it wasn't fun, either."

That's certainly the unvarnished truth, he thought. He called on every ounce of expertise he possessed to bring her to pleasure, and when he succeeded, he again felt that odd combination of power and control. He loved the way she shuddered in her climax, the way her eyes blurred over, the way she burrowed against him as if she wanted to get inside him.

As for Daphne, she was in a daze. She felt like a limp dishcloth, wrung out and used up. She hadn't understood his wildman performance, or the gleam of satisfaction in his eyes when she'd arched and whimpered in her release.

"Are you all right, sweetheart?" she heard him whisper softly against her temple. His hand, big and warm, was still cupped over her, lightly pressing and stroking, as if he wanted more from her. She could feel the wetness from both of them on his fingers.

But she didn't have anything more to give him. She wondered if she'd ever understand men, this one man in particular. She managed to nod against his shoulder before she fell into an exhausted sleep.

CHAPTER SEVENTEEN

Damnation! Hold it! I want the tree thinned, not denuded!''

The tree man turned off his electric saw and stared down at Lord Asherwood. ''What did you say, sir?''

Brant lowered his voice. ''I'll point to the branches I want you to take off, okay?''

Daphne, who was coming around from her now-budding rose garden, stopped and grinned. The tree man, Tommy Orville, had a wounded look on his round face. She stood quietly, watching Brant point patiently to a particular dried up branch. He looked so bloody handsome, she thought, her eyes roving over his body. He was wearing a red-and-white Astros sweatshirt, and a pair of very well worn and tight jeans. His thick dark hair shone in the bright afternoon sunlight. Passion was such a nice thing, she reflected, glad she'd discovered it before she'd gotten too much older. She'd asked Brant once after recovering from what she termed bouts of marriage, if it was always like this, and if it was, why people ever got divorced. He'd given her a long, lazy look and assured her that she was the luckiest woman he knew.

''Because you're the world greatest lover?'' she'd said with laughing sarcasm.

''You'd give me your vote, wouldn't you?''

When she'd paused, trying to come up with a retort, he had gently begun to caress her breast and nibble on that very sensitive spot just below her right ear. ''I give up,'' she'd giggled. ''You're the world's greatest everything!''

''You ain't so bad yourself, cookie,'' he'd said.

She wondered, though, gazing at him now, if he were as pleased with her as she was with him. Shut away at Asherwood as they had been for three months now, he certainly seemed to be contented. The restoration of the Hall took up a great deal of their time, but they had taken off days at a time to travel, once to Glasgow to visit Aunt Cloe, another up to York, another to the Lake District to stay on Lake Widemere. He seemed fascinated with Daphne's historical tales of all the sites they visited. Stonehenge had been his favorite. "Like huge football players in a huddle," he'd announced. It was like the continuation of their honeymoon.

The electric saw died once again, for the last time. Tommy climbed carefully down and cocked a faded brown eyebrow at Brant.

"That'll be all, thank you," Brant said. "Great job. Hey, Daph, what do you think?"

"Magnificent. Say hello to your sister for me, Tommy."

"Sure thing, Daphne," Tommy said.

"I'm so glad you're using local talent," Daphne said to her husband.

"It was a close thing. I'm glad I came out in time to save the tree from getting a flat top. How's your rose garden coming?"

"Come and see." She tucked her hand in his and lengthened her stride to match his. "Can we afford a gardener to keep things in shape after we go home?"

Home, he thought, smiling down at her. So New York was now home to her, was it? "Yes," he said, "I think we can manage it. I'll probably have to sell the condo and the Porsche, but roses are important, I know, and I wouldn't—"

She poked him in the ribs. "I'll pay for it once I liquidate some of my investments. Hmmm," she added, running her hands over his ribs, "nice."

In the next instant she was squealing. Brant's hand was under her loose top, inching around to cup her breast. "Brant, stop it! What if someone—"

"Just returning the favor, ma'am. You're not bad yourself, and no bra." He felt her quicken and grinned wickedly down at her. "You sure you want to show me the roses now? There's that other lovely garden you just might invite me to play in."

"You're terrible! So you did read some Greek plays in college. All right, I've decided it's time to have my way with you."

She did, to Brant's exhausted delight.

Daphne eased out of bed, leaving Brant sprawled on his back, beautifully naked and asleep. Just like in Hawaii, she thought, studying him in the dying afternoon light. I sure know a lot more about things than I did then, she thought, smiling. Well, she was no longer a naive twit, she thought as she climbed back onto the bed, leaned down on her hands and knees, and rained light kisses over his belly. He mumbled something in his sleep, and she kept kissing, lower. She was totally absorbed in her explorations when she heard him say softly, "Lovely view," and felt his hand lightly stroke over her bottom. He moaned suddenly, his body jerking, and she forgot her temporary embarrassment at him gazing at her backside, her legs slightly parted.

"Daph, sweetheart, you'd better stop before it's too late." He tangled his fingers in the veil of hair that covered her face, and tugged, but she wouldn't release him. "Daph," he managed once again, then gave up, expelling a sigh of pure pleasure.

"What's Winterspoon making for dinner?" he asked her sometime later. He'd wondered for a while if he'd ever be able to talk again.

"I haven't the vaguest idea," Daphne said, burrowing closer. "Sex and food. Is that all you jocks think about?"

"Just food, for the moment. I'll eat anything that doesn't bounce around on my plate. Woman, you wore me out."

"You deserved it," she said, her voice complacent. "I didn't want you to get the idea that only you could initiate…things."

"I swear that's the kind of idea men hate. Anytime you want to ravish my poor body, you go right ahead." She ran her palm down his chest to his belly. "But not right at this moment," he added. "The spirit is willing, but nothing else, I'm afraid."

"I love your spirit," she giggled. "And everything else."

"Good. We're leaving for Paris tomorrow. Say for a week?"

"Brant!" She threw herself on top of him and planted a wet kiss on his mouth.

His hand gently cupped her. "There are so many beautiful gardens in Paris, after all."

"Jerk."

Daphne's feelings were mixed when they returned to New York in mid-June. It was the real world, and she wasn't at all sure that she was ready for it. They flew back on the Concord, a special treat for both of them, and arrived shortly after they'd left London.

"Sir, ma'am," Winterspoon greeted them, flourishing a silver tray of canapés for their welcome home. He'd flown back a week earlier to "set everything to rights," he'd told Brant.

"And champagne, Winterspoon?" Brant asked.

"Champagne!" Daphne exclaimed. "Is this going to be an orgy or something?"

"Well, almost," Brant said, smiling down at her. "One glass and I've got a something to show you."

"Oh?" she asked, slanting him a provocative look.

The something was a new Mercedes 380 SL, silver body with black leather interior. Daphne stared at it, then at her husband. "So that's what your mysterious phone calls were all about."

"Yep."

"And all your ever-so-subtle questions about my preferences about this and that?"

"Yep. If you'll remember, I always asked after we'd made love. I knew your mind would be well beyond suspicious thoughts."

"Very low, Brant, very low."

"That too. You've got to name her and take me for a ride."

By the time Brant left for training camp in upstate New York, nearly every member of the Astros and their spouses had ridden in Gwendolyn, and the car and Daphne were a well-known sight to the doorman, Max.

"I wish," Daphne said on a small sigh to Tiffy Richardson one afternoon as she was cruising Gwendolyn toward Tiffy's home in Westchester, "that we could go up to the training camp."

"I used to wish the same thing," said Tiffy, patting Daphne's knee, "but Guy assured me, as I'm sure Brant did you, that there's absolutely nothing to do, since they're stuck out in the middle of nowhere, and after practice they're all dead.''

"Still…'' Daphne began.

"You miss him, I know. But it won't be much longer now. The first exhibition game is August 14, against the Lions.''

"We'll butcher them,'' Daphne said with relish. "Their offense relies primarily on the running game, and their defense stinks against the pass. Tiny was telling me—''

"Good grief, Daph! You've really gotten into football, haven't you?''

"I love the game, it's true, and I bought lots of books on football at Barnes and Noble, and Brant's got a huge video collection of games. I'm talking too much, aren't I?''

Tiffy laughed. "No, not at all. I love to hear your starchy English accent when you talk about football. Tell me,'' she continued without a pause, "how do you like marriage to Brant Asher?''

"Former playboy of the western world?''

"I believe former is the operative world,'' said Tiffy.

Daphne looked straight ahead at the highway and chewed a moment on her lower lip. "I think the question should be how does he like marriage to me? He's a gentleman, you know. Always says and does the right thing, sticks to his bargain and all that.''

"No,'' Tiffy repeated, "how do you like marriage to him?'' Bargain? she wondered silently. What bargain?

"I guess,'' Daphne said on a long sigh, "that I love him dearly.''

"I'm glad to hear it. Brant deserves the best, and I think you're it, Daph.''

"The best? Me? I'm really not sure of that, Tiffy. As I said, Brant's a gentleman.'' And he's never told me he loves me. She thought of all his love words, sometimes slurred when his need for her was great, but never a simple declaration over dinner, say, with Winterspoon in the kitchen. *Well, you haven't said anything either, idiot!* But she'd wanted to. Coward, that's what she was. He was such a gentleman that he'd probably say it back to her out of politeness and concern for her feelings.

"You're not still worried about Marcie, are you?''

"Oh no. I saw her last week at the theatre—I was with Brant's mother—and she was really quite nice. She's been a real brick. Brant's mother, that is."

"You're lucky. My mother-in-law is the martyr type. Drives me nuts. And, of course, whenever she visits us, she treats Guy like he's God's gift to the universe. He's impossible for a good two weeks after she leaves."

They spoke of Tiffy's two children and her interior decorating business, a growing concern in the past year.

"Will you be flying to Detroit for the game?" Daphne asked.

"Oh no. It's just an exhibition game. Guy shouldn't play more than two quarters at most. Sam'll want to give the new guys a chance to perform. Even Brant shouldn't play all that much. Evan Murphy has got to have some practice quarterbacking."

"Yes, I know." *In case Brant ever gets injured.* "But I'm going. I think even Winterspoon wants to give it a try. 'Bloody barbaric,' he calls it, but I've seen him reading some of my books."

"An English butler!" Tiffy laughed.

"It does boggle the mind, doesn't it?"

Daphne spent the final week before Brant's return from training camp with Alice Asher in Connecticut. And on a side street in Stamford one hot afternoon she nearly met her Waterloo, as she later told Alice in the hospital.

"Broadsided by a truck carrying Miller beer as I tried to avoid that boy on his bike. There must be some irony in there somewhere. It's not fair. What will Brant say?" She turned alarmed eyes to her mother-in-law. "I'm okay, Alice, really. You won't call Brant, will you?"

"Hush now, honey. You're very lucky, only a couple of bruised ribs and a mild concussion. And of course I called Brant. You were dead to the world for quite a long time."

"Oh, I wish you hadn't. This is the last thing he needs. He's got to concentrate on football, not get sidetracked by me and Gwen."

"If Gwen looks as good as you do, sweetheart, I won't say a single word."

"Brant!"

He walked over to her bed, leaned down and carefully studied her face. "You all right, woman driver?"

"It wasn't my fault," she said indignantly. "I did everything right, and if it hadn't been for that stupid beer—" He kissed her pursed lips. "And Alice said that Gwen is an awful mess."

"I'll have a look at her later. Not to worry." He picked up her hand and absently began to stroke her fingers. "What's all this nonsense about sidetracking me from football? Don't be an idiot. You're my wife."

"But the game plan for the Lions!" she wailed. "Watching their tapes, strategy..."

"Shush. I left Evan Murphy chomping at the bit. I like that little bruise over your right eye. Gives you a rakish look." His voice was light, because he'd spoken to her doctor briefly before coming into her room and knew she was all right. "You scared the hell out of me, you know."

Daphne gave Alice a reproachful look. "You shouldn't have worried him," she said.

"That's what husbands are for, honey," Alice said. "Now, I'm going to leave you two alone for a little while. Not too long, Brant; she still has the remains of a concussion."

"You make it sound like the leftovers from a meal," Daphne said.

Brant waited until his mother had closed the hospital door behind her, then seated himself on the bed beside his wife. He pulled back the covers and eased up her hospital gown.

"Whatever are you doing?" Daphne asked, wondering crazily if he wanted to make love to her, here in the hospital, with the nurses clustered not ten feet away at their station.

"Your ribs," he said, and bared them. "Pretty impressive," he said finally, staring at the dark purple and yellow streaks below her left breast. Actually, he tried to keep from swallowing convulsively, even though he knew they weren't broken. His mother's telephone call had done more than scare the hell out of him. He'd felt cold, clammy and seared with fear until she'd finally managed to convince him that Daphne was all right.

"I'll be able to make the exhibition game, I promise," she said. "I won't let you down again, Brant."

He looked briefly at her flat stomach before he carefully eased her hospital gown down over her ribs and pulled the starchy sheet and light blanket back up.

"We'll see about the game," he said, briefly closing his eyes. He wondered if he should tell her that she'd miscarried. No, it wouldn't make any difference, and it would likely make her feel guilty. Early days, the doctor had told him. Barely seven weeks, if that. He shook his head, reaffirming his silent decision.

He felt her fingers tighten over his. "What's the matter, Brant? I'll bet you're very tired from your trip."

"I wish you'd think only about yourself for once. Who the hell cares if I'm tired or not?"

She started at his harsh tone, but her head had begun to ache with a vengeance. "I care," she said quietly. "I care very much."

He saw the brief look of pain in her eyes and rose. "Is it time for a pain pill?"

"Probably," she said, turning her head very slowly to look at him. "I'm feeling completely sober, and they don't seem to like that."

"I'll talk to the nurse. You rest now, love, and I'll see you this evening."

"Will you go look at Gwen?"

"I'll even make sure she gets a pain pill."

Daph had been lucky, very lucky, he thought later as he eyed her Mercedes. The beer truck had hit the passenger side. He started to sweat again, and the humid Connecticut weather had nothing to do with it. He rubbed his hand over his forehead, and the ignoble thought occurred to him that he wouldn't be able to make love to her for a good three weeks. How to convince her not to, he wondered. He shook his head to clear it when he saw the bodyshop owner walking toward him.

Brant flew back to training camp three days later with Daphne's promise that she would remain with his mother and take it easy.

"You can't do anything else anyway," he told her. "Gwendolyn won't be ready to hit the road again for another week."

She hugged him exuberantly and promptly winced from the pain in her ribs. He stroked his fingertips over her smooth cheek. "I'll call you tonight, sweetheart, okay?"

Winterspoon closed up the condo and arrived in Connecticut that afternoon. "You will take care of Miss Daphne," he told Alice Asher, "and I'll see to the meals."

"It beats me how he only had to say that and I folded my tent and retired from the field," Alice said later to Daphne.

"Winterspoon is an autocrat, but a benign one," Daphne said, smiling. She knew not to laugh; it still hurt.

During the next week Alice was to shake her head several times. Daphne had been so unsure of herself, but the constant stream of visitors, all wives of the football players, made Alice realize soon enough that her daughter-in-law was very well-liked indeed.

On August 13, she blinked in surprise upon entering Daphne's bedroom. Daphne was packing.

"I'm going to Detroit to see Brant play," Daphne said firmly.

"Shouldn't you talk to the doctor—"

"Winterstoon is driving me over in about thirty minutes for a final checkup. I'm fine, Alice, really."

"But what will Brant say?"

Daphne twinkled at her. "He doesn't know. It's a surprise."

CHAPTER EIGHTEEN

Dr. Lowery was running late, and Daphne fidgeted in the waiting room, thumbing through one magazine, then another. Not one sports magazine, she thought, disgruntled.

"Mrs. Asher?"

"Yes," Daphne said, rising to face the nurse.

"Dr. Lowery will be with you in just a few minutes. Why don't you come with me to the examining room?"

Daphne dutifully followed the nurse into a small, sterile room and sat down on the single chair. The nurse handed her a paper gown and fiddled with instruments while Daphne stripped.

"Why do I have to change into this thing?" Daphne asked, looking askance at the paper gown. "It's just my ribs and head."

"Dr. Lowery will want to do a quick internal exam," said the nurse.

"Why?" Daphne asked, frowning. "I had a complete exam just about six months ago."

"I'm sure she'll want to check that you're all right after the miscarriage."

Daphne stared at her. "Miscarriage?" Her voice was thin and high.

The nurse turned and smiled at her. "Not to worry, Mrs. Asher. It's standard procedure, you know, and you were only about seven weeks along. I'm certain you're just fine."

She gave Daphne a reassuring pat on the shoulder and left the small room. Like an automaton, Daphne changed into the ridiculously embarrassing paper gown and perched on the edge of the examining table. *I lost a baby and nobody bothered to tell me about it. Dear God, I didn't even know I was pregnant.* She reviewed the previous weeks before the accident in her mind, realizing that she had missed a period. But she hadn't really thought about it. And she'd never felt ill. She stared at the white walls, her eyes widening. Did Brant know?

"Good afternoon, Mrs. Asher. My, but you're looking lovely and tiptop again."

Daphne said, without preamble, "Why didn't you tell me I'd miscarried, Dr. Lowery?"

Lorraine Lowery knew it had been a mistake to keep that information from Daphne. She should never have let Brant Asher talk her into it. And Jane Coggins, her talkative nurse, must have inadvertently spilled the beans. She sighed and sat down, gathering words together. "You were out of things for quite a while," she said finally, deciding she'd assume the responsibility for the omission. "We asked your mother-in-law if you were pregnant, and she said no, of course. That's standard procedure before we order any x-rays. The accident caused you to miscarry, but we would have had to abort in any case after the series of x-rays were completed. There was nothing anyone could have done. I'm sorry, Mrs. Asher."

Daphne nodded, mute. *You caused it, you fool, in that damned accident!*

Daphne knew about x-rays and pregnant women. She silently endured the examination, answering Dr. Lowery's questions in terse monosyllables.

"Why don't you get dressed and come into my office?" Dr. Lowery said when she was done. Daphne nodded, waiting until she was alone to scoot off the table and change.

When she was sitting across from the doctor, she wanted desperately to ask if Brant knew of the miscarriage, but she was afraid to hear the answer. Of course he didn't know, or else he would have said something to her.

"Your ribs are just fine. You no longer look like a foreign flag. You said you no longer have any headaches, so we can safely assume everything is back to normal there." She paused a moment, tapping her pen on her desktop. "If you wish to become pregnant again, Mrs. Asher, I would advise that you wait for another three months or so. We want your body to have time to heal itself.''

"It will be longer than that," Daphne said. "Football season starts in a couple of weeks. I don't want to be pregnant and traveling all over the country at the same time."

"You had no idea you were pregnant?"

Daphne shook her head, her eyes on her fingernails.

"Well, these things happen. Be thankful you weren't farther along. As to sexual relations with your husband, I suggest you wait another week or so.'' Dr. Lowery rose and extended her hand. Daphne shook it silently. "Have a visit with Dr. Mason in New York in three months, okay? She'll just doublecheck for you. Good luck to your husband and the Astros, Mrs. Asher.''

Sure, Daphne thought as she left the doctor's office. Easy for her to say. Good luck to the football team. Case closed. Too bad, but it was all for the best. Daphne closed her eyes against the bright sunlight. She wouldn't tell Brant. She couldn't. She didn't know how he would react. Did her mother-in-law know? She wouldn't ask her. She wouldn't mention it to anyone. It was done, over with. She would forget it, in time.

"Are you all right, ma'am?" Winterspoon asked as he opened the passenger door for her.

"What? Oh yes, Winterspoon, I'm fine. Just fine."

The game wasn't even a contest, Daphne thought in disgust as the final seconds ticked off. The Astros won 35 to 7, the Lions' only score coming on a thirty-yard run in the third quarter. Brant had played magnificently, his body agile, the announcers applauding his talent and throwing arm. She'd yelled herself hoarse. She hadn't sat with the few wives present, most of them rookies' wives, not wanting to chance any of the players looking at their special section and telling Brant she was there.

She walked down the stadium steps and positioned herself outside the Astros' locker room. A smile tugged at her lips as she thought of the look on Brant's face when he saw her. She couldn't wait to tell him that no pro football player could be better than number 12, or more handsome in the white uniform with its red lettering.

A man asked, ''Are you a wife of one of the players, ma'am?'' She turned and her radiant smile encompassed him. ''Yes. I'm Mrs. Asher.''

''Ah, the English heiress,'' the man said, enthusiasm over his surprise discovery raising his voice a half octave.

''No, the English *wife*. Wasn't that Lions' fumble crazy? It looked like that game—hot potato—for a few minutes.'' Her eyes began to shine. ''Brant is in excellent shape, isn't he? So graceful. It's as if the ball is an extension of his arm. And he runs as swiftly as any of the backs. Lloyd's three touchdown catches—he must have jumped a good three feet to bring the ball in.'' She continued speaking to her increasingly appreciative audience of one, recounting points of strategy, the performance of the different players in exquisite detail, the obvious outcome. ''We're going to the Superbowl this year. Yes, we are.''

Mac Dreyfus wrote as quickly as he could. The girl was a natural. She knew the game. And she was English. It was amazing. Absolutely amazing. He waved to his partner, Tim Maloney. Neither of them had wanted to cover the exhibition game. Lord, what a great break! When Brant finally emerged from the locker room he was met by a brilliantly smiling wife who threw herself into his arms. He kissed her and heard the flashbulb go off.

''Great game, Brant,'' Mac said jovially. ''And a great wife. Nice to have met you, ma'am.''

Other players gathered around Daphne, and Brant heard her giving them all a rundown on the health, current moods and thoughts of their wives, children and pets. He saw Mac Dreyfus turn in his tracks, an arrested look in his eyes. Brant found himself wondering if she ever forgot anything as he listened to her compliment each player on a specific play in which he had been the key. They basked in her praise.

It was close to thirty minutes before they were alone. Daphne hugged him again. ''I love Detroit,'' she said. ''I want to stay a day or two and visit one of the automobile places.''

"This is quite a surprise," he said once he could get in a word edgewise.

"Yes, isn't it?" Her smile was sunny, guileless.

"Are you sure you're all right?"

"Winterspoon gave me his stamp of approval," she said. "You were truly brilliant, Brant. It was such a thrill to watch you play in person. I've already arranged for us to get our own tape of the game in less than a week. You know, though, that new pass interference rule is going to cause some problems for a while, I think. You must remind the guys to be sure to *look* back toward the ball before they cream the receiver. Danny looked so furious when he got called, but it was legitimate."

He stopped a moment and gazed down at her. "You're something else, you know that?"

"Just don't squeeze me too hard for a while, okay?" She grinned, wrapping her arms around his waist and hugging.

To her surprise, his eyes darkened with worry.

"My ribs are fine," she said. "Please, there's nothing more to worry about, Brant."

He wasn't thinking about her ribs, but, of course, she couldn't know that. How, he wondered, am I going to keep her from love-making tonight? He was certain he shouldn't touch her for another week or so. She had to have time to heal.

"God, I'm happy to see you," he said, and kissed her deeply. "Now, wife, you're going to get your first dose of after-the-game aches and pains from your husband." He flexed his throwing arm.

"I'll rub you all over, I promise," Daphne said. "You only got sacked once. You hurt from that?"

"Nothing a little wifely tender loving care won't cure. You wanna play in the Jacuzzi, little girl?"

"We don't even have to go to California."

It was, of course, a mistake, but Brant figured the only obvious part of him was underwater, if Daphne would only keep her hands to herself. She did for a while, gently massaging his shoulders, but when she climbed into the swirling water with him, gorgeously naked, he groaned mentally. Distract her and yourself, you idiot, he thought, aware only of her beautiful breasts pressing against his chest.

"Mom's okay?"

"Humm? Oh yes, she's just fine and sends her love. Cloe called and wished you luck, and Winterspoon watched the game on TV."

I don't feel sore at all, Daphne was thinking. And I haven't for days now. No, not sore at all. Dr. Lowery's instruction had just been a suggestion, at least that was how she now chose to interpret it. She wanted her husband, very much, and made no attempt to stem her rising desire for him. She also had a supply of pills, so there was no danger of her getting pregnant until it was safe to do so. Her palm glided down her husband's chest to his belly, paused just a moment, and found him. Ah, she thought, smiling, he wasn't at all indifferent.

"Daph, don't," Brant said, his teeth gritted.

"Why? Haven't you missed me?"

"I'm tired and sore, and only interested locally. Please, sweetheart, not tonight. I feel like I'm an old man."

"I understand," she said, but he saw the confusion in her eyes.

He cursed fluently in his mind. Deception led to ridiculous problems. Here he was, ready to ravish her, yet he couldn't but she didn't know he couldn't. Damn.

"I'm glad you came," he said, drawing a deep breath. "Mac Dreyfus is probably half in love with you. I saw him staring at you in the most fascinated way."

"He just wanted to talk about the game after he got over that stupid English heiress bit. So we did. I probably bored him silly. Is he a sports writer?"

"Yeah, with the Chicago *Sun*. Let's get out of this thing before we turn into prunes."

She insisted on drying him, trying him to the limit. And she wore no nightgown to bed. He groaned when she wrapped herself around him. He could feel her heartbeat, erratic and fast. At least he could ease her, he thought, smiling into the darkness. He pressed her onto her back, balancing himself on his elbow beside her. "Just hold still," he said, and kissed her mouth at the same time his fingers found her. Her quick, surprised intake of breath delighted him. Lord but she was responsive. He wished the light was on when he felt her body begin to quiver. He wanted to see her face. She clutched at him frantically, her last rational thought being that if he was too tired to make love to her, where was he getting the energy for this?

She cried out, and he covered her, taking her moans into his mouth.

"You are the most perfect husband in the whole world," she murmured vaguely as she nestled against him.

He grinned, a bit painfully, and kissed her temple. "You're right," he said.

He awoke from the most intense erotic dream he'd ever experienced, only to realize that it was all too real. Early morning sunlight was filtering through the shades of their hotel room, but it took a moment for him to focus on his wife, who was covering his lower body with her own, her soft mouth caressing him. He couldn't hold back, and his moan of raw pleasure filled the silent room.

"Now, Brant, aren't I the most perfect wife in the whole world?" she asked, grinning up the length of his body.

"I'll let you know when and if I come back from the dead."

She giggled. "You only have about thirty minutes. I ordered breakfast from room service."

It was closer to fifteen minutes later when they were sitting on the bed, breakfast trays on their laps. Brant drank some of the hot black coffee and absently turned the pages of the Detroit paper to the sports section. He set down his coffee cup, very slowly and very carefully. There was a good-sized picture of Daphne kissing him enthusiastically, the caption beneath: "English Wife All-American."

"Good grief," he said, and handed Daphne the paper.

"That's a pun, isn't it? That All-American bit?" she asked in the most pleased voice he'd ever heard.

"Yes," he said, "it is. Mac likes that sort of thing."

"Listen to this, Brant. 'Daphne Asher is probably giving tips to her quarterback husband as well as all the other Astros players. Her understanding of the game is astounding, given the fact she only heard of football six months ago. Take this in, coaches—'" Daphne paused, quickly scanning the rest of the article. "I don't believe this, Brant, he's practically quoted me! It's crazy."

She handed the paper back. Brant read quickly, feeling somewhat dazed. He laid the paper on the bed and asked, "I knew you were learning at a great rate, but this—"

"I've been doing quite a bit of reading," she interrupted him, her voice demure, "and watching lots of films."

"It looks like the world is changing fast. My world, that is."

"Yes," she said, forking down a bite of scrambled eggs, "you're a married man. It's gotta change."

Gotta he thought. How long before she lost her English accent?

He enjoyed her growing popularity with the press until after the game with the Cowboys.

CHAPTER NINETEEN

Brant, sore, bruised and bone-weary from the hard game with the Cowboys, a game they'd lost, stood staring at Daphne, unable to take in what she was saying. He wondered vaguely if Winterspoon, cooking something very English in the kitchen, was listening.

"...so first I'd be doing straight interviews, then by season, if everything goes well, I'll actually be involved in the halftime talks."

Daphne, so excited she could barely talk straight, continued after a tiny pause, "And you'll not believe this, Brant! Maybe, just maybe, I'll be the first woman to actually do the play-by-play. Actually cover the games while they're happening! Joe Namath. Frank Gifford. O.J.—"

"Good God, Daph, hold it a minute." He shook his head, trying to get his mental bearings. "What the hell are you talking about? A network has offered you a sports job?"

"Yes, and they want me to interview my husband, Brant the Dancer, first! Oh, Brant, can you just imagine it? Interviewing you, and we can talk about all the players and your going to the Superbowl! Mr. Irving said that—"

"I don't believe this," he interrupted her in a stunned, incredulous voice. "Why the hell would they offer you a job like that?"

"A Scotch, neat, sir."

"What? Oh, Winterspoon. Thanks." Thank the Lord he'd made it a double.

"Just the thing, sir, to clear away confusion."

"A start, in any case." Brant downed the Scotch and wiped the back of his hand across his mouth. "I'm going to the Jacuzzi," he said. "To clear away more confusion."

Daphne blinked at his back and opened her mouth, only to be

forestalled by Winterspoon's calm reflections. "You know how he is after a game, Miss Daphne, and that sack in the third quarter by that brute probably shook his insides."

"But this is important, Winterspoon!" She rushed toward the bedroom after her husband. She saw a trail of clothes leading to the bathroom and grinned, momentarily diverted. His socks were always the last item to go, the left one specifically. He was standing in front of the mirror, slowly and carefully flexing his throwing arm. Daphne bit down on her enthusiasm.

"I've got to talk to the guys on the line, Brant," she said, pursing her lips. "It was Phil, mainly. He left a hole as wide as the Lincoln Tunnel. That's why they made a sandwich of you."

"Daphne," he said, and she started at the use of her full name. "You won't talk to Phil or anyone. You got that?"

"You're just tired and...cranky," she said, giving him a maternal pat on his shoulder. "Come on into the Jacuzzi."

"I am tired, but I'm not a damned five-year-old! Now, why don't you exit and go flutter around Winterspoon? You can offer to threaten the potatoes for him."

She stiffened, watching him with quickly narrowing eyes as he climbed into the swirling hot water. "You don't have to be nasty," she said, her voice as stiff as her back. "And I wasn't *fluttering*; I was trying to be nice and understanding."

Brant closed his eyes and leaned his head back against the tub. "Well, from the sound of it, I won't have to endure your niceness much longer, will I?"

"Just what is that supposed to mean?"

He cocked an eye open to see her standing, hands on hips, beside the tub. "It means that you'll cease being a wife when and if you accept this TV deal."

"What a stupid, mean thing to say! Of course I'm your wife. If I weren't, I doubt anyone would be interested in anything I had to say, regardless of whether I knew a smidgeon about football or not."

"A smidgeon is about all you do know, and I'm glad you finally realize why anyone would offer you anything!"

"Oh, I see now," she said, fury rising to the boiling point. "If it weren't for the great Brant Asher, shortened from Asherwood—the way you Americans shorten and change and butcher everything—I'd still be counting eggs and pruning roses at the Hall, afraid of my own shadow!"

"You got it, lady. Now, will you please just leave me alone?"

Daphne grabbed a washcloth and flung it at him, striking his face. Brant peeled it off and tossed it to the bathroom floor. "Talk about five-year-olds," he muttered.

"I'm not leaving," Daphne said between gritted teeth. "And I'm beginning to think that it would be just great if I didn't have to put up with your wretched aches and pains after every bloody game!"

"You won't, if you take that job. That kind of thing is demanding as hell. You'd barely have time to send me mailgrams."

"I'd be earning a lot of money, Brant. I could even afford to call you once in a while."

"I got it now. How many more credit cards do you want? How many more little pieces of paper that prove you're worth something?"

"I am worth something, you...you cad!"

"Back to the 19th century again." He sighed. "Why does it bother you so much that I'm the breadwinner in this family? We have a very comfortable life; Gwen will be back on her wheels in no time—"

"I don't understand why you're not thrilled about all this. And this has nothing to do with you making all the money. What do you want, a—a stick in the dirt?"

"Mud," he said. "You've been about as much a stick as I've been a hockey player."

He rose, reaching for a towel. "You wanna be a good little wife and dry my back for me?"

"I'd rather cut your throat!"

"So much for pleasant married life."

"I'm leaving," Daphne said, her body rigid with anger.

"As I recall, I asked you to several times." He continued drying himself, then tossed the towel on the floor and strode back to the bedroom. He eased onto the bed and stretched his arms above his head. "You still here?" he asked.

"Is this how you treated Marcie and all your other women?" she asked, her voice trembling with an effort at sarcasm.

"No. If you weren't here and Marcie were, she'd be doing all sorts of marvelous things to make me forget my aches and pains."

Daphne sucked in her breath. "I can do those things, too."

"Then why aren't you? Why are you harping on that ludicrous plan of yours to gain fame and fortune off your husband's name?"

It was cruel, and he knew it, but her next words made him forget every conciliatory word he'd ever considered saying.

"Damn you, Brant Asher! I don't need your name! I can and will do it all myself!"

"How can you be so damned stupid?" He jerked upright, anger and frustration churning in him. "If I hadn't agreed to marry you, you'd be whatever Lucilla told you to be, a wretched little file clerk, probably, in a dingy London office. That, or you'd be buried away in Glasgow with Aunt Cloe while she, poor lady, would be trying to marry you off to some unsuspecting soul with credit cards and a profession you'd try to dominate."

"I could marry anyone I wanted to! Dominate! God, I just don't believe you. Ha! You begged me to marry you."

"Begged, hell. It did, I'll admit, seem like quite a good idea at the time. Here was poor little Daphne, helpless, insecure, with about as much confidence as a drowned rat—"

"Stop it!"

"Why should I? It's the truth, isn't it?"

"I'm not insecure anymore! I'm competent now, and I can do anything, and—"

"Damn it, you couldn't even manage to drive competently enough to keep from losing the baby!"

She froze, her eyes glazing in shock and pain.

Brant cursed himself royally. He rose quickly from the bed, and, to his shock, she backed away from him. He stretched out his hand toward her. "Daph, I'm sorry. I didn't mean that. I've got a big mouth and—"

"You knew," she said dully, turning away from him, her arms clutched about her chest. "And you didn't tell me. I had to find out from a big-mouthed nurse."

He went after her and pulled her rigid body against him. "It was my decision not to tell you, love. The doctor thought you should know, but I insisted. I didn't want you to feel guilty or anything. I'm sorry, but when I get mad I shoot my mouth off. Please, Daph, forgive me."

"That's why you didn't make love with me in Detroit."

"You had to heal. Besides, I did give you pleasure, and I thought you enjoyed it."

He felt her hands flutter against her chest, but she said nothing.

"We can have kids, love, whenever you want."

"Don't call me *love*," she said, her voice steely. "Ours was an old-fashioned marriage of convenience; you know it as well as I do. You saved me from a wretched life; you don't have to remind me of that fact. And you're right. It's not proper of me to take advantage of you and your profession, to dominate, to stick myself in where I obviously don't belong."

He'd rather have her mad and spitting at him, he realized, listening to her emotionless voice against his shoulder. He felt like a prize jerk, a 19th-century cad, and he wished he had another Scotch, neat. What to say to her, what to do? Why had he flown off the handle at her like that? Dumb bastard! He stroked his hands down her arms.

"Daph, about that offer from the network, forget all that nonsense I spouted, please. It's your decision. Really."

She felt his hands move from her arms to begin gently massaging her shoulders, then rove down her back, hugging her more tightly against him. How stupid she'd been to believe he'd be as excited as she was over the offer. He'd kept to his part of the bargain, treating her well, staying faithful to her even when she'd acted like a total twit and nitwit. Why isn't it nit-twit? she thought crazily. But she'd seen what he really thought of her, despite his reassurances now. She understood. Slowly she eased away from him.

"Thank you," she said, not meeting his eyes. "Would you like to rest before dinner? I'll tell Winterspoon to hold it back for as long as you want. I think it's a pot roast, so it shouldn't be a problem. He's...teaching me how to cook, a bit. I'll call you in an hour?''

He let her go, watched her walk to the bedroom door. He stared after her, feeling utterly helpless. "An hour," he repeated. She didn't slam the bedroom door. He wished she had. No, she just slipped through it like a lifeless ghost. He threw himself back down on the bed and stared at the ceiling. Why don't you just admit the truth, at least to yourself, you idiot? Your overblown reaction was because you're afraid of losing her. You want all of her—her zest, her excitement, her caring, her *presence*—you want to know that she's cheering or booing in the stands while you're playing. You don't want her leaving you. You love her, fool. The admission made his guts churn. He'd believed he was immune, and he'd been more or less content to have that vague emptiness in his life. Until Daphne. He wondered now how long he'd loved her. This love business was sneaky, consuming him before he'd realized he'd been had. Oh yes, he'd loved her a long time, but had just been too blind and insensitive to realize it. He started to jump out of bed, to yell it to her, hell, to yell it to all New York. He stopped cold, falling back. She'd never believe him now.

She probably believed now that he was so small-minded, so much a male chauvinist, that he couldn't bear the thought of his wife having a life apart from him. Dog-in-the-manger syndrome, one of his shrink friends had tagged such behavior. No, he was certain he wasn't guilty of that. It wasn't that he was at all threatened by the notion of her success. He remembered Jayne, a professional model who at the time had earned more money than he had. It hadn't bothered him a bit. And Lisa Cormanth, a computer genius. And Marcie Ellis, a very successful journalist. No, boiled down to a proper pulp, he simply wanted his wife with him. He wanted to wallow in his good fortune. Some good fortune his mouth had provided him with now. She was probably ready to toss him out the door and good riddance to him.

And he'd thrown up her miscarriage at her. It occurred to him to wonder why she hadn't told him about it—unless, of course, she'd already known that he'd known. He saw again the pain in her eyes. She'd been carrying around that damned misery by herself, never letting on to him, not worrying him, protecting him, not wanting him to feel pain. And guilt? No, that was ridiculous. The accident hadn't been her fault.

Maybe she's still insecure enough to think you'd hate her if you knew about the miscarriage. That's why she never discussed it with you.

He groaned. He knew her thinking processes well enough to realize it was a possibility, a definite possibility.

But maybe, just maybe, she wanted to be away from him. After his sterling performance in the bathroom, maybe she couldn't wait to sign a contract with the network. Maybe she didn't feel anything close to what he felt about her.

When he emerged from the bedroom thirty minutes later, his agile tongue was a lead weight in his mouth. There was too much at stake, too much to lose, to go spouting off without careful consideration. He'd never felt so scared, so emptied of confidence, in his life.

What he managed to say over dinner, apart from chirpy comments on the weather, was, "Will you please come to Houston next week for the game with the Oilers? We can see Dusty, Lily and the kids while we're there, maybe stay for Thanksgiving."

Daphne looked up from her boiled potatoes after carefully shoving aside sprigs of parsley. Winterspoon loved greenery on a plate. She felt the tension radiating from him, though he spoke calmly, with no emotion in his voice. She studied the stark lines of his face, the high cheekbones, the rakish slant of his dark eyebrows. She loved him so much it hurt.

"Daphne?"

"Yes," she said finally, "I'll be there." Her voice was as calm and flat as his, but with new eyes he saw the uncertainty, the insecurity, in hers.

What to say? What to do?

He was a very physical man. Every woman he'd known intimately had teased him about being oversexed. He'd show her his love for her in bed. But later. Sex simply postponed problems; it didn't solve them.

He watched the distance stretch between them all evening. Her marvelous vivacity, her delightful laugh, had become tense wariness. They played three-handed Hearts with Winterspoon, and the supposed neophyte trounced both of them. "Well, sir," Winterspoon said, "it's only ten dollars, after all."

Much later, after careful and thorough foreplay, Brant watched her face as her body clenched with convulsive pleasure. "God, you're beautiful," he whispered. Daphne, whose body had unconsciously fought against satisfaction, felt as though she were drowning. When he entered her, gently, fully, she gasped with the wonder of it. "Brant, I—"

"I want you to be happy," he said into her mouth as he moved over her. "I want you to be happy with me."

She moaned softly against his shoulder, arching up, bringing him deeper, making him one with her.

"I want you to be happy," he said again, his words widely spaced as he gritted his teeth on the brink of his own release.

Only an absolute fool could be unhappy with him, she thought, dazed. "I want that, too," she whispered, her voice lost and helpless. She hugged him tight, feeling him explode deep within her.

CHAPTER TWENTY

Houston was warm, too warm, Daphne thought, for the end of November, and so humid that within ten minutes of meeting the climate, she felt as though her hair had turned to damp strings about her face.

"Lily! Dusty! Good grief, the whole brood!"

Daphne smiled as she was engulfed first by Lily, then by Dusty, aware that Danny, Keith and Patricia were dancing around them. She dropped all confusing thoughts and swallowed her unhappiness, giving in to the rambunctious greetings.

"Are you still going to keep this sister of mine, Dusty?" she heard Brant asking her brother-in-law as he poked him in the ribs.

"Brant, this little gal is a dynamo. Houston wouldn't be the same without her. Yep, old boy, I'll keep her."

"Ha! Why don't you ask me, brother dear?"

Brant grinned down at his beautiful sister. "You're so easy, Lily, it never occurred to me. Besides, Dusty is so much of a man, I always knew he'd keep you in line."

While Lily was punching Brant, Dusty turned to Daphne. "And how's my gorgeous little English gal?"

Daphne felt warmed by his good nature and grinned up at him. "How about two out of four?"

"Which two?" Dusty asked.

"I never get specific about a compliment," Daphne said, giggling.

"And I'll never get another word in edgewise, not with all these hellions around. All right, kids, let's get out of here. Brant, you're staying with the team until after the game?"

"Yep, then Daph and I will invade you for a couple of days. Okay?"

"You got it. Lily and I've planned a real Texas barbecue for you right after the game. But I swear it'll be turkey and all the fixings for Thanksgiving."

After another round of hugs, Brant and Daphne took the team bus to the hotel. In the lobby, fans and reporters alike surrounded the men. Daphne shrank against Brant when a reporter she'd seen at the Dallas game spotted her and yelled out, "Mrs. Asher! Welcome to Houston! You wanna give me your prediction for the game?"

Brant felt her tension and cursed himself yet again, silently. Very gently he said, "Go ahead, love. You're loaded with predictions; give them what they want."

Brant watched her from the corner of his eye as he spoke to another reporter. She seemed at first very shy and tongue-tied; then she came alive, and he smiled to see her gesticulate as she made a point, heard her sweet laughter, her starchy English accent. He felt himself swell with pride. You utter ass, he told himself. She's a natural, and you wanted to mold her into whatever it was you wanted. Hoard was more like it. He'd wanted her only for himself. He felt sick with self-disgust.

It wasn't long before other reporters converged on her, as did teammates. It was probably the most fun pre-game interviewing he'd ever been witness to. Even Sam Carverelli was grinning like a besotted hen over his little chick.

There was only one fly in the ointment, and his name was Richard Monroe, a big sports writer from Los Angeles. He was a bastion of male chauvinism in sports and became livid when a "girl" tried to swish her tail around athletes. Brant found himself inching away from his teammates, ready to pounce if the man gave Daphne a bad time.

Which he was prepared to do. Rich Monroe had eyed Daphne's performance and felt his lips thin. He was willing to agree that she was charming, lovely, but hell, let her model if she wanted to show off. He shoved his way into the group of fools surrounding her and asked, "Do you miss all your athletes in England, Mrs. Asher? The rugby season in full swing?"

"I don't know any, and I have no idea, sir," Daphne said, turning her sunny smile and wary eyes to the tall, gaunt-faced man.

"What?" he asked, his voice dripping sarcasm. "You mean you've left all your rugby heroes for our American athletes?"

Oh no, Daphne thought, studying the man with the gleaming blue eyes and ready-to-pounce voice. He thinks I'm some sort of groupie. "Yes, sir, I did, but I don't think they'll miss me." Take that, you ill-bred jerk.

"Are rugby players so much less...inviting than our American football players? Surely you must have *known* some of them in England."

"Not more than half a dozen," Daphne said, praying he wouldn't notice that her hands had clenched at her sides. "They're not nearly as...inviting as, for example, Lloyd here, or Tiny, or Guy."

"You're a team player, then," Rich Monroe said, his pencil poised over his pad. "The more the merrier. Perhaps a team play-erette."

"Perhaps, sir, you should look more closely at my husband, Brant Asher. Then, I promise you, you won't ask any more ignorant questions like that." She heard Lloyd groan in mock sorrow and tossed him a grin. Brant was at her elbow then, and she said, "My husband, sir."

Brant towered over Rich Monroe, and for a brief moment the sportswriter felt a frisson of fear at the barely veiled murderous look in Asher's eyes. Hell, he should have gotten her away from her brute of a husband.

Daphne willingly withdrew, watching Brant cut up the obnoxious man in his pleasant, utterly terrifying calm way.

"Good show, Daph," Brant said to her later. "Want me to break his neck?"

"Just his mean mouth, which you did quite nicely, thank you, Brant."

She hugged him, giving him her sweet smile, and Brant realized that she would never allow any problems between them to interfere with his game and concentration.

They beat Houston 21 to 14 in a wild and woolly fourth quarter that left Daphne hoarse from yelling, and Brant sore as hell.

"Daphne, we've got to talk."

She turned from the mirror, her pearls fastened. She gave him her special, intimate smile and said, "You are the most insatiable man! Here I am still recovering from terminal pleasure, and you—"

He slashed his hand through the air. "Cut it out, Daph. That's not what I meant, and you know it."

Oh yes, she knew it. She lowered her eyes a moment to her elegant Italian leather heels. "I don't want to be late for the barbecue. Lily was in a tizzy when I spoke to her. Really, Brant, Dusty is sending the limo, and it's probably here by now."

Brant frowned, then sighed. He saw the pleading look in her eyes and held his tongue. Later, he thought. They had to clear the air, get things straightened out between them. She had been all that was charming and supportive, wild in bed—and closed up like a clam. The wall she'd put up between them was as firm and immovable as the best offensive line.

"All right," he said. He started to pick up their suitcases, then changed his mind. No, he thought, he wanted to bring her back to the hotel. They had to talk, to be alone, with no interruptions from his well-meaning sister, equally well-meaning brother-in-law, and three oblivious nieces and nephews.

Lily and Dusty lived in a three-story white colonial house in the exclusive River Oaks section of Houston. The grounds were extensive, the swimming pool opulent, and the circular driveway bumper-to-bumper with cars. Almost immediately Daphne was gone from him, willingly or unwillingly he didn't know. He was, he supposed, afraid to find out.

The mood was festive, the guests in all stages of pleasant inebriation, many of them cavorting in the kidney-shaped pool.

Daphne smiled until she felt her face would crack from the effort. And she kept her distance from Brant. She'd just dipped a tortilla chip into a green substance that a guest told her was guacamole—whatever that was—when Lily said from behind her, "Daphne, why don't you come upstairs with me for a minute? I've got to make repairs to my poor face.''

Daphne studied her sister-in-law's exquisite face and blinked. ''What kind of repairs?''

''You'll see,'' Lily said briefly and, taking her arm, firmly steered her away from the crowd.

''You have a beautiful home,'' Daphne said as she followed in Lily's wake up the vast circular stairway.

''Yes,'' Lily said absently.

''The dinner was delicious.''

''Yes,'' Lily said again. ''In here, Daphne.''

It was the spacious master suite, and Daphne's jaw dropped in awe. She was so used to Brant's condo. The entire five rooms could fit into this one huge L-shaped suite.

''I want to know what's going on,'' Lily said without preamble, waving away what she knew would be more complimentary words from her sister-in-law.

''I don't know what you mean, Lily,'' Daphne said, resentment clear in her voice.

''Now, don't be like that,'' Lily pleaded, touching her arm. ''I love my brother dearly, and I thought you and he were perfect together. I know he loves you.''

Daphne's eyes met hers. ''I don't think so,'' she said quietly.

That was a shocker. ''Goodness, how can you be so blind, Daph? I've been watching his eyes following you all afternoon. And you've purposely avoided being with him.'' Daphne said nothing, and Lily said a bit hesitantly after a few moments, ''Mom told me about the miscarriage. It's a shame, but if you want children, you can have them. Is that the problem?''

Daphne raised her chin. ''Brant is a very honorable, kind man. And I, well, I fully intend now to keep up my end of the bargain. I'd already decided that, regardless of what he felt or didn't feel about me. I wanted to. He's been upset that I might not...keep to my end, that is. In fact, I just realized that I'm—'' She broke off. That news was for Brant first.

"What are you talking about?" Lily's voice was clearly bewildered.

"You'll see soon enough," was all Daphne would say. Lily, frustrated, allowed her to leave. Suddenly Daphne turned to face her sister-in-law again. "Do you really think so, Lily?"

"Think what?"

"That Brant loves me?"

"Don't be an ass, Daphne. I heard him tell Dusty that he was the luckiest man in the world. If I recall correctly, he said, 'And to think I almost didn't go to England. Jesus, I must have been born under a lucky star.' Does that convince you?"

Daphne thought her heart would gallop off into the sunset without her. She laughed, and at the same time a tear trickled down her cheek. She hugged Lily tightly, then skipped down the hall. She'd never been one for the grand gesture, but why not? She found Dusty, and he took her into his study, then left her alone. She picked up the phone without a moment's hesitation. It was Sunday, but why not give it a try?

Brant downed another beer. Why the hell couldn't things at least become a little blurry? All around him people were laughing, drinking, swapping jokes and unbelievable stories. It had cooled down considerably, and the Texas sky, true to legend, was clear and gleaming with stars. He watched a beautiful woman pull herself out of the swimming pool nearly as naked as the sunlit day she was born. He objectively noted her lovely breasts and long legs. They didn't do a bloody thing for him. Where was Daphne?

He saw her talking earnestly to a man Dusty had invited from one of the networks. Hell, *the* network. He watched the man shake his head and lean closer. Brant realized his hand was clutching his empty beer can, bending it out of shape, and that his knuckles were white. They'd work it out, he thought. He'd do anything not to lose her, anything.

It was Dusty who called out some ten minutes later, "Hey, folks, we've got an announcement for all of you. Come on, heads up!"

Brant felt the excitement radiating from his teammates as they shoved forward, bringing him with them. The word had leaked out sometime before. How, Brant didn't know. He hadn't said anything. "Hell," Guy had told him, "I don't mind at all if Daph sees me draped in a towel! Tiffy's accusing me of growing a fat gut, and Daph will tell the world the truth."

"I'd like to thank Mr. Donaldson," he heard Daphne say in her clear, precise voice, "and all the people who wanted to take a chance on me."

Wanted?

"I've given it a lot of thought and have decided that, as a new American, I still have so much to learn about my new home and about football. Perhaps if anyone is still interested in the next couple of years, I'll be there in the locker room to pour champagne on all your heads." She paused a moment, her eyes locked on her husband's face. "But for now, I realize that I want only to tell people just how great you guys are. Mr. Donaldson has agreed that a few short, special interviews with the Astros players is the way we'll go this year. After the Superbowl I won't be in any shape to see anyone, so we've got only the next two months."

There was a babble of comment. "That's great—just us!"

"Lordie, an interview in English English!"

Shape? Brant stared at her, his mind refusing to function.

"Thank you all so much. You're all such good friends, and I'll do my best to see that everyone knows just how great each of you is."

There was applause, the sound of glasses clinking in toast, people crowding around Daphne. Brant forced a smile to his lips, accepted handshakes, and couldn't keep his eyes off his wife.

How the hell could he get her alone? Brant smiled grimly. He eased his way through the crowd to Sam Carverelli, clapped his arms about his coach's waist, hefted him up and, amid curses from Sam and boisterous, surprised laughter from everyone else, lifted him high and tossed him into the pool.

He was at his wife's side in the next minute. "Let's go," he said. "Now."

"But, Brant, what about Lily? And poor Sam—"

"Shut up."

Her eyes sparkled, and she said in a mocking voice, "Will you toss me into the pool if I refuse?"

"No, I'll toss you flat on your back." He dragged her out without another word.

Her laughter rang out, sweet and pure and happy.

Brant didn't say a word until they'd reached their hotel room. He closed the door, locked it, then turned to face his wife.

"Your shape is beautiful. What the hell did you mean?"

"Didn't you see how much I ate? And that guacamole stuff...I really pigged in."

"Out," he said automatically.

"But we just got here! Where do you want to go now?"

"No, damn it, pig *out*. That's how you say it."

"Oh."

Brant studied her for a long moment, his fingers stroking his jaw thoughtfully. "Take off your clothes. Now."

Daphne's fingers went to her strand of pearls.

"You can leave those on."

"But why?"

"They won't interfere with anything. I want to see your shape."

"But you saw my shape last night, this morning—"

He was beside her in an instant, his fingers on the single button at the neck of her gray wool dress. She stood quietly as he pulled the dress over her head. Bra, slip and panty hose quickly followed.

Daphne said very softly, "Are you angry with me about my decision?"

"What decision?" he managed to ask, his eyes on her breasts.

"Just to do a few interviews this season. As for the rest, well, that could be, or then again, wouldn't have to be..."

"You sound breathless, Daph." He raised his eyes to her face. "When?" he asked softly.

"Well, first you, of course—"

"That's it!" He picked her up, but unlike his rough treatment with his coach, he laid her very gently on the bed. "Now, wife, enough B.S."

"But Brant, I don't have a degree and if I did, it would have to be a B.A. I don't—"

"I guess we're going to have to retire Gwen. A station wagon, perhaps? A move to Connecticut? A shaggy dog?"

"Winterspoon isn't allergic to dogs, thank goodness."

"Do you think our baby will call him Uncle Oscar? Uncle Spoon?"

"I love you, Brant."

His eyes gleamed, and he gave her a slow, intimate smile. There was a good deal of satisfied triumph in that smile, and she poked him in the stomach.

He didn't give her the satisfaction of a perfunctory grunt. "It's about time, lady. You've had me hanging over a damned cliff so long, well, my fingers are numb."

"Just so long as that's the only part of you that hasn't any feeling left."

"Lord, would you stop treating me like your straight man?"

"I'm scared."

Brant lay down beside her, drawing her close against him. His fingers tangled in her hair and the pearls. "I feel great," he said, burying his face in a mass of hair.

Daphne felt his hand slip between them and gently rove over her stomach. She no longer questioned her intense response to him, just arched more closely against him, her fingers searching out the buttons of his shirt.

He clasped her hand. "No, love, not until you hear what I've got to say."

Daphne arched back so she could see his face. He saw her tongue nervously glide over her lower lip. "No, it's nothing dreadful, I swear. I want you, sweetheart. Now, tomorrow, in the year two thousand and twenty-five. I think I've loved you forever. It took me a long time because I just didn't know what the hell was wrong with me. I want you to be happy. I want you to keep loving me."

"I don't think I could ever stop that. Brant, I'd made the decision a while ago, but I didn't know what to do, so I didn't say anything to anybody, even the network people. I thought maybe I'd end up being a single parent and would have to earn my own living. Then Lily hauled me upstairs and told me that you said you'd been born under a lucky star."

"I said that?"

"Yes, you did, you jerk! And I was under that star, too, waiting for you."

"Forget the damned star; just make it me you're under." He lightly kissed the tip of her nose, then continued in a very serious voice, "If you want to take over Joe Namath's job as announcer, I'll be your loudest supporter. What do you say? Will you keep me around as your straight man?"

Her lashes swept down, and he couldn't see her eyes. "How straight?" came her demure question.

He groaned and kissed her.

"I love you," he said into her mouth. "Even though you've become a smart-mouthed broad."

"Bird," she said. "That's how we say it in England."

Loving Evangeline
Linda Howard

CHAPTER ONE

Davis Priesen didn't think of himself as a coward, but he would rather have had surgery without anesthesia than face Robert Cannon and tell him what he had to tell him. It wasn't that the majority stockholder, CEO and president of Cannon Group would hold him responsible for the bad news; Cannon had never been known to shoot the messenger. But those icy green eyes would become even colder, even more remote, and Davis knew from experience that he would feel the frigid touch of fear along his spine. Cannon had a reputation for scrupulous fairness, but also for unmatched ruthlessness when someone tried to screw him. Davis couldn't think of anyone he respected more than Robert Cannon, but that didn't relieve his dread.

Other men in Cannon's position, with his power, insulated themselves behind layers of assistants. It was a measure of his own control and personal remoteness that only Cannon's personal assistant guarded the gates to his inner sanctum. Felice Koury had been Cannon's PA for eight years and ran his office with the precision of a Swiss watch. She was a tall, lean, ageless woman with iron-gray hair and the smooth complexion of a twenty-year-old. Davis knew that her youngest child was in his mid-twenties, putting Felice at least in her mid-forties, but it was impossible to guess her age from her appearance. She was cool under fire, frighteningly efficient and had never shown a hint of nervousness around her boss. Davis wished he had a little of that last ability.

He had called beforehand to make certain Cannon could see him, so Felice wasn't surprised when he entered her office. "Good morning, Mr. Priesen." She reached immediately for the phone and punched a button. "Mr. Priesen is here, sir." She replaced the receiver and stood. "He'll see you now." With the smooth efficiency that always intimidated him, she was at the door of the inner office before he could reach it, opening it for him, then firmly closing it when he was inside. There was nothing subservient in Felice's attention; rather, he felt as if she controlled even his entrance into Cannon's office. Which, of course, she did.

Cannon's office was huge, luxurious and exquisitely decorated. It was a tribute to his taste that the effect was relaxing, rather than overwhelming, even though original oil paintings hung on the walls and a two-hundred-year-old Persian rug was underfoot. To the right was a large sitting area, complete with entertainment center, though Davis doubted that Cannon ever used the large-screen television or VCR for anything other than business. Six Palladian windows marched along the wall, framing the matchless views of New York City as if they were six paintings. The windows were works of art in themselves, beautifully fashioned panes of cut glass that took the light streaming through them and splintered it into diamonds.

Cannon's massive desk was another antique, a masterpiece of carved black wood that supposedly had belonged to the eighteenth-century Romanovs. He looked very at home behind it.

He was a tall, lean man, with the elegant grace and power of a panther. There was something pantherish about his coloring, too, with his sleek black hair and pale green eyes. One might even think of Robert Cannon as indolent. One would be dangerously mistaken.

He rose to his feet to shake hands, his long, well-shaped fingers gripping Davis's with surprising strength. Davis was always taken aback by the steeliness of that grip.

On some occasions Cannon had invited him to the sitting area and asked if he would like coffee. This was not one of those occasions. Cannon hadn't reached his position by misreading people, and his eyes narrowed as he examined the tension in Davis's face. "I would say it's good to see you, Davis," he remarked, "but I don't think you're here to tell me something I'm going to like."

His voice had been easy, almost casual, but Davis felt his tension go up another ten notches. "No, sir."

"Is it your fault?"

"No, sir." Then, scrupulously honest, he admitted, "Though I probably should have caught it sooner."

"Then relax and sit down," Robert said gently as he reseated himself. "If it isn't your fault, you're safe. Now, tell me what the problem is."

Davis nervously took a seat, but relaxing was out of the question. He perched on the edge of a soft leather chair. "Someone in Huntsville is selling our software for the space station," he blurted.

Cannon was never a restless man, but now he became even more still, and those green eyes took on the glacial look that Davis dreaded. "Do you have proof?" he asked.

"Yes, sir."

"Do you know who?"

"I think so, sir."

"Fill me in." With those abrupt words, Cannon leaned back, his gaze focused on Davis like a pale green laser.

Davis did, stumbling several times as he tried to explain how he had become suspicious and done a bit of investigating on his own to verify his suspicions before he accused anyone. Cannon listened in silence, and Davis wiped the sweat from his brow as he described the results of his sleuthing. The Cannon Group company, PowerNet, located in Huntsville, Alabama, was currently working on highly classified software developed for NASA. That software was definitely showing up in the hands of a company affiliated with another country. This wasn't just industrial espionage, which would have been enough; this was treason.

His suspicions had centered on Landon Mercer, the company manager. Mercer had divorced the year before, and his style of living had gone noticeably upward. His salary was very good, but not good enough to support a family and live the way he had been living. Davis had discreetly hired an investigation service that had discovered large deposits into Mercer's bank account. After following him for several weeks, they had reported that he regularly visited a marina in Guntersville, a small town nearby, situated on Guntersville Lake, an impoundment of the Tennessee river.

The owner/operator of the marina was a woman named Evie

Shaw; the investigators hadn't yet been able to find out anything substantive from her bank accounts or spending habits, which could mean only that she was smarter than Mercer. On at least two occasions, however, Mercer had rented a motorboat at the marina, and shortly after he had left in the boat, Evie Shaw had closed the marina, gotten into her own boat and followed him. They had returned separately, some fifteen minutes apart. It looked as if they were meeting somewhere on the big lake, where they would find it very easy both to conceal their actions, and to see and hear anyone approaching them. It was much safer than trying to conduct clandestine business in the busy marina; in fact, the popularity of the marina made it all the odder that she would close it down in the middle of the day.

When Davis had finished and sat nervously cracking his knuckles, Cannon's face was hard and expressionless. "Thank you, Davis," he said calmly. "I'll notify the FBI and take it from here. Good work."

Davis flushed as he got to his feet. "I'm sorry I didn't catch it sooner."

"Security isn't your area. Someone was falling down on the job. I'll take care of that, too. We're lucky that you're as sharp as you are." Robert made a mental note to both increase Davis's salary, which was already healthy, and begin grooming him for more responsibility and power. He had shown a sharpness and initiative that shouldn't go unrewarded. "I'm sure the FBI will want to speak with you, so stay available for the rest of the day."

"Yes, sir."

As soon as Davis had left, Robert used his private line to call the FBI. The bureau maintained a huge force in the city, and he had had occasion to work with them before. He was put through immediately to the supervisory agent. His control was such that none of his rage was revealed in his voice as he requested that the two best agents come to his office as soon as possible. His influence was such that no questions were asked; he was simply given the quiet assurance that two agents would be there within the half hour.

That done, he sat back and considered all the options open to him. He didn't allow his cold fury to cloud his thinking. Uncontrolled emotion was not only useless, it was stupid, and Robert never allowed himself to do anything stupid. He took it personally that someone at one of his companies was selling classified computer programs; it was a blemish on his own reputation. He had nothing but contempt for someone who would sell out his own country merely for the money involved, and he would stop at nothing to halt the theft and put the perpetrator behind bars. Within fifteen minutes, he had formulated his plan of action.

The two agents arrived in twenty minutes. When Felice buzzed him, he told her to send them in, and that he wanted no interruptions of any kind until the gentlemen had left. A perfect secretary to the bone, she asked no questions.

She ushered the two conservatively dressed men into his office and firmly closed the door behind them. Robert stood to welcome them, but all the while he was assessing them with his cool, unreadable gaze. The younger man, about thirty, was immediately recognizable as a midlevel civil servant, but there was also a certain self-assurance in the man's eyes that Robert approved of. The older man, perhaps in his early fifties, had light brown hair that had gone mostly gray. He was not quite of average height, and was stocky of build. The blue eyes, behind metal-framed glasses, were tired, but nevertheless sparkled with intelligence and authority. No junior agent, this.

The older man held out his hand to Robert. "Mr. Cannon?" At Robert's nod, he said, "I'm William Brent, senior agent with the Federal Bureau of Investigation. This is Lee Murray, special agent assigned to counterespionage."

"Counterespionage," Robert murmured, his eyes cool. The presence of these two particular agents meant that the FBI had already been investigating PowerNet. "Good guess, gentlemen. Please sit down."

"It wasn't much of a guess," Agent Brent replied ruefully, as they took the offered seats. "A corporation such as yours, which handles so many government contracts, is unfortunately a prime target for espionage. I'm also aware that you have some experience in that area yourself, so it followed that you might need our particular talents, so to speak.''

He was good, Robert thought. Just the type of person to inspire trust. They wanted to know if he knew anything, but they weren't going to tip their own hand if he didn't mention PowerNet. That little charade was a screen of innocence, behind which they could exhibit surprise and consternation if he informed them that he had discovered a leak at the company, or hide their own knowledge if he didn't mention the matter.

He didn't let them get away with it. "I see you've picked up some disquieting information yourselves," he said remotely. "I'm interested in knowing why you didn't contact me immediately."

William Brent grimaced. He had heard that nothing got by Robert Cannon, but still, he hadn't expected the man to be so acute.

Cannon was looking at him with a slight, cool lift of his eyebrow that invited explanations, an expression most people found difficult to resist.

Brent managed to control the inclination to rush into speech, mingling explanation with apology; he was astonished that the impulse even existed. It made him study Robert Cannon even more closely. He already knew a lot about the man, as he had made it his business to find out. Cannon came from a cultured, moneyed background, but had made himself much wealthier with his own astute business sense, and his reputation was impeccable. He also had a lot of friends in both the State and Justice departments, powerful men in their own right, who held him in the greatest respect. "Look, here," one of those men had said. "If something crooked is going on with any of the Cannon Group companies, I'd take it as a personal favor if you'd let Robert Cannon know about it before you do anything."

"I can't do that," Brent had replied. "It would compromise the investigation."

"Not at all," the man had said. "I would trust Cannon with the country's most sensitive intelligence. As a matter of fact, I already have, on several occasions. He's done some…favors for us."

"It's possible he could be in on it," Brent had warned, still resisting the idea of briefing a civilian outsider on the situation developing down in Alabama.

But the other man had shaken his head. "No. Not Robert Cannon."

After learning something about the nature and magnitude of the "favors" Cannon had done, and the dangers involved, Brent had reluctantly agreed to apprise Cannon of the situation before they put any plans into operation. Cannon had derailed that by calling first, and they hadn't been certain if he already knew, or not. The plan had been to keep quiet until they found out why he had called. It hadn't worked. He'd seen through them immediately.

Brent was used to reading men, but he couldn't read Cannon. His persona was that of a wealthy, cultured, sophisticated man, and Brent supposed he was all that, but nevertheless, it was only the first layer. The other layers, whatever they were, were so well hidden that he only sensed their existence, and even that was due only to his own access to privileged information. Watching Cannon's leanly handsome face, he couldn't catch so much as a flicker of expression; there were only those remote eyes watching him with unlimited patience.

Making a swift decision, William Brent leaned forward. "Mr. Cannon, I'm going to tell you a lot more than I had originally planned. We have a definite problem at one of your companies, a software company down in Alabama—"

"Suppose I tell you what I know?" Robert interrupted in an even tone. "Then you can tell me if you have anything to add."

With calm, precise sentences, he recounted what Davis Priesen had told him. The two agents shared one startled, involuntary glance that revealed they hadn't discovered as much as Davis had, which upped that young man's stock with Robert even more.

When he had finished, William Brent cleared his throat and leaned forward. "Congratulations. You're a bit ahead of us. This will help us considerably in our investigation—"

"I'm flying down there tomorrow morning," Robert said.

Brent looked disapproving. "Mr. Cannon, I appreciate your desire to help, but this is best handled by the bureau."

"You misunderstand. I don't intend to *help*. This is my company, my problem. I'll take care of it myself. I'm merely apprising you of the situation and my intentions. I don't have to take the time to set up a cover and get inside the operation, because I own it. I will, of course, keep you informed."

Brent was already shaking his head. "No, it's out of the question."

"Who better? I not only have access to everything, my presence wouldn't be as alarming as that of federal investigators." He paused, then said gently, "I'm not a rank amateur."

"I'm aware of that, Mr. Cannon."

"Then I suggest you talk this over with your superiors." He glanced at his watch. "In the meantime, I have arrangements to make."

He had no doubt that when Brent took this to his superiors, he would be surprised and chagrined to be told to back off and let Robert Cannon handle this problem on his own. They would provide every assistance, of course, and have backup in place if he needed it, but Agent Brent would find that Robert was calling the shots.

He spent the rest of the day clearing his calendar. Felice made the open-ended flight arrangements and his hotel reservation in Huntsville. Just before leaving that night, he checked his watch and took a chance. Though it was eight o'clock in New York, it was only six in Montana, and the long summer daylight hours meant ranch work went on for much longer than during the winter.

To his delight, the phone was picked up on the third ring and his sister's lazy drawl came over the line. "Duncans' Madhouse, Madelyn speaking."

Robert chuckled. He could hear in the background the din his two young nephews were making. "Had a busy day, honey?"

"Robert!" Pleasure warmed her voice. "You might say that. Would you be interested in having your nephews for a prolonged visit?"

"Not until they're housebroken. I won't be at home, anyway."

"Where are you off to this time?"

"Huntsville, Alabama."

She paused. "It's hot down there."

"I'm aware of that."

"You might even *sweat*," she warned him. "Think how upset you'd be."

His firm mouth twitched at the amusement in her voice. "That's a chance I'll have to take."

"It must be serious, then. Trouble?"

"A few glitches."

"Take care."

"I will. If it looks as though I'll be down there for any length of time, I'll call you and give you my number."

"All right. Love you."

"Love you, too." He smiled a bit as he hung up. It was typical of Madelyn that she hadn't asked questions but had immediately sensed the seriousness of the situation awaiting him in Alabama. In six words she had given him her blessing, her support and her love. Though she was actually only his stepsister, the affection and understanding between them were as strong as if they had been connected by blood.

Next he called the woman he had been escorting rather regularly lately, Valentina Lawrence. The relationship hadn't progressed far enough that he would expect her to wait until his return, so the easiest thing for both of them was if he made it clear that she was free to see anyone she wished. It was a pity; Valentina was too popular to remain unattached for long, and he suspected he would be in Alabama for several weeks.

She was just the sort of woman Robert had always been most attracted to: the thoroughbred racehorse type—tall, lean, small-breasted. Her makeup was always impeccable and understated, her clothing both stylish and tasteful. She had a genuinely pleasant personality, and enjoyed the theater and opera as much as he did. She would have been a wonderful companion, if this problem hadn't interfered.

It had been several months since he had ended his last relationship, and he was feeling restless. He much preferred living with a woman to living alone, though he was perfectly content with his own company. He deeply enjoyed women, both mentally and physically, and he normally preferred the steadiness of a long-term relationship. He didn't do one-nighters and disdained those who were so stupid. He refrained from making love to a woman until she had committed herself to a relationship with him.

Valentina accepted the news of his prolonged absence with grace; after all, they weren't lovers and had no claim on each other. He could hear the gentle regret in her voice, but she didn't ask him to call when he returned.

That final piece of business concluded, he sat for several minutes, frowning as he allowed himself to think about the relationship that hadn't quite developed into intimacy, and how long it would be before he had time to attend to the sexual part of his life again. He wasn't pleased at the prospect of a long wait.

He wasn't casual about sex in any way. His intense sexuality was always under strict control; with the difference between a man's strength and a woman's, a man who *wasn't* in control could easily brutalize a woman, something that disgusted him. He tempered both his sexual appetite and his steely strength, reining them in with the icy power of his intellect. He never pressured a woman, though he always made it clear when he was attracted, so she would know where she stood. But he let his lady set the pace, let the intimacy progress at her speed. He respected a woman's natural caution about opening her tender, vulnerable body to a much bigger, stronger male. When it came to sex, he treated women gently and took his time so they could become fully aroused. Such control was no hardship; he could spend hours caressing soft, feminine skin and intriguing curves. Lingering over the lovemaking helped satisfy his own hunger, while intensifying his partner's.

There was nothing like making love that first time with a new partner, he mused. Never again was the experience so intense and hungry. He always tried to make it special for his lady, to make *her* feel special. He never stinted on the little details that made a woman feel treasured: romantic dinners for two, candlelight, champagne, thoughtful gifts, his complete attention. When the time finally came to retire to the bedroom, he would use all of his skill and control to satisfy her again and again before he allowed release for himself.

Thinking about what the problem in Alabama was causing him to miss made him irritated.

He was roused by a knock on his door. He looked up as Felice stuck her head in. "You should have gone home," he reproved. "You didn't have to stay."

"A messenger brought this envelope for you," she said, approaching to place it on his desk. She ignored his comment. No matter how late, she seldom left before he did.

"Go home," he said calmly. "That's an order. I'll call you tomorrow."

"Do you need anything before I go? A fresh pot of coffee?"

"No, I won't be staying much longer myself."

"Then have a good trip." She smiled and left the room. He could hear her in the outer office gathering together her possessions and locking everything up for the night.

He doubted that anything about the trip would be good. He was in a vengeful mood and out for blood.

He noticed that the manila envelope had no return address. He opened it and slid several pages out. There was one grainy, photostated picture, a recap of the situation and what they already knew about it, and a brief message from Agent Brent, identifying the woman in the picture and informing Robert that the bureau would cooperate with him in all matters, which was only what he had expected.

He picked up the reproduced photograph and studied it. It was of very poor quality, but pictured a woman standing on a dock, with motorboats in the background. So this was Evie Shaw. She was wearing sunglasses, so it was difficult to tell much about her, other than she had blondish, untidy hair and seemed to be rather hefty. No Mata Hari there, he thought, his fastidious taste offended by her poor choice of clothes and her general hayseed appearance. She looked more like a female mud wrestler, a coarse hick who was selling out her country for greed.

Briskly he returned the papers to the envelope. He looked forward to bringing both Landon Mercer and Evie Shaw to justice.

CHAPTER TWO

It was a typically hot, sultry Southern summer day. The sky overhead was a deep, rich blue, dotted with fat white clouds that lazily sailed along on a breeze so slight it barely rippled the lake's surface. Gulls wheeled overhead and boats bobbed hypnotically in their slips. A few diehard fishermen and skiers dotted the water, ignoring the heat, but most of the fishermen who had gone out that morning had returned before noon. The air was heavy and humid, intensifying the odors of the lake and the surrounding lush, green mountains.

Evangeline Shaw looked out over her domain from the big plate-glass windows at the rear of the main marina building. Everyone on earth needed his own kingdom, and hers was this sprawling skeletal maze of docks and boat slips. Nothing within these few square acres escaped her attention. Five years ago, when she had taken over, it had been run-down and barely paying expenses. A sizable bank loan had been required to give it the infusion of capital it had needed, but within a year she had had it spruced up, expanded and bringing in more money than it ever had before. Of course, it took more money to run it, but now the marina was making a nice profit. With any luck she would have the bank loan paid off in another three years. Then the marina would be completely hers, free and clear of debt, and she would be able to expand even more, as well as diversify her holdings. She only hoped business would hold up; the fishing trade had slacked off a lot, due to the Tennessee Valley Authority's "weed management" program that had managed to kill most of the water plants that had harbored and protected the fish.

But she had been careful, and she hadn't overextended. Her debt was manageable, unlike that of others who had thought the fishing boom would last forever and had gone deeply into debt to expand. Her domain was secure.

Old Virgil Dodd had been with her most of the morning, sitting in the rocking chair behind the counter and entertaining her and her customers with tales of his growing-up days, back in the 1900s. The old man was as tough as shoe leather, but almost a century weighed on his inceasingly frail shoulders, and Evie was afraid that another couple of years, three at the most, would be too much for him. She had known him all her life; he had been *old* all her life, changing little, as enduring as the river and the mountains. But she knew all too well how fleeting and uncertain human life was, and she treasured the mornings that Virgil spent with her. He enjoyed them, too; he no longer went out fishing, as he had for the first eighty years of his life, but at the marina he was still close to the boats, where he could hear the slap of the water against the docks and smell the lake.

They were alone now, just the two of them, and Virgil had launched into another tale from his youth. Evie perched on a tall stool, occasionally glancing out the windows to see if anyone had pulled up to the gas pump on the dock, but giving most of her attention to Virgil.

The side door opened, and a tall, lean man stepped inside. He stood for a moment before removing his sunglasses, helping his eyes adjust to the relative dimness, then moved toward her with a silent, pantherish stroll.

Evie gave him only a swift glance before turning her attention back to Virgil, but it was enough to make her defenses rise. She didn't know who he was, but she recognized immediately *what* he was; he was not only a stranger, he was an outsider. There were a lot of Northerners who had retired to Guntersville, charmed by the mild winters, the slow pace, low cost of living and natural beauty of the lake, but he wasn't one of them. He was far too young to be retired, for one thing. His accent would be fast and hard, his clothes expensive and his attitude disdainful. Evie had met his kind before. She hadn't been impressed then, either.

But it wasn't just that. It was the other quality she had caught that made her want to put a wall at her back.

He was dangerous.

Though she smiled at Virgil, instinctively she analyzed the stranger. She had grown up with bad boys, daredevils and hell-raisers; the South produced them in abundance. This man was something different, something...more. He didn't embrace danger as much as he *was* danger. It was a different mind-set, a will and temperament that brooked no opposition, a force of character that had glittered in those startlingly pale eyes.

She didn't know how or why, but she sensed that he was a threat to her.

"Excuse me," he said, and the deepness of his voice ran over her like velvet. A strange little quiver tightened her belly and ran up her spine. The words were courteous, but the iron will behind them told her that he expected her to immediately attend to him.

She gave him another quick, dismissive glance. "I'll be with you in a minute," she said, her tone merely polite, then she turned back to Virgil with real warmth. "What happened then, Virgil?"

No hint of emotion showed on Robert's face, though he was a bit startled by the woman's lack of response. That was unusual. He wasn't accustomed to being ignored by anyone, and certainly not by a woman. Women had always been acutely aware of him, responding to the intense masculinity he kept under ruthless control. He wasn't vain, but his effect on women was something he largely took for granted. He couldn't remember ever wanting a woman and not having her, eventually.

But he was willing to wait and use the opportunity to watch this woman. Her appearance had thrown him a little off balance, also something unusual for him. He still hadn't adjusted his expectations to the reality.

This was Evie Shaw, no doubt about it. She sat on a stool behind the counter, all her attention on an old man who sat in a rocking chair, his aged voice gleeful as he continued to recount some tall tale from his long-ago youth. Robert's eyes narrowed fractionally as he studied her.

She wasn't the thick-bodied hayseed he had expected. Or rather, she wasn't thick-bodied; he reserved judgment on the hayseed part. The unflattering image he'd formed must have been caused by the combination of bad photography and poorly fitting clothes. He had walked in looking for a woman who was coarse and ill-bred, but that wasn't what he'd found.

Instead, she...glowed.

It was an unsettling illusion, perhaps produced by the brilliant sunlight streaming in through the big windows, haloing her sunny hair and lighting the tawny depths of her hazel eyes. The light caressed her golden skin, which was as smooth and unblemished as a porcelain doll's. Illusion or not, the woman was luminous.

Her voice had been surprisingly deep and a little raspy, bringing up memories of old Bogie and Bacall movies and making Robert's spine prickle. Her accent was lazy and liquid, as melodious as a murmuring creek or the wind in the trees, a voice that made him think of tangled sheets and long, hot nights.

Watching her, he felt something inside him go still.

The old man leaned forward, folding his gnarled hands over the crook of his walking cane. His faded blue eyes were full of laughter and the memories of good times. "Well, we'd tried ever way we knowed to get John H. away from that still, but he weren't budging. He kept an old shotgun loaded with rat shot, so we were afeard to venture too close. He knowed it was just a bunch of young'uns aggravating him, but *we* didn't know he knowed. Ever time he grabbed that shotgun, we'd run like jackrabbits, then we'd come sneakin' back...."

Robert forced himself to look around as he tuned out the rest of Virgil's tale. Ramshackle though the building was, the business seemed to be prospering, if the amount of tackle on hand and the number of occupied boat slips were any indication. A pegboard behind the counter held the ignition keys to the rental boats, each key neatly labeled and numbered. He wondered how she kept track of who had which boat.

Virgil was well into his tale, slapping his knee and chortling. Evie Shaw threw back her head with a shout of pure enjoyment, her laughter as deep as her speaking voice. Robert was suddenly aware of how accustomed he had become to carefully controlled social laughter, how shrill and shallow it was compared to her unabashed mirth, with nothing forced or held back.

He tried to resist the compulsion to stare at her, but, to his surprise, it was like resisting the need to breathe. He could manage it for a little while, but it was a losing battle from the start. With a mixture of fury and curiosity, he gave in to the temptation and let his gaze greedily drink her in.

He watched her with an impassive expression, his self-control so absolute that neither his posture nor his face betrayed any hint of his thoughts. Unfortunately, that self-control didn't extend to those thoughts as his attention focused on Evie Shaw with such intensity that he was no longer aware of his surroundings, that he no longer heard Virgil's cracked voice continuing with his tale.

She wasn't anything like the women he had always found most attractive. She was also a traitor, or at least was involved in industrial espionage. He had every intention of breaking her, of bringing her to justice. Yet he couldn't take his eyes off her, couldn't control his wayward thoughts, couldn't still the sudden hard thumping in his chest. He had been sweating in the suffocating heat, but suddenly the heat inside him was so blistering that it made the outer temperature seem cool in comparison. His skin felt too tight, his clothing too restrictive. A familiar heaviness in his loins made the last two sensations all too real, rather than products of his imagination.

The women he had wanted in the past, for all the differences in their characters, had shared a certain sense of style, of sophistication. They had all looked—and been—expensive. He hadn't minded, and had enjoyed spoiling them more. They had all been well dressed, perfumed, exquisitely turned out. His sister Madelyn had disparagingly referred to a couple of them as mannequins, but Madelyn herself was a clotheshorse of the highest order, so he had been amused rather than irritated by the comment.

Evie Shaw, in contrast, evidently paid no attention to her clothes. She wore an oversize T-shirt that she had knotted at the waist, a pair of jeans so ancient that they were threadbare and almost colorless, and equally old docksiders. Her hair, a sun-streaked blond that ranged in color from light brown to the palest flax, and included several different shades of gold, was pulled back and confined in an untidy braid that was as thick as his wrist and hung halfway down her back. Her makeup was minimal and probably a waste of time in this humidity, but with her complexion, she didn't really need it.

Damn it, how could she glow like that? It wasn't the sheen of perspiration, but the odd impression that light was attracted to her, as if she forever stood in a subtle spotlight. Her skin was lightly tanned, a creamy golden hue, and it looked like warm, living satin. Even her eyes were the golden brown hazel of dark topaz.

He had always preferred tall, lean women; as tall as he was himself, he had felt better matched with them on the dance floor and in bed. Evie Shaw was no more than five-four, if that. Nor was she lean; rather, the word that came to mind was *luscious,* followed immediately by *delicious.* Caught off guard by the violence of his reaction, he wondered savagely if he wanted to make love to her or eat her, and the swift mental answer to his own question was a flat, unequivocal "yes." To both choices.

She was a symphony of curves, not quite full-figured, but sleek and rounded, the absolute essence of femaleness. No slim, boyish hips there, but a definite flare from her waist, and she had firm, round buttocks. He had always adored the delicacy of small breasts but now found himself entranced by the soft globes that shaped the front of the annoyingly loose T-shirt. They weren't big, heavy breasts, though they had a slight bounce that riveted his attention whenever she moved; they weren't exactly voluptuous, but were just full enough to be maddeningly tempting. Their soft, warm weight would fill his hands, hands that he tightened into fists in an effort to resist the urge to reach out and touch her.

Everything about her was shaped for a man's delight, but he wasn't delighted by his reaction. If *he* could respond to her like this, maybe Mercer was her pawn rather than the other way around. It was a possibility he couldn't ignore.

Not only was she nothing like the women he had previously desired, he was furious with himself for wanting her. He was down here to gather evidence that would send her to prison, and he couldn't let lust make him lose sight of that. This woman was wading hip-deep in the sewer of espionage, and he shouldn't feel anything for her except disgust. Instead he was struggling with a physical desire so intense that it was all he could do to simply stand there, rather than act. He didn't want to court her, seduce her; he wanted to grab her and carry her away. His lair was a hideously expensive Manhattan penthouse, but the primitive instinct was the same one that had impelled men to the same action back when their lairs were caves. He wanted her, and there was nothing civilized or gentle about it. The urge made a mockery of both his intellect and his self-control.

He wanted to ignore the attraction, but he couldn't; it was too strong, the challenge too great. Evie Shaw was not just ignoring him, she was totally oblivious to the pure male intent that was surging through him. He might as well have been a post for all the attention she was paying to him, and every aggressive cell in his body was on alert. By God, he *would* have her.

The door behind him opened, and he turned, grateful for the interruption. A young woman, clad in shorts, sandals and a T-shirt, smiled at him and murmured, "Hello," as she approached. Both the smile and the look lingered for just a moment before she turned her attention to the two people behind the counter. "Have you enjoyed your visit, PawPaw? Who all has been in today?"

"Had a good time," Virgil said, slowly getting to his feet with a lot of help from the cane. "Burt Mardis spent some time with us, and both of the Gibbs boys came by. Have you got the young'uns rounded up?"

"They're in the car with the groceries." She turned to Evie. "I hate to run, but it's so hot I want to get the food put up before it spoils."

"Everything I can, I put off until night," Evie said. "Including buying groceries. Bye, Virgil. You take care of that knee, all right? And come back soon."

"The knee feels better already," he assured her. "Getting old ain't no fun, but it's better than dying." He winked and steadily made his way down the aisle, using the cane but otherwise not making much allowance for his noticeable limp.

"See you later, Evie," the young woman said as she turned to go. She gave Robert another smile in passing.

When the old man and young woman had left and the door had closed behind them, Robert leaned negligently against the counter and said in a mild tone, "I assume she's his granddaughter."

Evie shook her head and turned away to check the gas pumps again. She was too aware of being alone with him, which was ridiculous; she was alone with male customers several times a day and had never felt the least hint of uneasiness—until now. She had felt a subtle alarm the second he had walked in the door. He hadn't said or done anything untoward, but still, she couldn't shake that feeling of wariness. "Great-granddaughter. He lives with her. I apologize for making you wait, but I'll have other customers, while Virgil is ninety-three, and he may not be around much longer."

"I understand," he said calmly, not wanting to antagonize her. He held out his hand, a gesture calculated to force her to look at him, truly acknowledge him, *touch* him. "I'm Robert Cannon."

She put her hand in his, just slowly enough to let him know that she was reluctant to shake hands with him and did it only to be polite. Her fingers were slim and cool and gripped his with surprising strength. "Evie Shaw," she said. He made certain his own grip was firm, but not enough to hurt, and promptly released her. The contact was brief, impersonal…and not enough.

Immediately she turned away and said briskly, "What is it you need, Mr. Cannon?"

He came up with several graphic ideas but didn't give voice to them. Instead he thoughtfully eyed her slim back, rapidly adjusting his impressions. He had thought her oblivious to him, but she was too studiously ignoring him for that; no, quite the contrary, she was very aware of him, and very on edge. In a flash, all of his plans changed.

He had entered the marina wanting only to look around a little, get an idea of the security and layout of the place, maybe buy a fishing license or map, but all of that had changed in the past few minutes. Rather than shadow Mercer, he now intended to stick to Evie Shaw like glue.

Why was she so wary of him? She had been, right from the beginning, even before he had introduced himself. The only explanation that came to mind was that she had already known who he was, had somehow recognized him, and she could only have done that if she had been briefed. If so, this operation was more sophisticated than he had expected. It wouldn't be beyond his capabilities, but it would certainly be more of a challenge. With one of his lightning-fast decisions, he changed the base of his investigation from Huntsville to Guntersville. Before the fall of the Soviet Union, he had, on a couple of memorable occasions, found himself attracted to female operatives; taking them to bed had been a risk, but a delightful one. Danger certainly added to the excitement. Bedding Evie Shaw, he suspected, would be an event he would never forget.

"First, I need information," he said, irritated because she still wasn't looking at him, but not a hint of it sounded in his voice. He needed to lull her suspicions, make her comfortable with him. Gentling women had never been difficult for him before, and he didn't expect it to be now. As far as anyone outside a few government officials knew, he was nothing more than a very wealthy businessman; if she was as smart as he now suspected her to be, she would soon see the benefits in becoming close to him, not only for what he could give her but for the information she could get from him. A summer fling would be perfect for her needs, and he intended to give her just that.

"Perhaps you should go to the Visitors' Center," she suggested.

"Perhaps," he murmured. "But I was told that you can help me."

"Maybe." Her tone was reluctant. She certainly wasn't committing herself to anything. "What kind of information do you need?"

"I'm taking a long vacation here, for the rest of the summer," he said. "My second reason for coming here is to rent a boat slip, but I also want someone to show me around the lake. I was told that you know the area as well as anyone."

She faced him, her gaze hooded. "That's true, but I don't guide. I can help you with the boat, but that's all."

She had thrown up a wall as soon as she had seen him, and she had no intention of being cooperative about anything. He gave her a gentle smile, one that had been soothing nervous women for years. "I understand. You don't know me."

He saw the involuntary reaction to that smile in the way her pupils flared. Now she looked uncertain. "It isn't that. I don't know a lot of my customers."

"I believe the going rate for guides is a hundred a day, plus expenses. I'm willing to pay twice that."

"It isn't a matter of money, Mr. Cannon. I don't have the time."

Pushing her now wouldn't accomplish anything, and he had a lot to get in place before he could really pursue her. He had made certain she wouldn't forget him, which was enough for a first meeting. "Can you recommend a guide, then?" he asked, and saw her relax a little.

She reeled off several names, which he committed to memory, for he fully intended to learn the river. Then she said, "Would you like to look at the boat slips that are available now?"

"Yes, of course." It would give him a chance to inspect her security arrangements, too.

She picked up a portable phone and clipped it to a belt loop, then came out from behind the counter. Robert fell into step slightly behind her, his heavy-lidded gaze wandering over her curvy hips and heart-shaped bottom, clearly outlined by the snug jeans. Her sun-streaked head barely reached the top of his shoulder. His blood throbbed warmly through his veins as he thought of cupping her bottom in his hands. It was an effort to wrench his attention away from the image that thought provoked.

"Do you just leave the store unattended?" he asked as they walked down the dock. The sunlight was blinding as it reflected off the water, and he slipped his sunglasses into place again. The heat was incredible, like a sauna.

"I can see from the docks if anyone drives up," she replied.

"How many others work here?"

She gave him a curious glance, as if wondering why he would ask. "I have a mechanic, and a boy who works mornings for me during the summer, then shifts to afternoons during the school year."

"How many hours a day are you open?"

"From six in the morning until eight at night."

"That's a long day."

"It isn't so bad. During the winter, I'm only open from eight until five."

Four of the docks were covered, and most of the slips were occupied. A variety of crafts bobbed in the placid water: houseboats, cabin cruisers, pontoon boats, ski boats, sailboats. The four covered docks were on the left, and the entrance to them was blocked by a locked gate. To the right were two uncovered docks, for use by general traffic. The rental boats were in the first row of boat slips on the secured dock closest to the marina building.

Evie unlocked the padlock that secured the gate, and they stepped onto the floating dock, which bobbed gently on the water. Silently she led him down the rows of boats, indicating which of the empty slips were available. Finally she asked, "What size boat do you have?"

He made another instant decision. "I intend to buy a small one. A speedboat, not a cabin cruiser. Can you recommend a good dealership in the area?"

She gave him another of those hooded looks, but merely said in a brisk tone, "There are several boat dealerships in town. It won't be hard to find what you want." Then she turned and started back toward the marina office, her steps sure and graceful on the bobbing dock.

Again Robert followed her, enjoying the view just as much as he had before. She probably thought she was rid of him, but there was no way that would happen. Anger and anticipation mingled, forming a volatile aggression that made him feel more alert, more on edge, than he ever had before. She would pay for stealing from him, in more ways than one.

"Will you have dinner with me tonight?" he asked, using a totally unaggressive tone. She halted so abruptly that he bumped into her. He could have prevented the contact, but deliberately let his body collide with hers. She staggered off balance, and he grabbed her waist to steady her, easing her back against him before she regained control. He felt the shiver that ran through her as he savored the heat and feel of her under his hands, against his thighs and loins and belly. "Sorry," he said with light amusement. "I didn't realize having dinner with me was such a frightening concept."

She should have done a number of things. If reluctant, she should have moved away from the subtle sexuality of his embrace. If compliant, she should have turned to face him. She should have hastened to assure him that his invitation hadn't frightened her at all, then accepted to prove that it hadn't. She did none of those things. She stood stock-still, as if paralyzed by his hands clasping her waist. Silence thickened between them, growing taut. She shivered again, a delicately sensual movement that made his hands tighten on her, made his male flesh quiver and rise. Why didn't she move, why didn't she say something?

"Evie?" he murmured.

"No," she said abruptly, her voice raspier than usual. She wrenched away from him. "I'm sorry, but I can't go out to dinner with you."

Then a boat idled into the marina, and he watched her golden head turn, her face light with a smile as she recognized her customer. Sharp fury flared through him at how easily she smiled at others, but would scarcely even glance at him.

She lifted her left arm to wave, and with shock Robert focused on that slim hand.

She was wearing a wedding ring.

CHAPTER THREE

Evie tried to concentrate on the ledgers that lay open on her desk, but she couldn't keep her mind on posting the day's income and expenses. A dark, lean face kept forming in her mind's eye, blotting out the figures. Every time she thought of those pale, predatory eyes, the bottom would drop out of her stomach and her heart would begin hammering. Fear. Though he had been polite, Robert Cannon could no more hide his true nature than could a panther. In some way she could only sense, without being able to tell the exact nature of it, he was a threat to her.

Her instincts were primitive; she wanted to barricade herself against him, wall him out. She had fought too long to put her life on an even keel to let this dark stranger disrupt what she had built. Her life was placid, deliberately so, and she resented this interruption in the even fabric of days she had fashioned about herself.

She looked up at the small photograph that sat on the top shelf of her old-fashioned rolltop desk. It wasn't one of her wedding photos; she had never looked at any of those. This photo was one that had been taken the summer before their senior year in high school; a group of kids had gotten together and spent the whole day on the water, skiing, goofing off, going back on shore to cook out. Becky Watts had brought her mother's camera and taken photos of all of them that golden summer day. Matt had been chasing Evie with an ice cube, trying to drop it down her blouse, but when he finally caught her, she had struggled and made him drop it. Matt's hands had been on her waist, and they had been laughing. Becky had called, ''Hey, Matt!'' and snapped the photo when they both automatically looked over at her.

Matt. Tall, just outgrowing the gangliness of adolescence and putting on some of the weight that came with maturity. That shock of dark hair falling over his brow, crooked grin flashing, bright blue eyes twinkling. He'd always been laughing. Evie didn't spare any looks for the girl she had been then, but she saw the way Matt had held her, the link between them that had been obvious even in that happy-go-lucky moment. She looked down at the slim gold band on her left hand. *Matt.*

In all the years since, there hadn't been anyone. She hadn't wanted anyone, had been neither interested nor tempted. There were people she loved, of course, but in a romantic sense her emotional isolation had been so complete that she had been totally unaware if any man had been attracted to her…until Robert Cannon had walked into her marina and looked at her with eyes like green ice. Though his expression had been impassive, she had felt his attention focus on her like a laser, had felt the heated sexual quality of it. That, and something else. Something even more dangerous.

He had left immediately after looking at the boat slips, but he would be back. She knew that without question. Evie sighed as she got up and walked to the French doors. She could see starlight twinkling on the water and stepped out onto the deck. The warm night air wrapped around her, humid, fragrant. Her little house sat right on the riverfront, with steps leading down from the deck to her private dock and boathouse. She sat in one of the patio chairs and propped her feet on the railing, calmed by the peacefulness of the river.

The summer nights weren't quiet, what with the constant chirp of insects, frogs and night birds, the splash of fish jumping, the rustle of the trees, the low murmur of the river itself, but there was a serenity in the noise. There was no moon, so the stars were plainly visible in the black bowl of the sky, the fragile, twinkling light reflected in millions of tiny diamonds on the water. The main river channel curved through the lake not sixty feet from her dock, the current ruffling the surface into waves.

Her nearest neighbors were a quarter of a mile away, out of sight around a small promontory. The only houses she could see from her deck were on the other side of the lake, well over a mile away. Guntersville Lake, formed when the TVA had dammed the Tennessee River back in the thirties, was both long and wide, irregularly shaped, curving back and forth, with hundreds of inlets. Numerous small, tree-covered islands dotted the lake.

She had lived here all her life. Here was home, family, friends, a network of roots almost two hundred years old that spread both wide and deep. She knew the pace of the seasons, the pulse of the river. She had never wanted to be anywhere else. The fabric of life here was her fortress. Now, however, her fortress was being threatened by two different enemies, and she would have to fight to protect herself.

The first threat was one that made her furious. Landon Mercer was up to no good. She didn't know the man well, but she had a certain instinct about people that was seldom wrong. There was a slickness to his character that had put her off from the start, when he had first begun renting one of her boats, but she hadn't actually become suspicious of him for a couple of months. It had been a lot of little things that had gradually alerted her, like the way he always carefully looked around before leaving the dock; it would have made sense if he'd been looking at the river traffic, but instead he'd looked at the parking lot and the highway. And there was always a mixture of triumph and relief in his expression when he returned, as if he'd done something he shouldn't have and gotten away with it.

His clothes were wrong, somehow. He made an effort to dress casually, the way he thought a fisherman would dress, but never quite got it right. He carried a rod and reel and one small tackle box, but from what Evie could tell, he never used them. He certainly never came back with any fish, and the same lure had been tied onto the line every time he went out. She knew it was the same one, because it was missing the back set of treble hooks. No, Mercer wasn't fishing. So why carry the tackle? The only logical explanation was that he was using it as a disguise; if anyone saw him, they wouldn't think anything about it.

But because Evie was alert to anything that threatened her domain, she wondered why he would need a disguise. Was he seeing a married woman? She dismissed that possibility. Boats were noisy and obvious; using them wasn't a good way to sneak around. If his lover's house was isolated, a car would be better, because then Mercer wouldn't have to worry about the vagaries of the weather. If the house had neighbors within sight, then a boat would attract attention when it pulled up to the dock; river people tended to notice strange boats. Nor was an assignation in the middle of the lake a good idea, given the river traffic.

Drugs, maybe. Maybe the little tackle box was full of cocaine, instead of tackle. If he had a system set up, selling in the middle of the river would be safe; the water patrol couldn't sneak up on him, and if they did approach, all he had to do was drop the evidence over the side. His most dangerous time would be before he got out on the water, while he could be caught carrying the stuff. That was why he never examined the parking lot when he returned; the evidence was gone. For all intents and purposes, he had just been enjoying a little fishing.

She had no hard evidence. Twice she had tried to follow him, but had lost him in the multitude of coves and islands. But if he was using one of her boats to either sell or transfer drugs, he was jeopardizing her business. Not only could the boat be confiscated, the publicity would be terrible for the marina. Boat owners would pull out of the slips they rented from her; there were enough marinas in the Guntersville area that they could always find another place to house their boats.

Both times Mercer had headed toward the same area, the island-dotted area around the Marshall County Park, where it was easy to lose sight of a boat. Evie knew every inch of the river; eventually she would be able to narrow down the choices and find him. She didn't have any grandiose scheme to apprehend him, assuming he *was* doing something illegal. She didn't even intend to get all that close to him; she carried a pair of powerful binoculars with her in the boat. All she wanted to do was satisfy her suspicions; if she was correct, then she would turn the matter over to the sheriff and let him work it out with the water patrol. That way, she would have protected both her reputation and the marina. She might still lose the boat, but she didn't think the sheriff would confiscate it if she were the one who put him onto Mercer to begin with. All she wanted was to be certain in her own mind before she accused a man of something as serious as drug dealing.

The problem with following Mercer was that she never knew when to expect him; if she had customers in the marina, she couldn't just drop everything and hop in a boat.

But she would handle that as the opportunity presented itself. Robert Cannon was something else entirely.

She didn't want to handle him. She didn't want anything to do with him—this man with his cold, intense eyes and clipped speech, this stranger, this Yankee. He made her feel like a rabbit facing a cobra: terrified, but fascinated at the same time. He tried to hide his ruthlessness behind smooth, cosmopolitan manners, but Evie had no doubts about the real nature of the man.

He wanted her. He intended to have her. And he wouldn't care if he destroyed her in the taking.

She touched her wedding ring, turning it on her finger. Why couldn't Matt have lived? So many years had passed without him, and she had survived, had gotten on with her life, but his death had irrevocably changed her. She was stronger, yes, but also set apart, isolated from other men who might have wanted to claim her. Other men had respected that distance; *he* wouldn't.

Robert Cannon was a complication she couldn't afford. At the very least, he would distract her at a time when she needed to be alert. At the worst, he would breach her defenses and take what he wanted, then leave without any thought for the emotional devastation he left behind. Evie shuddered at the thought. She had survived once; she wasn't sure she could do it again.

Today, when he had put his hands on her waist and pulled her against his lean, hard body, she had been both shocked and virtually paralyzed by the exquisite pleasure of the contact. It had been so many years since she had felt that kind of joy that she had forgotten how enthralling, how potent, it was to feel hard male flesh against her. She had been startled by the heated strength of his hands and the subtle muskiness of his scent. She had been swamped by the sensations, by her memories. But her memories were old ones, of two young people who no longer existed. The hands holding her had been Matt's; the eager, yearning kisses had been from Matt's lips. Time had dulled those memories, the precious ones, but the image of Robert Cannon was sharp, almost painful, in its freshness.

The safest thing would be to ignore him, but that was the one thing she was sure he wouldn't allow.

Robert strolled into the offices of PowerNet the next morning and introduced himself to the receptionist, a plump, astute woman in her thirties who immediately made a phone call and then personally escorted him to Landon Mercer's office. He was in a savage mood, had been since he'd seen the wedding ring on Evie Shaw's hand, but he gave the receptionist a gentle smile and thanked her, making her blush. He never took out his temper on innocents; in fact, his self-control was so great that the vast majority of his employees didn't know he even *had* a temper. The few who knew otherwise had learned it the hard way.

Landon Mercer, however, was no innocent. He came swiftly out of his office to meet Robert halfway, heartily greeting him. "Mr. Cannon, what a surprise! No one let us know you were in Huntsville. We're honored!"

"Hardly that," Robert murmured as he shook hands with Mercer, deliberately modifying his grip to use very little strength. His mood deteriorated even further to find that Mercer was tall and good-looking, with thick blond hair and a very European sense of style. Expertly Robert assessed the cost of the Italian silk suit Mercer was wearing, and mentally he raised his eyebrows. The man had expensive tastes.

"Come in, come in," Mercer urged, inviting Robert into his office. "Would you like coffee?"

"Please." The acceptance of hospitality, Robert had found, often made subordinates relax a little. Landon Mercer would be edgy at his sudden appearance, anyway; it wouldn't hurt to calm him down.

Mercer turned to his secretary, who was making herself very busy. "Trish, would you bring in two coffees, please?"

"Of course. How do you take yours, Mr. Cannon?"

"Black."

They went on into Mercer's office, and Robert took one of the comfortable visitors' chairs, rather than automatically taking Mercer's big chair behind the desk to show his authority. "I apologize for just dropping in on you without warning," he said calmly. "I'm in the area on vacation and thought I'd take the opportunity to see the operation, since I've never personally been down here."

"We're pleased to have you anytime," Mercer replied, still in that hearty tone of voice. "Vacation, you say? Strange place to take a vacation, especially in the middle of summer. The heat is murderous, as I'm sure you've noticed."

"Not so strange." Robert could almost hear Mercer's furiously churning, suspicious thoughts. Why was Robert here? Why now? Were they on to Mercer? If they were, why hadn't he been arrested? Robert didn't mind Mercer being suspicious; in fact, he was counting on it.

There was a light knock on the door; then Trish entered with two cups of steaming coffee. She passed Robert's to him first, then gave the other cup to Mercer. "Thank you," Robert said. Mercer didn't bother with the courtesy.

"About your vacation?" Mercer prompted, when Trish had closed the door behind her.

Robert leaned back in the chair and indolently crossed his legs. He could feel Mercer sharply studying him and knew what he would see: a lean, elegantly dressed man with cool, slightly bored eyes, certainly nothing to alarm him, despite this unexpected visit. "I have a house on the lake in Guntersville," he said in a lazy, slightly remote tone. It was a lie, but Mercer wouldn't know that. "I bought it and some land several years ago. I've never been down here before, but I've let several of my executives use the place, and they've all returned with the usual exaggerated fishing stories. Even allowing for that, they've all been enthusiastic about coming back, so I thought I'd try out the fishing for myself."

"I've heard it's a good lake," Mercer said politely, but the mental wheels were whirling faster than before.

"We'll see." Robert allowed himself a slight smile. "It seems like a nice, quiet place. Just what the doctor ordered."

"Doctor?"

"High blood pressure. Stress." Robert shrugged. "I feel fine, but the doctor insisted that I needed a long vacation, and this seemed like the perfect place to avoid stress."

"That's for sure," Mercer said. Suspicion still lingered in his eyes, but now it was tempered with relief at the plausible explanation for Robert's presence.

"I don't know how long I'll stay," Robert continued in an indifferent tone. "I won't be dropping in on you constantly, though. I'm supposed to forget about work for a while."

"We'll be glad to see you anytime, but you really should listen to your doctor," Mercer urged. "Since you're here, would you like a tour of the place? There isn't much to see, of course, just a lot of programmers and their computers."

Robert glanced at his watch, as if he had somewhere else to go. "I believe I have time, if it wouldn't be too much trouble."

"No, not at all." Mercer was already on his feet, anxious to complete the tour and send Robert on his way.

Even if he hadn't already known about Mercer, Robert thought, he would have disliked him; there was a slickness to him that was immediately off-putting. Mercer tried to disguise it with a glib, hearty attitude, but the man thought he was smarter than everyone else, and the contempt slipped through every so often. Did he treat Evie with the same attitude? Or was she, despite her relative lack of sophistication, cool and discerning enough that Mercer watched his step with her?

They were probably lovers, he thought, even though she was married. When had marital vows ever prevented anyone from straying, if they were so inclined? And why would a woman involved in espionage hesitate at cheating on her husband? Odd that her marital status hadn't been included in the information he'd received on her, but then, why would it be, unless her husband was also involved? Evidently he wasn't, but nevertheless, as soon as Robert had returned to his hotel room in Huntsville the afternoon before, he had called his own investigative people and asked for information concerning the man. He was coldly furious; he had never, under any circumstances, allowed himself to become involved with a married woman, and he wasn't going to lower his standards now. But neither had he ever wanted another woman as violently as he wanted Evie Shaw, and knowing that he had to deprive himself made his temper very precarious.

Mercer was all smooth bonhomie as he escorted Robert through the offices, pointing out the various features and explaining the work in progress. Robert made use of the tour to gather information. Calling on his ability to totally concentrate on one thing at a time, he pushed Evie Shaw out of his mind and ruthlessly focused on the business at hand. PowerNet was housed in a long, one-story brick building. The company offices were in front, while the real work, the programming, was done in the back, with computer geniuses working their peculiar magic. Robert quietly noted the security setup and approved; there were surveillance cameras, and motion and thermal alarms. Access to the classified material could be gained only by a coded magnetic card, and the bearer still had to have the necessary security clearance. No paperwork or computer disks were allowed to leave the building. All work was logged in and placed in a secure vault when the programmers left for the day.

For Robert, the security measures made things simple; the only way the system could have been breached without detection was by someone in a position of authority, someone who had access to the vault: Landon Mercer.

He made a point of checking his watch several times during the tour, and as soon as it was completed, he said, "I've enjoyed this very much, but I'm supposed to meet with a contractor to do a few repairs on the house. Perhaps we could get together for a round of golf sometime."

"Of course, anytime," Mercer said. "Just call."

Robert allowed himself a brief smile. "I'll do that."

He was satisfied with the visit; his intention hadn't been to do any actual snooping but rather to let Mercer know he was in town and to see for himself the security measures at PowerNet. He had the security layout from the original specs, of course, but it was always best to check out the details and make certain nothing had been changed. He might have to slip into the building at night, but that wasn't his primary plan, merely a possibility. Catching Mercer on-site with classified data didn't prove anything; the trick was to catch him passing it to someone else. Let his presence make Mercer nervous. Nervous people made mistakes.

An envelope from his personal investigators was waiting for him at the desk when he returned to the hotel. Robert stepped into the empty elevator and opened the envelope as the car began moving upward. He quickly scanned the single sheet. The information was brief. Matt Shaw, Evie's husband, had been killed in a car accident the day after their wedding, twelve years before.

He calmly slid the sheet back into the envelope, but a savage elation was rushing through him. She was a widow! She was avail-able. And, though she didn't know it yet, she was his for the taking.

Once in his hotel room, he picked up the phone and began mak-ing calls, sliding the chess pieces of intrigue into place.

CHAPTER FOUR

Evie stuck her head out the door. "Jason!" she bellowed at her fourteen-year-old nephew. "Stop horsing around. *Now!*"

"Aw, okay," he grudgingly replied, and Evie pulled her head back inside, though she kept an eye on him, anyway. She adored the kid but never forgot that he *was* just a kid, with an attention span that leaped around like a flea and all the ungovernable energy and awkwardness that went with early adolescence. Her niece, Paige, was content to sit inside with her, in the air-conditioning, but a couple of Jason's buddies had come by, and now they were out on the docks, clowning around. Evie expected any or all of the boys to fall into the water at any time.

"They're so jerky," Paige said with all the disdain a thirteen-year-old could muster, which was plenty.

Evie smiled at her. "They'll improve with age."

"They'd better," Paige said ominously. She pulled her long, coltish legs up into the rocking chair and returned to the young-adult romance she was reading. She was a beautiful girl, Evie thought, studying the delicate lines of the young face, which still wore some of the innocence of childhood. Paige had dark hair, like her father, and a classic bone structure that would only improve with age. Jason was more outgoing than his sister, but then, Jason was more outgoing than just about everyone.

A boat idled into the marina and pulled up to the gas pumps. Evie went outside to take care of her customers, two young couples who had already spent too much time on the water, judging by their sunburns. After they had paid and left, she checked on Jason and his friends again, but for the time being they were ambling along one of the docks and refraining from any rough horseplay. Knowing teenage boys as she did, she didn't expect that state of affairs to last long.

The day was another scorcher. She glanced up at the white sun in the cloudless sky; no chance of rain to cool things off. Though she had been outside for only a few minutes, she could already feel her hair sticking to the back of her neck as she opened the door to the office and stepped inside. How could the boys stand even being outside in this heat, much less doing anything as strenuous as their energetic clowning around?

She paused as she entered, momentarily blinded by the transition from bright sunlight into relative dimness. Paige was chatting with someone, her eager tone unusual in a girl who was normally quiet except with family members. Evie could see a man standing in front of the counter, but it was another minute before her vision cleared enough for her to make out his lean height and the width of his shoulders. She still couldn't see his features clearly, but nevertheless a tiny alarm of recognition tingled through her, and she drew a controlled breath. "Mr. Cannon."

"Hello." His pale green gaze slipped downward, leisurely examined her legs, which were exposed today, because the heat had been so oppressive that she had worn shorts. The once-over made her feel uncomfortable, and she slipped behind the counter to ring up the gas sale and put the money in the cash drawer.

"What may I do for you?" she asked, without looking at him. She was aware of Paige watching them with open interest, alerted perhaps by the difference in Evie's manner from the way she usually treated customers.

He ignored the distance in her tone. "I've brought my boat." He paused. "You *do* still have an available slip?"

"Of course." Business was business, Evie thought. She opened a drawer and pulled out a rental agreement. "If you'll complete this, I'll show you to your slip. When you were here the other day, did you see any particular location that you'd like?"

He glanced down at the sheet in his hand. "No, any one of them will do," he absently replied as he rapidly read the agreement. It was straightforward and simple, stating the rental fee and outlining the rules. At the bottom of the sheet was a place for two signatures, his and hers. "Is there an extra copy?" he asked, the businessman in him balking at signing something without keeping a record of it.

She shrugged and pulled out an extra copy of the rental agreement, took the one he held from his hands and slipped a sheet of carbon paper between the two sheets. Briskly she stapled them together and handed them back to him. Controlling a smile, Robert swiftly filled out the form, giving his name and address and how long he intended to rent the slip. Then he signed at the bottom, returned the forms to her and pulled out his wallet. The small sign taped to the counter stated that the marina accepted all major credit cards, so he removed one and laid it on the counter.

She still didn't look at him as she prepared a credit-card slip. Robert watched her with well-hidden greed. In the three days since he'd first met her, he had decided that she couldn't possibly have been as lovely as he had first thought or have such an impact on his senses. He had been wrong. From the moment he had entered the marina and watched her through the plate-glass window as she pumped gas, tension had twisted his guts until he could barely breathe. She was still as sleek and golden and sensual as a pagan goddess, and he wanted her.

He had accomplished a lot in those three days. In addition to making the first chess move with Mercer, he had bought a boat, a car and a house on the river. It had taken two days for the dealership to rig the boat, but he had taken possession of the house faster than that, having moved in the afternoon before. The Realtor still hadn't recovered from his blitzing style of decision making. But Robert wasn't accustomed to being thwarted; in record time the utilities had been turned on, the paperwork completed, a cleaning service from Huntsville dragooned into giving the place a thorough cleaning, and new furniture both selected and delivered. He had also put another plan into progress, one that would force Evie Shaw and Landon Mercer into a trap.

Silently Evie handed him the credit-card slip to sign. He scrawled his signature and returned it to her just as shouts from outside made her whirl.

Robert glanced out the window and saw several teenage boys roughhousing on the docks. "Excuse me," Evie said, and went over to open the door.

"They're going to get it now," Paige piped up with obvious satisfaction, getting to her knees in the rocking chair.

Just as Evie reached the door, Jason laughingly pushed one of his buddies, who immediately returned the shove, with interest. Jason had already turned away, and the motion propelled him forward; his sneakers skidded on a wet spot perilously close to the edge of the dock. His gangly arms began windmilling comically as he tried to reverse direction, but his feet shot out from under him and he flew into the air, over the water.

"Jason!"

He was too close to the dock. Evie saw it even as she raced through the door, her heart in her mouth. She heard the sickening crack as his head hit the edge of the dock. His thin body went limp in midair, and a half second later he hit the water, immediately slipping beneath the surface.

One of the boys yelled, his young voice cracking. Evie caught only a glimpse of their bewildered, suddenly terrified faces as she fought her way through the thick, overheated air. The dock looked so far away, and she didn't seem to be making any progress, even though she could feel her feet thudding on the wood. Frantically she searched the spot where Jason had gone under, but there was nothing, nothing....

She hit the water in a long, flat dive, stroking strongly for where she had last seen him. She was dimly aware of a distant splashing, but she ignored it, all her attention on reaching Jason in time. Don't let it be too late. Dear God, don't let it be too late. She could still hear the sodden *thunk* of his head hitting the dock. He could already be dead, or paralyzed. No. Not Jason. She refused to lose him; she couldn't lose him. She couldn't go through that again.

She took a deep breath and dived, pushing her way through the water, her desperately searching hands reaching out. Visibility in the river wasn't good; she would have to locate him mostly by touch. She reached the muddy bottom and clawed her way along it. He had to be here! There was the dark pillar of the dock, telling her that she wasn't too far away from where he had gone in.

Her lungs began to ache, but she refused to surface. That would use precious seconds, seconds that Jason didn't have.

Maybe the wave motion had washed him *under* the dock.

Fiercely she kicked, propelling herself into the darker water under the dock. Her groping hands swept the water in front of her. *Nothing.*

Her lungs were burning. The need to inhale was almost impossible to resist. Grimly she fought the impulse as she forced her way down to feel along the bottom again.

Something brushed her hand.

She grabbed, and clutched fabric. Her other hand, groping blindly, caught an arm. Using the last of her strength, she tugged her limp burden out of the shadow of the docks and feebly kicked upward. Progress was frustratingly, agonizingly slow; her lungs were demanding air, her vision fading. Dear God, had she found Jason only to drown with him, because she lacked the strength to get them to the surface?

Then strong hands caught her, gripping her ribs with bruising force, and she was propelled upward in a mighty rush. Her head broke the surface, and she inhaled convulsively, choking and gasping.

"I have you," a deep, calm voice said in her ear. "I have both of you. Just relax against me."

She could hardly do anything else. She was supported by an arm as unyielding as iron as he stroked the short distance to the dock. The boys were on their knees, reaching eager hands down toward him. "Just hold him," she heard Cannon order. "Don't try to pull him out of the water. Let me do it. And one of you go call 911."

"I already have," Evie heard Paige say, the girl's voice wavery and thin.

"Good girl." His tone changed to brisk command, the words

close by her ear. "Evie. I want you to hang on to the edge of the dock. Can you do that?"

She was still gasping, unable to talk, so she nodded.

"Let go of Jason. The boys are holding him, so he'll be okay. Do it now."

She obeyed, and he placed her hands on the edge of the dock. Grimly she clung to the wood as he heaved himself out of the water. She pushed her streaming hair out of her eyes with one hand as he knelt down and slipped both hands under Jason's arms. "He might have a spinal-cord injury," she croaked.

"I know." Robert's face was grim. "But he isn't breathing. If we don't get him up here and do CPR, he won't make it."

She swallowed hard and nodded again. As gently as possible, Robert lifted Jason out of the water, the muscles in his arms and shoulders cording under the wet shirt. Evie took one agonized look at Jason's still, blue face, and then she hauled herself out of the water, using strength she hadn't known she still possessed. She collapsed on the dock beside Jason, then struggled to her knees. "Jason!"

Robert felt for a pulse in the boy's neck and located a faint throb. Relieved, he said, "He has a heartbeat," then bent over the sprawled, limp body, pinching the boy's nostrils shut and using his other hand to press on his chin, forcing his mouth open. He placed his own mouth on the chill blue lips and carefully, forcefully, blew his breath outward. The thin chest rose. Robert lifted his mouth, and the air sighed out of the boy, his chest falling again.

Evie reached out, then forced herself to draw back. She couldn't do anything that Robert wasn't already doing, and she was still so weak and shaky that she couldn't do it nearly as well. She felt as if she were choking on her pain and desperation, on the overwhelming need to do *something,* anything. Her ears were buzzing. She would rather die herself than helplessly watch someone else she loved slowly die before her eyes.

Robert repeated the process again and again, silently counting. Fiercely he focused on what he was doing, ignoring the terrified kids grouped around them, not letting himself think about Evie's silence, her stillness. The kid's chest was rising with each breath forced into him, meaning oxygen was getting into his lungs. His heart was beating; if he didn't have a serious head or spinal injury, he should be okay, if he would just start breathing on his own. The seconds ticked by. One minute. Two. Then abruptly the boy's chest heaved, and he began choking. Quickly Robert drew back.

Jason suddenly convulsed, rolling to his side and knocking against Evie as he choked and gagged. She lurched sideways, off balance, unable to catch herself. Robert's hand shot out across Jason to steady her, the lean fingers catching her arm and preventing her from going into the water a second time. With effortless strength, he dragged her across Jason's legs, pulling her to him.

Water streamed from Jason's nostrils and open mouth. He gulped and coughed again, then abruptly vomited up a quantity of river water.

"Thank God," Robert said quietly. "No paralysis."

"No." Evie pulled loose from his grip. Tears burned her eyes as she crouched once again by Jason's side. Gently she touched the boy, soothing him, and noticed that the back of his head was red with blood. "You'll be okay, honey," she murmured as she examined the cut. "Nothing that a few stitches won't fix." She glanced up and saw Paige's white, tear-streaked face. "Paige, get a towel for me, please. And be careful! Don't run."

Paige gulped and headed back toward the marina. She didn't exactly run, but it was close.

Jason's coughing fit subsided, and he lay exhausted on his side, gulping in air. Evie stroked his arm, repeating that he was going to be all right.

Paige returned with the towel, and gently Evie pressed it to the deep cut, stanching the flow of blood. "A-aunt Evie?" Jason croaked, his voice so hoarse it was almost soundless.

"I'm here."

"Can I sit up?" he asked, beginning to be embarrassed by the attention.

"I don't know," she replied neutrally. "Can you?"

Slowly, cautiously, he eased himself into a sitting position, but he was weak, and Robert knelt down to support him, shifting so that one strong thigh was behind Jason's back. "My head hurts," Jason groaned.

"I imagine so," Robert said in a calm, almost genial voice. "You hit it on the edge of the dock." Sirens wailed, swiftly coming closer. Jason's eyes flickered as he realized a further fuss was going to be made.

Gingerly he reached back and touched his head. Wincing, he let his hand fall to his side. "Mom's going to be peed off," he said glumly.

"Mom isn't the only one," Evie replied. "But we'll settle that between ourselves later."

He looked abashed. He tried to move away from Robert's support but didn't quite make it. Then the paramedics were there, hurrying down the dock, carrying their tackle boxes of medical equipment. Robert drew back and pulled Evie with him, giving the paramedics room to work. Paige sidled over and slipped her arms around Evie's waist, burrowing close and hiding her face against Evie's wet shirt in a child's instinctive bid for reassurance. It was a simple thing for Robert to put his arms around both of them, and Evie was too tired, too numb, to resist. She stood docilely in his embrace. His strength enfolded her; his heat comforted her. He had saved Jason's life, and maybe even her own, because she wasn't certain she could have gotten Jason to the surface without his help. If so, she would simply have drowned with him rather than let him go and try to save her own life at the expense of his.

Jason was quickly checked; then the paramedics began preparations to transport him to the hospital. "That cut will have to be stitched," one of them said to Evie. "He probably has a concussion, too, so I wouldn't be surprised if they keep him overnight, at least."

Evie stirred in Robert's embrace. "I have to call Rebecca," she said. "And I want to ride with him to the hospital."

"I'll drive you," he said, releasing her. "You'll need a way back."

"Rebecca can bring me," she said as she hurried to the office,

Robert and Paige both following her inside. She reached for the phone, then halted, rubbing her forehead. "No, she'll stay with Jason. Never mind. I can drive myself."

"Of course you can," he said gently. "But you won't, because I'm driving you."

She gave him a distracted look as she dialed her sister's number. "That isn't necessary—Becky. Listen, Jason slipped on the dock and cut his head. He's going to be okay, but he needs stitches, and the paramedics are taking him to the hospital. They're leaving now. I'll meet you there. Yes, I'm bringing Paige with me. Okay. Bye."

She hung up, then lifted the receiver and dialed another number. "Craig, this is Evie. Can you take over the marina for a couple of hours? Jason's had an accident, and I'm going with him to the hospital. No, he'll be okay. Five minutes? Great. I'm leaving now."

Then, moving swiftly, she got her purse from under the counter and fished out her keys. Like lightning, Robert caught her hand and calmly removed the keys from her grasp. "You're too shaky," he said in a gentle, implacable tone. "You came close to drowning yourself. Don't fight me on this, Evie."

It was obvious that she lacked the strength to physically fight him for the keys. Frustrated, she gave in rather than waste more time. "All right."

She drove a sturdy, serviceable four-wheel-drive pickup, handy for pulling boats up a launch ramp. Paige raced ahead to scramble inside, as if afraid she would be left behind if she didn't beat them to the vehicle. Evie was only grateful that the child automatically slid to the middle of the seat, positioning herself between Evie and Robert and hastily buckling herself in.

"It's a straight shift," she blurted unnecessarily as she buckled her own seat belt.

He gave her a gentle smile as he started the engine. "I can manage."

Of course, he did more than manage. He shifted gears with the smooth expertise of someone who knew exactly what he was doing. Evie's heart gave a little thump as she tried to imagine Robert Cannon being awkward at anything.

She forced herself to watch the road, rather than him, as she gave directions to the hospital. She didn't want to look at him, didn't want to feel that primal pull deep inside her. He was dripping wet, of course, his black hair plastered to his head and his white silk shirt clinging to his muscled torso like a second skin. His leanness was deceptive; the wet shirt revealed the width of his shoulders and chest, and the smooth, steely muscles of his abdomen and back. She thought the image of him, the outline of his body, was probably branded on her mind for all eternity, as was everything else that had happened in the last fifteen minutes. Only fifteen minutes? It felt like a lifetime.

He drove fast, pulling into the hospital parking lot right behind the ambulance. The hospital was small but new, and he couldn't fault the staff's response. Jason was whisked into an examining room before Evie could reach his side to speak to him.

Firmly Robert took her arm and ushered both her and Paige to seats in the waiting area. "Sit here," he said, and though his voice was mild, that implacable tone was in it again. "I'll get coffee for us. How about you, sweetheart?" he asked Paige. "Do you want a soft drink?"

Dumbly Paige nodded, then shook her head. "May I have coffee, too, Aunt Evie?" she whispered. "I'm cold. Or maybe hot chocolate."

Evie nodded her agreement, and Robert strode to the vending machines. She put her arm around Paige and gathered her close, knowing that the girl had suffered a shock at seeing her brother almost die. "Don't worry, honey. Jason will be home by tomorrow, probably, griping about his headache and driving you up the wall."

Paige sniffed back tears. "I know. I'll get mad at him then, but right now I just want him to be okay."

"He will be. I promise."

Robert returned with three cups, one filled with hot chocolate and the other two with coffee. Evie and Paige took theirs from him, and he settled into the chair on Evie's other side. When she sipped the hot brew, she found that he had liberally dosed it with sugar.

She glanced at him and found him watching her, gauging her re-action. "Drink it," he said softly. "You're a little shocky, too."

Because he was right, she obeyed without argument, folding her cold fingers around the cup in an effort to warm them. Her wet clothes were uncomfortably chilly here in the air-conditioned hos-pital, and she barely restrained a shiver. He should be cold, too, she thought, but knew that he wasn't. His arm touched hers, and she felt heat radiating through his wet clothing.

As slight as it was, he felt the shiver that raced through her. "I'll get a blanket for you," he said, rising to his feet.

She watched him approach the desk and speak to the nurse. He was courteous, restrained, but in about thirty seconds he was re-turning with a blanket in his hands. He had an air of natural com-mand, she thought. One look into those icy green eyes and people scurried to do his bidding.

He bent over her to tuck the blanket around her, and she let him. Just as he finished, the emergency room doors swung open and her sister, Rebecca, hurried inside, looking tense and scared. Seeing Evie and Paige, she changed her direction to join them. "What's happening?" she demanded.

"He's in the treatment room now," Robert answered for Evie, his deep voice as soothing as when he'd talked to Paige. "He'll have a few stitches in the back of his head, and a bad headache. They'll probably keep him overnight, but his injuries are relatively minor."

Rebecca turned her shrewd brown eyes on him and bluntly de-manded, "Who are you?"

"This is Robert Cannon," Evie said, making an effort to appear calm as she made the introductions. "He dragged both Jason and me out of the water. Mr. Cannon, this is my sister, Rebecca Wood."

Rebecca took in Robert's wet clothes, then looked at Evie, seeing the strain on her sister's pale face. "I'll see about Jason first," she said in her usual decisive manner. "Then I want to know exactly what happened." She turned and marched toward a nurse, identified herself and was directed to the treatment room where Jason was located.

Robert sat down beside Evie. "What branch of the military was your sister in?" he asked, provoking a nervous giggle from Paige.

"I think it's called motherhood," Evie replied. "She began practicing on me at an early age."

"She's older, I presume."

"Five years."

"So you've always been 'baby sister' to her."

"I don't mind."

"I'm sure you don't. Drink your coffee," he admonished, lifting the cup himself and holding it to her lips.

Evie drank, then gave him a wry glance. "You aren't bad at the mother-hen routine yourself."

He allowed himself a slight smile. "I take care of my own." The words were a subtle threat—and a warning, if she were astute enough to hear it.

She didn't make the obvious retort, that she wasn't "his"; instead she withdrew, sinking back in her chair and staring straight ahead. Jason's close call had brought too many old memories to the surface, making it difficult for her to deal with anything just now, much less Robert Cannon. Right now, what she wanted most of all was to crawl into bed and pull the covers over her head, shutting out the world until she felt capable of facing it again. Maybe by the time night came, certainly by tomorrow, she would be all right. Then she would worry about the way he had taken over and about the gentle possessiveness that she couldn't fight. With Cannon, Evie was beginning to link gentleness with an implacable force of will that let nothing stand in his way. He would be tender and protective, but he would not be thwarted.

They sat in silence until Rebecca came out of the treatment room to rejoin them. "They're keeping him overnight," she said. "He has a slight concussion, a big shaved spot on the back of his head and ten stitches. He also won't say exactly what happened, other than mumbling that he fell. What's he trying to hide from me?"

Evie hesitated, trying to decide exactly what to tell Rebecca, and that gave Paige enough time to pipe up. "Scott and Jeff and Patrick came by the marina, and they were all acting silly out on the docks. Aunt Evie yelled at Jason to settle down, but they didn't. Jason pushed Patrick, and Patrick pushed him back, and Jason slipped and fell, and hit his head on the dock, then went into the water. Aunt Evie went in after him, and she was under forever and ever, and Mr. Cannon tried to find both of them. Then Aunt Evie came up, and she had Jason, and Mr. Cannon pulled them to the dock. Jason wasn't breathing, Mom, and Aunt Evie nearly drowned, too. Mr. Cannon had to do that artificial breathing stuff on Jason, and then Jason started coughing and puking, and the paramedics came. I called 911," she finished in a rush.

Rebecca looked a bit bemused at this flood of words from her quiet child but heard the fear still lurking under the loquaciousness. She sat down beside Paige and hugged her. "You did exactly right," she praised, and Paige gave a little sigh of relief.

Rebecca examined Evie's pale, drawn face. "He's all right," she said reassuringly. "At least for now. As soon as he's recovered, I'm going to kill him. Better yet, I think I'll ground him for the rest of the summer. *Then* I'll kill him."

Evie managed a smile. "If he lives through all that, I want a turn at him."

"It's a deal. Now, I want you to go home and get out of those wet clothes. You look worse than Jason does."

The smile, this time, was easier. "Gee, thanks." But she knew that Rebecca's sharp eyes had seen below the surface and recognized the strain that she was under.

"I'll see to her," Robert said, standing and urging Evie to her feet. She wanted to protest, she really did, but she was so tired, her nerves so strained, that it was too much effort. So she managed to say goodbye to Rebecca and Paige, and tell them to kiss Jason for her; then she gave in and let him usher her out of the building and across the parking lot to the truck. She had left the blanket behind, but the searing afternoon heat washed over her like a glow, and she shivered with delight.

Robert's arm tightened around her waist. "Are you still cold?"

"No, I'm fine," she murmured. "The heat feels good."

He opened the truck door and lifted her onto the seat. The strength in his hands and arms, the ease with which he picked her up, made her shiver again. She closed her eyes and let her head rest against the window, as much from a desire to shut him out as from an almost overpowering fatigue.

"You can't go to sleep," he said as he got in on the driver's side, amusement lacing his tone. "You have to give me directions to your house."

She forced herself to open her eyes and sit up, and gave him calm, coherent directions. It didn't take long to get anywhere in Guntersville, and less than fifteen minutes later he stopped the truck in her driveway. She fumbled with the door but was so clumsy that he was there before she managed it, opening it and supporting her with a firm hand under her elbow. She got out, reluctant to let him inside her house but accepting the inevitable. Best just to go shower and change as fast as she could, and get it over with.

He entered right behind her. "Have a seat," she invited automatically as she headed toward her bedroom. "I'll be out in about fifteen minutes."

"I'm still too wet to sit down," he said. "But take your time. I'll go out on the deck, if that's okay with you."

"Of course," she said, giving him a polite smile without really looking at him, and escaped into the privacy of her bedroom.

Robert eyed the closed door thoughtfully. She was so wary of him that she wouldn't even look at him if she could help it. It wasn't a response he was accustomed to from a woman, though God knew she had reason to be wary, given his assumption that she knew of his connection to PowerNet. She couldn't have acted any more guilty if he had caught her red-handed. He could opt for patience and let time disarm her, but he already had plans in motion that would force the issue, so he decided to allay her suspicions in another manner, by making a definite, concerted effort to seduce her. He had planned to seduce her, anyway; he would simply intensify the pressure.

He heard the shower start running. He couldn't have asked for a better opportunity to look around, and he took advantage of it. The house was probably forty years old, he thought, but had been remodeled so the interior was open and more modern, with exposed beams and gleaming hardwood floors. She had a green thumb; indoor plants of all sizes occupied every available flat surface. He could see into the kitchen from where he stood in the living room, and beyond that was the deck, with double French doors opening onto it. A dock led from the deck down to a boathouse.

Her furnishings were neat and comfortable, but certainly not luxurious. Without haste, he went over to the big, old-fashioned rolltop desk and methodically searched it, unearthing nothing of any great interest, not that he had expected to find anything. It wasn't likely she would have been fool enough to leave him in the room with an unlocked desk if the desk contained anything incriminating. He looked through her bank statement but found no unusually large deposits, at least at this particular bank or on this particular statement.

There was a small, framed photograph on the desk. He picked it up and examined the two people pictured. Evie, defintiely—a very young Evie, but already glowing with seductiveness. The boy, for he was nothing more than that, was probably her husband, dead now for twelve years. Robert studied the boy's face more closely, seeing laughter and happiness and yes, devotion. But had the boy any idea how to handle the sensual treasure that the girl in his arms represented? Of course not; what teenage boy would? Still, Robert felt an unexpected and unpleasant twinge of jealousy for this long-dead boy, for the riches that had so briefly been his. Evie had loved him, enough that she still wore his wedding ring after all these years.

He heard the shower shut off and replaced the photograph, then quietly walked out onto the deck. She had a nice place here, nothing extravagant, but cozy and homey. There was plenty of privacy, too, with no houses visible except for those on the far side of the lake. The water was very blue, reflecting both the green of the mountains and the deep blue bowl of the sky. The afternoon was slipping away, and the sun was lower now, but still white and searing. Soon it would begin to turn bronze, and the lush scents of the heavy greenery would grow stronger. By the time purple twilight brought a respite from the heat, the air would be redolent with honeysuckle and roses, pine and fresh-cut grass. Time was slower here; people didn't rush from one occupation to another. He had actually seen people sitting on their front porches, reading newspapers or shelling peas, occasionally waving to passersby. Of course, people from New York and other large cities would say that the locals here had nothing to rush *to*, but from what he'd seen they stayed busy enough; they just didn't get in any great hurry.

He heard Evie come to the open French door. "I'm ready," she said.

He turned and looked at her. Her newly washed hair was still wet, but she had braided it and pinned the braids up so they wouldn't get her shirt damp. She had exchanged the shorts for jeans, and had on a pink T-shirt that made her golden skin glow. But her cheeks were still a bit pale, and her expression was strained.

"You have a nice place," he said.

"Thanks. I inherited it from my in-laws."

Though he knew the answer, now was the time to ask for information; it would be odd if he didn't. "You're married?" he asked.

"Widowed." She turned and retreated into the house, and Robert followed her.

"Ah. I'm sorry. How long has it been?"

"Twelve years."

"I saw the picture on the desk. Is that your husband?"

"Yes, that's Matt." She stopped and looked toward the photograph, and an ineffable sadness darkened her eyes. "We were just kids." Then she seemed to gather herself and walked briskly to the door. "I need to get back to the marina."

"My house is about five miles from here," he said. "It won't take long for me to shower and change."

She carried a towel out to the truck and dried the seat before she got inside. She didn't even bother protesting his continued possession of her keys; it would be pointless, though she was now obviously calm enough to drive safely.

His clothes had dried enough that they were merely damp now, rather than dripping wet, but she knew they had to be uncomfortable. Hers certainly had been. Her conscience twinged. He had not only saved Jason's life but likely hers, as well, and had put himself to a great deal of trouble to see that she was taken care of. No matter how he alarmed her, she knew that she would never forget his quick actions or his cool decisiveness.

"Thank you," she said softly, staring straight ahead. "Jason and I probably wouldn't have made it without you."

"The likelihood was unnerving," he said, his tone cool and even. "You'd pushed yourself so far that you couldn't have gotten him out of the water. Didn't it occur to you to let go of him and come up for another breath?"

"No." The single word was flat. "I couldn't have done that."

He glanced at her profile, saw the deepening strain in her expression and deftly changed the subject. "Will your sister really ground him for the rest of the summer?"

Evie was startled into a laugh, a rusty little sound that went right to his gut. "I'd say he'll be lucky if that's all she does. It isn't that he was fooling around, but that I'd already told him to stop and he disobeyed me."

"So he broke a cardinal rule?"

"Just about."

Robert intended to have a few words with the young man himself, about acting responsibly and the possible consequences of reckless actions, but he didn't mention it to Evie. She was obviously very protective of her niece and nephew, and though she couldn't say that it wasn't any of his business, she wouldn't like it. His conversation with Jason would be private.

When he stopped in the driveway of his new house, Evie looked around with interest. "This place has been on the market for almost a year," she said.

"Then I'm lucky no one beat me to it, aren't I?" He got out and walked around the truck to open the door for her. Though she hadn't waited for him to perform the service at the hospital, that had been an emergency; nor would she have waited when they had reached her house, if she had been able to get the door open in time. He'd had the strong impression then that she had wanted to bolt inside and lock him out. Now, however, she waited with the natural air of a queen, as if he were only doing what he should. She might be dressed in jeans, sneakers and a T-shirt, but that didn't lessen her femininity one whit; she *expected* that male act of servitude. Robert had always preferred to treat women with the small courtesies but hadn't insisted on them when his partner had protested. He was both amused and charmed by Evie's rather regal, very Southern attitude.

He mused about this subtle signal as he ushered her into the house. Though she was still very wary of him, obviously on some level her resistance had weakened. Anticipation tightened his muscles, but he deliberately resisted it. Now was not the time. Not quite yet.

"Make yourself at home while I shower," he invited, smiling faintly as he walked toward his bedroom, which was down the hallway to the right. He had no doubt that she would do exactly as he had done, take full advantage of the opportunity to do a quick search.

Evie stood in the middle of the living room after he had gone, too tense to "make herself at home." She looked around, trying to distract herself. The house was sprawling and modern, one story of brick and redwood, easily three times the size of her own. A huge rock fireplace dominated the left wall, the chimney soaring upward to the cathedral ceiling. Twin white ceiling fans stirred a gentle breeze. The furniture was chic but comfortable-looking, sized to fit a man of his height.

The living room was separated from the dining room by a waist-high planter in which luxurious ferns flourished. Huge double windows revealed a deck, furnished with comfortable chairs, an umbrella table and even more plants. Hesitantly she walked into the dining room for a better view. The kitchen opened up to the right, an immaculate oasis gleaming with the most modern appliances available. Even the coffeemaker looked as if the user would need a degree in engineering to work the thing. There was a breakfast nook on the far side of the kitchen, occupied by a smallish table with a white ceramic tile top. She could see him sitting there in the mornings, reading a newspaper and drinking coffee. Double French doors, far more ornate and stylish than her own, led from the breakfast nook onto the deck. She would have liked to explore further but felt too constrained here on his territory. Instead she retreated to the living room once more.

Robert took his time showering and dressing. Let her look around all she wanted; the fact that she wouldn't find anything alarming would help allay her suspicions. She would begin to relax, which was exactly what he wanted.

A lot of men, maybe most of them, would have made a move while they had been at her house; she had been more off-balance, vulnerable. He had even had the opportunity, had he chosen to take it, of walking in on her while she was unclothed. But he had elected to wait, knowing she would be more at ease now that the most provocative and dangerous circumstances were past. He hadn't made a pass at her then, so she wouldn't be expecting him to do so now. And since she wouldn't be mentally prepared to handle an advance, her response would be honest, unguarded.

Finally he stopped dawdling and returned to the living room. To his surprise, she was still standing almost exactly where he had left her, and little of the strain had faded from her face. She turned to watch him. Her lovely golden brown eyes were still dark with some inner distress that went far deeper than the episode with Jason, traumatic as that had been.

Robert paused while still several feet from her, studying those somber eyes. Then he simply moved forward with a graceful speed that gave her no time to evade him, and took her in his arms. He heard her instinctive intake of breath, saw the alarm widening her eyes as she lifted her head to protest, a protest that was smothered when his mouth covered hers.

She jerked in his arms, and he gently controlled the action, pulling her even more firmly against him. He took care not to hurt her but deepened the insistent pressure of his mouth until he felt her own mouth yield and open. The sweetness of her lips sent an electrical thrill along his nerves, tightening his muscles and swelling his sex. He took her mouth with his tongue, holding her still for the imitative sexual possession, repeating the motion again and again, until she shivered and softened in his arms, her lips beginning to cling to his.

Her tentative response made his head swim, and to his surprise he had to struggle to maintain his control. But she felt perfect in his arms, damn her, all those soft, luscious curves molding to the hard, muscled planes of his body. Her mouth was sweeter than any he had ever tasted before, and the simple act of kissing her was arousing him to an unbelievable degree.

He didn't want to stop. He hadn't planned to do more than kiss her, but he hadn't expected the intensity of his own response. His mouth crushed fiercely down on hers, demanding even more. He heard the soft, helpless sound she made in her throat; then her arms lifted around his neck, and she pressed full length against him. Pure, primitive male triumph roared through him at this evidence of her own arousal. He could feel her breasts, round and firm, the nipples hard against his chest, and he slipped his hand under her shirt to cup one of them, his thumb rubbing across the peaked nipple through the thin lace of her bra. Her body arched, her hips pressing hard against his...and then suddenly she was fighting, panicked, trying to squirm free.

He let her go, though every cell in his body was screaming for more. "Easy," he managed to say, but the word was low and rough and his breath was uneven. He tried for a more controlled reassurance. "I won't hurt you, sweetheart."

Evie had backed away from him, her face pale but her lips swollen and red from his kisses. She forced herself to stop retreating, to stand her ground and face him. The sensual pull of his masculinity was almost overwhelming, tempting her to go back into those arms, to yield to that fierce domination. She felt a sense of doom; he was far more dangerous to her than she had first suspected.

"Yes, you will," she whispered. Her teeth were chattering. "Why are you doing this? What do you want from me?"

CHAPTER FIVE

She looked ready to bolt. To soothe her, he moved back a few paces and let his hands relax at his sides. His eyes gleamed with faint irony. "You're a lovely woman, sweetheart. Surely you aren't surprised that I'm attracted to you? As for what I want from you, I was holding you closely enough that the answer to that question should have been obvious."

She didn't respond to his gentle teasing. Instead her somber gaze remained locked on his face, trying to probe beneath that smooth, urbane sophistication. He was very cosmopolitan, beyond a doubt, but he used that slick surface as a shield to hide the real man, the man who had kissed her with such ruthless passion. There were many hidden layers to him, his motives complex and unfathomable. Yes, he was attracted to her, as she was to him. It would be foolish to deny her own participation, and Evie wasn't a foolish woman. But she always had the feeling that he was studying her, manipulating her in some subtle manner. From the very first she had sensed his determination to force himself into her life, and he was doing exactly that with a calm force of will that refused to be denied. Whatever his motive, it was something that went beyond the physical.

"I don't have casual sex," she said.

He almost smiled. It was merely an expression in those pale eyes, rather than an actual movement of his mouth. "My dear, I promise you there wouldn't be anything *casual* about it." He paused. "Are you involved with someone else?"

She shook her head. "No."

He wasn't surprised that she had denied any involvement with Mercer. "Then we don't have a problem, do we? You can't say that you aren't attracted to me, too."

She lifted her chin, and his pale eyes gleamed at that proud motion. "That velvet glove covers an iron fist, doesn't it?" she commented neutrally. "No, I can't say that I'm not attracted to you."

Her perception disturbed him, a reaction that he didn't allow to surface. "I can be determined when I want something...or someone."

She made an abrupt motion, as if tiring of the verbal jousting. "I phrased it wrong. I don't have affairs, either."

"A wise decision, but in this case too restrictive." He approached her now, and she didn't retreat. Gently he cupped her face with one long-fingered hand, his fingers stroking over the velvety texture of her cheek. God, she was lovely, not classically beautiful, but glowing with an intensely female seductiveness that made him think her name was very apt indeed. So must Eve have been, glorious in her nudity. No wonder Adam had been so easily led, a weakness he wouldn't allow himself, though he intended to fully enjoy Evie's sensuality. Her sweet, warm scent wafted up to him. "I won't force you," he murmured. "But I will have you."

"If you won't use force, how do you intend to go about it?" she asked.

His eyebrows lifted. "You think I should warn you?"

"Yes."

"An interesting notion, but one I'm going to leave untried." He rubbed his thumb over her lower lip. "For now, sweetheart, we'd better get back to the marina. You have a business to run, and I have a boat to get into a slip."

He let his hand drop as he spoke, and Evie turned from him with relief, as if she had been released from a force field. Her face tingled where he had touched her, and she remembered the electric sensation when he had put his hand on her breast. His boldness spoke of vast experience and self-confidence with women, something that put her at a disadvantage.

They were both silent on the drive back to the marina. She was vaguely surprised to see how late it was, the sun dipping low even for these long summer days. The sultry heat hadn't abated, though there was a hint of purple on the horizon that gave the promise of a cooling rain shower.

Robert's speedboat, a sleek, dark eighteen-footer, was still where he had left it, hitched to a black Jeep Renegade. Thank heavens it hadn't been blocking the launch ramps, or Craig would have had a mess on his hands. She hurried into the marina office, and Craig looked up from the sports magazine he was reading. "Is everything okay?" he asked, getting to his feet. "The kids said that Jason nearly drowned."

"He has a concussion, but he'll go home tomorrow," she said. "Thanks for coming in. I'm sorry for wrecking your day."

"No problem," he said cheerfully. He was seventeen, a tall, muscular, dark-haired kid who would be a senior when the new school year started. He had been working part-time for her for almost two years and was so steady that she had no qualms about leaving him in charge. "Say, what about that new boat outside?"

"It's mine," Robert said, stepping inside. "I'll be renting a slip here." He held out his hand. "I'm Robert Cannon."

Craig took his hand with a firm grip. "Craig Foster. Glad to meet you, Mr. Cannon. You must be the guy who pulled Evie and Jason out of the water. The kids said it was a tall Yankee."

"I'm the guy," Robert affirmed, amusement in his eyes.

"Thought so. Want me to help you get the boat into a slip?"

"I can do it," Evie said. "I've taken enough time out of your day."

"You pay me for it," Craig replied, grinning. "I might as well, since I'm already here. Mom won't be expecting me back until supper, anyway." He and Robert left, chatting companionably.

Kids seemed to like Robert, Evie thought, watching them from the window. Even shy Paige had been at ease with him. He didn't treat kids as equals—he was the adult, his was the authority—but at the same time he didn't dismiss them. Authority and responsibility sat easily on those broad shoulders, she mused. He was obviously accustomed to command.

For her own sake, her own protection, she had to hold him at bay, and she didn't know if she could. Today, with a few kisses and frightening ease, he had shown her that he could arouse her beyond her own control. She could love him, and that was the most terrifying prospect of all. He was a strong man, in mind and soul as well as body, a man worthy of love. He would steal her heart if she weren't careful, if she didn't keep her guard up at all times.

She turned away from the window. Twelve years ago, love had almost destroyed her, leaving only a forlorn heap of ashes from which she had laboriously rebuilt a controlled, protected life. She couldn't do that again; she didn't have the strength to once more live through that hell and emerge victorious. She had already lost too many people to believe that love, or life, lasted forever. She couldn't do anything about the people she already loved, the ones already in her heart: her family, old Virgil, a very few close friends, but she hadn't allowed anyone new to stake a claim on her emotions. She had already paid out too much in pain and had precious little reserve of spirit left. She had almost lost Jason today, and the pain had been overwhelming. Rebecca knew, had realized that if Evie hadn't been able to find Jason, she would now be mourning a sister as well as a son. That was the real basis for her sister's fury with Jason.

And Evie knew that Robert Cannon planned to force his way into her life. He would be here for the summer, he'd said; he wouldn't be looking for anything more than a pleasant affair, companionship during the long, lazy weeks. If she fell in love with him, that would make the affair sweeter. But at the end of summer he would go back to his real life, and Evie would have to continue here, with one more wound on a heart that had barely survived the last blow. Emotionally, she couldn't afford him.

There were always a hundred and one things to be doing around the marina, but suddenly she couldn't think of a single one. She felt oddly disoriented, as if the world had been turned upside down. Maybe it had.

She called the hospital and was put through to Jason's room. Her sister answered the phone on the first ring. "He's grouchy and has a throbbing headache," Rebecca cheerfully announced when Evie asked his condition. "I have to wake him every couple of hours tonight, but if he does okay, then he can go home in the morning. Paul left just a few minutes ago to take Paige to his mother's, then he's coming back here. How about you? Nerves settled down yet?''

''Not quite,'' Evie said truthfully, though Jason's close call wasn't all that had unsettled her. ''But I'm over the shakes.''

''Are you at home, I hope?''

''You know better than that.''

''You should have taken it easy for the rest of the day,'' Rebecca scolded. ''I had hopes that Mr. Cannon would take you in hand. He seems good at giving orders.''

''World-class champion,'' Evie agreed. ''I'll come by to see Jason after the marina closes. Do you want me to bring you anything? A pillow, a book, a hamburger?''

''No, I don't need anything. Don't come here. Jason's okay, and you need to go home and rest. I mean it, Evie.''

''I'm okay, too,'' Evie calmly replied. ''And I want to see Jason, even if just for a few minutes—'' She cried out in surprise as the phone was plucked from her hand. She whirled as Robert lifted the receiver to his ear.

''Mrs. Wood? Robert Cannon. I'll see that she goes straight home. Yes, she's still a little wobbly.''

''I am not,'' Evie said, narrowing her eyes at him. He reached out and gently stroked her cheek. Deliberately she stepped back, out of his reach.

''I'll take care of her,'' he firmly assured Rebecca, never moving his gaze from Evie's face. ''On second thought, I'll take her out to dinner before I take her home. I think so, too. Goodbye.''

As he hung up, Evie said in a cold voice, ''I despise being treated as if I'm a helpless idiot.''

''Hardly that,'' he murmured.

She didn't relent. ''I suppose you thought that I would feel safe and protected, to have you take over and make my decisions for me. I don't. I feel insulted.''

Robert lifted an inquisitive brow, hiding his true reaction. He had indeed hoped to provoke exactly that response from her and felt an uneasy surprise that she had so easily gone straight to the truth of the matter. She was proving to be uncomfortably astute. "What I think," he said carefully, "is that you were in more danger than you want your sister to know, and that you're still shaky. If you go to the hospital again, you'll have to put up a front to keep from scaring both her and Jason, and that will put even more strain on you."

"What *I* think," she replied, standing with her fists clenched at her sides, "is that I'm in far more danger from you than I ever was from the water." Her golden brown eyes were cool and unwaveringly level.

Again he felt a twinge of discomfort at her insight. Still, he was certain he could soften her stand, and his tone turned gently cajoling. "Even if I offer you a truce for tonight? No kisses, not even any hand-holding. Just dinner, then I'll see you safely home, and you can get a good night's rest."

"No, thank you. I won't have dinner with you, and I can get home by myself."

He gave her a considering look. "In that case, the offer of a truce is null and void."

His tone was so calm that she listened to it first, rather than to the actual words. She hesitated only a split second, but that was enough for him to have her in his arms again, and again she felt overcome by his steely, deceptive strength. His body was unyielding, his grip careful but unbreakable. The male muskiness of his clean, warm skin made her head swim. She had the dizzy impression that his mouth was lowering to hers and quickly ducked her head to rest it against his chest. It was disconcerting to hear a quiet chuckle over her head.

"Such a cowardly act, from one who isn't," he murmured, the words rich with amusement. "But I don't mind simply holding you. It has its own compensations."

She *was* a coward, though, Evie thought. She was terrified of him, not in a physical way, but emotional fear was just as weighty a burden to carry. She was handling him all wrong; he wouldn't be accustomed to rejection, so every time she turned him down it made him just that much more determined to have his way. If she had played up to him from the beginning, gushed over him, he would have been bored and left her alone. Hindsight, though, despite its acuity, was depressingly useless.

His hand moved soothingly over her back, subtly urging her closer. It was so easy to let him take more of her weight, so easy to give in to the strain and fatigue she had been successfully fighting until now. She resisted the urge to put her arms around him, to feel the heated vibrancy of his body under her hands, but she could hear the strong, steady thumping of his heartbeat beneath her ear, feel the rise and fall of his chest as he breathed, and that was enough to work its own seduction. The forces of life were strong in him, luring women to that intense strength. She was no different from all those countless, nameless others.

"Robert," she whispered. "Don't." A cowardly, shameless, useless plea.

That hand stroked up to her shoulder blades, rubbed the sensitive tendons that ran from her neck to her shoulders, massaged her tender nape. "Evie," he whispered in return. "Don't what?" He continued without waiting for a reply. "Is Evie your real name, or is it a nickname for Eve? Or possibly Evelyn? No matter, it suits you."

Her eyes drifted shut as his warmth and strength continued to work their black magic on her nerves, her will. Oh God, it would be so foolishly easy just to give in to him. His skill was nothing short of diabolical. "Neither. It's short for Evangeline."

"Ah." The short sigh was one of approval. He truly hadn't known her full name; none of the reports he had seen had called her anything except Evie. "Evangeline. Feminine, spiritual, sensual...sad."

Evie didn't respond outwardly to that analysis of her name, but the last word shook her. Sad...yes. So sad that for several long, bleak years she couldn't have said if the sun ever shone or not, because with her heart she had seen only gray. She could see the sunshine now; the relentless current of life as a whole had swept her out of the darkness, but there was never a day when she didn't realize how closely the shadows lurked. They were always there, a permanent counterpoint to life. If there was light, there had to be darkness; joy was balanced by pain, intimacy by loneliness. No one sailed through life untouched.

He was subtly rocking her with his body, a barely perceptible swaying that nevertheless urged her deeper and deeper into his embrace. He was aroused again; there was no mistaking that. She thought she should move away, but somehow in the past few minutes that had ceased to be an option. She was so tired, and the gentle motion of his body was soothing, like the swaying of a boat at anchor. The ancient rhythms were difficult to resist, linked as they were to instincts aeons beyond her control.

After several minutes he murmured, ''Are you going to sleep?''

''I could,'' she replied, not opening her eyes. Beyond the danger, there was deep comfort in his embrace.

''It's almost six-thirty. Under the circumstances, I'm sure your customers would understand if you closed a little early.''

''An hour and a half isn't a 'little' early. No, I'll stay until eight, as usual.''

''Then so will I.'' He stifled his surge of annoyance. He himself let very few things interfere with his work—in actuality, only Madelyn and her family—but he didn't like the idea of Evie pushing herself into exhaustion at the marina.

''It isn't necessary.''

''I rather believe it is,'' he replied thoughtfully.

''I still won't go out to dinner with you.''

''Fair enough. I'll bring dinner to you. Do you have any preferences?''

She shook her head. ''I'm not very hungry. I was going to have a sandwich when I got home.''

''Leave it all to me.''

She said against his chest, ''You take charge very naturally. I suppose this is normal behavior for you.''

''I'm decisive, yes.''

''Don't forget autocratic.''

''I'm sure you'll remind me if I forget.''

She heard the undertone of amusement in his voice. Damn him, why couldn't he be nasty in his bullying, rather than relentlessly, gently cosseting? She never allowed herself to rely on anyone, though Rebecca had been trying to take care of her for years, but Robert simply ignored her resistance.

"I realize I'm rushing you," he murmured into her hair. "Today is only the second time we've met. I'll back off, sweetheart, and give you time to get to know me better and feel more comfortable around me. Okay?"

Her head moved up and down. She didn't want to agree to have anything to do with him, but right now she would grasp at any offer to cool down the situation. He had knocked her off balance, and she still hadn't regained it. Yes, she needed time, a lot of it.

Robert cupped her chin in his hand and forced her to lift her head away from the shelter of his chest. His pale green eyes were glittering with intensity. "But I won't go away," he warned.

Evie slept heavily that night, exhausted by the stress of the day. When she woke at dawn at the far-off roar of an early fisherman's outboard motor, she didn't rise immediately as was her habit but lay watching the pearly light spread across the sky.

For twelve years she had kept herself safe inside her carefully constructed fortress, but Robert was storming the walls. *Had* stormed them, if she was honest with herself. He was already in the inner court, though he hadn't yet managed to breach the defenses of the keep. Since Matt's death, she hadn't really *seen* any man, but Robert had forced her to see him. She was attracted to him, mentally as well as physically; it was only with effort that she had kept her emotions still safely locked away. She didn't want to love him and knew she risked doing exactly that if she continued to see him.

But she *would* see him, time and again. He had warned her—or was it a promise?—that he wasn't going to leave her alone, and he wasn't a man who could be easily distracted from his purpose.

He would kiss her, hold her, caress her. Eventually, she knew, all of her caution would vanish under the sheer force of physical desire, and she wouldn't be able to stop him—or herself.

She closed her eyes and relived the way he had kissed her the afternoon before, the way he had tasted, the calm expertise with which he had deepened the kiss. She thought of his lean fingers on her breast, and her nipples throbbed. For the first time since Matt, she wondered about making love in relation to herself. She thought of the feel of Robert's hard weight pressing down on her, of his hands and mouth moving over her bare skin, of his muscled thighs spreading hers apart as he positioned himself to take her. The appeal of her fantasy was strong enough to make her entire body clench with desire. Yes, she wanted him, as much as she feared the pain he would leave behind when he walked out of her life.

A prudent woman would immediately see a doctor about birth control, and Evie was a prudent woman. She could protect herself in that way, at least.

CHAPTER SIX

Evie slid two food-filled plates onto the table, one in front of Rebecca and the other in front of her own seat, then refilled their coffee cups. "Thanks." Rebecca sighed, picking up her fork. Her eyes were dark-circled after the long, sleepless night spent with Jason in the hospital.

Evie sat down. After making a doctor's appointment for the next day, she had called the hospital to check on Jason. He was fine, but Rebecca had some definitely frayed edges. Not only had she been awake all night to keep watch on him and wake him regularly, evidently Jason had become as fractious and ill-tempered as he'd been as a baby whenever he was ill. He had complained about everything, griping about being woken every hour, even though both the doctor and Rebecca had explained the reason for it. In short, his mother's wrath was about to come down hard on his sore head.

So Evie had gone up to the hospital to take care of the myriad details involved in releasing Jason. Then she'd followed them home, helped get the restless teenager settled, pushed Rebecca into a chair and set about making breakfast for them all. She knew her way around Rebecca's kitchen as well as she did her own, so the work went smoothly, and in no time at all they were digging into scrambled eggs, bacon and toast. Jason was enthroned on the couch with a tray on his lap and the television blaring.

The coffee revived Rebecca enough that her big-sister instincts kicked in. She gave Evie a shrewd look over the rim of her cup. "Where did you have dinner last night?"

"At the marina. Sandwiches," Evie clarified.

Rebecca sat back, looking disgruntled. "He said he would take you out to dinner, then make sure you got home okay."

"I didn't want to go out."

"Really," Rebecca grumbled, "I'd thought the man was made of stronger stuff than that."

If he'd been any stronger, Evie thought wryly, she would have slept in *his* bed last night. "I was too tired to go out, so he brought sandwiches there. It was kind of him to do everything he did yesterday."

"Especially hauling both you and my brat out of the river," Rebecca said judiciously as she demolished a slice of bacon. "I need to thank him again for you. I'm reserving judgment on the wisdom of saving Jason."

Evie chuckled at Rebecca's sardonic statement. A sharp turn of phrase was a family trait that she shared with her sister, and even Paige had been exhibiting it for some time now.

"However," Rebecca continued in the same tone, "I know a man on the hunt when I see one, so don't try to throw me off the subject by telling me how *kind* he was. Kindness was the last thing on his mind."

Evie looked down at her eggs. "I know."

"Are you going to give him a chance, or are you going to look straight through him, like all the others?"

"What others?" Evie asked, puzzled.

"See what I mean? They were invisible to you. You've never even noticed all the guys who would have liked to go out with you."

"No one's ever asked me out."

"Why would they, when you never notice them? But I'll bet Robert asked you out, didn't he?"

"No." He'd *told* her that she was going out to dinner with him, and he had told her that he intended to make love to her, but he'd never actually asked her out.

Rebecca looked disbelieving. "You're pulling my leg."

"I am not. But he'll probably ask the next time he comes to the marina, if that's any consolation to you."

"The real question," her sister said shrewdly, "is if you'll go with him."

"I don't know." Evie propped her elbows on the table, the coffee cup cradled in her palms as she sipped the hot liquid. "He excites me, Becky, but he scares me, too. I don't want to get involved with anyone, and I'm afraid I wouldn't be able to stop myself with him."

"This is bad?" asked her sister with some exasperation. "Honey, it's been twelve years. Maybe it's time you became interested in men again."

"Maybe," Evie said in qualified agreement, though privately she didn't think so at all. "But Robert Cannon isn't the safest choice I could make, not by a long shot. There's something about him... I don't know. I just get the feeling that he's coming on to me for another reason besides the obvious. There's a hidden agenda there somewhere. And he puts up a good front, but he's *not* a gentleman."

"Good. A gentleman would probably take you at your word and never bother you again, after a hundred or so refusals. I have to admit, though, he struck me as being both gentle and protective."

"Possessive," Evie corrected. "And ruthless." No, he wasn't a gentleman. That cold force of will in his green diamond eyes was the look of an adventurer with a predator's heart. A hollow look of fear entered her own eyes.

Rebecca leaned forward and touched Evie's arm. "I know," she said gently. And she did, because Rebecca had been there and seen it all. "I don't want to push you into doing something you'll regret, but you never know what's going to happen. If Robert Cannon is someone you could love, can you afford to pass up that chance?"

Evie sighed. Rebecca's arguments to the contrary, could she afford to *take* that chance? And was she going to have the choice?

To her relief, Robert wasn't at the marina when she arrived to relieve Craig. Huge, black-bellied clouds were threatening overhead, and a brisk, cool wind began to blow, signaling one of the tempestuous thunderstorms so common during summer. Both pleasure-boaters and fishermen began coming in off the lake, and for an hour she didn't have a moment's rest. Lightning forked downward over the mountains, a slash of white against the purplish black background. Thunder boomed, echoing over the water, and the storm broke with blinding sheets of rain blowing across the lake.

With all of the fishermen who had put in at the marina safely off the water and the other boats snugly in their slips, Evie gladly retreated to the office where she could watch the storm from behind the protection of the thick, Plexiglass windows. She hadn't quite escaped all the rain, though, and she shivered as she rubbed a towel over her bare arms. The temperature had dropped twenty degrees in about ten minutes; the break from the heat was welcome, but the abrupt contrast was always chilling.

She loved the energy and drama of thunderstorms, and settled contentedly into her rocking chair to watch this one play out against the background of lake and mountains. Listening to the rain was unutterably soothing. Inevitably she became drowsy and got up to turn on the small television she kept to entertain Paige and Jason. A small logo at the bottom of the television screen announced "T'storm watch."

"I'm watching, I'm watching," she told the television, and returned to the rocking chair.

Eventually the violence of the storm dissipated, but the welcome rain continued, settling down to a steady soaker, the kind farmers loved. The marina was deserted, except for the mechanic, Burt Mardis, who was contentedly working on an outboard motor in the big metal building where he did all the repairs. She could see him occasionally through the open door as he moved back and forth. There wouldn't be any more business until the weather cleared, which it showed no signs of doing. At the top of the hour the local television meteorologist broke in on the normal programming to show the progression of the line of thunderstorms that were marching across the state, as well as the solid area of rain they had left behind, stretching all the way back into Mississippi. Rain was predicted well into the night, tapering off shortly before midnight.

It looked like a long, lazy afternoon ahead of her. She always kept a book there for such times and pulled it out now, but so much time had lapsed since she had started the thing that she didn't remember much about it, so she had to start over. Actually, this was the third time she had started over; she would have to carry it home if she ever hoped to finish it.

But she was already fighting drowsiness and after ten minutes she knew that reading was going to tip the scales in favor of sleep. Regretfully she put the book aside and looked around for some chores to do. Craig, however, had cleaned up that morning; the floors were freshly swept and mopped, the merchandise impeccably straight on the shelves or hanging on pegboard hooks.

She yawned and desperately turned the television channel to rock music videos. That should jar her awake.

When Robert walked in half an hour later, she was standing in front of the television, watching with a sort of amazed disbelief. Turning to him, she said in bemusement, "I wonder why bird-legged, sunken-chested musicians feel compelled to show their bodies to the audience?"

He was startled into a deep chuckle. He almost never laughed aloud, his amusement normally expressed, at most, by a twinkle in his eyes. This was twice, though, that Evie had charmed him into laughter. No one would ever suspect her of espionage, he thought suddenly, perhaps because of that very charm. It would be almost impossible for anyuone who knew her at all to think ill of her. Even he, who was well aware of her activities, couldn't keep himself from wanting her with a violence that both angered him and made him uneasy, because he couldn't control it.

He pushed those thoughts away as he walked toward her. If he let himself think about it now he would become enraged all over again, and Evie was so astute that he might not be able to hide it from her. When he reached her, though, and encircled her with his arms, forgetting about the other was laughably easy.

She blinked up at him, startled. Automatically she put her hands against his chest in a defensive movement. "You said you were going to back off and give me time," she accused.

"I am," Robert replied, lifting her left hand and pressing his warm, open mouth to the tender flesh on the inside of her wrist. Her pulse fluttered and raced beneath his lips. The scent of her skin was fresh and elusively, lightly fragrant, teasing him far more than if she had dabbed herself with perfume, no matter how expensive. He touched the tip of his tongue to the delicate blue veins that traced just under her skin and felt the throb of her blood beneath his touch.

Evie trembled at the subtle caress, her knees weakening. He felt that betraying quiver and gathered her more firmly against him, then lightly bit the pad at the base of her thumb. She swallowed a gasp; dear God, she hadn't known that could be so erotic.

"Will you go out to dinner with me tonight?" he murmured as his lips traveled on to her palm. Again his tongue flicked out, tasting her. Her hand trembled at the sensation.

"No, I can't." The instinctive denial was out before she could stop it, the habits of a dozen years firmly ingrained. Stunned, she realized that she *had* wanted to accept, much as a moth yearned toward the flame.

"Do you have another date?"

"No. It—it's difficult." He had no idea how difficult. She took a deep breath. "I haven't dated since my husband died."

Robert lifted his head, a slight frown drawing the black wings of his eyebrows together. "What did you say?"

She flushed and tugged her hand free. She started to wipe her palm against her jeans but instead tightly closed her fingers to hold the feel of his kiss. "I haven't gone out with anyone since Matt died."

He was silent, digesting this information, weighing it for truth. It was difficult to believe of anyone, but especially of a woman who looked like Evie. It was possible, of course, that she wasn't having an affair with Mercer after all, but to have lived like a nun for twelve years just didn't seem feasible. Still, he wasn't about to infuriate her by suggesting she was a liar.

Instead he gently stroked the underside of her jaw with the back of one finger and was immediately absorbed with the velvety texture of her skin. "Why is that?" he murmured a bit absently. "I know all the men down here can't be blind."

She bit her lip. "It was my choice. I...wasn't interested, and it didn't seem fair to waste a man's time under those circumstances."

"Reasonable, for a while. But twelve years?"

Restlessly she tried to pull away from him, but he stilled the movement, tightening the arm that remained around her. They were pressed firmly together from waist to knees, his muscled thighs hard and warm against hers. A man's strength was wonderful, she thought, inviting a woman to relax against him. Until Robert had taken her in his arms, she hadn't realized how very much she needed to be held. But not by just any man; only by him. In that moment Evie knew for certain that she had lost the battle. There was no use trying to evade him; not only would he refuse to let her get away with it, but she didn't *want* to get away with it, not any longer. For better or worse, and with dizzying speed, she had gotten herself involved with Robert Cannon. Dear God, she didn't know if she had the strength to do this, but she knew she had to try.

She didn't try to explain those twelve years. Instead she said, to his chest, "All right. I'll go out with you. Now what?"

"For starters, you could raise your head."

Slowly she did, mentally bracing herself as she met his crystalline eyes. She had expected to see amusement in them, but it was triumph glittering there rather than mirth. She shivered, more from sudden alarm than from the coolness brought by the steady rain.

"Cold?" he asked softly, rubbing his warm hands up the length of her arms.

"No. Afraid," she admitted, with painful candor. "Of you, of getting involved with you." Her eyes were deep and mysterious with shadows as she looked up at this man who had so inexplicably forced himself into her life. If he insisted on establishing some kind of romantic relationship with her, he should know up front how she felt about a few things. "I'm not good at games, Robert. Don't kiss me unless it's for real. Don't come around unless you mean to stay."

"Do you mean marriage?" he asked coolly, his expressive eyebrows lifting.

Her cheeks burned at his tone. Of course it was ridiculous to think of marriage; that wasn't at all what she had meant. At least, not the legality of marriage, the institution itself. Mentally she shied from the notion, unable to even think of it. "Of course not! I never want to get married again. But the stability, the emotional security, what I had with Matt...well, I won't settle for anything less than that, so if you're looking for a summer affair, I'm not your woman."

His mouth twisted as an unreadable expression crossed his face. "Oh, but you are. You just haven't admitted it to yourself yet."

She shivered again, but her gaze didn't waver. "I want emotional commitment. Under those terms, if you're still willing to get involved with me, I'll go out with you. I'm not comfortable with you, but I expect that will change as we get to know each other. And I don't want to sleep with you. That would just be too risky." He probably thought she meant physically, but for her the emotional risk was by far more dangerous.

He studied her face for a long moment before saying calmly, "All right, we'll take our time and get to know each other. But I *do* want to make love with you, and I'm not going to take a vow of chastity." He cupped her face in his hands, and the glitter in his eyes became more pronounced as his head began to slowly descend. "All you have to do to stop me, at any time," he whispered as his mouth touched hers, "is say no."

Her breath sighed out of her, as soft as a night breeze. The freedom to enjoy him was glorious; it felt as if she had long been frozen and was now thawing, growing warm with life again. For the first time her mouth opened welcomingly beneath his, and he took it with a calm mastery that liquefied her bones. He could give lessons in kissing, she thought hazily. His tongue probed and stroked, enticing her into a like response, so that their tongues touched and curled and petted. It was surprisingly sweet, and totally erotic.

It seemed as if he kissed her like that for a long time, simply holding her face between his palms, her body still pressed full against his. The play of his lips and tongue was both lulling and arousing. Her anxiety faded even as warmth slowly spread through her breasts and loins, making her feel as soft as butter. Her left hand was closed around his right wrist, but her right hand was leisurely stroking his back, feeling the firm, hard layers of muscle, the hollow of his spine, instinctively learning some of the details of how he was made.

The television played on unnoticed. No one came to the door on this rainy day; they stood alone in the office, oblivious to the music and the steady patter of the rain, hearing only each other's breathing and the soft, unconscious sounds of pleasure. Like a morning glory opening its shy face to the sun, Evie slowly bloomed in his arms, her golden sensuality growing in confidence. He was painfully aroused but held himself under strict control, ignoring his own condition so that she didn't feel pressured. She felt...safe, free to relax, and let herself feel the new sensations, explore the limits of her own desire. It was very different from the way it had been with Matt. She had been a girl then, and now she was a woman, with a woman's deeper and richer passion.

Though he had kissed her before, she had been distracted by the dangerous desire she felt for this man. Now, having given in, she could concentrate on the little details. She reveled in his taste, as the coolness of his lips rapidly became warm, then hard and hot. She measured the broadness of his shoulders, her palms smoothing over the curve of the joint and feeling the hardness of his solid bones covered by pads of muscle. She touched his hair, feeling it thick and silky and cool, warmer underneath, where it lay close to his skull. She felt the rasp of his five o'clock stubble against her cheeks. She inhaled the clean, musky scent of his maleness, a faint odor of soap, the fresh smell of rain on his clothes and skin.

"God." Abruptly he drew away, letting his head fall back as he drew in a deep breath. Her response had been hesitant at first, but then she had come alive in his arms, and he felt singed, as if he had been holding the sweetest of fires. His own response to her shook him with its violence. It was difficult to think of anything but taking her, and only their present location kept him from trying. "I'm the one calling a halt this time, sweetheart. We either have to stop or find a more private place."

She felt bereft, suddenly deprived of his touch. Her heart was pounding, and her skin felt as if it glowed with heat. Still, he was right. This wasn't the place for making out like teenagers. "There isn't a more private place," she said as she reached out to turn the television from rock to a country video station. The music abruptly changed from rap to a hauntingly passionate love song, and that was even more jarring to her nerves. She punched the Off button, and in the sudden quiet the rain sounded heavier than before. She looked out the window at the gray curtain that veiled the lake, obscuring the far bank.

"No one will be using their boats for the rest of the day," Robert said. "Why don't you close early and we'll go to Huntsville for dinner."

She considered how his questions and suggestions sounded like statements and demands. Had no one before her ever said no to this man? "I can't close early."

"The rain is supposed to last halfway through the night," he said reasonably.

"But that won't stop people from coming in to buy tackle. Granted, there probably won't be many, maybe not any, but the sign says that I'm open until eight."

And she would be, he thought, exasperated by the difficulty of courting a woman who refused to make time for him. He had certainly never had that problem before. In fact, he couldn't say that he'd ever had a problem with a woman at all—until Evie. Getting close to her presented him with as many obstacles as a mine field. Ruefully he thought that if he was going to spend any time with her, most of it would obviously be here at the marina.

Rather than become angry, which would only make her more obstinate, he said, "Could Craig swap shifts with you occasionally, if we give him advance notice?"

A tiny smile lifted the corners of her mouth, telling him that he was learning. "I suppose he could. He's generally accommodating."

"Tomorrow?"

This time she almost laughed aloud. "I can't tomorrow." She had an appointment with her doctor at ten in the morning. Though she had told Robert that she didn't want to sleep with him, he had said only that he would stop if she told him to. The ''if'' told her that she should be prudent, because his physical effect on her was potent. Of course, she wasn't going to tell Robert that she was arranging birth control; he would consider it a green light to making love.

He sighed. ''The day after tomorrow?''

''I'll ask him.''

''Thank you,'' he said with faint irony.

Robert received two phone calls the next morning. He was out on the deck, reading a sheaf of papers that Felice had faxed to him; it was remarkably easy, he'd found, to keep abreast of things by way of phone, computer and fax. The first call was from Madelyn. ''How are things in Alabama?''

''Hot,'' he replied. He was wearing only gym shorts. The rain of the day before had made everything seem even more green and lush, the scents more intense, but it hadn't done anything to ease the heat. If anything, the heat was worse. The morning sun burned on his bare chest and legs. Luckily, with his olive complexion, he didn't have to worry about sunburn.

''The weather is perfect here, about seventy-five degrees. Why don't you fly up for the weekend?''

''I can't,'' he said, and realized how much he sounded like Evie. ''I don't know how long I'll be down here, but I can't leave until everything is tied up.''

''The invitation stands,'' Madelyn said in her lazy drawl. A funny pang went through him as he realized how similar Madelyn's accent was to Evie's. ''If you do happen to find a couple of days free, we'd love to see you.''

''I'll try to get up there before I go back to New York,'' he promised.

''Try really hard. We haven't seen you since spring. Take care.''

The phone rang again almost immediately. This time it was the man he had hired to keep watch on Landon Mercer. ''He had a visitor last night. We followed the visitor when he left, and we're working on identifying him. There hasn't been anything of interest on the phones.''

''All right. Keep watching and listening. Has he spotted his tail yet?''

''No, sir.''

''Anything in his house?'' Robert was briefly thankful that he was a civilian and didn't have to follow the same tortuous rules and procedures that cops did, though it could have been sticky if his men had been caught breaking and entering. They hadn't seized any evidence, merely looked for it. Information was power.

''Clean as a whistle. Too clean. There's not even a bank statement lying around. We found out that he has a safety deposit box, so he might keep his paperwork in it, but we haven't been able to get into it yet. I'm working on getting a copy of his bank statement.''

''Keep me informed,'' Robert said, and hung up. In a few days Mercer would start feeling a slight squeeze. He wouldn't think much of it at first, but soon it would become suffocating. Robert's plans for Evie, both personal and financial, were moving along nicely, too.

CHAPTER SEVEN

Robert didn't intend to see Evie at all that day. He was an expert strategist in the eternal battle between men and women; after his determined pursuit of her, she would be expecting him to either call or come to the marina, and the lack of any contact with him would knock her slightly off balance, further weakening her defenses. He had often thought that seduction was similar to chess, in that the one who could keep the other guessing was the one in control of the game.

He was in control of the seduction. His instincts in that part of the game were infallible. It might take him a few weeks of gentling, but Evie would end up in his bed. Not long after that, he would have this entire mess cleaned up; Mercer and Evie would be arrested, and he would go back to New York.

Damn.

That was the problem, of course. He didn't want Evie in jail. He had been furious when he had come down here, determined to put both her and her lover away for a very long time. But that was before he had met her, before he had held her and tasted the heady sweetness of her. Before he had seen the underlying sadness in those golden brown eyes, and wondered if he would cause that expression to deepen. The thought made him uneasy.

Was she even guilty? At first he had been convinced that she was; now, even after such a short acquaintance, he was no longer certain. No criminal was untouched by his deeds. There was always a mark left behind, perhaps in a certain coldness in the eye, a lack of moral concern in certain matters. He hadn't been able to find any such mark in Evie. He had often thought that those who dealt in espionage, in the betrayal of their own country, were some of the coldest people ever born. They lacked the depth of emotion that others had. That lack of feeling wasn't evident in Evie; if anything, he would say that she felt far too much.

She hadn't hesitated at all in going into the river after Jason. That in itself wasn't unusual; any number of strangers would have done the same thing, much less a relative. But, knowing that every second counted, she had stayed down far too long herself in the effort to find the boy. He knew as surely as he knew the sun was in the sky that she would not have been able to make it back to the surface without his help…and that she had been willing to die rather than release Jason and save herself. Even now, the memory made his bones turn cold.

He had gone inside to work at the computer, but now he got up and restlessly walked out onto the deck, where the burning sun could dispel his sudden chill.

Only a person of deep emotion was capable of that kind of sacrifice.

He braced his hands on the top railing and stared out at the river. It wasn't green today, but rather a rich blue, reflecting the deep blue of the cloudless sky. There was little, if any, breeze, and the water's surface was calm. It lapped gently against the dock and the bank with a sound that tugged at something deep within him. All life had originated in the sea; perhaps it was an echo of that ancient time that made people respond so to water. But this river, peaceful as it was now, had almost taken Evie's life.

He shivered from another chill. He couldn't remember, he thought absently, when he had been so enraged…or so afraid. He had ruthlessly controlled both emotions, allowing no hint of them to surface, but they had roiled deep within him. It hadn't been an intellectual anger, but rather a gut-level rage at fate, at chance, which had seemed to be snatching Evie out of his grasp before he could…what? Have her indicted? He snorted mirthlessly at that idea. The thought hadn't entered his mind. No, he had been furious that he wouldn't be able to hold her, make love to her, that the endless stretch of his days wouldn't have her in them.

Was Evie the type of person who could betray her country? He was beginning to doubt his own information.

Indecision wasn't normally part of Robert's makeup, and he was impatient with himself now. He couldn't allow his doubts about Evie's guilt to alter his plans. If she was innocent, then she wouldn't be harmed. She would have some uncomfortable moments, she would be worried, but in the end he would take care of the situation, and she would be okay.

Thinking about her made him edgy. He glanced at his watch; it was a little after noon. She should be at the marina now, and he should already have heard from the tail that he had assigned to follow her every move.

Right on cue, the phone rang, and he stepped inside to pick it up.

"She went to Huntsville this morning," a quiet female voice reported. "Her destination was an office building. The elevator closed before I could get on it with her, so I don't know where she went. I waited, and she returned to the lobby after an hour and twenty-three minutes. She drove straight home, changed clothes and then went to the marina. Mercer was in his office at PowerNet the entire time, and they didn't talk on the phone. There was no contact between them at all."

"What kind of tenants are in the office building?"

"I made a list. There are two insurance firms, a real estate office, four medical doctors, four lawyers, three dentists, an office temp company and two computer programming firms."

Damn, Robert thought bleakly. Aloud he said, "Find out where she went. Concentrate first on the two programming firms."

"Yes, sir."

He swore as he hung up. Why couldn't she have spent the morning shopping, or paying bills?

He wanted to see her. He wanted to shake her until her teeth rattled. He wanted to whisk her away to some secluded place and keep her locked up there until he had this mess settled. He wanted to ride her until she wept with submission. The violence of all those longings was alien to him, but he couldn't deny it. She had definitely gotten under his skin in a way no other woman had ever done.

Temper and frustration merged, and with a muttered curse he gave in. After swiftly dressing, he left the house and climbed in the black Jeep. Damn it, he wanted to see her, so he would.

Virgil was visiting with Evie again that day. His knee was better, he said, and indeed, he was walking with less effort. The day had been fairly busy, with customers in and out on a regular basis, and Virgil had passed the time with several old friends and casual acquaintances.

She was busy ringing up a fisherman's purchase of gas, a soft drink and a pack of crackers when the door opened. Without looking, she knew Robert had entered. Her skin tingled, and she felt an instant of panic. She had hoped, foolishly, that she wouldn't see him that day, that her frazzled nerves would have a chance to recover somewhat before she actually went out with him the next night. On the other hand, she thought wryly, time and distance probably wouldn't help at all. Even if he wasn't there personally, he was in her mind, dominating both her thoughts and dreams.

Her customer taken care of, she allowed herself to look at him as he genially introduced himself to Virgil, who remembered him, of course. Very little got by that old man.

Robert was wearing jeans and a loose, white cotton shirt. A khaki baseball cap covered his black hair, and a pair of expensive sunglasses dangled from one hand. Her blood raced through her veins in excitement; even in such casual dress, there was something elegant and dangerous about him. The jeans were soft and faded with age, and he was as at home in them as he was in his silk shirts.

Then he was touching her on the arm, and it was like being burned with a tiny spark of electricity. "I'm going to take the boat out for a while, run the river and learn something about it."

So he wasn't going to be hanging around the marina all day. She was both relieved and disappointed. "Have you hired a guide?"

"No, but the river channel's marked, isn't it?"

"Yes, there shouldn't be any problem, unless you want to explore out of the channel. I'll give you a map."

"Okay." Thoughtfully Robert looked at Virgil. "Would you like to show me around the lake, Mr. Dodd? That is, if you don't have plans for the afternoon.''

Virgil cackled, his faded eyes suddenly gleaming with enthusiasm. ''Plans?'' he snorted. ''I'm ninety-three years old! Who in tarnation makes plans at my age? I could stop breathin' any minute now.''

Amusement danced in Robert's eyes, making them look like pale green diamonds. ''I'm willing to take the chance if you are, but I warn you, a corpse in the boat would be a real inconvenience.''

Virgil hauled himself out of the rocking chair. ''Tell you what, son. For the chance to park myself in a boat again, I'll try real hard not to put you to the trouble of havin' to call the coroner.''

''It's a deal.'' Robert winked at Evie as he turned away.

Evie shook her head as she smiled at Virgil. She knew better than to try talking him out of going. Besides, he deserved to enjoy an hour or so on the river he loved, and she had faith that Robert would be as skillful at handling a boat as he was at everything else he did. How had he guessed, on such short acquaintance, that Virgil would dearly love getting out on the water again?

''Both of you be careful,'' she admonished. ''Virgil, don't forget your cap.''

''I won't, I won't,'' he said testily. ''Think I'm fool enough to go out without somethin' on my head?''

''I'll bring the boat around to the dock,'' Robert said, and she was grateful to him for sparing Virgil the longer walk to the boat slip. He reached the door, stopped and came back to her. ''I forgot something.''

''What?''

He cupped her chin in one hand, leaned down and calmly kissed her. It wasn't a passionate kiss; it was almost leisurely. Still, when he lifted his head, her heart was pounding and her thoughts scattered. ''That,'' he murmured.

She heard Virgil's cracked laughter and became aware of the interested gazes of the two customers who were browsing among the hooks and spinner baits. Her cheeks burned with a blush, and she turned away to fiddle with some papers until she could regain her composure.

Virgil patted her on the arm. Though stooped under the weight of nine decades, he was still taller than she, and he grinned at her. "Heard tell that young feller made hisself useful the other day, when Becky's boy fell in."

She cleared her throat. "Yes. If he hadn't been there, Jason and I both would probably have drowned."

"Fast mover, is he?"

She found herself blushing again and waved Virgil off with shooing motions. Why on earth had Robert kissed her in public? She would never have thought that he was given to public displays of affection; there was something too contained about him. But he had certainly done just that!

She watched out the window as he idled the sleek black boat around to the dock, the powerful motor rumbling like thunder. The sunglasses were in place on the high-bridged nose, giving him a remote, lethal air. She had seen soldiers with that exact expression, and she wondered at it. With a start, she realized how little she knew about Robert Cannon. What did he do for a living? She knew he had to have some money to be able to afford that house, a new boat and the new Jeep. Where was he from? Did he have family, had he been married before, was he married *now*, did he have children? A chill went through her as she thought of all she didn't know about him.

And yet, in a way, she knew the man. He was cool and complicated, a private man who kept a subtle but permanent distance between himself and everyone else. The distance wasn't physical, God knows; he was the most physical, *sensual* man she'd ever met. Emotionally, though, he always held something back, keeping the inner man untouched. Probably most people thought of him as very controlled and unemotional; Evie agreed with the controlled part, but there was a ferocity lurking beneath the control that alarmed her even as it called to her own inner fire. He was ruthless, he was autocratic...and he had seen, almost at a glance, how much an old man would love to take a boat ride on his beloved river once more.

Her breath caught, and there was a pain in her chest. Panic filled her as she watched Virgil hobble out to the dock as Robert brought the boat alongside. Robert held out a strong hand, and Virgil gripped it and stepped aboard the craft. There was a wide smile on his face as he settled onto the seat. Robert handed him a life jacket, and obediently Virgil slipped it on, though Evie was fairly certain he'd never worn one before in his life.

The panic that almost suffocated her was comprised of equal parts terror and tenderness. She *couldn't* feel this much for him, not so soon. You had to know someone for that, and she had just been thinking how little she knew about him. She was fascinated by him, that was all. It was understandable. He was the first man in her life since Matt's death, twelve long, desolate years ago. He had brought passion alive in her again, with his skillful kisses and determined pursuit.

She had never felt so violently attracted to a man before.

With Matt...they had grown up together, they'd been in the same class in school, from first grade through graduation. She had known Matt as well as she knew herself; they'd been like two halves of a whole. The love had grown gradually between them, pure and steady, like a candle flame. Robert...Robert was an inferno, and the heat between them could leave her in ashes.

Robert and Virgil had been gone for over an hour when Landon Mercer strolled into the marina. "Hi, doll," he said jovially. "How's the prettiest woman in this part of the state?"

Evie's expression was impassive as she glanced at him. Unfortunately, business had slowed down and she was there alone. She always preferred to have company around when she had to deal with him. Of course, being alone meant that she would have the opportunity to follow him again. Her thoughts began to hum. "Hello, Mr. Mercer."

"Landon," he said, as he always did. He leaned against the counter in a negligent pose, one designed to show off his physique. Mercer was a good-looking man, she admitted, but he left her cold.

"Do you want to rent a boat today?" she asked, turning to check which ones were available, though she knew without looking. She had quickly discovered that the best way to deflect his attention was to appear oblivious to it.

"Sure do. It's been a while since I've done any fishing, so I decided to play hooky from work this afternoon." He laughed at his own pun.

Evie managed a polite smile. He had brought in a small tackle box and one rod and reel, the same rig he always carried. The same lure was tied to the line.

"Do you want any particular boat?"

"No, any of them will do." He leaned closer. "When I get back, why don't we go out to dinner tonight? Not anywhere here. We'll go someplace nice, maybe in Birmingham."

"Thanks, but I'm busy tonight," she replied, her tone conveying no interest at all. Unfortunately, he was so taken with his own charm that he was oblivious to her lack of response to him.

"Tomorrow night, then. It's Saturday night. We can even go to Atlanta for some real fun, since we wouldn't have to be back for work."

"The marina's open seven days a week."

"Oh. Okay, we'll go to Birmingham."

"No, thank you, Mr. Mercer. I'm busy tomorrow night, too."

"C'mon, how busy can you be? Whatever it is, you can put it off."

Her teeth were on edge. She barely managed to be polite as she said, "I have a date tomorrow night."

"Now I'm jealous. Who's the lucky man?"

"No one you know." She took an ignition key from the pegboard and slid it across the counter to him. "There you go. Number five, the one at the end of the dock."

He took out his wallet and extracted a couple of twenties. "I'll have it back in two hours." He picked up the ignition key.

"Fine." She mustered a smile. "Have a good time. Hope you catch a lot."

"I never do, but it's fun to try," he said breezily as he picked up his tackle and went out the door.

Evie put the money into the cash drawer and locked it, all the while eyeing Mercer as he walked down the dock. He was looking around, studying the parking lot and the traffic on the street out front, as well as on the bisecting causeway.

Swiftly she picked up the phone and buzzed Burt in the maintenance building. He picked up just as Mercer was getting into the boat.

"Burt, I'm taking the boat out for a while," Evie said swiftly. "I'm locking the store, but keep an eye on the gas pumps while I'm gone."

"Sure," he said, as unquestioning as ever. Burt Mardis didn't have a curious bone in his body.

Mercer was idling away from the dock. Evie jammed a ball cap on her head, grabbed her sunglasses and hurried from the building. She locked the door behind her, then sprinted for her own boat.

He was beyond the wave breakers by the time she reached her boat, and she heard the roar as he opened up the throttle. She all but threw herself into the boat and turned the key in the ignition. The motor coughed to life with a satisfying roar. Her boat was faster than any of the rentals, but on the water, and at speed, it was difficult to distinguish one vessel from another.

She had to idle away from the marina, because a fast takeoff would make waves large enough to violently rock the boats in their slips, possibly damaging them. Swearing at every lost second, she waited until she was past the wave breakers before pushing the throttle forward. The motor roared, and the front end of the boat lifted in the air as the vessel shot forward. It planed off almost immediately, the nose dropping into the running position.

She scanned the water for Mercer; unfortunately, he had gained enough distance that she couldn't positively identify him, and there were three boats speeding away from her, small specks that bobbed slightly as they cut through the waves. Which one was Mercer?

The sun wasn't far past its apex, and the glare turned the lake into a mirror. Hot air hit her, pulling tendrils of hair loose around her face. The scent of the river filled her head and lungs, and a quiet exultation spread through her. This was a part of her life that she loved—the wind in her face, the sense of speed, the feel of the boat as it glided over calm water and bumped over waves. Though there were other boats on the lake, and houses visible all along the shoreline, when she was speeding across the water it was like being alone with God. She would have been perfectly content, if only she knew what Mercer was up to.

After a minute one boat slowed and turned toward another marina. As she neared, she could tell that it held two passengers.

That left two. The throttle was full forward, and she was gaining on one, while the other, probably a speedy bass boat, was pulling away. Since her boat was faster than the rental, the one she was overtaking had to be Mercer. Cautiously she throttled back, enough to stay at a pace with him but not so close that he would see and identify her. Just about everyone on the water would be wearing a ball cap and sunglasses, and her hair was pulled back in a braid rather than flying loose, so she felt fairly confident that he wouldn't recognize her.

He was heading toward the same area, where there were a lot of small islands dotting the lake. She wouldn't be able to get very close, because once he cut his speed he would be able to hear other boats. Her best bet, she thought, was to stop some distance away and pretend to be fishing.

The boat ahead slowed and cut between two islands. Evie kept her speed steady and cruised on past. There was a distance of over two hundred yards between them, but she could tell that now he was idling closer to the bank of the island on the right.

She turned in the opposite direction, away from him. A barge was coming downriver, heavily loaded and settled deep into the water, pushing out a wave as it plowed forward. If she let the barge come between her and Mercer, it would block his activities for almost half a minute, plenty long enough for her to lose him. But if she moved inside the barge's path, it would put her closer to him than she wanted to be.

There was no help for it. She tucked her long braid inside her shirt to hide that identifying detail and turned the boat to angle back across the river ahead of the barge.

"Guntersville Lake's easy to learn," Virgil stated. "'Course, I was fishin' the river back before the TVA built the dam, so I knowed the lay of the land before the water backed up and covered it. Not many of us around now remembers the way it used to be. River used to flood a lot. So Roosevelt's boys decided we needed us a dam, so there wouldn't be no more floods. Well, hell, 'course there ain't, 'cause now the land that flooded ever now an' then is permanently under water. The government calls it flood control. They throwed around words like eminent domain, but what they did is take people's land, turn them off their farms, and put a lot of good land under water.''

''The TVA brought electricity to the Tennessee River Valley, didn't it?'' Robert asked. He was holding the boat to around twenty miles an hour, not much more than idling speed to the powerful motor behind them, but the slow speed made conversation possible. They had to raise their voices, but they could hear each other.

Virgil snorted. ''Sure it did. Glad to have it, too. But nobody ever thought the TVA built that dam to make our lives easier. Hell, we knew what was goin' on. It was the Depression, and Roosevelt would have built the second Tower of Babel to make jobs for folks, for all the good it did to the economy. It took the war to kick-start things again.''

''Did you fight in the war?''

''Too old for that one.'' Virgil cackled with glee. ''Imagine that! Over fifty years ago, they said I was too old! But I was in the first one. Lied about my age to get in. Not that they checked too close, 'cause they needed men could hit the broad side of a barn with a rifle slug. During the second one, I volunteered to help train the younger fellers with their rifles, but that was all stateside. Suited me. My wife weren't none too pleased with me, anyway, leavin' her to handle five young'uns on her own. She'd have been mad as hell if I'd gone overseas. Our oldest boy, John Edward, was seventeen when it all started, and he joined the navy. It fretted her enough that he was gone. He made it back fine, though. Imagine that. The boy went through a war in the Pacific without a scratch, then come home and died two years later with the pneumonia. Life's got a lotta strange turns in it. Don't guess I'll see too many more of them, but then, I didn't plan on hangin' around this long to begin with.''

The old man lapsed into silence, perhaps remembering all the people who had come and gone through his life. After a minute he roused himself. "Got a lot of creeks emptyin' into the lake. We passed Short Creek a ways back. This here's Town Creek.''

Robert had studied maps of the lake, so when Virgil identified the creeks he was able to pinpoint their location. Since the river channel was marked, staying in safely deep water was no problem. It was when he ventured out of the river channel that Virgil's expertise came in handy, because he knew where it was shallow, where the hidden stump rows were lurking just under the surface, ready to tear the bottom out of a boat if the driver wasn't careful. For several more minutes, Virgil devoted himself to his appointed task, pointing out quirks of the lake.

Then he said, "I've lost a lot of folks over the years. My own mama and pa, of course, and all my brothers and sisters. There were sixteen of us, and I'm the only one left. Got a piss pot full of nieces and nephews, though, and all of their kids, and their kids' kids. My wife passed on in sixty-four. Lord, it don't seem like it's been that long. I've lost three of my own kids. Parents ought not to outlive their kids. It ain't right. And all my friends that I growed up with, they're long gone.

"Yep, I've had to bury many a loved one, so I get right protective of the ones I got left." Faded blue eyes were suddenly piercing as he turned them on Robert. "Evie's a special woman. She's had enough sorrow in her young life, so if you don't mean to do right by her, it would be a kindness if you'd leave her alone and haul your ass back up north.''

Robert's face was impassive. "Evie's related to you?" he asked neutrally, ignoring Virgil's rather combative statement. He wasn't about to get into an argument with a ninety-three-year-old man.

Virgil snorted. "Not by blood. But I've knowed her all her life, watched her grow up, and there's not a finer woman in this town. Now, I watch television, so I know times have changed from when I was young enough to court a woman. Back then we had enough respect for womenfolk not to do nothing to cause them harm. But, like I said, times have changed. I know young folks now get serious about things without tyin' the knot proper, and that ain't what I'm talkin' about. Thing is, if you're just lookin' for a good time, then find some other woman. Evie ain't like that.''

Robert had to struggle with several conflicting emotions. Foremost was his cold, instinctive anger at Virgil's scolding interference. In neither his business nor his personal life was he accustomed to being taken to task. Right after that, though, was amusement. He was thirty-six and, moreover, an extremely wealthy man who wielded a great deal of power in both financial and political circles. He almost smiled at Virgil lumping him in with ''young folks.''

What took most of his attention, though, was this second warning that Evie wasn't a good-time girl. Evie herself had issued the first warning: *Don't kiss me unless it's for real.* After Virgil's little speech, the underlying meaning of those warnings was clear, though the reason wasn't.

''I don't usually discuss my relationships,'' he finally said in a faintly distant tone, just enough to signal his displeasure. ''But my interest in Evie isn't casual.'' *In any way.* ''What did you mean, she's had enough sorrow in her life?'' Because that had been the basis of the talk: *Don't hurt her.*

''I mean, life ain't been easy on her. Grief comes to everybody, if they live long enough. Some folks, though, it hits harder than others. Losin' Matt the way she did, the day after they got married…well, it changed her. There ain't no sunshine in her eyes now, the way there used to be. She never looked at another man since Matt died, until you. So don't disappoint her, is what I'm sayin'.''

Robert was knocked off balance by the surge of jealousy that seared through him. Jealousy? He'd never been jealous in his life, especially where a woman was concerned. Either his women were faithful to him or the relationship ended. Period. How could he be jealous of a boy who had been dead for a dozen years? But Evie still wore Matt Shaw's wedding ring on her finger and had evidently remained faithful to him even after all this time. Forget Mercer; that had obviously been an error. An understandable one, but still an error. He was both glad that she wasn't involved with Mercer, at least on that level, and furious that she was determined to waste herself on a memory. *I don't want to sleep with you,* she'd said. She was still trying to be faithful to a dead husband.

"What kind of person was Matt?" he asked. He didn't want to know, didn't want to talk about the boy, but he felt compelled to find out.

"He was a fine boy. Would have been a good man, if he'd had the chance. Good-natured, honest. Kindhearted, too. Can't say that about too many folks, but Matt didn't have a mean bone in his body. He never dated anybody but Evie, and it was the same with her. They planned to marry each other from the time they started high school together. Never saw two kids love each other the way they did. It was a shame that they didn't have no more time together than what they had. She didn't even have his child to keep part of him alive. Damn shame. She needed somthing to live for, back then."

Robert had had enough. He couldn't listen to much more about how wonderful Matt Shaw had been, and how much Evie had loved him, without losing his temper. He couldn't remember the last time he had lost control, but there was a deep-seated fury in him now that was surging forward. He didn't try to analyze his anger; he simply and ruthlessly contained it, shoving it down as he turned the boat downriver and headed back toward the marina. He eased the throttle forward so the noise would make conversation impossible.

Fifteen minutes later they were idling up to the docks. At the sound of the motor, a man wearing grease-covered coveralls came out of the maintenance building and walked out on the dock. He nodded a greeting to Robert and said to Virgil, "Come in outta the sun and keep me company for a while. Evie closed the office and took her boat out for a while." As he talked, he extended a muscular arm to steady Virgil as he climbed out of the boat onto the dock.

"When was this?" Robert asked sharply.

The mechanic shrugged. "An hour, maybe. I didn't pay no attention to the time."

She had refused to close the marina early one rainy late afternoon, when there had been no customers, but now she had closed it not long after lunch on a beautiful, sunny, *busy* day. Robert's eyes narrowed. He looked at the parking lot. He knew the make, model and color of Mercer's car, and there it sat.

Damn her. She had left to meet with the traitorous bastard.

CHAPTER EIGHT

Robert was standing on the dock when Evie eased her boat into its regular slip. He was wearing those extra dark sunglasses that completely hid his eyes, but she didn't need to see them to know that they were icy with rage. Maybe it was the way he moved, very deliberately, every action contained, that alerted her to his mood. An uncontrollable shiver ran over her, despite the heat. There was something far more alarming about that cold, ruthless control than if he had been violent. Again she had the thought that he was the most dangerous man she'd ever seen. But what had put him in such a menacing mood?

She tied off and leapt up onto the dock. "Did Virgil enjoy himself?" she asked as she stepped around Robert, heading toward the office. He wasn't the only one who had self-control. Right now she had other concerns besides dealing with his temper. She could hear the roar of a boat coming closer; that might or might not be Mercer, but she wasn't taking any more chances. When Mercer returned to the marina, she intended to be inside the office building, doing business as usual.

"Just a minute," Robert said, his tone clipped, and reached for her.

Evie evaded his grasp. "Later," she said, and hurried up the dock.

He was right behind her when she unlocked the door, but he didn't have a chance to say anything. Virgil had seen her boat and was slowly making his way across the lot. Robert eyed the old man's progress; he wouldn't have time to get any answers out of her before Virgil was there, so it would be better to wait, as she'd said, until later. Once more he controlled his anger and frustration, but the fury in him remained hot. If anything, he was becoming even angrier.

Virgil reached the doorway and gave a sigh of pleasure as the cool air-conditioning washed over him. "Got spoiled in my old age," he griped. "The heat didn't used to bother me none."

"No point in letting it bother you back then," Evie pointed out, smiling at him. "There wasn't any air-conditioning, so we all had to put up with it."

The old man eased into the rocking chair. "Spoiled," he repeated contentedly.

She went over to a vending machine and fed in the change for three soft drinks. She kept the machine's temperatre set low enough to form ice crystals in the drinks, to the delight of her customers. She popped the tops off the bottles and thrust one into Robert's hands, then gave another to Virgil. The third she drank herself, turning up the bottle for a long, cold swallow of the crisp, biting liquid.

She saw Robert eye the hourglass bottle in his hand with a less-than-thrilled expression; then he, too, took a drink. His tastes were probably too sophisticated to run to soft drinks, she thought, but if he was going to live here for the summer, he should do as the natives did. One of the front lines of defense against the heat was to consume cola every day as coolant for the insides.

A boat was idling in past the wave breakers. A quick glance told Evie that it was the rental boat. Mercer had seen her, she knew, but she didn't think he had recognized her. Wearing the universal ball cap and sunglasses, with her hair tucked in, she could have been anyone. It was doubtful that he had even been able to tell she was a woman.

Robert hitched one hip onto the counter, a sockless, docksider-clad foot swinging as he nursed the soft drink. His expression didn't give anything away, but she had the strong impression that he was...waiting. Until they could talk? No. It was more immediate than that.

She watched Mercer tie up the boat and walk jauntily along the dock, tackle box in one hand and useless tackle in the other. Then the door opened and he breezed in, all ego and self-satisfaction. "Nothing today, doll," he said in his obnoxious, too-hearty manner. "Maybe I'd have better luck if you went along. What do you say?"

"I'm not much for fishing," she lied without compunction, causing Virgil to almost choke on his drink.

Robert's back, as he sat on the counter, had been half-turned toward Mercer. Now he shifted around to face the other man. "Hello, Landon," he said coolly. "I'd like to go fishing with you the next time you take the afternoon off."

Evie was startled to hear Robert call Mercer by his first name, and a mental alarm began clanging. *How did Robert know the man?*

But if she was startled, the effect on Mercer was electric. He froze in place, his face draining of color as he gaped at Robert. "M-Mr. Cannon," he shuttered. "I—uh, how—w-what are you doing here?"

The black slashes of Robert's eyebrows rose in that sardonic way of his. Mercer was totally aghast at having run into him, Evie saw, and the tension in her relaxed. Whatever the connection, Robert wasn't in league with Mercer, or the other man wouldn't have been so taken aback at his presence.

The most obvious answer to Mercer's question would have been that he kept his boat here; that wasn't, however, what Robert said. Instead he looked deliberately at Evie and said, "The place has a certain attraction."

She felt silly, but she couldn't stop the color from heating her face. Mercer looked even more aghast, for some reason.

"Oh," he mumbled. "Yeah, sure." With an effort, he regained a bit of control and managed a sickly smile. "It's getting late. I should be going. Call me when you're free, Mr. Cannon, and we'll get in that game of golf we talked about."

"Or some fishing," Robert suggested, his voice like silk.

"Uh…yeah. Yes, we'll do that. Anytime." Mercer tossed the boat keys onto the counter and hastily left.

"Wonder what set his britches on fire," Virgil mused.

"Perhaps it was his bad luck in taking an afternoon off from

work to go fishing and running into his employer at the marina,''
Robert suggested, his eyes hooded.

Virgil leaned back in the rocker, wheezing with laughter. ''Well,
I'll be! He works for you, eh? Bet that ruined his fun for the day.''

''I'm certain it did.''

Evie stood motionless, absorbing all the nuances of the brief
scene with Mercer, and also the silkiness of Robert's murmured
reply. He had taken a great deal of pleasure in watching Mercer
squirm. He had also made that remark about her being the reason
for his presence for the same reason: to make Mercer squirm. After
all, what man would feel comfortable to find out he had just come
on to the boss's woman…in front of the boss? This was in addition
to being caught playing hooky from work.

Mercer probably didn't realize it, but it had been plain to Evie
that Robert disliked him. He had been perfectly cordial, but the
dislike had been there, underlying every word. She was enormously
relieved. For a horrible moment she had been afraid that Robert
was involved with whatever crooked deal Mercer had going on, but
Mercer's manner certainly hadn't been that of someone who had
met a friend. She was worried, though, to find that Mercer worked
for Robert. Just as she didn't want his dirty waves to touch the
marina, she also didn't want him to somehow harm Robert.

She hadn't been successful in finding out any more about what
Mercer was up to; he had idled a twisting path around several of
the islands, finally stopping for a moment on the back side of one
of the larger ones. She hadn't been able to see what, if anything,
he was doing. If she had had a trolling motor, she would have been
able to get much closer without him hearing her, but her boat
wasn't equipped with one. Then Mercer had started his motor again
and resumed his weaving in and out of the islands. She had watched
him as best she could, but there was no way to keep him in sight
all the time. When he had finally left the islands, it had taken all
the speed her boat was capable of to outpace him and reach the
marina far enough in advance that he wouldn't see her.

So she still had nothing but suspicion. While she was wondering
whether or not to confide in Robert when she had nothing of sub-

stance to tell him, Virgil's great-granddaughter came in. This time she was carrying a wide-eyed, eleven-month-old girl on her hip, and was followed by two towheaded boys, ages four and six. "PawPaw, PawPaw," both boys yelled. They ran toward the rocking chair, climbing up on Virgil's lap with a naturalness that suggested they had been doing it all their lives.

"Well, how'd it go?" Virgil asked, gathering both small bodies against him. "Did the dentist give you a sucker?"

"Yep," said the oldest one, pulling a bright red lollipop from his pocket. "Mom says it's okay, because it's sugarless. You want it?" His expression said that he was disappointed by the sugarless state of the candy.

"It's tempting," Virgil allowed, "but you keep it."

Evie smiled as she watched Virgil with his great-great- grandchildren, then turned back to their mother. "Sherry, this is Robert Cannon. He and Virgil have been out running the river today. Robert, Virgil's great-granddaughter, Sherry Ferguson."

"Pleased to meet you," Sherry said with her friendly smile. She obviously remembered Robert from the first time he had come to the marina. She shifted the baby onto her other hip and held out her hand.

Robert reached to shake Sherry's hand, and the baby evidently thought he was reaching for her; with a gurgle of pleasure she released her grip on Sherry's blouse and lunged forward, both dimpled little arms outstretched. Sherry made a startled grab for the child, but Robert was faster, scooping the baby into his arms almost before she had left the safety of her mother's.

"Allison Rose!" Sherry gasped, staring at the baby. "I'm sorry," she apologized to Robert as she reached to retrieve her child. "I don't know what got into her. She's never gone to a stranger like that before."

Allison Rose wouldn't have any of it; she shrieked and turned away from her mother's hands, clinging to Robert's shirt with all her might.

"She's all right," Robert said, his wonderful deep voice now holding a soothing tone to calm both mother and daughter. One powerful hand steadied the baby's back as his eyes smiled at Sherry. "I've always had a way with women."

That was nothing less than the truth, Evie thought, her blood moving in a slow throb through her veins as she watched him cradle the baby as comfortably as if he had a dozen of his own. Was there anything the man couldn't do? Sherry was all but melting under that smiling look, and tiny Allison was in heaven.

Perched on his arm, Allison looked around with a beatific expression, as if she were a queen surveying her subjects. Robert bent his head to brush his nose against the soft blond curls and reflected that girls were different from boys even at this young age. He had rocked Madelyn's two boys when they were infants and played with them as toddlers, but they hadn't been quite as soft as the baby girl in his arms, and her scent was indefinably sweeter. He found himself enchanted by the tiny sandals on her feet and the ruffled sundress she wore. The feel of her chubby, dimpled arms clinging to him was strangely satisfying.

Oh God, Evie thought. Her chest was so tight she could barely breathe. She had to turn away to hide the shattered look in her eyes. Why couldn't he have been uncomfortable with babies? Why did he have to cradle Allison so tenderly and close his eyes with delight at her sweet baby scent? The emotion swelling in her was so overwhelming that she couldn't think, couldn't function.

For the rest of her life she would remember the exact moment when she fell in love with Robert Cannon.

She busied herself fiddling with papers, though she couldn't have said what those papers were. As if from a distance, she could hear Sherry asking about Virgil's excursion on the river, could hear the enthusiasm in Virgil's reply and Robert's comments. The calm, soothing tone was still there, she noticed. How could Sherry fail to be reassured about the safety of the outing when his utter placidity and self-confidence said that he had taken every care without appearing to fuss over Virgil's safety?

He did it deliberately, she realized as she listened to them talk. She felt oddly detached, not really hearing words, but rather the way things were said, the underlying emotion. Robert was a master at reading people, then using his voice and manner with uncanny accuracy to manipulate them into the response he desired. It was almost as if he were a puppeteer, pulling everyone's strings so subtly that they never noticed they were being directed by his will.

And if he manipulated *them,* then it followed that he manipulated *her.*

There was a dull roaring in her ears, as if she might faint. Evie flatly refused to do something that silly and concentrated on breathing deeply. As she sucked in the first breath, she discovered that it was the first time she had done so for some time, judging by the acute relief in her lungs. She had simply stopped breathing, probably about the time Robert had rubbed his face against Allison's curls. No wonder she had felt faint.

Emotionally she had been groping for solid ground, had felt her fingers finally brush against something to which she had thought she could hold. Now she felt as if that lifeline had been jerked away from her and she was lost again, swirling away. Had anything Robert said to her been the truth, or had every word been a subtle manipulation, designed to…what? Get her into his bed? Was the thrill, for him, in the chase? The problem was that he could just as easily be sincere. How was she to tell the difference?

The answer, she thought painfully, was that she couldn't. Only time would tell if she could depend on him, entrust her heart to him, and she doubted that the time was there. He'd said he was here for the rest of the summer, and summer was half-over. He would be here another six, maybe seven, weeks.

"Evie." Her name was spoken quietly, almost in her ear. She felt his heat against her back, smelled the fresh, clean sweat on his body. His hand touched her arm. "Sherry and Virgil are leaving."

She turned, summoning both a smile and self-control. No one else had noticed her preoccupation, she saw, but Robert had, another disturbing example of his acute perception. Allison had been enticed, with one of the red suckers as bait, back into Sherry's arms, where she was engrossed with turning the cellophane-wrapped candy around and around, trying to find access. Finally she simply popped it into her mouth, cellophane and all. Virgil was standing, and the boys were already at the door, shouting that they wanted a Blizzard before they went home, while Sherry insisted that she wasn't driving all the way to Boaz to get one, at which Virgil added that he wouldn't mind having a Blizzard, himself. That, of course, settled the issue.

Evie added her voice to all the rowdy commotion, telling them goodbye, telling Virgil to take care. The boys raced out the door and headed toward the docks. Sherry stepped out and said, "Y'all get back here, *now!*" in a tone that stopped them in their tracks and brought them, pouting, back to her. It took another few minutes to get everyone settled in the station wagon, and through it all Evie was acutely aware of Robert standing very close behind her, his hand on the small of her back. Neither Sherry nor Virgil would have missed the body language, much less the touch, that stated his claim on her.

The silence after their departure was almost deafening. She closed the door and tried to slide past him, but his hands closed on her waist, and, with a dizzy whirl, she found herself plunked down on the counter with him standing between her legs to prevent her from getting down. She stared at the center of his chest, refusing to look up at him. She didn't want this, didn't want to confront him when she was still reeling from the jolting realization that she loved him and could trust him even less than she had thought.

"Damn it," he said very softly. Then, "Look at me."

"Why?"

"Because I don't want to talk to the top of your head."

"I can hear you just fine the way I am."

He hissed a curse just under his breath and caught her face between his hands, tilting it up. He was careful not to hurt her, but there was no resisting the easy strength of that grip. She tried to concentrate on his nose, but the pale green glitter of his eyes dominated his face, drawing her attention. There was no way *not* to see the cold fury there.

"Where did you go?"

The question was deceptively calm, almost idle. If she hadn't been able to see his eyes, if she hadn't been able to feel the roiling anger in him, she might have been fooled. "I had an errand to run."

"Ah." His hands tightened on her face. "Were you meeting Landon Mercer?" he asked abruptly. "Are you having an affair with him?"

She stared at him, stupefied. For several moments she was unable to formulate a single thought, her mind a total blank. How on earth had he managed to link her to Mercer? He had been gone when she had left, and she and Mercer had not come back at the same time. But she *had* left because of Mercer, even though she hadn't been with him. She could feel her cheeks heating and knew that she looked guilty, but she still couldn't seem to manage a coherent reply. Then the last question sank in, and she snapped, "No, I'm not having an affair with him! I *detest* the man!"

Robert's lips were thin. "Then why did you sneak off to meet with him?"

"I didn't sneak anywhere," she flared. "And I did *not* meet him!"

"But you closed the office in the middle of a busy day," he said relentlessly. "When you wouldn't close it a little early on a rainy afternoon when there weren't any customers at all."

"I told you, I had an errand."

"So you went in a boat?"

"I live on the water," she pointed out, light brown eyes glowing more golden by the second. "I can cross the lake faster than I can drive to my house. Sometimes, if the weather is good and I'm in the mood, I use the boat, anyway, rather than driving."

The dangerous look hadn't faded from his eyes. "Are you saying that you went home?"

Very deliberately she caught his wrists and removed his hands from her face. "I had an errand," she repeated. "I didn't meet Mercer. I'm not having an affair with him. And what in hell makes you think you have the right to interrogate me?" The last sentence was shouted as she tried to shove him away.

He didn't move, not an inch. "This," he said in a stifled tone, then moved forward as he bent his head to her.

She caught her breath at the heat of his mouth, the ravaging pressure. His movement had forced her thighs even wider, and he settled his hips in the notch. Evie quivered at the hard thrust of his sex against the vulnerable softness of her private body, alarmed by the contact even through several layers of cloth. The passion in him was as overwhelming as his anger had been, buffeting her, bending her under his will. His arms were painfully tight, and she tried to push him away once more, with the same result. "Stop it," he muttered against her mouth, and one arm dropped to encircle her bottom and pull her closer against him, rubbing her against the ridge beneath his jeans.

Unexpected, acute, the pleasure that shot through her loins made her cry out, the sound muffled by his lips. He repeated the motion, rocking his pelvis against her in a fury of jealousy and desire. The jolt was even stronger, and she arched in his arms, her hands lifting to cling to his shoulders. The transition from anger to desire was so swift that she couldn't control it, and the current of pleasure leaped within her. Every move he made increased the sensation, pushed her higher, as if she were being forced up a mountain and the purpose, once she reached the peak, was to hurl her over. The dizzying, panicked sensation was the same, and she clutched at him as the only anchor.

It had never been like this with Matt, she thought dimly. Their youthful passion had been shy, untutored, sweet but hesitant. Robert was a man who knew exactly what he was doing.

Though he hadn't touched them, her breasts were throbbing, the nipples tightly drawn and aching. She arched again, a soft, frantic sound in her throat as she tried to ease the ache by rubbing them against his chest. He knew, and whispered, "Easy," just as his hand closed over one firm, jutting mound.

She whimpered at the heat, the delicious pressure. She knew she should stop him, but putting an end to this ecstasy was the last thing she wanted to do. Her body was pliant, voluptuous with need, glowing with heat. He put his hand under her shirt and deftly opened the front snap of her bra. The cups slid apart, and then his fingers were on her naked flesh. He stroked the satin curves, then circled the tight nipples until she writhed in an agony of unfulfillment. "Is this what you want?" he murmured, and lightly pinched the distended tips. She moaned as a river of heat ran through her, gathering moisture to deposit between her thighs.

He bent her backward over his arm, the position thrusting her breasts upward. Her shirt was pulled up to completely bare them, she realized, wondering when that had happened. She saw her nipples, as red as berries; then his mouth closed over one, and her eyes closed as her head fell back.

He was going to take her right here, on the counter. She felt his determination, his own rampant desire. Panic surged through her, combating the heat that undermined her own will and common sense. He would take her here, where anyone could walk in and see them. He would take her without any thought for birth control. And she, besides risking her reputation and the chance of pregnancy, would lose the last bit of protection she retained for her heart.

His mouth was tugging at her nipple, drawing strongly on it before moving to the other one. And his hands were working at the waistband of her jeans, unsnapping and unzipping.

Desperately she wedged her arms between their bodies and stiffened them. "No," she said. The word was hoarse, barely audible. "Robert, no! Stop it!"

He froze, his muscled body taut as he held himself motionless for a long moment. Then, very slowly, he lifted his hands from her and moved back, one step, then two. His breathing was fast and audible.

Evie couldn't look at him as she slid from the counter and hastily fumbled her clothing back into presentable shape, fastening her bra, smoothing her shirt down, snapping and zipping her jeans. Her own breath was coming light and fast.

"Don't look so scared," he said calmly. "I gave you my word that I'd stop, and I did."

No, the problem wasn't with his willpower, she thought wildly, but with hers. Had they been anywhere else but in the marina, she didn't know if she could have made herself say no.

"Nothing to say?" he asked a moment later, when she remained silent.

She cleared her throat. "Not yet."

"All right." He still sounded far too calm and in control. "We'll talk tomorrow. I'll pick you up at seven o'clock."

"Seven," she echoed as he left.

Robert was on the secure mobile phone in the Jeep by the time he had pulled out of the marina's parking lot. "Did you follow him from the time he left work?" he asked as soon as the phone was answered.

"Yes, sir, we did. We saw your Jeep at the marina and pulled back."

"Damn. I was out in my boat. He rented a boat and met someone out on the lake, possibly Evie, because she left the marina in her boat, too. Was he carrying anything when he left work?"

"Not that we could tell, but he could easily have had a disk in his coat pocket."

"He didn't fish in his suit. Where did he change clothes?"

"At his house. He was there for not quite five minutes, then came out carrying a tackle box and a fishing rod."

"If he had a disk at all, it would have been in the tackle box."

"Yes, sir. We didn't have a chance to get to it."

"I know. It wasn't your fault. First thing, though, I'm going to have a secure phone put in the boat. That way, if I'm out on the water, you can get in touch with me."

"Good idea. We went through his house again while we had the chance. Nothing."

"Damn. Okay, continue to watch him. And send someone out to Evie's house tonight."

"The matter we discussed?"

"Yes," Robert replied. It was time for the pressure to begin.

CHAPTER NINE

The next morning was awful. Evie hadn't slept well—had scarcely slept at all. She had set the alarm for four-thirty, and when it went off she had been asleep for less than two hours. Dreaming about Robert was one thing, but she had been wide-awake and hadn't been able to get him out of her mind. Her thoughts had darted from the seething passion of his lovemaking, incomplete as it had been, to the unease she felt every time she thought of how he so skillfully manipulated people. She tried to analyze what he did and couldn't find any time when he had been malicious, but that didn't reassure her.

Sometime after midnight, lying in the darkness and staring at the ceiling, she realized what it was that so bothered her. It was as if Robert allowed people to see and know only a part of him; the other part, probably the closest to being the real man, was standing back, inviolate, carefully watching and analyzing, gauging reactions, deciding which subtle pressures to apply to gain the results he wanted. Everyone was shut away from that inner man, the razor-sharp intelligence functioning almost like a computer, isolated in a sterile environment. What was most upsetting was to realize that this was how he wanted it, that he had deliberately fashioned that inner isolation and wasn't about to invite anyone inside.

What place could she hope to have in his life? He desired her; he would be perfectly willing to make her the center of his attention for a time, in order to gain what he wanted: a carnal relationship. But unless she could break through into that fiercely guarded inner core, she would never reach his emotions. He would be fine, but she would break her heart battering against his defenses.

She, better than others, knew how important emotional barriers were. She had propped herself up with her own defenses for many years, until she had slowly healed to the point where she could stand on her own. How could she condemn him for staying within his own fortress? She didn't know if she should even try to get inside.

The thing was, she didn't know if she had a choice any longer. For better or worse, this afternoon he had slipped through her defenses. Such a little thing: playing with a baby. But it was the little things, rather than the watershed events, on which love was built. She had softened toward him when he had saved her and Jason's lives, but her heart had remained her own. Today she had fallen in love; it wasn't something she could back away from and ignore. It might be impossible to breach Robert's defenses and reach his heart, but she had to try.

Finally she drifted into sleep, but the alarm too soon urged her out of bed. Heavy-eyed, she put on the coffee and showered while it was brewing. Then, as she absently munched on a bowl of cereal and poured in the caffeine, a dull cramp knotted her lower belly. "Damn it," she muttered. Just what she needed; she was going out with Robert for the first time that night, and her period was starting. She had thought she had another couple of days before it was due. She made a mental note that in a few days she should begin taking the birth-control pills the doctor had just prescribed.

Normally her period didn't bother her, but the timing of this one, added to lack of sleep, made her cranky as she left the house in the predawn darkness and climbed into the truck.

The sturdy pickup, usually so reliable despite its high mileage, made some unfamiliar noises as she drove along the dark, deserted side road. "Don't you dare break down on me now," she warned it. She was just getting on a firm financial footing; a major repair job right now was just what she didn't need.

She reached U.S. 431 and turned onto it. The truck shuddered and began making loud clanging noises. Startled, she slowed and swept the gauges with a quick glance. The temperature was fine, the oil— Oh God, the oil gauge was red-lining. She slammed on the brakes and started to veer toward the shoulder, and that was when the engine blew. There were more clanging and grinding noises, and smoke boiled up around the hood, obscuring her vision. She steered the truck off the highway, fighting the heavy wheel as, deprived of power, the vehicle lurched to a halt.

Evie got out and stood looking at the smoking corpse as it pinged and rattled, the sounds of mechanical death. Her language was usually mild, but there were some occasions that called for swear words, and this was one of them. She used every curse word she had ever heard, stringing them together in rather innovative ways. That didn't bring life back to the motor, and it didn't make her bank account any healthier, but it relieved some of her frustration. When she ran out of new ways to say things, she stopped, took a deep breath and looked up and down the highway. Dawn was lightening the sky, and traffic was picking up; maybe someone she knew would come by and she wouldn't have to walk the full two miles to a pay phone. With a sigh she got the pistol out from under the truck seat, slipped it into her purse, then locked the truck—though obviously anyone who stole it would have to haul it away—and began walking.

It was less than a minute when another pickup rolled to a stop beside her. She glanced around and saw the boat hitched up behind. Two men were in the truck, and the one on the passenger side rolled down his window. "Havin' trouble?" Then he said, a bit uncertainly, "Miss Evie?"

With relief she recognized Russ McElroy and Jim Haynes, two area fisherman whom she had known casually for several years. "Hi, Russ. Jim. The motor in my truck just blew."

Russ opened the door and hopped out. "Come on, we'll give you a ride to the marina. You don't need to be out by yourself like this. There's too much meanness goin' on these days."

Gratefully she climbed into the cab of the truck and slid to the middle of the seat. Russ got back in and closed the door, and Jim eased the rig onto the highway. "You got a good mechanic?" Jim asked.

"I thought I'd have Burt, the mechanic at the marina, take a look at it. He's good with motors."

Jim nodded. "Yeah, I know Burt Mardis. He's real good. But if he can't get to it, there's another guy, owns a shop just off Blount, who's just as good. His name's Roy Simms. Just look it up in the phone book, Simms' Automotive Repair.''

"Thanks, I'll remember that.''

Jim and Russ launched into a discussion of other good mechanics in the area, and soon they reached the marina. She thanked them, and Russ got out again to let her out. They probably hadn't intended to put in at her marina, but since they were there they decided they might as well. As she unlocked the gate that blocked the launch ramp, Jim began to maneuver the truck so he could back the boat into the water. Next she unlocked the office and turned on the lights. Just as Jim and Russ were idling away from the dock, Burt drove up, and she went to tell him about the demise of her truck.

It wasn't long after dawn when the phone rang. Robert opened one eye and examined the golden rose of the sky as he reached for the receiver. "Yes.''

"The truck didn't make it into town. It blew just as she reached the highway. She caught a ride to the marina.''

Robert sat up in bed. He could feel the fine hairs on the back of his neck prickling with mingled anger and alarm. "Damn it, she hitchhiked?''

"Yeah, I was a little worried about that, so I followed to make certain she didn't have any trouble. No problem. It was a couple of fishermen who picked her up. I guess she knew them.''

That wasn't much better. Guntersville wasn't exactly a hotbed of crime, but anything could happen to a woman alone. Neither did it soothe him that she had been followed, that help was right behind if she'd needed it. The situation shouldn't have arisen in the first place. "Why was the timing off?''

"The hole in the oil line must have been bigger than West thought. Probably there's a big oil puddle in her driveway. She would have seen it if it hadn't still been dark when she left the house.''

In a very calm, remote voice Robert said, "If anything had happened to her because of his mistake, I wouldn't have liked it.''

There was a pause on the other end of the line. Then, "I understand. It won't happen again."

Having made his point, Robert didn't belabor it. He moved on. "Be careful when you're in the house tonight. I don't want her to notice anything out of place."

"She won't. I'll see to it myself."

After hanging up the phone, Robert lay back down and hooked his hands behind his head as he watched the sun peek over the mountains. The day before had made him more uncertain than ever of Evie's connection with Mercer. He was fairly certain she had rendezvoused with Mercer out on the water, but either she hadn't told Mercer of his presence, or she had been unaware of his own connection with PowerNet. This appeared to be an efficient espionage ring, to have escaped notice and capture for as long as they had; given that, Evie should have known of him. At the very least, Mercer should have notified her of his presence. What reason could they have had for keeping her in the dark about his identity, unless her participation was very peripheral and no one had thought she needed to know?

The other possibility was that Evie had indeed recognized his name, or been notified, but for reasons of her own had chosen not to pass on the information that he had leased a slip at her marina and appeared to have formed an intense personal interest in her.

Either way, it followed that Evie wasn't on good terms with the others in the espionage ring. On the one hand, it gave him a weakness he could exploit. On the other, her life could be in danger.

Evie made arrangements to have a wrecker tow the truck to the marina. That accomplished, Burt stuck his head under the hood to begin the examination. Next he lay down on a dolly and rolled underneath for another view. When he emerged, he wasn't optimistic about rebuilding the motor. "Too much damage," he said. "You'd be better off just buying another motor."

She had been expecting that, and she had already been mentally juggling her finances. The payment on the bank loan for the marina would be late this month, and then she would have to put off other payments to make the one on the loan. She could get by without transportation for a few days by using the boat to go back and forth from home to the marina. If she absolutely needed to go somewhere, she could borrow Becky's car, though she didn't like to.

"I'll call around and try to find one," she said. "Will you have time to put it in for me?"

"Sure," Burt said easily. "It's a little slow right now, anyway."

By the time Craig arrived to relieve her, it was all arranged. She had located an engine, and Burt would begin work putting it in as soon as it arrived. Depending on how much marina work came in, she might be driving home the next afternoon.

In Evie's experience, things didn't generally work that well. She wouldn't be surprised if Burt was suddenly flooded with a lot of boats needing attention.

The trip across the lake was enjoyable, despite her worries. The water was green, the surrounding mountains a misty blue, and fat, fluffy clouds drifted lazily across the sky, offering an occasional brief respite from the blazing sun. Gulls wheeled lazily over the water, and an eagle soared high in the distance. It was the kind of day when being inside was almost intolerable.

With that thought in mind, once she arrived home she put her financial worries on hold and got out the lawn mower to give her yard a trimming. She glared at the big black oil stain on the driveway where the truck had been parked. If it had been daylight when she'd left this morning, if she hadn't swapped shifts with Craig, she would have seen the oil and not have driven the truck; the motor would still be intact, and the repair bill would be much smaller.

Just simple bad timing.

The yard work finished, she went inside to cool off and tackle the housework, which was minimal. By three o'clock she was back outside, sitting on the dock with her feet in the water and a sweat-dewed glass of ice tea beside her. Fretting about the truck wouldn't accomplish anything. She would handle this just as she had handled every other money crisis that had arisen over the years, by strict economizing until all bills were paid. She couldn't do anything more than that, since it wasn't likely a good fairy would drop the money into her lap. Though there might be the possibility of taking a part-time job in the mornings at one of the fast-food restaurants serving breakfast. Forty dollars a week was a hundred and sixty dollars a month, enough to pay the power bill, with a little left over for the gas bill. But for now all she wanted was to sit on the dock with her feet in the water and gaze at the mountains, feeling contentment spread through her.

That was how Robert found her. He came around the side of the house and paused when he saw her sitting on the weathered dock, her eyes closed, face lifted to the sun. The long, thick, golden braid had been pulled forward over one shoulder, revealing the enticing, delicate furrow of her nape. She was wearing faded denim shorts and a white chemise top, hardly a sophisticated outfit, but his pulse began to throb as he studied the graceful curve of her shoulders, the delectable roundness of her slender arms, the shapeliness of her legs. Her skin glowed with a warm, pale gold luminescence, like a succulent peach. His eyes, his entire body, burned as he stared at her. His mouth was literally watering, and he had to swallow. He had never felt such urgent lust for any other woman. What he wanted was to simply throw himself on her and have her right here, right now, without thought or finesse.

She was unaware of his presence until the dock vibrated when he stepped onto it. There was no alarm in her eyes as she turned her head to see who had come visiting, only lazy curiosity followed by a warm look of welcome. Even the average five-year-old in a large city was more wary than the people around here, he thought as he sat down beside her and began taking off his shoes.

"Hi," she said, a sort of smiling serenity in that one word, which was drawled so that it took twice as long for her to say than it did for him.

He found himself smiling back, actually smiling, his mouth curved into a tender line as his heart pounded inside his chest. He had wanted her from the moment he'd first seen her; he'd been, several times, unexpectedly charmed by her. Both reactions were acute at this moment, but even more, he was enchanted.

He had whirled across countless dance floors with countless

beautiful women in his arms, women who could afford to pamper themselves and wear the most expensive gowns and jewelry, women whom he had genuinely liked. He had made love to those women gently, slowly, in luxurious surroundings. He had taken women when the added fillip of danger made each encounter more intense. But never had he felt more enthralled than he was right now, sitting beside Evie on a weathered old dock, with a blazing afternoon sun, almost brutal in its clarity, bathing everything in pure light. Sweat trickled down his back and chest from the steamy heat, and his entire body pulsed with life. Even his fingertips throbbed. It took all of his formidable self-control to prevent himself from pushing her down on the dock and spreading her legs for his entry.

And yet, for all the intensity of his desire, he was oddly content to wait. He would have her. For now he was caught in the enchantment of her slow smile, in the luminous sheen of her skin, in her warm, female scent that no perfume could match. Simply to sit beside her was to be seduced, and he was more than willing.

Having removed his shoes, he rolled up the legs of his khaki pants and stuck his feet into the water. The water was tepid, but refreshing in contrast to the heat of his skin. It made him feel almost comfortable.

"It isn't seven o'clock yet," she pointed out, but she was smiling.

"I wanted to make sure you hadn't chickened out."

"Not yet. Give me a couple of hours."

Despite the teasing, he was certain she wouldn't have stood him up. She might be nervous, even a little reluctant, but she had agreed, and she would keep her word. Her lack of enthusiasm in going out with him might have been insulting if he hadn't known how potent her physical reaction to him was. Whatever reasons she had for being wary of him, her body was oblivious to them.

She lazily moved her feet back and forth, watching the water swirl around her ankles. After a minute of wondering about the advisability of bringing up the subject that had been bothering her so much, she decided to do so, anyway. "Robert, have you ever let anyone really get close to you? Has anyone ever truly known you?''

She felt his stillness, just for a split second. Then he said in a light tone, ''I've been trying to get close to you from the moment I first saw you.''

She turned her head and found him watching her, his ice-green eyes cool and unreadable. ''That was a nice evasion, but you just demonstrated what I meant.''

''I did? What was that?'' he murmured indulgently, leaning forward to press his lips to her bare shoulder.

She didn't let that burning little caress distract her. ''How you deflect personal questions without answering them. How you keep everyone at arm's length. How you watch and manipulate and never give away anything of your real thoughts or feelings.''

He looked amused. ''You're accusing *me* of being difficult to get to know, when you're as open as the Sphinx?''

''We both have our defenses,'' she admitted readily.

''Suppose I turn your questions around?'' he said, watching her intently. ''Have you ever let anyone get close to you and really get to know you?''

A pang went through her. ''Of course. My family…and Matt.''

She lapsed into silence then, and Robert saw the sadness move over her face, like a cloud passing over the sun. Matt again! What had been so special about an eighteen-year-old boy that twelve years later just the mention of his name could make her grieve? He didn't like himself for the way he felt, violently jealous and resentful of a dead boy. But at least Matt's memory had diverted Evie from her uncomfortable line of questioning.

She seemed content to sit in silence now, dabbling her feet in the water and watching the sunlight change patterns as it moved lower in the sky. Robert left her to her thoughts, suddenly preoccupied with his own.

Her perception was disturbing. She had, unfortunately, been dead on the money. He had always felt it necessary to keep a large part of himself private; the persona he presented to the world, that of a wealthy, urbane businessman, was not false. It was merely a small part of the whole, the part that he chose to display. It worked very well; it was perfect for doing business, for courting and seducing the women he wanted, and was an entrée into those parts of the world where his business was not quite what it seemed.

None of his closest associates suspected that he was anything other than the cool, controlled executive. They didn't know about his taste for adventure, or the way he relished danger. They didn't know about the extremely risky favors he had done, out of sheer patriotism, for various government departments and agencies. They didn't know about all the ongoing, specialized training he did to keep himself in shape and his skills sharp. They didn't know about his volcanic temper, because he kept it under ruthless control. Robert knew himself well, knew his own lethal capabilities. It had always seemed better to keep the intense aspects of his personality to himself, to never unleash the sheer battering force of which he was capable. If that meant no one ever really *knew* him, he was content with that. There was a certain safety in it.

No woman had ever reached the seething core of his emotions, had ever made him lose control. He never wanted to truly love a woman in the romantic sense, to find himself open to her, vulnerable to her. He planned to marry someday, and his wife would be supremely happy. He would treat her with every care and consideration, pleasing her in bed and cosseting her out of it. She would never want for anything. He would be a tender, affectionate husband and father. And she would never know that she had never truly reached him, that his heart remained whole, in his isolated core.

Madelyn, of course, knew that there were fiercely guarded depths to him, but she had never probed. She had known herself to be loved, and that was enough for her. His sister was a formidable person in her own right, her lazy manner masking an almost frightening determination, as her husband had discovered to his great surprise.

But how could Evie, on such short acquaintance, so clearly see what others never did? It made him feel exposed, and he didn't like it one damn bit. He would have to be more careful around her.

The sun was shining full on his back now, and his spine was prickling with sweat. Deciding that the silence had gone on long enough, he asked in an idle tone, "Where's your truck?"

"I'm having a new motor put in it," she replied. "I might have it back by tomorrow afternoon, but until then I'm using the boat to get to the marina and back."

He waited, but there was no additional explanation. Surprised, he realized that she wasn't going to tell him about the motor blowing, wasn't going to broadcast her troubles in any way. He was accustomed to people bringing their problems to him for deft handling. He had also thought it possible that Evie would ask him for a loan to cover the repairs. They hadn't discussed his financial status, but she had seen the new boat, the new Jeep, the house on the waterfront, and she was far from stupid; she had to know he had money. He wouldn't have given her a loan, of course, because that would have defeated his subtle maneuvering to put financial pressure on her, but still, he wouldn't have been surprised if she'd asked. Instead, she hadn't even planned to tell him that her truck had broken down.

"If you need to go anywhere, call me," he finally offered.

"Thanks, but I don't have any errands that can't be put off until I get the truck back."

"There's no need to put them off," he insisted gently. "Just call me."

She smiled and let the subject drop, but he knew she wouldn't call. Even if he installed himself at the marina until her truck was repaired, she wouldn't tell him if she needed anything.

He took her hand and gently stroked her fingers. "You haven't asked me where we're going tonight."

She gave him a surprised look. "I hadn't thought about it." That was the truth. Where they went was inconsequential; the fact that she would be with *him* was what had occupied her mind.

"That isn't very flattering," he said with a faint smile.

"I didn't say I hadn't thought about going out with you. It's just that the *where* never entered my mind."

The sophisticated socialites he normally squired about New York and the world's other major cities would never have made such an artless confession. Or rather, if they had, it would have been in an intimately flirtatious manner. Evie wasn't flirting. She had simply stated the truth and let him take it as he would. He wanted to kiss her for it but refrained for now. She would be more relaxed if she didn't have to deal with a seduction attempt every time she saw him.

Then she turned to him, brown eyes grave and steady. "I answered your question," she said. "Now answer mine."

"Ah." So she had been delayed but not diverted. Swiftly he decided on an answer that would satisfy her but not leave him open. It had the advantage of being the truth, as far as it went. "I'm a private person," he said quietly. "I don't blurt out my life story to anyone who asks. You don't either, so you should understand that."

Those golden brown eyes studied him for another long moment; then, with a sigh, she turned away. He sensed that his answer hadn't satisfied her, but that she wasn't going to ask again. The sensation of being given up on wasn't a pleasant one, but he didn't want her to keep prying, either.

He checked his watch. There were a few calls he had to make before picking her up for the evening, not to mention showering and changing clothes. He kissed her shoulder again and got to his feet. "I have to leave or I'll be late to an appointment. Don't stay out much longer or you'll get a sunburn. Your shoulders are already hot."

"All right. I'll see you at seven." She remained sitting on the dock, and Robert looked down at her streaked tawny head with stifled frustration. Just when he thought he was finally making serious progress with her, she mentally retreated again, like a turtle withdrawing into its shell. But this afternoon's mood was an odd blend of contentment, melancholy and resignation. Maybe she was worried about the truck; maybe she was nervous about their first date, though why she should be, when he'd already had her half-naked, was beyond his comprehension.

The truth was that she was as opaque to him as he was to others.

He had always had the ability to read people, but Evie's mind was either closed to him or she reacted in a totally unexpected way. He couldn't predict what she would do or tell what she was thinking, and it was slowly driving him mad. He forced himself to walk away, rather than stand there waiting for her to look up at him. What would that accomplish? It was likely that she would figure out why he was waiting and look up just to get it over with, so he would go. Little mind games were only for the insecure, and Robert didn't have an insecure bone in his body. Nevertheless, he was reluctant to leave her. The only time he wasn't worried about what she was doing was when he was with her.

As he climbed into the Jeep, he wryly reflected that it was a sad state of affairs when he was so obsessed with a woman he couldn't trust out of his sight.

Evie remained where she was until long after the sound of the Jeep's engine had faded in the distance. Robert had stonewalled her questions, and sadly she realized that he simply wasn't going to allow her to get close to him. She supposed she could make a pest of herself and keep yammering at him, but that would only make him close up more. No, if she wanted a relationship with him, she would have to content herself with the litte he was comfortable in giving. She had known Matt to the bone and loved him as deeply. How ironic it was that now she had fallen in love with a man who allowed her to touch only the surface.

Finally she pulled her feet out of the water and stood. This had been a day of fretting, though she had tried not to. She would be better off getting ready for her big date. She had the feeling she would need every bit of preparation she could manage.

CHAPTER TEN

A woman couldn't have asked for a more perfect escort, she realized about halfway through the evening. For all his sophistication, or perhaps because of it, there was something very old-fashioned in the courtesy and protectiveness with which he treated her. Everything was arranged for *her* pleasure, *her* comfort, and she herself was old-fashioned enough, Southern enough, to accept it as the way things should be. Robert Cannon was courting her, so of course he should make certain she was pleased by the evening.

His attention was solely on her. He didn't eye other women, though she noticed other women watching him. He held her chair for her whenever she got up or sat down, poured wine for her and asked the maitre d' to turn up the thermostat when he noticed her shivering. It was a matter of his own presence that his request was instantly honored. Whenever they walked, his hand rested warmly on the small of her back in a protective, possessive touch.

In no time, he had put her at ease. It was only natural that she had been nervous about the evening; after all, she hadn't been on a date in twelve years, and there was a great deal of difference between eighteen and thirty. Back then a date had been a hamburger and a movie, or just getting together with a bunch of friends at the skating rink. She wasn't at all certain what one did on a date with a man who was used to the most cosmopolitan of entertainments.

As she watched his dark, lean face, she realized how truly sophisticated he was. He had brought her to a very nice restaurant in Huntsville, but she was well aware that it didn't compare to the sort of establishments available in New York or Paris or New Orleans. Not by even a hint, though, did he indicate that the standards were less than those to which he was accustomed. Others, worldly but less sophisticated—and certainly less polite—would have subtly tried to impress by describing the *truly* good restaurants where they'd eaten. Not Robert. She doubted that he even thought of it, for he had the true sophisticate's knack of being at home in any surrounding. He didn't rate or compare; he simply enjoyed. He would have been as happy eating barbecue with his fingers as he was dining with gold flatware and blotting his mouth with a starched linen napkin.

Oh, God. Not only did he play with babies, he was totally comfortable in her world. Just one more thing to love.

He waved his fingers in front of her face. "You've been watching me and smiling for about five minutes," he said with amusement coloring his tone. "Ordinarily I'd be flattered, but somehow it makes me uneasy."

Her mouth quirked as she picked up her fork. "It shouldn't, because actually it was flattering. I was thinking how comfortable you are down here, despite how different things are."

He shrugged and said gently, "The differences are mostly good ones, though I admit I wasn't prepared for the heat. Somehow, ninety degrees in New York is different from ninety degrees here."

Her brows lifted delicately. "Ninety degrees isn't all that hot."

He chuckled and again wondered briefly at her ability to amuse him. It wasn't anything overt, just the subtle differences in her outlook and the way she phrased it. "That's the difference, one of attitude. Though, of course, it gets hotter than that occasionally, to a New Yorker ninety degrees is *hot*. To you, it's a nice day."

"Not exactly. Ninety degrees is hot to us, too. It's just that, compared to a hundred degrees, it isn't bad."

"Like I said, attitude." He sipped his wine. "I like New York for what it is. I like it down here for the same reason. In New York there's an air of excitement and energy, the opera and ballet and museums. Here, you have clean air, no overcrowding, no traffic jams. No one seems to hurry. People smile at strangers." His eyes lingered on her face, and when he continued his voice was a little deeper. "Though I admit I've been disappointed that I haven't heard you say 'y'all' at all. In fact, I've heard it very few times since I've been here."

She hid her smile. "Why would I say it to you? Y'all is plural. You're singular."

"Is it? That minor detail had escaped me."

"That you're singular?" She paused, aware that she was trespassing into his private life and that he might well shut down as he had that afternoon. "Have you ever been married?"

He sipped his wine again, and his eyes glittered at her over the rim of the glass. "No," he replied easily. "I was engaged once, when I was in college, but we both realized in time that getting married—particularly to each other—would have been a stupid thing to do."

"How old are you?"

"Thirty-six. To satisfy any other pertinent questions you may have, my sexual interest is exclusively in women. I've never done drugs, and I don't have any communicable diseases. My parents are dead, but I have a sister, Madelyn, who lives in Montana with her husband and two sons. There are a few distant cousins, but we don't keep in touch."

She regarded him calmly. He was totally relaxed, telling her that he didn't regard those details of his life as being particularly revealing. They were simply facts. She listened, though, because such minutiae made up the skeleton of his life. "Becky and I have relatives scattered all over the state," she said. "One of my uncles has a huge farm down around Montgomery, and every June we get together there for a family reunion. We aren't a close family, but we're friendly, and it's a way to stay in touch. If it wasn't for the reunion, Jason and Paige would never know Becky's side of the family, only their father's, so we make an effort to go every year."

"Your parents are dead?" He knew they were, for that had been in the supplementary report he had received.

"Yes." The golden glow in her eyes dimmed. "Becky is the only immediate family I have. When Mom died, I lived with Becky and Paul until Matt and I married." Her voice faltered, just a little, at the end.

"What about afterward?" he asked gently.

"Then I lived with Matt's parents." The words were soft, almost soundless. "Where I live now. It was their house. The marina was theirs, too. Matt was their only child, and when they died, they left everything to me."

Robert was pierced by another arrow of jealousy. She was still living in the house where Matt had grown up; there was no way she could walk into that house without being reminded of him at every turn. "Have you ever thought of moving? Of buying a more modern house?"

She shook her head. "Home is important to me. I lost my home when Mom died, and though Becky and Paul made me welcome, I was always aware that it was their home and not mine. Matt and I were going to live in a trailer, at first, but after he died I couldn't.... Anyway, his parents asked me to live with them, and they needed me as much as I needed company. Maybe because they needed me, I felt comfortable there, more like it really was my own home. And now," she said simply, "it is."

He regarded her thoughtfully. He had never felt that sort of attachment for a place, never felt the tug of roots. There had been a large country estate in Connecticut, when he was growing up, but it had simply been the place where he lived. Now his penthouse served the same emotionless function. Evie wouldn't like it, though it was spacious and impeccably decorated. Still, he was comfortable there, and the security was excellent.

The restaurant featured a live band, and they were really very good. In keeping with the image of the place, they played old standards, meant for real dancing rather than solitary gyrations. He held out his hand to Evie. "Would you like to dance?"

A glowing smile touched her face as she placed her hand in his, but then she hesitated, and a look of uncertainty replaced the pleasure. "It's been so long," she said honestly, "that I don't know if I can."

"Trust me," he said, soothing her worries. "I won't let you come to grief. It's like riding a bicycle."

She went into his arms. She was stiff at first, but after several turns she relaxed and let the pleasure of the music and the movement sweep through her. Robert was an expert dancer, but then, she hadn't expected anything else. He held her closely enough that she felt secure, but not so close as to touch intimately. More of those exquisite manners, she thought.

As the music continued, she realized that he didn't have to be blatant. Dancing was its own seduction. There was the tender way he clasped her hand, the warm firmness of his other hand on her back. His breath brushed her hair; the clean scent of his skin teased her nostrils. This close, she could see the closely shaven stubble of his beard, dark against his olive skin. Occasionally her breasts brushed against his chest or arm, or their thighs slid together. It was stylized, unconsummated lovemaking, and she wasn't immune to it.

They left at midnight. During the forty-minute drive back to Guntersville, Evie sat silently beside him as he competently handled the black Renegade. They didn't speak until he pulled into her driveway and turned off the ignition, flooding the sudden darkness with silence. As their eyes adjusted, they could see the river stretching, soundless and glistening, behind her house.

"Tomorrow night?" he asked, turning toward her and draping one arm over the steering wheel.

She shook her head. "I can't. I haven't arranged for Craig to take over my shift, so he'll open the marina in the morning as usual. I wouldn't, anyway. That isn't the deal we made."

He sighed. "All right, we'll compromise. How about swapping shifts with him once a week? Would that be acceptable to your strange scruples? He works for you, rather than the other way around, you know."

"He's also a friend, and he does a lot of favors for me. I won't take advantage of him." The coolness in her voice told him that he had offended her.

He got out and walked around to open the door for her. As he lifted her to the ground, he said with a touch of whimsy, "Will you try to make a little time for me, anyway?"

"I'll talk to Craig about it," she replied noncommittally.

"Please."

She extracted her house key from her purse, and Robert deftly lifted it out of her fingers. He unlocked the door, reached inside to turn on a light, then stepped back. "Thank you," she said.

He delayed her with his hand on her arm as she started to go inside. "Good night, sweetheart," he murmured, and placed his mouth over hers.

The kiss was slow and warm and relatively undemanding. He didn't touch her, except for his hand on her arm and his lips moving over hers. Unconsciously she sighed with pleasure, opening her mouth to the warmth of his breath and the leisurely penetration of his tongue.

When he lifted his head, her breasts were tingling, her body was warm, and she was breathing faster than normal. It gratified her to notice that his breath, too, was a little rough. "I'll see you tomorrow," he said. Then he kissed her again and walked back to the Jeep.

She closed the door, locked it and leaned against it until she heard the sound of the Jeep fade in the distance. Her chest felt tight, her heart swollen and tender. She wanted to weep, and she wanted to sing.

Instead, she kicked off her shoes and walked into the kitchen to get a drink of water. Her left foot landed solidly in something wet and cold, and she jumped in alarm. Quickly she turned on the kitchen light and stared in dismay at the puddle around the bottom of the refrigerator. Even more ominously, there was no faint humming sound coming from the appliance. She jerked the door open, but no little light came on. The interior remained dark.

"Oh no, not now," she moaned. What a time for the refrigerator to die! She simply couldn't afford to get it repaired now. She supposed she could buy a new one on credit, but she hated to add another payment to the monthly load. The refrigerator had been elderly, but why couldn't it have lasted another year? By then she would have paid off a couple of debts and had more ready cash. Another six months would have made a difference.

There was nothing, however, that she could do about the refrigerator at nearly one in the morning. She was drooping with fatigue, but she mopped up the water and put down towels to catch any additional leaks.

When she finally got into bed, she couldn't sleep. That part-time job she had thought about during the afternoon now looked like a necessity, rather than an option. Her lower abdomen was dully aching. The evening with Robert, about which she had been so nervous, had turned out to be the best part of the day.

At seven o'clock she was on the phone to Becky. While Becky was calling around to her friends, Evie began systematically calling in response to every Refrigerator For Sale ad in the paper. As she had suspected, even at that early hour there were a number of calls that weren't answered. One, which had seemed the most promising, had sold the refrigerator as soon as the ad appeared.

By nine o'clock, she and Becky had located a good refrigerator for sale. At a hundred dollars, it was more than she could readily afford, but considerably less than a new one would cost. Becky came to get her, and they drove out together to look at it.

"It's ten years old, so it probably has another five to seven years," the woman said cheerfully as she showed them into the kitchen. "There isn't anything wrong with it, but we're building a new house, and I wanted a big side-by-side refrigerator. We were getting one, anyway, but last week I found just what I wanted, on sale at that, so I didn't wait. As soon as I get this one sold, I can have the new one delivered."

"It's sold," Evie said.

"How are you going to get it home?" asked Becky practically. "Until your truck is fixed, you don't have any way to haul it." Having stated the problem, she set about trying to solve it, running down the list of everyone she knew who owned a pickup truck and might be available.

Evie's own list was formidable. After all, she knew a lot of fishermen. Half an hour later, Sonny, a friend who worked second shift and had his mornings free, was on his way.

Time was running short for Evie by the time they got the refrigerator to her house. She called Craig to let him know what was going on and that she might be a few minutes late. "No sweat," was his easygoing reply.

Sonny hooked up the ice maker while Evie and Becky hurriedly transferred what food had survived from the old refrigerator into the new one. The frozen stuff was okay, and since she hadn't opened the door, most of the food in the other compartment was still cool and salvageable. She threw away the eggs and milk, just to be on the safe side.

"Do you want me to haul off the old one?" Sonny asked.

"No, you need to go to work. Let's just push it out onto the deck, and I'll take care of getting rid of it when I get my truck back. Thanks, Sonny. I don't know what I'd have done without you today."

"Anytime," he said genially, and bent his muscles to the job of getting the old refrigerator outside.

After that was accomplished and Sonny had left, Becky grinned at her sister "I know you're in a hurry to get to the marina, so I'll call you tonight. I can't wait to hear all the juicy details about your evening with Robert."

Evie blew a wisp of hair out of her face. "It was fine," she said, smiling because she knew the answer would disappoint Becky. "I was worried for nothing. He was a perfect gentleman all night long."

"Well, damn," muttered her once-protective big sister.

With Murphy's Law in full effect, when Evie arrived at the marina she found that the afternoon before had indeed brought Burt several repair jobs on boats that had to be done before he could get to her truck. Because the people who used the marina were her livelihood, she didn't protest the delay. Financially, it would be better for her if even more repair jobs came in. Enough of them would pay for fixing her truck.

Craig met her at the dock, took one look at her and said, with his tongue firmly planted in his cheek, "Boss, you need to stop all this carousing and get a good night's sleep."

"That bad, huh?"

"Not really. Dark circles are in this month."

"If one more thing tears up," she said direly, "I'm going to shoot it."

He put his brawny young arm around her shoulders. "Aw, everything will be okay. Chin up, boss. You're just tired. If you want to take a nap, I'll hang around for another couple of hours. I've got a date tonight, but I'm free this afternoon."

She smiled at him, touched by his offer. "No, I'm fine. You go on home, and I'll see about getting a morning job to help pay for all this stuff that's going kablooey."

"What stuff?" asked a deep voice behind them. She and Craig turned. A boat had been idling outside, and the noise had masked the sound of Robert's arrival. Unlike her, he looked well rested. His expression didn't give anything away, but she sensed that he didn't like Craig putting his arm around her.

"My refrigerator died last night," she replied. "I spent the morning locating a good used one and getting it home."

That seemed to give him pause, for some reason. Then he gave her a considering look and said, "You didn't get much sleep, did you?"

"A few hours. I'll sleep like a log tonight, though."

Craig said, "If you're sure you don't want me to stay for a while…?"

"I'm sure. I'll see you tomorrow."

"Okay." He took off, whistling. Robert turned to watch him go, a tall, well-built boy who gave the promise of being an outstanding man.

"You don't have any reason to be jealous of Craig," Evie said coolly as she brushed by him, heading toward the office and the promise of air-conditioning.

Robert's eyebrows climbed as he followed her. When they were inside, he murmured, "I don't recall saying anything."

"You didn't, but it was plain what what you were thinking."

He was taken aback. God, her perception was expanding into mind reading. He didn't like the feeling of transparency.

"I've known Craig since he was a child. There's absolutely nothing sexual in our relationship."

"Maybe not from your perspective," he said calmly, "but I was a teenage boy once myself."

"I don't want to hear about raging hormones. If all you can do is criticize, then leave. I'm too tired to deal with it right now."

"So you are." He took her in his arms and tucked her head into the hollow of his shoulder. With one hand he stroked her sun-warmed hair, which was restricted into its usual braid. The night before, she had worn it in an elegant twist. One day soon—or rather, one night—he was going to see it down and spread across his pillow.

Gently he swayed, rocking her. The support of his hard, warm body was so delicious that Evie felt her eyes drifting shut. When she realized that she actually was dozing off, she forced herself to lift her head and step away. "Enough of that or I'll be asleep in your arms."

"You'll sleep there eventually," he said. "But in different surroundings."

Her heart gave a great thump. What he so effortlessly did to her simply wasn't fair. Unbidden, she thought of the one night she had slept in Matt's arms, the sweetness that had so shortly been overlaid with bitterness and regret when his life had ended the next day. Sleeping with Robert wouldn't be anything like that long-ago night....

He saw the sadness darken her eyes again, and he felt like swearing savagely. Every time he thought he was making progress, he slammed into Matt Shaw's ghost, standing like an ethereal wall between Evie and any other man. As unlikely—as damned *ridiculous*—as it seemed, he couldn't doubt that she'd been entirely chaste during her widowhood. Her connection with Landon Mercer, whatever else it was, certainly wasn't physical.

Her relationship with *him,* on the other hand, certainly would be.

"Did you come by for any particular reason?" she asked.

"Just to see you for a moment. Would you like to get a quick bite to eat tonight before you go home?"

"I don't think so. I'm so tired I just want to go home and get some sleep."

"All right." Gently he touched her cheek. "I'll see you tomorrow, then. Take care going across the lake tonight."

"I will. The days are so long, I'll be home before it gets dark."

"Take care, anyway." He leaned over and kissed her, then left.

As soon as he was out of her sight, his black brows pulled together in a frown. Last night's ploy hadn't worked all that well because of something he simply hadn't considered, and he was impatient with himself. He'd been born into money and had made even more, so the option of buying a second-hand refrigerator hadn't occurred to him. He had no idea what she'd paid for it, but he assumed that it was considerably less than a new one, even the cheapest model, would have cost. Though a little more financial pressure had been brought to bear on her, it hadn't been as much as he'd planned.

Mercer was beginning to find the financial waters a little choppy these days, too. It wasn't anything for him to worry about…yet. Soon he would find himself in a pinch with a growing need for ready cash. The next time he made a move, Robert would be ready for him. The net was slowly closing.

He estimated another two weeks, three at the most. He could make things move faster, but he was oddly reluctant to bring everything to a close just yet. If Mercer tried to make another sale, of course he would have to act, but until then, he intended to use the time to complete Evie's seduction.

That was, if he could keep her mind off her dead husband. Robert's jealous fury was banked, but glowing hotly under the restraint. It was ironic that he, of all people, should be jealous. It wasn't an emotion that he'd ever felt before, and he'd been coolly contemptuous of those who allowed someone to become that important to them. But he had never wanted a woman so violently, nor found himself up against such a formidable rival. That, too, was a new experience for him. If a woman had been interested in another man, he had simply moved on, on the theory that battling for her affections was too much trouble and complicated what was, for him, a fairly simple issue.

But then he'd met Evangeline. Her name whispered through his mind, as musical and elegant as the wind sighing in the trees. Evangeline. A poetic name, associated with undying love.

He couldn't accept that she was Matt Shaw's forever, that he might never have her.

Damn it, what was this appeal that teenage boys had for her? He had wanted to punch Craig in the jaw for daring to touch her, but his own sense of fair play had restrained him. Craig looked to be as strong as a young ox, but Robert knew his own capabilities. He could easily have killed the boy without meaning to.

Because Matt had died so young, was Evie's taste forever frozen at that age? The idea was distasteful. He was disgusted with himself for even thinking it. He had no basis for the ugly speculation; he knew very well that there was nothing sexual between Evie and Craig. It was his own jealousy that had spurred the thought.

He had to have her. Soon.

CHAPTER ELEVEN

Evie slept soundly for ten hours that night, from nine until seven the following morning. She woke feeling much better, though she was groggy from sleeping so hard. She stumbled through the house toward the kitchen, keeping her fingers crossed that nothing else had gone on the fritz during the night, especially the coffeemaker. Everything seemed to be in working order, though, so she put on a pot of coffee and headed back toward the bathroom while it was brewing.

Fifteen minutes later, semidressed and with hair and teeth brushed, she was contentedly curled in a chair on the deck, sipping her first cup of coffee. She closed her eyes as the morning sun bathed her with soothing heat. It was a perfect morning, clear and still and fragrant. The birds were singing madly, and the temperature was still comfortable, probably in the high seventies.

She heard tires singing on the road, the particular note that meant four-wheel drive, and a few seconds later Robert pulled into her driveway. Though she couldn't see either the driveway or the road from the deck, and though she knew any number of people who had four-wheel-drive vehicles, she had no doubt of her visitor's identity. Her blood had started moving faster, her skin tingled, and a subtle heat that had nothing to do with either the sun or the coffee had begun spreading through her body.

How many women had loved him? Instinct told her that she was far from the first. Poor creatures. They, like her, had been unable to resist that gentle, ruthless charm. She knew just as certainly that he had never loved any of them in return.

Through the open patio door she heard the knock at the front. "Robert?" she called. "I'm on the deck."

His footsteps in the grass were silent as he walked around, but in fifteen seconds he was coming up the three shallow steps onto the deck. He stopped, his eyes kindling as he stared at her.

Surprised, she curled a little tighter in the chair. "What have I done now?"

His expression relaxed as he moved to take the chair beside her. "You mistake the matter. That was lust, not anger."

"Ah." She used the cup to hide her face as she took another sip. "That should tell you something."

"Should it?"

"That I see anger from you more often than I do lust." Her heart was pounding even harder. My God, she was *flirting*. She was stunned by the realization. She had never in her life engaged in suggestive banter with a man, especially not to discuss his lust for her. She didn't think she had ever even flirted with Matt; somehow things had always seemed settled between them, and they hadn't gone through that dizzying, intense stage of courtship before commitment. They had grown up committed to each other.

"Again you mistake the matter," Robert said idly.

"In what way?"

"The lust is always there, Evangeline."

The quiet, almost casual, statement left her breathless. This time she took refuge in good manners, unwinding her legs to stand up as she said, "Would you like a cup of coffee?"

"I'll get it," he said, stopping her with a hand on her shoulder. His touch lingered, his fingertips lightly caressing the curve of the joint. "You look as contented as a cat. Just tell me where the cups are."

"In the cabinet directly over the coffeemaker. I don't have any cream, only skim milk—"

"It doesn't matter. I drink it black, like you. While I'm in there, would you like a refill?"

Silently she handed him her cup, and he disappeared into the house.

As Robert got a cup from the cabinet, he noticed that his hand was shaking slightly. He was both amused and amazed at the force of his reaction to her, though he had gotten used to being at least semi-aroused whenever he was in her company. But when he had first seen her this morning...well, he had wanted to see her with her hair down, and now he had gotten his wish.

He just hadn't expected the potency of his response, hadn't expected that thick, tawny-gold, streaky mantle flowing halfway down her back, the sunlight glinting along the strands like precious metal. Only the ends curled, frothing in delight at having been released from the confines of her habitual braid. One lock hung over her shoulder and breast, the curl wrapping around her nipple as perfectly as if it had been created to do just that. It had taken only a glance for him to tell that she wasn't wearing a bra under the pale peach camisole top with the tiny tucks down the front that she probably thought disguised her braless state.

He should have become accustomed by now to the luminosity of her skin. He hadn't. Every time he saw her anew, he was struck by the way she seemed to glow. This morning the effect had been particularly acute. She had been curled in the chair like a cat, sleepy and slightly tousled, her shapely legs and delicate feet bare, the bright sunlight somehow lighting her from within.

He wanted to pick her up and carry her back into the dim coolness of her bedroom, strip her naked and sate himself on the golden pearl of her flesh. But he remembered, with an unpleasant jolt, that this was the house where Matt had grown up. He didn't want to take her here, where the memories of the boy abounded.

"Robert?" Her tone was questioning at his long delay.

"I'm just reading your coffee cups," he called back, and heard her chuckle in reply.

He chose the cup that said, "I'm forty-nine percent sweet. It's the other fifty-one percent you have to worry about," and poured coffee into it, then refilled her cup. He carried both of them out onto the deck and carefully gave hers to her, not wanting even a drop of the hot liquid to spill on her bare legs.

"That's quite a collection of cups."

"Isn't it? Jason and Paige are the culprits. Every birthday, every Christmas, they give me a cup as a gag gift. It's become tradition. They put so much time and effort into picking the cup that it's gotten to where unwrapping it is the highlight of the occasion. They don't let Becky or Paul see it beforehand, so it's always a surprise to them, too."

"Some of them are rather suggestive."

She grinned. "Paige's doing. She's an expert at finding them."

He raised his eyebrows. "That delicate, innocent child?"

"That precocious, inventive child. Don't let the shyness fool you."

"She didn't seem shy to me. She started talking to me right away when I first met her."

"Blame your own charm. She isn't that open with most people. But considering the way Sherry's baby took to you," she said judiciously, "it seems that little girls have an affinity for you."

"That's all well and good," he replied, watching her calmly over the rim of his cup, "but what about the grown-up ones?"

"I'll bring you a big stick tomorrow so you can keep them beat off." Very calmly he leaned over to place his cup on the deck, then took her cup from her hand and put it beside his. She eyed him warily. "What are you doing?"

"This." With one swift, deft movement, he scooped her out of her chair, and settled down in his again with her on his lap. She sat stunned, stiffly erect, her eyes big with surprise. He retrieved her cup and placed it in her hands, then shifted her so she was off balance and had to relax against his chest.

"Robert," she said in a weak protest.

"Evangeline." His voice lingered over the long *i*.

She couldn't think of anything else to say. She sat there wrapped by his strength, his warmth, his scent. She could feel the steady thumping of his heart. She had known that he was tall, but even now, with her sitting on his lap, her head wasn't as high as his. She felt physically overwhelmed and remarkably safe. Not from him, but from the rest of the world.

His thighs were hard under her, and something else was, too.

"Finish your coffee," he said, and unthinkingly she raised the cup to her lips.

They sat there in peaceful silence as the heat grew and the traffic on the river increased. When their cups were empty, he set them aside, then caught her face in his hand and turned it up for his slow, deep kiss.

Like a flower turning toward the sun, she shifted toward him, fitting herself more firmly against him. The taste of coffee was in his mouth and hers. His tongue gently explored, and she trembled, her arms lifting to encircle his neck. How long he drank from her mouth she didn't know; time was measured only by the heavy pulse of her blood, throbbing through every inch of her body.

His hand brushed across her breast, pushing her hair aside, then returned to firmly cup the soft mound. Evie stiffened slightly, but he soothed her with a deep murmur, not really a word, only a calming sound. He had had his hands and his mouth on her breasts before, but he could sense that she was still uncertain about allowing the caress. He petted her, gently circling her nipples with one fingertip until they stood temptingly erect, stroking the lush curves with tender care. He wanted her to relax, but instead the tension in her changed, became more finely charged, and he knew that he was arousing her instead.

Deliberately he unbuttoned the first three buttons of the camisole and slid his hand inside. With a sharply indrawn breath, she turned her face into his neck, but she didn't say the one word that would stop him. Her satiny flesh was cool to his touch, the small nipples puckered and tight. He played with them, rubbing them between his fingers, lightly pinching as he watched her with acute attention to learn exactly what she liked. Slowly her breasts grew warm from his touch, the paleness taking on a pinkish glow.

Evie held herself very still, barely breathing, her eyes closed as she tried to deal with the delicate, exquisite pleasure sweeping through her. She knew she was playing with fire, but she couldn't seem to make herself stop. What if he carried her inside? She would have to call a halt then, because she was still having her period, and she was neither sophisticated nor experienced enough to either let him proceed or tell him, without embarrassment, why he couldn't.

"Shall I stop?" he asked, the sound very low.

She swallowed. "I think you should." But she didn't lift her face, and that wasn't the agreed signal. He shifted her, lifted her, and the shocking heat of his mouth closed over the distended nipple of her exposed breast. She cried out, her nipple prickling at the sensation, and fire shot straight through to her loins.

Then, incredibly, his mouth left her body and he was sitting her up on his lap. "We have to stop," he was saying with gentle regret. "I don't think you're ready to give me the go-ahead, and I don't want to push my self-control much further."

Evie bent her head, struggling with a mixture of relief and chagrin as she fumbled with her buttons, restoring her clothing to order. He was right, of course. She didn't want their intimacy to go any further than it already had, though she intended to be prepared if it did.

She managed to smile at him as she scrambled out of his lap and bent down to get the coffee cups. "Thank you," she said, and carried the cups inside.

Robert rubbed his hand over his eyes. God, that had been closer than he'd let on, at least for him. Would she have let him make love to her, after all? Somehow he didn't think so; he could still sense reluctance in her. In a few more minutes she would have said no, and the way he felt now, the strain might well have killed him. Even if she had said yes, he didn't want to make love to her in this house, so it was just as well he'd had the sense to stop.

They spent the morning together without a repeat of the scene on the deck. He'd already had enough frustration for one day, he decided. When it was time for her to cross the lake to work, he kissed her goodbye and left.

The wind blowing in her face helped clear Evie's mind as she sped across the water. What did he do for most of the day? she wondered. He'd said that he was on vacation, but a person, especially a man like Robert, could take only so much relaxation.

To her relief, Burt had made real progress on the marina jobs and thought he would be able to get started on her truck that afternoon. The prospect of having a vehicle to drive home the next day made her cheerful. Perhaps the run of bad luck was over.

She called the local fast-food restaurants to ask about a part-time job in the mornings, but with school out for the summer, none of them needed any help, all of the part-time jobs being filled by teenagers. Call again after school starts, she was told.

"Well, that was a dead end," she muttered to herself as she hung up from the last call. It looked as if the pendulum of luck hadn't swung back her way, after all.

On the other hand, she had the knack of existing on practically nothing when she had to. Over the next few days Evie cut operating expenses where she could and her personal expenses to the bone. She ate oatmeal or cold cereal for breakfast, and allowed herself one sandwich for lunch and one for supper. There were no snacks, no soft drinks, nothing extra. She turned off the air-conditioning at home, making do with the ceiling fans and drinking a lot of ice water. She was pragmatic enough that she didn't feel particularly deprived by these cost-cutting measures. It was simply something that had to be done, so she did it and didn't think much about it one way or the other.

For one thing, Robert occupied a great deal of her thoughts. If he didn't drop by the house in the morning, he came by the marina in the afternoon. He often kissed her, whenever they were alone, but he didn't pressure her for sex. The more he refrained, the more confused she became about whether she wanted to make love with him or not. She had never bemoaned her lack of practical experience before, but now she did; she needed every bit of help she could muster in handling her feelings for him. With every passing day she wanted him more physically, but caution kept warning her away from letting him become more important to her than he already was. She loved him, but somehow, if she didn't make love with him, some small part of her heart remained hers. If he claimed her body, he would claim all of her, and she would have no reserve to fall back on when the end came.

Still, she was acutely aware of how gradually and skillfully he was undermining her resolve. Every day she became more accustomed to his kisses, to the touch of those lean hands, until he had only to look at her and her breasts would tighten in anticipation.

Frightened of the consequences if her willpower faltered, she began taking the birth-control pills on schedule, and as she did so, she wondered if she wasn't actually weakening her own position, for knowing that she was protected might make her less inclined to say no. She was well and truly caught on the horns of that particular dilemma, afraid not to take the pills and afraid of what would happen if she did. In the end, the deciding factor had been that she would rather gamble with her own well-being than that of a helpless baby.

When the next weekend came, Robert once again asked her to swap shifts with Craig so they could have an evening out. Remembering with pleasure the first time she'd had dinner with him, and the dancing afterward, she quickly agreed.

When he picked her up the next night, a slow fire lit the green of his eyes as he looked her up and down. Evie felt a very female gratification at his response. She knew she was looking particularly good, her hair and makeup just as she had wanted, and her dress was very flattering. It was the only cocktail dress she owned, purchased three years before, when the chamber of commerce had organized a party for the local businessmen and women to meet some manufacturing representatives who were thinking about locating in Guntersville.

The deal had fallen through, but the cocktail dress was still smashing. It was teal green, a shade that did wonders for her complexion. There was a full, flirty skirt that swirled just above her knees, a sweetheart bodice supported by thin straps, and it was very low-cut in the back. She had pinned up her hair in a loose twist, with several tendrils left around her ears. Simple gold hoop earrings and her wedding band were the only jewelry she wore, but she had never liked a lot of jewelry weighing her down, so she was satisfied.

Robert was wearing an impeccable black suit with a snowy white silk shirt, but with the heat so oppressive, she wondered how he could stand it. Not that he looked hot; on the contrary, he was as cool and imperturbable as ever, except for the expression in his eyes.

"You're lovely," he said, touching her cheek and watching her bloom at the compliment.

"Thank you." She accepted his verbal appreciation with serene dignity as he drew her outside and locked the door behind them.

He helped her into the Jeep, and as he got in on the other side he said, "I think you'll like the club we're going go. It's quiet, has good food and a wonderful patio for dancing."

"Is it in Huntsville?"

"No, it's here. It's a private club."

She didn't ask how, if it were private, he had managed to get reservations for them. Robert didn't make a show of being wealthy and influential, but he obviously was, given the quality of his clothing, the things he'd bought. Any local bigwig worth his salt would be more than willing to extend an invitation for Robert to join his club.

There was no place in Guntersville that couldn't be gotten to rather quickly. Robert turned the Jeep off of the highway onto a small private road that wound toward the river and soon was parking in a paved lot. The club was a sprawling one-story cedar-and-rock affair, with manicured grounds and a soothing atmosphere. She had seen it before only from the water which glistened just beyond the club. It was only seven-thirty, still daylight, but already the parking lot was crowded.

Robert's hand was firm and very warm on Evie's bare back as he ushered her inside, where they were met by a smiling, very correct maitre d'. They were seated in a small horseshoe booth, upholstered in buttery soft leather.

They ordered their meals, and Robert requested champagne. Evie didn't know anything about wines, period, but his choice brought a spark to the waiter's eyes.

The only time she had tasted champagne had been at her wedding, and that had been an inexpensive brand. The pale gold wine that Robert poured into her glass had nothing in common with that long-ago liquid except its wetness. The taste was dry and delicious, the bubbles dancing in her mouth and exploding with flavor. She was careful to only sip it, not knowing what effect it would have on her.

As before, the evening was wonderful, so wonderful that it was half-over before Evie realized that Robert was herding her toward some swiftly nearing conclusion as implacably as a stallion herded the mare he had chosen to breed, keeping after her, blocking all retreat, until she was cornered. Robert was unfailingly gentle and courteous, but nevertheless relentless. She could see it in those pale eyes, in which a fire smoldered. He intended to have her before the evening was finished.

It was evident in the way he touched her almost constantly, small touches that looked casual but were not. They were seductive touches, light caresses that both gentled her and accustomed her to his hand on her body, while at the same time patiently beginning the process of arousing her.

When they danced, his fingertips moved over her bare back, leaving a trail of heat behind and making her shiver in response. His body moved against hers in rhythm with the music, with her heartbeat, until it seemed as if the music flowed through her. And when they returned to their booth, he was close beside her. Several times she shifted uncomfortably, putting more distance between them, but he was inexorable; he would move closer, so that she could feel the heat of his body, smell the faint, spicy scent of his cologne and the muskiness of his skin. He would lightly stroke her arm, or trace the line of her jaw with one long finger, or rub his thumb over the curve of her collarbone. His leg would slide along hers, and then she would feel the hard curve of his arm behind her back, the firm clasp of his hand at her waist. With every move he made her more aware of him and at the same time broadcast his posession of her to any male in the vicinity who might be thinking of poaching.

Evie was both alarmed and excited, and therefore couldn't get her thoughts in order. She managed to retain an outward calm, but inside she was quietly panicking. Robert had always presented the image of an urbane, eminently civilized man, but from the beginning she had seen beneath the cosmopolitan surface to a far more primitive man, a man of swift and ruthless passion. Now she saw that she had underestimated that volatile streak. He meant to take her to bed with him that very night, and she didn't know if she could stop him.

She didn't even know if she *wanted* to stop him. Was it the champagne, or the fever of desire he had been expertly feeding, not just tonight, but from the moment he'd first kissed her? Her usually clear thought processes kept getting tangled by the slowly increasing heat and hunger of her own body. She tried to think why she should say no, why he was so dangerous for her, but all she could bring to mind was his mouth on her breasts, the way it felt when he touched her.

Physically...oh God, physically he had destroyed all the years of control, of peaceful solitude. She had wanted no man since Matt—until Robert—and she had never wanted Matt this much. Matt had died on the verge of manhood and was forever frozen in her memory as a laughing, wonderful boy. Robert was a man, in the purest sense of the word. He knew the power of the flesh. He knew that, in the taking of her body, he would also be forging a claim, a possession as old as time. His experience far exceeded hers, and he wanted all of her. She would never be able to hold herself, her inner self, inviolate against his taking. A small voice in her cried out in abject fear, and she struggled toward control.

But he seemed to sense whenever that clear inner voice would gather itself, whenever she would panic as she realized anew what he was doing, and with a warm, lingering touch and the brush of his hard body against her soft curves, he would fan the flames of physical desire to overcome the voice of sanity. He was too good at seduction; even though she recognized it, she couldn't stop it. She had the bitter realization that he could have had her any time he'd wanted, that her will was proving no match for his expertise. He had held back only for some reason of his own, and now he had decided that he wasn't waiting any longer.

He asked her to dance again, and helplessly she went into his arms. She felt too warm, her skin too sensitive. She could feel the fabric of her dress sliding over her body, rasping her nipples, caressing her belly and thighs. Whenever he touched her, her entire body seemed to clench. They moved across the dance floor on the patio, and he held her close while his powerful legs slid against hers, sometimes thrusting his thigh between hers, and she began to throb with a hollow ache between her legs. In the distance, heat flashes lit the sky over the mountains with flickers of purple and gold. There was a sullen rumble of thunder, and the air was humid and still, waiting.

She felt weak, physically weak. She hadn't known that desire robbed the muscles of power. She melted against him, flowed against him, until she felt as if only his arm around her was holding her up.

He brushed his hard mouth over the fragile skin at her temple, his warm breath stirring her hair, touching her ear. "Shall we go home?"

A last, small vestige of caution cried, "No!" but she was so caught in his sensual web that she could only nod her head, and the cry remained unvoiced. She leaned against him as he walked her out to the Jeep.

Not even on the way home did he ease the relentless pressure. After he had shifted gears, he put his right hand on her thigh, sliding it up under her skirt, and the heat of his palm on her naked flesh almost made her moan aloud. She didn't even realize where he was taking her until he parked in front of his house, rather than hers.

"This isn't—" she blurted.

"No," he said quietly. "It isn't. Come inside, Evie."

She could say no. Even now, she could say no. She could insist that he take her home. But even if she did, she suspected, the outcome would be the same. All she would be changing was the location.

He held out his hand. The intent behind it was ruthless. She could feel the heavy arousal and hunger that tightened his lean, powerful frame. He was going to take her.

She put her hand in his.

Even though she sensed his savage satisfaction at her tacit surrender, he remained gentle. If he had not, perhaps her common sense would have won after all. But he was too experienced to make that mistake, and she found herself standing in his moonlit bedroom with his big bed looming behind her. She looked out the French doors to the lake, a black mirror reflecting the cool, pale moon. Another low rumble of thunder reached her ears, and she knew that the heat flashes were continuing, bright bursts of light that teased with their promise of rain but never delivered.

Robert put his hands on her waist and turned her to him. Her heart thudded painfully against her ribs as he bent his head and his mouth claimed hers. His kisses were slow, so slow, and devastatingly thorough. His tongue probed, and his mouth drank deeply from hers as his hands leisurely moved over her body, unzipping, loosening, removing. The bodice of her dress fell to her waist, and beyond. He paused a moment to caress her smooth back, the inward curve of her waist; then he gently removed the dress and tossed it aside.

She stood before him wearing only high heels and panties. He caught her to him for more kisses, his tongue stroking deeply within. His hands moved over her breasts, molding them under his lean fingers. Desperately Evie clung to his broad, muscled shoulders, trying to steady her spinning senses. His silk shirt slid across her tightly budded nipples, making her whimper. He murmured soothingly as he unbuttoned his shirt and shrugged out of it, dropping it, too, to the floor. Then her naked breasts were pressed full against his bare chest, nestled into the curly black hair, and she heard herself make a low, hungry sound.

''Easy, darling,'' he whispered. He kicked out of his shoes and unfastened his pants, letting them drop. His thick sex extended the front of his short, snug boxers. She arched against him, blindly thrusting her pelvis forward to nestle that rigid length. His breath hissed inward, and his control cracked. Fiercely he crushed her to him, his arms tightening until pain made her cry out, the sound stifled against his shoulder.

He lowered her to the bed, the sheets cool against her heated flesh. In a swift movement he divested himself of his shorts. Evie's eyes flared as she saw him totally naked, aroused, the muscles in his body taut with desire and the strain of control. His leanness was dangerously deceptive, for it was all steely muscle, the graceful strength of a panther rather than the bulk of a lion. He lowered himself beside her, one arm cradling her head, while his other hand efficiently removed her shoes and panties. Her total nudity was suddenly startling; she made a brief movement to cover herself, a movement that he halted by catching her wrists and pinning them on each side of her head. Then, very deliberately, he mounted her.

Evie couldn't catch her breath. He was heavier, much heavier, than she had imagined. The sensations were alarming, jarring through her consciousness, coming too swiftly on waves of pleasure that both panicked and beguiled. She was violently aware of his muscled thighs pushing between hers, holding them apart, of his furry, ridged abdomen rubbing against her much softer belly, of the hard press of his chest on her breasts. Between her legs, on her bare loins, she could feel the insistent push of his naked sex against her. Her own sex felt swollen and hot, throbbing in rhythm to her own heartbeat.

He loomed over her in the darkness, much bigger, much stronger. The moonlight was sufficient for her to see the pale glitter of his eyes, the hard planes of his face. His expression was stamped with savage male triumph.

Then he released her wrists and cupped her jaw in one hard, hot hand, turning her face up to him. He held her for the deep thrust of his tongue, the blatant domination of his mouth. Helplessly she responded, caught in the heated madness.

He suckled her breasts, lingering over them and making her writhe with pleasure, and all the while she could feel that hard length impatiently nudging her softest flesh.

The moment came too soon, and not fast enough. He braced himself over her on one arm and reached between their bodies with the other. She felt his lean fingers on her sex, gently parting the folds, finding and stroking her soft, wet entrance. Her hips strained instinctively upward. Her entire body was throbbing. "Robert," she whispered. The single word was taut with strain.

He guided his rigid shaft to her, leaning over and into her as he tightened his buttocks and increased the pressure against the tender opening, forcing it to widen and admit him.

Evie stiffened, her breath quickening. The pressure swiftly became burning pain, real pain. He rocked against her, forcing himself fractionally deeper with every controlled thrust. Her fists knotted the sheet beneath her. She turned her head away, closing her eyes against the hot tears that seeped out beneath her lashes.

He froze as realization hit him.

He turned her head so that she faced him. Her eyes flew open, brilliant with tears in the silver moonlight, and then she couldn't look away. His chest was heaving with the force of his breathing, the sound loud in the quiet, still bedroom. There was nothing of the urbane sophisticate in the man who leaned over her, his face hard with desire. For a split second she saw straight into his soul, into the frighteningly intense, primitive core of him. He held her, forced her to look at him, and with a guttural, explosive sound of control breaking, thrust hard into the depths of her silky body, forcing his way past the barrier of her virginity. She cried out, her body arching under the deep lash of pain. Beyond the pain was the stunning shock of invasion, worse than she had imagined, her delicate inner tissues shivering as they tried to adjust to and accommodate the hard bulk of the intruder.

A rough, deep growl sounded in his throat as he gripped her hips, pulling her more tightly into his possession.

He rode her hard, thrusting heavily, his hips hammering and recoiling as he imprinted his physical brand on her flesh. He had never before been less than gentle with a woman, but with Evie he was ferocious in his need. He couldn't be gentle, not with his head and heart reeling, his entire body exploding with savage pleasure. She was hot and tight, silky, wet...and his. No one else's. Ever. *His.*

He shuddered, gasping, convulsing, and she felt the hot wash of his seed deep inside her. Then he slowly collapsed, shaking in every muscle, blindly groping for support. His heavy weight settled over her, pressing her into the mattress.

Dazed, Evie lay beneath him. She felt shattered, unable to form a coherent thought.

And then she found that it wasn't over.

CHAPTER TWELVE

Slowly Robert surfaced from the depths of pure physical sensation, his mind sluggishly beginning to function once more. The power of what he had experienced left him shaken, with a sense of being outside himself, not quite connected. He was intensely aware of his own body in a way he never had been before. He could feel the warmth of his blood pumping through his veins with the heavy, slowly calming beats of his heart. He could feel the harsh bellowing of his lungs decreasing to a more normal pace, feel the intense sexual satisfaction relaxing his muscles, feel the hot, delicious clasp of Evie's body as he remained firmly inside her, satisfied but not yet sated. She was naked beneath him, just the way he had wanted.

Then, with an abrupt shift, the sluggishness was gone from his brain and reality settled in with ruthless clarity. Robert tensed, appalled at himself. He had lost control, something that had never happened before. Gentleness on his part had never been more needed, and instead he had taken her like a marauder, intent only on his own pleasure, on the conquest and possession of her silky flesh.

She lay motionless beneath him, holding herself in a sort of desperate stillness, as if to avoid attracting his attention again. His heart squeezed painfully. Robert shoved aside the matter of her virginity—he would know the answer to that puzzle later—and concentrated instead on the task of reassuring her. His mind was racing. If he let her escape him now, he would have a hell of a time getting anywhere near her again, and he couldn't blame her for being wary. Wary, hell. She would probably be downright scared, and with good reason.

He had shown her the relentless drive of passion but none of the pleasure. She had known nothing but pain, and the scale was dangerously tilted; unless he could balance the pain with pleasure, he was afraid he would lose her. It was the first time Robert had felt that sort of fear, but a sensation of panic seized him and mixed with his determination. A part of his brain remained blindingly clear. He knew exactly how to bring a woman to climax in a variety of ways: fast or slow, using his mouth or hands or body. He could gently take her to ecstasy with his mouth, and that way would perhaps be the kindest, but his instinct rejected it. He had to do it fast, before she recovered enough to begin fighting—God, he couldn't bear that—and he had to do it the same way that had caused her the pain to begin with. He wanted her to find pleasure in his body rather than dread the thrust that brought their flesh together.

He was still hard, and once more he began moving, slowly, within her. She tensed, and her hands flattened against his chest as if she would try to shove him off. "No," he said harshly, forestalling her resistance. "I won't stop. I know I'm hurting you now, but before I'm finished I'm going to make you like having me inside you."

She stared up at him, her eyes darkened with distress. But she didn't say anything, and he gathered her close, adjusting their positions so she would have the maximum sensation. He could feel her thighs quivering alongside his hips.

He took a deep breath and gentled his voice, wanting to reassure her. "I can make it good for you," he promised, brushing her soft mouth with kisses and feeling it tremble beneath his. "Will you trust me, Evangeline? Will you?"

Still she didn't say anything, hadn't spoken a word since whispering his name at the beginning. Robert hesitated for half a heartbeat, then lifted her hands and put them around his neck. After a moment her fingers shifted slightly to press against him, and relief shuddered through him at that small gesture of permission.

Evie closed her eyes again, gathering herself to once more endure this painful use of her body. At the moment, that was the limit of her capability; she couldn't act, couldn't think, could only endure. She wanted to curl herself into a protective ball and weep in shock and pain and disappointment, but she couldn't do that, either. She was helpless, her body penetrated; she was dependent on his mercy, and he seemed to have none.

At first there was only more pain. But then, abruptly, the twisting thrust of his hips made her arch off the bed with something that wasn't pain, but was just as sharp. There was no warning, no gradual lessening of pain and buildup of pleasure, only that jolt of sensation that made her cry out. He did it again, and with a strangled moan she discovered that her body was even less under her control than she had thought.

She had been cold, but now she was suffused with heat, great waves of it, rolling up from her toes until she felt as if her entire body glowed. It concentrated between her legs, increasing with each inward thrust. Her hands slid from his neck to his shoulders, clinging now, her nails biting into the hard layer of muscle. He was gripping her buttocks, lifting her up to meet him, moving her, rocking her subtly back and forth, and each tiny movement set off new explosions of pleasure within her. She had the sensation of being relentlessly driven up an internal mountain toward some point she couldn't see, but now she was straining to reach it. He pushed her further with each hard recoil of his hips until she was panting and desperate, sobbing as she arched tightly into him. And then he forced her over the edge, and Evie screamed as her senses shattered.

She shuddered and bucked, trying to meld into his flesh, as devastated by the paroxysms of pleasure as she had been by the pain that went before. Robert held himself still and deep, gritting his teeth, but the frantic milking of her internal muscles was more than he could stand, and with a groan he gave himself over, pulsing with release. Somehow he forced himself not to thrust, to let her take her pleasure and not intrude with his, and that only intensified the sensation. From a distance he heard himself groan again as he dissolved, collapsing heavily in her arms.

If Evie had been dazed before, she was even more so now. She lay limply beneath him, drifting in and out of a haze. The demands he'd made on her body, the roller-coaster succession of pain and shock and ecstasy, had left her with neither mind nor body functioning. Perhaps she dozed; she knew she dreamed, flickering images that faded too swiftly to grasp as she surfaced into foggy consciousness once more. She felt him separate himself from her, knew he was trying to be careful, but couldn't prevent a moan at the pain of his withdrawal. She didn't open her eyes as he paused, then murmured softly, a soothing sound that also held a note of apology, and completed the motion. She felt instantly bereft, cold in the air-conditioned darkness. She would have curled protectively on her side, but her limbs were too heavy. The next moment the dark fog closed about her again.

A light snapped on, blindingly bright against her eyelids. She flinched away from it, but he stilled her with a touch. The mattress shifted as he sat down beside her and firmly parted her thighs. Evie made a faint sound of protest and tried to struggle upward, but again the effort was too much.

"Shh," he whispered, a mere rustle of reassurance. "Let me make you more comfortable, sweetheart. You'll sleep better."

A cool wet cloth touched her between her legs. Deftly, tenderly, he cleaned away the evidence of their lovemaking, then dried her with a soft towel. Evie gave a soft sigh of pleasure. He returned the washcloth and towel to the bathroom, and when he came back to turn out the lamp and slide into bed beside her, she was asleep. She didn't rouse even when he turned her into his arms, cradling her protectively against him.

Evie woke in the still, dark silence before dawn. The moon had long since set, and even the stars seemed to have given up their twinkling efforts. The darkness that pressed against the patio doors was more complete than at any other time of night, in the last moments before being dispelled by the first graying that heralded the approach of the sun. She was still sleepy, exhausted by the tumultuous night in Robert's arms. It was as if her body was no longer hers, the way he called forth and controlled her responses. He had seduced her past caring about fear, about pain, so that her body arched eagerly into his possessive thrusts.

Robert lay beside her, his breathing slow and deep. One arm was curled under her head, the other lay heavily across her waist. His heat enveloped her, welcome in the cool night. The strangeness of his presence beside her made her breath catch.

She didn't want to think about the night that had just passed, or the things that had happened between them. She was too tired, too off balance, to handle the riot of impressions and thoughts that whirled in her brain, but she was also too tired to fend them off. She gave up the effort and instead tried to make sense of what she was feeling.

She had never thought that giving herself to the man she loved would prove so traumatic, but it had. The physical pain, oddly, was the least of it, the most understandable. She had known that, under his urbane manner, Robert had the soul of a conqueror. She had also known that he had been sexually frustrated from the time they'd met. It would have made her very uneasy if, under those circumstances, his control *hadn't* wavered. She hadn't expected such a complete collapse, but then, to be perfectly fair, he hadn't expected everything that had happened, either.

She should have told him that she was a virgin, she knew, but the telling would have required an explanation that she simply hadn't been able to give. Talking about Matt, reliving those brief hours of their marriage, was too painful. Her throat tightened with dread, knowing that Robert would demand that explanation soon. She had hoped—foolishly—that he wouldn't be able to tell, that her first time would provide no more than a momentary discomfort that she could easily disguise or ignore. She felt like weeping and laughing at the same time. Had she told him, that might well have been the extent of her pain. As it was, she had paid dearly for keeping her secret, only to have it known, anyway.

The two most difficult things for her to deal with, however, were mingled grief and terror. She had known that sleeping with Robert would destroy her defenses, but she hadn't known how panicked she would feel, or that giving herself to him would call up such poignant memories of Matt. She couldn't distance herself from the grief; loving Matt, and losing him the way she had, had shaped her life and her soul. He had, in effect, made her into the woman she was now.

For twelve years she had been faithful to him, and his memory had wrapped around her like an invisible shield, protecting her. But now she had given herself irrevocably to another man, in both heart and body, and there was no going back. She loved Robert with an intensity that swelled in her chest and made her breath catch. For better or worse, *he* filled her life now. She would have to let Matt go, surrender his memory so that it became only a small, indelible part of her, rather than a bulwark between her and the world. It was like losing him twice.

"Goodbye, Matt," she whispered in her mind to the image of the laughing, dark-haired boy she carried there. "I loved you...but I'm his now, and I love him, too, so much." The image stilled, then nodded gravely, and she saw a smile, a blessing, move across the young face as it faded away.

She couldn't bear it. With a low, keening sound of grief she surged out of bed, awakening Robert. He shot out a hand to catch her, but she evaded it and stood in the middle of the floor, looking wildly around the dark bedroom, her fist pressed to her mouth to stop the sobs that pressed for release.

"What's wrong?" he asked softly, every muscle in his body tense and alert. "Come back to bed, sweetheart."

"I—I have to go home." She didn't want to turn on a light, feeling unable to bear his too-discerning gaze, not now, with her emotions stripped bare. But she needed to find her clothes, get dressed.... There was a dark heap on the carpet, and she snatched it up, touch telling her that it was her dress. Oh God, her muscles protested every move she made, his lovemaking during the night echoing now in her flesh. A deep internal ache marked where he had been.

"Why?" His voice remained soft, compelling. "It's early yet. We have time."

Time for what? she wanted to ask, but she knew, anyway. If she got back into that bed, he would make love to her again. And again. Shaking with grief, caught in the transition between the old love and the new, she thought she would break into pieces if he touched her. She was irrevocably passing from one phase of her life into another, traumatic enough under any circumstances, but she had the sensation of leaving a secure fortress and plunging headlong into unknown danger. She needed to be alone to deal with what she was feeling, to get herself back.

"I have to go," she repeated in a ghostly voice, tight with suppressed tears.

He got out of bed, his naked body pale in the shadowy darkness. "All right," he said gently. "I'll take you home." She watched in bewilderment as he stripped the top sheet from the bed. His next movement was a blur, so swift that she couldn't tell what he was doing until it was too late. With two quick steps he was beside her. He swathed the sheet tightly around her, then lifted her in his arms. "Later," he added as he opened the patio doors and stepped outside with her.

The early morning was silent, as if all God's creatures were holding their breath, waiting for first light. Not even a cricket chirped. The water lapped at the bank with only a slight rustling sound, like silk petticoats. Robert sat down in one of the deck chairs and held her cradled on his lap, the sheet protecting her from the cool, damp air.

Evie tried to hold herself tight, all emotion contained. She managed for a few minutes. Robert simply held her, not saying anything, looking out over the dark water as if he, too, were waiting for the dawn. It was his silence that defeated her; if he had talked, she could have concentrated on her replies. Faced with nothing but her own thoughts, she lost the battle.

She turned her face into his neck as hot tears ran down her cheeks and her body shook with sobs.

He didn't try to hush her, didn't try to talk to her, simply held her more closely to him and gave her the comfort of his body. It was, despite her chaotic emotions, a considerable comfort. The bonds of the flesh that he had forged during the night were fresh and strong, her senses so attuned to him that it was as if his breath were hers, her jerky inhalations gradually slowing and taking on the steady rhythm of his.

When she had calmed, he used a corner of the sheet to dry her face. He didn't bother to wipe her tears from his neck.

Exhausted, empty of emotion, her eyes burning and grainy feeling, she stared out at the lake. In a tree close by, a bird gave a tentative chirp, and as if that were a signal, in the next moment hundreds of birds began singing madly, delirious with joy at the new day. In the time while she had wept, the morning had grown perceptibly lighter, the darkness fading to a dim gray that gave new mystery to details that had been hidden before. That dark hump out in the water—was that a stump, a rock or a magical sea creature that would vanish with the light?

Robert was very warm, the heat of his powerful, naked body seeping through the sheet in animal comfort. She felt the steely columns of his thighs beneath her, the solid support of his chest, the secure grasp of his arms. She rested her head against that wide, smoothly muscled shoulder and felt as if she had come home.

"I love you," she said quietly.

Foolish of her to admit it; how many other women had told him the same thing, especially after a night in his arms? It must be nothing new to him. But what would she gain by holding it back? It would allow a pretense, when he left, that he had been nothing more than a summer affair, but she couldn't fool herself with a sop to her pride. Probably she couldn't even fool him, though he would be gentleman enough to allow her the pretense.

All the same, she was glad of his self-possession. He didn't parrot the words back to her; she would have known he was lying, and she would have hated that. Nor did he act uncomfortable or nervous. He merely gave her a searching look and asked in a level tone, "Then why the tears?"

Evie sighed and returned to staring at the water. He was due some explanation, would probably insist on one, but even though she loved him, she simply couldn't strip her soul bare and blurt out everything. She had a deeply private core, and even if she remained Robert's lover for years, there would be some things she wouldn't be able to tell him, memories that brought up too much pain.

"Evie." It wasn't a prompt but a gentle, implacable demand.

Sadness haunted her eyes and trembled around her mouth. She was very familiar with it, had walked with it for twelve years, gone to bed with it at night, awakened with it on countless mornings. Sadness and a deep lonelines that neither friends nor family had been able to dispel had been her constant, invisible companions. But Robert wanted an answer. A man who had held a woman through such a bout of bitter weeping should at least know the reason for her tears.

"I realized," she finally said in a low, shaking voice, "that Matt is truly gone now."

Cradled against him as she was, she felt the way his muscled body tightened. His words, however, were still controlled. "He's been gone for a long time."

"Yes, he has." Only she knew exactly how long those twelve years had been. "But until last night, I was still his wife."

"No," he said flatly. "You weren't." He put one finger under her chin and tilted it up, forcing her to look at him. It was light enough now for her to see those pale eyes glittering. "You were never his wife. You never slept with him. I hope you aren't going to try to pretend you weren't a virgin, because I'm not a fool, and the stain on the sheet isn't because you're having your period."

Evie flinched. "No," she whispered. God, it was eerie how he had gone straight to the secret she had kept for so long.

"You married him," he continued relentlessly. "How is it that I'm the only man who's ever had you?"

Sadness still darkened her eyes, but she said, "I had a June wedding," and a wealth of grief and irony lay in those brief words.

He didn't understand, but he lifted his dark brows, inviting her to continue.

"It's impossible to book a church for a wedding in June unless you do it about a year in advance," she explained. "Matt and I picked the day when we were still juniors in high school. But there's no way to do any personal planning that far ahead of time." Evie turned her head away from him once more, toward her private solace, the water. "It was a beautiful wedding. The weather was perfect, the decorations were perfect, the cake was perfect. Everything went off without a hitch. And my period started that morning.''

Robert was silent, still waiting. Evie swallowed, aching inside as she looked back at the innocent girl she had been. ''I was so embarrassed that night, when I had to tell Matt that we couldn't make love. We were both miserable.''

''Why didn't you—'' he began, but then stopped as he realized that two teenagers wouldn't have the ease and experience of two adults.

''Exactly,'' Evie said, as if he had put his thoughts into words. ''We had never made love, obviously. Matt didn't have any more experience than I did. What experience we had, we'd gotten together, but we'd both wanted to wait until after we were married. So there we were, two eighteen-year-olds on our wedding night, and all we could do was neck and hold hands. Matt was so miserable that we didn't even do much of that.

''But he was basically such a cheerful person that nothing depressed him for long. He was making jokes about it the next morning, making me laugh, but we both agreed that it was something we'd *never* tell our kids when we got old.'' Her voice wavered and faded until it was almost soundless. ''He died that day.''

Gently Robert pushed a strand of hair away from her face. So she had never made love with her young husband, but for over a decade had kept herself untouched for him. With an acuteness of insight that often made people uncomfortable, he saw exactly how it had been. Traumatized by Matt's death, she had doubly mourned the fact that they had never been able to make love and had sealed herself off from other men. If her first time couldn't be with Matt, it would be with no one. She had existed ever since as an animated Sleeping Beauty whose body had kept on functioning while her emotions had been suspended.

Robert felt a deep, savage satisfaction. Despite that enormous barrier, he had succeeded where others hadn't even been able to begin. Her first time had been *his*. She was *his*.

He had always despised promiscuity but hadn't prized virginity. It had seemed to him the height of hypocrisy to demand something from a woman that he himself lacked. All of his sophisticated affairs, however, had nothing in common with the powerful, primitive sense of jealous possessiveness that had swept over him the moment he had realized that he was the only man ever to make love to Evie.

Her association with Landon Mercer, whatever it was, was certainly not romantic in any sense. Sitting there in the early dawn, with Evie cradled on his lap, Robert made a swift decision. He wouldn't stop the investigation, wouldn't warn her in any way, because the espionage had to be halted before it did irreparable harm to both the space station and national security. But when the net was tightened and all the traitorous little fish caught, he would step in and use his influence to shield Evie from prosecution. She wouldn't escape punishment, but the punishment would be his, and his alone, to mete out. The simple truth was that he couldn't bear for her to go to prison. He was astonished at himself, but there it was.

He didn't know why she was involved in something so vile. He was a very good judge of people, and he would have sworn that honor was a cornerstone of her character. Therefore, she had to be doing it for what she considered a good reason, though he couldn't imagine what that could be. It was possible she didn't realize exactly what was going on; that explanation fit better than any other, and made him all the more determined to protect her. As he had told her once, he was good at taking care of his own, and last night Evie had become his in the most basic of ways.

He was fiercely glad that nature's rhythm had interfered with her wedding night all those years ago. Poor Matt. A lot of his jealousy for the boy faded away, and a rather poignant pity took its place. Matt Shaw had died without ever tasting the perfection of his young wife's body.

Robert remembered the moment the night before when he had removed her last garment and seen her totally naked, nothing left to his imagination any longer. To his numb surprise, his imagination had fallen short. He had seen her breasts before, but each time he had marveled at how firm and round they were, delightfully upright, the nipples small and a delectable shade of dark pink. Her body curved in to a lithe waist, then flared again to very womanly hips. Her skin, in the silver moonlight, had glowed like alabaster. Instead of being model thin, like the women he had been accustomed to, her curves had been lush and sensual. He hadn't been able to wait but had mounted her immediately.

A gentleman would have been far more considerate of her than he had been, but he had always been wryly aware that, despite what all his acquaintants thought, he was definitely *not* a gentleman. He was controlled and intelligent and not a cruel man, but that wasn't the same thing as being gentlemanly. Where Evie was concerned, though, his control went right out the window. His mouth took on a grim line as he remembered the wild rush of passion, the primitive instinct to make her his, that had blotted out all reason. Not only had he hurt her, he hadn't used a condom. He, who had never before neglected to make certain some form of protection was used, hadn't even given a thought to birth control.

She might be pregnant. He allowed the possibility to seep into his mind just as the golden light began to seep over the ridge of mountains. To his surprise, he didn't feel any panic or disgust at his stupidity. Rather, he felt pleased—and intrigued.

He put his hand inside the sheet, resting it on her cool, flat belly. "We may be parents. I didn't wear a condom."

"It's all right." She gave him a composed look. The tears and grief were now well under control. "I went to my doctor in Huntsville and got a prescription for birth-control pills."

He felt a not altogether pleasant jolt. He should have been relieved, but instead he was strangely disappointed. Common sense prevailed however. "When?"

"Not long after meeting you," she said wryly.

Robert almost snorted at the amount of work he'd had his people doing, trying to find out what she had been doing, whom she had seen, that day in Huntsville. He would pull them off that particular job now, but he would be damned if he'd tell them what she *had* been doing.

He lifted his eyebrows at her, a sardonic look on his face. "I distinctly remember you saying that you didn't intend to sleep with me.''

"I didn't. But that doesn't mean I'd leave something that important to chance, because you were determined, and I wasn't entirely sure of my willpower.''

"Your willpower would have been fine," he said, "if you hadn't wanted me, too.''

"I know," she admitted softly.

Dawn was well and truly upon them now, golden light spilling across the water. The roar of outboard motors broke the serene hush of the morning, and soon the river would be crowded with fishermen and pleasure boaters. Though Evie's position on his lap would keep anyone from seeing he was naked, Robert thought it best not to chance shocking the locals. After all, she ran a business here, and she might be recognized. He stood up easily, still cradling her securely in his arms, and carried her back through the open patio doors.

He had never been more content than he was at this moment. Evie probably didn't know what was really going on with Mercer and was involved only peripherally; he would be able to protect her without much problem. He had taken her to bed, and now he knew what had lain beneath her mysterious sadness. He doubted that Evie would ever completely stop thinking about Matt, but that was okay now, because Matt Shaw's ghost had been banished and she had emerged from her emotional deep freeze. She had said that she loved him, and he knew instinctively that she hadn't been mouthing the words merely to rationalize their lovemaking. If she hadn't already loved him, he would never have been able to seduce her.

Some of the women who had come before had also told him that they loved him—most of them, in fact. The declarations had never elicited more from him than a rather tender pity for their vulnerability. Though he had liked and enjoyed all his lovers, none of them had ever managed to pierce his shell; he doubted any of them had even known the shell existed.

Evie's simple statement, though, had filled him with a satisfaction so fierce that his blood had thrummed through his veins. She hadn't expected him to respond. Now that he thought about it, she expected less from him than anyone else ever had. It was a startling realization to a man accustomed to having people come to him with their problems, expecting him to make decisions that would affect thousands of workers and millions of dollars. Evie expected nothing. How was it, then, that she gave so much?

He carried her into the bathroom and stood her on her feet, then unwrapped her from the sheet. The sight of her creamy golden flesh aroused him again, drew his hands to cup her breasts and feel the cool, silky weight of them. His thumbs rubbed across her nipples, making them tighten. Evie's eyes were wide with alarm as she stared at him.

His mouth quirked into a crooked smile. "Don't look so worried," he said as he bent down to press his lips to her forehead. "I'll restrain myself until you've had time to heal. Get in the tub, sweetheart, while I put on the coffee. A bath will relieve some of the soreness."

"Good idea," she said with absolute sincerity.

He chuckled as he left her there. The feeling of contentment was even deeper. She was *his*.

CHAPTER THIRTEEN

How could experiencing such a night not leave an imprint on her face? Evie wondered as she got ready for work. After her leisurely soak in the soothing hot water and an equally leisurely breakfast, which Robert had cooked with the same easy competence with which he handled everything else, he had driven her home and reluctantly kissed her goodbye for the day, saying that he had some business to attend to in Huntsville but would try to get back before she closed the marina. If not, he would come to her house.

She had forced herself to do the normal things, but she felt as if her entire life had been turned upside down, as if nothing were the same. *She* wasn't the same. Robert had turned her into a woman who actively longed for his possession, despite the discomfort of her newly initiated body. She hadn't known, hadn't even suspected, that passion could be so savage and all-encompassing, that the pain would be as nothing before the need to link her body with his.

She wanted him even more now than before. He had brought up the long-buried sensuality of her nature and made it his, so that she responded to the lightest touch of his hand. When she thought of him, her body throbbed with the need to wrap her legs around him and take him inside her, to cradle his heavy weight, accept and tame the driving need of his masculinity. The scent of his skin, warm and musky, aroused her. Her memory was filled now with details that she hadn't known before, like the guttural growl of his words and the way his neck corded when he threw his head back in the arching frenzy of satisfaction.

She stared at her face in the mirror as she swiftly braided her hair. Her eyes had shadows under them, but she didn't look tired. She simply looked...like herself. If there was any change at all, it was in the expression in her eyes, as if there was a spark that had been missing before.

But if her face was the same, her body bore the signs of his lovemaking. Her breasts were pink and slightly raw from contact with his beard stubble, her nipples so sensitive from his mouth that the soft fabric of her bra rasped them. There were several small bruises on her hips, where he had gripped her during his climax, and her thighs ached. She was sore enough that every step reminded her of his possession and awakened echoes of sensation that made her acutely aware of her body.

It was much earlier than usual when she drove to the marina, but she needed the distraction to take her mind off Robert. If she was lucky, Sherry would bring Virgil by to spend the day with her.

Craig was gassing up a boat when she arrived. When he had finished, he came in and rang up the sale, putting the money in the cash drawer. "How come you're in so early? Have a nice time last night?"

Her nerves jumped, but she managed a composed smile. "Yes, we did. We went to a private club for dinner and dancing. And I came in early...just because."

"That's a good enough reason for me." He brushed his dark hair out of his eyes and gave her an urchin's grin. "I'm glad you're going out with him. You deserve some fun, after the way you've worked to build up this place."

"Thanks for swapping shifts with me."

"You bet."

Another customer idled up to the docks, and Craig went out again. Evie picked up the morning mail and began sorting through it. The junk mail and sales papers went into the trash. The bills went to one side, to be juggled later. One letter was from a New York bank she'd never heard of, probably wanting her to apply for a credit card. She started to toss it without opening it, but on second thought decided to see what it was about. She picked up the pen-knife she used as a letter opener and slit the envelope.

Thirty seconds later, her brows knit in puzzlement, she let the single sheet of paper drop to the desk. Somehow this bank had gotten her confused with someone else, though she couldn't think how they had gotten her name on one of their files when she had never done business with them. The letter stated, in brisk terms, that due to a poor payment record they would be forced to foreclose on her loan unless it was paid in full within thirty days.

She would have ignored it except that the amount noted was the same as what she owed her bank for the loan against the marina. She knew that figure well, had struggled to get it down to that amount. Each payment brought it even lower. She didn't know how, but obviously her file had gotten into this other bank's computers, and they wanted her to pay fifteen thousand, two hundred and sixty-two dollars within thirty days.

Well, it was obviously something she would have to clear up before it got even more tangled. Evie called her bank, gave her name and asked for her loan officer, Tommy Fowler, who was also an old school friend.

The line clicked, and Tommy's voice said, "Hi, Evie. How're you doing?"

"Just fine. How are you and Karen doing, and the kids?"

"We're doing okay, though Karen says the kids are driving her crazy, and if school doesn't start soon she's going to get herself arrested, so she can have some peace and quiet."

Evie chuckled. The Fowler kids were known for their frenetic energy.

"What can I help you with today?" Tommy asked.

"There's been a really strange mix-up, and I need to know how to straighten it out. I got a letter today from a bank in New York, asking for payment in full on a loan, and it's the same amount as the one I took out from you, on the marina."

"Is that so? Wonder what's going on. Do you have your account number handy?"

"Not with me, no. I'm at work, and all my bookkeeping is at home."

"That's okay, I'll pull it up under your name. Just a minute."

She could hear the tapping of computer keys as he hummed softly to himself. Then he stopped humming and silence reigned, stretching out for so long that Evie wondered if he'd left the room. Finally a few more keys were tapped, then more silence.

He fumbled with the receiver. "Evie, I—" Reluctance was heavy in his voice.

"What's wrong? What's happened?"

"There's a problem, all right, hon. A big one. Your loan was bought by that bank."

Evie's mind went blank. "What do you mean, bought?"

"I mean we sold off some of our loans. It's a common practice. Banks do it to reduce their debt load. Other financial institutions buy them to diversify their own debt load. According to the records, this transaction took place ten days ago."

"Ten days! Just ten days, and already they're demanding payment in full? Tommy, can they do that?"

"Not if you've fulfilled the terms of the loan. Have you... ah...were you late with the payment?"

She knew he must have her payment record there in front of him, showing that she had been late several times, though she had never fallen a full month behind and had always gotten back on schedule. "It's late now," she said numbly. "I had an unexpected expense, and it'll be next week before I can."

She heard him exhale heavily. "Then they're legally within their rights, though the normal procedure would be to make an effort at collecting the payment, rather than the full amount."

"What do I do?"

"Call them. It should be fairly easy to straighten out. After all, you're a good risk. But be sure to follow up by letter, so you'll have a record in writing."

"Okay. Thanks for the advice, Tommy."

"You're welcome. I'm sorry about this, hon. It never would have happened if we'd still held the loan."

"I know. I'll see what I can do."

"Call me if there's anything I can do to help."

"Thanks," she said again and hung up.

Her heart was pounding as she dialed the number on the letterhead. An impersonal voice answered and nasally requested her business. Evie gave the name of the man who had signed the letter, and the connection was made before she could even say please.

The call was brief. Mr. Borowitz was as brisk as his letter had been and as impersonal as the operator. There was nothing he could do, nor did he sound interested in trying. The outstanding amount was due in full by the time limit set forth in the letter, or the loan would be foreclosed and the property forfeit.

Slowly she hung up and sat there staring out the window at the blindingly bright day. The lake was crowded with boaters, people laughing, having fun. The marina was busy, with owners cleaning their craft, others using her ramps to launch their boats, still others idling in for gas. If she didn't somehow come up with over fifteen thousand dollars within the next thirty days, she would lose it all.

She loved the marina. Because she and Matt had been playmates before they had become sweethearts, she had spent a lot of time here even as a child. She had spent hours playing on the docks, had grown up with the smell of the water in her nostrils. The rhythms of the marina were as much a part of her as her own heartbeat. She had helped Matt work here, and later, after his death, had taken over the lion's share of the work from his parents. When they had left the marina to her, she had channeled all her energy and efforts into making it prosperous, but it had been a labor of love. The marina, as much as her family, had given her a reason for going on when she had been doubtful that she wanted to even try.

This was her kingdom, her home, as much or more than the house in which she lived. She couldn't bear to lose it. Some way, any way, she would find the money to pay off the loan.

The most obvious solution was to borrow against the house. The amount of the debt would be the same, but it would be stretched out over a longer period of time, and that would actually lower the payments. She felt giddy for a moment as the shock and horror lifted from her shoulders. She would be in even better shape than before, with more free cash every month.

She called Tommy again and got the ball rolling. He agreed that a mortgage was the perfect solution. He would have to get an okay on the loan, but he didn't foresee any problems and promised to call her as soon as permission came through.

When she hung up, Evie sat with her head in her hands for a long moment. She felt as if she had just survived combat. She was shaky, but elated at her victory. If she had lost the marina... She couldn't let herself imagine it.

When she finally lifted her head and looked out the window, driven by a need to see her domain still safe and secure, still hers, her face broke into a smile. Business was good today. So good, in fact, that Craig desperately needed a hand and was probably wondering why she wasn't out there helping him. Evie bounded to her feet, energy restored, and rushed out to help him with the sudden glut of customers.

Robert arrived at the marina just after seven that evening. It had been busy all day, and she was on the dock selling gas and oil to yet another happy, sun-roasted boater. Alerted by a sensitivity to her lover's presence, Evie looked around and saw him standing just outside the door, watching her. She lifted her hand. "I'll be there in a few minutes."

He nodded and stepped inside, and she turned her attention back to her customer.

Robert watched her through the big window as he stepped behind the counter. He had been notified that she had received the letter and called the bank that he had arranged to buy her loan, and that, as instructed, they had been totally unwilling to cooperate on the matter. Glancing down, he saw the letter lying on top of the stack of mail, the single sheet of paper neatly folded and stuffed back into the envelope.

She had to be uspet. He regretted the need for it, but he had decided to see the plan through. Though he was almost certain she didn't know exactly what Mercer was doing, that she was more of an unwitting accomplice than anything else, there was still the small chance that she was involved up to her pretty neck. Because of that, he couldn't relent in his financial pressure. If she *was* involved, she would be forced into another sale just to raise the money to pay the loan. If she wasn't involved, he would take care of her money problems just as soon as he had Mercer in jail. There were others, and he would get them, too. But Evie was his, one way or the other.

Since he had left her that morning, he had several times been struck with amazement that he wouldn't see her sent to jail, even if she was guilty. This was his country's security at stake, something he took very seriously indeed. He had risked his life more than once for the same principle. He had relished the adventure, but the underlying reason for taking those risks had been a simple, rock-solid love of country. If Evie had betrayed it, she deserved prison. But acknowledging that in no way changed his decision. He would protect her from prosecution.

The sunburned customer and his trio of friends, all young men in their early twenties, were obviously in no hurry to stop chatting with Evie. Robert scowled out the window, but he couldn't blame them. Only a dead man wouldn't respond to her curvy, glowing femininity.

He slipped the letter out of the envelope and unfolded it. There was no reason for doing so, except a meticulous attention to detail. He wanted to know exactly what it said. Swiftly he scanned the contents, satisfied with the way it had been handled. Then he read Evie's notes, hastily scribbled in the margin.

She had written down the name ''Tommy Fowler,'' with a phone number beside it. Underneath she had written ''mortgage house'' and circled that.

A smile tugged at his mouth. She was certainly a resourceful, common-sense woman. Relief welled up in him. If she was truly involved in stealing the NASA computer programs, she wouldn't be trying to mortgage her house to pay the loan; she would simply arrange another buy. In his experience, criminals didn't think of things like honest work to pay off debts; they were leeches, living off the effort of others, and would simply steal again.

Robert returned the letter to the envelope. More than ever, he regretted the need to play out what he had begun, but he never left anything to chance, certainly not in a matter this serious. He would have to squash any attempt to mortgage the house, of course. Evie would be worried sick, but he would make it up to her afterward.

He sat down on the high stool and watched her as she finally got rid of the four admiring young men. She was dressed much as she had been the first time he'd seen her, in jeans and a T-shirt with her tawny blond hair in a thick, loose braid. His reaction, too, was almost the same: he was poleaxed with lust. The only difference was that it was more intense now, and he hadn't thought that possible. But now he knew exactly how she looked naked, knew all the delectable textures and curves of her body, and the hot, tight clasp of being sheathed deep inside her. He shivered with desire, his burning gaze locked on her as she walked up the dock. He knew the sounds she made at the peak of pleasure, knew how she clung to him, the way her legs locked convulsively around him, and how her nipples hardened to tight little raspberries. He knew the taste of her, the scent, and wanted to have it again.

She came inside, glanced at him and froze in place. He saw the shudder of awareness that rippled over her as she sensed his arousal. God, was she even more attuned to him than she had been before? The thought was unsettling.

"Come here," he said softly, and she blindly walked into his arms.

He didn't rise from the stool but pulled her between his thighs. Her arms circled his shoulders as he bent his mouth to hers. He kissed her for a long time, so hungry for her that he couldn't be gentle. Evie moved against him, her hips rolling in a languorous, wanton manner that made his heart almost stop in his chest. Kissing her when her response was reluctant had been intoxicating enough; now that she was willing, her mouth clung to his in a way that made him forget about Mercer and the stolen computer programs, about the mess she was embroiled in, even where he was, everything but the hot joy of holding her.

But she would be too sore for any more lovemaking today, and reluctantly he eased away from her mouth, trailing kisses across her temple and the curve of her jaw. He would have to restrain himself for a while yet.

"How did your day go?" he murmured, opening the door for her to tell him about the problem with the bank loan.

"It was as busy today as I've ever seen it," she replied, leaning back in the circle of his arms. Her eyes were soft and sleepy. "How about yours?"

"Tedious. I had some boring details to handle." That was a lie. No detail was boring to him.

"I wish you had been here today, I'd have put you to work. I think everyone who owns a boat was on the water today." She glanced over his shoulder. "There's another one," she said as she slipped out his arms.

This group didn't need any gas but trooped inside in search of some snacks and cold drinks. They had the ruddiness of people who had been out in the sun and wind all day, and brought with them the coconut scent of sunscreen lotion. Once inside, they seemed reluctant to leave the air-conditioning and milled around looking at the fishing tackle. Evie didn't try to hurry them, instead chatting pleasantly. They were two couples about her age, out for a day of relaxation on the lake. One of the women mentioned how nice it was to have a day away from the kids, and for a while the conversation centered on the antics of their children. When the group finally left, it was with friendly goodbyes.

"Alone at last," Robert said, glancing at his watch. "It's closing time, anyway."

"Thank goodness." Evie stretched and yawned, catching herself in midstretch with a wince that she quickly covered, but not quickly enough. He saw that slight hesitation. He would indeed have to exercise self-control.

He helped her to close up, then sent her home while he stopped for takeout. They ate dinner together, then sat out on the deck in the cooling night, talking softly about routine things. But Evie soon became sleepy, a direct result of not sleeping much the night before. On her third yawn, Robert stood up and held out his hand. "That's it, sleepyhead. Bedtime."

She put her hand in his and let him pull her to her feet. He led her to the bedroom and gently began undressing her.

"Robert, wait," she said uneasily, trying to draw away from him. "I can't—"

"I know," he said, and kissed her forehead. "I told you I'd give you time to heal. I didn't say anything about not sleeping together, but *sleep* is the operative word."

She relaxed into his arms again, and he finished the task of undressing both of them. It was too warm in the house for him to be comfortable, but when they were both naked and lying on the bed, the ceiling fan wafted a cooling breeze over them, and he began to get drowsy, anyway. They lay nestled spoon fashion, his hard thighs under her round bottom, one hand possessively covering a breast.

He lay quietly. She was already asleep, her breathing slow and even. All his objections to staying in this house had faded when he had found that Evie had never truly been Matt's wife. He would still have preferred being in his own house; the bed was much bigger, for one thing. But Evie would be more comfortable in her own home, and that was the most important thing. He had notified his people where he would be, just as he had notified them that Evie would be staying with him the night before.

He had given her every opportunity to tell him about the bank loan, but she hadn't said a word about it. Just as she had with the blown motor in her truck, she kept her trouble to herself rather than running to him for help or even emotional support. For someone who was so open and friendly, Evie was a very solitary person, accustomed to handling everything on her own. Though he would have had to turn her down if she'd asked for help, he wanted her to confide in him, to let him far enough into her life that he knew about the problems as well as the pleasures. When they were married, he would make damn certain he knew every time she stubbed her toe.

Until that moment, he hadn't let his plans for the future progress that far, but suddenly it seemed the thing to do. He had never wanted any other woman the way he wanted Evie, and he sincerely doubted that he ever would. After this mess was settled, he intended to keep her close by, which would mean taking her to New York with him. And he knew Evie. Though she had given herself to him, she was essentially a conventional soul. She would want the security of marriage; therefore, he would marry her. Other women had wanted marriage from him, but this was the first time in his life he'd been willing to give it. He couldn't imagine ever becoming bored with Evie, which had always happened with other lovers. Even more, he couldn't imagine letting any other man have the chance to marry her.

He didn't regret the impending loss of freedom. He thought of dressing her in silk gowns and expensive jewelry, of settling her in the lap of luxury—his—so that she wouldn't have to work seven days a week or worry about paying bills. She wouldn't have to make do with a secondhand refrigerator or drive around in a beat-up old truck. She wouldn't be so tired that dark smudges lay under her eyes. He would take her with him on his business trips, show her Paris and London and Rome, and they would take vacations on the ranch in Montana. Madelyn, he suspected, would gloat because he had finally been caught, but she would like Evie. Evie, despite that glowing sensuality, wasn't the type of woman that other women disliked on sight. She was friendly and courteous and unselfconscious about her looks. He had seen a lot of women who were far more vain than Evie, and with a lot less reason.

Within a month, perhaps even sooner, all of this would be behind them and they would be in New York. He fell asleep, thinking with pleasure of having her all to himself.

As usual, Evie woke at dawn. Robert lay close beside her, his body heat bathing her in warmth, despite the fact that the sheet had been kicked completely off the bed. He had done that, she supposed, because he wasn't accustomed to doing without air-conditioning. His arm was draped heavily across her hips, and his breath stirred the hair at the back of her neck.

She had slept with him for two nights in a row now and wondered how she would be able to bear the desolation when he was no longer there.

She turned within the circle of that enveloping arm and rose up on one elbow. He woke immediately. "Is anything wrong?" he asked, and just for a moment there was something feral and frightening in his eyes, and an instant tension in his muscles, as if he were poised to attack.

Quickly she shook her head to reassure him. "No. I just wanted to see you."

He relaxed at her words, lying back on the pillows. His olive-toned skin was dark against the whiteness. His thick black hair was tousled, and his jaw darkened by a heavy stubble. She was entranced by his sheer, uncomplicated masculinity, not yet smoothed over with grooming and clothes that somewhat obscured his true nature. Lying there with his iron-hard body naked and relaxed, he looked like what he was, a warrior honed down and redefined by years of battle.

She put her hand on his chest, and he lay quietly, watching her from beneath lowered lids but content to let her do as she wished. She didn't whisper her love to him; she had already told him how she felt and didn't intend to badger him about it. She concentrated, instead, on learning as much as she could about him. She had spent the first eighteen years of her life gathering memories about Matt, but she would have a much shorter time with Robert, and she didn't want to waste a minute.

She bent over him, her long hair trailing across his chest and shoulder as she planted a line of gentle kisses down his body. He smelled delicious in the morning, she thought, all warm and sleepy. The crispy curls of black hair on his chest invited her to rub her cheek against them, catlike. His nipples, tiny and brown, were almost hidden in the hair. She sought them out, tickled by the minute points that stood out when she rubbed her fingertip across them. Robert flexed restlessly on the sheet as desire tightened his muscles, then forced himself to relax again to better enjoy her attentions.

"I wonder if that's the same expression a pasha would have, lying back and letting his favorite concubine pleasure him," she murmured.

"Probably." He put his hands on her head, fingers sliding beneath the heavy fall of hair to massage her scalp. "You do pleasure me, Evangeline."

She continued her dreamy exploration, down the furry ridged abdomen toward his hips and thighs, detouring around his early morning erection. Something high on the inside of his left thigh caught her eye, and she bent closer to examine the mark. The morning sunlight clearly revealed a stylized outline of an eagle, or perhaps a phoenix, with upswept wings. The tattoo was small, not even an inch in length, but so finely made that she could see the fierceness of the raptor.

She was startled by the tattoo—not the design, but its very presence. Lightly she traced her finger over it, wondering why he had it. After all, Robert hardly seemed the type of man who would have a tattoo; he was too polished and sophisticated. But for all that sophistication, he wasn't quite civilized, and the tattoo matched that part of him. This was perhaps the only overt signal he permitted himself that he was more than what he seemed.

"How long have you had it?" she asked, looking up at him.

He was watching her with piercingly intent eyes. "Quite a while."

It was a very inexact answer, but she sensed that it was all she would get from him, at least for now. Slowly she leaned down and licked the tattoo, her tongue gently caressing the sign in his flesh that signaled the presence of the inner man.

A low, rough sound vibrated in his throat, and his entire body tightened.

"Do you want me?" she whispered, licking him again. She felt very warm, and slightly drunk with her feminine power. Desire was unfurling inside her, opening like a flower. Her breasts throbbed, and she rubbed them against his leg.

He gave a strangled laugh, almost undone by her natural sensuality. "Look a few inches to your right and tell me what you think."

She did, turning her head with slow deliberation to survey the straining, pulsing length of his sex. "I believe you do."

"The sixty-four-thousand-dollar question is, how do *you* feel?"

Evie gave him a slow, luminous smile of desire that promised him more than he thought he could survive. "I feel...willing," she purred, crawling up the length of his body to lie on him as she wound her arms around his neck.

His face was strained as he rolled, placing her beneath him. "I'll be careful," he promised in a rough whisper.

She reached up to touch his beard-roughened cheek and opened her thighs to clasp them around him. Her heart was in her eyes as he began slowly, with almost agonizing care, to enter her. "I trust you," she said, giving him her body as surely as she had given him her heart.

CHAPTER FOURTEEN

Landon Mercer caught himself wearing a habitually worried expression whenever he glanced into a mirror. Nothing was going right, for no particular reason that he could tell. One day he had been feeling pretty damn good about himself and the way everything was going, and the next it all began to go to hell. It was just little things at first, like that bastard Cannon showing up and nearly giving him a heart attack, though it turned out that Cannon had been the least of his worries. The big boss's reputation had been vastly overstated; he was nothing more than another lazy playboy, born into money, without any real idea of what it was like to get out and hustle for what he had.

Sometimes, though, Cannon had a cold look in his eyes that was downright spooky, as if he could see right through flesh. Mercer wouldn't soon forget the panic he'd felt when Cannon had caught him in Shaw's Marina. For one terror-stricken minute, Mercer had thought he was caught, that they'd somehow managed to find out what he was doing. But all Cannon had seemed interested in was that he'd taken off from work for the afternoon, something he'd been careful not to do again. Of all the damn luck! There were plenty of marinas in Guntersville; why had Cannon picked Shaw's? It wasn't the biggest, or the best run. In fact, for him, its major attraction was that it was small, a bit out of the way and basically a one-horse outfit. Evie Shaw didn't have time to pay attention to everything going on around her.

Of course, once Cannon had seen Evie, it was understandable why he kept hanging around. Mercer had been trying for months to get her to go out with him, but she was as standoffish as she was stacked. He just didn't have enough money, he supposed; she had latched on to Cannon fast enough.

Of course, if things had worked out, he *would* have had enough money to interest her. He wasn't stupid. He hadn't blown the pay-offs; he'd invested them. The ventures he'd picked had all seemed sound. He'd stayed away from the high-interest but volatile money markets and opted for slower but more secure returns. In a few years, he'd figured, he would have enough money invested to be on easy street.

But stocks that had looked good one day went sour the next, prices going on a steady slide as other investors dumped their shares. In one terrible week the tidy little nest egg he'd built up had decreased in value to less than half of what it had been before. He had sold out, taking a loss, and in a desperate move to recoup his money had invested it all in the money markets. The money market had promptly plummeted, almost wiping him out. He felt like King Midas in reverse; everything he touched turned to dross.

When he was contacted about another sale, he was so relieved that he almost thanked them for calling. If his bank account didn't get a cash transfusion soon, he wouldn't be able to make his car payment, or the payments on all his credit cards. Mercer was horrified at the thought of losing his beloved Mercedes. There were more expensive cars, and he intended to have them eventually, but the Mercedes was the first car he'd had that said he was *somebody*, a man on the way up. He couldn't bear to go back to being nothing.

Evie felt as if she had been split into two separate beings. Half of her was deliriously happy, overwhelmed by the intoxication of having Robert for a lover. She had never dreamed she could be so happy again, or feel so whole, but the great emptiness that had lurked in her heart for so long had been filled. Robert was both passionate and considerate, paying her so much attention that she felt as if she were the center of his universe. He never ignored her, never took anything about her for granted, always made her feel as if she were the most desirable woman he'd ever seen. Whenever they went out, his attention never wandered to other women, though she was well aware of other women looking at him.

She saw him every day, slept with him almost every night. As she became more at ease with her own body and the passion he aroused, their lovemaking became more leisurely, and even more intense, until sometimes she screamed with the force of it. He was a sophisticated lover, leading her into new positions, new variations, new sensations, and he was so skilled that he didn't make her feel awkward or ignorant. He made love to her almost every night. Only once, but that once was long and complete, leaving her sated and sleepy. Then, in the morning when they woke, they would make love again, silently, drifting in that half-awake state when dreams still shadow consciousness.

His mastery of her body was so complete that thoughts of him were always with her, lurking just under the surface, ready to come to the fore and bringing desire with them. She didn't know which she enjoyed most, the intense sessions at night or the dreamy ones of early morning. It was amazing how quickly her body had learned to crave sexual pleasure with him, so that, as the afternoon hours advanced, she would become jittery with anticipation and need. He knew it, surely. She could see him watching her, as if gauging her readiness. Sometimes she had a violent desire to pin him to the floor and have her way with him, but she always restrained herself, because the buildup of desire, though maddening, was equally delicious.

She had become accustomed to containing her thoughts and emotions, guarding them behind a wall of reserve, but Robert drew her out. They had long, involved discussions about a wide variety of subjects. Sitting out on the deck at night, staring up at the stars, they would discuss astronomy and various theories, from the big bang to black holes, dark matter and the relativity of time. His intelligence and the scope of his interests were almost frightening. Without giving any indication of restlessness, his mind was always working, looking for new facts to absorb or arranging those he already had. They would trade sections of the newspaper, and debate politics and national events. They swapped childhood stories, she telling him about growing up with an older sister as bossy as Becky, he making her laugh with stories of his indomitable younger sister, Madelyn. He told her about the ranch in Montana, which he owned in partnership with Reese Duncan, Madelyn's husband, and about their two rowdy little boys.

The sense of closeness with Robert was at once seductive and terrifying. There was a powerful lure that drew her to him, creating an intimacy as much of the mind as of the body, so that she was no longer a solitary creature but half of a *couple,* her entire sense of being altering to include him. Sometimes, in the back of her mind, she wondered how she would survive if he were to leave— she had to think of it as *if* now, rather than *when*—and the thought of losing him made her almost sick with terror.

She couldn't let herself worry about that. Loving him now, in the present, demanded all her attention. She couldn't hold anything back; she was helpless to even try.

At the same time, the other part of her, the part that wasn't preoccupied with Robert, worried incessantly about the bank loan and the mortgage on the house. Tommy hadn't called her back. She had called the bank twice; the first time he said that permission simply hadn't come through yet, but he didn't think there was any problem and that she should just be patient. The second time she called, he was out of town.

She couldn't wait much longer. It had already been eleven days, leaving just nineteen until the loan had to be paid. If her bank couldn't give her a loan, she would have to find a bank that would, and if all banks moved so slowly, she could find herself running out of time. Just thinking of the possibility was enough to make her break out in a cold sweat.

She tried to think of other options, of some way to quickly raise the money in case the loan didn't go through fast enough. She could put her boat up for sale, but it wasn't worth even half the amount that she needed and might not sell in time, anyway. Asking Becky and Paul for a loan was out of the question; they had their own financial responsibilities, and supporting two teenagers was expensive.

She could sell the rental boats, which would raise enough money but deprive her of a surprisingly tidy bit of income. Of course, with the loan paid, and if she didn't have to take out another one, she would have much more available cash and would soon be able to acquire more boats for rent. The only problem with that was time—again. In her experience, people took their time buying boats. Boats, even in a town like Guntersville that was geared toward the river, weren't a necessity of life. People looked at them, thought about it, discussed it over the dinner table, checked and double-checked their finances. It was possible, but unlikely, that she would be able to sell enough of them to raise the money she needed in the time she had.

Of the limited options available to her, however, that was the best one. She put a sign that read Used Boats For Sale in front of the marina and posted other notices in the area tackle stores. Even if she sold only one, that would lower the amount of money she would need to borrow.

Robert noticed the sign immediately. He walked in late that afternoon, removed his sunglasses and pinned her with a pale, oddly intense look. "That sign out front—which boats are for sale?"

"The rental boats," she calmly replied and returned her attention to waiting on a customer. Once she had made the decision to sell the boats, she hadn't allowed herself any regrets.

He moved behind the counter and stood in front of the window with his hands in his pockets, looking out at the marina. As she had known he would, he waited until the customer had left before turning to ask, "Why are you selling them?"

She hesitated for a moment. She hadn't told him anything about her financial worries and didn't intend to do so now, for a variety of reasons. One was simply that she was reticent about personal problems, disinclined to broadcast her woes to the world. Another was that she was fiercely possessive about the marina, and she didn't want word to get around that it was on shaky financial ground. Yet another was that she didn't want Robert to think she was obliquely asking for a loan, and she would be distressed if he offered one. He was obviously wealthy, but she didn't want the issue of money to become a part of their relationship. If it did, would he ever be certain, in his own mind, that her attraction to him wasn't based on his wealth? Still another reason was that she didn't want anyone else to have a share, and thus a say-so, in the marina. Banks were one thing, individuals another. The marina was *hers*, the base on which she had rebuilt the ruins of her life. She simply couldn't give up any part of it.

So when she answered, she merely said, "They're getting old, less reliable. I need to buy newer ones."

Robert regarded her silently. He didn't know whether to hug her or shake her, and in fact he could do neither. It was obvious that she was trying to raise money by any means available, and he wanted to put his arms around her and tell her it would be all right. But his instinct to protect his own had to be stifled, at least for now. Despite his decision that she was largely innocent in Mercer's espionage dealings, the small chance that he was wrong about her wouldn't let him relent. Soon he would know for certain, one way or the other. But if she sold the rental boats, what means would Mercer use to deliver the goods? Every one of those rental boats was now equipped with tiny electronic bugs that would allow them to be tracked; if Mercer was forced to use some other boat, or even change his method of delivery entirely, Robert would lose his control of the situation.

On the plus side, he was certain Mercer would act soon. They had intercepted a very suspicious phone call, putting them on the alert. It didn't matter if Evie managed to sell a couple of boats, or even most of them, so long as she had one remaining when Mercer made his move. He would simply have to monitor the situation and step in to prevent a sale if it looked as if she would manage to unload all of them.

Aloud he asked, "Have you had any offers yet?"

She shook her head, a wry smile curving her mouth. "I just put the sign up this morning."

"Have you put an ad in any of the newspapers?"

"Not yet, but I will."

That might bring in more customers than he could block, he thought with a sigh. The easiest way would be to stop the ads from being printed; there weren't that many area newspapers. The phones both here and at her house were being monitored, so he would know which papers she called. Somehow he hadn't expected to have so much trouble keeping abreast of her maneuvers. Evie was a surprisingly resourceful woman.

Five days later, Evie rushed in from overseeing a delivery of gas to answer the phone. She pushed a wisp of hair out of her face as she lifted the receiver. "Shaw's Marina."

"Evie? This is Tommy Fowler."

As soon as she heard his voice, she knew. Slowly she sank down onto the stool, her legs so weak that she needed the support. "What's the verdict?" she asked, though she knew the answer.

He sighed. "I'm sorry, hon. The board of directors says we already have too many real-estate loans. They won't okay the mortgage."

Her lips felt numb. "It isn't your fault," she said. "Thanks, anyway."

"It isn't a lost cause. Just because we aren't making that type of loan right now doesn't mean other banks aren't."

"I know, but I have a deadline, and it's down to fourteen days. It's taken you longer than that to tell me no. How long would it take to process a loan at any other bank?"

"Well, we took longer than usual. I'm sorry as hell about it, Evie, but I had no idea the okay wouldn't go through. Go to another bank. Today, if possible. An appraiser will have to make an estimate of the house's value, but it's waterfront property and in good shape, so it's worth a lot more than the amount you want to mortgage. Getting an appraiser out there is what will take so much time, so get started as soon as you can."

"I will," she said. "Thanks, Tommy."

"Don't thank me," he said glumly. "I couldn't do anything. Bye, hon."

She sat there on the stool for a long time after she hung up the phone, trying to deal with her disappointment and sense of impending disaster. Though she had been worried, the worry had been manageable, because even though she had been making contingency plans, she had been certain the mortgage would go through.

She hadn't sold a single boat.

Time was of the essence, and she didn't have a lot of faith in getting a loan through any other bank. It was as if an evil genie was suddenly in control of things, inflicting her with malfunctioning machinery and uncooperative banks.

Still, she had to try. She couldn't give up and perhaps lose the marina from lack of effort. She *wouldn't* lose the marina. No matter what, she simply refused to let it go. If she couldn't get a mortgage, if she couldn't sell the boats, she had one other option. It was strictly last-resort, but it was there.

She picked out a bank with a good reputation and called to make an appointment with a loan officer for the next morning.

The heat was already intense the next day when she was getting ready. Despite the ceiling fans, her skin was damp with perspiration, making her clothes cling to her. Robert hadn't asked why her house was so hot, but the past three nights he had insisted on taking her to his home and bringing her back after breakfast. This morning she had showered at his house as she usually did, then asked him to bring her home earlier than usual because she had a business appointment at nine. He hadn't asked any questions about that, either.

She retrieved her copy of the deed from the fireproof security box under the bed and braced herself like a soldier going to war. If this bank wouldn't give her a loan, she wasn't going to waste any more time going to another one. Time was too short. She would rather be too hasty than take the chance of losing the marina.

She rolled the truck window down, and the wind blowing in her face cooled her as she drove to the bank. The heat was building every day, and soon it would be unbearable in the house if she didn't turn on the air-conditioning. She smiled grimly. She might as well turn it on; one way or the other, she would have the money to pay the power bill.

Her appointment was with a Mr. Waldrop, who turned out to be a stocky, sandy-haired man in his late forties. He gave her a strangely curious look as he led her into his small office. Evie took one of the two comfortable chairs arranged in front of the desk, and he settled into the big chair behind it.

"Now then, Mrs. Shaw, what can we do for you today?"

Concisely, Evie told him what she needed, then pulled the copy of the deed from her purse and placed it on his desk. He unfolded it and looked it over, pursing his lips as he read.

"It looks straightforward enough." He opened his desk and extracted a sheet of paper. "Fill out this financial statement, and we'll see what we can do."

Evie took the sheet of paper and went out to one of the small seating areas off the lobby. While she was answering the multitude of questions, her pen scratching across the paper, someone else came in to see Mr. Waldrop. She glanced up automatically, then realized she knew the newcomer, not an unusual occurrence in a small town like Guntersville. He was Kyle Brewster, a slightly shady businessman who owned a small discount store, dealing in seconds and salvage material. He was also known as a gambler and had been arrested once, several years back, when the back room of a pool hall had been raided on the information that an illegal game was being conducted there. Evie supposed that Kyle was fairly successful in his gambling; his style of living was considerably higher than the income from the discount store could provide.

The door to Mr. Waldrop's office was left open. She couldn't hear what Kyle was saying, only the indistinct drawl of his voice, but Mr. Waldrop's voice was more carrying. "I have the check right here," he was saying cheerfully. "Do you want to cash it, or deposit it into your account?"

Evie returned her attention to the form, feeling slightly heartened. If the bank would lend money to Kyle Brewster, she saw no reason why it wouldn't lend money to her. Her business was more profitable, and her character was certainly better.

Kyle left a few minutes later. When Evie completed the form, someone else had come in and was with Mr. Waldrop. She sat patiently, watching the hour hand on the clock inch to ten o'clock, then beyond. At ten-thirty, the other customer left and she carried the form in to Mr. Waldrop.

"Have a seat," he invited as he looked over the information she had provided. "I'll be back in a few minutes." He carried the form out with him.

Evie crossed her fingers, hoping the loan would be okayed that morning, pending an appraisal of the property. She would get the bank's appraiser out to the house if she had to call him ten times a day and hound him until he appeared.

More time ticked by. She shifted restlessly in the chair, wondering what was taking so long. But the bank seemed busy this morning, so perhaps the person Mr. Waldrop had taken the form to was also tied up, and Mr. Waldrop was having to wait.

Forty-five minutes later Mr. Waldrop returned to his office. He settled into his chair and tapped his fingertips together. "I'm sorry, Mrs. Shaw," he said with real regret. "We simply aren't making this type of loan right now. With the economy the way it is…"

Evie sat up straight. She could feel the blood draining from her face, leaving the skin tight. Enough was enough. "The economy is fine," she interrupted sharply. "The recession didn't hit down here the way it did in other parts of the country. And your bank is one of the strongest in the country. There was an article in one of the Birmingham papers just last week about this bank buying another one in Florida. What I want to know is why you would lend money to someone like Kyle Brewster, a known gambler with a police record, but you won't make a loan on a property worth five or six times that amount."

Mr. Waldrop flushed guiltily. A distressed look came into his eyes. "I can't discuss Mr. Brewster's business, Mrs. Shaw. I'm sorry. I don't make the decisions on whether or not to okay a loan."

"I realize that, Mr. Waldrop." She also realized something else, something so farfetched she could hardly believe it, but it was the only thing that made any sense. "I didn't have a chance of getting the loan, did I? Having me fill out that form was just for show. Someone is stepping in to block the loan, someone with a lot of influence, and I want to know who it is."

His flush turned even darker. "I'm sorry," he mumbled. "There's nothing I can tell you."

She stood and retrieved the deed from his desk. "No, I don't suppose you can. It would mean your job, wouldn't it? Goodbye, Mr. Waldrop.''

She was almost dizzy with fury as she went out to the truck. The heat slammed into her like a blow, but she ignored it, just as she ignored the scorching heat of the truck's upholstery. She sat in the parking lot, tapping her finger against the steering wheel as she stared unblinkingly at the traffic streaming by on U.S. 431.

Someone wanted the marina. No one had made an offer to buy it, so that meant whoever it was knew she wasn't likely to sell. This mysterious someone was powerful enough, well-connected enough with the local bankers, to block her attempts to get a loan. Not only that, the original transfer of the loan from her bank to the New York bank had probably been arranged by this person, though she couldn't think of anyone she knew with that kind of power.

She couldn't think why anyone would want her little marina enough to go to such an extreme. Granted, she had made a lot of improvements in it, and business was better every year. When she paid off the outstanding debt, the marina would turn a healthy profit, but it wouldn't be the kind of money that would warrant such actions from her unknown enemy.

Why didn't matter, she thought with the stark clarity that comes in moments of crisis. Neither did *who*. The only thing that mattered was that she kept the marina.

There was one move she could make that wouldn't be blocked, because she wouldn't be the one obtaining the loan. She wouldn't breathe a word about this to anyone, not even Becky, until it was a done deal.

Numbly she started the truck and pulled out into traffic, then almost immediately pulled off again when she spotted a pay phone outside a convenience store. Her heart was thudding with slow, sickening power against her ribs. If she let herself think about it, she might not have the nerve to do it. If she waited until she got back home, she might look around at the dear, familiar surroundings and not be able to make the call. She had to do it now. It was a simple choice. If she lost the marina, she stood to lose everything, but if she sacrificed the house now, she would be able to keep the marina.

She slid out of the truck and walked to the pay phone. Her legs seemed to be functioning without any direction from her brain. There was no phone book. She called Information and got the number she wanted, then fed in another quarter and punched the required numbers. Turning her back on the traffic, she put her finger in her other ear to block out noise as she listened to the ringing on the other end of the line.

"Walter, this is Evie. Do you and Helene still want to buy my place on the river?"

"She stopped at a convenience store immediately after leaving the bank and made a call from a pay phone," the deep voice reported to Robert.

"Could you tell what number she called?"

"No, sir. Her position blocked the numbers from view."

"Could you hear anything she was saying?"

"No, sir. I'm sorry. She kept her back turned, and the traffic was noisy."

Robert rubbed his jaw. "Have you checked to see if it was the marina she called?"

"First thing. No such luck. She didn't call Mercer, either."

"Okay. It worries me, but there isn't anything we can do about it. Where is she now?"

"She drove straight home from the convenience store."

"Let me know if she makes any more calls."

"Yes, sir."

Robert hung up and stared thoughtfully out at the lake as he tried to imagine who she had called, and why. He didn't like the angry little suspicion that was growing. Had she called the unknown third party to whom Mercer had been selling the stolen computer programs? Was she involved up to her pretty little neck after all? He had backed her up against a financial wall, just to find out for certain, but he had a sudden cold, furious feeling that he wasn't going to like the results worth a damn.

CHAPTER FIFTEEN

"Would you like to go fishing this morning?" Robert asked lazily, his voice even deeper than usual. "We've never been out in a boat together."

It was six-thirty. The heat wave was continuing, each day seeing temperatures in the high nineties, and it was supposed to reach the hundred mark for the next few days, at least. Even at that early hour, Evie could feel the heat pressing against the windows.

It was difficult to think. Robert had just finished making love to her, and her mind was still sluggish with a surfeit of pleasure. He had awakened her before dawn and prolonged their loving even more than usual. Her entire body still throbbed from his touch, the echoes of pleasure still resounding in her flesh. The sensation of having him inside her lingered, though he had withdrawn and moved to lie beside her. Her head was cradled on one muscled arm, while his other arm lay heavily across her lower abdomen. She would have liked nothing better than to snuggle against him and doze for a while, then wake to even more lovemaking. It was only when she was sleeping, or when Robert was making love to her, that she was able to forget what she was doing.

But the throb of pleasure was lessening, and a dull ache resumed its normal place in her chest. "I can't," she said. "I have some errands to run." Errands such as finding a place to live. Walter and Helene Campbell had jumped at the chance to buy her house. They had wanted it for years and had decided to pay cash for it and worry about the financing later, afraid she would change her mind if she had a chance to think about it. Evie had promised she would be out within two weeks.

She couldn't bring herself to tell Robert, at least, not yet. She was afraid he would feel pressured to ask her to live with him, when he seemed perfectly satisfied with things the way they were now. It was difficult to think of anyone pressuring Robert to do anything he didn't want to do, and he might not offer, but neither did she want him to think she was hinting that he should. It would be best to find an apartment or house for rent first, then tell him about it.

For that matter, she hadn't told Becky, either. She hadn't told anyone. She had made her decision, but hadn't managed to come to terms with it yet. Every time she thought about moving, tears burned in her eyes. She couldn't bear to go into the explanations and listen to the arguments.

She didn't let herself think about who was behind all these financial maneuverings. First she had to concentrate on saving the marina and finding a place to live. After that was settled, she would try to find out who had been doing this to her.

"What kind of errands?" Robert asked, nuzzling her ear. His hand stroked warmly over her stomach, then covered her left breast. Her nipple, still sensitized from the strong suckling he had subjected it to a short while ago, twinged with a sharp sensation and immediately puckered against his palm. Her breathing deepened. Rather than becoming less intense with familiarity, his sensual power over her body seemed to increase each time he took her.

"I have to pay a few bills and do some shopping," she lied, and wondered why he'd asked. He had no compunction about taking over every facet of her private life but seldom inquired about what she did when they weren't together.

"Why not put it off until tomorrow?" His nuzzling was growing a bit more purposeful, and she closed her eyes as pleasure began to warm throughout her body again.

"I can't," she repeated regretfully. He rolled her nipple between this thumb and forefinger, making it even harder. She caught her breath at the tug of desire, as if the nerves of her nipples were directly connected to those in her loins.

"Are you certain?" he murmured, pressing his open mouth against the rapid pulse at the base of her throat.

Going fishing didn't tempt her, at least not in this heat. Lying in bed with him all morning, though, was so tempting it took all of her willpower to resist. "I'm certain," she forced herself to say. "It has to be done today."

Another man might have turned surly at having his advances refused, but Robert only sighed as he rested his head once again on the pillow. "I suppose we should get up, then."

"I suppose." She turned into him, pressing her face against his chest. "Hold me, just for a minute."

His arms tightened around her, satisfyingly tight. "What's wrong?"

"Nothing," she whispered. "I just like for you to hold me."

She felt his muscles tense. Abruptly he rolled on top of her, his hair-roughened thighs pushing hers apart. Startled, she looked up into slitted green eyes, glittering beneath those heavy black lashes. She couldn't read his expression but sensed his tightly contained violence.

"What—" she began to ask.

He thrust heavily into her, the power of his penetration making her body arch and shudder. He had had her only a little while before, but he was as hard as if that had never happened, so hard that she felt bruised by the impact of his flesh against hers. She gasped and clutched his shoulders for support. Not since the first time he'd taken her had he moved so powerfully. A primal feminine fear beat upward on tiny wings and mingled with an equally primitive sense of excitement. He wasn't hurting her, but the threat was there, and the challenge was whether she could handle him in this dangerous mood, all raw, demanding masculinity.

Desire flooded through her. She dug her nails into his muscular buttocks, pulling him deeper, arching her hips higher to take all of him. He grunted, his teeth clenched against the sound. Evie locked him to her, as fiercely female as he was dominatingly male, not only accepting his thrusts but demanding them. The sensation spiraled rapidly inside her, burning out of control, and she bit his shoulder. He cursed, the word low and hoarse, then slid his arms under her bottom to lift her even more tightly against him. All of his heavy weight bore her into the mattress as they strained together.

The sensation peaked, and Evie cried out as she shuddered wildly in the throes of pleasure. His hips hammered three more times; then he stiffened and began to shake as satisfaction took him, too. He ground his body against hers, as if he could meld their flesh.

The room slowly stopped spinning about her. She heard the twin rhythms of their panting breaths begin to calm. His heartbeat seemed to be thudding through her body, until it was in sync with her own. Their bodies were sealed together with sweat, heat rolling off them in waves.

Their first lovemaking of the morning had lasted an hour. This time, it hadn't taken even five minutes. The fury and speed of it, the raw power, left her even more exhausted than she'd been before.

What had aroused him so violently? After their first night Robert had been a slow, considerate lover, but he had just taken her like a marauder.

He was very heavy on top of her, making breathing difficult. She gasped, and he shifted his weight to the side. Pale green eyes opened, the expression still shuttered. His mouth had a ruthless line to it. "Stay with me today," he demanded.

Regret pierced her, sharp and poignant. "I can't," she said. "Not today."

For a split second something frightening flickered in his eyes, then was gone. "I tried," he said with rueful ease, rolling off her and sitting up. He stretched, rolling his shoulders and lifting his muscled arms over his head. Evie eyed his long, powerful back with pleasure and approval. The layered muscles were tight and hard, the deep hollow of his spine inviting kisses, or clutching hands. He was wide at the shoulders, his body tapering in a lean vee to his hips. She reached out and ran a lingering hand over the round curve of his buttocks, loving the cool resilience of his flesh.

He looked at her over his shoulder, and she saw a smile come into those green eyes. He leaned over to kiss her, his mouth lingering warmly for a moment; then with a yawn he was off the bed and heading toward the shower. She watched him until he closed the bathroom door behind him, drinking in his tall, naked body. She felt like smacking her lips, like a child drooling after a tasty treat. He was a fine figure of a man, all right. Sometimes, when she saw him sprawled naked and sleepy beside her, it was all she could do to keep from attacking him. She lay in bed for a while, listening to the shower run and entertaining a wicked, delicious fantasy in which he was tied to the bed and totally at her mercy.

But a glance at the clock told her that time was still ticking away. Sighing, she got out of bed and slipped into his shirt, then went to the kitchen to make coffee.

When she returned, he was just coming out of the bathroom, a towel draped around his neck but otherwise still completely naked. His skin was glowing from the shower, his black hair wet and slicked back.

"I put on the coffee," she said as she went to take her turn in the shower.

"I'll start breakfast. What do you want this morning?"

The thought of what she had to do that day killed her appetite. "I'm not hungry. I'll just have coffee."

But when she had showered and dressed, she went into the kitchen to find that he had his own ideas about what she was having for breakfast. A bowl of cereal, as well as a glass of orange juice and the requested coffee, was sitting at her customary place at the table. "I'm really not hungry," she repeated, lifting the coffee cup and inhaling the fragrant steam before sipping.

"Just a few bites," he cajoled, taking his own place beside her. "You need to keep up your strength for tonight."

She gave him a heated, slumberous look, remembering her fantasy. "Why? Are you planning something special?"

"I suppose I am," he said consideringly. "It's special every time we make love."

Her heart swelled in her chest, making it impossible for her to speak. She simply looked at him, her golden brown eyes glowing.

He picked up the spoon and put it into her hand. "Eat. I've noticed you haven't been eating much while it's been so hot, and you're losing weight."

"Most people would consider that a good thing," she pointed out.

His black eyebrows lifted. "I happen to like your butt as round as it is now, and your breasts perfectly fit my hands. I don't want to sleep with a stick. Eat."

She laughed, amused by his description of her rear end, and dipped the spoon into the cereal. It was her favorite brand, of course; once he had seen the box in her cabinets, a box of the same cereal had taken up residence in his.

She managed to choke down a few bites, more than she wanted and not enough to satisfy him, which was a reasonable compromise. The cereal felt like a lump in her stomach.

Less than an hour later he kissed her goodbye at her door. "I'll see you tonight, sweetheart. Take care."

As she entered the house, she thought it a little odd for him to have added that last admonition. What on earth did he think she would be doing?

Sadly she dressed for work, so she wouldn't have to come back to the house before going to the marina. She wouldn't be braiding her hair in front of this mirror very many more times, she thought. After this afternoon, the house would no longer belong to her. Walter and Helene were getting a real estate agent, a friend of theirs, to handle the transaction immediately. They were supposed to bring all the paperwork to the marina this afternoon, along with a cashier's check in the specified amount. Evie was taking the deed to the property, the surveyor's report that she had had done when she inherited the house, as well as the certification of the title search that had also been done at that time. It was a measure of their trust in her that they were willing to forgo another title search, probably against their agent friend's advice.

She addressed an envelope to the bank in New York, stamped it and added it to her stack of papers. She would take the cashier's check immediately to her bank, desposit it and have another cashier's check made out in the amount of the outstanding loan against the marina. Then she would express-mail that check to New York, to Mr. Borowitz's attention. All her financial troubles would be over.

She wouldn't have her home any longer, but she could live any-where, she told herself. The marina was more important, the means of her support. With it, she could someday buy another house. It wouldn't hold the memories this one did, but she would make it into a home.

She took a last look in the mirror. "Standing here won't get anything done," she said softly to herself and turned away.

She spent the morning driving around Guntersville. She had checked a few of the rental ads in the newspaper but didn't want to call them yet, preferring to see the houses and the neighborhoods before calling. She knew she was just stalling, despite the urgency of the situation, but somehow actually making contact was beyond her at the moment. She gave herself a stern talking-to, but it didn't help much. She didn't like any of the houses she saw.

It was almost noon when she came to a decision. She made an abrupt turn, causing a car behind her to squeal its tires and the irate driver to lean on the horn. Muttering an apology, she cut through a shopping-center parking lot and back onto the highway, but in the opposite direction.

The apartment complex she had chosen was new, less than two years old, incongruously known as the Chalet Apartments. She stopped the truck outside the office and went inside. Twenty minutes later she was the new resident of apartment 17, which consisted of a living room and combination dining room/kitchen downstairs, along with a tiny laundry area just big enough to hold a washer and dryer, and two bedrooms upstairs. There were no one-bedroom apartments available. She paid a deposit, collected two sets of keys and went back out to the truck.

It was done. She doubted she would be happy there, but at least she would have a roof over her head while she took her time look-ing for a house.

The cellular phone beeped, and Robert answered it as he threaded his way through the traffic on Gunter Avenue, the one-way street that bisected Guntersville's downtown area and also ran through a neighborhood of grand old houses that looked turn-of-the-century.

"I think she spotted me."

"What happened?" he asked in a clipped tone.

"First she just drove around, all over town. I had to hang back so I wouldn't be as easy to spot. She slowed down several times but didn't stop anywhere. Maybe she was looking for something. Then she got on the highway, going south toward Albertville. She was on the inside lane, I was on the outside. All of a sudden, without a turn signal, she whipped the truck into a parking lot and nearly got hit doing it. I was in the wrong lane and couldn't follow her. By the time I got turned around, she'd vanished."

"Damn." Robert felt both tired and angry. Just when he'd been convinced of Evie's innocence, she was suddenly doing some very suspicious things. She was obviously worried about the marina, but there was something else on her mind, something she was trying to keep hidden. This mornng, in bed, he had been seized by the urgent need to keep her with him all day, thereby preventing her from doing anything foolish. He wasn't used to women refusing any request he made, but Evie didn't appear to have any trouble doing it. She had said no with insulting ease.

Furious, he had even tried to seduce her into staying with him, only to lose his control, something he'd sworn wouldn't happen again. And afterward she'd still said no.

"I'll pick her up again when she comes to the marina," the man said in his ear. "I'm sorry, sir."

"It wasn't your fault. No tail's perfect."

"No, sir, but I should have been more careful about letting her see me."

"Have two cars next time, so you can swap."

"Yes, sir."

Robert ended the call and replaced the receiver. It took all his self-control to keep from driving to the marina to wait for her so he could shake some sense into her as soon as he saw her. But he had to play this through to the end.

As mundane as it was, he had his own errand to run that day:

grocery shopping. It wasn't something he normally did for himself, but it wasn't an onerous duty. Despite its strangeness, or perhaps because of it, he didn't mind doing it. Southerners imbued grocery shopping with the same casualness that characterized almost everything else they did. Shoppers ambled down the aisles, stopping to talk with chance-met acquaintances or to strike up conversations with strangers. The first time he had gone into the big grocery store, he had been amused by the thought that a New Yorker relaxed in the park with more energy than Southerners shopped. But when in Rome... He had learned to slow his own pace, to keep from smashing into old ladies who had stopped to pass the time of day.

Today, though, he wasn't in the mood to be amused. It went against his protective, controlling nature to leave Evie to hang herself with all the evidential rope he was feeding to both her and Mercer. He wanted to snatch her away from here, kidnap her if necessary. But if she *were* involved with Mercer, that would scare off the others and they might never be caught. Not knowing for certain, one way or the other, was driving him crazy with frustration.

Two more days. From the telephone calls they had intercepted, they knew that Mercer would transfer more stolen data the day after tomorrow. Evie hadn't been able to sell any of the rental boats, so that was one less problem for Robert. It didn't matter which boat Mercer took, since they were all wired. As a precaution, he had also had Evie's boat wired. In two days it would all be over except for the cleanup. In three days, if all went on schedule, he would be back in New York, and Evie would be with him.

He wouldn't need many groceries, just enough for three days, but he was completely out of coffee and almost out of food, and he didn't want to eat in restaurants for three days. He strode through the aisles of the grocery store, his expression remote as he planned the damage-control measures he would use. Operating with his usual efficiency, he was in and out of the store within fifteen minutes. As he walked out the automatic doors with a grocery bag in his arms, though, the woman just entering through the other set of doors stopped and stared at him.

"Robert."

He paused, immediately recognizing Evie's sister, Becky. Another shopper was exiting behind him, and he stepped out of the way. "Hello, Becky. How are you?" He smiled faintly. "And how's Jason? I haven't seem him at the marina again."

"Didn't Evie tell you? He can't come back to the marina for the rest of the summer. That's a real punishment to him," Becky said dryly. "The marina's one of his favorite places." She too, stepped away from the doors. "There's no sense standing here blocking traffic. I'll walk you to your car."

They strolled across the hot, sticky pavement. The heat was smothering, and sweat began to gather almost immediately on his skin. Wryly he waited, seeing Becky's determination plain on her face. The protective older sister wanted to have a heart-to-heart talk with him, to make certain he didn't hurt Evie.

They reached the Jeep, and he stored the groceries inside, leaving the door open so some of the heat inside could dissipate. He leaned against the vehicle and calmly eyed her. "You worried about Evie?" he prompted.

She flashed him a rueful look. "Am I that easy to read?"

"She mentioned that you're a bit protective," he murmured.

Becky laughed and pushed her hair out of her face. Her hair was darker than Evie's, but in that moment Robert saw a flash of resemblance, a similarity in expression and in the husky tone of their voices. "The big-sister syndrome," she said. "I didn't use to be this bad, only since—"

She stopped, and Robert felt his curiosity stir. "Since when?"

Becky didn't answer immediately, instead turning her gaze to the traffic on the highway. It was a delaying tactic, to give her time to think and organize her answer. He waited patiently.

"Are you serious about her?" she asked abruptly.

He wasn't accustomed to being interrogated about his intentions, serious or otherwise, but he quelled his surge of irritation. Becky was asking only out of concern for Evie, an emotion he shared. In a very level tone he said, "I intend to marry her."

Becky closed her eyes on a sigh of relief. "Thank God," she said.

"I didn't realize the state of our relationship was so critical," he said, still in that cool, dead-level tone.

Becky's eyes opened, and she gave him a considering look. "You can be very intimidating, can't you?"

He almost smiled. If he could, it obviously wasn't working on her. He'd never managed to intimidate Evie, either.

Becky sighed and looked again at the traffic. "I was worried. I didn't know how important Evie is to you, and…well, the success of your relationship *is* critical to her."

His curiosity became intense. "In what way?"

Becky didn't answer that directly, either. Instead she asked, "Has she told you about Matt?"

Robert's eyes glittered suddenly. "Probably more than even you know," he said, his voice deepening as he remembered the first time he'd made love to Evie.

"About how he died?"

Sweat trickled down his back, but suddenly nothing could have moved him from the scorching asphalt parking lot. "He died in a car accident, didn't he?" He couldn't remember if Evie had told him that, or if it had been in the report he'd requested on Matt Shaw.

"Yes, the day after they married." She paused, organizing her thoughts, and again she made what appeared to be a shift in topic. "Our father died when Evie was fifteen. I was twenty, already married, already about to be a mother. A year later our mother died. Can you understand the difference in the way losing our parents affected us?" she asked, her voice strained. "I loved them both dearly, but I had built my home with Paul. I had him, I had my son, I had an entire life away from my parents. But losing Daddy shook Evie's foundations, and then when Mother died…Evie didn't just lose Mother, she lost her home, too. She came to live with Paul and me, and we loved having her, but it wasn't the same for her. She was still just a kid, and she had lost the basis of her life."

Robert stood silently, all his attention on this insight into Evie's past life. She didn't talk about her childhood much, he realized. They had talked about a lot of things, sitting on the deck at night with all the lights off and the starry sky spread like a quilt overhead, but it was as if Evie had closed a mental door on her life before Matt's death.

"But she had Matt," Becky said softly. "He was a great kid. We'd known him all his life, and I can't remember when they hadn't been inseparable, first as buddies, then as sweethearts. They were the same age, but even as young as he was, when Daddy died, Matt was right there beside Evie. He was there with her when Mother died. I think he was her one constant, the only person other than me who had been there for as long as she could remember. But I had my own family, and Evie had Matt. He put a smile back in her eyes, and because she had him, she weathered the loss of our parents. I remember what she was like back then, a giggling teenager as rowdy as Jason is now, and full of mischief."

"I can't picture Evie as rowdy," he commented, because Becky's voice had become strained, and he wanted to give her a moment to compose herself. "There's something so solemn about her."

"Yes, there is," Becky agreed. "Now."

The jealousy he thought he had banished swelled to life again. "Because of Matt's death."

Becky nodded. "She was in the car with him." Tears welled in her eyes. "For the rest of my life, I'll carry two pictures of Evie in my mind. One is of her on her wedding day. She was so young and beautiful—so *glowing*—that it hurt to look at her. Matt couldn't take his eyes off her. The next time I saw her, she was in a hospital bed, lying there like a broken doll, her eyes so empty that—" She stopped, shuddering.

"They had spent the night in Montgomery and were going on to Panama City the next morning. It was raining. It was Sunday, and they were in a rural area. There wasn't much traffic. A dog ran out into the highway, and they hit it, and Matt lost control of the car. The car left the road and rolled at least twice, then came to a stop, on its right side, in a stand of trees. Evie was pinned on the bottom. Matt was hanging in his seat belt above her. She couldn't get out, couldn't get to him, and he b-bled to death in front of her, his blood dripping down on her. He was conscious, she said." Furiously Becky dashed the tears from her cheeks. "No one saw the car for a long time, what with the rain and the trees blocking the view. He knew he was dying. He told her he loved her. He told her goodbye. He'd been dead for over an hour before anyone saw the car and came to help."

Robert turned to stone, his eyes burning as he pictured, far too clearly, what a young girl had gone through that rainy Sunday. Then he reached out automatically and took Becky in his arms, holding her head against his shoulder while she wept.

"I'm sorry," she finally managed, lifting her head and wiping her eyes yet again. "It's just that, when I let myself think about it, it tears my heart out all over again."

"Yes," he said. Still holding her with one arm, he fished his handkerchief out of his pocket and gently wiped her face.

"She's never let herself love anyone else," she said fiercely. "Do you understand? She hasn't risked letting anyone else get close to her. She's stuck with the people she already loved, before the accident—Paul and me, Jason and Paige, and a few, very few, special friends, but no one else. If you hadn't pulled her and Jason out of the river, she would have drowned rather than let him go, because she couldn't have stood to lose anyone else she loves. She's been so...so *solitary,* keeping everyone a safe distance from her heart."

"Until me," he said.

Becky nodded and managed a wavery little smile. "Until you. I didn't know whether to be glad or terrified, so I've been both. I want her to have what I've got, a husband I love, kids I love, a family that will give her a reason to go on living when someone else dies." She saw the sudden flare in Robert's eyes and said quickly, "No, she never said anything about suicide, not even right after Matt died. That isn't what I meant. She recovered from her injuries—both legs were broken, some ribs, and she had a concussion—and did exactly what the doctors told her, but you could see that she wasn't interested. For *years,* life for her was just going through the motions, and every day was an effort. It took a long time, but finally she found a sort of peace. Evie's incredibly strong. In her place, I don't know if I could have managed it.''

Robert kissed Becky's forehead, touched and pleased by this fiercely competent woman's concern for her sister. He would, he realized, like having her for a sister-in-law. ''You can put down your shield and sword, and rest,'' he said gently. ''I'll take care of her now.''

''You'd better,'' Becky said, her fierceness not one bit abated. ''Because she's already paid too much for loving people. God only knows where she found the courage to love you. I've been terrified that you didn't care about her, because if you waltzed out of here at the end of the summer, it might well destroy her.''

Robert's eyes glittered. ''When I waltz out of here,'' he said, ''I'm taking her with me.''

CHAPTER SIXTEEN

Walter and Helene Campbell were in their mid-sixties, retired, comfortable but not wealthy. Evie's house was just what they wanted, well-built and maintained, but old enough and small enough that her asking price was much less than what they would have paid for a new house on the lakefront. They were both thrilled to the point of giddiness at their unexpected good fortune, for though they had asked several times if she would sell, they had long since given up hope that she would.

They arrived at the marina over half an hour early, their estate agent in tow and bearing a huge sheaf of papers. Having never bought or sold a house before, Evie was struck by the amount of paperwork it evidently required and amazed that the agent had managed to get it all prepared in less than a day.

There weren't sufficient chairs for everyone to sit down, so they stood grouped around the counter. The agent explained the purpose of each document as he presented it first for her signature, then the Campbells'. After an hour of dedicated document-signing, it was finished. Evie had sold her house, and the check was in her hand.

She managed a smile to send the joyous Campbells on their way, but as soon as the door had closed behind them, her smile collapsed. She closed her eyes and shuddered in an effort to control the grief that had been growing since she had made the phone call the day before. No matter that she had told herself it was just a house and she could live anywhere, it was her *home*, and she had just lost part of herself. No, not lost it—sold it.

But the marina was a more important part of her foundation, and the green cashier's check in her hand had just saved it.

She wiped the betraying moisture from her eyes and braced her shoulders. She called Burt and told him she had to go to the bank and would be back in about half an hour. "Okay," he said, as laconic as ever, when she asked him to watch for customers.

The transaction at the bank took very little time. The Campbells' cashier's check was deposited and a new cashier's check cut in the amount she owed on the loan. Tommy Fowler saw her standing at the counter and came out to speak to her, his eyes anxious.

"How're you doing, Evie?"

She heard the worry in his tone and managed a version of the same smile she had given the Campbells. "I'm okay. I have the money to pay the loan."

Relief flooded his face. "Great! That didn't take long. So another bank gave you the mortgage?"

"No, I sold my house."

The relief faded, and he stared at her, aghast. "Sold your house? But, Evie…God, why?"

She wasn't about to tell him, with the teller and other customers listening, that she suspected someone of blocking the mortgage. "It was something I'd been thinking about," she lied. "Now my bank account is healthy, the marina is out of debt and will turn a pure profit, and I can take my time looking for another house."

Varying expressions were flickering across Tommy's face like slides. The final one, a rather uneasy relief, was testament to his belief in her pragmatic lie. "I guess it's worked out, then," he said.

She kept her smile intact with an effort. "Yeah, I guess it has."

The teller handed the check over the counter to her, and she slipped it into the envelope. "I'm getting this mailed today," she said to Tommy. "Thanks for all you did."

"I didn't manage to do anything," he replied.

"Well, no, but you tried."

She left the bank and drove straight to the post office, where the precious envelope was dispatched by express mail. She felt a sense of finality. It was done; she had gotten past this. It hadn't been easy, but now she could move on.

Robert was waiting at the marina when she got back. "Where have you been?" he demanded, striding up as she slid out of the truck.

She blinked at the unguarded fierceness of his tone. Robert was seldom overt in his reactions, except in bed. "The bank and the post office. Why?"

He didn't answer but caught her shoulders in a hard grasp and pulled her to him. His mouth was heavy and hungry, demanding rather than seducing a response from her. Evie made a muffled sound of surprise, her hands lifting to rest against his chest, but she gave him what he wanted, her mouth opening to admit the thrust of his tongue, her lips shaping to the pressure of his.

Passion rose sharply between them, strong and heady. She hadn't recovered her balance after the difficult events of the day and she melted against him, drawn irresistibly to the whipcord strength of his body. Although a whirlwind was tossing the rest of her life about, he wasn't swayed but remained solidly on his feet and in control. Though she had bitterly resisted—and feared—coming to depend on him, his very presence now made her feel better. She was both aroused and comforted by the familiarity of his body, his warm animal scent, all the subtle details by which she knew her mate.

He drew back, hampered by the public nature of the parking lot. Inside wouldn't be much better, with people coming and going. He threaded his hands through her hair, tilting her face back so he could read every nuance of her expression. He must have been pleased by the drowning look of desire he saw there, for his fingers tightened on her scalp. "Not here, damn it. But as soon as I get you home..." He didn't have to finish the sentence. Raw lust was on his face and in his voice, violent and intense.

Recalled to where she was, Evie cast a half-embarrassed look around and touched his hand as she slipped from his grasp. How many hours until they could go home? She didn't know if she could wait that long. Her body was throbbing.

The long afternoon was an exercise in self-control, and she wished the summer days weren't quite so long. She needed Robert, needed his driving presence within her, taking her into oblivion so she could forget everything but the almost narcotic pleasure of making love with him. She felt raw, her emotions sharp and too near the surface.

It was difficult, when she was finally able to close the marina that night, to hold to the schedule they had established. Robert wanted to take her straight to his house, but she resisted. "I don't want to leave my truck here overnight," she said. "You'd either have to bring me to pick it up in the morning or waste your morning hanging around so you could drive me to work."

"It wouldn't be a waste," he growled, his lean face taut, and she knew what he envisioned them doing to pass the time.

Temptation weakened her, but she shook her head again. "It would be so blatant, if my truck was still here and you brought me to work. Craig—"

"You're worried about Craig knowing that we sleep together?" he asked, amusement lighting his eyes. "He's seventeen, sweetheart, not seven."

"I know, but…this isn't New York. We're more conventional down here."

He was still smiling, but he gave in with good grace. "All right, protect his tender sensibilities, though I have to tell you that most teenage boys have the sensibility of a rhino in heat."

She laughed, and it felt good, her heart lightening. "Then let's just say that *I* wouldn't feel comfortable."

He kissed her forehead. "Then go home, sweetheart. I bought some fillets this afternoon, and I'll get them ready to grill before I pick you up."

"I have a better idea," she said. "You start grilling, and I'll drive over. That will save even more time."

He smiled again as he rubbed his thumb over her lower lip in a gentle caress. "You make me feel like a teenage rhino myself," he murmured, and she blushed.

Anticipation heated her blood as she drove home, preoccupying her so much that she showered and dressed without more than a twinge of sadness. Her heartbeat pounded in the rhythm of his name.

It was still hot, so hot that she couldn't bear the idea of encasing her legs in clothing, but she didn't want to wear shorts. She opted instead for a gauzy blue skirt and a sleeveless, scoop-necked chemise, with her breasts unconfined beneath. The floaty skirt was virtually transparent, clearly showing her legs, but allowed air to filter through the flimsy fabric and cool her skin. She would never have worn it out in public, but to Robert's house…yes, definitely.

He came to the door when he heard the truck in his driveway. His face tightened as he watched her walk toward him. "God," he muttered. As soon as she was inside, he slammed the door and caught her arm, pulling her rapidly down the hall to the bedroom.

"What about the steaks?" she cried, startled by his haste despite the pleasant frustration of the afternoon.

"Screw the steaks," he said bluntly, wrapping his arms around her and falling across the bed. His heavy weight crushed her into the mattress. With a quick motion he flipped the skirt to her waist and caught the waistband of her panties, tugging them down her legs. When her feet were free, he tossed her underwear aside and pulled her thighs apart, kneeling between them.

Evie laughed, the sound low and provocative. He hadn't even kissed her, and her entire body was throbbing. He was tearing at his belt buckle with impatient fingers, and she added her hands to the confusion, trying to find the tab of his zipper and pull it down. She could feel the hard, swollen ridge of his sex, pushing at his clothing. He grunted as his length sprang free and lowered himself between her legs.

No matter how many times he took her, she always felt a small sense of surprise at his size and heat, and a flutter of uncertainty at the stretching sensation that followed the initial pressure as he sank deep within. She gasped, her entire body lifting to the impact. She was tender from the unbridled lovemaking of the morning, his thrusting sex rasping against inner tissues that were sensitive to the least touch. Intense pleasure rippled through her, tossing her unprepared into paroxysms of satisfaction. She cried out, her hands digging into his back as the shivery delight went on and on, past bearing, until she thought she would die if he didn't let the pleasure ebb. He was muttering hotly in her ear, sex words, the sound indistinct but the meaning clear.

And then he shuddered, too, holding himself deep as the spasms took him. Afterward, he lay heavily on her, both of them breathing deeply in the exhausted aftermath. Drowsily she let her eyes drift shut, only to open them again as he suddenly chuckled, the small movement shaking them both. "Definitely like a teenager," he murmured, nuzzling the lobe of her ear before taking it between his teeth and gently biting it. "No matter how often I have you, I want you again almost as soon as I move off you. The only time I'm satisfied is when we're like this." He thrust lazily, their bodies still linked.

"Then let's stay like this." She ran her hands down his muscular back, feeling the heat of him through the fabric of his shirt. "Someone will find us in a couple of weeks."

He laughed and kissed her. "They'd probably think, wow, what a way to go, but I'd prefer both of us being warm and pliable. If I want to keep you that way, I suppose I'd better feed you, hadn't I?" He kissed her again and rolled away to sit up.

She stretched, replete, the afternoon's aching frustration relieved. Even the hollowness in her chest had faded, though by no means vanished. She had never had this before, she thought dimly, this bone-deep sense of connection. And she wouldn't have it now if Robert had been less ruthlessly determined to have his way.

They spent the next couple of hours grilling the steaks, then sitting out on the deck after they had eaten and cleaned the kitchen. The night was thick and warm, the temperature still in the high eighties. Robert stretched out on a chaise longue and pulled Evie down on top of him. There were no lights on in the house, and the concealing darkness was like a blanket. They lay there in the heavy, peaceful silence, with his hand slowly moving over her back. Slowly his caresses grew more purposeful, and Evie melted against him. Her chemise top was lifted off over her head and dropped to the deck. She hadn't put her underwear back on, so when his hand moved under the gauzy skirt, he touched only the bare flesh of her thighs and buttocks. He cupped the twin mounds in his hands and held her hard against him, nestling his arousal in the soft junction of her thighs.

"You have on too many clothes," she murmured, kissing the underside of his jaw.

"You, on the other hand, hardly have on any."

"Whose fault is that?" Her wandering mouth nibbled down his neck. "I was completely dressed when I arrived here."

"I wouldn't say that, sweetheart. Even if your nipples hadn't been sticking out like little berries, the delicious jiggle of your breasts when you walked made it obvious you weren't wearing anything under your top. And this thing," he continued lazily, grasping a handful of material, "doesn't qualify as a skirt." Tiring of her mouth being on his throat rather than his own mouth, he pulled her up for a long kiss, during which his own clothing was opened and removed. Sighing with pleasure, she lifted the skirt out of the way and settled over him, gasping a little as he slid inside her.

Then they lay quietly again, bodies linked, content with the sensation as it was. The lights of a night fisherman drifted by on the lake, but they were shielded by the darkness. Sometime later it became difficult to lie still. Hidden impulses twinged deep inside, inviting undulating movement. She resisted, but knew he was feeling the same compulsion. He was growing even harder, reaching deeper into her, and a fine tension invaded his muscles as he lay motionless beneath her.

She pressed her forehead hard against his jaw, fighting not to move. He throbbed inside her, and she moaned softly. Her inner muscles clenched in helpless delight on his invading length, then did so again, and her soft cries floated in the night air as the moment took her. In an effort to control his own reaction, Robert gripped her bottom hard, his teeth clenched against the almost overwhelming need to give in. He won, but sweat beaded on his forehead from the struggle.

When she stilled, he lifted her from him and bent her over the end of the chaise. He knelt behind her, his thighs cupping hers, and thrust heavily into her moist, relaxed sheath. She clung to the chaise, unable to stifle her moans of pleasure as his rhythmic motion increased in speed and power. He convulsed, flooding her with warmth, and lay heavily over her for a long time, while his breathing slowed and his heartbeat returned to normal.

Recovered, he gathered their scattered clothing and pushed it into her arms, then lifted her and carried her inside, to the big bed that awaited them.

They slept late the next morning, until after nine o'clock. She yawned and stretched like a sleepy cat, and Robert held her close, stroking her tangled hair away from her face. As usual, he had awakened her at dawn with silent, drowsy lovemaking; then they had both gone back to sleep.

With a quick kiss and a lingering pat on her bare bottom, he left the bed and headed toward his shower. Evie yawned again and got up herself. She slipped into his shirt as she went to the kitchen to make coffee. ''Robert, you need an automatic timer on your coffeemaker,'' she muttered to herself as she scooped the coffee into the round filter. Not that they would ever remember to prepare the coffee and set the timer before they went to bed.

Standing there in the sun-drenched kitchen, listening to the coffeemaker pop and hiss, she became aware that she felt strangely light, almost carefree. She hugged herself in an effort to contain the elusive feeling. She was happy, she thought with some surprise. Despite selling the house, she was happy. She had saved the marina, and she had Robert. Most of all, she had Robert.

Her love for him quietly grew each time she was with him. He was such a complicated, controlled, private man; no matter how often he made love to her, he still kept that inner core of himself inviolate, not allowing her or anyone else inside. Knowing that had no effect on the way she felt about him. He hadn't opened his heart to her, but that in no way made him less worthy of love. He might never love her, she realized. But if this was all he could give a woman, then she would take it.

A ringing interrupted the quiet. It sounded like a telephone, but the phone there in the kitchen definitely wasn't ringing, and this sound was muffled, as if it were in a different room. The line in

Robert's office must be a different number, she realized. He was in the shower and wouldn't be able to hear it. It rang only once, though, and she realized that the answering machine there must have picked up the call.

She walked down the hall to the office and opened the door. The whirring sound of the fax machine greeted her. So it hadn't been a call, after all, but a fax.

The machine stopped whirring and lapsed into silence after having spat out only one sheet of paper. As she turned to go, her eye was caught by a name on the page, and curiously she turned back.

It was her name that had caught her attention.

The message was brief. "Mr. Borowitz just reported that a cashier's check from E. Shaw, in full payment of the outstanding amount, was delivered by express mail and received by him. His hands are tied. Further instructions?" The scrawled signature looked like "F. Koury."

Evie picked up the page and read it again. At first she was merely puzzled. Why would this F. Koury be telling Robert that she had paid the loan? And why would Mr. Borowitz be reporting it at all? Robert didn't even know about the loan, much less the threat of foreclosure.

Her mind stopped, along with her breathing. She hung there, paralyzed by a sickening realization. Robert knew all about it because he was the one who had been blocking her efforts to mortgage the house. He was also the reason why her loan had been bought, and why Mr. Borowitz had been so intractable in demanding full payment. He had been instructed to give her no cooperation at all, instructed by Robert Cannon. Her lover was her enemy.

Her chest was hurting. She gasped and resumed breathing, but the pain remained, a cold, heavy lump in her chest. The sense of betrayal was suffocating.

Obviously Robert was far wealthier and more powerful than she had imagined, to have this much influence, she thought with detached calm. She didn't know why he wanted her marina, but he obviously did. There were a lot of why's she couldn't comprehend, particularly right now. Maybe later, when she could think better, some of this would make sense.

Right now, all she could think was that Robert had tried to take over her marina and had cost her her home.

That distance she had sensed in him had been all too real. He hadn't committed his heart because, for him, it had all been business. Had he seduced her simply so he could stay close and keep tabs on what she was doing? Given what else he had done, that seemed to her like a reasonable assumption.

Her lips felt numb, and her legs moved like an automaton's as she left the office, carefully closing the door behind her. The damning fax was still in her hand as she returned to the kitchen.

The hopeless enormity of the situation overwhelmed her. How ironic that she had fallen in love with the man who was coolly trying to destroy her! Oh, she doubted he looked at it in such melodramatic terms, but then, he probably saw the whole thing as a successful business takeover, rather than a love affair.

She heard the shower cut off. With slow, achingly precise movements, she folded the fax and dropped it into the trash, then poured a cup of coffee. She desperately needed the caffeine, or anything, to bolster her. Her hands were shaking slightly as she lifted the cup to her lips.

She was standing in front of the window when Robert came into the kitchen a few moments later, wearing only a pair of jeans and still rubbing a towel across his chest. He stopped, his entire body clenching at the sight of her. God, she was breathtaking, with her mane of tawny gold hair loose and tousled. She was wearing only his shirt, and it was unbuttoned. There had never been another garment invented, he thought with a surge of desire, that looked better on a woman than a man's shirt. She was sipping coffee and looking out the window, lost in thought, her expression as calm and remote as a statue's.

He dropped the towel and went to her, sliding one arm around her as he took the cup and lifted it to his own lips. He imagined he could taste her on the rim, but then, his senses were so attuned to her that he could pick her out of a crowd blindfolded.

No woman had ever responded to him the way Evie did. She was pure fire in his arms, reveling in every thrust, tempting more from him. If he was gentle, she melted. If he was rough in his passion, she clung to him, clawed at him, her soaring desire feeding his own until they were both frenzied with need. He wanted her incessantly.

He smoothed his hand over the curve of her bottom, delighting in the silky texture of her flesh. ''The shower's all yours, sweetheart.''

''All right,'' she said automatically, but he had the impression she didn't really hear him. She was still looking out the window.

He tipped his head to see if he could tell what had her so interested. He saw only a wide expanse of lake, dotted with a few boats. ''What are you looking at?''

''Nothing. Just the lake.'' She turned away from his embrace and left the kitchen.

Robert's brows briefly knit in puzzlement, but he was hungry, and breakfast took precedence at the moment. He had scarcely gotten the bacon started when Evie reappeared in the kitchen, fully dressed, and with her keys in her hand.

''A fax came in while you were in the shower,'' she said quietly.

He turned, going still at what he saw in her face—or rather, what he didn't see. She was pale and expressionless, her eyes empty. With a chill, he remembered how Becky had described the look in Evie's eyes after the accident and he knew it must have been something like this. She looked so terribly remote, as if she had somehow already left.

''Who was it from?'' he asked, keeping his voice gentle while his mind raced, sorting through the possibilities, all of them damning. The worst-case scenario was if she was indeed working with Mercer and had found out that the trap was closing tight about them.

''An F. Koury.''

''Ah.'' He nodded, concealing a sense of relief. ''My secretary.'' Probably it had nothing to do with Mercer, then, but why was Evie looking so frozen?

"It's there in the trash, if you want to read it, but I can tell you what it said."

He leaned against the cabinet and crossed his arms, eyeing her carefully. "All right. Tell me."

"Mr. Borowitz notified your secretary that he'd received a cashier's check from E. Shaw for payment in full of the loan, and that his hands were tied. She asked for further instructions."

Robert's expression didn't change, but inwardly he was swearing viciously. Of all the things for Evie to stumble onto! It was less damaging, from a security standpoint, than anything connected with Mercer would have been, but a hell of a thing to try to explain to a lover. He'd never intended her to know about it. The pressure had been real, but he would never have let it go to foreclosure. He didn't rush into explanations but waited for her reaction so he could better gauge what to say to her. And how in hell had she managed to get the money to pay the loan?

"You're the reason I couldn't get a mortgage on my house," she said, her voice so strained it was almost soundless.

She'd put it together quickly, he thought. But then, from the beginning, she'd proven herself to be uncomfortably astute. "Yes," he said, disdaining to lie.

"You're behind the loan being sold to another bank in the first place."

He inclined his head and waited.

She was gripping the keys so tightly that her fingers were white. He noted that small giveaway of emotion held in check. She took several shallow breaths, then managed to speak again. "I want your boat gone from my marina by the end of the day. I'll refund the balance of the rent."

"No," he said gently, implacably. "I'm holding you to the agreement."

She didn't waste her breath on an argument she couldn't win. She had hoped he would have the decency to do as she asked, but given his ruthless streak, she hadn't really expected it.

"Then leave it there," she said, her voice as empty as her eyes.

"But don't call me again, because I don't want to talk to you. Don't come by, because I don't want to see you."

Sharply he searched her expression, looking for a way to penetrate the wall she had thrown up between them. "You won't get rid of me that easily. I know you're angry, but—"

She laughed, but it was raw and hollow, not a sound of amusement. Robert winced. "Is that how you've decided to 'handle' me? I can see you watching me, trying to decide which angle to take to calm me down," she said. "You never just react, do you? You watch and weigh other people's reactions so you can manipulate them." She heard the strain in her voice and paused to regain control of it. "No, I'm not angry. Maybe in fifty years or so, it'll just be anger." She turned on her heel and started for the door.

"Evie!" His voice cracked like a whiplash, and despite herself, she stopped, shivering at the force of will he commanded. This wasn't the cool strategist speaking but the ruthless conqueror.

"How did you pay off the loan?" The words were still sharp.

Slowly she looked at him over her shoulder, her eyes dark and unguarded for a moment, stark with pain. "I sold my house," she said, and walked out.

Robert started to go after her, then stopped. Instead he swore and hit the countertop with his fist. He couldn't explain anything to her, not yet. Every instinct in his body screamed for him to stop her, but he forced himself to let her go. He stood rigidly, listening as the truck door slammed and the motor started. She didn't spin the wheels or anything like that; she simply backed out of the driveway and drove away without histrionics.

God! *She had sold her house.* The desperation of the action staggered him, and with sudden, blinding clarity he knew, beyond the faintest doubt, that she wasn't involved with Mercer in any way. A woman who could make money by espionage would never have sold her home to pay a debt. She had appeared to be leaving the marina and meeting with Mercer on the lake, but it must have been nothing more than damnable coincidence. Evie was totally innocent, and his machinations had cost her her home.

She wouldn't listen to anything he said right now, but after he had the espionage ring broken up and Mercer safely behind bars, he would force her to understand why he had threatened foreclosure on her loan. That he had suspected her of espionage was another rocky shoal he would have to navigate with care. He didn't imagine it would be easy to get back into her good graces, but in the end he would have her, because he didn't take no for an answer when he really wanted something. And he wanted Evie as he had never wanted anything or anyone else in his life.

He would have to make amends, of course, far beyond apologies and explanations. Evie was the least mercenary person he'd ever met, but she had a strong sense of justice, and an offer of reparation would strike a chord with her. He could buy her house from the new owners—they probably wouldn't be willing to sell at first, but he cynically suspected that doubling the price would change their minds—and present her with the deed, but he far preferred that she have a newer, bigger house. The simplest thing would be to deed over his own house to her. It meant nothing to him, he could buy a house anywhere he wanted, but Evie needed a base that was hers and hers alone. It would be a vacation home, a getaway when they needed a break from the hubbub of New York, a place for her to stay when she wanted to visit Becky.

He fished the damning fax out of the trash and read it. Three concise sentences, Felice at her most efficient. There was nothing more he could do about the loan; realizing that, she had deprioritized it and sent the information by fax so he could have it immediately but respond at his leisure, rather than calling and wasting both his time and hers. Felice was a genius at whittling precious seconds here and there so she would have more time to devote to the truly important matters. In this instance, however, her knack for superefficiency had worked against him and perhaps cost him Evie.

No. No matter what, he wouldn't let Evie go.

Evie drove automatically, holding herself together with desperate control. She tried to empty her mind, but it wasn't possible. How could she be so numb but hurt so much at the same time? She literally ached, as if she had been beaten, yet felt somehow divorced from her body. She had never felt as remote as she did now, or as cold and hollow. The heat of the sun washed over her, but it didn't touch her. Even her bones felt cold and empty.

Why? She hadn't asked him that and couldn't think of a reason that would matter. The why of it wasn't important. The hard fact was that he had sought her out for a reason that had nothing to do with love or even attraction, used the intimacy he had deliberately sought as a means to gather information that he wanted, and then turned that knowledge against her. How had he known about the loan in the first place? She supposed it was possible a credit report would have given him the information, but a far more likely explanation was that he had simply taken a look through the papers in her desk at home. There had been ample opportunity for him to do so; the very first time he had been in her house, she remembered, was when he had brought her home to change clothes after Jason had fallen in the water, and she had left him alone while she showered and changed.

She didn't know why he had targeted her marina, and she didn't care. She marked it down to simple avarice, the greedy impulse to take what belonged to others.

She hadn't known him at all.

She was still calm and dry-eyed when she reached her house. No—not her house any longer, but the Campbells'. Dazed, she unlocked the door and walked inside, looked at the familiar form and content of her home, and bolted for the bathroom. She hung over the toilet and vomited up the little coffee she had swallowed, but the dry, painful heaves continued long after her stomach was emptied.

When the spasms finally stopped, she slumped breathless to the floor. She had no idea how long she lay there, in a stupor of exhaustion and pain, but after a while she began to cry. She curled into a ball, tucking her legs up in an effort to make herself as small as possible, and shuddered with the violent, rasping sobs that tore through her. She cried until she made herself sick and vomited again.

It was a long time before she climbed shakily to her feet. Her eyelids were swollen and sore, but she was calm, so calm and remote that she wondered if she would ever be able to feel anything again. God, she hoped not!

She stripped, dropping her clothes to the floor. She would throw them out later; she never wanted to see that skirt again, or any other garment she had worn that night. She was shivering as she climbed into the shower, where she stood for a long time, letting the hot water beat down on her, but the heat sluiced off her skin just like the water, none of it soaking in to thaw the bone-deep cold that shook her.

She would have stood there all day, paralyzed by the mind-numbing pain, but at last the hot water began to go and the chill forced her out. She wanted nothing more than to crawl into bed, close her eyes and forget, but that wasn't an option. She wouldn't forget. She would never forget. She could stay in the shower forever, but it wouldn't wash his touch off her flesh or his image out of her mind.

He had never wanted her at all. He had wanted the marina.

The marina. Her mind fastened on it with desperate gratitude. She still had the marina, had salvaged something from the ruin Robert Cannon had made of her life. No matter how much damage he had done, he hadn't won.

The habits of years took over as she moved slowly about, getting ready to go to work. After towel-drying her hair, she stood in front of the bathroom mirror to brush out the tangles and braid it. Her own face looked back at her, white and blank, her eyes dark, empty pools. Losing Matt had been devastating, but she had carried the knowledge of his love deep inside. This time she had nothing. The care Robert had shown her had been an illusion, carefully fostered to deceive her. The passion between them, at least on his part, had been nothing more than a combination of mere sex and his own labyrinthine plotting. The man could give lessons to Machiavelli.

He had destroyed the protective shield that had encased her for so many years. She had thought she couldn't bear any more pain, but now she was learning that her capacity for pain went far beyond imagination. She wouldn't die from it, after all; she would simply rebuild the shield, stronger than before, so that it could never be penetrated again. It would take time, but she had time; she had the rest of her life to remember Robert Cannon and how he had used her.

She hid her sore, swollen eyes behind a pair of sunglasses and carefully drove to the marina, not wanting to have an accident because she wasn't paying attention. She refused to die in a car accident and give Cannon the satisfaction of winning.

When she drove up to the marina, everything looked strangely normal. She sat in the truck, staring at it for a few seconds, bewildered by the sameness of it. So much had happened in such a short time that it seemed as if she had been gone for weeks, rather than overnight.

No matter what, she still had this.

Robert prowled the house like a caged panther, enraged by the need to wait. Waiting was alien to him; his instinct was to make a cold, incisive decision and act on it. The knowledge of the pain Evie must be feeling, and what she must be thinking, ate at him like acid. He could make it up to her for the house, but could he heal the hurt? Every hour he was away from her, every hour that passed with her thinking he had betrayed her, would deepen the wound. Only the certainty that she would refuse to listen to him now kept him from going after her. When Mercer was in jail, when he had the proof of what he'd been doing and could tell her the why, then she would listen to him. She might slap his face, but she would listen.

It was almost three o'clock when the phone rang. "Mercer's moving early," his operative barked. "He panicked and called them from the office. No dead drop this time. He told them that he needed the money immediately. It's a live handoff, sir. We can catch the bastards red-handed!"

"Where is he now?"

"About halfway to Guntersville, the way he was driving. We have a tail on him. I'm on the way, but it'll take me another twenty-five minutes to get there."

"All right. Use the tracking device and get there as fast as you can. I'll go to the marina now and get ahead of him. He's never seen my boat, so he won't spot me."

"Be careful, sir. You'll be outnumbered until we can get there."

Robert smiled grimly as he hung up the phone. Everything he needed was in the boat: weapons, camera, binoculars and tape recorder. Mercer's ass was in a sling now.

He drove to the marina, ignoring the speed laws. He only hoped Evie wouldn't come out when she saw him and do something foolish like cause a scene. He didn't have time for it, and he sure as hell didn't want to attract any attention. He tried to imagine Evie causing a scene, but the idea was incongruous. No, she wouldn't do that; it wasn't her style at all. She would simply look through him as if he didn't exist. But when he reached the marina, he didn't take any chances. He went straight to the dock where his boat was moored, not even glancing at the office.

Evie heard him drive up. She knew the sound of that Jeep as intimately as she knew her own heartbeat. She froze, trying to brace herself for the unbearable, but the seconds ticked past and the door didn't open. When she forced herself to turn and look out the window, she caught a glimpse of his tall, lean figure striding purposefully down the dock toward his boat. A minute later she heard the deep cough of the powerful motor, and the sleek black boat eased out of its slip. As soon as he was out of the Idle Speed Only zone, he shoved the throttle forward, and the nose of the boat rose like a rearing stallion as the craft shot over the water, gaining speed with every second.

She couldn't believe how much it hurt just to see him.

Landon Mercer walked in ten minutes later. Loathing rose in her throat, choking her, and it was all she could do to keep from screaming at him. Today, though, there was none of the slimy come-on attitude he thought was so irresistible; he was pale, his face strained. He was wearing slacks and a white dress shirt, the collar unbuttoned. Sweat beaded on his forehead and upper lip. He carried the same tackle box, but no rod and reel.

"Got a boat for me, Evie?" he asked, trying to smile, but it was little more than a grimace.

She chose a key and gave it to him. "Use the one on the end."

"Thanks. I'll pay you when I get back, okay?" He was already going out the door when he spoke.

Something in her snapped. It was a quiet snap, but suddenly she had had enough. Mercer was definitely up to no good, and today he hadn't even made the pretense of going fishing. The marina was all she had left, and if that bastard was dealing drugs and dragged her into it by using her boats, she might lose the marina after all.

Over her dead body.

It was too much, all the events of the day piling on top of her. She wasn't thinking when she strode out to the truck and retrieved her pistol from under the seat, then hurried to her own boat. If she had been thinking, she would have called the police or the water patrol, but none of that came to mind. Still reeling from shock, she could focus on only one thing—stopping Mercer.

Robert had positioned his boat where he could see Mercer leave the marina and fall in behind him without attracting his notice. The tracking device was working perfectly, the beeping increasing in speed as Mercer approached his position, then decreasing as the rental boat sped past. Not wanting to get too close and scare off the people Mercer was meeting, he started the motor and began idling forward, letting Mercer put more distance between them.

Another boat was coming up fast on the left, intersecting his path at a right angle. There was enough space that Robert didn't have to back off his speed, and he kept his eye on the diminishing dot on Mercer's boat. Then the other boat flashed across his line of vision, and he saw a long blond braid bouncing as the boat took the waves.

Evie! His heart leapt into his throat, almost choking him. Her appearance stunned him; then, suddenly, he knew. *She was following Mercer!* That was what she'd been doing all along. With that unsettling intuition of hers, she had known that Mercer was up to no good and had taken it upon herself to try to find out what it was. He even knew her reasoning: by using one of her boats, Mercer was involving her marina. Robert knew better than most to what lengths she would go to protect that place. She would give up her home, and she would risk her life.

Swearing savagely, he picked up the secure phone and punched in the number even as he pushed the throttle forward. "Evie is following Mercer," he snarled when the call was answered on half a ring. "She's on our side. Pass the word and make damn sure no one fires on her by mistake!"

His blood ran cold at the thought. None of his people would shoot at her, but what about the others?

Mercer was heading toward the islands again, as she had known he would. She kept about five hundred yards between them, enough distance that her presence wouldn't worry him, at least not yet. She would close the gap in a hurry when he reached the islands and slowed down.

The pistol lay in her lap. It was a long-barreled .45 caliber, very accurate, and she not only had a license to carry it, she knew how to use it. Whatever Mercer was doing, it was going to stop today.

There was another boat anchored between two of the smaller islands, two men inside it. Mercer didn't take his usual circuitous route around and through the islands, but headed straight toward the other boat. Grimly Evie increased her speed and followed.

Mercer pulled up alongside the other boat and immediately passed the tackle box over. Evie saw one of the men point to her as she neared, and Mercer turned to look. She wasn't wearing a hat or sunglasses, and though her hair was braided, she knew she was easily recognizable as a woman. But she didn't care if Mercer recognized her, because the time for stealth was past.

The fact that she was a woman, and alone, made them less cautious than they should have been. Mercer was standing, his feet braced against the gentle rocking of the boat. Confident that they hadn't been caught doing anything suspicious, he said something in a low tone to the two other men, then raised his voice to call to her. "Evie, is something wrong?"

She waved to allay any suspicions. She was still twenty yards away. She eased the throttle into neutral, knowing that the boat would continue nosing forward for several yards even without power. Then, very calmly, she lifted the pistol and pointed it at the man holding the tackle box.

"Don't make me nervous," she said. "Put the tackle box down."

The man hesitated, darting a petrified look at his partner, who was still behind the wheel of the boat. Mercer was frozen, staring at her and the huge pistol in her hand.

"Evie," he said, his voice shaking a little. "Listen, we'll cut you in. There's a hell of a lot of money—"

She ignored him. "I told you to put the box down," she said to the man who was holding it. Her mind still wasn't functioning clearly. All she could think was that if he dropped the tackle box into the river, the evidence would sink and there wouldn't be any way of proving what he was doing. She had no idea how she would manage to get three men and three different boats to the authorities, but there was a lot of boat traffic on the river this afternoon, and eventually someone would come over this way.

Another boat was coming up behind her already, way too fast. Mercer's attention switched to it, and a sick look spread over his face, but Evie didn't let her attention waver from the man holding the tackle box. A sleek black boat appeared in her peripheral vision, nosing up to the side of the boat holding the two men. Robert rose from the seat, holding the steering wheel steady with his knee as he leveled a pistol on the three men, his two-fisted grip holding the weapon dead level despite the rocking of the boat.

"Don't even twitch a muscle," he said, and the tone of his voice made Evie risk a quick glance at him. The facade of urbanity had fallen completely away, and he made no attempt now to disguise his true nature. The lethal pistol in his hand looked like a natural extension of his arm, as if he had handled weapons so often it was automatic to him now. His face was hard and set, and his eyes held the cold ferocity of a hunting panther.

The waves made by Robert's boat were washing the others closer together, inexorably sweeping Evie's boat forward to collide with them. "Look out," she warned sharply, dropping one hand to the throttle to put her motor into reverse, to counteract the force of the waves. The two other boats bumped together with staggering force, sending Mercer plunging into the river. The man holding the tackle box cursed and flailed his arms, fighting for balance, and dropped the box. It fell into the bottom of the boat. Robert's attention was splintered, and in that instant the driver of the boat reached beneath the console and pulled out his own weapon, firing as soon as he had it clear. Evie screamed, her heart stopping as she tried to bring her pistol around. Robert ducked to the side, and the bullet tore a long gouge out of the fiberglass hull. Going down on one knee, he fired once, and the driver fell back, screaming in pain.

The second man dived sideways into the rental boat. Mercer was clinging to the side, screaming in panic as the man hunched low in the boat and turned the ignition key. The motor coughed into life, and the boat leapt forward. Knowing she couldn't get a good shot at a moving target, especially with her own boat still rocking, Evie dropped the pistol and shoved the throttle back into forward gear. The two boats collided with a grinding force that splintered the fiberglass of both craft, her more powerful motor shoving her boat on top of the other. The impact tossed her out of the seat, and she hit the water with a force that knocked her senseless.

She recovered consciousness almost immediately but was dazed by the shock. She was underwater, the surface only a lighter shade of murky green. There was a great roaring in her ears, and a vibration that seemed to go straight through her. Boats, she thought dimly, and terror shot through her as she realized how much danger she was in. If the drivers couldn't see her, they might drive right over her, and the propeller would cut her to pieces.

She clawed desperately for the surface, kicking for all she was worth. Her head cleared the water, and she gulped in air, but there was a boat almost on top of her, and she threw herself to the side. Someone in the boat yelled, and she heard Robert's deep voice roaring, but she couldn't understand his words. Her ears were full of water, and dizziness made everything dim. If she passed out, she thought, she would drown. She blinked the water out of her eyes and saw the wreckage of the two boats, not five yards away. She struggled toward it and shakily hooked her arm over the side of the rental boat. It was very low in the water and would probably sink within half an hour, but for now it was afloat, and that was all that mattered.

The boat that had almost hit her was idling closer. Two men were in it, dressed in jeans and T-shirts. The driver brought the boat around sideways to her, and the other man leaned out, his arm outstretched to her. The sunlight glinted off a badge pinned to the waistband of his jeans. Evie released the rental boat and swam the few feet to the other craft. The man caught her arms, and she was hauled out of the water and into the boat.

She sank down onto the floor. The man knelt beside her. His voice was anxious. "Are you all right, Mrs. Shaw?"

She was panting from exertion, gulping air in huge quantities, so she merely nodded. She wasn't hurt, just dazed from the impact, so dazed that it was a minute before she could wonder how he knew her name.

"She's okay!" she heard him yell.

Gradually her confusion faded, and things began to sort themselves out. She remained quietly in the bottom of the boat, propped against one of the seats, and watched as the two men in the water were hauled out and roughly handcuffed, and the man Robert had shot was given medical aid. Though pale and hunched over, he was still upright and conscious, so Evie assumed he would live.

Four more boats had arrived, each of them carrying a team of two men, and all of those men wore badges, either pinned to their jeans or hung around their necks. She heard one of them briskly identify himself to Mercer as FBI and assumed that they all were.

Other boats who had seen the commotion on the water were approaching but stopped at a short distance when they noticed the badges. "Y'all need any help with those boats?" one fisherman called. "We can keep 'em afloat and haul 'em to a marina, if you want."

She saw one agent glance at Robert, as if for permission, then say, "Thanks, we'd appreciate your help." Several of the fishermen idled foward and added their boats to the snarl.

Evie resisted the urge to look at Robert, though she could feel his hard, glittering gaze on her several times. For the rest of her life she would remember the cold terror she'd felt when that man had shot at him and she had thought she would have to watch another man she loved die in front of her. The devastation she'd been feeling all day, bad as it was, paled in comparison to that horror. Robert didn't want her, had used her, but at least he was alive. Reaction was setting in, and fine tremors were starting to ripple through her body.

The mopping-up seemed to take forever, so long that her sopping clothes began to dry, as stiff as cardboard from the river water. The wounded man was placed in another boat and taken for further medical attention, with two agents in attendance. Mercer and the other man were taken away next, both of them handcuffed. There was a lot of maneuvering around the two wrecked boats as the salvaging continued. Gathering her strength, she took control of the boat she was in, while the driver added his efforts to the job. Finally, though, it all seemed to be winding down. Robert brought his boat alongside the one Evie was handling.

"Are you all right?" he asked sharply.

She didn't look at him. "I'm fine."

He raised his voice. "Lee, get this boat. I'm taking Evie back to the marina."

Immediately the agent clambered back into the boat, and Evie relinquished her place behind the wheel. She didn't want to go anywhere with Robert, however, and looked around for anyone else she knew.

"Get in the boat," he said, his voice steely, and rather than make a fool of herself, she did. There was no way to avoid him, if he was determined to force the issue. If he wanted to discuss private matters, then she would prefer that they were private when he did.

Nothing was said on the ride back to the marina. The black boat moved like oiled silk over the choppy waves, but still every small bump jolted her head. She closed her eyes, trying to contain the nausea rising in her throat.

As Robert throttled down to enter the marina, he glanced over at her and swore as he took in her closed eyes and pale, strained face. "Damn it, you *are* hurt!"

Immediately she opened her eyes and stared resolutely ahead. "It's just reaction."

Coming down off an adrenaline high could leave a person feeling weak and sick, so he accepted the explanation for now but made a mental note to keep an eye on her for a while.

He idled the boat into his slip, and Evie climbed onto the dock before he could get out and assist her. True daughter of the river that she was, she automatically tied the lines to the hooks set in the wood, the habits of a lifetime taking precedence over her emotions. The boat secured, she turned without a word and headed toward the office.

Burt was behind the counter when she entered, and a look of intense relief crossed his lined face, followed by surprise and then concern when he saw her condition. It went against his grain to ask personal questions, so the words came reluctantly out of his throat, as if he were forcing them. "Did the boat flip? Are you all right?"

Two questions in a row from Burt? She needed to mark this date on her calendar. "I'm all right, just a little shaken up," she said, wondering how many more times that day she would have to say those words. "The boat's wrecked, though. Some guys are bringing it in."

Robert opened the door behind her, and Burt's expression went full cycle, back to relief. "I'll get back to the shop, then. How long do you reckon it'll take 'em to get the boat here?"

"About an hour," Robert answered for her. "They'll have to idle in." He went to the soft-drink machine and fed in quarters, then pushed the button. With a clatter, the bottle rolled down into the slot, and he deftly popped off the top.

"Well, don't make no difference. I reckon I'll stay until they get here." Burt left the unnatural surroundings of the office and headed back to where he felt most comfortable, leaving the oily smell of grease behind.

Evie walked behind the counter and sat down, wanting to put something between herself and Robert. It didn't work, of course; he knew all the moves, all the stratagems. He came behind the counter, too, and propped himself against it with his long legs outstretched and crossed at the ankle.

He held out the Coke. "Drink this. You're a little shocky and need the sugar."

He was probably right. She shrugged and took the bottle, remembering another time when she'd been fished out of the water, and how he had insisted she drink very sweet coffee. The last thing she wanted to do was faint at his feet, so she tilted the bottle and drank.

He watched until he was satisfied that she was going to follow his orders, then said, "Mercer was manager of my computer programming firm in Huntsville. We've been working on programs for the space station, as well as other things, and the programs are classified. They began turning up where they shouldn't. We figured out that Mercer was the one who was stealing them, but we hadn't managed to catch him at it, so we didn't have any proof.''

"So that's what was in the tackle box," she said, startled. "Not dope. Computer disks.''

His dark eyebrows rose. "You thought he was a drug dealer?"

"That seemed as plausible as anything. You can't sneak up on anyone in the middle of the river. He must have been weighting the package and dropping it in a shallow spot between the islands, and the others were picking it up later.''

"Exactly. But if you thought he was a drug dealer," he said, his voice going dangerously smooth, "why in hell did you follow him today?"

"The federal seizure law," she replied simply. "He was in my boat. I could have lost everything. At the very least, he could have given the marina a bad reputation and driven away business.''

And she would do anything to protect the marina, he thought furiously, including sell her house. Of course she hadn't balked at following a man she suspected of being a drug dealer! She had been armed, but his blood ran cold at the thought of what could have happened. She had been outnumbered three to one. In all honesty, however, she had had the situation under control until the waves from his boat had washed them all together.

"You could have killed yourself, deliberately ramming the boat like that.''

"There wasn't much speed involved," she said. "And my boat was bigger. I was more afraid of the gas tanks exploding, but they're in the rear, so I figured they'd be okay.''

She hadn't had time to consider all that, he thought; her reaction had been instantaneous and had nearly given him a heart attack. But a lifetime spent around boats had given her the knowledge needed to make such a judgment call. She hadn't known that reinforcements were almost there, she had simply seen that one of them was about to escape, and she had stopped him. Robert didn't know if she was courageous or foolhardy or both.

She still hadn't so much as glanced at him, and he knew he had his work cut out for him. Carefully choosing his words, he said, "I've been working with the FBI and some of my own surveillance people to set a trap for Mercer. I soured some deals he had made, put some financial pressure on him, to force him to make a move."

It didn't take more explanation than that. Watching her face, he saw her sort through the implications and the nuances of what he had just said, and he knew the exact moment when she realized he had also suspected her. A blank shield descended over her features. "Just like you did with me," she murmured. "You thought I was working with him, because he was using my boats, and because I'd been following him, trying to find out what he was doing."

"It didn't take me long to decide that if you were involved at all, you probably didn't realize what was going on. But you kept doing suspicious things, just enough that I didn't dare relax my pressure on you."

"What sort of suspicious things?" she asked, a note of disbelief entering her flat tone.

"Leaving the marina in the middle of the day to follow him. The day before yesterday, when you left the bank, you immediately stopped at a pay phone and made a call that we couldn't monitor. Yesterday you led the guy following you all over Guntersville, then ditched him by making an abrupt turn across traffic, and we weren't able to find you again until you came to work."

Evie laughed, but the sound was bitter and disbelieving. "All that! It's amazing how a suspicious mind can see suspicious actions everywhere. When the mortgage was turned down a second time, I realized there had to be someone behind it, someone who was blocking the loans. I couldn't lose the marina. The only thing left to do was sell the house, and I knew if I didn't make the call right then, I'd lose my nerve. So I stopped at the first pay phone I came to and called some people who have tried several times to buy the house, to see if they were still interested. They were so interested that they decided to pay me immediately rather than take a chance that I'd change my mind.

"Yesterday," she said softly, "I was looking for a place to live.

But I knew I was just dithering, and that the longer I put it off, the worse it would be. So I made a quick turn, drove to an apartment complex and rented an apartment.''

Yes, he thought, watching her colorless face. A quick, sharp pain was better than endless agony. Innocent actions based on desperate decisions.

She shrugged. ''I thought you wanted the marina. I couldn't figure out why. It means a lot to me, but if you were looking for a business investment, there are bigger, more profitable ones around. Instead, you thought I was a traitor, and what better way to keep tabs on me than to start a bogus relationship and push it until we were practically living together?''

This was the tricky part, he thought. ''It wasn't bogus.''

''The moon isn't round, either,'' she replied, and turned to look out the windows at her kingdom, saved at such cost to herself.

''I wasn't going to go through with the foreclosure,'' he said. ''It was just a means of pressure. Even if you'd been guilty, I'd already decided to prevent them from prosecuting you.''

''How kind of you,'' she murmured.

He uncrossed his ankles and left the support of the counter, moving until he was directly in front of her. He put his hands on her shoulders, warmly squeezing. ''I know you're hurt and angry, but until Mercer was caught, I didn't dare ease up on the pressure.''

''I understand.''

''Do you? Thank God,'' he said, closing his eyes in relief.

She shrugged, her shoulders moving under his hands. ''National security is more important than hurt feelings. You couldn't have done anything else.''

The flat note was still in her voice. He opened his eyes and saw that he hadn't cleared all the hurdles. The issue of the house was still between them.

''I'm sorry about your house,'' he said gently. ''I would never have let you sell it if I'd known that was what you were planning.'' He cupped her cheek with one hand, feeling the warm silkiness of her skin under his fingers. ''I can't get your house back, but I can give you mine. I'm having the deed made over in your name.''

She stiffened and jerked her face away from his hand. "No, thank you," she said coldly, standing up and turning to stare out the window, her back to him.

Of course she had jumped to the wrong conclusion, he thought, annoyed with himself that he had brought up the house before settling the other issue. "It isn't charity," he said in a soothing tone, putting his hand on the nape of her neck and gently rubbing the tense muscles he found there. "It isn't even much of a gesture, come to that, since it will be staying in the family. Evie, sweetheart, will you marry me? I know you love it here, but we can compromise. I won't take you completely away from your family. We can use the house for vacations. We'll come down every summer for a long vacation, and of course we'll visit several times during the year."

She pulled away from him and turned to face him. If she had been white before, she was deathly pale now. Her golden brown eyes were flat and lusterless, and with a chill he remembered how Becky had said she'd looked after Matt had died. What he saw in Evie's eyes was an emotional wasteland, and it froze him to the bone.

"Just like everything else, your *compromises* are heavily in your favor," she said, a rawness in her voice that made him flinch. "I have a better one than that. Why don't you stay in New York, and I'll stay here, and that way we'll both be a lot happier."

"Evie…" He paused, forced himself to take a deep breath and reached for control. She was wildly off balance, of course, with everything that had happened today. She loved him, and he had hurt her. Somehow he had to convince her to trust him again.

"No!" she said violently. "Don't try to decide how you're going to manipulate me into doing what you want. You're too intelligent for your own good, and too damn subtle. Nothing really reaches you, does it?" She spread her hands far apart and gestured. "You're over here, and everyone else is way over here, and never the twain shall meet. Nobody and nothing gets close to you. You're willing to marry me, but nothing would change. You'd still keep yourself closed off, watching from the distance and pulling strings to make all the puppets do what you want. What I had with Matt was *real*, a relationship with a person instead of a facade! What makes you think I'd settle for what you're offering?'' She stopped, shuddering, and it was a moment before she could speak again. ''Go away, Robert.''

CHAPTER EIGHTEEN

Evie's absence left a great, gaping hole in his life. Robert had never before in his life missed a woman or let one assume enough importance to him that he was lonely without her, but that was the predicament he found himself in now. After her flat rejection of his marriage proposal, he'd returned to New York the next day and immediately taken up the threads of his business concerns, but the social whirl he had enjoyed before seemed simultaneously too frantic and too boring. He didn't want to attend the opera or the endless parade of dinner parties; he wanted to sit out on the deck in the warm, fragrant night, listening to the murmur of the river and enjoying the array of stars scattered across the black sky. He wanted to lie naked on the chaise with Evie, motionless, their bodies linked, until their very stillness was unbearably erotic and they both shattered with pleasure.

Sex had always been a controlled but extremely important part of his life, but now he found himself unresponsive to the lures cast his way. His sex drive hadn't abated; it was driving him crazy. But he didn't want the controlled pleasure he'd known before, his mind staying remote from his body. He hadn't been remote when he'd made love with Evie, and several times he hadn't been controlled, either. Having her naked under him, thrusting into her tight, unbelievably hot sheath, and feeling her turn into pure flame in his arms...

The carnal image brought him to full arousal, and he lunged to his feet to prowl restlessly around the apartment, swearing between his teeth with every step. Nothing else made him hard these days, but just the thought of Evie could do it. He wanted her, and her absence was like acid, eating away at his soul.

He still couldn't decide what had gone wrong. He sensed the

answer, but it was an ethereal thing, always floating just beyond his comprehension. His inability to understand the problem was as frustrating, in its own way, as his hunger for Evie. He had always been able to grasp nuances, see clearly to the crux of any problem, with a speed that left others in the dust. Now it was as if his brain had failed him, and the thought infuriated him.

It wasn't the house. As much as that had hurt her, she had understood his explanation; he had seen that in her eyes. Balanced against national security, her house was nothing, and she had believed him when he'd told her that he'd never intended to go through with the foreclosure. It was a dreadful miscalculation on his part, and though it chafed that he had made such a mistake, Evie had made a move that no one could have anticipated. Mortgage the house, yes, but not *sell* it. He was still stunned by the solution she had chosen.

But she had forgiven him for that, had even forgiven him for suspecting that she might be a traitor.

Why in hell, then, had she refused to marry him? The expression in her eyes still haunted him, and he lay awake nights aching with the need to put the glow back into her face. His golden, radiant Evie had looked like…ashes.

She loved him. He knew that as surely as he knew his heart beat in his chest. And still she had turned him down. "Go away, Robert," she'd said, and the finality in her voice had stunned him. So he had gone away, and he felt as if, every day away from her, he died a little more.

Madelyn had called several times, and she was becoming insistent that he come to Montana for a visit. Knowing his sister as he did, he was ruefully aware that he had maybe two more days to get out there before she turned up on his doorstep, holding one toddler by the hand and the other balanced on her hip, a ruthless expression in those lazy gray eyes. She knew him well enough to sense that something was wrong, and she wouldn't rest until she knew what it was. Her determination had been a fearsome thing when she'd been a child, and it had gotten worse as she'd grown older.

Robert swore in frustration, then made a swift decision. Other than Evie, Madelyn was the most astute woman he knew. Maybe, as a woman, she could put her finger on the reason that was eluding him. He called Madelyn to let her know he was coming.

With the time difference, it was still early the next morning when his plane landed in Billings. The ranch was another hundred and twenty miles, and had its own airstrip, so he had long since developed the habit of renting a small plane and flying the rest of the way, rather than making the long drive. As he banked to align the Cessna with the runway, he saw Madelyn's four-wheel drive Explorer below; she was leaning against the hood, her long hair lifting in the breeze. The color of her hair was lighter and cooler than Evie's tawny-blond mane, but still his heart squeezed at the similarity.

He landed the plane and taxied it close to the vehicle. As he cut the engine, he could see the two lively little boys bouncing in the cargo area, and a rueful smile touched his eyes. He had missed the little hooligans. He wanted some of his own.

As he crossed the pavement, Madelyn came to meet him, her lazy stroll fluid and provocative. "Thank God you're here," she said. "The imps of Satan have been driving me crazy since I told them you were coming. Did you know that when a one-year-old says Uncle Robert, it sounds remarkably like Ali Baba? I've heard it fifteen thousand times in the past hour, so I'm an expert."

"Dear God," he murmured, looking past her to where the two imps of Satan were shrieking what was undoubtedly their version of his name.

She went up on tiptoe to kiss his cheek and he hugged her to him. Something guarded inside him always relaxed when he set foot on the ranch. The sense of nature was much closer here, just as it had been in Alabama.

Madelyn waited until after lunch before broaching the subject he knew had been eating her alive with curiosity. The boys had been put down for their afternoon naps, and he and Reese were sitting at the table, relaxing over coffee. Madelyn came back into the dining room, sat down and said, "All right, what's wrong?"

He gave her a wry smile. "I knew you couldn't wait much longer. You've always been as curious as a cat."

"Agreed. Talk."

So he did. It felt strange. He couldn't remember ever needing help before in deciding what to do. He concisely outlined the situation with Mercer, explaining Evie's suspected involvement and the method he had used to force them into action. He described Evie, unaware of the aching hunger in his eyes as he did so. He told them everything—how Evie had sold her house to stop the foreclosure on the marina, how she had discovered that he was behind it all, and how Mercer had been caught. And how she had turned down his marriage proposal.

He was aware that Madelyn had stiffened during his recital of events, but she was looking down at the table, and he couldn't read her expression. When he finished, however, she lifted her head, and he was startled to see the molten fury in her eyes.

"Are you that dense?" she shouted, jumping to her feet with a force that overturned her chair. "I don't blame her for not marrying you! I wouldn't have, either!" Infuriated, she stomped out of the dining room.

Bemused, Robert turned to stare after her. "I didn't know she could move that fast," he murmured.

Reese gave a startled shout of laughter. "I know. It took me by surprise the first time I made her lose her temper, too."

Robert turned back to his brother-in-law, a big, tough rancher as tall as himself, with dark hair and hazel-green eyes, coloring that he had passed on to his two sons.

"What set her off?"

"Probably the same thing that set her off when I was being that dense, too," Reese explained, amusement in his eyes.

"Would someone please explain it to me?" Robert asked with strained politeness. On the surface he was still in complete control, but inside he was dying by inches. He didn't know what to do, and that had never happened to him before. He was at a complete loss.

Reese leaned back in his chair, toying with the handle of his cup. "I almost lost Madelyn once," he said abruptly, looking down. "She probably never told you, but she left me. She didn't go far, just into town, but it might as well have been a million miles, the way I felt."

"When was this?" Robert asked, his eyes narrowing. He didn't like knowing that Madelyn had had problems and hadn't told him about them.

"When she was pregnant with Ty. I tried everything I could think of to convince her to come back, but I was too stupid to give her the one reason that mattered."

Reese was going somewhere with this, Robert realized. He was a private man and not normally this talkative. "Which reason was that?"

Reese lifted his gaze to meet Robert's, and hazel-green eyes met ice-green ones, both stark with emotion.

"It isn't easy to give someone else that kind of power over you," Reese said abruptly. "Hell, it wasn't easy to even admit it to myself, and you're twice as bad as I ever was. You're a tough son of a bitch, more dangerous than you want people to know, so you keep it all under control. You're used to controlling everything around you, but you can't control this, can you? You probably don't even know what it is. I practically had to be hit in the head before I saw the light. You love her, don't you?"

Robert froze, and his eyes went blank with shock. Love? He'd never even thought the word. He wanted Evie, wanted to marry her, wanted to have children with her. God, he wanted all of that with a fierce passion that threatened to destory him if he didn't get it. But everything in him rebelled at the thought of being in *love*. It would mean a terrible helplessness; he wouldn't be able to hold himself apart from her, to keep uncompromised the basic invulnerability that was at the core of him. He was well aware of his true nature, knew the savage inside. He didn't want to unleash that kind of raw passion, didn't want anyone to even know it existed.

But Evie knew, anyway, he realized, and felt another shock. She had seen through him right from the beginning. With that maddening intuition of hers, she sometimes went straight into his thoughts. He could shut everyone else out, but he had never been able to shut out Evie, and he had spent the entire time they were together trying to regain control over himself, over the situation, over her. She knew him for what he was, and she loved him, anyway.

He swore, running a shaking hand over his face, blinding truth staring him in the eye. Evie wouldn't have loved him if that savage intensity hadn't been there. She had known real love with Matt, and lost it; only something incredibly powerful could take her beyond that. Loving Evangeline couldn't be a civilized, controlled affair; she would want him heart and soul, nothing held back.

The house hadn't been the issue. Neither had suspecting her of a crime. He could offer her a hundred houses, all the power his wealth could bring, and none of that would tempt her. What she wanted was the one thing he hadn't offered: his love.

"It was that simple," Reese said softly. "I told Maddie that I love her. More importantly, I admitted it to myself."

Robert was still stunned, still turned inward. "How do you know?" he murmured.

Reese made a low, harsh sound. "Do you feel as if you can never get enough of her? Do you want to make love to her so much that the ache never quite leaves your gut? Do you want to protect her, carry her around on a satin cushion, give her everything in the world? Are you content just being with her, listening to her, smelling her, touching her hand? Do you feel as if someone's torn your guts out, you miss her so much? When Maddie left me, it hurt so damn bad I could barely function. There was a big empty hole in me, and it ached so much I couldn't sleep, couldn't eat. The only thing that could make it better was seeing her. Is that the way it feels?"

Robert's green eyes were stark. "Like I'm bleeding to death inside."

"Yep, that's love," Reese said, shaking his head in sympathy.

Robert got to his feet, his lean face setting in lines of determination. "Kiss Madelyn goodbye for me. Tell her I'll call her."

"You can't wait for morning?"

"No," Robert said as he took the stairs two at a time. He couldn't wait another minute. He was on his way to Alabama.

Evie didn't like her new home. She felt hemmed in, though she had a corner apartment and neighbors on only one side. When she looked out the window, she saw another apartment building, rather than the river sweeping endlessly past. She could hear her neighbors through the thin walls, hear them arguing, hear their two small children whining and crying. They were out until all hours, children in tow, and came dragging the poor little tykes in at one or two in the morning. The commotion inevitably woke her, and she would lie in bed staring at the dark ceiling for hours.

She could look for another place, she knew, but she couldn't muster enough energy or interest to do it. She forced herself to go to the marina every day, and that was the limit of what she could do. She was going through the motions, but each day it took more and more effort, and soon she would collapse under the strain.

She felt cold, and she couldn't get warm. It was an internal cold, spreading out from the vast emptiness inside, and no amount of heat could get past it. Just thinking his name was like having a knife jabbed into her, shards of pain splintering in all directions, but she couldn't get him out of her mind. A glimpse of black hair brought her head snapping around; a certain deep tone of voice made her heart stop for an instant—a precious instant—as uncontrollable joy shot through her and she thought, *He's back!* But he never was, and the joy would turn to ashes, leaving her more desolate than before.

The sun burned down, the heat wave continuing, but she couldn't feel its heat or see its bright light. The world was colored in tones of cold gray.

I got through this before, she would think on those mornings when there didn't seem to be any reason to get out of bed. *I can do it again.* But the fact was, doing it before had nearly killed her, and the depression that sucked all the spirit out of her was getting deeper every day. She didn't know if she had the strength to fight it.

Becky had gone ballistic when she found out Robert had left town. "He told me he was going to ask you to marry him," she'd roared, so enraged her hair had practicallly been standing on end.

"He did," Evie had said listlessly. "I said no." And she had refused to answer any more questions; she hadn't even told Becky why she'd sold the house.

Summer was coming to an end, burning itself out. It was almost time for school to start. The calendar said that fall was a month away, but the scent of it was in the air, crisp and fresh, without the redolent perfumes of summer. She was burning herself out, too, Evie thought, and didn't much care.

She went to bed as soon as it was dark, hoping to get a few hours' sleep before her noisy neighbors came home. It was usually a useless effort. Whenever she stopped, she couldn't keep the memories at bay; they swarmed at her from all the corners of her mind. Lying in bed, she would remember Robert's warm presence beside her, feel his weight compressing the mattress, and the memory was so real that it was almost as if she could reach out and touch him. Her body throbbed, needing his touch, the exquisite relief of having him inside her. She would relive every time he had made love to her, and her breasts would grow heavy with desire.

He was gone, but she wasn't free of him.

That night was no different; if anything, it was worse. She tossed about, trying to ignore the fever in her flesh and the misery in her heart. The T-shirt she wore rasped her aching nipples, tempting her to remove it, but she knew better. When she had tried to sleep nude, her skin had become even more sensitive.

Someone banged on the door, startling her so much that she bolted upright in bed. She glanced at the clock. It was after ten.

She got up and slipped on a robe. The banging came again, as thunderous as if someone was trying to beat down her door. She paused to turn on a lamp in the living room. "Who is it?"

"Robert. Open the door, Evie."

She froze, her hand on the knob, all the blood draining from her face. For a moment she thought she would faint. "What do you want?" she managed, the words so low that she wasn't sure he could hear them, but he did.

"I want to talk to you. Open the door."

The deep, rich voice was the same, the tone as controlled as ever. She leaned her head against the door facing, wondering if she had the strength to send him away again. What remained to be said? Was he going to try to make her accept the house? She couldn't live there; the memories of him were too strong.

"Evangeline, *open the door.*"

She fumbled with the lock and opened the door. He stepped in immediately, tall and overwhelming. She was swamped by her reactions as she fell back a pace. The scent of him was the same, the leashed vitality of his tall, lean body slamming against her like a blow. He closed the door and locked it, and when he turned back to her she saw that his black hair was tousled, and a dark shadow of beard covered his cheeks. His eyes were glittering like green fire as they fastened on her. He didn't give the apartment a glance.

"I'm only going to ask you once more," he said abruptly. "Will you marry me?"

Evie shuddered with the strain, but slowly shook her head. She could have married him before, when she'd thought he cared for her at least a little, but when she had realized he'd only been using her... No, she couldn't do it.

A muscle clenched in his jaw. She could feel the tension in him, like some great beast coiled to jump, and she took another step back. When he spoke, however, his voice was almost mild. "Why not?"

The contrast of his voice to the energy she could feel pulsing in him was maddening. All the misery of the past weeks congealed inside her, and she felt herself splintering inside. "Why not?" she cried incredulously, her voice shaking. "My God, look at yourself! Nothing touches you, does it? You'd take everything I have to give, but you'd never let me inside where you really live, where I could reach the real man. You keep yourself behind a cold wall, and I'm tired of bruising myself against it!''

His nostrils flared. ''Do you love me?''

''Is that what you came for?'' Tears welled in her eyes, rolled slowly down her cheeks. ''A sop to your ego? Yes, I love you. Now *get out!*''

She saw his powerful muscles tense, saw his eyes flare with something savage. Her heart leapt, and too late she saw the danger. She turned to run, but Robert grabbed her, whirling her to face him. Confused, Evie thought at first it was one of his carefully gauged actions, designed to impress upon her how serious he was, but then she saw his eyes. The pupils were contracted to tiny black points, the irises huge and glittering like pale fire. His face was tight and pale, except for two spots of color high on the blades of his cheekbones. Not even Robert, she thought dazedly, could control those physical reactions.

His hands tightened on her waist until his fingers dug painfully into her soft flesh, a grip that she knew would leave bruises. ''You're right,'' he said almost soundlessly. ''I've never wanted anyone to get close to me. I've never wanted to care this much for anyone, to let you or anyone else have this kind of power over me.'' His lips drew back over his teeth, and he was breathing hard. ''Shut you out? My God, I've tried to, but I can't. You want the real man, sweetheart? All right, I'm yours. I love you so much it's tearing me apart. But there's a flip side to it,'' he continued harshly. ''I'll give you more than I've ever given any other human being, but by God, I'll take more, too. You don't get to pick and choose which qualities you like the best. It's a package deal. You get all the bad with the good, and I warn you now, I'm not a gentleman.''

''No,'' she whispered, ''you're not.'' She hung in his grip, her eyes fastened on his face, seeing the sheen of sweat on his forehead and the ferocity of his expression. Her heart thundered at what he had just said, her mind reeling with joy. He loved her? She almost couldn't take it in, couldn't believe he'd actually said it. She stared up into those fiery eyes, too dazed to say anything else.

"I'm jealous," he muttered, still in that tone of stifled violence. "I don't want you even looking at another man, and if any fool tries to come on to you, he'll be lucky if I only break his arm." He shook her with enough force to make her teeth snap together. "I want you all the time, and now, damn it, I'll take you. I'll be on you so often, four and five times a day, that you'll forget what it's like not to have me inside you. No more being a gentleman and restricting myself to twice a day."

Her golden brown eyes widened. "No," she said faintly. "I wouldn't want you to restrict yourself." There were no controls on him now; she could feel the passion surging through him, a wild and savage force that caught her up in its tide and swept her along with him.

"I'll want you at my beck and call. I can't ignore the business, so I'll expect you to fit your schedule around mine, to be available whenever I'm home." As he talked, he moved her backward and roughly pushed her against the wall. His hands tugged at her panties, stripping them down her legs. He leaned against her, his heavy weight pinning her to the wall as he tore his pants open. She gave a brief, incoherent prayer of thanks that her neighbors were gone, then clung to his shoulders as he hooked one arm under her bottom and lifted her. Her heart pounding, her blood rushing through her veins on a giddy tide of joy, she parted her thighs, and he shoved himself between them. His penetration was fast and rough. She bit back a cry and buried her face against his neck. She could feel his own heartbeat thudding against her breast.

They were both motionless, overwhelmed by the stunning relief and pleasure of their bodies being joined once more, she trying to adjust to the hard fullness of him, he groaning at the tightness of her inner clasp on his sex. Then, still caught in the savage exaltation of emotional freedom, he drove mercilessly into her.

"I don't want to wear a condom," he said fiercely, his breath hot against her ear. "I don't want you to take birth-control pills. I don't want you to act like my semen is some hostile marauder that you have to protect yourself against. I want to give it to you. I want you to want it. I want you to have my babies. I want a house full of kids.'' With each word he thrust, pushing himself deeper and deeper into her.

She moaned, shuddering around him with the force of her pleasure. ''Yes.'' She had unleashed a monster of passion, a total dictator, but she could meet his power with her own. This was the real man, the one who made her feel alive again, who sent heat throbbing through every cell of her body. She wasn't cold any longer, but radiant with vibrant life.

''I want marriage.'' His teeth were ground together, and a drop of sweat ran down his temple. ''I want you tied to me—legally, financially, every way I can devise. I want you to take my name, Evangeline, do you understand?''

''Yes,'' she said, and splintered with joy. ''Robert, *yes!*''

He bucked violently against her with his climax, flooding her with moisture and heat. Evie locked her legs around him and took him deep within, her senses whirling and fading, all consciousness gone except for the primal awareness of him inside her.

Some endless time later, she realized that she was on the bed and he was stretched out naked beside her. She hadn't fainted, but neither had she been aware of anything else but him. He hadn't released her during the entire time he had stripped both her and himself, struggling out of clothing while still keeping her in his grasp. She turned to snuggle closer, and the lure of his body, after the long deprivation, was too great. She found herself on top of him, wriggling to find the right contact and nestle his sex against the soft heat between her legs. He caught his breath, and she felt him begin to harden again.

''You might get started on that house full of kids sooner than you thought,'' she murmured, moving against him again in voluptuous delight. ''I stopped taking the birth-control pills the day you left.''

''Good.'' He caressed her bottom and hip, urging her closer to him. ''I don't want to hurt you,'' he said even as he slipped inside her.

She heard the worry in his voice and knew that he was uneasy with releasing all the force he'd kept contained for so long. She kissed him and bit his lip as his subtle movements made her nerve endings riot with pleasure. "You can't hurt me by loving me," she said.

His eyes glittered in the faint light coming from the lamp in the living room. "That's good," he murmured. "Because God knows I do."

EPILOGUE

Evie heard the elevator arrive and crouched down beside the tiny, adorable creature who was clinging unsteadily to the chair in the entrance hall. "There's Daddy," she whispered, and watched her daughter's big eyes go round with delight. She barely restrained herself from gathering the baby into her arms; sometimes the surge of love was so strong that she thought she would burst from the force of it.

The elevator doors slid open, and Robert stepped out, an indescribable light flaring in his pale green eyes as he saw them waiting for him. With a joyous gurgle, the baby let go of the chair and hurled herself toward him, every toddling step teetering on the edge of disaster. Robert turned absolutely white, dropped his briefcase with a thud, and went down on one knee to swoop her into his arms. "My God," he said, shocked. "She's walking!"

"For a couple of hours now," Evie said, smiling as Angel caught her father's silk tie in one tiny, chubby hand and began babbling at him. "It makes my heart stop every time she lurches across the floor."

"She's too young to walk. She's only seven months old." Aghast, he stared down at the small head, covered with downy dark hair, that butted against his chest. He had been just as aghast when she had started crawling at five months. If he could, Robert would have kept his darling offspring as a babe in arms for the first five years of her life. She, however, was blissfully oblivious of his panic at her daring.

Still holding the baby, he hugged Evie close for a long kiss, one that quickly grew heated despite his squirming burden, who tried to poke her fingers between their mouths. They had named her Jennifer Angelina, intending to call her Jenna, but instead she had been Angel from the day she'd been born. She was angelic only when she was asleep, however; during waking hours, she had the fearless spirit of a daredevil.

Evie clung to his mouth for a long time, her hand clenching his hair to hold him in place. She had been waiting all day for him to come home, feeling shivery and excited and a little frightened.

"You were right," she murmured.

He lifted his head, and the green eyes gleamed. "I was, huh?"

She laughed and pinched him. "You knew you were." They had decided to have another baby as soon as possible. Both pregnancy and delivery had been easy for her, and though they had decided that two children would fill the house they were building just fine, they had both wanted to have them close together.

Three weeks ago, they had spent the night locked together, lost in the passion that hadn't faded during the sixteen months of their marriage. When they had awakened at dawn, for their ritual of morning love, Robert had looked down at her with his sleepy green eyes barely open and said, "We made a baby last night."

She had thought so, too, her instincts certain even before the early pregnancy test she'd taken just that morning had confirmed it. Already it was as if she could feel that hot, tiny weight in her womb, pulsing with life.

She leaned her head against his broad shoulder, remembering the sheer terror she'd felt when she had realized that she was pregnant the first time. Taking a chance on loving Robert had required all her courage, but now there was to be someone else to love, someone who was part of her, part of Robert. She would have no defense against this new little person, and she had thought she would shatter from the fear. But Robert had known how she was feeling, had seen the raw fear in her eyes and hadn't left her side all day. He had called Felice and announced that he wouldn't be in, cancel everything, and had spent the day holding Evie on his lap or making love to her. His solution, she thought wryly, had been to overwhelm her with what had gotten her in that condition to begin with; the tactic had been amazingly successful.

Angel was trying to throw herself bodily out of his arms. Sighing, he released Evie to bend down and set the baby on her chubby feet. As soon as he released her, she was off like a wobbly rocket. Evie went back into his arms, but they both kept a weather eye on their precocious daughter as she began investigating a fascinating crack in the hardwood floor.

Evie rested her head on his chest, reassured by the strong, steady thump of his heart beneath her ear. Far from losing himself in his work and demanding that she structure her time around him, as he'd said he would, Robert had instead ruthlessly reorganized his office schedule so he could spend every available moment with her and Angel. She had known that he was a man of alarming intensity, but instead of being frightened when he focused it on her, she had bloomed. Robert wasn't a man who loved lightly; when he loved, it was with every fiber of his being.

His hand moved to Evie's belly and pressed in gentle reassurance. "Are you all right?" he asked softly.

She lifted her head and gave him a luminous smile. His love had renewed her strength, banished the shadows. "I've never been better."

Robert kissed her, savoring her sweet taste and the familiar, delicious tension of desire that quivered in their bodies. "I love you, Evangeline," he said, gathering her close to him. Loving her was the most joyous, satisfying thing he'd ever done. She demanded everything from him and gave him all of herself, and sometimes he was staggered by the richness of the bond between them. He'd been right; loving Evangeline took everything he had, heart and soul.

*   *   *   *   *

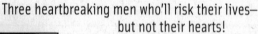

HARLEQUIN® *Presents*

The world's bestselling romance series.

Pick up a Harlequin Presents® novel and you will enter a world of spine-tingling passion and provocative, tantalizing romance!

2002 offers an exciting selection of titles by all your favorite authors.

Are you looking for...?

Cole Cameron's Revenge
#2223, January
by Sandra Marton

The Bellini Bride #2224, January
by Michelle Reid
The Italian's Wife #2235, March
by Lynne Graham

LONDON'S MOST
ELIGIBLE PLAYBOYS

by Sharon Kendrick
The Unlikely Mistress
#2227, January
Surrender to the Sheikh
#2233, February
The Mistress's Child #2239, March

Passion™

His Miracle Baby #2232, February
by Kate Walker
A Secret Vengeance #2236, March
by Miranda Lee
The Secret Love Child
#2242, April
by Miranda Lee

MISTRESS
TO A
MILLIONAIRE

The Billionaire Affair
#2238, March
by Diana Hamilton

**Seduction and
passion guaranteed!**

*Available wherever
Harlequin books are sold.*

HARLEQUIN®
Makes any time special ®